ALCATRAZ

ALSO BY BRANDON SANDERSON
FROM GOLLANCZ:

MISTBORN

The Final Empire
The Well of Ascension
The Hero of Ages

The Alloy of Law

THE STORMLIGHT ARCHIVE
The Way of Kings Part One
The Way of Kings Part Two

Elantris
Warbreaker

ALCATRAZ

Alcatraz versus the Evil Librarians
Alcatraz versus the Scrivener's Bones
Alcatraz versus the Knights of Crystallia
Alcatraz versus the Shattered Lens

BRANDON SANDERSON

GOLLANCZ
LONDON

First published in Great Britain in 2012 by Gollancz
An imprint of the Orion Publishing Group
Orion House, 5 Upper St Martin's Lane, London WC2H 9EA
An Hachette UK Company

A CIP catalogue record for this book
is available from the British Library

ISBN 978 0 575 13133 0 (Cased)
ISBN 978 0 575 13134 7 (Trade Paperback)

1 3 5 7 9 10 8 6 4 2

Typeset by Deltatype Ltd, Birkenhead, Merseyside

Printed in Great Britain by Clays Ltd, St Ives plc

The Orion Publishing Group's policy is to use papers
that are natural, renewable and recyclable products and made
from wood grown in sustainable forests. The logging and
manufacturing processes are expected to conform to
the environmental regulations of the country of origin.

www.brandonsanderson.com
www.orionbooks.co.uk

ALCATRAZ VERSUS THE EVIL LIBRARIANS

For my father, Winn Sanderson, who bought me books

AUTHOR'S FOREWORD

I am not a good person.

Oh, I know what the stories say about me. They call me Oculator Dramatus, Hero, Savior of the Twelve Kingdoms ... Those, however, are just rumors. Some are exaggerations; many are outright lies. The truth is far less impressive.

When Mr. Bagsworth first came to me, suggesting that I write my autobiography, I was hesitant. However, I soon realized that this was the perfect opportunity to explain myself to the public.

As I understand it, this book will be published simultaneously in the Free Kingdoms and Inner Libraria. This presents something of a problem for me, since I will have to make the story understandable to people from both areas. Those in the Free Kingdoms might be unfamiliar with things like bazookas, briefcases, and guns. However, those in Libraria – or the Hushlands, as they are often called – will likely be unfamiliar with things like Oculators, Crystin, and the depth of the Librarian conspiracy.

To those of you in the Free Kingdoms, I suggest that you find a reference book – there are many that would do – to explain unfamiliar terms to you. After all, this book will be published as a biography in your lands, and so it is not my purpose to teach you about the strange machines and archaic weaponry of Libraria. My purpose is to show you the truth about me, and to prove that I am not the hero that everyone says I am.

In the Hushlands – those Librarian-controlled nations such as the United States, Canada, and England – this book will be published as a work of fantasy. Do not be fooled! This is no work of fiction, nor is my name really Brandon Sanderson. Both are guises to hide the book from Librarian agents. Unfortunately, even with these precautions, I suspect that the Librarians will discover the book and ban it. In that case, our Free Kingdom agents will have to sneak into libraries and bookstores to put it on shelves. Count yourself lucky if you've found one of these secret copies.

For you Hushlanders, I know the events of my life may seem wondrous and mysterious. I will do my best to explain them, but please remember that my purpose is not to entertain you. My purpose is to open your eyes to the truth.

I know that in writing this I shall make few friends in either world. People are never pleased when you reveal that their beliefs are wrong.

But that is what I must do. This is my story – the story of a selfish, contemptible fool.

The story of a coward.

1

So, there I was, tied to an altar made from outdated encyclopedias, about to get sacrificed to the dark powers by a cult of evil Librarians.

As you might imagine, that sort of situation can be quite disturbing. It does funny things to the brain to be in such danger – in fact, it often makes a person pause and reflect upon his life. If you've never faced such a situation, then you'll simply have to take my word. If, on the other hand, you *have* faced such a situation, then you are probably dead and aren't likely to be reading this.

In my case, the moment of impending death made me think about my parents. It was an odd thought, since I hadn't grown up with them. In fact, up until my thirteenth birthday, I really only knew one thing about my parents: that they had a twisted sense of humor.

Why do I say this? Well, you see, my parents named me Al. In most cases, this would be short for Albert, which is a fine name. In fact, you have probably known an Albert or two in your lifetime, and chances are that they were decent fellows. If they weren't then it certainly wasn't the name's fault.

My name isn't Albert.

Al also could be short for Alexander. I wouldn't have minded this either, since Alexander is a great name. It sounds kind of regal.

My name isn't Alexander.

I'm certain that you can think of other names Al might be short for. Alfonso has a pleasant ring to it. Alan would also be acceptable, as would have been Alfred – thought I really don't have an inclination toward butlery.

My name is not Alfonso, Alan, or Alfred. Nor is it Alejandro, Alton, Aldris, or Alonzo.

My name is Alcatraz. Alcatraz Smedry. Now, some of you Free Kingdomers might be impressed by my name. That's wonderful for you, but I grew up in the Hushlands – in the United States itself. I didn't know about Oculators or the like, though I did know about prisons.

And that was why I figured that my parents *must* have had a twisted sense of humor. Why else would they name their child after the most infamous prison in U.S. history?

On my thirteenth birthday, I received a second confirmation that my parents were indeed cruel people. That was the day when I unexpectedly received in the mail the only inheritance they left me.

It was a bag of sand.

I stood at the door, looking down at the package in my hands, frowning as the postman drove away. The package looked old – its string ties were frayed, and its brown paper packaging was worn and faded. Inside the package, I found a box containing a simple note.

> Alcatraz,
> Happy thirteenth birthday!
> Here is your inheritance, as promised.
> Love, Mom and Dad

Underneath the note, I found the bag of sand. It was small, perhaps the size of a fist, and was filled with ordinary brown beach sand.

Now, my first inclination was to think that the package was a joke. You probably would have thought the same. One thing, however, made me pause. I set the box down, then smoothed out its wrinkled packaging paper.

One edge of the paper was covered with wild scribbles – a little like those made by a person trying to get the ink in a pen to flow. On the front there was writing. It looked old and faded – almost illegible in places – and yet it accurately spelled out my address. An address I'd been living at for only eight months.

Impossible, I thought.

Then I went inside my house and set the kitchen on fire.

Now, I warned you that I wasn't a good person. Those who knew me when I was young would never have believed that one day *I* would be known as a hero. *Heroic* just didn't apply to me. Nor did people use words like *nice* or even *friendly* to describe me. They might have used the word *clever*, though I suspect that *devious* may have been more correct. *Destructive* was another common one that I heard. But I didn't care for it. (It wasn't actually all that accurate.)

No, people never said good things about me. Good people don't burn down kitchens.

Still holding the strange package, I wandered toward my foster parents' kitchen, lost in thought. It was a very nice kitchen, modern looking with white wallpaper and lots of shiny chrome appliances. Anyone entering it would immediately notice that this was the kitchen of a person who took pride in their cooking skills.

I set my package on the table, then moved over to the kitchen stove. If you're a Hushlander, you would have thought I looked like a fairly normal American boy, dressed in loose jeans and a T-shirt. I've been told I was a handsome kid – some even said that I had an 'innocent face.' I was not too tall, had dark brown hair, and was skilled at breaking things.

Quite skilled.

When I was very young, other kids called me a klutz. I was always breaking things – plates, cameras, chickens. It seemed inevitable that whatever I picked up, I would end up dropping, cracking, or otherwise mixing up. Not exactly the most inspiring talent a young man ever had, I know. However, I generally tried to do my best despite it.

Just like I did this day. Still thinking about the strange package, I filled a pot with water. Next I got out a few packs of instant ramen noodles. I set them down, looking at the stove. It was a fancy gas one with real flames. My foster mother Joan wouldn't settle for electric.

Sometimes it was daunting, knowing how easily I could break

things. This one simple curse seemed to dominate my entire life. Perhaps I shouldn't have tried to fix dinner. Perhaps I should simply have retreated to my room. But what was I to do? Stay there all the time? Never go out because I was worried about the things I *might* break? Of course not.

I reached out and turned on the gas burner.

And, of course, the flames *immediately* flared up around the sides of the pan, far higher that should have been possible. I quickly tried to turn down the flames, but the knob broke off in my hand. I tried to grab the pot and take it off of the stove. But, of course, the handle broke off. I stared at the broken handle for a moment, then looked up at the flames. They flickered, catching the drapes on fire. The fire gleefully began to devour the cloth.

Well, so much for that, I thought with a sigh, tossing the broken handle over my shoulder. I left the fire burning – once again, I feel I must remind you that I'm not a very nice person – and picked up my strange package as I walked out into the den.

There, I pulled out the brown wrapper, flattening it against the table with one hand and looking at the stamps. One had a picture of a woman wearing flight goggles, with an old fashioned airplane in the background behind her. All of the stamps looked old – perhaps as old as I was. I turned on the computer and checked a database of stamp issue dates and found that I was right. They had been printed thirteen years ago.

Someone had taken quite a bit of effort to make it *seem* like my present had been packaged, addressed, and stamped over a decade earlier. That, however, was ridiculous. How would the sender have known where I'd be living? During the last thirteen years, I'd gone through dozens of sets of foster parents. Besides, my experience has been that the number of stamps it takes to send a package increases without warning or pattern. (The postage people are, I'm convinced, quite sadistic in that regard.) There was no way someone could have known, thirteen years, ago, how much postage it would cost to send a package in my day.

I shook my head, standing up and tossing the M key from the computer keyboard into the trash. I'd stopped trying to stick the keys back on – they always fell off again anyway. I got the fire extinguisher from the hall closet, then walked back into the kitchen, which was now quite thoroughly billowing with smoke. I put the box and extinguisher on the table, then picked up a broom, holding my breath as I calmly knocked the tattered remnants of the drapes into the sink. I turned on the water, then finally used the extinguisher to blast the burning wallpaper and cabinets, also putting out the stove.

The smoke alarm didn't go off, of course. You see, I'd broken *that* previously. All I'd needed to do was rest my hand against its case for a second, and it had fallen apart.

I didn't open a window but did have the presence of mind to get a pair of pliers and twist the stove's gas valve off. Then I glanced at the curtains, a smoldering ashen lump in the sink.

Well, that's it, I thought, a bit frustrated. *Joan and Roy will never continue to put up with me after this.*

Perhaps you think I should have felt ashamed. But what was I supposed to do? Like I said – I couldn't just hide in my room all the time. Was I to avoid living just because life was a little different for me than it was for regular people? No. I had learned to deal with my strange curse. I figured that others would simply have to do so as well.

I heard a car in the driveway. Finally realizing that the kitchen was still rank with smoke, I opened the window and began using a towel to fan it out. My foster mother – Joan – rushed into the kitchen a moment later. She stood, horrified, looking at the fire damage.

I tossed aside the towel and left without a word, going up to my room.

'That boy is a disaster!'

Joan's voice drifted up through the open window into my room. My foster parents were in the study down on the first floor, their favorite place for 'quiet' conferences about me. Fortunately, one of the first things that I'd broken in the house had been the study's window rollers, locking the windows permanently open so that I could listen in.

'Now, Joan,' said a consoling voice. It belonged to Roy, my foster father.

'I can't take it!' Joan sputtered. 'He destroys everything he touches!'

There was that word again. *Destroy*. I felt my hair bristle in annoyance. *I don't destroy things*, I thought. *I break them. They're still there when I'm finished, they just don't work right anymore.*

'He means well,' Roy said. 'He's a kindhearted boy.'

'First the washing machine,' Joan ranted. 'Then the lawn mower. Then the upstairs bath. Now the kitchen. All in less than a year!'

'He's had a hard life,' Roy said. 'He just tries too hard – how would you feel, being passed from family to family, never having a home . . . ?'

'Well, can you blame people for getting rid of him?' Joan said. 'I—'

She was interrupted by a knock on the front door. There was a moment of silence, and I imagined what was going on between my foster parents. Joan was probably giving Roy 'the look'. Usually, it was the husband who gave 'the look', insisting that I be sent away. Roy had always been the soft one here, however. I heard his footsteps as he went to answer the door.

'Come in,' Roy said, his voice faint, since he now stood in the entryway. I remained lying on my bed. It was still early evening – the sun hadn't even set yet.

'Mrs. Sheldon,' a new voice said from below, acknowledging Joan. 'I came as soon as I heard about the accident.' It was a woman's voice, familiar to me. Businesslike, curt, and more than a little condescending. I figured those were all good reasons why Ms. Fletcher wasn't married.

'Ms. Fletcher,' Joan said, faltering now that the time had come. They usually did. 'I'm . . . sorry to—'

'No,' Ms. Fletcher said. 'You did well to last this long. I can arrange for the boy to be taken tomorrow.'

I closed my eyes, sighing quietly. Joan and Roy had lasted quite long – longer, certainly, than any of my other recent sets of foster parents. Eight months was a valiant effort when taking care of *me* was concerned. I felt a little twist in my stomach.

'Where is he now?' Ms. Fletcher asked.

'He's upstairs.'

I waited quietly. Ms. Fletcher knocked but didn't wait for my reply before pushing open the door.

'Ms. Fletcher,' I said. 'You look lovely.'

It was a stretch. Ms. Fletcher – my personal caseworker – *might* have been a pretty woman, had she not been wearing a pair of hideous hornrimmed glasses. She perpetually kept her hair up in a bun that was only slightly less tight than the dissatisfied line of her lips. She wore a simple white blouse and a black ankle-length skirt. For her, it was a daring outfit – the shoes, after all, were maroon.

'The kitchen, Alcatraz?' Ms. Fletcher asked. 'Why the kitchen?'

'It was an accident,' I mumbled. 'I was trying to do something nice for my foster parents.'

'You decided that you would be kind to Joan Sheldon – one of the city's finest and most well-renowned chefs – by burning down her kitchen?'

I shrugged. 'Just wanted to fix dinner. I figured even *I* couldn't mess up ramen noodles.'

Ms. Fletcher snorted. Finally, she walked into the room, shaking her head as she strolled past my dresser. She poked my inheritance package with her index finger, harrumphing quietly as she eyed the crumpled paper and worn strings. Ms. Fletcher had a thing about messiness. Finally, she turned back to me. 'We're running out of families, Smedry. The other couples are hearing rumors. Soon there won't be any place left to send you.'

I remained quiet, still lying down.

Ms. Fletcher sighed, folding her arms and tapping her index finger against one arm. 'You realize, of course, that you are worthless.'

Here we go, I thought, feeling sick. This was my least favorite part of the process. I stared up at my ceiling.

'You are fatherless and motherless,' Ms. Fletcher said, 'a parasite upon the system. You are a child who has been given a second, third, and now *twenty-seventh* chance. And how have you received this generosity? With indifference, disrespect, and *destructiveness!*'

'I don't destroy,' I said quietly. 'I break. There's a difference.'

Ms. Fletcher sniffed in disgust. She left me then, walking out and pulling the door closed with a snap. I heard her say good-bye to the Sheldons, promising them that her assistant would arrive in the morning to deal with me.

It's too bad, I thought with a sigh. *Roy and Joan really are good people. They would have made great parents.*

2

Now, you're probably wondering about the beginning of the previous chapter, with its reference to evil Librarians, altars made from encyclopedias, and its general feeling of 'Oh, no! Alcatraz is going to be sacrificed!'

Before we get to this, let me explain something about myself. I've been many things in my life. Student. Spy. Sacrifice. Potted plant. However, at this point, I'm something completely different from all of those – something more frightening than any of them.

I'm a writer.

You may have noticed that I began my story with a quick, snappy scene of danger and tension – but then quickly moved on to a more boring discussion of my childhood. Well, that's because I wanted to prove something to you: that *I am not a nice person.*

Would a nice person begin with such an exciting scene, then make you wait almost the entire book to read about it? Would a nice person write a book that exposes the true nature of the world to all of you ignorant Hushlanders, thereby forcing your lives into chaos? Would a nice person write a book that proves that Alcatraz Smedry, the Free Kingdoms' greatest hero, was just a mean-spirited adolescent?

Of course not.

I awoke grumpily that next morning, annoyed by the sound of some banging on my downstairs door. I climbed out of bed, then threw on a bathrobe. Though the clock read 10:00 A.M., I was still tired. I had stayed up late, lost in thought. Then Joan and Roy had tried to say goodbye. I hadn't opened my door to them. Better to get things over without all that gushing.

No, I was not happy to be reawoken at 10:00 A.M. – or, actually, *any* A.M. I yawned, walking downstairs and pulling open the door, prepared to meet whichever assistant Ms. Fletcher had sent to retrieve me. 'Hell—' I said. (I hadn't intended to swear, but a boisterous voice cut me off before I could get to the 'o.')

'Alcatraz, my boy!' then man at the doorway exclaimed. 'Happy Birthday!'

'—o,' I said.

'You shouldn't swear, my boy!' the man said, pushing his way into the house. He was an older man who was dressed in a sharp black tuxedo and wore a strange pair of red-tinted glasses. He was quite bald save for a small bit of white hair running around the back of his head, and this puffed out in an unkempt fashion. He wore a similarly bushy white mustache, and he smiled quite broadly as he turned to me, his face wrinkled but his eyes alight with excitement.

'Well, my boy,' he said, 'how does it feel to be thirteen?'

'The same as it did yesterday,' I said, yawning. 'When it was *actually* my birthday. Ms. Fletcher must have told you the wrong date. I'm not packed yet – you're going to have to wait.'

I tiredly began to walk toward the stairs.

'Wait,' the old man said. 'Your birthday was ... yesterday?'

I nodded. I'd never met the man before, but Ms. Fletcher has several assistants. I didn't know them all.

'Rumbling Rawns!' then man exclaimed. 'I'm late!'

'No,' I said, climbing the stairs. 'Actually, you're early. As I said, you'll need to wait.'

The old man rushed up the stairs behind me.

I turned, frowning. 'You can wait downstairs.'

'Quickly, boy!' the old man said. 'I can't wait. Soon you'll be getting a package in the mail, and—'

'Stop. You know about the package?'

'Of course I do, of course I do. Don't tell me it already came?'

I nodded.

'Blistering Brooks!' the old man exclaimed. 'Where, lad? Where is it?'

I frowned. 'Did Ms. Fletcher send it?'

'Ms. Fletcher? Never heard of her. Your parents sent that box, my boy!'

He's never heard of her? I thought, realizing that I'd never verified the man's identity. *Great. I've let a lunatic into the house.*

'Oh, blast!' the old man said, reaching into his suit pocket and pulling out a pair of yellow-tinted glasses. He quickly exchanged the light red ones for these, then looked around. 'There!' he said, rushing up the stairs, pushing past me.

'Hey!' I called, but he didn't stop. I muttered quietly to myself, following. The old man was surprisingly spry for his age, and he reached the door to my room in just a few heartbeats.

'Is this your room, my boy?' the old man asked. 'Lots of footprints leading here. What happened to the doorknob?'

'It fell off. My first night in the house.'

'How odd,' the old man said, pushing the door open. 'Now, where's that box ...?'

'Look,' I said, pausing in the doorway. 'You have to leave. If you don't, I'm going to call the police.'

'The police? Why would you do that?'

'Because you're in my house,' I said. 'Well ... my ex-house, at least.'

'But you let me in, lad,' the old man pointed out.

I paused. 'Well, now I'm telling you to leave.'

'But why? Don't you recognize me, my boy?'

I raised an eyebrow.

'I'm your grandfather, lad! Grandpa Smedry! Leavenworth Smedry, Oculator Dramatus. Don't tell me you don't remember me – I was there when you were born!'

I blinked. Then frowned. Then cocked my head to the side. 'You were there ...?'

'Yes, yes,' the old man said. 'Thirteen years ago! You haven't seen me since, of course.'

'And I'm supposed to remember you?' I said.

'Well, certainly! We have excellent memories, we Smedrys. Now, about that box ...'

Grandfather? The man had to be lying, of course. *I don't even have parents. Why would I have a grandfather?*

Now, looking back, I realize that this was a silly thought. Everybody has a grandfather – two of them, actually. Just because you haven't seen them doesn't mean they don't exist. In that way, grandfathers are kind of like kangaroos.

At any rate, I most certainly *should* have called the police on this elderly intruder. He has been the main source of all my problems ever since. Unfortunately, I didn't throw him out. Instead, I just watched him put away his yellow-tinted spectacles, retrieving the reddish-tinted ones again. Then he finally spotted the box on my dresser, scribbled-on brown paper still sitting beside it. The old man rushed over eagerly.

Did he send it? I wondered.

He reached into the box, taking out the note with an oddly reverent touch. He read it, smiling fondly, then looked up at me.

'So, where is it?' Grandpa Smedry – or whoever he really was – asked.

'Where is what?'

'The inheritance, lad!'

'In the box,' I said, pointing at the package.

'There isn't anything in here but the note.'

'What?' I said, walking over. Indeed, the box was empty. The bag of sand was gone.

'What did you do with it?' I asked.

'With what?'

'The bag of sand,' I said.

The old man breathed out in awe. 'So, it really came?' he whispered, eyes wide. 'There was actually a bag of sand in this box?'

I nodded slowly.

'What color was the sand, lad?'

'Um ... sandy?'

'Galloping Gemmells!' he exclaimed. 'I'm too late! They must have gotten here before me. Quickly, lad. Who's been in this room since you received the box?'

'Nobody,' I said. By this point, as you can imagine, I was

growing a little frustrated and increasingly confused. Not to mention hungry and still a bit tired. And a little sore from gym class the previous week – but that isn't exactly all that relevant, is it?

'Nobody?' the old man repeated. 'Nobody else has been in this room?'

'Nobody,' I snapped. 'Nobody at all.' Except ... I frowned. 'Except Ms. Fletcher.'

'Who *is* this Ms. Fletcher you keep mentioning, lad?'

I shrugged. 'My caseworker.'

'What does she look like?'

'Glasses,' I said. 'Snobbish face. Usually has her hair in a bun.'

'The glasses,' Grandpa Smedry said slowly. 'Did they have ... horn rims?'

'Usually.'

'Hyperventilating Hobbs!' he exclaimed. 'A Librarian! Quickly, lad, we have to go! Get dressed; I'll go steal some food from your foster parents!'

'Wait!' I said, but the old man had already scrambled from the room, moving with a sudden urgency.

I stood, dumbfounded.

Ms. Fletcher? I thought. *Take the inheritance? That's stupid. Why would she want a silly bag of sand?* I shook my head, uncertain what to make of all this. Finally, I just walked over to my dresser. Getting dressed, at least, seemed like a good idea. I threw on a pair of jeans, a T-shirt, and my favorite green jacket.

As I finished, Grandpa Smedry rushed back into the bedroom, carrying two of Roy's extra briefcases. I noticed a leaf of lettuce sticking halfway out of one, while the other seemed to be leaking a bit of ketchup.

'Here!' Grandpa Smedry said, handing me the lettuce briefcase. 'I packed us lunches. No telling how long it will be before we can stop for food!'

I raised the briefcase, frowning. 'You packed lunches inside of briefcases?'

'They'll look less suspicious that way. We have to fit in! Now, let's get moving. The Librarians could already be working on the sand.'

'So?' I said.

'So!' the old man exclaimed. 'Lad, with those sands, the Librarians could destroy kingdoms, overthrow cultures, dominate the world! We need to get them back. We'll have to strike quickly, and possibly at great peril to our lives. But that's the Smedry way!'

I lowered the briefcase. 'If you say so.'

'Before we leave, I need to know what our resources are. What's your Talent, lad?'

I frowned. 'Talent?'

'Yes,' Grandpa Smedry said. 'Every Smedry has a Talent. What is yours?'

'Uh ... playing the oboe?'

'This is no time for jokes, lad!' Grandpa Smedry said. 'This is serious! If we don't get that sand back ...'

'Well,' I said, sighing. 'I'm pretty good at breaking things.'

Grandpa Smedry froze.

Maybe I shouldn't play with the old man, I thought, feeling guilty. *He may be a loon, but that's no reason to make fun of him.*

'Breaking things?' Grandpa Smedry said, sounding awed. 'So it's true. Why, such a Talent hasn't been seen in centuries ...'

'Look,' I said, raising my hands. 'I was just joking around. I didn't mean—'

'I knew it!' Grandpa Smedry said eagerly. 'Yes, yes, this improves our chances! Come, lad, we have to get moving.' He turned and left the room again, carrying his briefcase and rushing eagerly down the stairs.

'Wait!' I cried, chasing after the old man. However, when I reached the doorway, I paused.

There was a car parked on the curb outside. An old car. Now, when you read the words *old car*, you likely think of a beat-up or rusted vehicle that barely runs. A car that is old, kind of in the same way that cassette tapes are old.

This was not such a car. It was not old like cassette tapes are old – it wasn't even old like records are old. No, this car was old like Beethoven is old. Or, at least, so it seemed. To me – and, likely, to most of you living in the Hushlands – the car looked like an antique. Kind of like a Model-T.

But that was just my assumption.

The point is that many times, the first thing a person presumes about something – or someone – is inaccurate. Or, at the very least, incomplete. Take the young Alcatraz Smedry, for instance. After reading my story up to this point, you have probably made some assumptions. Perhaps you're – despite my best efforts – feeling a bit of sympathy for me. After all, orphans usually make very sympathetic heroes.

Perhaps you think that my habit of using sarcasm is simply a method of hiding my insecurity. Perhaps you've decided that I wasn't a cruel boy, just a very confused one. Perhaps you've decided, despite my feigned indifference, I didn't *like* breaking things.

Obviously, you are a person of very poor judgment. I would ask you to kindly refrain from drawing conclusions that I don't explicitly tell you to make. That's a very bad habit, and it makes authors grumpy.

I was none of those things. I was simply a mean boy who didn't really care whether or not he burned down kitchens. And that mean boy was the one who stood on the doorstep, watching Grandpa Smedry waving eagerly for him to follow.

Now, *perhaps* I'll admit that I felt just a little bit of longing. A … wishfulness, you might say. Getting a package that claimed to be from my parents had made me remember days long ago – before I realized how foolish I was being – when I had yearned to know my real parents. Days when I had longed to find someone who *had* to love me, if only because they were related to me.

Fortunately, I had outgrown those feelings. My moment of weakness passed quickly, and I slammed the door closed and locked the old man outside. Then I went to the kitchen to get some breakfast.

That, however, is when someone drew a gun on me.

3

I'd like to take this opportunity to point out something important. Should a strange old man of questionable sanity show up at your door – suggesting that he is your grandfather and that you should accompany him upon some quest of mystical import – you should flatly refuse him.

Don't take his candy either.

Unfortunately, as you will soon see, I was quickly forced to break this rule. Please don't hold it against me. It was done under duress. I'm really not used to being shot at.

I walked tiredly into the kitchen – which still smelled of smoke – hoping that the strange old man wouldn't take to pounding on the door. I didn't really want to call the police on him – not only would I likely break the telephone in the process (I'm particularly bad with phones) but I really didn't want the old loon carted away in a police car. That would have been—

'Alcatraz Smedry?' a voice suddenly asked.

I jumped, turning from the half-burned cupboard, a box of cornflakes in my hand. A man stood in the doorway behind me, wearing slacks and a button-down shirt. I frowned, realizing that I recognized the symbol on the man's shirt pocket and standard-issue attaché case. He was a foster care caseworker – *this* was the man that Ms. Fletcher had sent to pick me up from the house. I realized that when I'd originally gone chasing the old man up to my room, I'd left the front door open. The caseworker must have come in looking for me while I was upstairs chatting with the lunatic.

'Hi,' I said, putting down the box. 'I'll be ready in a bit – let me have breakfast first.'

'You're him, then?' the caseworker asked, adjusting his horn-rimmed glasses. 'The Smedry kid?'

I nodded.

'Good,' the man said, then pulled a gun out of his attaché case and raised it toward me. It had a silencer on the barrel.

I froze, shocked. (And don't try to claim that you did anything different the first time a government bureaucrat pulled a gun on you.)

Fortunately, I eventually found my tongue. 'Wait!' I said, raising my hands. 'What are you doing?'

'Thanks for the sands, kid,' the man said, and moved as if to pull the trigger.

At that moment something massive crashed through the wall of my house – something that looked a lot like the front end of an old Model-T Ford. I cried out, dodging to the side, and the caseworker stumbled to the ground in the chaos.

The man who called himself Grandpa Smedry sat happily in the driver's seat. A chunk of smoke-damaged ceiling fell down onto the hood of the car, throwing up a puff of white dust. The old man poked his head out the window.

'Lad,' he said, 'might I point out that you have two choices right now? You can get in the car with me, or you can stay here with the man holding a gun.'

I stood, dazed.

'You really don't have much time to decide,' Grandpa Smedry said, leaning toward me, speaking in a kind of half whisper, as if he were sharing some kind of great secret.

Now, I'd like to pause here and note that Grandpa Smedry was lying to me. I didn't have only two choices at that point – I had quite a few more than that. True, I could have chosen to stay in the room and get shot. I also could have chosen to get in the car. However, there were lots of other things I could have done. For instance, I could have run around the house flapping my arms and pretending that I was a penguin. The logical choice to make in this situation would have been to call the police on both of those maniacs.

Unfortunately, I didn't think of penguins or police and instead did as Grandpa Smedry said, scrambling over and getting into the car.

As I stated at the beginning of the chapter, I really shouldn't have done this. I was soon to learn the dangers involved in following strange old men on quests. I don't want to give away any more of the story, but let me say that my fate at this point took a sharp turn toward altars, sacrifices, and evil Librarians.

And possibly some sharks.

The car backed out of the house, the tires leaving tracks in the lawn. I sat in the front passenger seat, still stunned, looking at the wreckage of the Sheldons' house. Bits of siding were falling off the outside wall, crushing Roy's prize tulips. This was more damage than I'd ever done to any foster home. This time it wasn't directly my fault, but ... well, that didn't change the fact that the kitchen was no longer just burned but also had quite a large hole in it.

We turned onto the street in front of the house – the car puttering along at a modest speed. The caseworker didn't chase after us, but that didn't stop me from watching anxiously until the house disappeared in the distance.

Someone just tried to kill me, I thought, feeling numb. You may find it hard to believe – considering the number of things I'd broken in my life – but this was the first time someone had actually tried to shoot me. It was an unsettling feeling. A little like the way you feel when you have the flu, actually.

Maybe there's a connection.

'Well, that was exciting!' Grandpa Smedry said.

I was still staring out the window. The street passed outside, a suburban neighborhood distinctive only in that it looked pretty much like every other one in the nation. Calm two-story houses. Green lawns. Oak trees, shrubs, flower beds, all carefully maintained.

'He tried to kill me,' I whispered.

Grandpa Smedry snorted. 'Not very well. You'll understand eventually, lad, but pulling a gun on a Smedry isn't exactly the smartest thing a man can do. But that's behind us. Now we have to decide what to do next.'

'Next?'

'Of course. We can't just let them have those sands!' Grandpa Smedry raised a hand and pointed at me. 'Don't you understand, lad? It's not just your life that's in danger here. This is the fate of an entire *world* we're juggling! The Free Kingdoms are already losing their war against the Librarians. With a tool like the Sands of Rashid, the Librarians will have just the edge they need to win. If we don't get the sands back before they're smelted – which will only take a few hours – it could lead to the overthrow of the Free Kingdoms themselves! We are civilization's only hope.'

'I ... see,' I said.

'I don't think you do, lad. The Lenses smelted from that sand will contain the most powerful Oculatory Distortions either land has ever seen. Gathering those sands was your father's life's work. I can't believe you let the Librarians steal them. I'll be honest, lad – I had higher hopes for you. I really expected better. If only I hadn't come so late ...'

I sat quietly, looking out the windshield. Now, it's time you understood something about me. Despite what the stories like to say about my honor and my foresight, the truth is that I possess neither trait in large amounts. One trait I've *always* possessed, however, is rashness. Some call it irresponsibility; others call it spontaneity. Either way, I could rightly be called a somewhat reckless boy, not always prone to carefully considering the consequences of my actions.

In this case, of course, there was something more behind the decision I made. I had seen some very odd things that day. It occurred to me that if something as crazy as a gunman showing up in my house could happen, perhaps it could be true that this old man was my grandfather.

Someone had tried to kill me. My house was in a shambles. I was sitting in a hundred-year-old car with a madman. *What the heck,* I thought. *This might be fun.*

I turned, focusing on the man who claimed to be my grandfather. 'I ... didn't *let* them steal the sand,' I found myself saying.

Grandpa Smedry turned to me.

'Or, well, I *did*,' I said, 'but I let them take the sand on purpose, of course. I wanted to follow them and see what they tried to do with it. After all, how else are we going to uncover their dastardly schemes?'

Grandpa Smedry paused, then he smiled. His eyes twinkled knowingly, and I saw for the first time a hint of wisdom in the old man. Grandpa Smedry didn't seem to believe what I had said, but he reached over anyway, clapping me on the arm. 'Now *that's* talking like a Smedry!'

'Now,' I said, holding up a finger. 'I want to make something very clear. I do not believe a word of what you have told me up to this point.'

'Understood,' Grandpa Smedry said.

'I'm only going with you because someone just tried to kill me. You see, I am a somewhat reckless boy and am not always prone to carefully considering the consequences of my actions.'

'A Smedry trait for certain,' Grandpa Smedry noted.

'In fact,' I said, 'I think that you are a loon and likely not even my grandfather at all.'

'Very well, then,' Grandpa Smedry said, smiling.

I paused as the old car turned a corner, moving with a very smooth speed. We were leaving the neighborhood behind, turning onto a commercial street. We began to pass convenience stores, service stations, and the occasional fast-food restaurant.

It was at that point that I realized Grandpa Smedry had taken his hands off the wheel sometime during the conversation, and now sat with his hands in his lap, smiling happily. I jumped in surprise.

'Grandpa!' I yelped. 'The steering wheel!'

'Drastic Drakes!' Grandpa Smedry exclaimed. 'I nearly forgot!' He grabbed the steering wheel as the car turned another corner. Grandpa Smedry proceeded to turn the wheel back and forth, seeming in random directions, as a child might play with a toy steering wheel. The car didn't respond to his motions but moved smoothly along the street, picking up speed.

'Good eye, lad!' Grandpa Smedry said. 'We always have to keep up appearances, eh?'

'Um … yes,' I said. 'Is the car driving itself, then?'

'Of course. What good would it be if it didn't? Why, you'd have to concentrate so much that it wouldn't be worth the effort. Might as well walk, I say!'

Right, I thought.

Those of you from the Free Kingdoms might be familiar with silimatic engines and can – perhaps – determine how they could be used to mimic a car. Of course, if you're from the Free Kingdoms, you probably have only a vague idea what a car is in the first place, since you're used to much larger vehicles. (It's kind of a like a silimatic crawler with wheels instead of legs, though people treat them more like horses. Only, unlike horses, they aren't alive – and when they poop, environmentalists get mad.)

'So,' I asked, 'where are we going?'

'There's only one place the Librarians would have taken an artifact as powerful as the Sands of Rashid,' Grand Smedry said. 'Their local base of operations.'

'That would be … the library.'

'Where else? The downtown library, to be exact. We'll have to be very careful infiltrating that place.'

I cocked my head. 'I've been there before. Last I checked, it wasn't too hard to get in.'

'We don't have to just get in,' Grand Smedry said. 'We have to *infiltrate*.'

'And the difference is …?'

'One requires far more sneaking.' Grandpa Smedry seemed quite delighted by the prospect.

'Ah,' I said. 'Right, then. Are we going to need any … I don't know, special equipment for this? Or, perhaps, some more help?'

'Ah. A very wise idea, lad,' Grandpa Smedry said.

And the car suddenly jerked, turning onto a larger street. Cars passed on either side, whizzing off to their separate destinations, Grandpa Smedry's little black automobile puttering along happily in the center lane. Grandpa gave the wheel a few good twists, and we rode in silence.

I kept glancing at the steering wheel, trying to sort out exactly what mechanism was controlling the vehicle. In my world, vehicles don't drive themselves, and men like Grandpa Smedry are generally kept in small padded rooms with lots of crayons.

Eventually (partially to keep myself from going mad from frustration) I decided to try conversation again. 'So,' I said, 'why do you think that man tried to kill me?'

'Because the Librarians got what they wanted from you, lad,' Grandpa Smedry said. 'They have the sands, which we all knew would make their way to you eventually. Now that they have your inheritance, you're no longer an asset to them. In fact, you're a threat! They were right to be afraid of your Talent.'

'My Talent?'

'Breaking things. All Smedrys have a Talent, my boy. It's part of our lineage.'

'So ... you have one of these Talent things?' I asked.

'Of course I do, lad!' Grandpa Smedry said. 'I'm a Smedry, after all.'

'What is it?'

Grandpa smiled modestly. 'Well, I don't like to brag, but it's quite a powerful Talent indeed.'

I raised a skeptical eyebrow.

'You see,' Grandpa Smedry said, 'I have the ability to arrive late to things.'

'Ah,' I said. 'Of course.'

'I know, I know. I don't deserve such power, but I try to make good use of it.'

'You are completely nuts, you know.' It's always best to be blunt with people.

'Thank you!' Grandpa Smedry said as the car began to slow. The vehicle pulled up to the pumps at a small gas station. I didn't recognize the brand – the sign hanging above the ridiculously high prices simply depicted the image of an upside-down teddy bear.

Our doors swung open on their own. Grandpa hopped out of

his seat and rushed over to meet the station attendant, who was approaching to fill up the tank.

I frowned, still sitting in the car. The attendant was dressed in a pair of dirty overalls and no shirt. He was chewing on the end of a piece of straw, as one might see a farmer doing in old Hushlander movies, and he had on a large straw hat.

Grandpa Smedry approached the man with an exaggerated look of nonchalance. 'Hello, good sir,' Grandpa Smedry said, glancing around. 'I'd like a Philip, please.'

'Of course, good sir,' the attendant said, tipping his hat and accepting a couple of bills from Grandpa Smedry. The attendant approached the car, nodding to me, then took out one of the gasoline hoses and held it up against the side of the car, whistling pleasantly to himself.

'Come, Alcatraz!' Grandpa Smedry said, walking up to the gas station's store. 'There isn't time!'

Finally, I just shook my head and climbed out of the car. Grandpa Smedry went inside, the screen door slamming behind him. I walked up, pulled open the screen door – threw the door handle over my shoulder as it broke off – then stepped inside after Grandpa Smedry.

Another attendant – also with straw in his mouth and a large hat on his head – stood leaning against the counter. The small 'store' consisted of a single stand of snacks and a wall-sized cooler. The cooler was stocked completely with cans of motor oil, though a sign said ENJOY A COOL REFRESHING DRINK!

'Okay,' I said, 'where exactly are you people finding straw to chew on in the middle of the city? It can't be all that easy to get.'

'Quickly, now. Quickly!' Grandpa Smedry gestured frantically from the back of the store. Glancing to either side, he said in a louder voice, 'I think I'll have a cool refreshing drink!' Then he pulled open the cooler door.

I froze in place.

Now, it's very important to me that you understand that I am not stupid. It's perfectly all right if you end this book convinced that I'm not the hero that some reports claim me to be. However,

I'd rather not everyone I meet presume me to be slow-witted. If that were the case, half of them would likely try and sell me insurance.

The truth is, however, that even clever people can be taken by surprise so soundly that they are at a loss for words. Or, at least, at a loss for words that make sense.

'Gak!' I said.

You see. Now, before you judge me, place yourself in my position. Let's say that you had watched a crazy old man open up a cooler full of oilcans. You would have undoubtedly expected to see ... well, a cooler full of oilcans on the other side.

You would *not* expect to see a room with a large hearth at the center, blazing with a cheery reddish-orange fire. You would not expect to see two men in full armor standing guard on either side of the door. Indeed, you would not expect to see a room – instead of a cooler full of oilcans – at all.

Perhaps you would have said 'Gak' too.

'Gak!' I repeated.

'Would you stop that, boy?' Grandpa Smedry said. 'There are absolutely *no* Gaks here. Why do you think we keep so much straw around? Now, come on!' He stepped through the doorway into the room beyond.

I approached slowly, then glanced at the other side of the open glass door – and saw oilcans cooling in their wall racks. I turned, looking through the doorway. It seemed as if I could see much more than I should have been able to. The two knights standing on either side of such a small doorway should have left no room to walk through, yet Grandpa Smedry had passed easily.

I reached out, rapping lightly on one of the knight's breastplates.

'Please don't do that,' a voice said from behind the faceplate.

'Oh,' I said. 'Um, sorry.' Still frowning to myself, I stepped into the room.

It was a large chamber. Far larger, I decided than could have possibly fit in the store. I could now see a rug set with thronelike chairs arranged to face the hearth in a homey manner (if your home is a medieval castle …). To my left, there was a long, broad table, also set with chairs.

'Sing!' Grandpa Smedry yelled, his voice echoing down a hallway to the right. 'Sing!'

If he breaks into song, I think I might have to strangle myself … I thought, cringing.

'Lord Smedry?' a voice called from down the hallway, and a huge figure rushed into sight.

If you've never seen a large Mokian man in sunglasses, a tunic, and tights before—

Okay. I'm going to assume that you've never seen a large Mokian man in sunglasses, a tunic, and tights. I certainly hadn't.

The man – apparently named Sing – was a good six and a half feet tall, and had dark hair and dark skin. He looked like he could be from Hawaii, or maybe Samoa or Tonga. He had the mass and girth of a linebacker and would have fit right in on the football field. Or, at least, he would have fit right in if he'd been wearing a football uniform, rather than a tunic – a type of garment that I still think looks silly. Bastille has pictures of me wearing one. If you ask her, she'll probably show them to you gleefully.

Of course, if you do that, I'll probably have to hunt you down and kill you. Or dress you in a tunic and take pictures of you. I'm still not sure which is worse.

'Sing,' Grandpa Smedry said. 'We need to do a full library infiltration. *Now.*'

'A library infiltration?' Sing said excitedly.

'Yes, yes,' Grandpa Smedry said hurriedly. 'Go get your cousin, and both of you get into your disguises. I need to gather my Lenses.'

Sing rushed back the way he had come. Grandpa Smedry walked over to the wall on the other side of the hearth. Not sure what else to do, I followed, watching as Grandpa Smedry knelt beside what appeared to be a large box made entirely of black glass. Grandpa Smedry put his hand on it, closed his eyes, and the front of the box suddenly shattered.

I jumped back, but Grandpa Smedry ignored the broken shards

of black glass. He reached into the chest and pulled out a tray wrapped in red velvet. He set this on top of the box, unwrapping the cloth and revealing a small book and about a dozen pairs of spectacles, each with a slightly different tint of glass.

Grandpa Smedry pulled open the front of his tuxedo jacket, then began to slip the spectacles into little pouches sewn into the lining of the garment. They hung like the watches on the inside of an illegal street peddler's coat.

'Something very strange is going on, isn't it?' I finally asked.

'Yes, lad,' Grandpa Smedry said, still arranging the spectacles.

'We're really going to go sneak into a library?'

Grandpa Smedry nodded.

'Only, it's not really a library. But someplace more dangerous.'

'Oh, it's really a library,' Grandpa Smedry said. 'What you haven't realized before is that *all* libraries are far more dangerous that you've always assumed.'

'And we're going to break into this one,' I repeated. 'A place filled with people who want to kill me.'

'Most likely,' Grandpa Smedry said. 'But what else can we do? We either infiltrate, or we let them make those sands into Lenses.'

This isn't a joke, I began to realize. *This man isn't actually crazy. Or, at least, the craziness includes much more than just him.* I stood there for a moment, feeling overwhelmed, thinking about what I had seen.

'Well, all right, then,' I finally said.

Now, you Hushlanders may think that I took all of these strange experiences quite well. After all, it isn't every day that you get threatened with a gun, then discover a medieval dining room hiding inside the beverage cooler at a local gas station. However, maybe if *you'd* grown up with the magical ability to break almost anything you touched, then you would have been just as quick to accept unusual circumstances.

'Here, lad,' Grandpa Smedry said, standing and picking up the final pair of spectacles. They were reddish tinted, like the pair Grandpa Smedry was currently wearing. 'These are yours. I've been saving them for you.'

I paused. 'I don't need glasses.'

'You're an Oculator, lad,' Grandpa Smedry said. 'You'll *always* need glasses.'

'Can't I wear sunglasses, like Sing?'

Grandpa Smedry chuckled. 'You don't need Warrior's Lenses, lad. You can access abilities far more potent. Here, take these. They're Oculator's Lenses.'

'What are Oculators?' I asked.

'We are, my boy. Put them on.'

I frowned, but took the glasses. I put them on, then glanced around. 'Nothing looks different,' I said, feeling disappointed. 'The room doesn't even look ... redder.'

'Of course not,' Grandpa Smedry said. 'The tints come from the sands they're made of and help us keep the Lenses straight. They're not intended to make things look different.'

'I just ... thought the glasses would do something.'

'They do,' Grandpa Smedry said. 'They show you things that you need to see. It's just subtle, lad. Wear them for a while – let your eyes get used to them.'

'All right ...' I glanced over as Grandpa Smedry knelt to put the tray back inside the broken box. 'What's that book?'

Grandpa Smedry looked up 'Hmmm? This?' He picked up the small book, handing it to me. I opened to the first page. It was filled with scribbles, as if made by a child.

'The Forgotten Language,' Grandpa Smedry said. 'We've been trying to decipher it for centuries – your father worked on that book for a while, before you were born. He thought its secrets might lead him to the Sands of Rashid.'

'This isn't a language,' I said. 'It's just a bunch of scribbles.'

'Well, any language you don't understand would just look like scribbles, lad!'

I flipped through the pages of the book. It was filled with completely random circles, zigzags, loop-dee-loops, and the like. There were no patterns. Some of the pages only had a couple marks on them; others were so black with ink that they looked like a child's rendition of a tornado.

'No,' I said. 'No, I don't think so. A language has to make patterns! There's nothing like that in here.'

'That's the big secret, lad,' Grandpa Smedry said, taking back the book. 'Why do you think nobody, despite centuries of trying, has managed to break the code? The Incarna people – the ones who wrote in this language – held vast secrets. Unfortunately, nobody can read their records, and the Incarna disappeared many centuries ago.'

I wrinkled my brow at the strange comments. Grandpa Smedry stood up, stepping away from the glass box. And, suddenly, the shattered front of the box melted and reformed its glassy surface.

I stepped back in shock. Then I reached up, suspiciously pulling off my glasses. Yet the box still sat pristine, as if it hadn't been broken in the first place.

'Restoring Glass,' Grandpa Smedry said, nodding toward the box. 'Only an Oculator can break it. Once he moves too far away, however, it will reform into its previous shape. Makes for wonderful safes. It's even stronger than Builder's Glass, if used right.'

I slipped my Lenses back on.

'Tell me, lad,' Grandpa Smedry said, laying a hand on my shoulder, 'why did you burn down your foster parents' kitchen?'

I started. That wasn't the question I'd been expecting. 'How did you know about that?'

'Why, I'm an Oculator, of course.'

I just frowned.

'So why?' he asked. 'Why burn it down?'

'It was an accident,' I replied.

'Was it?'

I looked away. *Of course it was an accident,* I thought, feeling a bit of shame. *Why would I do something like that on purpose?*

Grandpa Smedry was studying me. 'You have a Talent for breaking things,' he said. 'Or so you have said. Yet lighting fire to a set of drapes and ruining a kitchen with smoke doesn't seem like a use of that Talent. Particularly if you let the fire burn for a while before putting it out. That's not breaking. That seems more like destroying.'

'I don't destroy,' I said quietly.

'Why, then?' Grandpa Smedry said.

I shrugged. What was he implying? Did he think I *liked* messing things up all the time? Did he think I liked being forced to move every few months? It seemed that every time I came to love someone, they decided that my Talent was just too much to handle.

I felt a stab of loneliness but shoved it down.

'Ah,' Grandpa Smedry said. 'You won't answer, I see. But I can still wonder, can't I? Why would a boy do such damage to the homes of such kind people? It seems like a perversion of his Talent. Yes, indeed ...'

I said nothing. Grandpa Smedry just smiled at me, then straightened his bow tie and checked his wristwatch. 'Garbled Greens! We're late. Sing! Quentin!'

'We're ready, Uncle!' a voice called from down the hallway.

'Ah, good,' Grandpa Smedry said. 'Come, my boy. Let me introduce you to your cousins!'

4

Hushlanders, I'd like to take this opportunity to commend you for reading this book. I realize the difficulty you must have gone through to obtain it – after all, no Librarian is likely to recommend it, considering the secrets it exposes about their kind.

Actually, my experience has been that people generally don't recommend this kind of book at all. It is far too interesting. Perhaps you have had other kinds of books recommended to you. Perhaps, even, you have been given books by friends, parents, or teachers, then told that these books are the type you 'have to read.' Those books are invariably described as 'important' – which, in my experience, pretty much means that they're boring. (Words like *meaningful* and *thoughtful* are other good clues.)

If there is a boy in these kinds of books, he will not go on an adventure to fight against Librarians, paper monsters, and one-eyed Dark Oculators. In fact, the lad will not go on an adventure or fight against anything at all. Instead, his dog will die. Or, in some cases, his mother will die. If it's a *really* meaningful book, both his dog *and* his mother will die. (Apparently, most writers have something against dogs and mothers.)

Neither my mother nor my dog dies in this book. I'm rather tired of those types of stories. In my opinion, such fantastical, unrealistic books – books in which boys live on mountains, families work on farms, or anyone has *anything* to do with the Great Depression – have a tendency to rot the brain. To combat such silliness, I've written the volume you now hold – a solid, true account. Hopefully, it will help anchor you in reality.

So, when people try to give you some book with a shiny round award on the cover, be kind and gracious, but tell them that you don't read 'fantasy,' because you prefer stories that are real. Then come back here and continue your research on the cult of evil Librarians who secretly rule the world.

'This,' Grandpa Smedry proclaimed, pointing to Sing, 'is your cousin Sing Sing Smedry. He's a specialist in ancient weapons.'

Sing nodded modestly. He had exchanged his tunic for what appeared to be a formal kimono – though he still wore his dark sunglasses. The kimono was of a very rich dark blue silk and, though it fit him quite well, there was something … wrong about the entire presentation. More than just the fact that the kimono itself wasn't something a regular person in America wore. Sing's chest parted the front of the silk, and the loose garment hung tied about the waist with a large sash tucked beneath his massive stomach.

'Uh, nice to meet you Sing … Sing,' I said.

'You can just call me Sing,' the large man replied.

'Ask him what his Talent is,' Grandpa whispered.

'Oh,' I said. 'Um, what's your Talent, Sing?'

'I can trip and fall to the ground,' Sing said.

I blinked. *That's* a Talent?'

'It's not as grand as some, I know,' Sing said, 'but it serves me well.'

'And the kimono?' I asked.

'I come from a different kingdom than your grandfather,' Sing said. 'I am from Mokia, while your grandfather and Quentin are from Melerand.'

'Okay,' I said. 'But what difference does that make?'

'It means I have to wear a different disguise from the rest of you,' Sing explained. 'That way, I won't stand out as much. If I look like a foreigner to America, people will ignore me.'

I paused. 'Whatever,' I finally said.

'It makes perfect sense,' Grandpa Smedry said. 'Trust me. We've researched this.' He turned and pointed to the other man. 'Now, this is your cousin Quentin Smedry.' Short and wiry, Quentin wore a sharp tuxedo like that of Grandpa Smedry, complete with a red carnation on the lapel. He had dark brown hair, pale skin, and freckles. Like Sing, he looked to be about thirty years old.

'Well met, young Oculator,' Quentin said from behind his dark sunglasses.

'And what is your Talent?' I dutifully asked.

'I can say things that make absolutely no sense whatsoever.'

'I thought everyone here had that Talent,' I noted.

Nobody laughed. Free Kingdomers never get my jokes.

'He's also really sneaky,' Grandpa Smedry said.

Quentin nodded.

'Great,' I said. 'So, are both of you ... Oculators?'

'Oh, goodness no,' Sing said. 'We're cousins to the Smedry family, not members of the direct line.'

'Didn't you notice the glasses?' Grandpa Smedry asked. 'They're wearing Warrior's Lenses, one of the only kinds of Lenses that a non-Oculator can use.'

'Um, yes,' I said. 'Actually, I did notice the glasses. I ... noticed the tuxedos too. Is there a reason you dress like that? If we go out like this, we'll kind of stand out, right?'

'Maybe the young lord has a point,' Sing said, rubbing his chin.

Lord? I thought. I had no idea what to make of that.

'Should we get Alcatraz a disguise too, Lord Smedry?' Quentin asked my grandfather.

'No, no,' Grandpa Smedry said. 'He isn't supposed to wear a suit at his age. At least, I don't think ...'

'I'm fine,' I said quickly.

The collection of Smedrys nodded.

Now, many of you Hushlanders may be scoffing at the disguises used by the Smedry group. Before you pass judgment on them, realize that they were somewhat out of their element. Imagine if you were suddenly thrust into a different culture, with very little knowledge of its customs or fashions. Would you know the difference between a Rounsfield tunic and a Larkian tunic? Would you be able to distinguish when to wear a batoled and when to wear a carfoo? Would you even know *where* you wrap a Carlflogian wickerstrap? No? Well, that's because I just made all of those items up. But you didn't know that, did you?

Therefore, my point is proven. All things considered, I think the Smedrys did quite well. I've seen other infiltration teams – ones *without* Grandpa Smedry, who is widely held as the Free Kingdoms' foremost expert on American culture and society. The last group that tried an infiltration without him ended up trying to sneak into the Federal Reserve Bank disguised as potted plants.

They got watered.

'Are we ready, then?' Grandpa Smedry said. 'My grandson will be leading this infiltration. Our target is the central downtown library.'

Sing and Quentin glanced at each other, looking a bit surprised. Grandpa had mentioned a library infiltration to Sing, but apparently the *downtown* library was not what he'd expected. It made me wonder, once again, what I was getting myself into.

'I realize this will be a most ambitious mission, gentlemen,' Grandpa Smedry said. 'But we have no choice. Our goal is to recover the legendary Sands of Rashid, which the Librarians have acquired through some very clever scheming and plotting.'

Grandpa Smedry turned, nodding to me. 'The sands belong to my grandson, and so he will be lead Oculator on this mission. Once we breach the initial stacks, we'll split into two groups and search for the sands. Gather as much information as you can, and recover the sands at all costs. Any questions?'

Quentin raised his hand. 'What exactly does this bag of sand *do?*'

Grandpa Smedry wavered. 'We don't actually know,' he admitted. 'Before this, nobody had ever managed to gather enough of them to smelt a Lens. Or, at least, nobody had managed to do it during *our* recorded history. There are vague legends, however. The Lenses of Rashid are supposed to be *very* powerful. They will be a great danger to the people of the Free Kingdoms if they are allowed to fall into Librarian hands.'

The room fell silent. Finally, Sing raised a meaty hand. 'Does this mean I can bring weapons?'

'Of course,' Grandpa Smedry said.

'Can I bring *lots* of weapons?' Sing asked carefully.

'Whatever you deem necessary, Sing,' Grandpa Smedry said.

'You're the specialist. But go quickly! We're going to be late.'

Sing nodded, dashing back down his hallway.

'And you?' Grandpa Smedry asked of Quentin.

'I'm fine,' the short man said. 'But … my lord, don't you think we should tell Bastille what we're doing?'

'Jabbering Jordans, no!' Grandpa Smedry said. 'Absolutely not. I forbid it.'

'She's not going to be happy …' Quentin said.

'Nonsense,' Grandpa Smedry said. 'She enjoys being ignored – it gives her an excuse to be grumpy. Now, since we have to wait for Sing to get his weapons, I'm going to go get something to eat. I was clever enough to pack some lunches for myself and the lad. Coming, Alcatraz?'

I shrugged, and we made our way out though the cooler – passing the armored knights – and walked back into the shop. Grandpa Smedry nodded to the two hillbilly attendants, then walked out toward his car, apparently going to grab the briefcases stuffed with food.

I didn't follow him. At that point, I still felt a little overwhelmed by what was happening to me. Part of me couldn't believe what I had seen, so I decided to see if I could figure out how they were hiding that huge room inside. I turned, wandering around to the back of the small service station, then I carefully paced off the lengths of its walls.

The building was a rectangle, ten paces long on two sides, eighteen paces long on the other two. Yet the room inside had been far larger. A *basement?* I wondered. (Yes, I realize that it took me quite some time to accept that the place was magical. You Free Kingdomers really have no idea what it's like to live in Librarian-controlled areas. So, stop judging me and just keep reading.)

I kept at it, trying to figure out some logical explanation. I squatted down on the hot, tar-stained concrete, trying to find a slope in the ground. I stood up, eyeing the back of the building, which was set with a small window. I grabbed a broken chair from a nearby Dumpster, then climbed up to peek in the window.

I couldn't see anything through the dark glass. I pressed my face against it – bumping my glasses against the window – and shaded the sunlight with my hand, but I still couldn't see inside.

I leaned back, sighing. But ... then it seemed as if I *could* see something. Not through the window, but alongside it. The edges of the window seemed to fuzz just a little bit, and I got the distinct, *strange* impression that I could see through the wall's siding.

I pulled off my glasses. The illusion disappeared, and the wall looked perfectly normal. I put them back on, and nothing really changed. Yet, as I stared at the wall, I felt the odd sense again. As if I could just *barely* see something. I cocked my head, teetering on the broken chair. Finally, I reached up a hand, laying it against the white siding.

Then I broke it.

I didn't really do much. I didn't have to twist, pull, or yank. I just rested my hand against the wall for a moment, and one of the siding planks popped free and toppled to the ground. Through the broken section, I could see the true wall of the building.

Glass. The entire wall was made of a deep lavender glass.

I saw through the siding, I thought. *Was it my glasses that let me do that?*

A footstep sounded on the gravel behind me.

I jumped, almost slipping off the chair. And there he was: the man from my house, the caseworker – or whatever he was – with the suit and the gun. I wobbled, feeling terror rise again. Of course he would chase us. Of course he would find us. What was I thinking? Why hadn't I just called the police?

'Lad?' Grandpa Smedry's voice called. He appeared around the corner, holding an open briefcase smeared with ketchup. 'Your sand-burger is ready. Aren't you hungry?'

The man with the gun spun around, weapon still raised. 'Don't move!' he yelled nervously. 'Stay right there!'

'Hmm?' Grandpa Smedry asked, still walking.

'*Grandpa!*' I screamed as the caseworker pulled the trigger.

The gun went off.

There was a loud crack, and a chunk of siding blew off the

building right in front of Grandpa Smedry. The old man continued to walk along, smiling to himself, looking completely relaxed.

The caseworker fired again, then again. Both times, the bullets
hit the wall right in front of Grandpa Smedry.

Now, a true hero would have tackled the man who was shooting his grandfather, or done something else equally heroic. I am
not a true hero. I stood frozen with shock.

'Here now,' Grandpa Smedry said. 'What's going on?'

Looking desperate, the caseworker pointed his gun back at
me and pulled the trigger. The consequences, of course, were
immediate.

The clip dropped out of the bottom of the gun.

The top of the weapon fell off.

The gun's trigger popped free, propelled by a broken spring.

The screws fell out of the gun's sides, dropping to the pavement.

The caseworker widened his eyes in disbelief, watching as the
last part of the handle fell to pieces in his hand. In a final moment
of indignity, the dying gun belched up a bit of metal – an unfired
bullet – which spun in the air a few times before clicking down
to the ground.

The man stared at the pieces of his weapon.

Grandpa Smedry paused beside me. 'I think you broke it,' he
whispered to me.

The caseworker turned and scrambled away. Grandpa Smedry
watched him go, a sly smile on his lips.

'What did you do?' I asked.

'Me?' Grandpa Smedry said. 'No, *you're* the one who did that! At
a distance, even! I've rarely seen a Talent work with such power.
Though it's a shame to ruin a good antique weapon like that.'

'I ...' I looked at the gun pieces, my heart thumping. 'It couldn't
have been me. I've never done anything like that before.'

'Have you never been threatened by a weapon before today?'
Grandpa Smedry asked.

'Well, no.'

Grandpa Smedry nodded. 'Panic instinct. Your Talent protects you – even at a distance – when threatened. It's a good thing that he attacked with such a primitive weapon; Talents are much more powerful against them. Honestly, you'd think the Librarians would know not to send someone with a *gun* against a Smedry of the true line. They obviously underestimate you.'

'What am I doing here?' I whispered. 'They're going to kill me.'

'Nonsense, lad,' Grandpa Smedry said. 'You're a Smedry. We're made of tougher stuff than the Librarians give us credit for. Ruling the Hushlands for so long has made them sloppy.'

I stood quietly. Then I looked up. 'We're really going to go *into* the library? The place where these guys come from? Isn't that kind of ... stupid?'

'Yes,' Grandpa Smedry said, speaking – for once – with a quiet solemnity. 'You can stay back, if you wish. I know how this must all seem to you. Overwhelming. Terrifying. Strange. But you must understand me when I say our task is *vital*. We've made a terrible mistake – *I've* made a terrible mistake – by letting those sands get into the wrong hands. I'm going to make it right, before thousands upon thousands of people suffer.'

'But ... isn't there anyone else who could do this?'

Grandpa Smedry shook his head. 'Those sands will be forged into Lenses before the day is out. Our only chance – the world's only chance – is to get them before that happens.'

I nodded slowly. 'Then I'm going,' I said. 'You can't leave me behind.'

'Wouldn't dream of it,' Grandpa Smedry said. Then he glanced up at the wall where I had broken it. 'You do that?'

I nodded again.

'Nagging Nixes! You really *do* have quite the skill for breaking things,' Grandpa Smedry said. 'Must have been hard for you when you were younger.'

I shrugged.

'What kinds of things can you break?' Grandpa Smedry asked.

'All kinds of things,' I said. 'Doors, electronics, tables. Once I broke a chicken.'

'A *chicken*?'

I nodded. 'It was on a field trip. I got ... kind of frustrated, and I picked up a chicken. When I put it down, it immediately lost all of its feathers, and from then on refused to eat anything but cat food.'

'Breaking living things ...' Grandpa Smedry mumbled to himself. 'Extraordinary. Untamed, yes, but extraordinary nonetheless ...'

I pointed at the building, hoping to change the subject. 'It's a glass box.'

'Yes,' Grandpa Smedry said. 'Expander's Glass – if you make space inside of it, you can push out the walls inside without pushing out the walls on the outside.'

'That's impossible. It disobeys the laws of physics.' (We Hushlanders pay a *lot* of attention to physics.)

'That's just Librarian talk,' Grandpa Smedry said. 'You've got a lot to learn, lad. Come on, we need to get moving. We're late!'

I allowed myself to be led away, past the three bullet holes in the siding. 'They missed,' I said, almost to myself. 'It's a good thing that man had such bad aim.'

Grandpa Smedry laughed. 'Bad aim! He didn't have a chance of hitting me. I arrived late to every shot. Your Talent can do some great things, my boy, but it's not the only powerful ability around! I've been arriving late to my own death since before you were born. In fact, once I was so late to an appointment that I got there before I left!'

I paused, trying to work through that last statement, but Grandpa Smedry waved me on. We rounded the building. Quentin and Sing stood with one of the station attendants, talking quietly. Sing had a good dozen different guns strapped to his body. He wore two holsters on each leg, one holster around each upper arm, and one underneath each arm. These were complemented by a couple of uzis tucked into his sash, and what looked like a shotgun tied to his back in a kind of swordlike fashion.

'Oh, dear,' Grandpa Smedry said. 'He's not supposed to show them off like that, is he?'

'Um, no,' I said.

Could we peace bond them, you think?'

'I don't know what that is,' I said, 'but I doubt it would help.' Still, after getting shot at, the sight of Sing with all those weapons did make me feel a little more comfortable. Until I realized that, if we were going to be bringing an arsenal like that, what would our *enemies* have?

'Ah, well,' Grandpa Smedry said. 'I already told him he could bring them. We can hide them in a bag or something. They're really not that dangerous – it's not like he's got a sword or something. Anyway, we need to get moving, we're—'

'—late,' I said. 'Yes, I know.'

'Good, then let's—'

At this point, you should be very annoyed with people getting interrupted midsentence. I assure you that I feel the same way. In fact, I think—

A silver sports car screeched into the parking lot. Its windows were tinted the deepest black – even the windshield – and it had a sleek, ominous design, the make and model of which I couldn't quite place. It was like every spy car I'd ever seen melded into one.

The door burst open, and a girl – about my age – jumped out. Her hair was silvery, matching the car's paint, and she wore a fashionable black skirt and silver jacket, and carried a black handbag.

She appeared to be very, *very* angry.

'Smedry!' she snapped, swatting her purse at Sing as he moved too slowly to get out of her way.

'What?' I asked, jumping back slightly.

'Not you, lad,' Grandpa Smedry said with a sigh. 'She means me.'

'What?' I asked. 'What did you do?'

'Nothing much,' Grandpa Smedry said. 'I just kind of left her behind. That's Bastille, lad. She's our team's knight.'

If I'd had any sense, I'd have run away right then.

5

At this point, perhaps you Hushlanders are beginning to doubt the truth of this narrative. You have seen several odd and inexplicable things happen. (Though, just as a warning, the story so far has actually been quite tame. Just wait until we get to the part with the talking dinosaurs.) Some readers might even think that I'm just making this story up. You might think that everything in this book is dreamy silliness.

Nothing could be further from the truth.

This book is serious. Terribly serious. Your skepticism results from a lifetime of training in the Librarians' school system, where you were taught all kinds of lies. Indeed, you'd probably never even heard of the Smedrys, despite the fact that they are the most famous family of Oculators in the entire world. In most parts of the Free Kingdoms, being a Smedry is considered equivalent to being nobility.

(If you wish to perform a fun test, next time you are in history class, ask your teacher about the Smedrys. If your teacher is a Librarian spy, he or she will get red-faced and give you a detention. If, on the other hand, your teacher is innocent, he or she will simply be confused, then likely give you a detention.)

Remember, despite the fact that this book is being sold as a 'fantasy' novel, you must take all of the things it says extremely seriously, as they are quite important, are in no way silly, and always make sense.

Rutabaga.

'*That* is a knight?' I asked, pointed at the silver-haired girl.

'Unfortunately,' Grandpa Smedry said.

'But she's a girl!' I said.

'Yes,' Grandpa Smedry said. 'and a very dangerous one, I might add. She was sent to protect me.'

'Sent?' I said. 'Who sent her, then?' *And is she supposed to protect you from Librarians, or from yourself?*

Bastille stalked right up to Grandpa Smedry, placed her hands on her hips, and glared at him. 'I'd stab you with something if I didn't know that you'd arrive too late to get hurt.'

'Bastille, my dear,' Grandpa Smedry said. 'How pleasant. Of course I didn't *mean* to leave you behind. You see, I was running late, and I needed to go—'

Bastille held up a hand to silence Grandpa, then glared at me. 'Who is he?'

'My grandson,' Grandpa Smedry said. 'Alcatraz.'

'*Another* Smedry?' she asked. 'I have to try to protect *four* of you now?'

'Bastille, dear,' Grandpa Smedry said. 'No need to get upset. He won't be much trouble. Will you, Alcatraz?'

'Uh ... no,' I said. That was, of course, an absolute lie. But would you have said anything different?

Bastille narrowed her eyes. 'Somehow I doubt that. What are you planning, old man?'

'Nothing to worry about,' Grandpa Smedry said. 'Just a little infiltration.'

'Of?' Bastille asked.

'The downtown library,' Grandpa Smedry said, then smiled innocently.

'*What?*' Bastille said. 'Honestly, can't I even leave you alone for half a day? Shattering Glass! What would make you want to infiltrate *that* place?'

'They have the Sands of Rashid,' Grandpa Smedry said.

'So? We've got plenty of sand.'

'These sands are very important,' Grandpa Smedry said. 'It's an Oculator sort of thing.'

Bastille's expression darkened a bit at that comment. She threw her hands into the air. 'Whatever,' she said. 'I assume we're late.'

'Very,' Grandpa Smedry said.

'Fine.' She stabbed a finger at me; I barely suppressed a tense jump. 'You, get in my car. You can fill me in on the mission. We'll meet you there, old man.'

'Lovely,' Grandpa Smedry said, looking relieved.

'I—' I began.

'Must I remind you, Alcatraz,' Grandpa Smedry said, 'that you shouldn't swear? Now, we're late! Get moving!'

I paused. 'Swear?' I said. However, my confusion gave Grandpa Smedry a perfect chance to escape, and I caught sight of the man's eyes twinkling as he jumped into his car, Quentin and Sing joining him.

'For an old man who arrives late to everything,' I noted, 'he certainly is spry.'

'Come on, Smedry!' Bastille growled, climbing back into her sleek car.

I sighed, then rounded the vehicle and pulled open the passenger side door. I tossed the handle to the side as it broke off, then climbed in. Bastille rapped her knuckles on the dashboard, and the car started. Then she reached for the gear shift, throwing it into reverse.

'Uh, doesn't the car drive itself?' I asked.

'Sometimes,' Bastille said. 'It can do both – it's a hybrid. We're trying to get closer to things that look like real Hushlander vehicles.'

With that, the car burst into motion.

Now, I had been very frightened on several different occasions in my life. The most frightening of these involved an elevator and a mime. Perhaps the second most frightening involved a caseworker and a gun.

Bastille's driving, however, quickly threatened to become number three.

'Aren't you supposed to be some sort of bodyguard?' I asked, furiously working to find a seat belt. There didn't appear to be one.

'Yeah,' Bastille said. 'So?'

'So, shouldn't you avoid *killing me in a car wreck*?'

Bastille frowned, spinning the wheel and taking a corner at a ridiculous speed. 'I don't know what you're talking about.'

I sighed, settling into my seat, telling myself that the car probably had some sort of mystical device to protect its occupants. (I was wrong, of course. Both Oculator powers and silimatic technology have to do with glass, and I seriously doubt that an air bag made of – or filled with – glass would be all that effective. Amusing, perhaps, but not effective.)

'Hey,' I said. 'How old are you?'

'Thirteen,' Bastille replied.

'Should you be driving, then?' I asked.

'I don't see why not.'

'You're too young,' I said.

'Says who?'

'Says the law.'

I could see Bastille narrow her eyes, and her hands gripped the wheel even tighter. 'Maybe *Librarian* law,' she muttered.

This, I thought, *is probably not a topic to pursue further.* 'So,' I said, trying something different. 'What is your Talent?'

Bastille gritted her teeth, glaring out through the windshield.

'Well?' I asked.

'You don't have to rub it in, Smedry.'

Great. 'You ... don't have a Talent, then?'

'Of course not,' she said. 'I'm a Crystin.'

'A what?' I asked.

Bastille turned – an action that made me rather uncomfortable, as I thought she should have kept watching the road – and gave me the kind of look that implied that I had just said something very, very stupid. (And, indeed, I had said something very stupid. Fortunately, I made up for it by doing something rather clever – as you will see shortly.)

Bastille turned her eyes back on the road just in time to avoid running over a man dressed like a large slice of pizza. 'So you're really *him*, then? The one old Smedry keeps talking about?'

This intrigued me. 'He's mentioned me to you?'

Bastille nodded. 'Twice a year or so we have to come back to this area and see where you've moved. Old Smedry always manages to lose me before he actually gets to your house – he claims I'll stand out or something. Tell me, did you really knock down one of your foster parents' houses?'

I shifted uncomfortably. 'That rumor is exaggerated,' I said. 'It was just a storage shed.'

Bastille nodded, eyes narrowing, as if for some reason she had a grudge against sheds to go along with her apparent psychopathic dislike of Librarians.

'So ...' I said slowly. 'How does a thirteen-year-old girl become a knight anyway?'

'What's that supposed to mean?' Bastille asked, taking a screeching corner.

And here's where I proved my cleverness: I remained silent.

Bastille seemed to relax a bit. 'Look,' she said. 'I'm sorry. I'm not very good with people. They annoy me. That's probably why I ended up in a job that lets me beat them up.'

Is that supposed to be comforting? I wondered.

'Plus,' she said, 'you're a Smedry – and Smedrys are trouble. They're reckless, and they don't like to think about the consequences of their actions. That means trouble for me. See, *my* job is to keep you alive. It's like ... sometimes you Smedrys try to get yourselves killed just so I'll get in trouble.'

'I'll try my best to avoid something like that,' I said honestly. Though her comment did spark a thought in my head. Now that I had begun to accept the things happening around me, I was actually beginning to think of Grandpa Smedry as – well – my grandfather. And that meant ... *My parents,* I thought. *They might actually be involved in this. They might actually have sent me that bag of sands.*

They would have been Smedrys too, of course. So, were they some of the ones that 'got themselves killed,' as Bastille so nicely put it? Or, like all these other relatives I was suddenly learning I had, were my parents still around somewhere?

That was a depressing thought. A lot of us foster children don't like to consider ourselves orphans. It's an outdated term, in my opinion. It brings to mind images of scrawny, dirty-faced thieves living on the street and getting meals from good-hearted nuns. I wasn't an orphan – I had lots of parents. I just never stayed with any of them all that long.

I'd rarely bothered to consider my real parents, since Ms. Fletcher had never been willing to answer questions about them. Somehow, I found the prospect of their survival to be even more depressing than the thought of them being dead.

Why did you burn down your foster parents' kitchen, lad? Grandpa Smedry had asked. I quickly turned away from that line of thinking, focusing again on Bastille.

She was shaking her head, still muttering about the Smedrys who get themselves into trouble. 'Your grandfather,' she said, 'he's the worst. Normal people avoid Inner Libraria. The Librarians have enough minions in our own kingdoms to be plenty threatening. But Leavenworth Smedry? Fighting them isn't *nearly* dangerous enough for him. He has to live as a spy inside of the shattering Hushlands themselves! And, of course, he drags me with him.

'Now he wants to infiltrate a *library*. And not just any library but the regional headquarters – the biggest library in three states.' She paused, glancing at me. 'You think I have good reason to be annoyed?'

'Definitely,' I said, again proving my cleverness.

'That's what I thought,' Bastille said. Then she slammed on the brakes.

I smashed against the dash, nearly losing my glasses. I groaned, sitting back. 'What?' I asked, holding my head.

'What what?' Bastille said, pushing open the door. 'We're here.'

'Oh.' I opened my door, dropping the inside handle to the street as it came off in my hand. (This kind of thing becomes second nature to you after you break off your first hundred or so door handles.)

Bastille had parked on the side of the street, directly across from the downtown library – a wide, single-story building set on a street corner. The area around us was familiar to me. The downtown wasn't extremely huge – not like that of a city like Chicago or L.A. – but it did have a smattering of large office buildings and hotels. These towered behind us; we were only a few blocks away from the city center.

Bastille rapped the hood of her car. 'Go find a place to park,' she told it. It immediately started up, then backed away.

I raised an eyebrow. 'Handy, that,' I noted. Like Grandpa Smedry's car, this one had no visible gas cap. *I wonder what powers it.*

The answer to that, of course, was sand. Silimatic sand, to be precise – sometimes called steamsand. But I really don't have room to go into that now – even if its discovery was what eventually led to the break between silimatic technology and regular Hushlander technology. And that was kind of the foundation for the Librarians breaking off of the Free Kingdoms and creating the Hushlands.

Kind of.

'Old Smedry won't be here for a few more minutes,' Bastille said, standing with her handbag over her shoulder. 'He'll be late. How does the library look?'

'Umm ... like a library?' I said.

'Funny, Smedry,' she said flatly. 'Very funny.'

Now, I generally know when I'm being funny. At this moment, I did not believe that I was. I looked over at the building, trying to decide what Bastille had meant.

And, as I stared at it, something seemed to ... *change* about the library. It wasn't anything I could distinctly put my finger on; it just grew *darker* somehow. More threatening. The windows appeared to curl slightly, like horns, and the stonework shadows took on a menacing cast.

'It looks ... dangerous,' I said.

'Well, of course,' Bastille said. 'It's a *library.*'

'Right,' I said. 'What else should I look for, then?'

'I don't know,' she said. 'I'm no Oculator.'

I squinted. As I watched, the library seemed to ... stretch. 'It's not just one story,' I said with surprise. 'It looks like three.'

'We knew that already,' Bastille said. 'Try for less permanent auras.'

What does that mean? I wondered, studying the building. It now looked far larger, far more grand, to my eyes. 'The top two floors look ... thinner than the bottom floor. Like they're squeezing in slightly.'

'Hmm,' Bastille said. 'That's probably a population aura – it means the library isn't very full today. Most of the Librarians must be out on missions. That's good for us. Any dark windows?'

'One,' I said, noticing it for the first time. 'It's jet-black, like it's tinted.'

'Shattering Glass,' Bastille muttered.

'What?' I asked.

'Dark Oculator,' Bastille said. 'What floor?'

'Third,' I said. 'North corner.'

'We'll want to stay away from there, then.'

I frowned. 'I'm guessing a Dark Oculator is something dangerous, right?'

'They're like *super* Librarians,' Bastille said.

'Not all Librarians are Oculators?'

She rolled her eyes at me. 'Of course not,' she said. 'Very few people are Oculators. Smedrys on the main line and ... a few others. Regardless, Dark Oculators are very, very dangerous.'

'Well, then,' I said. 'If I had something valuable – like the Sands of Rashid – then I'd keep them with him. So, that's probably the first place we should go.'

Bastille looked at me, eyes narrowing. 'Just like a Smedry. If you die, I'm *never* going to get promoted!'

'How comforting,' I said, then nodded at the library. 'I'm seeing something else about the building. I think ... some of the windows are glowing just a bit.'

'Which ones?'

'All of them, actually,' I said, cocking my head. 'Even the black one. It's ... a little strange.'

'There's a lot of Oculatory power in there. Strong Lenses,

powerful sands, that sort of thing. They're making the glass charge with power by association.'

I reached up, sliding the glasses down on my nose. I still couldn't quite tell if I was seeing actual images, or if the light was just playing tricks on me. The changes were so subtle – even the stretching – that they didn't even seem like changes at all. More like impressions.

I pushed the glasses back up, then glanced at Bastille. 'You certainly seem to know a lot about this – especially for someone who says she's no Oculator.'

Bastille folded her arms, looking away.

'So how do you know all of this?' I asked. 'About the Dark Oculator and the library seeming empty?'

'Anyone would know those auras,' she snapped. 'They're simple, really. Honestly, Smedry. Even someone raised by *Librarians* should know that.'

'I wasn't raised by Librarians,' I said. 'I was raised by regular people – good people.'

'Oh?' Bastille said. 'Then why did you work so hard to destroy their houses?'

'Look, aren't knights supposed to be a little less ... annoying?'

Bastille stood upright, sniffing angrily. Then she swung her purse straight at my head. I started but remained where I was. *The handbag's strap will break,* I thought. *It won't be able to hit me.*

And so, of course, it smashed right into my face. It was surprisingly heavy, as if Bastille had packed a brick or two inside, just in case she had to whack the odd Smedry in the head. I stepped backward – half from the impact, half from surprise – and stumbled, falling to the ground. My head banged against the streetlamp, and I immediately heard a crack up above.

The lamp's bulb shattered on the ground beside me.

Oh, sure, I thought, rubbing my head. *That breaks.*

Bastille sniffed with satisfaction, as she looked down at me, but I caught a glimmer of surprise in her eyes – as if she too hadn't expected to be able to hit me.

'Stop making so much noise,' she said. 'People will notice.'

Behind her, Grandpa Smedry's little black car finally puttered up the street, coming to a stop beside us. I could see Sing smushed into the backseat, obscuring the entire back window.

Grandpa Smedry climbed perkily out of the car as I stood rubbing my jaw. 'What happened?' he asked, glancing at the broken light, then at me, then at Bastille.

'Nothing,' I said.

Grandpa Smedry smiled, eyes twinkling, as if he knew exactly what had happened. 'Well,' he said, 'should we be off, then?'

I nodded, straightening my glasses. 'Let's go break into the library.'

And once again, I considered just how strange my life had become during the last two hours.

Rutabaga.

6

Kindly pretend that you own a mousetrap factory.

Now, I realize that some of this narrative still might feel a little far-fetched to you. For instance, you might wonder why the Librarians haven't captured Grandpa Smedry and his little team of spies long before they attempted this particular infiltration. My friends do – as you have undoubtedly noticed – stand out, with their self-driving cars, odd disguises and near-lethal handbags.

This brings us back to your mousetrap factory. How is it doing? Are profits up? Ah, that's very pleasant.

A mousetrap factory – as you well know, since you own one – creates mousetraps. These mousetraps are used to kill mice. However, your factory is in a very nice, clean part of town. That area itself has never had a problem with mice – your mousetraps are sold to people who live near fields, where mice are far more common.

So, do you set mousetraps in your own factory? Of course not. You've never seen any mice there. And yet, because of this, if a small family of mice *did* somehow sneak into your factory, they might have a very nice time living there, as there are no traps to kill them.

This, friends, is called irony. Your mousetrap factory could itself become infested with mice. In a similar way, the Librarians are very good at patrolling the borders of their lands, keeping out enemy Oculators like Grandpa Smedry. Yet they don't expect to find mice like Grandpa Smedry hiding in the centers of their cities.

And that is why two men in tuxedos, one very large Mokian in sunglasses and a kimono, one young girl with a soldier's grace, and a very confused young Oculator in a green jacket could walk right up to the downtown library without drawing *too* much Librarian attention.

Besides, you've seen the kinds of people who walk around downtown, haven't you?

'All right, Smedry,' Bastille said to Grandpa. 'What's the plan?'

'Well, first I'll take an Oculatory reading of the building,' Grandpa Smedry said.

'Done,' Bastille said tersely. 'Low Librarian population, high Oculatory magic content, and a very nasty fellow on the third floor.'

Grandpa Smedry squinted at the library through his reddish glasses. 'Why, yes. How did you know?'

Basille nodded to me.

Grandpa Smedry smiled broadly. 'Getting used to the Lenses this quickly! You show quite a bit of promise, lad. Quite a bit indeed!'

I shrugged 'Bastille did the interpreting. I just described what I saw.'

'Was this before or after she smacked you with her purse?' Quentin asked. The short man watched the conversation with amusement, while Sing poked around in the gutter. Sing had, fortunately, put away his weapons – and was now carrying them in a large gym bag, which clashed horribly with his kimono.

'Well,' Grandpa Smedry said. 'Well, well. Sneaking into the downtown library at last! I think our base infiltration plan should work, wouldn't you say, Quentin?'

The wiry man nodded. 'Cantaloupe, fluttering paper makes a duck.'

I frowned. 'What is that supposed to mean?'

'Don't mind him,' Bastille said. 'He says things that don't make sense.'

His Talent, I thought. *Right.*

'And what, exactly,' Bastille said to Grandpa Smedry, 'is your base infiltration plan?'

'Quentin takes a few minutes scouting and watching the lobby, just to make sure all's clear,' Grandpa Smedry said. 'Then Sing makes a distraction and we all sneak into the employee access corridors. There, we split up – one Oculator per team – and search out powerful sources of Oculation. Those sands should glow like nothing else!'

'And if we find the sands?' I asked.

'Take them and get out. Sneakily, of course.'

'Huh.' Bastille paused. 'Why, that actually sounds like a good plan.' She seemed surprised.

'Of course it is,' Grandpa Smedry said. 'We spent long enough working on it! I've worried for years that someday we might have to infiltrate this place.'

Worried? I thought. The fact that even Grandpa Smedry found the infiltration a bit unnerving made it seem even more dangerous than it had before.

'Anyway,' Grandpa Smedry said. 'Quentin, be off! We're late already!'

The short man nodded, adjusted the carnation on his lapel, then took a deep breath and ducked through the building's broad glass doors.

'Grandfather,' I said, glancing at Grandpa Smedry. 'These people want to kill me, right?'

'Don't feel bad,' he said, removing his Lenses. 'They undoubtedly want to kill *all* of us.'

'Right', I said. 'So, shouldn't we be … hiding or something? Not just standing on the street corner in plain sight?'

'Well, answer me this,' he said. 'That man with the gun – had you seen him before?'

'No.'

'Did he recognize you?'

'No, actually,' I said. 'He asked who I was before he tried to shoot me.'

'Exactly,' Grandpa Smedry said, strolling over to glance in the library window. 'You are a very special person, Alcatraz – and because of that, I suspect that those who watch over you didn't want their peers knowing where you were. You may be surprised to hear this, but there are a lot of factions inside the Librarian ranks. The Dark Oculators, the Order of the Shattered Lens, the Scrivener's Bones … though they all work together, there's quite a bit of rivalry between them.

'For the faction controlling your movements, the fewer people who knew about you – or recognized you – the better. That way, they could keep better control of the sands when they arrived.' He lowered his voice. 'I won't lie, Alcatraz. This mission will be very dangerous. If the Librarians catch us, they will likely kill us. Now that they have the sands, they have no reason to let you live – and every reason to destroy you. However, we have three things going for us. First, very few people will be able to recognize us. That should let us slip into the library without being stopped. Second – as you have noticed – most of the Librarians are out of the library at the moment. My guess is that they're actually searching for you and me, perhaps trying to break into our gas station hideout.'

'And the third thing we have going for us?'

Grandpa Smedry smiled. 'Nobody would expect us to try something like this! It's completely insane.'

Great, I thought.

'Now,' he said, 'you might want to take off those Oculator's Lenses – they're the only thing that makes you distinctive right now.'

I quickly did so.

'Quentin will stay in the lobby and inner stacks for a good five minutes or so – watching for any signs of unusual patterns in Librarian movement or security – meaning we have a little bit of time here. Try to wait without looking suspicious.'

I nodded, and Grandpa Smedry wandered over to peek through another window. I lounged with my back against a lamp pole, trying not to break it. It was hard to remain still, considering my anxiety. As I thought about it, the three things Grandpa said we had going for us didn't seem to provide much of an advantage at all. I tried to calm my nerves.

A few minutes later, a clink sounded behind me as Sing set down his gym bag of weaponry. I jumped slightly, eyeing the bag

– I wasn't really that fond of the idea of having my toes shot off by an 'ancient' weapon.

'Alcatraz,' Sing said. 'Your grandfather tells me that you grew up raised by Hushlander parents!'

'Um, yes,' I said slowly.

'Wonderful!' Sing said. 'Tell me, tell me. What is the significance of *this*?' He proffered something small and yellow which he had likely found in the gutter.

'Uh, it's just a bottle cap,' I said.

'Yes,' Sing said, peering at it through his sunglasses, 'I'm aware of your primitive liquid beverage packaging methods. But look, see here. What's this on the *underneath*?'

I accepted the bottle cap. On the underside, I could see printed the words YOU ARE NOT A WINNER.

'See what it says?' Sing asked, pointing with a chubby finger. 'Is it common for Hushlanders to print insults on their foodstuffs? What is the purpose of this advertising campaign? Is it to make the consumer feel less secure, so they purchase more highly caffeinated drinks?'

'It's just a contest,' I said. 'Some of the bottles are winners, some aren't.'

Sing frowned. 'Why would a bottle want to win a prize? In fact, how do bottles even go about *claiming* prizes? Have they been Alivened? Don't your people understand that Alivening things is *dark* Oculary?'

I rolled my eyes. 'It's not Oculary, Sing. If you open the bottle and the cap says you're a winner, then you can claim a prize.'

'Oh.' He seemed a bit disappointed. Still, he carefully tucked the cap inside a pouch at his waist.

'Why do you care about that anyway?' I asked. 'Aren't you an ancient weapons expert?'

'Yes, well,' Sing said, 'an ancient weapons expert, and an ancient clothing expert, and an ancient cultures expert.'

I frowned.

'He's an anthropologist, lad,' Grandpa Smedry said from beside the library window. 'One of the most famous ones at the Mokian Royal University. That's why he's part of the team.'

'Wait,' I said. 'He's a professor?'

'Of course,' Grandpa Smedry said. 'Who else would be able to work those blasted guns? The civilized world hasn't used such things for centuries! We figured that we should have someone who can use them – swords might be more effective, but nobody carries them in the Hushlands. It's better to have at least one person on the team who understands and can use local weapons, just to be sure.'

Sing nodded eagerly. 'But don't worry,' he said. 'I may not be a soldier, but I've practiced with the weapons quite a bit. I've ... never shot at something *moving* before, but how difficult can it be?'

I stood quietly, then turned to Grandpa Smedry. 'And what about Quentin? Is he a professor too?'

Sing laughed. 'No, no. He's just a graduate student.'

'He's quite capable, though,' Grandpa Smedry said. 'He's a language specialist who focuses on Hushlander dialects.'

'So,' I said, holding up a finger. 'Let me get this straight. Our strike team consists of a loony old man, an anthropologist, a grad student, and two kids.'

Grandpa Smedry and Sing nodded happily. Bastille, leaning against the library wall a short distance away, gave me a flat stare. 'You see what I have to work with?'

I nodded, beginning to understand where she might have gotten such a grumpy attitude.

'Oh, don't be like that,' Grandpa Smedry said. He walked over, putting his arm around my shoulders and pulling me aside. 'Here, lad, I've got some things I want to give you.'

Grandpa Smedry pulled open his tuxedo jacket and removed two pairs of spectacles. 'You'll recognize these,' he said, holding up a yellow-tinted pair. 'I used them back when I first picked you up from the house. They're fairly easy Lenses to wield – if you can already do readings like you did on the library building, you should be able to use these.'

I accepted the glasses, then covertly tried them on. At first, nothing changed – but then I thought I saw something. Footsteps, in various colors, fading slowly on the ground around me.

'Tracks,' I said with surprise, watching as Sing wandered over to another gutter, leaving a trail of blue footprints on the concrete behind him.

'Indeed, lad,' Grandpa Smedry said. 'The better you know a person, the longer the footprints will remain visible. Once we get inside, we'll split up – you and I are the only Oculators in the group, and so we're the only ones who will be able to sense where the sands are. But the inside of a library can be deceptively large. Sometimes the stacks form mazes, and it's easy to get lost. If you lose your way, you can use these Tracker's Lenses to retrace our footprints. Also, you can probably track me down, if necessary.'

I glanced down. Grandpa Smedry's footprints glowed a blazing white, like little bursts of flame on the ground. I could easily see the trail of white back to Grandpa Smedry's black car, still parked across the street.

'Thanks,' I said, still feeling a little apprehensive as I removed and pocketed the Tracker's Lenses.

'You'll do fine, lad,' Grandpa Smedry said, picking up a second pair of glasses. 'Remember, this is *your* inheritance we're searching for. You lost it, and you'll have to get it back. I can't hold your hand forever.'

I felt like noting that I had seen very little hand-holding in this adventure so far. I didn't really know what was going on, didn't quite trust my sanity anymore, and wasn't even convinced that I wanted my inheritance back. Grandpa Smedry, however, didn't give me an opportunity to complain. He held up the second pair of glasses – they had mostly clear Lenses, with a little dot of red at the center of each one.

'These,' he said, handing the Lenses to me, 'are one of the most powerful pairs of Oculatory Lenses I possess. However, they're also one of the easiest to use, which is why I'm loaning them to you.'

I eyed the glasses. 'What do they do?'

'You can use them for many purposes,' Grandpa Smedry said. 'Once you switch them on – you just have to concentrate a bit to do that – they'll begin gathering the light around you, then direct it out in concentrated beams.'

'You mean, like a laser?' I asked.

'Yes,' Grandpa Smedry said. 'These are *very* dangerous, Alcatraz. I don't carry many offensive Lenses, but I've found these too useful to leave behind. However, let me warn you – if there really is a Dark Oculator in there, he'll be able to sense when you activate these. Only use the Firebringer's Lenses in an emergency!'

Don't get too worried – this isn't the sort of story in which emergencies occur. Yes, it is highly unlikely that you will ever see those Firebringer's Lenses activated. So don't get your hopes up.

I accepted the Firebringer's Lenses from my grandfather and they immediately started glowing.

'Cavorting Cards!' Grandpa Smedry yelped, dodging to the side as the Lenses blasted a pair of intensely hot beams into the ground just in front of my feet. I hopped backward in shock, nearly dropping the Lenses in surprise.

Grandpa Smedry grabbed the Lenses from behind, deactivating them. The scent of melted tar rose in the air, and I blinked, my vision marked by two bright afterimages of light.

'Well, well,' Grandpa Smedry said. 'I *told* you they were easy to use.' He glanced up at the building. 'We should be too far away for that to have been sensed ...'

Great, I thought. As my vision cleared, I could see Bastille rolling her eyes.

Sing waddled over, raising his sunglasses and inspecting the three-foot-wide disk of blackened, half-melted concrete. 'Nice shot,' he noted. 'I think it's dead now.'

I blushed, but Grandpa Smedry just laughed. 'Here,' he said, slipping a small velvet bag around the Firebringer's Lenses. He pulled the drawstring tight at the top. 'This should keep them safe. Now, with these Lenses and your Talent, you should be able to handle pretty much anything the Librarians throw at you!'

I accepted the glasses back, and fortunately they didn't go off.

Now, as I was telling you previously, these Lenses will probably *never* get used in this story. You'll be lucky if you ever get to see them fired. Again.

'Grandfather,' I said quietly, eyeing Bastille, then stepping aside again with Grandpa Smedry. 'I'm not sure that I can do this.'

'Nonsense, lad! You're a Smedry!'

'But I didn't even know I was until earlier today,' I said. 'Or ... well, I didn't know what being a Smedry meant. I don't think ... well, I'm just not ready.'

'What makes you say that?' Grandpa Smedry asked.

'I tried to use my Talent earlier,' I said. 'To stop Bastille from smacking me with her purse. It didn't work. And that wasn't the first time – sometimes I just can't make things break. And when I *don't* want them to break, they usually do anyway.'

'Your Talent is still wild,' Grandpa Smedry said. 'You haven't practiced it enough. Being a Smedry isn't just about having a Talent, it's about finding out how to *use* that Talent. A clever person can make anything turn to his advantage, no matter how much a disadvantage it may seem at first.

'No Smedry Talent is completely controllable. However, if you practice enough, you'll begin to get a grasp on it. Eventually, you'll be able to make things break not just when and where you want, but also *how* you want.'

'I ...' I said, still uncertain.

'This doesn't sound like you, Alcatraz,' Grandpa Smedry said. 'Where's that spark of spirit – that stubbornness – that you're always tossing about?'

I frowned. 'How do you know what I'm like? You only just met me.'

'Oh? You think I've left you in Librarian hands all this time, never checking in on you?'

Of course he checked on me, I thought. *Bastille mentioned something about that.* 'But you don't know me,' I said. 'I mean, you didn't even know what my Talent was.'

'I suspected, lad,' Grandpa Smedry said. 'But I'll admit – I usually got to your foster homes *after* you'd moved somewhere else.

Still, I've been watching over you, in my own way.'

'If that's the case,' I said, 'then why—'

'Why did I leave you to the foster homes?' Grandpa Smedry asked. 'I'm not that great a parent. A boy needs somebody who can arrive on time to his birthdays and ball games. Besides, there were … reasons for letting you grow up in this world.'

That didn't seem like much of an explanation to me, but Grandpa didn't look like he'd say more. So, I just sighed. 'I just can't help feeling like I won't be much help in this fight. I don't know how to use my Talent, or these Lenses. Maybe I should get a gun or a sword or something.'

Grandpa Smedry smiled. 'Ah lad. This war we're fighting – it isn't about guns, or even about swords.'

'What is it about then? Sand?'

'Information,' Grandpa Smedry said. 'That's the real power in this world. That man who held a gun on us earlier – he had power over you. Why?'

'Because he was going to shoot me,' I said.

'Because you *thought* he could shoot you,' Grandpa Smedry said, raising a finger. 'But he had no power over me, because I *knew* that he couldn't hurt me. And when he realized that …'

'He ran away,' I said slowly.

'Information. The Librarians control the *information* in this city – in this whole country. They control what gets read, what gets seen, and what gets learned. Because of that, they have power. Well, we're going to break that power, you and I. But first, we need those sands.'

'Grandpa,' I said. 'You have to have *some* kind of idea what the sands do. You came to get them from me, after all. Didn't you have a plan to use them?'

'Pestering Pullmans, of course I did! I was going to smelt them into Lenses, just like the Librarians are probably doing now. Your father, lad – he was a sandhunter. He spent all his time searching out new and powerful types of sand, gathering the grains together, crafting Lenses like nobody had seen before. The Sands of Rashid were his crowning achievement. His greatest discovery.' Grandpa

Smedry's voice grew even quieter. 'He was convinced they had something to do with where the Smedry family gained its Talents in the first place. The Sands of Rashid are a key, somehow, to understanding the power and origin of our entire family. Can you understand, perhaps, why the Librarians might want them?'

I nodded slowly. 'The Talents.'

'Indeed, lad. The Talents. If they could find a way to arm their agents with Talents like ours, then the Free Kingdoms could very well be doomed. Smedry powers are a large part of what has kept the Librarians at bay for so long. But we're losing. The land you call Australia was lost to us only a few decades back – absorbed and added to the Hushlands. Now Sing's homeland has almost fallen. They've already taken some of the outlying Mokian islands – the places you call Hawaii, Tonga, Samoa – and added them to the Hushlands. I fear it will only be a few years before Mokia itself falls.'

He paused, then shook his head, looking just a little bit distant as he continued. 'Either the Free Kingdoms are going to fall – and everything will become Hushlands – or we're going to find a way to break the Librarians' power. The Smedry Talents, and the secrets these sands will reveal, are key to the next stage of the war. Things are changing ... things *have* to change. We can't just keep fighting and losing ground. That's why your father spent so much of his life gathering those sands. He felt it was time to go on the offensive.'

I felt a stab of anxiety, a question surfacing that I wasn't certain I wanted to know the answer to. Finally, I couldn't keep it down. 'Is he still alive, Grandpa?'

'I don't know,' he said, looking back at me. 'I honestly don't know.'

The comment hung in the air. Grandpa Smedry placed a hand on my shoulder. 'Alive or not, Attica Smedry was a great man, Alcatraz. An amazing man. And he, like you, was no warrior. We are Oculators. Our weapon is *information*. Keep your eyes, and your mind, open. You'll do just fine.'

I nodded slowly.

'Good lad, good lad. Ah, here's Quentin.'

The short, tuxedo-wearing man slipped quickly out of the library's front doors. 'Five Librarians in the main lobby,' he said quietly. 'Three behind the checkout desk, two in the stacks. Their patterns are right on schedule with what we've seen from them before. The entrance to the employee corridors is on the far south side. It isn't guarded right now, though a Librarian passes to check on it every few minutes or so.'

'All right, then,' Grandpa Smedry said. 'In we go!'

7

I seem to recall that last year a Free Kingdoms biographer wrote an article claiming I had spent my childhood performing a 'deep infiltration' of Library lands. I guess in his mind, playing video games counted as a 'deep infiltration.'

I hope you Free Kingdomers aren't *too* put out to discover that dragons didn't come and bow to me at my birth. I wasn't tutored by the spirits of my dead Smedry ancestors, nor did I kill my first Librarian by slitting his throat with his own library card.

This is the real me, the troubled boy who grew into an even more troubled young man. Now, I'm not a terrible person. I'm just not a particularly nice one either. If you'd been tied to altars, nearly eaten by walking romance novels, and thrown off a glass pillar taller than Mt. Everest, you might have turned out a little like me yourself.

Sing tripped.

Now, I've seen a lot of people trip in my lifetime. I've seen people stumble, tumble, and misstep. I once saw my foster brother fall down the stairs (not my fault) and I also saw a local bully belly flop when his diving board broke beneath him (I plead the Fifth on that one).

I have never, however, seen a trip quite so ... well executed as the one Sing performed in the library lobby that day. The hefty Mokian quite convincingly stumbled on the welcome mat just inside the doors. He cried out, hopping on one foot – a teetering, lumbering mound with the kinetic energy of a collapsing building.

People scattered. Children cried, clutching picture books about aardvarks in their terrified fingers. A Librarian raised her hand in warning.

With a weird mixture of skillful grace and a mad lack of control,

Sing fell over a comfortable reading chair and collided with a massive bookshelf. Those shelves – you may know – are usually bolted to the floor. That didn't matter. When confronted with a three-hundred-and-fifty-pound Mokian missile, iron bends.

And the bookshelf fell.

Books flew in the air. Pages fluttered. Metal groaned.

'Now's our chance,' Grandpa Smedry said. He dashed forward, just one more body in the flurry of lobby activity.

The rest of us followed, scooting past the horrified Librarians. Grandpa Smedry led us behind the children's section, through the media section, and to a pair of shabby doors at the back marked EMPLOYEES ONLY.

'Put your Oculator's Lenses back on, lad,' Grandpa Smedry said, sliding on his reddish pair.

I did so as well, and through those Lenses I could see a certain faint glow around the doors. Not a white or black glow, like I'd seen before. But instead … a bluish one. The power was focused on a square in the wall. On closer inspection, I could see that that section of the wall was inset with a small square of glass.

'A Hushlander handprint scanner,' Grandpa Smedry said. 'Kind of like Recognizer's Glass. How quaint. All right, lad, it's your turn.'

I gulped quietly, feeling nervous – both because of the Librarians so near and because everyone was counting on me. I reached out and pressed my hand against the door. There was a hum from the glass panel, but I ignored it. Instead I focused on myself.

I'd always known, instinctively, about my power. I'd always had it, but I'd rarely tried to control it specifically. Now I focused on it, and I felt a tingle – like the shock that comes from touching a battery to your tongue – pulse out of my chest and down my arm.

There was a crack from the door as the lock snapped. 'Masterfully done, lad!' Grand Smedry said. 'Masterfully done indeed.'

I shrugged, feeling proud. 'Doors have always been my specialty.'

Quentin quickly pushed open the door and waved everyone through. Grandpa Smedry's eyes twinkled as he passed me. 'I've *always* wanted to do this,' he whispered.

I could hear Bastille grumbling something under her breath as she joined us in the hallway, Sing's bag of guns slung over her shoulder. Quentin held the door open for a moment longer, and finally a puffing Sing rounded the bookshelves and joined us.

'Sorry,' he said. 'One of the female patrons insisted on wrapping my ankle for me.' Indeed, his sandal-shod right foot now bore a support bandage.

Quentin closed the door, then checked the handle, twisting it a few times. 'Coconuts, the pain don't hurt,' he said, then paused. 'Sorry,' he said, flushing. 'Sometimes the gibberish comes out when I don't want it to. Anyway, the lock is still broken – it will be suspicious next time someone comes through here.'

'Can't be helped,' Grandpa Smedry said, pulling out what appeared to be two small hourglasses. He gave them each a tap, and the sand started flowing. He handed one to me. The sand continued to flow at the same rate no matter which way I turned the device. *Nifty,* I thought. I'd always wanted a magical hourglass.

Well, not really. But if I'd *known* that there were such things as magical hourglasses, I'd have wanted one. Who wouldn't? I should note, however, that the Free Kingdomers would be offended by my calling the hourglass magical. They have very strange feelings on what counts as magical and what doesn't. For instance, Oculatory powers and Smedry Talents are considered a form of magic to most Free Kingdomers, since they are things that can only be performed or used by a few select people. The hourglasses, like the silimatic cars, Sing's glasses, or Bastille's jacket, can be used by anyone. That makes those things 'technology' in Free Kingdomer speak.

It's confusing, I know. However, you're probably smart enough to figure it out. And if you aren't, then I shall likely call you an insulting name. (Wait for Chapter Fifteen.)

'We'll meet here in one hour,' Grandpa Smedry said. 'Any longer than that, and we'll be getting close to closing time. When that happens, all those Librarians out on patrol will return to check in – and we'll be in serious trouble. Quentin is with me – Sing and Bastille, go with Alcatraz.'

'But—' Bastille said.

'No,' Grandpa Smedry interrupted. 'You're going with him, Bastille. I order you to.'

'I'm *your* Crystin,' she objected.

'True,' Grandpa Smedry said. 'But you're sworn to protect *all* Smedrys, especially Oculators. The lad will need your help more than I will.'

Bastille huffed quietly but made no further objections. As for myself, I wasn't really sure whether to be annoyed or glad.

'You three inspect this floor, then move up to the second one,' Grandpa Smedry said quietly. 'Quentin and I will take the top floor.'

'But,' Bastille said, 'that's where the Dark Oculator is!'

'That's where his lair is,' Grandpa Smedry corrected. 'That aura glows so brightly because he spends so much time there. You might be able to notice the Dark Oculator's own aura if he's nearby, Alcatraz, but it won't give you much advance warning. Stay quiet and unseen, all right?'

I nodded slowly.

Grandpa Smedry stepped a little closer, speaking quietly. 'If you *do* run into him, lad, make certain you keep those Oculator's Lenses on. They can protect you from an enemy's Lenses, if you use them right.'

'How ... how do I manage that?' I asked.

'It takes time to practice, lad,' Grandpa Smedry said. 'Time we don't have! But, well, it probably won't come to that. Just ... try to stay away from any rooms that shine black, okay?'

I nodded again.

'Well, then!' Grandpa Smedry said to the whole group. 'The Librarians will have to spend ages cleaning up that mess in the lobby. Hopefully, they won't even notice the door until we're gone. One hour! Quickly, now. We're late!'

With that, Grandpa Smedry spun to the left and began walking down the empty white hallway. Quentin waved good-bye. 'Rutabaga, fire over the inheritance!' he said, then rushed after the elderly Oculator.

Sing and Bastille turned to me. *It ... looks like I'm in charge,* I thought with surprise.

This was a strange realization. Yes, yes, I know – Grandpa Smedry had already said that I would have to lead my group. I shouldn't have been surprised to find myself in this situation.

The truth is, however, that I was never the sort of person that people put in charge. Those kinds of duties generally go to the types of boys and girls who deliver apples, answer questions, and smile a lot. Leadership duties do *not* generally go to boys whose desks collapse, who are often accused of playing pranks by removing the doorknobs of school bathrooms, and who once unwittingly made a friend's pants fall down while he was writing on the chalkboard.

I never did manage to get that stunt to work again.

'Um, I guess we go this way,' I said, pointing down the hallway.

'You think?' Bastille asked flatly, handing Sing his gym bag of guns. She pulled a pair of sunglasses – Warrior's Lenses, as the others called them – out of her jacket packet and slipped them on. Then she took off, walking down the hallway, handbag flipped around her shoulder.

If I ordered her to go back and follow Grandpa instead, I wonder if she'd go ... I decided that she probably wouldn't.

'Say, Alcatraz,' Sing said as we followed Bastille. 'What do you suppose this little wrap on my ankle means?'

I frowned, glancing down. 'The bandage?'

'Oh,' Sing said. 'Is *that* what it is? First aid, it is called, correct?'

'Yes,' I said. 'Why else would someone wrap your ankle like that?'

Sing glanced down, obviously trying to inspect the ankle bandage while still walking. 'Oh, I don't know,' he said, 'I thought maybe it was some preliminary courtship ritual ...' He trailed off, looking toward me hopefully.

'No,' I said. 'Not a chance.'

'That's sad,' Sing said. 'She was pretty.'

'Is that the sort of thing you should be thinking about?' I asked.

'I mean, you're an anthropologist – you study cultures. Are you allowed to interfere with the "natives" you meet?'

'What?' Sing said. 'Of course we can! Why, we're *here* to interfere! We're trying to overthrow Librarian domination of the Hushlands, after all.'

'Why not just let people live their lives, and live yours?'

Sing looked taken aback. 'Alcatraz, the Hushlanders are enslaved! They're being kept in ignorance, living only with the most primitive technologies! Besides, we need to do *something* to fight. Back at the Conclave of Kings, some people are starting to talk about surrendering to the Librarians completely!' He shook his head. 'I'm glad for people like your grandfather, people willing to take the fight into Librarian lands. It shows that we won't just sit back and slowly have our kingdoms taken from us.'

Up ahead, Bastille glared back at us. 'Would you two like to chat a little more?' she snapped. 'Perhaps sing a little tune? If there are any Librarians up ahead, we wouldn't want them to miss out on *hearing us coming.*'

Sing looked at his feet sheepishly, and we fell silent – though a part of me wanted to yell something like, 'What did you say, Bastille?' as loudly as I could. You see, that is the sad, sorry, terrible thing about sarcasm.

It's really funny.

But I just walked quietly, thinking about what Sing had said – particularly the part about the Librarians only letting Hushlanders have the most 'primitive' of technologies. It seemed ridiculous to me that the Free Kingdomers considered things like guns and automobiles to be 'primitive.' They weren't primitive, they were ... well, they were what I knew. Growing up in America, I'd come to assume that everything I had – and did -- was the newest, best, and most advanced in the world.

It was very unsettling to be confronted by people who weren't impressed by how advanced my culture was. I wanted to huff and think that whatever *they* had must not be all that good either. Except the problem was that I'd *seen* that they had self-driving cars, glasses that could track a person's footprints, and armored knights. All were, in one way or another, superior to what I'd known. (Admit it, knights are just cool.)

I was coming to realize something very difficult. I was slowly accepting that the way I did things – the way my people did things – might not actually be the best way.

In other words, I was feeling humility.

I sincerely hope that you never have to feel this emotion. Like asparagus and fish, it's not really as good for you as everyone says it is. Selfishness, arrogance, and callousness got me much further than humility ever did.

Have I mentioned that I'm not really a very good person?

Our small group reached the end of the unmarked hallway, Bastille still in the lead. She paused, holding up a hand, peeking around the corner. Then she continued onward, her platform sandals making a slight noise as she stepped onto a carpeted floor. Sing and I followed. The room beyond was filled with books.

Really filled.

Perhaps you've never experienced the full, suffocating majesty of a true library. You Hushlanders have probably visited your local libraries – you've perused the parts that normal people are allowed to see. These places tend to have row upon row of neat bookshelves, arranged nicely. They are presented attractively for the same reason that kittens are cute – so that they can draw you in, then pounce on you for the kill.

Seriously. Stay away from kittens.

Public libraries exist to entice. The Librarians want everyone to read their books – whether those books are deep and poignant works about dead puppies or nonfiction books about made-up topics, like the Pilgrims, penicillin, and France. In fact, the only book they *don't* want you to read is the one you're holding right now.

Those aren't real libraries, however. Real libraries take little concern for enticement. You who have visited the basement stacks of a university library's philosophy section know what I'm talking about. In such places, the shelves get squeezed closer and closer together, and they reach higher and higher. Piles of books appear randomly at the junctions and in corners waiting to be shelved, like the fourth-generation descendants of a copy of *Summa Theologica* and an edition of *Little Women*.

Dust settles on the books like a gray perversion of rain forest moss, giving the air a certain moldy, unwelcome scent faintly reminiscent of a baledragon's lair. At each corner, you expect to turn and see the withered, skeletal remains of some poor researcher who got lost in the stacks and never found his way out.

And even *those* kinds of libraries are but pale apprentices to the enormous cavern of books that I entered that day. We walked quietly, passing shelves packed so tightly together that only an anorexic racing jockey could have squeezed between them. The bookshelves were easily fifteen feet high, and enormous plaques on the ends proclaimed, in very small letters, the titles each one contained. Long wooden poles with pincerlike hooks leaned against some shelves, and I got the impression that they were used for reaching between the shelves to pull out books.

No, I thought, *it would take a ridiculous amount of practice to learn to do something like that. I must be wrong.*

You may have guessed that I wasn't actually wrong. You see, Librarian apprentices have plenty of time to practice things that are ridiculous. They really only have three duties: First, to learn the incredibly and needlessly complicated filing system used to catalog books in the back library stacks. Second, to practice with the book-hooks. Third, to plot ways to torture an innocent populace.

That third one is the most fun. Kind of like gym class for the murderously insane.

Sing, Bastille, and I crept along the rows, careful to keep an eye out for Librarian apprentices. This was undoubtedly the most dangerous thing I'd ever done in my short life. Fortunately, we were able to get to the eastern edge of the room without incident.

'We should move along the wall,' Bastille said quietly, 'so Alcatraz can look down each row of books. That way, he might see powerful sources of Oculation.'

Sing nodded. 'But we should move quickly. We need to find

the sands and get out fast, before the Librarians realize they've been infiltrated.'

They looked at me expectantly. 'Uh, that sounds good,' I finally said.

'You've got this leadership thing down, Smedry,' Bastille said flatly. 'Very inspiring. Come on, then. Let's keep moving.'

Bastille and Sing began to walk along the wall. I however, didn't follow. I had just noticed something hanging on the wall above us: a very large painting that appeared to be an ornate, detailed map of the world.

And it looked nothing like the one I was used to.

8

At this point, you're probably expecting to read something like, 'I suddenly realized that everything I *thought* I had known was untrue.'

Though I'll likely use that exact phrase, I should warn you that it is actually misleading. Everything I knew was *not* untrue. In fact, many of the things I'd learned about the world were quite true.

For instance, I knew that the sun came up every day. That was not untrue. (Though, admittedly, that sun shone on a geography I didn't understand.) I knew that my homeland was named the United States of America. That was not untrue. (Though the U.S.A. was not actually run by senators, presidents, and judges – but instead by a cult of evil Librarians.) I knew that sharks were annoying. This also was not untrue. (There's actually nothing witty to add here. Sharks *are* annoying. Particularly the carnivorous kind.)

You have been warned.

I stared up at the enormous wall map and suddenly realized something. Everything I thought I'd known about the world was untrue. 'This can't be real ...' I whispered stepping back.

'I'm afraid it is, Alcatraz,' Sing said, laying a hand on my shoulder. 'That's the world – the entire world, both the Hushlands and the Free Kingdoms. This is the thing that the Librarians don't want you to know about.'

I stared. 'But it's so ... big.'

And indeed it was. The Americas were there, represented accurately. The other continents – Asia, Australia, Africa, and the rest – were there as well. They were collectively labeled INNER LIBRARIA on the map, but I recognized them easily enough. The difference, then, was the *new* continents. There were three of them, pressed into the oceans between the familiar continents. Two of the new continents were smaller, perhaps the size of Australia. One, however, was very large. It sat directly in the middle of the Pacific Ocean, right between America and Japan.

'It's impossible,' I said. 'We would have noticed a landmass like that sitting in the middle of the ocean.'

'You *think* you would have noticed,' Sing said. 'But the truth is that the Librarians control the information in your country. How often have you personally been out sailing in the middle of what you call the Pacific Ocean?'

I paused. 'But ... just because *I* haven't been there doesn't mean anything. The ocean is like kangaroos and grandfathers – I believe that other people have seen it. Ship captains, airplane pilots, satellite images ...'

'Satellites controlled by the Librarians,' Bastille said, regarding the map through her sunglasses. 'Your pilots fly guided by instruments and maps that the Librarians provide. And not many people sail boats in your culture – particularly not into the deep ocean. Those who do are bribed, threatened, brainwashed, or – most often – carefully misled.'

Sing nodded. 'Those other continents make sense, if you think about it. I mean, a planet that is seventy percent water? What would be the point of so much wasted space? I'd *never* have thought people would buy that lie, had I not studied Hushlander cultures.'

'People go along with what they're told,' Bastille said. 'Even intelligent people believe what they read and hear, assuming they're given no reason to question.'

I shook my head. 'A hidden gas station I can believe, but *this*? This isn't some little cover-up or misdirection. There are *three new continents* on that map!'

'Not new,' Sing said. 'The cultures of the Free Kingdoms are quite well established. Indeed, they're far more advanced than Hushlander cultures.'

Bastille nodded. 'The Librarians conquered the backward

sections of the world first. They're easier to control.'

'But ...' I said. 'What about Columbus? What about history?'

'Lies,' Sing said quietly. 'Fabrications, many of them – the rest are distortions. I mean, haven't you always wondered why your people supposedly developed guns *after* more technology-advanced weapons, like swords?'

'No! Swords *aren't* more advanced than guns!'

Sing and Bastille shared a glance.

'That's what *they* want you to believe, Alcatraz,' Sing said. 'That way, the Librarians can keep the powerful technology for themselves. Don't you think it's strange that nobody in your culture carries swords anymore?'

'No!' I said, holding up my hands. 'Sing, most people don't need to carry swords – or even guns!'

'You've been beaten down,' Bastille said quietly. 'You're docile. Controlled.'

'We're happy!' I said.

'Yes,' Sing said. 'You're quiet, happy, and completely ignorant – just like you're supposed to be. Don't you have a phrase "Ignorance is bliss"?'

'The Librarians came up with that one,' Bastille said.

I shook my head. 'No,' I said. 'This is too much. I was willing to overlook the self-driving cars. The magic glasses ... well, they could be some kind of trick. Sneaking into a library, that sounded like fun. But this ... this is ridiculous. I can't accept it.'

And likely, you Hushlanders are thinking the very same thing. You are saying to yourself, 'The story just lost me. It degenerated into pure silliness. And since only silly people enjoy silliness, I'm going to go read a book about a boy whose dog gets killed by his mother. Twice.'

Before you embark upon your voyage into caninicide, I'd like to offer a single argument for your consideration: Plato.

Plato was a funny little Greek man who lived a long time ago. He is probably best known for two things: First, for writing stories about his friends, and second for philosophically proving that somewhere in the eternities there exists a perfect slice of cheesecake. (Read the *Parmenides* – it's in there.) At this moment, however, the reader should be less interested in cheesecake and more interested in caves.

One cave, to be specific. Plato tells a story about a group of prisoners who lived in a very special cave. The prisoners were tied up – heads held so they could only face one direction – and all they could see was the wall in front of them. A fire behind them threw shadows up on this wall and these shadows were the only things the prisoners ever knew. To them, the shadows *were* their world. As far as they knew, there was nothing else.

However, one of these prisoners was eventually released and saw that the world was much more than just shadows. At first, he found this new world very, very strange. Once he learned of it, however, he returned and tried to tell his friends about it. They, however, didn't trust him – and didn't want to listen to him. They didn't want to believe in this new world, because it didn't make sense to them.

You Hushlanders are like these people. You have, through no fault of your own, lived your entire life believing in the shadows the Librarians have shown you. The things I reveal in this narrative will seem like nonsense to you. There is no getting around this. No matter how logical my arguments are, they will seem illogical to you. Your mind – struggling to find ways to hold on to your Librarian lies – will think of all kinds of ridiculous concerns. You will ask questions such as, 'But what about tidal patterns?' Or, 'But how can you explain the lack of increased fuel costs created by airplanes flying around these hidden landmasses?'

Since nothing I can say would be able to pierce your delusions, let the fact that I make *no* arguments stand as ultimate proof that I am right. As Plato once said that his friend Socrates once said, 'I know that I'm right because I'm the only person humble enough to admit that I'm not.'

Or something like that.

I stood for a long moment, staring up at that map. Part of me – most of me – resisted what I was seeing. And yet, the things I had experienced bounced around in my head, reminding me that many things – like gas station coolers and young men who set fire to kitchens – were not always as simple as they appeared.

'I'll deal with this later,' I finally said, turning away from the map. 'Let's keep moving.'

'Finally,' Bastille said. 'You Hushlanders. Honestly, sometimes it seems like it would take a hammer to the face to get you to wake up and see the truth.'

'Now, Bastille,' Sing said as we walked by a long, low filing cabinet. 'That really isn't fair. I think young Lord Smedry is doing quite well, all things considered. It isn't every day that—'

'Gak!'

Sing said this last part as he suddenly and without apparent reason, tripped and fell to the ground. I frowned, looking down, but Bastille burst into motion. She hopped dexterously over Sing, then grabbed me by the arm and threw me to the ground behind the filing cabinet. She ducked down beside me.

'Why—' I began, rubbing my arm in annoyance. Bastille, however, clapped a hand over my mouth, shooting me a very hostile, very persuasive silencing look.

I fell quiet. Then I heard something. Voices approaching.

Bastille removed her hand, then carefully peeked out over the filing cabinet. I moved to do likewise, and Bastille shot me another glance – I could see the glare even through her sunglasses. This time, however, I refused to be cowed.

If she can look, so can I, I thought stubbornly. *I didn't spend thirteen years being a troublemaker so I can get pushed around by a girl my age. Even if she is a pretty good shot with that handbag of hers.*

I peeked over the cabinet. In the distance, moving between two lines of enormous bookshelves, I could see a group of figures. Most looked like they were wearing dark robes.

'Librarian apprentices,' Sing whispered, peeking up beside me. 'Doing their tasks. Somewhere in this room, the Master Librarians have placed one misfiled volume. The apprentices have to find it.'

I eyed the nearly endless rows of tightly packed bookshelves. 'That could take years!' I whispered.

Sing nodded. 'Some go insane from the pressure. They're usually the ones who get promoted first.'

I shivered as the group moved off. There were a couple of much larger figures following them, and these weren't dressed in robes. They were entirely white, and their bodies moved in a not-quite-natural manner. They lumbered as they stepped, arms held too far to the sides. They trailed behind the Librarian apprentices, moving with ponderous steps, some carrying stacks of books.

I squinted, looking closer. The whitish figures glowed slightly, giving off a dark haze. The apprentices and the white figures turned a corner, disappearing from view.

'What were those?' I whispered. 'Those white things that were with them?'

'Alivened,' Bastille said, shivering. She glanced at me, standing up. 'When Sing trips, Smedry, *always* duck.'

'You trip whenever there's danger?'

. 'Of course not,' Sing said. 'I only trip when there's danger and when tripping will be helpful. Or, at least, that's usually the way it works.'

'Better than your Talent, Oculator,' Bastille said with a snort. 'Do you want to tell me how you managed to *break* the carpet?'

I glanced down. The carpet lay unraveled around me, separated into individual strands of yarn.

'Come on,' Bastille said. 'We should keep moving.'

I nodded, as did Sing, and we continued along the perimeter of the musty library chamber. We walked in silence; the sight of the apprentices had reminded us of the need for stealth. However, it quickly grew apparent to me that searching through that room wouldn't lead us to the Sands of Rashid. Despite the room's many alcoves (the thousands upon thousands of bookshelves made it feel like a cubicle-filled office for demonic bibliophiles) it didn't seem like the kind of place where one kept objects of great power. I figured that the sands would be in a locked room, or perhaps a laboratory. Not a vast storage chamber.

I spotted a stairwell to the right, and I waved to the others. 'We should go up to the second floor.'

Bastille raised an eyebrow. 'We haven't finished checking this room yet.'

'We don't have time,' I said, glancing at the hourglass Grandpa Smedry had given me. 'This room is too big. Besides, it doesn't feel right.'

'We're going to let the fate of the world rest on your feelings?' she asked flatly.

'He *is* our Oculator, Bastille,' Sing reminded her. 'If he says we go up, then we go up. Besides, he's probably right – the sands aren't likely to be here in the stacks. Somewhere in this building should be a Lens forge. *That's* where they've probably got the sands.'

Bastille sighed, then shrugged. 'Whatever,' she said, pushing past me to lead the way toward the stairs.

I was a little bit surprised that they'd listened to me. I followed Bastille, and Sing took the rear. The stairwell was made of stone, and it reminded me distinctly of something one might find in a medieval castle. It wound in circles around itself and was encased entirely in a massive stone pillar, lit by little frosted windows that let in marginal amounts of daylight.

After several minutes of climbing the steep steps, I was puffing. 'Shouldn't we have reached the second floor by now?'

'Space distortion,' Bastille said from in front of me. 'You didn't honestly expect the Librarians to confine their entire base into a building as small as this one looks?'

'No,' I said. 'I saw the stretching aura outside. But, I mean, how far up can this stairwell go?'

'As far as it needs to,' Bastille said testily.

I sighed but continued to climb. By that logic, that stairwell could go on forever. I didn't however, want to contemplate that point. 'For how "advanced" you people always claim to be,' I noted, 'you'd think that the Librarians would have elevators in their buildings.'

Bastille snorted. 'Elevators? How primitive.'

'Well, they're better than stairs.'

'Of course they aren't,' Bastille said. 'It took society *centuries* to develop from the elevator to the flight of stairs.'

I frowned. 'That doesn't make any sense. Stairs are far less advanced that elevators.'

She glanced over her shoulder, looking at me over the top of her sunglasses. I was annoyed to note that she didn't seem the least bit winded.

'Don't be silly,' she said. 'Why would elevators be *more* advanced than stairs? Obviously, stairs take more effort to climb, are harder to construct, and are far more healthy to use. Therefore, they took longer to develop. Don't you realize how stupid you sound when you claim otherwise?'

'No,' I said, annoyed. 'The *opposite* is stupid to me. And does everything you say have to sound like an insult?'

'Only when I intend to be insulting,' she said, turning and resuming her climb.

I sighed, looking back at Sing, who just shrugged and smiled, still carrying his gym bag of guns. We kept moving.

Stairs are more advanced than elevators? I thought. *Ridiculous.*

Caves. Caves, shadows, and cheesecake.

We eventually reached the top of the stairwell, and it opened out into a long hallway constructed of stone blocks. Along this hallway was a line of large, thick, wooden doors set into stone archways.

'This is more like it,' I said. 'I'll bet the sands are behind one of these doors.'

'Well,' Bastille said, 'let's try one, then.'

I nodded, then walked up to the first door. I listened at it for a moment, but either there was no sound on the other side of the wood was so thick that I couldn't hear anything.

'See any darkness around the door?' Bastille whispered.

I shook my head.

'The Dark Oculator probably isn't in there, then,' Bastille said quietly.

'It could open into anything,' Sing said.

'Well, we'll never find the sands if we keep to the hallways,' Bastille said.

I glanced at the other doors. None of them seemed to glow any more than the others. Bastille was right – we had to start trying them, and any one was as good as the next. So, I took a breath and pushed against the door in front of me. I'd intended to move it open slightly, so we could peek in, but the door swung far more easily than I'd expected. It flew open, exposing the large room beyond, and I stumbled into the doorway.

The room was filled with dinosaurs. Real, live, moving dinosaurs. One of them waved at me.

I paused for a moment. 'Oh,' I finally said, 'is that all? I was worried that I might find something strange in here.'

9

I'd like you to realize two things at this point.

First, I want you to know that when I uttered the words 'Oh, is that all? I was worried I might find something strange in here,' I wasn't being sarcastic in the least. Actually, I was being quite serious. (Nearly as serious, even, as the moment when I would plead for my life while tied to an altar of outdated encyclopedias.)

You see, after all I'd seen that day, I was growing desensitized to strangeness. The realization that the world contained three new continents still had me in shock. Compared to that revelation, a room full of dinosaurs just couldn't compete.

'Why, hello, good chap!' cried a small green Peteridactyl. 'You don't look like a Librarian sort.'

Talking rocks might have gotten a reaction out of me. A talking slice of cheese definitely would have. Talking dinosaurs … meh.

The second thing I want you to realize is this: You were warned beforehand about the talking dinosaurs. (Kindly see page 40.) So no whining.

I stepped into the room. It was some sort of storage chamber and was filled with battered cages. Many of those cages contained … well, dinosaurs. At least, that's what they looked like to me.

Of course, they were quite different from the dinosaurs I'd learned about in school. For one thing, they weren't very big. (The largest one, an orange Tyrannosaurus Rex, was maybe five or six feet tall. The smallest looked to be only about three feet tall.) The vests, trousers, and British accents were unexpected as well.

'I say,' said a Triceratops. 'Do you think he's a mute? Does anybody by chance know sign language?'

'Which sign language do you mean?' asked the Pteridactle. 'American primitive, New Elshamian, or Librarian standard?'

'My hands aren't articulated enough for sign language,' noted the Tyrannosaurus Rex. 'That's always been rather a bother for deaf members of my subspecies.

'He can't be mute!' another said. 'Didn't he say something when he opened the door?'

Bastille poked her head into the room. 'Dinosaurs,' she said, noticing the cages. 'Useless. Let's move on.'

'I say!' said the Triceratops. 'Charles, did you hear that?'

'I did indeed!' replied the Pterydactle. 'Quite rude, if I do say so myself.'

I frowned. 'Wait. Dinosaurs are British?'

'Of course not,' Bastille said, stepping into the room with a sigh. 'They're Melerandian.'

'But they're speaking English with a British accent,' I said.

'No,' Bastille said, rolling her eyes. 'They're speaking *Meleran* – just like we are. Where do you think the British and the Americans got the language from?'

'Uh ... from Great Britain?'

Sing chuckled, stepping into the room and quietly shutting the door. 'You think a little island like that spawned a language used by most of the world?'

I frowned again. 'I say,' said Charles the Pterrodactlye. 'Do you suppose you could let us free? It's *terribly* uncomfortable in here.'

'No,' Bastille said curtly. 'We have to keep a low profile. If you escaped, you could give us away.' Then, under her breath, she muttered, 'Come on. We don't want to get involved.'

'Why not?' I asked. 'Maybe they could help us.'

Bastille shook her head. 'Dinosaurs are *never* useful.'

'She certainly is a rude one, isn't she?' asked the Triceratops.

'Tell me about it,' I replied, ignoring the dark look Bastille shot me. 'Why are you dinosaurs here anyway?'

'Oh, we're to be executed, I'm afraid,' Charles said.

The other dinosaurs nodded.

'What did you do?' I asked. 'Eat somebody important?'

Charles gasped. 'No, no. That's a Librarian myth, good sir. We don't eat people. Not only would that be barbaric of us, but I'm sure you would taste terrible! Why, all we did was come to your continent for a visit!'

'Stupid creatures,' Bastille said, leaning against the door. 'Why would you visit the Hushlands? You know that the Librarians have built you up as mythological monsters.'

'Actually,' Sing noted, 'I believe the Librarians claim that dinosaurs are extinct.'

'Yes, yes,' Charles said. 'Quite true. That's why they're going to execute us! Something about enlarging our bones, then putting them inside of rock formations, so that they can be dug out by human archaeologists.'

'Terribly undignified!' the T. Rex said.

'Why did you even come here?' Sing asked. 'The Hushlands aren't the type of place one comes on vacation.'

The dinosaurs exchanged ashamed glances.

'We ... wanted to write a paper,' Charles admitted. 'About life in the Hushlands.'

'Oh, for the love of ...' I said. 'Is *everybody* from your continent a professor?'

'We're not professors,' the T. Rex huffed.

'We're field researchers,' Charles said. 'Completely different.'

'We wanted to study primitives in their own environment,' the Triceratops said. Then he squinted, looking up at Sing. 'I say, don't I recognize you?'

Sing smiled modestly. 'Sing Smedry.'

'Why, it *is* you!' the Triceratops said. 'I absolutely *loved* your paper on Hushlander bartering techniques. Do they really trade little books in exchange for goods?'

'They call the books "dollar bills",' Sing said. 'They're each only one page long – and yes, they do use them as currency. What else would you expect from a society constructed by Librarians?'

'Can we go?' Bastille asked, looking tersely at me.

'What about freeing us?' the Triceratops asked. 'It would be terribly kind of you. We'll be quiet. We know how to sneak.'

'We're quite good at blending in,' Charles agreed.

'Oh?' Bastille asked, raising an eyebrow. 'And how long did you last on this continent before being captured?'

'Uh …' Charles began.

'Well,' the T. Rex said. 'We *did* get spotted rather quickly.'

'Shouldn't have landed on such a popular beach,' the Triceratops agreed.

'We pretended to be dead fish that washed up with the tide,' Charles said. 'That didn't work very well.'

'I kept sneezing,' said the T. Rex. 'Blasted seaweed always makes me sneeze.'

I glanced at Bastille, then back at the dinosaurs. 'We'll come back for you,' I told them. 'She's right – we can't risk exposing ourselves right now.'

'Ah, very well, then,' said Charles the Pterradactyl. 'We'll just sit here.'

'In our cages,' said the T. Rex.

'Contemplating our impending doom,' said the Triceratops.

The reader may wonder why one of the dinosaurs was consistently referred to by his first name, while the others were not. There is a very simple and understandable reason for this.

Have you ever tried to spell *Pterodactyl*?

We slipped out of the dinosaur room. 'Talking dinosaurs,' I mumbled.

Bastille nodded. 'I can only think of one group more annoying.'

I raised an eyebrow.

'Talking rocks,' she said. 'Where do we go next?'

'Next door.' I pointed down the hallway.

'Any auras?' Bastille asked.

'No,' I replied.

'That doesn't necessarily mean the sands won't be in there,' Bastille said. 'It would take some time for the sands to charge the area with a glow. I think we should check them.'

I nodded. 'Sounds good.'

'Let me open this one,' Bastille said. 'If there *is* something dangerous in there, it would be better if you didn't just stumble in and stare at it with a dumb look.'

I flushed as Bastille waved Sing and me back. Then she crept up to the door, placing her ear against the wood.

I turned to Sing. 'So ... do you really have talking rocks in your world?'

'Oh, yes,' he said with a nod.

'That must be odd,' I said contemplatively. 'Talking rocks ...'

'They're really not all that exciting,' Sing said.

I looked at him quizzically.

'Can you honestly imagine anything interesting that a rock might have to say?' Sing asked.

Bastille shot an annoyed look back at us, and we quieted. Finally, she shook her head. 'Can't hear anything,' she whispered, moving to push open the door.

'Wait,' I said, an idea occurring to me. I pulled out the yellow-tinted Tracker's Lenses and slipped them on. After focusing, I could see Bastille's footprints on the stone – they glowed a faint red. Other than that, the hallway was empty of footprints, except for mine and Sing's.

'Nobody's gone in the room recently,' I said. 'Should be safe.'

Bastille cocked her head, a strange expression on her face. As if she were surprised to see me do something useful. Then she quietly cracked the door open, peeking through the slit. After a moment she pushed it open the rest of the way, waving Sing and me forward.

Instead of dinosaur cages, this room held bookshelves. They weren't the towering, closely packed bookshelves of the first floor, however. These were built into the walls and made the room look like a comfortable den. There were three desks in the room, all unoccupied, though all of them had books open on top of them.

Bastille shut the door behind us. I glanced around the small den – it was well furnished and, despite the books, didn't feel cluttered. *This is more like it,* I thought. *This is the kind of place I might stash something important.*

'Quickly,' Bastille said. 'See what you can find.'

Sing immediately walked to one of the desks. Bastille began poking around, peeking behind paintings, probably looking for a hidden safe. I stood for a moment, then walked over to the bookshelves.

'Smedry,' Bastille hissed from across the room.

I glanced over at her.

She tapped her dark sunglasses. Only then did I realize that I was still wearing the Tracker's Lenses. I quickly swapped them for my Oculator's Lenses, then stepped back, trying to get a good view of the room.

Nothing glowed distinctly. The books, however ... the text on the spines seemed to *wiggle* slightly. I frowned, walking over to a shelf and pulling off one of the volumes. The text had stopped wiggling, but I couldn't read it anyway.

It was just like the book in Grandpa Smedry's glass safe. The pages were filled with scribbles, like a child had taken a fountain pen to a sheet of paper and attacked it in a bout of infantile artistic wrath. There was no specific direction, or reason, to the lines.

'These books,' I said. 'Grandpa Smedry has one like them in the gas station.'

'The Forgotten Language,' Sing said from the other side of the room. 'It doesn't look like the Librarians are having any luck deciphering it either. Look.'

Bastille and I walked over to the place where Sing was sitting. There, set out on the table, were pages and pages of scratches and scribbles. Beside them were different combinations of English letters, obviously written by someone trying to make sense of the scribbles.

'What would happen if they *did* translate it?' I asked.

Sing snorted. 'I wish them good luck. Scholars have been trying to do *that* for centuries.'

'But why?' I asked.

'Because,' Sing said. 'Isn't it obvious? There are important things hidden in those Forgotten Languages texts. If that weren't the case, the language wouldn't have been forgotten.'

I frowned. Something about that didn't make sense. 'It seems the opposite to me,' I said. 'If the language were all that important, then we wouldn't have forgotten it, would we?'

Both of them looked at me as if I were crazy.

'Alcatraz,' Sing said. 'The Forgotten Language wasn't just acci-dentally forgotten. We were *made* to forget it. The entire world somehow lost the ability to read it some three thousand years back. Nobody knows how it happened, but the Incarna – the people who wrote all of these texts – decided that the world wasn't worthy of their knowledge. We forgot all of it, as well as the method of reading their language.'

'Don't they teach you anything in those schools of yours?' Bastille said, not for the first time.

I gave her a flat look. 'Librarian schools? What do you expect?'

She shrugged, glancing away.

Sing glanced at me. 'It's taken us three thousand years to get back even a fraction of the knowledge we had before the Incarna stole it from us. But, there are still lots of things we've never discovered. And nobody has been able to crack the code of the Forgotten Language despite three thousand years of work.'

The room fell silent. Finally, Bastille glanced at me. 'Well?'

'Well what?' I asked.

She glanced at me over the top of her sunglasses, giving me a suffering look. 'The Sands of Rashid. Are they in here?'

'Oh,' I said. 'I don't see anything glowing.'

'Good enough. You would be able to see them glowing even if they were encased in Rebuilder's Glass.'

'I did notice something odd, though,' I said, glancing back at the bookshelves. 'The scribbles on the spines of those books started to wiggle the first time I looked at them.'

Bastille nodded. 'That's just an attention aura – the glasses were trying to get you to notice the text.'

'The *glasses* wanted me to notice something?' I asked.

'Well,' Bastille said. 'More like your subconscious wanted you to notice something. The glasses aren't alive, they just help you focus. I'd guess that because you've seen the Forgotten Language before, your subconscious recognized it on those spines. So, the glasses gave you an attention aura to make you notice.'

'Interesting,' Sing said.

I nodded slowly – then, curiously, Bastille's entire shape fuzzed just slightly. Another attention aura? If so, what as it I was supposed to notice about her?

How do you know so much about Oculator auras, Bastille? I thought, realizing what was bothering me. There was more to this girl than she liked to let people see.

Some things just weren't making sense to me. Why was Bastille chosen to protect Grandpa Smedry? Certainly, she seemed like a force to be reckoned with – but she was still just a kid. And for her to know so much about Oculating, when Sing – a professor, and a Smedry to boot – didn't seem to know much …

Well, it was odd.

You may think those above paragraphs are some kind of foreshadowing. You're right. Of course those thoughts weren't foreshadowing when they occurred to me. I couldn't know that they'd be important.

I tend to have a lot of ridiculous thoughts. I'm having some right now. Most of these certainly *aren't* important. And so, I usually only mention the ones that matter. For instance, I could have told you that many of the lanterns in the library looked like types of fruits and vegetables. But that has no real relevance to the plot, so I left it out. Likewise, I could have included the scene where I noticed the roots of Bastille's hair and wondered why she dyed it silver, rather than letting it grow its natural red. But since that part isn't relevant to the—

Oh. Wait. Actually, that *is* relevant. Never mind.

'Ready to go, then?' Bastille asked.

'I'm taking these,' Sing said. He unzipped his duffel bag, tossed aside a spare uzi, then stuffed in the translator's notes. 'Quentin would kill me if I left them behind.'

'Here,' I said, tossing a Forgotten Language book into the bag. 'Might as well take one of these for him too.'

'Good idea,' Sing said, zipping up his duffel.

'There's just one thing I don't get,' I said.

'*One* thing?' Bastille asked with a snort.

'Why do the Librarians work so hard to keep everything quiet?' I asked. 'Why go to all that trouble? What's the point?'

'Do you have to have a point if you're an evil sect of Librarians?' Bastille asked with annoyance.

I fell silent.

'They do have a point, Bastille,' Sing said. 'Everyone has a reason to do what they do. The Librarians, they were founded by a man named Biblioden. Most people just call him The Scrivener. He taught that the world is too strange a place – that it needs to be ordered, organized, and controlled. One of Biblioden's teachings is the Fire Metaphor. He pointed out that if you let fire burn free, it destroys everything around it. If you contain it, however, it can be very useful. Well, the Librarians think that other things – Oculatory powers, technology, Smedry Talents – need to be contained too. Controlled.'

'Controlled by those who supposedly know better,' Bastille said. 'Librarians.'

'So,' I said, 'all of this cover-up ...'

'It's to create the world The Scrivener envisioned,' Sing said. 'To create a place where information is carefully controlled by a few select people, and where power is in the hands of his followers. A world where nothing strange or abnormal exists. Where magic is derided, and everything can be blissfully ordinary.'

And that's what we fight, I thought, coming to understand for the first time. *That's what this is all about.*

Sing threw his duffel over his shoulder, adjusting his glasses as Bastille went back to the door, cracking it open to make certain nobody was in the hallway. As she did, I noticed the discarded uzi, lying ignored on the floor. Trying to look nonchalant, I wandered over to it, absently reaching down and picking it up.

This is, I would like to note, precisely the same thing *any* thirteen-year-old boy would do in that situation. A boy who wouldn't do such a thing probably hasn't been reading enough books about killer Librarians.

Unfortunately for me, I wasn't like most thirteen-year-old boys. I was special. And, in this case, my specialness manifested itself by making the gun break the moment I touched it. The weapon made a noise almost like a sigh, then busted into a hundred different pieces. Bullets rolled away like marbles, leaving me sullenly holding a piece of the gun's grip.

'Oh,' Sing said. 'I meant to leave that there, Alcatraz.'

'Yes, well,' I said, dropping scrap of metal. 'I thought I should ... uh, take care of the gun, just in case. We wouldn't want anyone to find such a primitive weapon and hurt themselves by accident.'

'Ah, good idea,' Sing said. Bastille held open the door, then we all moved into the hallway.

'Next door,' Bastille said.

I nodded, switching glasses. As soon as the Tracker's Lenses were on, I noticed something: bright black footprints, burning on the ground.

They were still fresh – I could see the trail disappearing as I watched. And there was a certain ... *power* to the footprints. I instantly knew to whom they belonged.

The footprints passed through the hallway, beside a yellowish-black set, disappearing into the distance. They burned, foreboding and dark, like gasoline dropped to the floor and lit with black fire.

As Bastille crept toward the next door in the hallway, I made a decision. 'Forget the room,' I said, growing tense. 'Follow me!'

10

A re you annoyed with me yet?

Good. I've worked very hard – perhaps I will explain why later – to frustrate you. One of the ways I do this is by leaving cliff-hangers at the ends of chapters. These sorts of things force you, the reader, to keep on plunging through my story.

This time, at least, I plan to make good on the cliff-hanger. The one at the end of the previous chapter is entirely different from the hook I used at the beginning of the book. You remember that one, don't you? Just in case you've forgotten, I believe it said:

'So, there I was, tied to an altar made from outdated encyclopedias, about to get sacrificed to the dark powers by a cult of evil Librarians.'

This sort of behavior – using hooks to start books – is inexcusable. In fact, when you read a sentence like that one at the beginning of a book, you should know *not* to continue reading. I have it on good authority that when an author gives a hook like this, he isn't ever likely to explain why the poor hero is tied to an altar – and, if the explanation *does* come, it won't arrive until the end of the story. You'll have to sit through long, laborious essays, wandering narratives, and endless ponderings before you reach the small bit of the story that you *wanted* to read in the first place.

Hooks and cliff-hangers belong only at the ends of chapters. That way, the reader moves on directly to the next page – where, thankfully, they can read more of the story without having to suffer some sort of mindless interruption.

Honestly, authors can be so self-indulgent.

'Alcatraz?' Bastille asked as I took off down the hallway following the footprints.

I waved for her to follow. The black footprints were fading

quickly. True, if the black ones disappeared, we could just follow the yellow ones, since they appeared more stable. But if I
didn't keep up with the black ones, I wouldn't know if the two
sets diverged.

Bastille and Sing hurried along behind me. As we moved,
however, the thought of what I was doing finally hit me: I was
chasing down the Dark Oculator. I didn't even really know what a
Dark Oculator was, but I was pretty certain that I didn't want to
meet one. This was, after all, probably the person who had sent a
gunman to kill me.

Yet I was also pretty certain that this Dark Oculator was the
leader of the library. The most important person around. That
made him the person most likely to know where the Sands of
Rashid were. And I intended to get those sands back. They were
my link to my parents, perhaps the only clue I would ever get to
help me know what had happened to them. So, I kept moving.

Now some of you reading this may assume that I was being
brave. In truth, my insides were growing sick at the thought
of what I was doing. My only excuse can be that I didn't really
understand how much danger I was in. Knowledge of the Free
Kingdoms and Oculators was still new to me, and the threat didn't
quite seem real.

If I'd understood the risk – the death and pain that pursuing
this course would lead to – I would have turned back right then.
And it would have been the right decision, despite what my bio-
graphers say. You'll see.

'What are we doing?' Bastille hissed, walking quickly beside
me.

'Footprints,' I whispered. 'Someone passed this way a short
time ago.'

'So?' she asked.

'They're black.'

Bastille stopped short, falling behind. She hurriedly caught up,
though. '*How* black?'

'I don't know,' I said. 'Blackish black.'

'But I mean …'

'It's him,' I said. 'The footprints seem like they're *burning*. Like they were seared into the stones and are slowly melting away the floor. That's how black they are.'

'That's the Dark Oculator, then,' Bastille said. 'We don't want to follow them.'

'Of course we do. We have to find the sands!'

Bastille grabbed my arm, yanking me to a halt. Sing puffed up behind us. 'Goodness!' he said. 'Ancient weapons certainly are heavy!'

'Bastille,' I said, 'we're going to lose the trail!'

'Smedry, *listen to me*,' she said, still gripping my arm. 'Your grandfather might be able to face a high-level Dark Oculator. *Might*. And he's one of the Free Kingdoms' most powerful living Oculators, with an entire repertoire of Lenses. What do you have? Two pairs?'

Three, I thought, reaching into my jacket pocket. *Those Firebringer's Lenses. If I could turn them on the Dark Oculator . . .*

'I know that look,' Bastille said. 'Your grandfather gets it too. Shattering Glass, Smedry! Is everyone in your family an idiot? Do your Talent genes replace the ones that give most people common sense? How am I supposed to protect you if you insist on being so foolish?'

I hesitated. Down the hallway, the last of the dark footprints burned away, leaving only the yellowish set. I looked down at them, frowning to myself.

I'm missing something, I thought.

Grandpa Smedry had explained about the Tracker's Lenses. He'd said . . . that the footprints would remain longer for people that I knew well. I glanced back down the way we had come. My own footprints, glowing a weak white, showed no signs of fading. Bastille and Sing's sets, however, were already beginning to disappear.

That yellow set of footprints, I realized, turning back toward the ways the Dark Oculator had gone. *They must belong to someone I know . . .*

That was too big a mystery for me to ignore.

I reached into my pocket, pulling out the small hourglass Grandpa Smedry had given me. 'Look, Bastille,' I said, holding it up before her. 'We only have a *half hour* until this place gets filled with Librarians back from patrolling. If that happens, we'll get caught, and those sands will fall permanently into Librarian hands. We don't have time to go poking around, looking in random doors. This place is *way* too big. There's only one way to find what we need.'

'The Dark Oculator might not even have the sands with him,' Bastille said.

'Perhaps,' I said. 'But he might know where to find them – or he might lead us to them. We at least have to try to follow him. It's our best lead.'

Bastille nodded reluctantly. 'Don't try to fight him, though.'

'I won't,' I said. 'Don't worry – it'll be all right.'

And if you believe that, then I have a bridge to sell you ... *on the moon*.

To my credit, I didn't really *want* to face down a Dark Oculator. I was half hoping that Bastille would talk me out of the decision. Usually when I tried to do reckless things, there had been adults around to stop me. But things were different now. By some act of fortune – perhaps even more strange than the appearance of talking dinosaurs and evil Librarians – I was in charge. And people listened to me. I was realizing that if I chose poorly, I would not only get myself into trouble but I might end up getting Bastille and Sing hurt as well.

It was a sobering thought. My life was changing, and so my view of myself had to change as well. You might think I was turning into a hero – however, the truth is that I was just setting myself up for an even greater fall.

'We'll stay out of sight,' I said. 'Eavesdrop and hope the Dark Oculator mentions where the sands are. Our goal is *not* to fight him. At the first sign of trouble – or, in Sing's case, tripping – we'll back out. All right?'

Bastille and Sing nodded. Then I turned. The yellowish footprints were still there. A little more cautious, I followed them down the hallway. We passed a couple more archways, set with solid wooden doors, but the footprints didn't lead into any of them. The hallway led deeper and deeper into the library.

Why build a library that looks like a castle inside? I thought, passing an ornate lantern bracket shaped like a cantaloupe. The lantern atop it burned a large flame, and – despite the tense situation – something occurred to me.

'Fire,' I said as we walked.

'What?' Bastille asked.

'You can't tell me that those lanterns are more "advanced" than electric lights.'

'You're still worried about *that*?'

I shrugged as we paused at an intersection, and Bastille peeked around it, then waved the all clear.

'They just don't seem very practical to me,' I whispered as we started again. 'You can turn electric lights on and off with a switch.'

'You can do that with these too,' Bastille said. 'Except without the switch.'

I frowned. 'Uh ... okay.'

'Besides,' Bastille whispered. 'You can light things on fire with these lamps. Can you do that with electric ones?'

'Well, not most of them,' I said, pointing as the footprints turned down a side corridor. 'But that's sort of the idea. Open flames like that can burn things down.'

I couldn't see because of the sunglasses, but I had the distinct impression that Bastille was rolling her eyes at me. 'They only burn things if you *want* them to, Smedry.'

'How does *that* work?' I whispered, frowning.

'Look, do we have time for this?' Bastille asked.

'Actually, no,' I said. 'Look up there.'

I pointed ahead, toward a place where the hallway opened into a large room. This diversion was actually quite fortunate for Bastille, for it meant that she didn't have to explain how silimatic lanterns work – something I now know that she couldn't have done anyway. Not that I'd point out her ignorance to her directly.

She tends to start swinging handbags whenever I do things like that.

Bastille went up the hallway first. Despite .myself, I was impressed by her stealth as she crept forward, close to the wall. The room ahead was far better lit than the hallway, and her movements threw shadows back along the walls. After reaching the place where the hallway opened into the room, she waved Sing and me forward. I realized that I could hear voices up ahead.

I approached as quietly as possible, creeping up next to Bastille. There was a quiet clink as Sing huddled beside us, setting down his gym bag. Bastille shot him a harsh look, and he shrugged apologetically.

The room at the end of the corridor was actually a large, three-story entryway. It was circular, and our corridor opened up onto a second-story balcony overlooking the main floor down below. The footprints turned and wound around a set of stairs, leading down. We inched forward to the edge of the balcony and looked down upon the people I had tracked.

One of them was indeed a person I knew. It was a person I had known for my entire life: Ms. Fletcher.

It made sense. After all, Grandpa Smedry had said that she'd been the one to steal the sands from my room. The idea had seemed silly to me at the time, but then a lot of things had been confusing to me back then. I could now see that he must have been right.

And yet, it seemed so odd to see a person from my regular life in the middle of the library. Ms. Fletcher wasn't a friend, but she was one of the few constants in my life. She had directed my moves from foster family to foster family, always checking in on me, looking after me ...

Spying on me?

Ms. Fletcher still wore her unflattering black skirt, tight bun, and horn-rimmed glasses. She stood next to a hefty man in a dark business suit with a black shirt and a red power tie. As he turned, conversing with Ms. Fletcher, I could see that he wore a patch over one eye. The other eye held a red-tinted monocle.

Bastille breathed in sharply.

'What?' I asked quietly.

'He only has one eye,' she said. 'I think that's Radrian Blackburn. He's a very powerful Oculator, Alcatraz – they say he put out his own eye to increase the power focused through his single remaining one.'

I frowned. 'Blackburn?' I whispered. 'That's an interesting name.'

'It's a mountain,' Bastille said. 'I think in the state you call Alaska. Librarians named mountains after themselves – just like they named prisons after us.'

I cocked my head. 'I'm pretty sure that Alcatraz Island is older than I am, Bastille.'

'You were named after someone, Alcatraz,' Sing said, crawling up next to us. 'A famous Oculator from long ago. Among people from our world – and among our opponents – names tend to get reused. We're traditional that way.'

I leaned forward. Blackburn didn't look all that threatening. True, he had an arrogant voice and seemed a bit imposing in his black-on-black suit.

Still, I had expected something more dramatic. A cape, maybe?

I was, of course, missing something very important. You'll see in a moment.

Beside me, Bastille looked *very* nervous. I could see her pulling her purse up, reaching one hand inside of it. An odd gesture, I thought, since I doubted there was anything inside that purse that could face down a Dark Oculator. Anyway, the voices from below quickly stole my attention. I could just barely hear what Blackburn was saying.

'. . . you hadn't scared him off last night,' the Oculator said, 'we wouldn't *be* in this predicament.'

Ms. Fletcher folded her arms. 'I brought you the sands, Radrian. That's what you wanted.'

Blackburn shook his head. Hands clasped behind his back, he began to stroll in a slow circle, his well-polished shoes clicking on the stones below.

'You were supposed to watch over the boy,' he said, 'not *just* collect the sands. This was sloppy, Shasta. Very sloppy. What possessed you to send a regular thug to go collect the child?'

Ms. Fletcher sent the gunman, I thought with a stab of anger. *She really was working for them, all this time.*

'That's what I've always done,' Ms. Fletcher snapped. 'I send one of my men to move the boy to another foster home.'

Blackburn turned. 'Your man drew a gun on a Smedry.'

'That wasn't supposed to happen,' Ms. Fletcher said. 'Someone must have bribed him – someone from one of the other factions, I'd guess. The Order of the Shattered Lens, perhaps? We won't know for certain until the interrogation is complete, but I suspect that they were afraid that you'd manage to recruit the boy.'

Recruit me? That comment made me cock my head. However, there was something more pressing in that statement. It implied that Ms. Fletcher *hadn't* wanted me killed. For some reason, that made me relieved, though I knew it was foolish.

Down below, Blackburn shook his head. 'You should have gone yourself to collect him, Shasta.'

'I intended to go along,' Ms. Fletcher said. 'But ...'

'But what?'

She was silent for a moment. 'I lost my keys,' she said.

I frowned. It seemed like an odd comment to make. Blackburn, however, simply laughed at this. 'It still has the better of you, doesn't it?'

I could see Ms. Fletcher flushing. 'I don't see what problem you have working with me. The man who tried to shoot the boy was working for someone else. We should be focusing on discovering what those sands do.'

'The problem is, Shasta,' Blackburn said, growing solemn again, 'this operation was sloppy. When my people are sloppy, it makes *me* look incompetent. I'm not very fond of that.' He paused, then looked at her. 'This is not a time we can spare mistakes. Old Smedry is in this town somewhere.'

Ms. Fletcher paused. 'Him? You think it was *him*?'

'Who else?' Blackburn asked.

'There are a lot of elderly Oculators, Radrian,' she said.

Blackburn shook his head. 'I should think that you, of all people, would recognize the Old One's handiwork. He's in the city, after the same thing that we were.'

'Well,' Ms. Fletcher said. 'If Leavenworth was here, he's gone now. He'll have the boy out of Inner Libraria before we can track him down.'

'Perhaps,' Blackburn said quietly.

I squirmed. As I listened, I'd revised my earlier opinion of Blackburn. I didn't like this man. Blackburn seemed too ... thoughtful. Careful.

Dangerous.

'I've always been curious,' Blackburn said, as if to himself. 'Why did they leave a Smedry of the pure line to be raised in Inner Libraria? Old Leavenworth must have known that we would find the boy. That we would watch him, control him. It seems like an odd move, wouldn't you say?'

Ms. Fletcher shrugged. 'Perhaps they just didn't want him. Considering his ... parentage.'

What? I thought. *Say more on that!*

But Blackburn didn't. He just shook his head thoughtfully. 'Perhaps. But then this child seems to have an inordinately power-ful Talent. And there were always the sands. Old Smedry must have known, as we did, that the sands would arrive on the boy's thirteenth birthday.'

'So, they used the boy as bait for the sands,' Ms. Fletcher said. 'But we got to them first.'

'And old Smedry ended up with the child. Who gained the bet-ter half of the deal, I wonder?'

Tell me where the sands are! I thought. *Say something useful!*

'As for the sands,' Ms. Fletcher said. 'There is the matter of payment ...'

Blackburn turned, and I caught a flash of emotion on his face. Anger?

Ms. Fletcher raised a finger. 'You don't own me, Blackburn. Don't presume to think that you do.'

'You'll get paid, woman,' Blackburn said, smiling.

It was not the type of smile one wanted to see. It was dark. Dark as the footprints I had followed. Dark as the hatred in a man's eyes the moment he does something terrible to another person. Dark as an unlit street on a silent night, when you know something is out there, watching you.

It was from this smile that I realized where Radrian Blackburn got the title 'Dark' Oculator.

'You would sell the child too, wouldn't you?' Blackburn said, still smiling as he removed his monocle, rubbed it clean, then placed it in his pocket. 'You would pass him off for wealth, as you did with the sands. Sometimes you impress even me, Fletcher.'

Ms. Fletcher shrugged.

Blackburn placed a different monocle onto his eye.

Wait, I thought. *What am I forgetting?*

And then I realized what it was. Ms. Fletcher's footprints, along with Blackburn's, shone below. I was still wearing the Tracker's Lenses. Cursing quietly, I pulled them off, then switched them for my Oculator's Lenses.

Blackburn glowed with a vibrant black cloud. He crackled with power, giving off an aura so strong that I had to blink against the terrible shining darkness.

If Blackburn gave off an aura like that … what did I give off?

Blackburn smiled, turning directly toward the place where I was hiding with the others. Then his monocle flashed with a burst of power.

I immediately fell unconscious.

11

You probably assume you know what is going to happen next: me, tied to an altar, about to get sacrificed. Unfortunately, you're wrong. The story hasn't gotten to that part yet.

This revelation may annoy you. It may even frustrate you. If it does, then I've achieved my purpose. However, before you throw this book against the wall, you should understand something about storytelling.

Some people assume that authors write books because we have vivid imaginations and want to share our vision. Other people assume that authors write because we are bursting with stories, and therefore *must* scribble those stories down in moments of creative propondidty.

Both groups of people are completely wrong. Authors write books for one, and only one, reason: because we like to torture people.

Now, actual torture is frowned upon in civilized society. Fortunately, the authorial community has discovered in storytelling an even more powerful – and more fulfilling – means of causing agony in others. We write stories. And by doing so, we engage in a perfectly legal method of doing all kinds of mean and terrible things to our readers.

Take, for instance, the word I used above. *Propondidty*. There is no such word – I made it up. Why? Because it amused me to think of thousands of readers looking up a nonsense word in their dictionaries.

Authors also create lovable, friendly characters – then proceed to do terrible things to them (like throw them in unsightly, Librarian-controlled dungeons). This makes readers feel hurt and worried for the characters. The simple truth is that authors *like* making people squirm. If this weren't the case, all novels would be filled completely with cute bunnies having birthday parties.

So, now you know the reason why I – one of the most wealthy and famous people in the Free Kingdoms – would bother writing a book. This is the only way I can prove to all of you that I'm not the heroic savior that you think I am. If you don't believe what I'm telling you, then ask yourself this: would any decent, kindhearted individual become a writer? Of course not.

I know how this story ends. I know what really happened to my parents. I know the true secret of the Sands of Rashid. I know how I finally ended up suspended over a bubbling pit of acid magma, tied to a flaming altar, staring at my reflection in the twisted, cracked dagger of a Librarian executioner.

But I am not a nice person. And so, I'm not going to reveal any of these things to you. Not yet, anyway.

So there.

'I can't believe how *stupid* I am!' Bastille snapped.

I blinked, slowly coming awake. I was lying on something hard.

'I should have realized that Alcatraz would have an aura,' Bastille continued. 'It was so obvious!'

'He only just started using Oculator's Lenses, Bastille,' Sing said. 'You couldn't have known he'd have an aura already.'

She shook her head. 'I was sloppy. I just … have trouble thinking of that idiot as an Oculator. He doesn't seem to know anything.'

I groaned and opened my eyes, discovering a bland stone ceiling above me. The something hard I was lying on turned out to be the ground. And no, it didn't want to be friends with me.

'What happened?' I asked, rubbing my forehead.

'Shocker's Lenses,' Bastille said. 'Or … well, *one* Shocker's Lens. They cause a flash of light that knocks out anyone who's looking at the Oculator.'

I grunted, sitting. 'I'll have to get a set of those.'

'They're *very* difficult to use,' Bastille said. 'I doubt you could manage it.'

'Thanks for the confidence,' I grumbled. We were in a cell,

apparently. It felt more like a dungeon than a prison. There was a pile of straw to one side, apparently to use for sleeping, and there didn't appear to be any 'facilities' besides a bucket by the wall.

It was certainly not a place I wanted to spend any extended period time. Especially in mixed company.

I stumbled to my feet. My jacket was gone, as were Sing's bag of weapons and Bastille's handbag. 'Is there anyone out there?' I asked quietly. The cell had three stone walls, while the front was set with more modern-style, cagelike bars.

'One guard,' Bastille said. 'Warrior.'

I nodded, then took a deep breath and walked up to the front of the cell. I put one hand on the bars and activated my Talent.

Or, at least, I tried to. Nothing happened.

Bastille snorted. 'It won't work, Smedry. Those bars are made from Reinforcer's Glass. Things like Smedry Talents and Oculator powers won't affect them.'

'Oh,' I said, lowering my hand.

'What did you expect to do anyway?' she snapped. 'Save us? What about the soldier out there? What about the Dark Oculator, who is in the room next door?'

'I didn't think—'

'No. No, you Smedrys *never* think! You make all this talk about "seeing" and "information," but you never do anything useful. You don't plan, you just *go*. And you drag the rest of us along with you!'

She spun and walked as far from me as she could, then sat down on the floor, not looking at me.

I stood silent, a little stupefied.

'Don't mind her, Alcatraz,' Sing said quietly, joining me at the front of the cell. 'She's just a little angry with herself for letting us get caught.'

'It wasn't her fault,' I said. 'It was mine.'

It was mine. Not words I'd often said. I was a little surprised to hear them come out of my mouth.

'Actually,' Sing said, 'it's really not *any* of our fault. You were right to suggest following Blackburn – he was probably our best chance of finding the sands. But, well, this is how things turned out.'

Sing sighed, running his hand along one of the bars. I reached out and felt one too, noting now that Bastille had been right – the bar didn't quite feel like iron. It was too smooth.

'There were a few Smedrys who could have gotten through these bars, Reinforcer's Glass or no,' Sing said. 'Ah, to have a Talent like that ...'

'I think your Talent is pretty useful,' I said. 'It saved us down below, and that stumble you did to create a distraction was great. I've never seen anything so amazing!'

Sing smiled. 'I know you're just saying that. But I appreciate it anyway.'

We stood quietly for a moment, and I found myself feeling frustrated, and more than a little guilty. Despite what Sing had said, I felt responsible for getting us captured. Slowly, the real weight of what was going on began to press against me.

I'd been imprisoned by the type of people who sent armed gunmen to collect young boys from their homes – people who included a man so evil, he left dark footprints burning on the ground. Blackburn obviously could have killed me if he'd wanted. That meant he had kept me alive for a reason. And I was growing more and more certain I didn't want to know what that reason was.

It had been a long time since I'd felt true dread. I'd learned over the years to be a bit callous – I'd had to, with my foster parents abandoning me so often. In that moment, however, dread pushed through my shell.

Bastille was still sulking in the back, so I glanced at Sing, looking for some sort of comfort. 'Sing? Our ancestors – could you tell me about some of them?'

'What would you like to know?'

I shrugged.

'Well,' Sing said, rubbing his chin. 'There was Libby Smedry – she was quite the capable one. I've often wished to have a Talent half as grand as hers.'

'And it was?'

'She could get impossible amounts of water on the floor when she did the dishes,' Sing said, sighing slightly. 'She single-handedly ended the drought in Kalbeeze during the fourth-third century – and she did it while keeping all their dishware sparkling clean!'

He smiled wistfully. 'Also, I suppose everyone knows about Alcatraz Smedry the Seventh – he would be about sixteen generations removed from you. The Librarians weren't around then, but Dark Oculators were. Alcatraz Seven had the Talent to make annoying noises at inappropriate times. He defeated enemy after enemy – you see, he distracted the Dark Oculators so much that they couldn't concentrate hard enough to work their Lenses!'

Sing sighed. 'Thinking about those kinds of Talents always makes tripping seem so bland.'

'Breaking things isn't all that great either,' I said.

'No, Alcatraz. Breaking things – now that's a *real* Talent. One of the great old talents, talked about in the legends. I know I shouldn't really complain about my power – I should be happy to have anything. But you … it would be a true shame to speak ill of a Talent like that. And it couldn't have been given to a better Smedry.

A better Smedry …

Sing smiled at me encouragingly, and glanced away. *I'm getting too attached to him,* I thought. *To all of them – Grandpa Smedry, Sing, even Bastille.*

'Come on,' Sing said. 'Don't look so glum.'

'You don't really know me, Sing,' I found myself saying. 'I'm not a good person.'

'Nonsense!' Sing said.

I leaned against the bars of the cell, glancing out – not that there was much to look at. A simple stone wall stood across from the cell. 'You don't know the things I've done, Sing. The … breaking. The pain I've brought to good people – people who just wanted to give me a home.'

Sing shrugged. 'Actually, Alcatraz, Grandpa Smedry spoke of you sometimes. He talked about the … mishaps that happened around you. He said he thought it might be related to your Talent, and turns out it was. Not your fault at all!'

Why did you burn down your foster parents' kitchen? Grandpa Smedry had asked. *It seems like a perversion of your Talent ...*

'No,' I said. 'It *was* my fault, Sing. I didn't break simple, ordinary things. I broke the things that were the most valuable to people who cared for me. I made them hate me. On purpose.'

'No,' Sing said. 'No, that doesn't sound like something a Smedry could do.'

'Every family has its black sheep, Sing,' I said. 'I'm a ... broken Smedry. Maybe that's why the Dark Oculator didn't kill me. Maybe he knows that I'm not noble like the rest of you. Maybe he knows that he might be able to pull me to his side. Perhaps I'd be better there.'

Sing fell silent. I waited for him to look horrified or betrayed.

After a few moments, Sing raised a hand and put it on my shoulder. 'You're still my cousin. Even if you've done bad things, that doesn't make you a Dark Oculator. Anything you've done, you can fix. You can change.'

It's not that easy, I thought. *Will Sing be that forgiving when I accidentally break something precious to him? His books perhaps? What will Sing Smedry do when he finds all that he loves broken and mangled, discarded at the feet of the disaster known as Alcatraz Smedry?*

Sing smiled, removing his hand from my shoulder, apparently thinking that the problem was resolved. But it wasn't, not for me. I sat down on the stones, arms around my knees. *What's wrong with me lately? Sing seems determined to like me. Why am I so concerned with making certain he knows what I've done?*

I turned away from Sing and, for some reason, found myself thinking about days long past.

I have trouble remembering the first things I broke. They were valuable, though – I remember that. Expensive crystal things, collected by my first foster mother. It seemed that I could barely walk by her room without one of them shattering.

That wasn't all either. Any room they locked me in I could

escape without even really trying. Anything they bought or brought into the home, the curious young Alcatraz would study and inspect.

And break.

So, they got rid of me. They hadn't been cruel people – I'd just been too much for them. I saw them once, on the street a few months later, walking with a little girl. My replacement. A girl who didn't break everything she touched, a girl who fit better into what they had imagined for their lives.

I shivered, sitting with my back to the glass bars of my prison cell. Sometimes I tried – I tried *so* hard – not to break anything. But it was like the Talent welled up inside of me when I did that. And then, when it burst free, it was even more powerful.

A tear rolled down my cheek. After moving from family to family enough times, I'd realized that they would all leave me eventually. After that, I hadn't worried as much about what I broke. In fact … I'd begun to break things more often – important things. The valuable cars of a father who collected vehicles. The trophies won by a father who played sports in college. The kitchen of a mother who was a renowned chef.

I'd told myself that these things were simply accidents. But now I saw a pattern in my life.

I broke things early, quickly. The most valuable, important things. That way, they'd know. They'd know what I was.

And they'd send me away. Before I could come to care for them. And get hurt again.

It felt safer to act that way. But what had it done to me? In breaking so many objects, had I broken myself? I shivered again. Sitting in that cold Librarian dungeon – faced by my first (but certainly not last) failure as a leader – I finally admitted something to myself.

I don't just break, I thought. *I destroy.*

12

At this point, perhaps you feel sorry for me. Or perhaps you feel that my suffering was deserved, considering what I'd done to all those families who tried to take me in.

I'd like to tell you that all of this soul-searching was good for me. And perhaps it did help in the short term. However, before you get your hopes up, let me promise you here and now that the Alcatraz Smedry you think you know is a farce. You may see some promising things developing in my young self, but in the end, none of these things were able to save those I love.

If I could go back, I'd drive Sing and the others away for good. Unfortunately, at that point in my life, I still had some small hope that I'd find acceptance with them. I should have realized that attachment would only lead to pain. Especially when I failed to protect them.

Still, it was probably good for me to realize that I was driving people away on purpose, for it let me understand just how bad a person I am. Perhaps more young boys should be captured by evil Librarians, forced to sit in cold dungeons, contemplating their faults as they wait for their doom. Perhaps I'll start a summer camp based on that theme.

The weirdest part about this all, I thought, *is that nobody yet has made a joke about a pair of kids named Alcatraz and Bastille getting locked in a prison.*

Of course, we weren't in a very jokey mood at that moment. I couldn't know for certain, since the hourglass – along with my jacket – had been taken from me, but I figured that our remaining half hour had passed, and then some. I tried very hard not to look at the latrine bucket, in the hopes that it wouldn't remind my body of any duties that needed to be done.

Yet as I sat and thought, some very strange things were happening to me. I'd always kind of thought of myself as a defiant rebel against the system. However, the truth was that I was just a whiny kid who threw tantrums and broke things because he wanted to make certain that he hurt others before they hurt him. It was that dreaded humility again, and it was having a very odd effect on me. It should have made me feel like a worm, crushing me down with shame. Yet for some reason, it didn't do that.

Realizing my faults didn't make my head bow but made me look up instead. Realizing how stupid I had been didn't cause me grief but made me smile at my own foolishness. Losing my identity didn't make me feel paranoid or worthless.

The truth was, I'd secretly felt all of those things – shame, grief, paranoia, insecurity – for most of my life. Now that I wasn't covering them up, I could begin to let go of them. It didn't make me a perfect person, and it didn't change what I'd done. However, it did let me stand up and face my situation with a little more determination.

I was a Smedry. And while I wasn't quite certain of all that meant, I was beginning to have a better idea. I crossed the room, passing Sing, and crouched down by Bastille.

'Bastille,' I whispered. 'We've waited long enough. We have to figure a way to get out of here.'

She glanced up at me, and I could see that her face was streaked with tears. I blinked in surprise. *Why has she been crying?*

'Get out?' she said. 'We can't get out! This cell was *built* to hold people like you and me.'

'There has to be a way.'

'I've failed,' Bastille said quietly, as if she hadn't heard me.

'*Bastille*,' I said. 'We don't have time for this.'

'What do you know?' she snapped. 'You've been an Oculator all of your life, and have you done anything with it? Never! You didn't even know. How is that fair?'

I paused, then reached up to touch my face. I hadn't even noticed – my glasses were gone.

Of course they are, I thought. *They took my jacket with the*

Tracker's Lenses and the Firebringer's Lenses in the pocket. They took Bastille's and Sing's Warrior Lenses. They would have taken my Oculator's Lenses.

'You didn't even notice, did you?' Bastille asked bitterly. 'They took your most powerful possession, and you didn't even notice.'

'I haven't been wearing them for long,' I said. 'Only a few hours, really. I guess it felt natural to me for them to *not* be there when I woke up.'

'Natural for them to not be there,' Bastille said, shaking her head. 'Why do *you* get to be an Oculator, Smedry? Why you?'

'Aren't all Smedrys Oculators?' I asked. 'Or, at least, all of those in the pure line?'

'Most of them are,' she said. 'But not all of them. And there are plenty of Oculators who *aren't* Smedrys.'

'Obviously,' I said, glancing over my shoulder, toward the room where Blackburn and Ms. Fletcher supposedly were.

Then I glanced back at Bastille, cocking my head. She stared at me defiantly. *That's it. That's what I've been missing.* 'You wanted to be one, didn't you?' I asked. 'An Oculator.'

'It's none of your business, Smedry.'

But it made too much sense to ignore. 'That's why you know so much about Oculator auras. And you were the one who identified the Lenses that Blackburn used on us. You must have studied a whole lot to learn so many things.'

'For all the good it did,' she said with a quiet snort. 'I learned that studying can't change a person, Smedry. I've always wanted to be something I wasn't – and the thing is, everyone supported me. "You can be anything you want, if you try hard enough!" they said.

'Well, you know what, Smedry? They lied. There are some things that you just *can't* change.'

I stood silently.

Bastille shook her head. 'You can't study yourself into being something you aren't. I won't ever be an Oculator. I'll have to settle for being what my mother always told me I *should* be. The thing I'm apparently "gifted" in.'

'And that is?' I asked.

'Being a warrior,' she said with a sigh. 'But I guess I'm not too good at that either.'

Now, you're probably expecting poor Bastille to 'learn something' by the end of this book. You probably expect to see her overcome her bitterness, to realize that she never should have given up on her dreams.

You think this because you've read too many silly stories about people who achieve things they previously thought impossible – deep and poignant books about trains that climb hills or little girls who succeed through sheer determination.

Let me make one thing very clear. Bastille will *never* become an Oculator. It's a genetic ability, which means you can only become an Oculator if your ancestors were Oculators. Bastille's weren't.

People can do great things. However, there are some things they just *can't* do. I, for instance, have not been able to transform myself into a Popsicle, despite years of effort. I could, however, make myself insane, if I wished. (Though if I achieved the second, I might be able to make myself *think* I'd achieved the first ...)

Anyway, if there's a lesson to be learned, it's this: Great success often depends upon being able to distinguish between the impossible and the improbable. Or, in easier terms, distinguishing between Popsicles and insanity.

Any questions?

I wanted to say something to help Bastille. After all, I'd just undergone a life-changing revelation, and I figured that there should be enough to go around. Unfortunately, Bastille wasn't exactly in a 'life-changing revelation' sort of mood.

'I don't need your pity, Smedry,' she snapped, swatting my arm away. 'I'm just fine as I am. There really isn't anything you could do to help anyway.'

I opened my mouth to reply, but at that moment, I heard a door open. I turned as Ms. Fletcher strolled into the hallway outside our cell.

'Hello, Smedry,' she said.

'Ms. Fletcher,' I said flatly. 'Or "Shasta," or whatever your real name is.'

'Fletcher will do,' she said, obviously trying to sound friendly. She couldn't quite pull it off. 'I've come to chat.'

I shook my head. 'I have little to say to you.'

'Come now, Alcatraz. I've always looked out for you, despite how difficult you made my life. Surely you can see that I have your best interests at heart.'

'Somehow I doubt that, Ms. Fletcher.'

She raised an eyebrow. 'That's all you have to say? I expected something a little more ... scathing, Smedry.'

'Actually, I've changed,' I said. 'You see, I just had a life-changing revelation and don't plan to make snide comments anymore.'

'Is that so?'

'Yes, it is,' I said firmly.

Ms. Fletcher cocked her head, a strange look on her face.

'What?' I asked.

'Nothing,' she said. 'You just ... reminded me of someone I used to know. Anyway, I don't care what game you are playing today. The time has come for us to deal.'

'Deal?'

Ms. Fletcher nodded, leaning in. 'We want the old man. The crazy one who came and got you this morning.'

'You mean Grandpa Smedry?' I asked, glancing at Sing, who was watching quietly. Apparently, he was content to let me take the lead in the conversation.

'Yes,' Ms. Fletcher said. 'Grandpa Smedry. Tell us where he is and we'll let you go.'

'Let me go? Let me go where?'

'Out,' Ms. Fletcher said, motioning with her hand. 'We'll find you another foster family and things can go back to the way they were.'

'That hardly seems compelling,' I said.

'Alcatraz,' Ms. Fletcher said flatly. 'You're in a Librarian dungeon, and you have Oculator blood. If you aren't careful, you'll end up as a sacrifice. I'd be a little more friendly if I were you – I'm likely the only ally you'll find in this place.'

This was, of course, the first time I ever heard about a ceremony involving sacrificial Oculators. I dismissed the comment as an idle threat.

Foolish, foolish Alcatraz.

'If you're the best ally I have, Ms. Fletcher,' I said, 'then I'm in serious trouble.'

'That sounded just a little bit snide, Alcatraz,' Sing said helpfully. 'You may want to back off a little.'

'Thank you, Sing,' I said, still watching Ms. Fletcher, my eyes narrowed.

'I can get you out, Alcatraz,' Ms. Fletcher said. 'Don't make me do something we'd both regret. I've watched over you for years, haven't I? You can trust me.'

Watched over you for years ... 'Yes,' I said. 'Yes, you *have* watched over me. And every time a family abandoned me, you told me I was useless. It was like you *wanted* me to feel abandoned and unimportant.' I met her eyes. 'That's it, isn't it? You were worried that I'd learn what it meant to be a Smedry. That's why you always treated me like you did. You needed me to be insecure, so that I would trust you – and distrust my Talent.'

Ms. Fletcher looked away. 'Look, let's just make a deal. Let me get you out, and we can forget about the past for now.'

'And these others?' I asked, nodding toward Sing and Bastille. 'If I go free, what happens to them?'

'What do you care?' Ms. Fletcher asked, looking back at me.

I folded my arms.

'You *have* changed,' Ms. Fletcher said. 'And not for the better, I'd say. Is this the same boy who burned down a kitchen yesterday? Since when did you start caring about the people around you?'

The answer to that question was actually 'About five minutes ago.' However, I didn't intend to share that information with Ms. Fletcher.

'Okay,' I said. 'We'll have an exchange. You want to know where the old man is? Well, I want to know some things too. Answer my questions, and I'll answer yours.'

'Fine,' Ms. Fletcher said, folding her arms.

Businesslike as always, I thought. 'How did you know about the Sands of Rashid?'

Ms. Fletcher waved an indifferent hand. 'Your parents promised them to you at your birth. It's a custom – to pronounce an inheritance upon a newborn and deliver it on the child's thirteenth birthday. Everyone knew that you were *supposed* to get those sands. Some of us are a little surprised that they actually made their way to you, but we were happy to see them nonetheless.'

'Did you know my parents, then?'

'Of course,' Ms. Fletcher said. 'Actually, I studied under them. I thought they might be able to train me to be an Oculator.'

I snorted. 'That's not something you can learn.'

'Yes, well,' Ms. Fletcher said, looking a little flustered, 'I was young.'

'Were you friends with them, then?' I asked.

'I got along better with your father than your mother,' Mr. Fletcher said.

'Did you kill them?' I asked, teeth gritted.

Ms. Fletcher laughed a flat, lifeless laugh. 'Of course not. Do I look like a killer?'

'You sent a man with a gun after me.'

'That was a mistake,' Ms. Fletcher said. 'Besides, your parents were Smedrys. They would be even harder to kill than you.'

'And why do you want Grandpa Smedry?' I asked.

'No, I think I've answered enough questions,' Ms. Fletcher said. 'Now, fulfill your end of the bargain. Where is the old man?'

I smiled. 'I forgot.'

'But ... our bargain!'

'I lied, Ms. Fletcher,' I said. 'I do that sometimes.'

See, I promised you. Life-changing revelation or not, I never was all that good a person.

Ms. Fletcher's eyes opened wide, and she displayed more emotion that I'd ever seen from her as she began muttering at me under her breath.

'Enough!' a new voice said. A dark-suited arm shoved Ms.

Fletcher away, and Blackburn moved over to stand in front of the cell.

'Tell me where the old fool is, boy,' Blackburn said quietly. He stared at me, his monocle glistening with a reddish color. Even without my Oculator's Lenses, I swear that I could see a little black cloud rising from him.

'If you don't talk willingly,' Blackburn said, reaching up to take off his monocle, 'I will *make* you.' He pulled another monocle from a vest pocket. It had green and black tints. 'This is a Torturer's Lens. By looking through it and focusing on a part of your body, I can make you feel intense agony. It makes the muscles begin to rip, and while it *probably* won't kill you, you will soon start to wish that it would.'

He reached up, putting the monocle in place. 'I've seen men permanently paralyzed by these things, boy. I've seen them break their own bones as they thrash about on the ground, crying out with such pain that they'd have killed themselves to stop it. Does that sound like fun? Well, if not, you should start talking. *Now!*'

It's funny what a little taste of leadership can do to someone. A shade of responsibility, a smidgen of self-understanding, and I was ready to stand up to a full-blooded Dark Oculator. I gritted my teeth, jutted out my chin defiantly, and stared him in the eye.

So, of course, I got my heroic little self blasted with a beam of pure pain.

This is supposed to be a book for all ages, so I won't go into details about how it felt to get hit by a Torturer's Lens. Just try and remember the worst wound you've ever felt. The most agonizing, most terrifying pain in your life. Remember it, hold it in your head.

Then imagine if a shark swam by and bit you in half while you were distracted. That's a little what it felt like. Only, add in swallowing a few grenades and suffering through a night at the opera too. (And don't *try* and tell me I didn't warn you about the sharks.)

The pain let up. I lay on the floor of the cell, though I didn't remember falling. Sing was at my side, and even Bastille was moving over to me, her face concerned. My agony faded slowly, and

I looked up, seeing Blackburn as a dark shadow standing before the cell.

There was a small twist of pleasure on his lips. 'Now, boy, tell me what I want to know.'

And I would have. This is your hero, Free Kingdomers. I broke that easily – I hadn't ever known pain; I was no soldier. I was just a kid trapped by forces he had no hope of understanding. I would have told Blackburn anything he wanted to know.

However, I didn't have a chance to spit it out. At that moment, you see, Grandpa Smedry poked his head into the dungeon hallway, smiling happily.

'Why, hello, Blackburn,' he said. Then he waved to me, holding up a pair of hands that were manacled together. He wasn't wearing his Oculator's Lenses, and a pair of beefy-looking men in dark robes and black sunglasses stood behind him, holding his arms.

'It appears that I've been captured,' Grandpa Smedry said, manacle chains clinking. 'I hope I'm not too late!'

13

We have now spent two complete chapters trapped in the dungeon. We're about to embark on our third chapter in there, assuming I ever finish with this introduction.

Three chapters is an awfully long time in book terms. You see, time moves differently in novels. The author could, for instance, say, 'And I spent fourteen years in prison, where I obtained the learning of a gentleman and discovered the location of a buried treasure.' Now, this sounds like it would be a great deal of time – fourteen *years* – but it actually only took one sentence to explain. So, therefore, it happened very quickly.

Three chapters, on the other hand, is a very long time. It is a longer time than I spent in my foster home. It is a longer time than I spent visiting the gas station. It's a longer time than I spent in childhood, which was covered in only about two sentences.

Why so long in prison? At that moment, I was struggling with the same question. Few things are more maddening than forced inactivity, and I had been forced into inactivity for two entire chapters. True, I'd made some good, deep, personal revelations – however, the time for those had passed. I would almost *rather* have been tied to an altar and sacrificed, as opposed to being forced to sit around and wait while my grandfather was towed off to be tortured.

For, you see, that was what happened in between chapters – a space of time so short that it's practically nonexistent. During that void of nothingness, Blackburn laughed evilly a couple of times, then pulled Grandpa Smedry off to the 'Interrogation Room.' Apparently, the Dark Oculator was overjoyed at the prospect of having a fully trained Smedry to torture.

But then again, who wouldn't be?

'Come back here!' Bastille screamed, pounding the latrine bucket repeatedly against the bars. I was now even more glad that I hadn't ended up needing to use it.

'Come back and fight me!' she yelled, slamming the bucket against the bars in one final overhand strike, venting her fury by smashing the wooden container into a dozen different pieces. She stood, puffing for a second, holding a broken handle.

'Well,' Sing whispered, 'at least she's getting back some of her good humor.'

Right, I thought. By then, my agony had faded almost to nothingness. (I later learned that I'd only been subjected to the Torturer's Lens for a period of three seconds. It takes at least five to do permanent damage.)

I empathized with Bastille – I even felt some of her same rage, even if I didn't express it by destroying innocent bucketry. The longer I sat, the more ashamed I felt at how quickly I'd broken. Yet remembering those three seconds of pain made me shudder.

And even worse than the memory was the knowledge that my grandfather – a man I barely knew, but one for whom I already felt a sincere affection – had been captured. At that very moment, the old man was probably being subjected to the Torturer's Lens. And *his* torture would last far longer than three seconds.

Bastille reached down, picking up a few bucket shards and tossing them in annoyance at the wall outside the cell.

'That isn't helping, Bastille,' I said.

'Oh?' she snapped. 'And what about sitting on the ground, looking stupid? How much good is *that* doing?'

I blinked, flushing.

'Bastille, lass,' Sing said quietly. 'That was harsh, even for you.'

Bastille puffed quietly for a few more moments, then turned away. 'Whatever,' she muttered, walking over to kick at the hay pile with a frustrated motion. 'It's just that … Old Smedry … I mean, he's a fool, but I think of him being tortured …'

She kicked at the hay again, tossing a pile into the air. The way it bounced off the wall and fell back on her might have been comical, had the situation been different.

'We all care for him, Bastille,' Sing said.

'You don't understand,' Bastille said, picking a few strands of hay out of her silvery hair. 'I'm a Knight of Crystallia! I'm sworn to protect the Oculators of the Free Kingdoms. And I was assigned to be *his* guard. I'm supposed to protect the old Smedry – keep him out of situations like this!'

'Yes, but—'

'No, Sing,' Bastille said. 'You really don't understand. Leavenworth is a fully trained Smedry of the pure line. Not just that, he's a member of the Oculator Council and is the trusted friend of *dozens* of kings and rulers. Do you have any idea the kinds of state secrets he knows?'

Sing frowned, and I looked up.

'Why do you think the Council insists that he *always* keep a Knight of Crystallia around to protect him?' Bastille asked. 'He complains – says he doesn't need a Crystin guard. Well, the Council would have conceded to him long ago, if it were just his life that he endangered. But he knows things, Sing. *Important* things. That's why I'm supposed to keep him out of trouble, why I'm supposed to do my best to protect him.' She sighed, slumping down beside the wall. 'And I failed.'

And at that moment, I probably said the dumbest thing I ever have.

'Why you?' I asked. 'I mean, if he's so important, why – of all people – did they choose *you* to protect him?'

Yes, it was very insensitive. No, it wasn't very helpful. However, it's what slipped out.

You know you were thinking the same thing anyway.

Bastille's eyes widened with anger, but she didn't snap at me. Finally, she just let her head slump against her knees. 'I don't know,' she whispered. 'They never told me – they never even explained. I had barely achieved knighthood, but they sent me anyway.'

We all fell silent.

Finally, I stood. I walked to the bars of the cell. Then I knelt. *I've broken cars, kitchens, and chickens,* I thought. *I've destroyed the homes and possessions of people who took me in. I've broken the hearts of people who wanted to love me.*

I can break the cell that is keeping me a prisoner.

I reached out, gripping the bars, then closed my eyes and focused.

Break! I commanded. Waves of power washed down my arms, tingling like jolts of electricity. They slammed into the bars.

And nothing happened.

I opened my eyes, gritting my teeth in frustration. The bars remained where they were, looking annoyingly unbroken. There wasn't even a crack in them. The lock was made of glass as well, and somehow I knew that it would react the same way to my Talent.

Again, I feel the need to point out the Popsicle lesson. Desire does not instantly change the world. Sometimes, stories gloss over this fact, for the world would be a much more pleasant place if you could obtain something simply by wanting it badly enough.

Unfortunately, this is a real and true story, not a fantasy. I couldn't escape from the prison simply because I wanted to.

Yet I would like to note something else at this point. Determination – true determination – is more than simply *wanting* something to happen. It's wanting something to happen, then finding a realistic way to make certain that what you want to happen, happens.

And that happened to be what was happening with the story's current happenings.

I ignored the bars, instead laying my palm flat against the stones of the cell floor. They were large, sturdy blocks, plastered together with a smooth mortar. The bars ran directly into holes in the stone.

I smiled, then closed my eyes again, focusing. I hadn't often used my Talent so intentionally, but I felt that I was gaining some skill with it. I was able to send a wave of power through my arms and into the rocks.

The mortar cracked quietly beneath my fingers. I focused harder, sending out an even larger wave of breaking power. There was a loud *crack*. When I opened my eyes, I found that I was kneeling in dust and chips, the stones beneath my knees reduced entirely to rubble.

I stared, a little shocked at just how much of the stone I had broken. Sing stood, looking on with a surprised expression. Even Bastille looked up from her mourning. Cracks in the stone twisted across the floor, spiderwebbing all the way to the back of the cell.

They keep saying that my Talent is powerful, I thought. *How much could I really break, if I set my mind to it?* Eagerly, I reached up, grabbing a bar and trying to pull it free from its now-rubbled mountings.

It remained firm. It didn't even budge a bit.

'Did you really think that would work?' an amused voice asked.

I looked up at the dungeon guard, who had walked over to watch me. He wore the clothing one might have expected of a Librarian – an unfashionable knit vest pulled tight over a buttoned pink shirt, matched by a slightly darker pink bow tie. His glasses even had a bit of tape on them.

Only one thing about him deviated from what I would have expected: He was huge. He was as tall as Sing, and easily twice as muscular. It was like a bodybuilder supersoldier had beaten up an unfortunate nerd and – for some inconceivable reason – stolen his clothing.

The guard punched a fist into his palm, smiling. He wore a sword tied at his waist, and his glasses – the taped ones – were dark, like the ones that Sing and Bastille wore. Once again, I was struck by the unfairness of letting the warriors wear sunglasses, while I was stuck with slightly pink ones.

That is one complaint, by the way, I still haven't gotten over.

'The stones are just there for show,' the Librarian said. 'The entire cage is made from Reinforcer's Glass – it's a box, with the bars at the front. Breaking the stones won't do any good. You think we aren't familiar with Smedry tricks?'

He's too far away to touch, I thought with frustration. *But ... what was it Grandpa Smedry said when I destroyed that gunman's weapon?*

The man had threatened me. And my Talent had worked pro-actively, instinctively.

At a distance.

I reached down, picking up a few pieces of wood from the broken bucket. The beefy Librarian snorted and turned to walk back to his post. I, however, tossed a piece of wood through the bars, hitting him in the back of the head.

The guard turned, frowning. I bounced another piece of wood off his forehead.

'Hey!' the Librarian snapped.

I threw harder, this time causing the Librarian to flinch as the bit of wood came close to his eyes.

'Alcatraz?' Sing asked nervously. 'Are you certain this is wise?' Bastille, however, stood up. She walked toward the front of the cell.

I threw again.

'Stop that!' the Librarian said, stepping forward, raising his fists.

I threw a fifth piece of wood, hitting him in the chest.

'All right,' the Librarian said, reaching down to unsheathe his sword. 'What do you think of this?' He stuck the sword forward, apparently intending to force me back with it.

Bastille, however, moved more quickly. I watched with shock as she grabbed the blade of the sword, somehow managing to keep from cutting herself as she yanked it forward. This threw the Librarian off balance, and he stumbled toward the cell, still holding on to his weapon.

Bastille snapped forward, reaching between the bars and grab-bing the Librarian guard by the hair. Then she yanked the man's head down and forward, slamming it against the glass bars.

The sword clanged to the ground. The guard's unconscious body followed a second later. Bastille knelt down, grabbing the guard's arm and pulling him up against the cell bars. Then she began fishing around in his pockets. 'All right, Smedry,' she ad-mitted, 'that was well done.'

'Uh, no problem,' I said. 'You . . . took him down pretty smoothly.'

Bastille shrugged, pulling something out of the man's pocket – a glass sphere. 'He's just a Librarian thug.'

'No match for a trained Knight of Crystallia,' Sing agreed. 'Yes, that was indeed quite clever, Alcatraz. How did you know he'd lose his temper and pull out the sword?'

'Actually,' I said, 'I was trying to get him to throw something at me.'

Bastille frowned. 'What good would that do?'

'I figured it would engage my Talent if he tried to hurt me.'

Sing rubbed his chin. 'That would probably have broken the thing he threw at you. But ... how was that going to get us out of the cell?'

I paused. 'I hadn't exactly gotten that far yet.'

Bastille placed the glass sphere against the lock. It clicked; the door swung open.

'Either way,' she said, 'we're out.' She glanced at me, and I could see something in her eyes. Relief, even a bit of gratitude. It wasn't an apology – but from Bastille, it was virtually the same thing. I took it for what it was worth.

Bastille left the cell and stooped down beside the unconscious Librarian. She pulled off his sunglasses, removed the tape – which was apparently there just for show – then slipped the glasses on her own face. After that, she grabbed the guard by one arm and pulled him into the cell. She quickly patted him down, pulling out a wallet and a dagger as Sing and I left the cell. Then she closed the door, using the glass sphere to lock it again.

She grinned and held up the sphere to me. 'Would you mind?'

I smiled as well, then reached out with one finger and touched the sphere. It shattered.

She dug in the wallet for a moment. 'Nothing useful in here,' she noted. 'Except maybe this.' She pulled out a small card.

'A library card?' I asked.

'What else?' she said. I took it from her fingers, turning it over.

'Hey, they're gone,' Sing said. He was peeking into the room beside the dungeon, the one where Grandpa Smedry, Ms. Fletcher, and the Dark Oculator had gone.

Bastille and I joined him. The room was indeed empty, except for our possessions, which had been carefully set out on a table.

'Thank the First Sands,' Bastille said with relief, tossing aside the guard's sword in favor of her handbag. 'I was worried that I'd be stuck with those common weapons. I'd almost rather have had some guns.'

'Now, that's not very nice,' Sing said, waddling forward to inspect his guns, which sat on the table beside the gym bag.

I joined the two of them at the table as Bastille replaced her silver jacket. 'There, Smedry,' she said. My three pairs of glasses sat on the table. I grabbed the Oculator's Lenses eagerly, slipping them on.

Of course, nothing really *changed*. And yet, it did. Even though I wasn't used to wearing glasses, I found myself comforted to feel their weight on my face. I grabbed the other two pairs, the Firebringer's Lenses still inside their small pouch.

'We have to move quickly,' Bastille said.

Sing nodded, checking the clip on a handgun. He tucked several uzis into the front of his kimono belt, threw on four separate handgun holsters, then strapped the shotgun onto his back. He soon looked like some bizarre fat Rambo samurai.

'We have to find the room where they took your grandfather,' Bastille said.

'No problem,' I said, slipping off my Oculator's Lenses, then putting on the Tracker's Lenses. Though Blackburn's footprints had disappeared, Grandpa Smedry's prints blazed a fiery white, still present. They led out the door on the far side of the room. Ms. Fletcher's diverged from them, heading in a different direction.

We'll have to worry about her later, I thought, nodding toward the other two. Sing slung the gym bag over his shoulder – it was still filled with ammunition – and we set off, moving quickly out after Grandpa Smedry's footprints.

And so, I managed to escape from my first dungeon. Determination can actually take you quite far – though, admittedly, you sometimes have to rely on the thirteen-year-old girl to knock out the guards.

14

Yes, you're very clever. You noticed a problem.

In the last chapter, Sing, Bastille, and I escaped from prison, then immediately rushed off to save Grandpa Smedry. But, of course, Grandpa Smedry was being tortured by the very same man who had captured Sing and Bastille and me in the first place.

That meant we were in vaguely the same position as before. How did we intend to defeat a master Oculator – a dark, powerful man with more experience than all of us combined? Well, the answer is simple.

While imprisoned, we had gained a newfound wisdom. We came to a greater understanding of the world around us and of our place in it. We gained insight regarding our ...

Oh, all right. None of us paused to think about what we were doing. In our defense, we were a little bit flustered at the time. Plus, two of us were Smedrys.

That ought to explain it.

'This way,' I said, pointing down another castlelike corridor, following Grandpa Smedry's footprints. And as we ran, something occurred to me. (No, not the fact that we were running after the man who had so easily captured us previously. Something else.)

'These corridors look familiar,' I said.

'That's because *all* the corridors in this place look the same,' Bastille said.

'No,' I said. 'It's not just that. That lantern bracket looks like a cantaloupe.'

'They're all designed to look like one fruit or another,' Bastille said.

'And we've passed this one before,' I said.

'You think we're going in circles?' Bastille asked.

'No,' I said. 'I think we passed it while chasing down Blackburn that first time. That's the lantern I saw that made me ask you about electric lights. That means—'

Sing tripped.

I stood for just a brief moment. Then I dove for the ground. Sing didn't even try to keep his balance, and he toppled like a felled tree. Bastille also threw herself down with a vengeance, as if determined to get to the floor first. All three of us hit, dropping as fast as a group of pathological martyrs at a grenade testing ground.

Nothing happened.

'Well?' I asked, glancing around.

'I don't see anything,' Bastille whispered. 'Sing?'

'I think I bruised something,' he muttered, rubbing his side. 'One of these pistols jammed me in the tummy!'

I snorted quietly. 'Be glad it didn't go off. Now, why did you trip?'

'Because my foot hit something,' Sing said. 'That's usually how it works, Alcatraz.'

'But there was nothing in this hallway to trip on!' I said. 'The floor is perfectly level.'

Sing nodded. 'You have to have a real Talent to trip like I do.'

'Which returns us to my original question,' I said. 'Is there a reason why we all had to hit the deck like that? This floor isn't very comfortable.'

'Floors rarely are,' Sing said.

'Hush!' Bastille said, scanning the corridor. 'I thought I heard something.'

We fell silent for a moment. Finally, Sing shrugged. 'Sometimes a trip is just a trip, I guess. Maybe I—'

The wall exploded.

It *really* exploded. Rubble flew across the corridor, bits of shattered rock spraying against the wall just above me. I cried out, covering my head with my arms as chips and pebbles showered down.

The explosion opened up a large section in the wall to my left. I could see through the opening to where a hulking shadow stood in the clearing dust.

'An Alivened!' Bastille yelled, scrambling up.

I stood, bits of broken stone tumbling off my clothing. The creature obviously wasn't human. It was misshapen – its arms were far too wide and long, and they jutted out of the body in a threatening posture. In a way, the upper half of its body looked like an enormous 'M,' though I had rarely seen a letter of the alphabet look quite so dangerous.

As the dust settled, I could see that the thing was pale white, with patterns of gray and black peppering its wrinkled skin. In fact, it looked like . . .

'Paper?' I asked. 'That thing is made of wadded-up pieces of paper?'

Bastille cursed, then grabbed me by the shoulder and shoved me down the corridor. 'Run!' she said.

The urgency in her voice made me obey, and I took off. Sing ran behind, and Bastille backed away from the broken wall, looking on warily as the lumbering paper monster pulled its way through the hole and into the corridor.

'Bastille!' I yelled.

'Come on lad!' Sing said from beside me. 'Regular Aliveneds are bad enough – but a Codexian . . . well, they're the most powerful of the lot.'

'But Bastille!'

'She'll follow, lad. She's just giving us a head start!'

I let myself get pulled along. However, I watched over my shoulder as I ran, keeping an eye on Bastille. She ducked a few swings from the massive creature. Then finally, she turned and began to run.

Fast.

You Hushlanders likely have never seen a Knight of Crystallia use her abilities to her fullest potential. People like Bastille spend years practicing inside of their city kingdom, training their bodies, bonding to their swords, learning to use Warrior's Lenses, and finally being implanted with a certain magical crystal. (Though, again, the Free Kingdomers consider this to be technology, rather than magic.) Only the best trainees are given the title of knight. To this day, Bastille holds the record for attaining the rank at the youngest age.

Regardless, all of this training and special preparation means that when Crystins want to run, they can really *run*. I was shocked as I saw Bastille take off after us, dashing with a speed that would have made any Olympic sprinter give up and become an accountant.

Sing yelled suddenly, lurching to a halt. I, unfortunately, was following right behind him, and, as I turnèd, I was met by a chestful of Mokian posterior. Sing wasn't a Crystin, but he was wearing Warrior's Lenses, which probably helped him keep his balance as I bounced off of him and fell back into the hallway.

'Sing?' I said. 'What—'

The large anthropologist reached to his waist, pulling out a pair of handguns. And then – with the flair of a man who had watched too many action movies – he began to unload them at something farther down the corridor. I twisted to the side and was met by the sight of another Alivened – also made completely from wadded-up pieces of paper – lumbering down the hallway in front of us.

Sing's guns had little effect on the creature. Bits of paper flipped into the air as the bullets tore through the Alivened's body. Each impact seemed to slow it a bit, but it still continued to move toward Sing at an unsteady pace.

Bastille pulled up beside me. 'Shattered Glass!' she cursed, turning. The Alivened behind us was quickly approaching. 'You'd better do something, Smedry,' she said, whipping her handbag off her shoulder. 'I don't know if I can handle these things on my own.'

With that, she reached into the purse and grabbed something inside. She whipped her hand out, throwing the bag aside as she drew forth a massive crystalline sword.

I blinked. Yes, the thing Bastille had pulled from her purse was, indeed, a sword. It was nearly as tall as Bastille was, and it glittered in the lantern light, refracting a spray of rainbow colors across the corridor.

The handbag, of course, couldn't have held something so long. However, if the pulling of a sword from a handbag is the thing in this story that stops you, then you likely need therapy. I could recommend a good psychologist. Of course, he's Librarian controlled. They all are.

It's a union thing.

Bastille jumped forward, her sword glistening as she charged the Alivened. It swung at her, and she rolled, just barely ducking beneath its massive arm. Then she sliced, shearing the thing's arm completely free.

The arm fell off, its wrinkled pages suddenly straightening and bursting into the air – like those of a book that had suddenly had its binding torn free. They fluttered as they fell. The Alivened, however, didn't seem to mind the missing limb – and I soon saw why. The lumps of paper in its body surged forward, forming a new arm to replace the one that Bastille had cut free.

I finally shook myself from my daze, scrambling to my feet. Behind me, Sing pulled out twin uzis. He knelt, holding the weapons with meaty hands, and automatic weapon fire echoed in the corridor. His Alivened paused from the shock, a flurry of paper scraps exploding from its body. It stumbled for a moment, then continued on despite the rain of bullets.

'Alcatraz!' Sing yelled over the gunfire. 'Do something!'

I ran to the side of the corridor, grabbing a lantern off the wall. The cantaloupe-shaped holder broke free easily beneath my Talent, and I turned, hurling it at Sing's Alivened as Sing ran out of bullets.

The lantern crashed into the Alivened, then bounced free. The creature did not catch on fire.

'Not like that!' Sing said, reloading his uzis. 'Nobody would build an Alivened out of paper without also making it resistant to a little fire!'

Sing raised the uzis and fired another spray of bullets. The thing slowed but pressed on, continuing its inevitable march.

Now, if you are ever writing a story such as this, you should know something. Never interrupt the flow of a good action scene by injecting needless explanations. I did this once, in Chapter Fourteen of an otherwise very exciting story. I regret it to this day.

Also, if you are ever attacked by unstoppable monsters created entirely from bad romance novels, you should do exactly what I did: Quickly reach into your pocket and pull free your Firebringer's Lenses.

Resistant to a little fire, eh? I thought, yanking open the velvet pouch. *What about a* lot *of fire?!*

I reached into the pouch with desperate fingers, whipping out the Lenses — yet, as before, my touch was too unpracticed, and I was too powerful for my own good. The Lenses activated as soon as I touched them.

They began to glow dangerously.

'Gak!' I said. I tried to get the Lenses turned around. However, I fumbled, spinning the Lenses so they pointed backward at me instead.

At that moment, my Talent proactively broke the spectacles' frames. Both Lenses fell to the ground, one shattering as it hit the stones, the other bouncing away and falling facedown. It fired, blasting a stream of concentrated light into the stones beneath it.

'Alcatraz!' Sing said desperately as his uzis ran out of bullets again. He dropped them, reaching over his shoulder to pull out the shotgun. He fired it with a loud boom. The Alivened's chest exploded with a burst of paper, spraying confetti across the corridor.

The creature stumbled, nearly falling as Sing hit it again. However, it righted itself and continued to walk toward him.

I reached for the intact Firebringer's Lens, but shied back from the heat. The Lens itself wasn't hot, of course — that would make it fairly difficult to wear on the face. However, it was superheating the stones around it, and I couldn't get close.

I turned urgently to check on Bastille, and I was just in time to see her ram her crystal sword directly into her opponent's chest. The Alivened, however, slammed its bulky arm into her, tossing her backward. The sword remained jutting ineffectively from its chest, and Bastille crashed into the stone wall of the corridor, crumpling.

'Bastille!' I shouted.

She did not move. The creature loomed over her.

Now, as I've tried to explain, I wasn't a particularly brave boy. But it has been my experience that doing something brave is much like saying something stupid.

You rarely plan on it happening.

I charged the Alivened monster. It turned toward me, stepping away from Bastille, and raised its arm to swing. I somehow managed to duck the blow. Stumbling, I reached up and grabbed the sword in the creature's chest. I pulled it free.

Or, rather, I pulled the hilt free.

I stumbled back, raising the hilt to swing before I realized that the crystal blade was still sticking in the monster's chest.

Behind me, Sing's shotgun began to click, out of ammunition.

I lowered my hand, staring at the hilt. My Talent, unpredictable as always, had broken the sword. I stood for a long moment – far longer, undoubtedly, that I should have in those circumstances. I gripped the broken hilt.

And began to grow angry.

All my life, my Talent had ruled me. I'd pretended to go along with it, pretended that I was the one in control, but that had been a sham. I'd purposely driven my foster families away because I'd known that sooner or later, the Talent would do it for me – no matter what I wanted.

It was my master. It defined who I was. I couldn't be myself – whoever that was – because I was too busy getting into trouble for breaking things.

Grandpa Smedry and the others called my Talent a blessing. Yet I had trouble seeing that. Even during the infiltration, it seemed like the Talent had been only accidentally useful. Power was nothing without control.

The Alivened stepped forward, and I looked up, teeth clenched in frustration. I gripped the sword hilt tightly.

I don't want this, I thought. *I never wanted any of this! Bastille wanted to be an Oculator ... well, I just wanted one thing.*

To be normal!

The hilt began to break in my hand, the carefully welded bits of steel falling free and clinking to the ground. 'You want breaking?' I yelled at the Alivened. 'You want *destruction?*'

The creature swung at me, and I screamed, slamming my hand palm-forward to the floor. A surge of Talent electrified my body, focusing through my chest and then down my arm. It was a jolt of power like I'd never summoned before.

The floor broke. Or perhaps *shattered* would be a more appropriate word. *Exploded* would have worked, except that I just used that one a bit earlier.

The stone blocks shook violently. The Alivened stumbled, the floor beneath it surging like waves on an ocean. Then the blocks dropped. They fell away before me, tumbling toward the level beneath. Bookshelves in the massive library room below were smashed as blocks of stone rained down, accompanied by an enormous paper monster.

The Alivened hit the ground, and there was a distinct shattering noise. It did not rise.

I spun wildly, dropping the last bits of the sword hilt. Sing was furiously reloading the shotgun. I brushed by him, charging the second Alivened. I reached to touch the ground, but the massive beast jumped, moving quickly out of the way. It was obviously smart enough to see what I had just done to its companion.

I raised a hand, slamming it into the jumping creature's chest. Then I released my Talent.

There was a strange, instant backlash – like hitting something solid with a baseball bat. I was thrown backward, my arm blazing with sudden pain.

The Alivened landed in a stumble. It stood for a moment, teetering. Then it exploded with a whooshing sound, a thousand crumpled sheets of paper erupting in an enormous, confetti-like burst.

I sat for a moment, staring. I blinked a few times, then lifted my hurt arm, wincing. Paper filled the corridor, bits fluttering around us.

'Wow,' Sing said, standing up. He turned around, looking at the massive pit I had created. 'Wow.'

'I ... didn't really do that intentionally,' I said. 'I just kind of let my power go, and that's what happened.'

'I'll take it, either way,' Sing said, resting the shotgun on his shoulder.

I climbed to my feet, shaking my arm. It didn't seem broken. 'Bastille,' I said, stumbling over to her. She was moving, fortunately, and as I arrived she groaned, then managed to sit up. Her jacket looked ... shattered. Like the windshield of a car after it collides with a giant penguin.

Blasted giant penguins.

I tried to help Bastille to her feet, but she shook off my hands with annoyance. She stumbled a bit as she stood, then pulled off her jacket, looking at the spiderweb of lines. 'Well, I guess that's useless now.'

'Probably saved your life, Bastille,' Sing said.

She shrugged, dropping it to the floor. It crackled like glass as it hit the stones.

'Your jacket was made of glass?' I asked, frowning.

'Of course,' Bastille said. 'Defender's Glass. Yours isn't?'

'Uh ... no,' I said.

'Then why wear something so atrocious?' she said, stumbling over to the hole in the floor. 'You did this?' she asked, looking over at me.

I nodded.

'And ... is that my sword down there, broken and shattered in a pile of books?'

'Afraid so,' I said.

'Lovely,' she grumbled.

'I was trying to save your life, Bastille,' I said. 'Which, I might point out, I *succeeded* in doing.'

'Yeah, well, next time try not to bring down half the building when you do.'

But I detected the barest hint of a smile on her lips when she said it.

15

Moron.

It has been my experience that most problems in life are caused by a lack of information. Many people just don't know the things they need to know.

Some ignore the truth; others never understand it.

When two friends get mad at each other, they usually do it because they lack information about each other's feelings. Americans lack information about Librarian control of their government. The people who pass this book on the shelf and don't buy it lack information about how wonderful, exciting, and useful it is.

Take, for instance, the word that started this chapter. You lacked information when you read it. You likely assumed that I was calling you an insulting name. You assumed wrong. *Moron* is actually a village in Switzerland located near the Jura mountain range. It's a nice place to live if you hate Librarians, for there is a well-hidden underground rebellion there.

Information. Perhaps you Hushlanders have read about Bastille and the others referring to guns as 'primitive,' and have been offended. Or, perhaps, you simply thought the text was being silly. In either case, maybe you should re-evaluate.

The Free Kingdoms moved beyond the use of guns many centuries ago. The weapons became impractical for several reasons – some of which should be growing apparent from this narrative. Smedry Talents and Oculator abilities are not the only strange powers in the Free Kingdoms – and most of these abilities work better on items with large numbers of moving parts or breakable circuits. Using a gun against a Smedry, or one similarly talented, is usually a bad idea.

(This comes down to simple probability. The more that can go wrong with an item, the more that will. My computer – when I used to use one – was always about one click away from serious meltdown. My pencil, however, remains to this day remarkably virus-free.)

And so, many of the world's soldiers and warriors have moved on from guns, instead choosing weapons and armors created from Oculatory sands or silimatic technology. They don't often associate these items with their ancient counterparts – the people of the Free Kingdoms never got much beyond muskets before they moved on to using sand-based weapons – and so they think that guns are the primitive weapons. It makes sense, if you look at it from their perspective.

And anyone who's not willing to do that ... well, they might just be a moron. Whether or not they live there.

'Sing, put those primitive guns away!' Bastille snapped, stepping away from the hole in the floor. 'Those shattering things are so loud that half the library must have heard your racket!'

'They're effective, though,' Sing said happily, changing the clips in a pair of his pistols. 'They stopped that Alivened long enough for Alcatraz to take it down. I didn't see your sword doing half as well.'

Bastille grumbled something, then paused, frowning. 'Why is it so hot in here?'

I cursed, turning toward the glowing, smoking stones around the Firebringer's Lens. The floor looked dangerously close to becoming molten.

'I still can't believe old Smedry gave you a Firebringer's Lens,' Bastille said. 'That's like ...'

'Giving a bazooka to a four-year-old?' I asked. I edged as close to the heated stones as I could stand. 'That's kind of what I feel like when I pick the thing up.'

'Well, turn it off!' Bastille said. 'Quickly! You think Sing's guns were loud – using an Oculatory Lens that powerful will draw Blackburn's attention for certain. The longer you leave it on, the more loud it will seem!'

The reference to loudness probably doesn't make much sense

to non-Oculators. After all, the Lens didn't make any noise. However, as I tried to figure out a way to turn off the Firebringer's Lens, I realized that I could *feel* it. Even though I'd only been aware of my Oculatory abilities for a short time, I was already getting in synch with them enough to sense when a powerful Lens was being used nearby.

The point is, I knew Bastille was right. I needed to turn that Lens off quickly. If Blackburn hadn't heard the gunfire, then he'd certainly notice the Lens 'noise'.

'Sing, loan me that shotgun,' I said urgently, waving with my hand.

Sing reluctantly relinquished the weapon. As soon as I touched it, the barrel fell off – but I was ready for that. I grabbed the tube of steel and used it to flip the Firebringer's Lens over. The Lens was convex, meaning it bulged out on one side, and now that it was flipped over it looked like a translucent eyeball staring up out of the ground. It continued to fire its superhot ray of light, which was now directed at the ceiling.

I used the barrel of the gun to scoot the Lens away from the heated section of the floor, then carefully reached out. I gritted my teeth – expecting to get burned – and touched the side of the Lens.

Remarkably (as I've mentioned before) the glass wasn't even hot. As soon as I touched it, the Lens shut off, the ray of light dwindling. I stepped back, surprised at how cold and dark the corridor now seemed by comparison.

'My shotgun,' Sing said despondently as I handed back the barrel. 'This was an antique!'

That's what happens when you stay around me, Sing, I thought with a sigh. *Things you love get broken. Even when I don't do it on purpose.*

'Oh, get off it, Sing,' Bastille said. 'I lost my sword – you can't even *understand* how much trouble I'll be in for that. I was already bonded to the shattering thing; now I'll have to start the process all over, if they even let me. Next to that, your gun is nothing.'

Sing sighed but nodded as Bastille reached into her handbag

and pulled out a large, crystalline knife. You may, by the way, have noticed the connection between the word Crystin and the weapons made of crystal that Bastille uses. This is actually just a coincidence. Crystin is the Vendardi word for 'grumpy,' which all Crystins tend to be. And I think ...

Nah, I'm just kidding. They got the name because they use crystal swords. Plus, they live in a big castle (dubbed Crystallia) made of – you guessed it – crystals. That clear enough? Crystal clear?

Ahem.

'I'm out of bullets for the Uzis too,' Sing said, looking in his bag. 'Small weapons for us both, I guess.'

I knelt down and tentatively poked the Firebringer's Lens, still trying to pick it up off the floor. It began to glow. *Blast!* I thought and touched it again. The glow dissipated.

'Try being dumb,' Bastille suggested.

'Excuse me?' I asked, frowning.

'Think dumb thoughts,' Bastille said. 'Or try not to think very much at all. The Lenses react to information and intelligence. So, it's easiest to handle them when there isn't much of either one around.'

I paused. Then I frowned and looked at the Lens trying my best to be ... well, stupid. I would like to note that this is quite a bit more difficult that it might sound. Particularly for a person like me, who can be (has this been mentioned?) rather clever.

Not only is it against a rashional purson's nature to try and convince himself that he is more stoopid than he thinks he is, it is quite dificult to not think about *anything* when one has been told not to. Only the trooly most briliant of peeple can purrtend stoopidity so sucessfuly.

Butt eet kan bee dun.

I closed my eyes and tried to empty my mind. Then I reached for the Lens. It started to glow. I frowned, then tapped it before it could go off.

'Maybe we should just leave it,' Sing said nervously. 'Before someone sees us.'

'Too late,' Bastille said, nodding down the hallway, to where a group of robed Librarians had just appeared around a corner. They looked quite anxious, and I suspected that Bastille had been right in her earlier comment. The gunfire had been heard.

Bastille glanced at them through her sunglasses, then flipped her knife in her hand, raising it to throw.

'No!' I said. 'Wait!'

Dutifully, she paused. The Librarians scattered, several racing back the way they had come.

'Why did you stop me?' Bastille asked testily.

'Those aren't paper monsters, Bastille,' I said. 'Those are unarmed people. We can't just kill them.'

'We're at war, Alcatraz. Those people are the enemy. Plus, they're going to alert Blackburn!'

I shrugged. 'It just didn't feel right. Besides, there were too many for you to kill them all. We can't keep our escape secret any longer.'

Bastille snorted but otherwise fell silent. Either way, I didn't have any more time for acting stupid. I grabbed the Lens – it began to glow – and quickly shoved it back inside its velvet pouch. Then I reached in and tapped it off with a finger. I pulled the bag shut, then stuffed it in my pocket.

'Let's go, then,' I said.

Bastille nodded. Sing, however, had moved over to the pile of ripped, shredded papers that were the remnants of the Alivened. 'Alcatraz,' he said. 'There's something here you should see.'

'What?' I asked, hurrying over. As I approached, I could see that in the center of the pile, Sing had found what appeared to be a portion of the Alivened that was still ... well, *alive*ned.

It sat up as I arrived, causing Sing to point a pistol at it. The creature was smaller now, and it was much more human-shaped. However, it was still made of crumpled-up paper, and now that I was close, I could see that it had two beady, glasslike eyes.

I frowned, looking at Sing. 'What's going on?'

'I don't know,' Sing said. 'Of course, I don't know a lot about Alivening. It's Dark Oculary.'

'Why?' I asked, watching the three-foot-tall paper man with suspicious eyes.

'Bringing an inanimate thing to life this way is evil,' Bastille said. 'To do it, the Oculator has to give up a bit of his own humanity and store it in Glass of Alivening. That's what those eyes are made of. Shoot it, Sing. If you hit it in the eye, you may be able to kill it.'

The little paper creature cocked its head, quizzically staring down the barrel of the gun.

I looked back at Bastille. 'They give up a bit of their own humanity? What does that mean?'

'They let the glass drain them of things,' Bastille explained.

'Things? That's specific.'

From the side, I could see Bastille narrow her eyes behind her sunglasses, staring at the little creature with suspicion. 'Human things, Alcatraz. Things like the capacity to love, protect others, and have mercy. Each time an Oculator creates an Alivened, he makes himself a little less human. Or, at least, he makes himself a little less like the kind of human the rest of us would want to associate with.'

Sing nodded. 'Most Dark Oculators think the transformation is an advantage.' He reached down with his free hand, still keeping his gun leveled at the small Alivened. He held up a ripped bit of paper.

'You'd think that by giving up part of his humanity,' the anthropologist said, 'the Dark Oculator would create a creature that possessed good emotions. But that's not the way it works. The process twists the emotions, creating a creature that has just enough humanity to live, but not enough of it to really function.'

I accepted the scrap of paper. I could read the text – it appeared to be prose. The title line at the top right corner read *The Passionate Fire of Fiery Passion*.

'You can make an Alivened out of virtually anything,' Sing said. 'But substances that soak up emotion tend to work the best. That's why a lot of Dark Oculators prefer bad romance novels, since the object used determines the Alivened's temperament.

'Romance novels make an Alivened very violent,' Bastille said. 'But rather dense in the intelligence department.'

'Go figure,' I said, dropping the scrap of paper. *They give up their own humanity* ... And this was the monster that had my grandfather held captive. 'Come on,' I said, standing. 'We've wasted too much time already.'

'And this thing?' Sing asked.

I paused. The Alivened looked up at me, its paper face somehow managing to convey a look of confusion.

I ... broke it somehow, I thought. *I thought I'd killed it – but that's not the way my Talent works.* I don't destroy, not when the Talent is in full form. I just break and transform. 'Leave it,' I said.

Sing looked up in surprise.

'We don't want any more gunshots,' I said. 'Come on.'

Sing shrugged, rising. Bastille moved down the hallway, checking the intersection. I quickly swapped my Oculator's Lenses for my Tracker's Lenses – fortunately, my grandfather's footprints were still glowing.

I didn't think I knew him that well, I thought.

I met Bastille at the intersection, pointing to the right branch. 'Grandpa Smedry went that way.'

'The same way the Librarians went,' she said. 'After they discovered us.'

I nodded, glancing in the other direction. I pointed. 'I see Ms. Fletcher's footprints that way.'

'She turned away from the others?'

'No,' I said. 'She didn't go with Grandpa Smedry from the dungeons. Those footprints I can see now are the original ones we followed – the ones that led us to the place where we got captured. I told you we were close to where we started.'

Bastille frowned. 'How well do you know this Ms. Fletcher?'

I shrugged.

'It's been hours,' Bastille said. 'I'm surprised her footprints are still glowing.'

I nodded. As I did, I noticed something else odd.

(If you haven't noticed, this is the chapter for noticing weird things. As opposed to the other chapters, in which only normal things were ever noticed. There is a story I could tell about that, but as it involves eggbeaters, it is not appropriate for young people.)

The normalcy-challenged thing that I had noticed was actually not all that odd, all things considered. It was a lantern holder – the ornate bracket that I'd ripped free when I'd thrown the lantern at the Alivened.

There was nothing all that unusual about this lantern bracket, except for the already-noted fact that it was shaped like a canta-loupe. For all I knew, cantaloupe-shaped library lanterns were quite normal. Yet the sight of this one sparked a memory in my head. *Cantaloupe, fluttering paper makes a duck.*

I glanced back at the hallway behind me, with its broken wall, *more* broken floor, and piles of paper that shuffled in the draft.

It's probably nothing, I thought.

You, of course, know better than that.

16

If you are anything like me – clever, fond of goat cheese, and devilishly handsome – then you have undoubtedly read many books. And, while reading those books, you likely have thought that you are smarter than the characters in those books.

You're just imagining things.

Now, I've already spoken about foreshadowing (a meddling literary convention of which Heisenberg would uncertainly be proud). However, there are other reasons why you only *think* that you're smarter than the characters in this book.

First off, you are likely sitting somewhere safe as you read the story. Whether it be a classroom, your bedroom, your aquarium, or even a library (but we won't get into that right now ...), you have no need to worry about Alivened monsters, armed soldiers, or straw-fearing Gaks. Therefore, you can examine the events with a calm, unbiased eye. In such a state of mind, it is easy to find faults.

Secondly, you have the convenience of holding this story in book form. It is a complete narrative, which you can look through at your leisure. You can go back and reread sections (which, because of the marvelous writing the book contains, you have undoubtedly done). You could even scan to the end and read the last page. Know that by doing so, however, you would violate every holy and honorable story-telling principle known to man, thereby throwing the universe into chaos and causing grief to untold millions.

Your choice.

Either way, since you can reread anytime you want, you could go back and find out *exactly* where I first heard cantaloupes mentioned. With such an advantage, it is very easy to find and point out things that my friends and I originally missed.

The third reason you think you are smarter than the characters is because you have me to explain things to you. Obviously, you don't fully appreciate this advantage. Suffice it to say that without me, you would be far more confused about this story than you are. In fact, without me, you'd probably be *very* confused as you tried to read this book.

After all, it would be filled with blank pages.

Two soldiers stood in the hallway, chatting with each other, obviously guarding the door that sat between them. Sing, Bastille, and I crouched around a corner just a short distance away, unnoticed. We'd followed Grandpa Smedry's footprints all the way here. His prints went through the door – and that, therefore, was the way we needed to go.

I nodded to Bastille, and she slipped quietly around the corner, moving with such grace that she resembled an ice-skater on the smooth stone floor. The guards looked over as she approached, but she was so quick that they didn't have time to cry out. Bastille elbowed one in the teeth, then caught his companion in a grip around the neck, choking him and keeping him quiet. The first guard stumbled, holding his mouth, and Bastille kicked him in the chest.

The first guard fell to the ground, hitting his head and going unconscious. She dropped the second guard a moment later, after he'd passed out from being choked. She hadn't even needed the dagger.

'You really *are* good at this,' I whispered as I approached.

Bastille shrugged modestly as I moved up to the door. Sing followed me, looking over his shoulder down the hallway, anxious.

I knew it wouldn't be long before the entire library was on alert. We didn't have much time. I didn't care about the Sands of Rashid. I just wanted to get my grandfather back.

'His footprints go under the door,' I whispered.

'I know,' Bastille whispered as she peeked through a crack in the door. 'He's still in there.'

'What?' I said, kneeling beside her.

'Alcatraz!' Bastille hissed. 'Blackburn's in there too.'

I paused beside the door, peeking through an open-holed knot in the wood. That was one thing that old-style wooden doors had over the more refined American versions. In fact, Bastille would probably have called this door more 'advanced,' since it had the advantage of holes you could look through.

The view in the room was exactly what I had feared. Grandpa Smedry lay strapped to a large table, his shirt removed. Blackburn stood in his suit a short distance away, an angry expression on his face. I twisted a bit, looking to the side. Quentin was there too, tied to a chair. The short, dapper man looked like he'd been beaten a bit – his nose was bleeding, and he seemed dazed. I could hear him muttering.

'Bubble gum for the primate. Long live the Jacuzzi. Moon on the rocks, please.'

The walls of the room were covered with various nasty-looking torture implements – the kinds of things one might find in a dentist's office. If that dentist were an *insane torture-hungry Dark Oculator*.

And there were also ... 'Books?' I whispered in confusion.

Bastille shuddered. 'Papercuts,' she said. 'The worst form of torture.'

Of course, I thought.

'Alcatraz,' Bastille said. 'You have to leave. Blackburn will see your aura again!'

'No he won't,' I said, smiling.

'Why not?'

'Because he made the same mistake I did before,' I said. 'He's not wearing his Oculator's Lens.'

Indeed he wasn't. In his single, monocle eye, Blackburn was *not* wearing his Oculator's Lens. Instead, as I had anticipated, he was wearing a Torturer's Lens – it was easy to distinguish, with its dark green and black tints.

Perhaps I wasn't as stupid as you thought.

'Ah,' Bastille said.

Blackburn turned, focusing on Grandpa Smedry. Even though I wasn't wearing my Oculator's Lenses, I could feel a release of power – the Dark Oculator was activating the Torturer's Lens. *No!* I thought, feeling helpless, remembering the awful pain.

Grandpa Smedry lay with a pleasant expression on his face. 'I say,' he said. 'I don't suppose I could bother you for a cup of milk? I'm getting a bit thirsty.'

'Turtlenecks look good when the trees have no ears,' Quentin added.

'Bah!' Blackburn said. 'Answer my questions, old man! How do I bypass the Sentinel's Glass of Ryshadium? How can I grow the crystals of Crystallia?' He released another burst of torturing power into Grandpa Smedry.

'I really need to get going,' Grandpa Smedry said. 'I'm late – I don't suppose we could call it a day?'

Blackburn screamed in frustration, taking off his Torturer's Lens and looking at it with an annoyed eye. 'You!' he snapped to a guard that I couldn't see.

'Uh ... yes, my lord?' a voice asked.

'Stand right there,' Blackburn said, putting on the monocle. I sensed another wave of power.

The guard screamed. I couldn't see him crumple, but I could hear it – and I could hear the pain, the utter agony, in the poor man's voice. I cringed, closing my eyes and gritting my teeth against the awful sound as I remembered that brief moment when I had felt Blackburn's fury.

I had to work hard to keep myself from fleeing right then. But I stayed. I'll point out that now, looking back, I don't consider this bravery – just stupidity.

The guard stopped screaming, then began to whimper.

'Hmm,' Blackburn said. 'The Lens works perfectly. Your Talent is stronger than I had anticipated, old man. But it can't protect you forever! Soon you'll know the pain!'

Bastille suddenly grabbed my arm – she was still watching through the crack beside me. 'He's arriving late for the pain!' she said in an excited whisper. 'Such power ... to put off an abstract sensation. It's amazing.'

I noted the look of relief in Bastille's face. *She does care*, I realized. *Despite all the grumbling, despite all the complaints. She really was worried about him.*

'What's going on?' Sing whispered. He was too big to fit beside the door with the two of us.

'Old Smedry is handling the torture with poise,' Bastille said. 'But Quentin looks like he's had a hard time.'

'Is he babbling?' Sing asked.

Bastille nodded.

'Then he's gone into anti-information mode,' Sing said. 'He can engage his Talent so that it translates *everything* he says into gibberish. He can't turn it off, even if he wants to – not until it wears off a day later.'

'That's why he makes such a good spy,' I realized. 'He can't betray secrets – they can't force him to talk, no matter how hard they try!'

Sing nodded.

Inside the room, Blackburn stomped around the table. He grabbed a knife from a rack of torturing implements, then rammed it toward Grandpa Smedry's leg.

It missed, sliding just to the side, and Blackburn swore in frustration. He held the knife up, steadied his hand, then carefully plunged it down again.

This time, it hit Grandpa's leg and jabbed directly into the flesh.

'Shattered Glass,' Bastille cursed. 'The knife is too advanced a weapon – it can get past old Smedry's Talent.'

I stared in shock at the cut in my grandfather's leg. No blood came out, however.

'It's a good thing I don't need to go to the bathroom,' Grandpa Smedry said in a cheerful voice. 'That would be embarrassing, wouldn't it?'

'We have to do something,' Bastille said urgently. 'He's powerful, but he can't hold back the pain – or the wounds – forever.'

'But we can't fight a Dark Oculator,' Sing said. 'Especially not without your sword, Bastille.'

I stood. 'Then we'll have to get him to leave Grandpa alone.

Come on!' With that, I rushed down the hallway. Bastille and Sing followed in a dash.

'Alcatraz!' Bastille said as soon as we were a safe distance from the torture room. 'What are you planning?'

'We need a distraction,' I said. 'Something that will draw Blackburn away long enough for us to get in and rescue Grandpa Smedry. And I think I know of one.'

Bastille was about to object, but at that moment Sing tripped. Bastille and I ducked to the side just as a pair of bow-tied, sword-carrying Librarian soldiers came up out of the stairwell ahead. Bastille cursed, dashing toward them with a sudden burst of Crystin speed.

The stairs they had come up were the very same stairs that we ourselves had come up a few hours before. That meant the door I wanted was—

I threw my weight against it, pushing open the door and stepping into a room filled with caged dinosaurs.

'Good day!' said Charles. 'I see that you have not ended up dead. What a pleasant surprise!'

'Did you bring us something to eat?' the Tyrannosaurus asked hopefully.

'Better,' I said, then rushed into the room, touching the cage locks as I moved. Each one my fingers brushed against snapped open, the complicated gears inside breaking easily before my Talent.

'Why, what a good chap you are!' Charles said. The group of twenty dinosaurs agreed with eager, loud voices.

'I've freed you,' I said. 'But I need something in return. Can you cause a disturbance downstairs for me?'

'Of course, my good fellow!' Charles said. 'We're *excellent* at creating disturbances, aren't we, George?'

'Indeed, indeed!' said the Stegosaurus.

With that, I stepped aside, waving eagerly, trying to begin a stampede of undersized dinosaurs. They, of course, filed out of the room in a very gentlemanly manner – for, as everyone knows, all British are refined, calm, and well-mannered. Even if they are a bunch of dinosaurs.

I followed the group out of the room, trying to whip them into a frenzy – or at least a mild agitation.

'*That's* your plan?' Bastille asked flatly, standing above two unconscious Librarians.

'They'll make a disturbance,' I said. 'I mean, they're *dinosaurs*.'

Bastille and Sing shared a look.

'What?' I said. 'Don't you think it'll work?'

'You know very little about dinosaurs, Alcatraz,' Bastille said as the dinosaurs went down the stairs to the first floor.

We waited. We waited for painful minutes, hiding in the Forgotten Language room. We heard no cried of panic. No yells for help. No sounds of people being chewed up by rampaging bloodthirsty reptiles.

'Oh, for goodness' sake!' I said, rushing from the room and running over to the hallway with the broken floor. I got on my hands and knees and peered through the opening, hoping to catch a glimpse of chaos below.

Instead, I saw the dinosaurs sitting in a group, several stacks of books settled around them. One of them – the Stegosaurus – appeared to be reading to the others.

'Dinosaurs,' Bastille said. 'Useless.'

'They are easily distracted by books, Alcatraz,' Sing said. 'I don't think they're going to help much.'

'Hey!' I called with an annoyed voice. 'Charles.'

The little Pterodactyl looked up. 'Ah, my good friend!'

'What about the chaos?' I demanded.

'Done!' Charles said.

'We each moved six books out of their proper places,' called George the Stegosaurus. 'It will take them *days* to find them all and put them back.'

'Though we did put them into place backward,' Charles said. 'You know, so they could be seen more easily. We wouldn't want it to be *too* hard.'

'Too hard?' I asked, stupefied. 'Charles, these are the people who were going to kill you and bury your bones in an archaeological dig!'

'Well, that's no reason to be uncivilized!' Charles said.

'Indeed!' called a duck-billed dinosaur.

I knelt, blinking.

'Dinosaurs,' Bastille said again. 'Useless.'

'Don't worry, my Oculator friend!' Charles called. 'We gave them a little extra kick! We had Douglas eat the entire science fiction section!'

'Well,' admitted Douglas the T. Rex, 'I only ate the "C" section. Honestly – claiming that Velociraptors were the smartest dinosaurs? I knew a Velociraptor in college, and he *failed* chemistry. Plus, resurrecting a character just because he didn't die in the movie? Poppycock, I say!'

I sat back. Bastille had the dignity not to say, 'I told you so.' Or, at least, she had the dignity not to say it a third time.

We need another plan. Another plan. Can't stop to think about the failure. We need to draw the Dark Oculator away. Need to ...

I stood, steeling my nerves.

'Another idea?' Sing asked, clearly a little apprehensive.

I took off again. Sing and Bastille followed reluctantly. But they hadn't come up with anything better. My failure with the dinosaurs had come from relying on misinformation. In most books, two dozen rampaging dinosaurs would have been a distraction worthy of even a Dark Oculator's attention.

That's why most books aren't true. Sorry, kids.

I dashed back toward the torturing room. The guards still lay unconscious in the hallway where Bastille had left them. I checked the knothole – Blackburn was still there inside, and he had apparently decided to rough up Grandpa Smedry with slaps to the face.

'I think I'll go for a walk ...' Grandpa Smedry said cheerfully.

'Wasing not of wasing is,' Quentin added.

I gritted my teeth. Then I pulled the velvet pouch out of my pocket and looked inside.

'Alcatraz ...' Bastille said carefully. 'You can't defeat him. You might have a powerful Lens, but that's not everything. Blackburn will be able to deflect that Firebringer's Lens with his Oculator's Lens.'

'I know,' I said. 'Sing, take these two unconscious men and hide them – with yourself – in the Forgotten Language room.'

My cousin opened his mouth as if to object, but then paused. Finally, he nodded. He easily lifted the two unconscious men, then left down the hallway.

'Alcatraz,' Bastille said. 'I know you want to protect your grandfather. But this is suicide.'

I waited a few moments for Sing to complete his task. Then I knelt down beside the door and looked through the knothole. Blackburn was raising a mallet, as if to break Grandpa Smedry's arm.

'You can't resist forever, old man,' Blackburn said.

I activated the Firebringer's Lens.

17

Immediately, the Dark Oculator looked up.

I smiled, watching Blackburn turn with a confused expression on his face. At that moment, he was sensing a very powerful Oculatory Lens coming in from the hallway outside. He took a step toward the door.

'Now,' I hissed. *'Run!'*

Bastille didn't need further command. She took off down the hallway, as did I. However, she obviously held back so that she didn't outstrip me.

I held the Firebringer's Lens before me, and it spewed forth it's powerful line of light. I ran on, aiming it at the side of the corridor.

'You're leading him away!' Bastille said. 'You're using us as bait.'

'Hopefully bait that escapes,' I said, ducking around a corner, then pausing to wait. The Firebringer's Lens continued to blast.

A door slammed in the distance. 'Smedry!' a voice bellowed. 'You can't run from me! Don't you realize that I can sense your power?'

'Go!' I said, taking off at a dash. Within seconds, we were at the section of the corridor with the broken floor.

'Charles!' I yelled down through the hole. 'Trouble is coming your way! I'd run if I were you!'

And then I took the Firebringer's Lens and tossed it through the hole. It bounced against a few books, then came to rest on the floor, still shooting a piercing-hot laser of heat up into the air, burning the ceiling, threatening to start several of the bookshelves on fire.

I grabbed Bastille by the arm, tugging her around the corner and into the Forgotten Language room. Sing jumped as we entered.

He had – for some reason that he never explained – propped both of the unconscious men in chairs at the desks.

Anthropologists are funny that way.

Now, I would like to take this opportunity to point out that I didn't take the opportunity to point out anything at the beginning of this chapter. Never fear; my editorial comments were simply delayed for a few moments.

You see, that last chapter ended with a terribly unfair hook. By now, it is probably very late at night, and you have stayed up to read this book when you *should* have gone to sleep. If this is the case, then I commend you for falling into my trap. It is a writer's greatest pleasure to hear that someone was kept up until the unholy hours of the morning reading one of his books. It goes back to authors being terrible people who delight in the suffering of others. Plus, we get a kickback from the caffeine industry.

Regardless, because of how exciting things were, I didn't feel comfortable interjecting my normal comments at the beginning of this chapter. So, I shall put them here instead. Prepare yourself.

Blah, blah, sacrifice, altars, daggers, sharks. Blah, blah, something pretentious. Blah, blah, rutabaga. Blah, blah, something that makes no sense whatsoever.

Now back to the story.

(And whoever put in that cliff-hanger at the end of the last chapter needs to be reprimanded. It's growing quite late here, and I really should be getting to bed, rather than writing this book.)

I crouched inside the Forgotten Language room with Bastille and Sing. I kept my Oculator's Lenses off, hoping that without them I wouldn't have as strong an aura. Sure enough, watching under the door, we saw a dark shadow pass by, and I felt a slight surge of power as an activated Oculatory Lens passed by. (Fortunately, Blackburn didn't appear to have a Tracker's Lens of his own.) His shadow didn't stop to check the Forgotten Language room, but instead continued on toward the stairwell.

'We have very little time,' I said, looking back at the other two.

We burst from the room and ran back toward the torture chamber. By the time we arrived, I was feeling a little out of breath.

Having never had to rescue anyone from torture before, I wasn't accustomed to so much running. Fortunately, Sing wasn't exactly in shape either, and so I didn't feel *too* bad lagging behind Bastille.

Once I reached the guard chamber, I noticed Bastille standing beside the door with the peephole. She gave the handle a good rattle. 'Locked,' she said.

'Move aside,' I said, walking up to the door. I rested a hand on the lock, jolting it with a bit of Breaking Talent. Nothing happened.

'Glass lock,' I said. I moved my hand up to the door's hinges, but they resisted too.

Bastille cursed. 'The whole door will be warded against your Talent. We'll have to try to break it down manually.'

I eyed the thick wooden door with a skeptical eye. Then, from behind me, there was a click. I turned to see Sing leveling one of the biggest, baddest handguns I'd ever seen. It was the kind of gun that took most men two hands to hold – the type of gun that used bullets so big that they could have doubled as paperweights.

Sing pulled out another gun, identical to the first, in his other hand. Then he took aim at the door handle – which sat directly between Bastille and me.

'Oh, put those antiques away,' Bastille said testily. 'This isn't the time for – Gak!'

This last part came as I grabbed her by the shoulder, yanking her with me as I took cover behind a table.

Sing pulled the triggers.

Wood chips sprayed across the room, mixing with shards of dark black glass. The booming sound of gunshots echoed in the small chamber – or, at least, the booming sound of *three* gunshots echoed in the small chamber. By the time Sing fired the fourth shot, I'd been deafened and couldn't tell whether or not the rest of the shots made any noise.

I couldn't hear any trees fall either.

When it was over, I peeked out from behind my table. Bastille remained stunned on the floor beside me. The door stood shattered and splintered, the remnants of its handle and lock hanging pitifully, surrounded by bullet holes. As I watched, the broken, bullet-shattered lock finally dropped to the floor, and the door quietly swung open – as if in surrender.

Now, after all our discussions of 'advanced' weapons and the like, you probably weren't expecting the guns to do much good. I certainly wasn't. One thing to remember is this: Primitive doesn't always mean useless. An old flintlock pistol may not be as advanced as a handgun, but both could kill you. Sitting there, I realized why Sing was insistent upon bringing the guns along, and why Grandpa Smedry had let him do so.

It seems to me that some people underestimate good, old-fashioned Hushlander technology a little too much. It was good to see something from my world prove so effective. Locks made from Oculator's Glass might be *resistant* to physical damage, but they certainly aren't completely indestructible.

'Nice shooting,' I said.

Sing shrugged, then said something.

'What?' I asked, still feeling a bit deaf.

'I said,' Sing said, speaking louder, 'even *antiques* have their uses every once in a while. Come on!' He waddled over to the door, pushing it open the rest of the way.

Bastille stumbled to her feet. 'I feel like a thunderstorm went off inside my head. Your people really use those things on the battlefield?'

'Only when they have to,' I said.

'How can you hear what your commanders are saying?' she asked.

'Uh ... helmets?' I said. The answer, of course, didn't make any sense. But I didn't care at the moment. I rose to my feet, rushing after Sing into the room. Inside, we found one guard on the ground, unconscious from Blackburn's use of the Torturer's Lens. Grandpa Smedry still lay tied to the table, Quentin in his chair.

'Alcatraz, lad!' Grandpa Smedry said. 'You're late!'

I smiled, rushing to the table. Bastille saw to Quentin, cutting the ropes that tied him to the chair.

'The manacles on my wrists are made of Enforcer's Glass, lad,'

Grandpa Smedry said. 'You'll never break it. Quickly, you have to leave! The Dark Oculator sensed you using the Firebringer's Lens!'

'I know,' I said. 'That was intentional. We distracted him with the Lens, then came in to get you.'

'You did?' Grandpa Smedry said. 'Whooping Williams, lad, that's brilliant!'

'Thank you,' I said, placing two hands against the wood of the table. Then I closed my eyes and channeled a blast of Talent into it. Fortunately, it wasn't warded as well as the door had been, even if the manacles were. Nails sprang free, boards separated, and legs fell off. Grandpa Smedry collapsed in the middle of it, crying out in surprise. Sing quickly rushed over to help him to his feet.

'Muttering Modesitts,' Grandpa Smedry said quietly, looking at the remnants of the table. The manacles and their chains now hung freely from his wrists and ankles, for the other ends had been affixed to the now-defunct table. Grandpa Smedry looked up at me. 'That's some Talent, lad. Some Talent indeed …'

Quentin walked over, rubbing his wrists. He had a few budding bruises on his face, but otherwise looked unharmed. 'Churches,' he said. 'Lead, very small rocks, and ducks.'

I frowned.

'Oh, he won't be able to say anything normal for the rest of the day,' Grandpa Smedry said. 'Sing, my boy, would you help me with …' He nodded downward, toward his leg – which, I now noticed, was still impaled by the torturing knife.

'Grandpa!' I said with concern as Sing reached down gingerly and pulled the knife free.

There was no blood.

'Don't worry, lad,' Grandpa Smedry said. 'I'll arrive late to that wound.'

I frowned. 'How long can you keep that up?'

'It depends,' Grandpa Smedry said, accepting his tuxedo shirt from Sing. He put it on, then began doing up the front. 'Arriving late to wounds requires a bit of effort – holding this one back, along with all the pains Blackburn gave me with his Torturer's Lenses, is already fatiguing. I can hold on for a little while longer, but I'll have to start letting the pain through eventually.'

Indeed, Grandpa Smedry looked far less spry now that he had earlier in the day. The torture might not have broken him, but it had certainly produced an effect.

'Oh, don't look at me like that,' Grandpa Smedry said. 'I can arrive at the pain in small, manageable amounts, once we're free. Bastille, dear, any luck?'

I turned. Bastille had apparently done a quick search of the room's tables and cabinets. She looked up from the last one and shook her head. 'If he took your Lenses, he didn't stash them in here, old man.'

'Ah, well,' Grandpa Smedry said. 'Good work anyway, dear.'

'I only searched the room,' she said, slamming the door, 'because I was so *furious* at you for getting yourself captured. I figured that if I walked over to help you, I'd end up punching you instead. That didn't seem fair in your weakened state.'

Grandpa Smedry raised a hand, whispering to me, 'This would probably be a bad time to remind her that *she* got captured too, eh?'

'My capture was a *different* Smedry's fault,' Bastille snapped, flushing. 'And that doesn't matter. We need to get out of here before that Dark Oculator comes back.'

'Agreed,' Grandpa Smedry said. 'Follow me – I know the way to a stairwell up.'

'*Up?*' Bastille asked incredulously.

'Of course,' Grandpa Smedry said. 'We came for the Sands of Rashid – and we're not leaving until we have them!'

'But they know we're here,' Bastille said. 'The entire library is on alert!'

'Yes,' Grandpa Smedry said. 'But *we* know where the sands are.'

'We do?' I asked.

Grandpa Smedry nodded. 'You don't think Quentin and I got ourselves captured for nothing, do you? We got close to the sands, lad. Very close.'

'But?' Bastille asked, folding her arms.

Grandpa Smedry blushed slightly. 'Snarer's Glass. Blackburn has that room so well trapped that it's a wonder he doesn't catch himself every time he walks into it.'

'And how are we going to get past the traps now, then?' Bastille asked.

'Oh, we won't have to,' Grandpa Smedry said. 'Quentin and I couldn't think of a way to get by the traps, so we just fell into them! The room should be completely free now. Each square of Snarer's Glass can only go off once, you know!'

Bastille huffed at him. 'You could have gotten yourself killed, old man!'

'Yes, well,' he said. 'I didn't! Now, let's get moving! We're going to be late.'

With that, he rushed out of the room. Bastille gave me a flat look. 'Next time, let's just leave him.'

I smiled wryly, moving to follow her out of the room. However, something caught my attention. I stopped beside it.

'Sing?' I asked as the large man walked past.

'Yes?'

I pointed at a lantern holder on the wall. 'What does this lantern holder look like to you?'

Sing paused, scratching his chin. 'A coconut?'

Coconut, I thought. 'Do you remember what Quentin said downstairs, just after we entered the library?'

Sing shook his head. 'What was it?'

'I can't quite remember,' I said. 'But it sounded like gibberish.'

'Ah,' Sing said. 'Quentin speaks in gibberish sometimes. It's a side effect of his Talent – like me tripping when I get startled.'

Or me breaking things I don't want to, I thought. But this seemed different. *Coconuts ... pain don't hurt. That's what it was.*

I glanced back at the broken table. The pain of torture hadn't hurt Grandpa Smedry.

'Come on, Alcatraz,' Sing said urgently, pulling on my arm. 'We have to keep moving.'

I allowed myself to be led from the room, but not before I took one last look at the wall bracket.

I had the feeling I was missing something important.

18

The book is almost done.

The ending of a book is, in my experience, both the best and the *worst* part to read. For the ending will often decide whether you love or hate the book.

Both emotions lead to disappointment. If the ending was good, and the book was worth your time, then you are left annoyed and depressed because there is no more book to read. However, if the ending was bad, then it's too late to stop reading. You're left annoyed and depressed because you wasted so much time on a book with a bad ending.

Therefore, reading is obviously worthless, and you should go spend your time on other, more valuable pursuits. I hear algebra is good for you. Kind of like humility, plus factoring. Regardless, you will soon know whether to hate me for not writing more, or whether to hate me for writing too much. Please confine all assassination attempts to the school week, as I would rather not die on a Saturday.

No need to spoil a good weekend.

'This is it,' Grandpa Smedry said, leading us through another hallway. 'That door at the end.'

The third floor was a little more lavish than the second floor: Instead of stark, unpleasant stones and blank walls, the third floor was lined with stark, unpleasant rugs and blank tapestries. The door had a large glass disc set into its front, and at first I thought the disc had a lightbulb in the middle. It certainly glowed sharply enough. Then I remembered my Oculator's Lenses and realized that the disc was glowing only to my eyes.

There had to be Lenses beyond that door – powerful ones.

Bastille caught Grandpa Smedry on the shoulder as he reached the door, then shook her head sharply. She pulled him back, moved up to the door, and tried to get a good look through the glass disc. Then she raised her crystal dagger to the ready and pushed open the door.

Light burst from the room, as if that door were the gate to heaven itself. I cried out, closing my eyes.

'Focus on your Lenses, lad,' Grandpa Smedry said. 'You can dim the effect if you concentrate.'

I did so, squinting. I managed, with some effort, to make the light dim down until it was a low glow. No longer blinded, I was awed by what I saw.

What I felt at this point is a little bit hard to describe. To Bastille and my cousins, the room would have been simply a medium-sized, circular chamber with little shelves built into the walls. The shelves held Lenses – hundreds of them – and each one had its own little stand, holding it up to sparkle in the light. It must have been a pretty sight, but nothing spectacular.

To me, the room looked *different*.

Perhaps you've owned something in your life to which you ascribed particular pleasure. A treasured toy, perhaps. Some photographs. The bullet that killed your archnemesis.

Now, imagine that you'd never before realized how important that item was to you. Imagine that your understanding of it – your feelings of love, pride, and satisfaction – suddenly hit you all at once.

That was how I felt. There was something *right* about all of those Lenses. I'd never been in the room before, but to me, it felt like home. And to a boy who had lived with dozens of different foster families, *home* was not a word to be used lightly.

Sing, Grandpa Smedry, Bastille, and Quentin moved into the room. I walked up to the doorway, where I stood for a few moments, basking in the beauty of the Lenses. There was a majesty to the room. A warmth.

This is what I was meant to be, I thought. *This is what I was always meant to be.*

'Hurry, lad!' Grandpa Smedry said. 'You have to find the sands.

I don't have my Oculator's Lenses! I'll try to find a pair in here, but you need to start looking while I do!'

I shocked myself into motion. We were still being chased. This wasn't my home – this was the stronghold of my enemies. I shook my head, forcing myself to be more realistic. Yet I would always retain a memory of that moment – the first moment when I knew for certain that I wanted to be an Oculator. And I would treasure it.

'Grandfather, *everything* in here is glowing,' I protested. 'How can I find the sands in all of this?'

'They're here,' Grandpa Smedry said, furiously looking through the room. 'I swear they are!'

'Golf the spasm of penguins!' Quentin said, pointing to a table at the back of the circular room.

'He's right!' Grandpa Smedry said. 'That's where the sands were before. Aspiring Asimovs! Where did they go?'

'Typically,' a new voice said, 'one uses sands to make Lenses.'

I spun. Blackburn stood in the hallway behind us. For some reason, the man's aura of darkness was far less visible than it had been before.

My Oculator's Lenses, I realized. *I turned them down.*

Blackburn smiled. He was accompanied by a large group of Librarians – not the skinny, robe-wearing kind but the bulky, overmuscled kind in the bow ties and sunglasses, as well as a couple of sword-wielding women wearing skirts, their hair in buns.

Blackburn had something in his hand. A pair of spectacles. Even with my Oculator's Lenses turned down, these spectacles glowed powerfully with a brilliant white light.

'Back away, lad,' Grandpa Smedry said quietly.

I did so, slowly backing into the room. *There are no other exits,* I thought. *We're trapped!*

Bastille growled quietly, raising her crystal dagger, stepping between Grandpa Smedry and the smiling Blackburn. Librarian thugs fanned into the room, moving to surround us. Sing watched warily, cocking a pair of handguns.

'Nice collection you have here, Blackburn,' Grandpa Smedry said, walking around the perimeter of the room. 'Frostbringer's Lenses, Courier's Lenses, Harrier's Lenses ... Yes, impressive indeed.' I noticed that my grandfather's hand was glowing slightly.

'I have a weakness for power, I'm afraid,' Blackburn said.

Grandpa Smedry nodded, as if to himself. 'Those Lenses in your hand. They come from the Sands of Rashid?'

Blackburn smiled.

'Why a pair? Why not just a monocle?' Grandpa Smedry asked.

'In case I choose to share these Lenses with others. Not everyone has realized the value of focusing power, as I have.'

'The torture, the chasing us,' Grandpa Smedry said. 'I was worried that we were taking too long – that you were just trying to distract us long enough for your lackeys to forge those Lenses.'

'Not *just*,' Blackburn said. 'I was sincerely hoping that I'd be able to break you with the torture, old man, and find the secret to the Smedry Talents that way. But you do have a point. I assumed that when I had these lenses, I could beat you for certain.'

Grandpa Smedry smiled. 'They don't do what you thought they would, do they?'

Blackburn shrugged.

Grandpa Smedry finally stopped strolling. He reached up and selected a Lens off of a shelf, then slipped it into his hand with several others he'd pilfered. He turned to look directly at Blackburn. 'Shall we, then?'

Blackburn's smile deepened. 'I'd like nothing better.'

Grandpa Smedry whipped his hand up, raising something to his eye – an Oculator's Lens. Blackburn raised his own hand, placing a monocle *over* the one he already wore.

Sing, of course, tripped.

'Shattering Glass!' Bastille swore, grabbing me by the arm and towing me to the side. The Librarian thugs all stooped down, bracing themselves.

And the air suddenly began to crackle with energy. My hair raised up on its ends, and each footstep zapped me slightly with a static charge.

'What's going on?' I cried to Bastille.

'Oculator's Duel!' she cried.

I noticed Grandpa Smedry raise another Lens to his eye. He kept his left eye closed, placing both lenses together over his right eye. The first Lens he had placed – the reddish pink Oculator's Lens – remained in place, hovering in front of his eye.

Blackburn raised a third Lens to his eye. The room surged with power, and Lenses on the walls started to rattle. I recognized this one – it was a Torturer's Lens. I could feel that it had been activated, yet it seemed to have no effect on Grandpa Smedry.

'Those Oculator's Lenses you wear,' Bastille said over the noise. 'They're the most basic Lenses for a good reason. A well-trained Oculator can use them to negate his enemy's attacks.'

Grandpa Smedry slowly raised a third Lens to his eye. All three remained hovering in the air in front of him. The new one made a screeching sound that hurt my ears, though most of the noise seemed directed at Blackburn.

'Why are they using multiple Lenses at once?' I said as Blackburn added a fourth Lens. The room grew colder and a line of frosty ice shot forward toward Grandpa Smedry.

Bastille crouched down farther. Wind began to churn in the room, ruffling my hair, whipping at my jacket.

'They're countering each other's attacks,' Bastille said.

'Adding Lens after Lens. However, it gets increasingly hard to focus your power through all those Lenses at once. The first one who loses control of his Lenses – or who fails to block an attack – will lose.'

Grandpa Smedry, arm beginning to shake, raised a fourth Lens to his eye. The hovering line of Lenses trembled in the wind. Grandpa Smedry was no longer smiling – in fact, he had one arm up, steadying himself against the wall.

Blackburn added a fifth Lens – one that I recognized. It didn't have a little monocle frame like the others, and it had a red dot at the center.

My Firebringer's Lens! I thought. *He* did *recover it.*

Sure enough, this Lens began to spit out a line of fire. The beam shot forward, moving alongside the line of ice. But, like the ice line, the Firebringer's line puffed into non-existence near Grandpa Smedry, as if hitting an invisible shield. Grandpa Smedry grunted quietly at the impact.

I could see Sing a short distance away, struggling to his knees. The large man raised a gun, then fired at Blackburn. I could barely hear the gunshots over the sound of wind.

Flashes of lightning shot from Blackburn's body, moving more quickly that I could track. I'm still not certain what happened to those bullets, but they obviously never reached their mark. I glanced at Sing, who sat cradling a burned hand, his gun smoking slightly on the floor.

Grandpa Smedry finally managed to place his fifth Lens. My ears popped, and it felt like the air was growing more pressurized – as if some force were pushing out from Grandpa Smedry, most of it slamming into Blackburn.

The Dark Oculator grunted, stumbling. However, I could see a glistening spot appear near the knife-hole on Grandpa Smedry's tuxedo pants, and a small pool of blood began forming at his feet.

The wound from the torture chamber, I thought. *He's too tired to hold it back any longer.* 'We have to do something!' I yelled over the wind. Lenses were toppling from their pedestals, some shattering to the ground, and scraps of paper were churning inside the vortex of the room.

Bastille shook her head. 'We can't interfere!'

'What?' I asked. 'Some stupid code of honor?'

'No! If we get too close to either of them, the power will vaporize us!'

Oh, I thought. Blackburn, whose arm had begun to tremble with strain, raised a sixth Lens to his eye. In his hand, he still held the spectacles he'd had forged from the Sands of Rashid. *Why doesn't he use those?* I wondered. *Is he saving the best for last?*

Sing managed to pull himself over to Bastille and me. 'Lord Leavenworth can't win this fight, Bastille! He's only using single-eye Lenses. Blackburn's trained on those – he put his eye out to increase his power with them. But Leavenworth is accustomed to two eyes. He can't—'

Grandpa Smedry suddenly let out a defiant yell. He raised his hand, gripping his sixth Lens in rigid fingers. He wavered for a moment.

Then dropped the Lens.

There was a flash of light and a blast of power. I cried out in shock as I was thrown backward.

And the winds stopped.

I opened my eyes to the sound of laughter. I rolled over, desperately looking for Grandpa Smedry. The old man lay on the ground, barely moving. Blackburn had been thrown backward as well, but he picked himself up without much trouble.

'Is that it?' Blackburn asked, brushing off his suit. He smiled, looking down at Grandpa Smedry through his single eye, an eye that now bore no Lenses. They had all dropped to the ground at his feet. 'You barely gave a fight, old man.'

Sing reached for another gun. Two beefy Librarians tackled him from behind. Bastille jumped the first one. Six more soldiers rushed at her.

Blackburn continued to chuckle. He walked slowly across the room, his feet crunching on shattered glass. He shook his head. 'Do you realize how much trouble it's going to be to gather up all these broken Lenses, have the shards sorted, then have them all reforged? My Librarians will spend months remaking my collection!'

I have to do something, I thought. Bastille continued to fight, but more and more Librarian thugs were surrounding her. They already had Quentin and Sing pinned. Nobody, however, seemed to notice me. Perhaps they thought me unthreatening because I had been knocked down.

I scanned the room. There, a short distance away, I saw them – the Lenses of Rashid, lying temptingly in the middle of a pile of discarded monocles. They had fallen to the ground during the blast along with the other Lenses Blackburn had held during the fight.

I gritted my teeth.

I have to use the Lenses of Rashid, I thought, crawling forward slowly. *I have to—*

Wait. I want you to do something for me. Try to recall the very *first* part of my story. It was way back in Chapter One, before I even told you about my name. Back then, I spoke about life-and-death situations, and how they make people think about some very odd subjects. The prospect of dying – or, in this case, watching someone dear to you die – does strange things to the mind. Makes it think along tangents.

Makes it remember things that it might have otherwise thought unimportant.

Grandpa Smedry was going to die. And, strangely, at that very moment, I noticed the lantern that still stood on a pole at the very center of the room. The lantern holder … it looked something like a rutabaga.

Rutabaga, I thought. *I've heard that word recently. Rutabaga … fire over the inheritance!*

I scrambled forward. Blackburn spun. I threw myself toward the Lenses of Rashid – but I didn't grab them. I grabbed a Lens sitting next to them.

The Firebringer's Lens.

Blackburn's foot came down on my arm. I cried out, dropping the Lens, and a pair of Librarian soldiers quickly grabbed me. They yanked me to my feet and pulled me backward, one holding each of my arms.

Blackburn shook his head. From the corner of my eye, I could barely make out a Librarian finally tackling Bastille. She struggled, but three others helped him hold her.

'My, my, my,' Blackburn said. 'And here you all are, captured again.' He looked over at Grandpa Smedry, but the old man was obviously no threat. Grandpa Smedry was dazed, his leg bleeding, his face puffing up from bruises he'd apparently been putting off since his torture.

Blackburn bent down, picking up the Firebringer's Lens. 'A Firebringer's Lens,' He said. 'You should have known better than to try and use one of these against me, boy. I'm far more powerful than you.'

Blackburn turned the Lens over in his fingers. 'I'm glad you brought me one, however. There weren't any in my collection – they're quite rare.' Then he picked up the Lenses of Rashid. 'And these. Supposedly the most powerful Lenses ever forged. Didn't your son spend his entire life gathering the sands to make these, old Smedry?'

Grandpa Smedry didn't answer.

'What a waste,' Blackburn said, shaking his head. Then he raised the Firebringer's Lens to his eye. 'Now, we're going to do this one more time. You are going to start answering my questions, old man. You're going to tell me the secrets of your order, and you're going to help me conquer the rest of the Free Kingdoms.'

Blackburn smiled. 'If you don't, I'm going to kill every one of your friends.' He looked around the room. My companions stood, held by Librarian thugs. Only Bastille still struggled – Sing and Quentin looked like they had been punched a few good times in the stomach to keep them quiet.

'No,' Blackburn said, 'not one of the Smedrys. Your blasted Talents are too protective. Let's start with the girl.' He smiled, focusing his single eye on Bastille.

'No!' Grandpa Smedry said. 'Ask your questions, monster!'

'Not yet, Smedry,' Blackburn said. 'I have to kill one of them first, you see. Then you will understand how serious this all is.'

The Firebringer's Lens began to glow.

'NO!' Grandpa Smedry screamed.

The Firebringer's Lens fired ...

...directly *back* into Blackburn's eye.

Taking advantage of the moment, I twisted with a sudden motion, raising my hands and grabbing the arms of my captors. I sent out shocks of Talent and felt bones snap beneath my fingers. My captors cried out, jumping back and cradling broken limbs. Blackburn fell to his knees, and the Firebringer's Lens fell free, leaving a smoking socket behind. He screamed in pain.

I stepped toward the now powerless Dark Oculator. 'When I

grabbed the Firebringer's Lens, Blackburn, I wasn't trying to use it on you,' I said. 'You see, I only needed to touch it for a moment – just long enough to break it.

'It shoots *backward* now.'

19

I apologize for that last chapter. It was far too deep and ponderous. At this rate, it won't be long before this story departs
speaking of evil Librarians, and instead turns into a terribly boring
tale about a lawyer who defends unjustly accused field hands.

What do mockingbirds have to do with that, anyway?

I scooped up the Firebringer's Lens, spinning toward the thugs
who still held my grandfather. The Librarians looked down at the
fallen Oculator, then back up at me. I raised the Lens.

The two men dashed away. In the fury of the moment, I didn't
even realize that I'd finally been able to pick up the Lens without
it going off.

Grandpa Smedry slumped back against the wall in exhaustion.
However, he smiled at me. 'Well done, lad. Well done. You're a
Smedry for certain!'

The other thugs in the room backed away, towing their hostages.

'There are two of us now,' Grandpa Smedry said, righting himself, staring down the Librarians. 'And your Oculator has fallen.
Do you *really* want to make us mad?'

There was a moment of hesitance, and Bastille seized it. She
swung up and slammed her feet into the back of the Librarian
in front of her. Then she pulled herself free from her surprised
captors.

The other thugs dropped Quentin and Sing, then dashed
away. Bastille chased after them, cursing and kicking at one as
he rushed out the door. But she let him go, grumbling quietly as
she turned to make certain Sing and Quentin were all right. Both
seemed well enough.

Blackburn groaned. Grandpa Smedry shook his head, looking
down at the Dark Oculator.

'Should we ... do something with him?' I asked.

'He's no threat now, lad,' Grandpa Smedry said. 'An Oculator without eyes is about as dangerous as a little girl.'

'Excuse me?' Bastille huffed, rolling over one of the Librarian thugs that she'd knocked out before. She pulled off his sword belt and tied it around her waist.

'I apologize, dear,' Grandpa Smedry said in his tired voice. 'It was just a figure of speech. Sing, would you do me a favor ...?'

Sing rushed over, steadying Grandpa Smedry. 'Ah, very nice,' Grandpa Smedry said. 'Quentin, gather up any unbroken Lenses you can find. Bastille, be a dear and watch for danger at the door – there are others in this library who won't be as easily intimidated as those thugs.'

'And me?' I asked.

Grandpa Smedry smiled. 'You, lad, should recover your inheritance.'

. I turned, noticing the glasses that still lay on the ground. I walked over, picking them up. 'Blackburn seemed disappointed in these.'

'Blackburn was a man who focused only on one kind of power,' Grandpa Smedry said. 'For a man whose abilities depended on seeing, he was remarkably shortsighted.'

'So ... what do these do?' I asked.

'Try them on,' Grandpa Smedry suggested.

I took off my Oculator's Lenses and put on the Rashid Lenses instead. I couldn't see any difference – no release of power, no amazing revelations.

'What am I looking for?' I asked.

'Quentin,' Grandpa Smedry said, turning toward the small grad student. 'What do you think?'

'I really wouldn't know,' Quentin said. 'The legends are all so contradictory.'

I started. 'Hey! I understood him!'

'That's impossible,' Quentin said, still gathering Lenses off the ground. 'I have my Talent on. I'm gibberish for the whole day.'

'Actually, you're not,' I said. 'And you weren't truly gibberish those other times either. Did you know that your Talent can predict the future?'

Quentin's jaw dropped. 'You can *understand* me?'

'That's what I just said. Thanks for the hint about the rutabaga, by the way.'

Quentin turned toward Grandpa Smedry, who was smiling. 'No, Quentin,' Grandpa Smedry said. 'I still can't understand you.'

I stood, shocked. *What in the world . . . ?*

Then I turned, rushing over to Sing's gym bag, which lay on the side of the room. I unzipped it, digging through the ammunition to find a particular object: the book I'd swiped from the Forgotten Language room.

I opened it up to the first page. *The mechanics of forging a Truefinder's Lens is complex,* it read, *but can be understood by one who takes the proper time to study.*

I looked up, staring over at Grandpa Smedry. The old man smiled. 'There are a lot of different theories about what the Sands of Rashid do, lad. Your father, however, believed in a specific theory. Translator's Lenses, they were once called – they gave the power to read, or understand, any language, tongue, or code.'

I looked back at the book.

'Yes,' Grandpa Smedry said tiredly. 'Just wait until we show these to your father – if we can ever find him.'

I spun. 'So you *do* think he's alive?'

'Perhaps, lad,' Grandpa Smedry said. 'Perhaps. Now that we have those Lenses, perhaps we can find out for sure. I wish I'd had a way to discover sooner. If I'd known for certain whether he was dead or not, do you think I'd have let you get raised by foster parents?'

I paused. *Well, I guess the Lenses won't help me when* he *makes no sense.*

I opened my mouth to demand more, but Bastille cut me off. 'Trouble coming! Librarian – the blond one.'

I rushed over to the corridor and saw Ms. Fletcher striding toward the room, a troop of at least fifty soldiers marching behind her. These men and women were armored with shiny breastplates. A few Alivened lumbered in the background.

'Time to go, I think,' I said, pushing Bastille back. Then I slammed my hand into the ground.

The floor just in front of me fell away, blocks tumbling down to the storey below us. I backed away from the hole with Bastille.

'Oh, very clever, Alcatraz,' Ms. Fletcher said, stopping at the pit's edge. 'Now you've trapped yourself.'

I smiled, raised an eyebrow, then pressed my hand against the back wall of the room. The bricks separated, mortar cracking. Sing came over and gave the wall a hefty push, topping the bricks into the next room.

I winked at Ms. Fletcher, then reached down to slide a sword from the sheath of a fallen soldier. Ms. Fletcher stood with arms crossed, regarding Blackburn with a sour expression as I ducked out the broken wall after Sing, who was carrying Grandpa Smedry.

'Quickly, now!' Grandpa Smedry said. 'We're late!'

'For what?' I asked, running beside Sing and Quentin. Bastille, of course, ran ahead of us, watching for danger.

'Why, for our dramatic exit, of course!' Grandpa Smedry said, sounding a bit tired. 'Ms. Surly back there will try and cut us off at the front doors of the library.'

'Well, I'll just make us another door,' I said. 'We'll bust out the back wall.'

'Ah, lad,' Grandpa Smedry said. 'Haven't you realized? This entire building is inside a box of Expander's Glass – just like the gas station. Expander's Glass is *very* hard to break, even with a Talent. Besides, if you did, we'd be crushed as the entire library tried to burst out of the hole you'd made.'

'Oh,' I said as we reached a stairwell. 'Well, then, I have another idea.'

'What?' Grandpa Smedry asked.

I smiled, then reached into my pocket. I pulled out a small white rectangle: the library card we had taken off of the dungeon guard.

*

The main lobby of the library was unusually busy for a weekday evening. People milled about, perusing stacks of books, completely unaware – of course – that everything they saw was filled with Librarian fabrications.

They knew nothing of Alivened, of Librarian cults, of Smedrys, or of Lenses. They just wanted a good book to read. (None of them were, unfortunately, able to check out this volume. Not because it was banned – which it is – but because it simply hadn't been written yet. Those poor people may never know the joy they missed out on.)

Small children looked through the picture books. Parents checked out the latest thrillers. The rebellious, trouble-making types looked through the fantasy section. A few unfortunate kids ended up with meaningful books about dysfunctional families.

Few of the people noticed the large number of Librarians gathering behind the front desk. Fewer still noticed that these Librarians were oddly muscular. What *nobody* noticed, however, were the weapons carefully stashed behind the counter. Ms. Fletcher stood at the front of the group. She wished to avoid making an incident – but when incidents *were* necessary, they could be contained. Smedrys were far more difficult.

Despite the buildup of Librarian troops, most of the people in the room went about their libraryish activities. All in all, there was a sense of peace about the room. It was the joy and simple contentment that comes from being around books, Librarian sanctioned or not.

That peace ended abruptly as a door at the back of the room burst open, and a group of dinosaurs rushed in.

It didn't matter that the dinosaurs carried books. It didn't matter that they were smaller than one might expect. It didn't matter that most of them wore clothing. They were dinosaurs – and they were very, *very* realistic.

The screaming started a second later.

Mothers grabbed children. Men cursed, demanding to know if this was 'some kind of a joke!' Librarians stood, shocked. Their hesitation cost them greatly, for within seconds there was an air of general chaos in the room.

That was when I burst through the door, carrying a sword (something I still figured I should have had all along). I was followed by Bastille Crystin, dressed in her stylish silver clothing. Quentin followed in his tuxedo, carrying Sing's gym bag, now filled with Oculator's Lenses. Sing came last, wearing his blue kimono and carrying Grandpa Smedry.

The dinosaurs dashed ahead of us, inadvertently crowding the people against the checkout counters. A few librarian thugs broke through, but the others got trapped behind the desk, blocked by a horde of frightened people and excited dinosaurs.

Bastille met the first Librarian thug. She ducked his sword swing, then shoved him aside. He fell as she hopped over him, waving her sword toward the crowd. The people shied back in confused fear.

A Librarian behind the counter raised a crossbow.

That's new, I thought, moving between the man and Bastille. I stared down the crossbow bolt, thinking about just how dangerous it was. This last bit was, of course, to convince myself. I was beginning to get the hang of my Talent. It only worked at a distance when—

The crossbow's bowstring snapped free, flipping the crossbow bolt uselessly into the air. The Librarian watched it, dumbfounded, and I smiled, leaving Bastille to intimidate the people – and therefore keep the Librarians trapped. I rushed over to pull open the front library door.

I held it for Sing and Quentin. Bastille left next, and I paused, turning and smiling at the packed room. One of the dinosaurs – the T. Rex – finally reached the checkout desk. He slammed down his pile of books, then placed the library card on top of it.

'I'd like to check these out!' he said eagerly.

Ms. Fletcher stood, arms folded as her soldiers tried to push through the crowd. She met my eyes, and I could see from her expression that she knew she was beaten.

I raised my sword to her in a gesture of farewell. The blade immediately fell free and dropped to the ground.

I stared at it for a moment. *What? I thought I was finally figuring out how to control my Talent!*

Ms. Fletcher gave me a curious expression, as if confused by my gesture, and I sighed, flipping the broken bit into the room. Then I stepped out onto the sidewalk. Sing (still carrying my grandfather) and Quentin ran ahead, moving toward Grandpa Smedry's little black car, which still waited where it had been parked.

Bastille still stood by the door. She met my eyes. 'All right, all right,' she said. 'You were right about the dinosaurs. This time.'

I stepped aside as some brave library patrons finally pushed past me out onto the street.

'Your dinosaur friends are just going to get caught again,' Bastille said.

'Charles said he'd try to get them to leave in the confusion,' I said, joining her as we ran across the street. 'It's the best we can do.'

And it really was. Honestly, you have no idea how hard it is to work with dinosaurs. It's no wonder the Librarians made up the myth about them going extinct – pretty much everyone in the Free Kingdoms wishes that one were true.

Sing set Grandpa Smedry in the passenger seat of the car, and Quentin squeezed into the backseat. Then Sing took the driver's seat – holding the useless steering wheel as the car took off. Bastille's silver sports car pulled up just a second later. She climbed in, but I paused. My door had no handle. Finally, Bastille opened the door by rapping on the inside dash. 'The inner door handle is gone,' she said, frowning.

'That's very strange,' I said sliding into the car. 'Now, can we get going?'

She smiled, throwing the car into gear, then she slammed down on the pedal. I turned, watching out the back window. Behind us, a bunch of Librarians had finally managed to push their way out of the building. They watched in dismay as Bastille's car squealed away.

I smiled, turning back around. 'I assume you have ways of making sure that the Librarians don't just have some of their police pick us up?'

'They don't work that way,' Bastille said. 'The Librarians keep as few people as possible informed about the true nature of the world. Most governments don't know that they're being manipulated. Now that we're outside of the Librarian central base, we should have a little breathing room. Especially since we neutralized their Oculator.'

I nodded, resting back in my chair. 'That's good to hear. I think I've had enough sneaking, chasing, and other ridiculousness for one day.'

Bastille smiled, taking a sharp corner. 'You know, Alcatraz, you're a bit less annoying than most Smedrys.'

I smiled. 'Guess I'll just have to practice some more, then.'

20

All right. It's true. I lied to you.

You have undoubtedly figured out that there is no altar made of outdated encyclopedias in this book. There is no harrowing situation where I lay, strapped to said altar, about to be sacrificed. There is no dagger-wielding Librarian about to slice me open and spill my blood into the void to complete a dark ritual. No sharks, no pit of acidic magma.

That's all in the sequel. You didn't really think I'd be able to tell my entire story in one book, did you?

Grandpa Smedry's car puttered along the street. It was dark out – after escaping the library, we had evacuated the gas station, then spent the night and entire next day recovering in the team's safe house (a mock hamburger stand called Sand-burgers).

'Grandfather?' I asked as we drove.

'Yes, lad?'

'What do we do now?'

Grandpa Smedry sat for a moment, turning the wheel in random directions. He looked far better after a night's rest – he had gained back enough strength to begin arriving late to his pain again, and now he was doling it out in very small amounts. He looked almost like his chipper old self.

'Well,' he finally said, 'there is a great deal to be done. The Free Kingdoms are losing the battle against the Librarians. Most of the outright fighting is happening in Mokia right now, though the work behind the scenes in other kingdoms is just as dangerous.'

'What will happen if Mokia does fall?' I asked.

'The Librarians will fold it into their empire,' Grandpa Smedry said. 'It will take a decade or two before it's fully integrated – the

Librarians will have to begin changing the history books across the entire world, making up a new history for the region.'

I nodded. 'And ... my parents are part of this war?'

'Very big parts,' Grandpa Smedry said. 'They're very important people.'

'So important,' I asked quietly, 'that they couldn't be bothered to raise me?'

Grandpa Smedry shook his head. 'No, lad. That's not it at all.'

'Then why?' I asked, frustrated. 'What was this all about? Why leave me to the Librarians all these years?'

'It will make sense if you think about it, lad.'

'I don't really want to think about it at the moment,' I snapped.

Grandpa Smedry smiled. 'Information, Alcatraz. It was all about information. Perhaps you've noticed, but the rest of us don't quite fit into your world.'

I nodded.

'You have information, lad,' Grandpa Smedry said. 'Important information. You understand the lies the Librarians are teaching – and you understand their culture. That makes you important. Very important.'

'So, my parents gave me up so that they could make a *spy* out of me?' I asked.

'It was a very hard decision, my boy,' Grandpa Smedry said quietly. 'And they did not make it lightly. But even when you were a baby, they knew you would rise to the challenge. You are a Smedry.'

'And there was no other way?' I demanded.

'I know it's hard to understand, lad. And, truth be told, I often questioned their decision. But ... well, how many people from other countries have you known who could speak your language perfectly?'

'Not many.'

'The more different a language is from your own,' Grandpa Smedry said, 'the more difficult it is to sound like a native. For some languages, I'm convinced it's impossible. The difference between our world and yours isn't as much a matter of language as it is a matter of understanding. I can see that I don't quite fit in here, but I can't see *why*. It's been the same for all of our operatives. We needed someone on the inside – someone who understood the way Librarians think, the way they live.'

I sat quietly for a long moment. 'So,' I finally said, 'why aren't my parents here? Why did you have to come get me?'

'I can't really answer that, Alcatraz. You know we lost track of your father some years ago, just after you were born. I kind of hoped I'd find him here, on your thirteenth birthday, come to deliver the sands himself. That obviously didn't happen.'

'You have no idea where he is, then?'

Grandpa Smedry shook his head. 'He is a good man – and a good Oculator. My instincts tell me that he's alive, though I have no real proof of that. He must be about something important, but for the life of me, I can't figure out what it is!'

'And my mother?' I asked.

Grandpa Smedry didn't reply immediately. So, I turned to a slight tangent – something that had been bothering me for some time. 'When I wore the Tracker's Lenses back in the library, I was able to see your footprints for a long, long time.'

'That's not surprising,' Grandpa Smedry said.

'And,' I said, 'when you came into my house, you identified my room with the Tracker's Lenses because you saw so many footprints leading into it. But I'd only walked out there once that day. So, the other sets of footprints must have been hours – or even days – old.'

'True,' Grandpa Smedry said.

'So,' I said, 'the Tracker's Lenses work differently for family.'

'Not differently, lad.' Grandpa Smedry said. 'Family members are part of you, and so they're a part of what you know best. Their tracks tend to hang around for a long time, no matter how little you think you know them.'

I sat quietly in my seat. 'I saw Ms. Fletcher's footprints hours after she'd made them.' I finally said.

'Not surprising.'

I closed my eyes. 'Why did she and my father break up?'

'He fell in love with a Librarian, lad,' Grandpa Smedry said. 'Marrying her wasn't the wisest decision he ever made. They thought they could make it work.'

'And they were wrong?'

'Apparently,' Grandpa Smedry said. 'Your father saw something in her – something that I've never been able to see. She isn't exactly the most loyal of Librarians, and your father thought that would make her more lenient to our side. But . . . I think she's only interested in herself. She married your father for his Talent, I'm convinced. Either way, I think that she was another reason that your father agreed to let you be raised in Librarian lands. That way, your mother could see you. He still loved her, I'm afraid. Probably still does, poor fool.'

I closed my eyes. *She sold the Sands of Rashid to Blackburn. My father's life's work, my inheritance. And . . . Blackburn implied that she would sell me too.* I didn't know how to think about what I felt. For some reason, all the danger – all the threats – I'd been through during the last few days hadn't felt as disturbing to me as the knowledge that my mother lived.

And that she was on the wrong side.

Grandpa Smedry's car puttered to a stop. I opened my eyes, looking out the window with a frown. I recognized the street we were on. Joan and Roy Sheldon – my latest foster family, the one whose kitchen I had burned – lived just a few houses down.

'Why are we here?' I asked.

'You remember when I first gave you your Oculator's Lenses, lad?'

'Sure.'

'I asked you a question then,' Grandpa Smedry said. 'I asked you why you had burned down your family's kitchen. You didn't answer.'

'I thought about it, though,' I said. 'I'm figuring things out. I'm getting better with my Talent.'

'Alcatraz, lad,' Grandpa Smedry said, laying a hand on my shoulder. 'That question wasn't just about your Talent. You keep asking about your parents, keep wondering why they were so willing to abandon you. Well, did you ever think to wonder why *you* abandoned so many families?'

'I have thought about it,' I said. 'Or, at least, I have recently. And perhaps I was a little hard on them. But it wasn't *only* my fault. They couldn't handle it when I broke things.'

'Maybe some of them,' Grandpa Smedry said. 'But how many of them did you really give a chance?'

I knew he was right, of course. And yet, knowing something is very different from feeling it. And at that moment, I was feeling all the same emotions I felt every time parents gave me away.

I felt a twist in my gut. It was happening again, and this time it wasn't my fault. I'd tried. I'd tried not to push Grandpa Smedry away. And now it was happening anyway.

'You're trying to get rid of me,' I whispered.

Grandpa Smedry shook his head. 'Information, lad! It's all about *information*. You thought those families were going to give you up, so you acted first. You *made* them get rid of you. But you had bad information.

'I'm not trying to abandon you. We have a lot of work to do, you and I. However, you need to go back and spend some time with those who have loved you. You need to make your peace with them if you're ever going to understand yourself well enough to help us win this war.'

'Blackburn didn't think information was all that important,' I snapped.

'And how'd he end up?' Grandpa Smedry said, smiling.

'But he beat you,' I said. 'In the Oculator's Duel. He was stronger.'

'Yes, he was,' Grandpa Smedry said. 'He worked very hard to be able to beat a person like me in a contest like that. He put out his eye so that he would be stronger with offensive Lenses, and he collected other Lenses that would let him fight effectively.

'But, in doing so, he gave up the ability to see as well. Alcatraz, everything we do is about seeing! If he'd *seen* just a little better, he would have noticed your trick. If he'd *seen* a little better, he'd have realized that by putting out his eye and focusing on the powers that let him win battles, he handicapped himself in larger, far more important ways. Perhaps if he'd *seen* a little more, he'd have realized that those Translator's Lenses you have are far more powerful that any Firebringer's Lens.'

I sat back, trying to sort out my thoughts – and my emotions. It was hard to focus on any one feeling – regret, anxiety, anger, confusion. I still couldn't believe that Grandpa wanted me to stay with Joan and Roy. I glanced at the house. 'Hey, there's no hole in the side of it!'

'The Librarians would have fixed that before your foster parents got home,' Grandpa Smedry said. 'They try to keep things quiet, work on the underground – something like that hole would have attracted too much attention to this house, and therefore to you.'

'Won't it be dangerous for me to be here?' I asked.

'Probably,' Grandpa Smedry said. 'But it will be dangerous for *you* everywhere. And, we have some ... means of keeping you safe here, for a little while, at least.'

I nodded slowly.

'They'll be happy to see you, lad,' Grandpa Smedry said.

'I don't know about that,' I said. 'I burned down their kitchen.'

'Try them.'

I shook my head. 'I still can't control it, Grandfather,' I said quietly. 'My Talent. I thought I was getting the hang of it, but I still break things all the time – things I don't wasn't to.'

Grandpa Smedry smiled. 'Perhaps. But when it counted, you broke that Firebringer's Lens in *exactly* the right way. You didn't just shatter it or make it stop working. You made it work wrong, but made it work right for you. That shows real promise, lad.'

I looked over at the Sheldons' house again. 'You'll ... come for me, won't you?'

'Of course I will, lad!'

I took a deep breath. 'All right, then. Do you want to take the Translator's Lenses with you?'

'They're your inheritance, lad. It wouldn't be right. You keep them.'

I nodded. Grandpa Smedry smiled, then reached over to give me a hug. I held on tight – tighter than I'd probably intended.

Grandfather, cousins, perhaps even my father, I thought. *I have family.*

Finally, I let go, then got out of the car. I looked up at the house again. *I've always had family,* I thought. *Not always the Sheldons, but someone.*

People willing to give me a home. I guess it's about time I admitted that.

I closed the door, then looked in through the window.

'Don't break anything!' Grandpa Smedry said.

'Just come for me,' I said. 'Don't be late.'

'Me?' Grandpa Smedry asked. 'Late?'

Then he rapped on the dash of the car, and it began to hum. I watched it pull away, watched it until it was gone. Then I walked up the street to the house. I paused on the doorstep.

I could still faintly smell smoke.

I knocked on the door. Roy opened it. He stood, stupefied, for a moment. Then he yelled in surprise, grabbing me in a hug. 'Joan!' he cried.

She rushed around the corner. 'Alcatraz?'

Roy handed me over to her. She grabbed me in a tight embrace.

'When the caseworker called,' Roy said, 'asking where you'd gone … well, we assumed you'd run off for good, kiddo.'

'You didn't get into trouble, did you?' Joan asked, looking at me sternly.

I shrugged. 'I don't know. I knocked down two floors, one wall, and a few doors, I think. Nothing too bad.'

Joan and Roy shared a look, then smiled, and took me in.

Hours later, after giving them some reasonable lies about where I'd been, after having a good meal, and after accepting their pleas that I stay with them for at least a little while longer, I walked up to my room.

I sat down on my bed, trying to think through the things that had happened to me. Oddly, I didn't find the Librarians, the Alivened, or the Lenses to be the most strange of the recent events. The strangest things to me were the changes I saw in myself.

I *cared*. And it had all happened because of a simple package in the mail …

My head snapped up. There, sitting on my desk, was the empty box, beside its brown wrapper. I stood and walked across the room. I flattened out the packaging noting the stamp that I'd investigated, the address written in faded ink … and the scribbles up the side of the paper. The ones I'd assumed had come from someone trying to get the ink in his pen to flow.

With trembling hands, I reached into my pocket and pulled out the Translator's Lenses – the Lenses of Rashid. I slipped them on. The scribble immediately changed into legible words.

Son,

Congratulations! If you can read this, then you have managed to craft Lenses of Rashid from the sands I sent you. I knew you'd be able to do it!

I must tell you that I am afraid. I fear that I've stumbled on something powerful — something more important, and more dangerous, than any of us expected. The Lenses of Rashid were only the beginning! The Forgotten Language leads to clues, stories, legends about the Smedry Talents and —

Well, I can't say more here. By the time you get this package, much time will have passed. Thirteen years. Perhaps I'll have solved the problem by then, but I suspect not. The Lenses that let me see where you will be living at age thirteen have also given me a warning that my task will not be done by then. But I can only see vaguely into the future — the Oracle's Lenses are far from perfect! What I see makes me even more worried.

Once I have confirmation that this box reached you without being intercepted, I will send you further information. I have the other set of Rashid Lenses — with them, I can write in the Forgotten Language, and only you will be able to read my messages.

For now, simply know that I'm proud of you, and that I love you.

Your father,
Attica Smedry

I put the paper down, stunned. It was at that moment that I heard a rapping on my window. Instead of a raven outside, however, I saw the mustached face of Grandpa Smedry.

I frowned, walking over and opening the window. Grandpa Smedry stood on a ladder that appeared to have extended from the back of his little black automobile.

'Grandpa?' I asked. 'What are you doing here?'

'What?' he asked. 'I came for you, as promised.'

'As promised?' I asked. 'But you only left me a few hours ago.'

'Yes, yes,' Grandpa Smedry said. 'I know, I'm late. Come on, lad! We've got work to do. Are you packed yet?'

Grandpa Smedry began to climb back down the ladder.

'Wait,' I said, sticking my head out the window. 'Packed? I thought I was staying here with Joan and Roy!'

'What?' Grandpa Smedry said, looking back up. 'Edible Eddings, boy! This city is crawling with Librarians. It was dangerous enough to give you a chance to come back and say good-bye!'

'But you said I had to spend some time with them!'

'A few hours, lad,' Grandpa Smedry said, 'to apologize for the trouble you'd given them. What did you expect? That I'd leave you here all summer, in the exact place where your enemies know where to look? With people that aren't even your family? In a place you don't really like, and that is depressingly normal compared to the world you've grown to love? Doesn't that sound a little stupid and contrived to you?'

I raised my hand to my head. 'Yeah,' I noted, 'now that you mention it, who *would* do something silly like that? Let me go get my things and write a note to Joan and Roy. Oh, and you have to see what's written on this package!'

I rushed back into the room, pulling out a gym bag to begin

packing. Outside, I heard Grandpa Smedry's car hum quietly to life.

I smiled. Everything felt right. Weird, true, but *right*.

It was about time.

EPILOGUE

So, that's how it began. Not as spectacular as some have claimed, I know, but it felt incredible enough to me at the time.

Now, I'll be the first to admit that those first couple of days had a profound effect on me, shaking me slightly out of the self-indulgent rebelliousness that I had fallen into. The thing is, if I could go back, I'd still tell myself not to go with Grandpa Smedry on that strange, unfortunate day.

The things I learned during that first infiltration – trust, self-confidence, bravery – might seem good at first glance. However, the changes I experienced were just setting me up for my eventual fall. you'll see what I mean.

For now, I hope this narrative was enough to show that even supposed heroes have flaws. Let this be your warning – I'm not the person that you think I am. You'll see.

With regret,
Alcatraz Smedry

And so, untold millions screamed out in pain, and then were suddenly silenced. I hope you're happy.

(This was included for anyone who skipped forward to read the last page of the book. For the rest of you – the ones who reached the last page in the proper, honorable, and Smedry-approved manner – those untold millions are cheering in praise of your honesty.

They'll probably throw you a party.)

ALCATRAZ VERSUS THE SCRIVENER'S BONES

*For Lauren, who somehow manages to be both the baby of
the family and the most responsible one of us all*

AUTHOR'S FOREWORD

I am a liar.

I realize that you may not believe this. In fact, I hope that you don't. Not only would that make the statement particularly ironic, but it means you have very far to fall.

You see, I know that you Free Kingdomers have heard stories about me. Perhaps you've seen a documentary or two about my life through a silimatic screen. I can understand why you might not believe that I'm a liar. You probably think that I'm just being humble.

You think you know me. You've listened to the storytellers. You've talked with your friends about my exploits. You've read history books and heard the criers tell of my heroic deeds. The trouble is, the only people who are bigger liars than myself are the people who like to talk about me.

You don't know me. You don't understand me. And you certainly shouldn't believe what you read about me. Except – of course – what you read in this book, for it will contain the truth.

Now, let me speak to the Hushlanders. That means those of you who live in places like Canada, Europe, or the Americas. Do not be fooled because this book looks like a work of fantasy! Like the previous volume, we are publishing this book as fiction in the Hushlands to hide it from the Librarians.

This is not fiction. In the Free Kingdoms – lands like Mokia and Nalhalla – it will be published openly as an autobiography. For that is what it is. My own story told – for the first time – to prove what really happened.

For once, I intend to cut through the falsehoods. For once, I intend to see the truth in print. My name is Alcatraz Smedry, and I welcome you to the second volume of my life story.

May you find it enlightening.

1

So, there I was, slumped in my chair, waiting in a drab airport terminal, munching absently on a bag of stale potato chips.

Not the beginning you expected, is it? You likely thought that I would start this book with something exciting. A scene involving evil Librarians, perhaps – something with altars, Alivened, or at least some machine guns.

I'm sorry to disappoint you. It won't be the first time I do that. However, it's for your own good. You see, I have decided to reform. My last book was terribly unfair – I started it with an intense, threatening scene of action. Then I cut away from it and left the reader hanging, wondering, and frustrated.

I promise to no longer be deceptive like that in my writing. I won't use cliff-hangers or other tricks to keep you reading. I will be calm, respectful, and completely straightforward.

Oh, by the way. Did I mention that while waiting in that airport I was probably in the most danger I'd ever been in my entire life?

I ate another stale potato chip.

If you'd passed by me sitting there, you would have thought that I looked like an average American boy. I was thirteen years old, and I had dark brown hair. I wore loose jeans, a green jacket, and white sneakers. I'd started to grow a bit taller during the last few months, but I was well within the average for my age.

In fact, the only abnormal thing about me were the blue glasses I was wearing. Not truly sunglasses, they looked like an old man's reading glasses, only with a baby-blue tint.

(I still consider this aspect of my life to be terribly unfair. For some reason, the more powerful a pair of Oculator Lenses is, the less cool they tend to look. I'm developing a theory about it – the Law of Disproportional Lameness.)

I munched on another chip. *Come on . . .*, I thought. *Where are you?*

My grandfather, as usual, was late. Now, he couldn't *completely* be blamed for it. Leavenworth Smedry, after all, is a Smedry. (The last name's a dead giveaway.) Like all Smedries, he has a magic Talent. His is the ability to magically arrive late to appointments.

While most people would have considered this to be a large inconvenience, it's the Smedry way to use our Talents for our benefit. Grandpa Smedry, for instance, tends to arrive late to things like bullet wounds and disasters. His Talent had saved his life on numerous occasions.

Unfortunately, he also tends to be late the rest of the time too. I think he uses his Talent as an excuse even when it isn't to blame; I've tried to challenge him on this several times, but always failed. He'd just arrive late to the scolding, and so the sound would never reach him. (Besides, in Grandpa Smedry's opinion, a scolding *is* a disaster.)

I hunched down a little bit more in the chair, trying to look inconspicuous. The problem was, anyone who knew what to look for could see I was wearing Oculatory Lenses. In this case, my baby-blue spectacles were Courier's Lenses, a common type of Lens that lets two Oculators communicate over a short distance. My grandfather and I had put them to good use during the last few months, running and hiding from Librarian agents.

Few people in the Hushlands understand the power of Oculatory Lenses. Most of those who walked through the airport were completely unaware of things like Oculators, silimatic technology, and the sect of evil Librarians who secretly ruled the world.

Yes. You read that right. Evil Librarians control the world. They keep everyone in ignorance, teaching them falsehoods in place of history, geography, and politics. It's kind of a joke to them. Why else do you think the Librarians named themselves what they did?

Librarians. LIE-brarians.

Sounds obvious now, doesn't it? If you wish to smack yourself in the forehead and curse loudly, you may proceed to do so. I can wait.

I ate another chip. Grandpa Smedry was supposed to have contacted me via the Courier's Lenses more than two hours before. It was getting late, even for him. I looked about, trying to determine if there were any Librarian agents in the airport crowd.

I couldn't spot any, but that didn't mean anything. I knew enough to realize that you can't always tell a Librarian by looking at one. While some dress the part – horn-rimmed glasses for the women, bow ties and vests for the men – others looked completely normal, blending in with the regular Hushlanders. Dangerous, but unseen. (Kind of like those troublemakers who read fantasy novels.)

I had a tough decision to make. I could continue wearing the Courier's Lenses, which would mark me as an Oculator to Librarian agents. Or, I could take them off, and thereby miss Grandpa Smedry's message when he got close enough to contact me.

If he got close enough to contact me.

A group of people walked over to where I was sitting, draping their luggage across several rows of chairs and chatting about the fog delays. I tensed, wondering if they were Librarian agents. Three months on the run had left me feeling anxious.

But that running was over. I would soon escape the Hushlands and finally get to visit my homeland. Nalhalla, one of the Free Kingdoms. A place that Hushlanders didn't even know existed, though it was a large continent that sat in the Pacific Ocean between North America and Asia.

I'd never seen it before, but I'd heard stories, and I'd seen some Free Kingdom technology. Cars that could drive themselves, hourglasses that could keep time no matter which direction you turned them. I longed to get to Nalhalla – though, even more desperately, I wanted to get out of Librarian-controlled lands.

Grandpa Smedry hadn't explained exactly *how* he planned to get me out, or even why we were meeting at the airport. It seemed unlikely that there would be any flights to the Free Kingdoms.

However, no matter what the method, I knew our escape probably wouldn't be easy.

Fortunately, I had a few things on my side. First, I was an Oculator, and I had access to some fairly powerful Lenses. Second, I had my grandfather, who was an expert at avoiding Librarian agents. Third, I knew that the Librarians liked to keep a low profile, even while they secretly ruled most of the world. I probably didn't have to worry about police or airport security – the Librarians wouldn't want to involve them, for that would risk revealing the conspiracy to people who were too low ranked.

I also had my Talent. But ... well, I wasn't really sure whether that was an advantage or not. It—

I froze. A man was standing in the waiting area of the gate next to mine. He was wearing a suit and sunglasses. And he was staring right at me. As soon as I noticed him, he turned away, looking too nonchalant.

Sunglasses probably meant Warrior's Lenses – one of the only kinds of Lenses that a non-Oculator could use. I stiffened; the man seemed to be muttering to himself.

Or talking into a radio receiver.

Shattering Glass! I thought, standing up and throwing on my backpack. I wove through the crowd, leaving the gate behind, and raised my hand to my eyes, intending to pull off the Courier's Lenses.

But ... what if Grandpa Smedry tried to contact me? There was no way he'd be able to find me in the crowded airport. I needed to keep those Lenses on.

I feel I need to break the action here to warn you that I frequently break the action to mention trivial things. It's one of my bad habits that, along with wearing mismatched socks, tends to make people rather annoyed at me. It's not my fault, though, honestly. I blame society. (For the socks, I mean. The breaking-the-action thing is *totally* my own fault.)

I hastened my pace, keeping my head down and my Lenses on. I hadn't gone far before I noticed a group of men in black suits and pink bow ties standing on a moving airport walkway a short distance ahead. They had several uniformed security guards with them.

I froze. *So much for not having to worry about the police* ... I tried to hold in my panic, turning – as covertly as I could – and hurrying in the other direction.

I should have realized that the rules would start changing. The Librarians had spent three months chasing Grandpa Smedry and me. They might hate the idea of involving local law enforcement, but they hated the idea of losing us even more.

A second group of Librarian agents were coming from the other direction. A good dozen warriors in Lenses, likely armed with glass swords and other advanced weapons. There was only one thing to do.

I stepped into the bathroom.

Numerous people were in there, doing their business. I rushed to the back wall. I let my backpack fall to the ground, then placed both hands against the wall's tiles.

A couple of men in the bathroom gave me odd looks, but I'd gotten used to those. People had given me odd looks for most of my life – what else would you expect for a kid who routinely broke things that weren't really all that breakable? (Once, when I was seven, my Talent decided to break pieces of concrete as I stepped on them. I left a line of broken sidewalk squares behind me, like the footprints of some immense killer robot – one wearing size six sneakers.)

I closed my eyes, concentrating. Before, I'd let my Talent rule my life. I hadn't known that I could control it – I hadn't even been convinced that it was real.

Grandpa Smedry's arrival three months earlier had changed all of that. While dragging me off to infiltrate a Library and recover the Sands of Rashid, he'd helped me learn that I could *use* my Talent, rather than just be used by it.

I focused, and twin bursts of energy pulsed from my chest and down my arms. The tiles in front of me fell free, shattering as they hit the ground like a line of icicles knocked off of a railing. I continued to focus. People behind me cried out. The Librarians would be upon me any moment.

The entire wall broke, falling away from me. A water line began to spray into the air. I didn't pause to look behind at the shouting men, but instead reached back and grabbed my backpack.

The strap broke loose. I cursed quietly, grabbing the other one. It broke free too.

The Talent. Blessing and curse. I didn't let it rule me anymore – but I wasn't really in control either. It was as if the Talent had joint custody over my life; I got it on every other weekend and some holidays.

I left the backpack. I had my Lenses in the pockets of my jacket, and they were the only things of real value I owned. I leaped through the hole, scrambling over the rubble and into the bowels of the airport. (Hmm. Out of the bathroom and into the bowels – kind of opposite of the normal way.)

I was in some kind of service tunnel, poorly lit and even more poorly cleaned. I dashed down the tunnel for several minutes. I think I must have left the terminal behind, traveling through some access passageway to another building.

At the end, there were a few stairs leading to a large door. I heard shouting behind me and risked a glance. A group of men were barreling down the passage toward me.

I spun and tugged on the doorknob. The door was locked, but doors have always been one of my specialties. The knob came off; I tossed it over my shoulder in an offhanded motion. Then I kicked the door open, bursting out into a large hangar.

Massive airplanes towered over me, their windshields dark. I hesitated, looking up at the enormous vehicles, feeling dwarfed as if by large beasts.

I shook myself out of the stupor. The Librarians were still behind me. Fortunately, it appeared as if this hangar was empty of people. I slammed the door, then placed my hand on the lock, using my talent to break it so that the deadbolt jammed in place. I hopped over the railing and landed on a short line of steps leading down to the hangar's floor.

When I reached the bottom, my feet left tracks in the dusty floor. Fleeing out onto the runway seemed like an easy way to get myself arrested, considering the current state of airport security. However, hiding seemed risky as well.

That was a good metaphor for my life, actually. It seemed that no matter what I did, I ended up in even more danger than I'd been in before. One might have said that I constantly went 'out of the frying pan and into the fire,' which is a common Hushlands saying.

(Hushlanders, it might be noted, aren't very imaginative with their idioms. Personally, I say, 'Out of the frying pan and into the deadly pit filled with sharks who are wielding chainsaws with killer kittens stapled to them.' However, that one's having a rough time catching on.)

Fists began to bang on the door. I glanced at it, then made my decision. I'd try hiding.

I ran toward a small doorway on the floor of the hangar. It had slivers of light shining in around it, and I figured it led out onto the runway. I was careful to leave big, long footprints in the dust. Then – my false trail made – I hopped onto some boxes, moved across them, then jumped onto the ground.

The door shook as the men pounded. It wouldn't hold for long. I skidded down next to the wheel of a 747 and whipped off my Courier's Lenses. Then, I reached into my jacket. I had sewn a group of protective pockets onto the inside lining, and each one was cushioned with a special Free Kingdoms material to protect the Lenses.

I pulled out a pair of green-Lensed spectacles and shoved them on.

The door burst.

I ignored it, instead focusing on the floor of the hangar. Then, I activated the Lenses. Immediately, a quick gust of wind blew from my face. It moved across the floor, erasing some of the footprints. Windstormer's lenses, a gift from Grandpa Smedry the week after our first Librarian infiltration.

By the time the Librarians got through the door, cursing and muttering, only the footprints I *wanted* them to see were still there. I huddled down beside my wheel, holding my breath and trying to still my thumping heart as I heard a fleet of soldiers and policemen pile down the steps.

That's when I remembered my Firebringer's Lens.

I peeked up over the top of the 747 wheel. The Librarians had fallen for my trick and were moving along the floor toward the door out of the hangar. They weren't walking as quickly as I would have wanted, though, and several were glancing around with suspicious eyes.

I ducked back down before I could be spotted. My fingers felt the Firebringer's Lens – I only had one left – and I hesitantly brought it out. It was completely clear, with a single red dot in the center.

When activated, it shot forth a super-hot burst of energy, something like a laser. I could turn it on the Librarians. They had, after all, tried to kill me on several different occasions. They deserved it.

I sat for a moment, then quietly tucked the Lens back in its pocket and instead put my Courier's Lenses back on. If you've read the previous volume of the autobiography, you'll realize that I had some very particular ideas about heroism. A hero wasn't the type of person who turned a laser of pure energy upon the backs of a bunch of soldiers, particularly when that bunch included innocent security guards.

Sentiments like this one eventually got me into a lot of trouble. You probably remember how I'm going to end up; I mentioned it in the first book. I'll eventually be tied to an altar made from outdated encyclopedias, with cultists from the Librarian Order of the Shattered Lens preparing to spill my Oculator's blood in an unholy ceremony.

Heroism is what landed me there. Ironically, it also saved my life that day in the airport hangar. You see, if I hadn't put on my Courier's Lenses, I would have missed what happened next.

Alcatraz? a voice suddenly asked in my mind.

The voice nearly made me cry out in surprise.

Uh, Alcatraz? Hello? Is anyone listening?

The voice was fuzzy and indistinct, and it wasn't the voice of my grandfather. However, it *was* coming from the Courier's Lenses.

Oh bother! The voice said. *Um. I've never been good with Courier's Lenses.*

It faded in and out, as if someone were speaking through a radio that wasn't getting good reception. It wasn't Grandpa Smedry, but at that moment, I was willing to take a chance on whoever it was.

'I'm here!' I whispered, activating the Lenses.

A blurry face fuzzed into existence in front of me, hovering like a hologram in the air. It belonged to a young girl with dark tan skin and black hair.

Hello? she asked. *Is someone there? Can you talk louder or something?*

'Not really,' I hissed, glancing out at the Librarians. Most of them had moved out the door, but a small group of men had apparently been assigned to search the hangar. Mostly security guards.

Um . . . okay, the voice said. *Uh, who is this?*

'Who do you think it is?' I asked in annoyance. 'I'm Alcatraz. Who are you?'

Oh, I – the image, and voice, fuzzed for a moment – *sent to pick you up. Sorry! Uh, where are you?*

'In a hangar,' I said. One of the guards perked up, then pulled out a gun, pointing it in my direction. He'd heard me.

'Shattering Glass!' I hissed, ducking back down.

You really shouldn't swear like that, you know . . . , the girl said.

'Thanks,' I hissed as quietly as possible. 'Who are you, and how are you going to get me out of this?'

There was a pause. A dreadful, terrible, long, annoying, frustrating, deadly, nerve-racking, incredibly wordy pause.

I . . . don't really know, the girl said. *I – wait just a second. Bastille says that you should run out somewhere in the open then signal us. It's too foggy down there. We can't really see much.*

Down there? I thought. Still, if Bastille was with this girl, that seemed like a good sign. Although Bastille would probably chastise me for getting myself into so much trouble, she did have a habit of being very effective at what she did. Hopefully that would include rescuing me.

'Hey!' a voice said. I turned to the side staring out at one of the guards. 'I found someone!'

Time to break some things, I thought, taking a deep breath. Then I sent a burst of breaking power into the wheel of the airplane.

I ducked away, leaping to my feet as lug nuts popped free from the airplane wheel. The guard raised his gun but didn't fire.

'Shoot him!' said a man in a black suit, the Librarian who stood directing things from the side of the room.

'I'm not shooting a *kid,*' the guard said. 'Where are these terrorists you were talking about?'

Good man, I thought as I dashed toward the front of the hangar. At that moment, the wheel of the airplane fell completely off, and the entire front of the vehicle crashed down against the pavement. Men cried out in surprise, and the security guards dived for cover.

The Librarian in black grabbed a handgun from one of the confused guards and pointed it at me. I just smiled.

The gun, of course, fell apart as soon as the Librarian pulled the trigger. My Talent protects me when it can – and the more moving parts a weapon has, the easier it is to break. I rammed my shoulder into the massive hangar doors and sent a shock of breaking power into them. Screws and nut and bolts fell like rain around me, hitting the ground. Several guards peeked out from behind boxes.

The entire front of the hangar came off, falling away from me and hitting the ground outside with a reverberating crash. I hesitated, shocked, even though that was exactly what I'd wanted to happen. Swirling fog began to creep into the hangar around me.

It seemed that my Talent was getting even more powerful. Before, I'd broken things like pots and dishes, with the very rare exception of something larger like the concrete I had broken when I was seven. That was *nothing* like what I'd been doing lately: taking the wheels off of airplanes and making entire hangar doors fall off. Not for the first time, I wondered just how much I could break if I really needed to.

And how much the Talent could break if *it* decided that it wanted to.

There wasn't much time to contemplate that, as the Librarians outside had noticed the ruckus. They stood, black upon the noon-day fog, looking back at me. Most of them had spread out to the sides, and so the only way for me to go was straight ahead.

I dashed out onto the wet tarmac, running for all I was worth. The Librarians began to yell, and several tried – completely inef-fectively – to fire guns at me. They should have known better. In their defense, few people – even Librarians – are accustomed to dealing with a Smedry as powerful as I was. Against the others, they might have been able to get off a few shots before some-thing went wrong. Firearms aren't *completely* useless in the Free Kingdoms, they're just much less powerful.

The shooting – or lack thereof – bought me just a few seconds of time. Unfortunately, there were a pair of Librarians in my path.

'Get ready!' I yelled into my Courier's Lenses. Then I whipped them off and put on the Windstormer's Lenses. I focused as hard as I could, blowing forth a burst of wind from my eyes. Both Librarians were knocked to the ground, and I leaped over them.

Other Librarians cried out from behind, chasing me as I moved out onto a runway. Puffing, I reached into a pocket and pulled free my Firebringer's Lens. I spun and activated the Lens.

It started to glow. The group of Librarians pulled to a halt. They knew enough to recognize that Lens. I held it out, then pointed it up into the air. It shot a line of red firelight upward, piercing the fog.

That had better be enough of a signal, I thought. The Librarians gathered together, obviously preparing to rush at me. Lens or no Lens. I prepared my Windstormer's Lenses, hoping I could use them to blow the Librarians back long enough for Bastille to save me.

The Librarians, however, did not charge. I stood, anxious, the

Firebringer's Lens still firing into the air. What were they waiting for?

The Librarians parted, and a dark figure – silhouetted in the muggy fog – moved through them. I couldn't see much, but something about this figure was *wrong*. It was a head taller than the others, and one of its arms was several feet longer than the other. Its head was misshapen. Perhaps inhuman. Most definitely dangerous.

I shivered, taking an involuntary step backward. The dark figure raised its bony arm, as if pointing a gun.

I'll be all right, I told myself. *Guns are useless against me.*

There was a crack in the air, then the Firebringer's Lens exploded in my fingers, hit square on by the creature's bullet. I yelled, pulling my hand down.

Shoot my lens rather than me. This one is more clever than the others.

The dark figure walked forward, and part of me wanted to wait to see just what it was that made this creature's arm and head so misshapen. The rest of me was just plain horrified. The figure started to run, and that was enough. I did the smart thing (I'm capable of that on occasion) and dashed away as quickly as I could.

Instantly, I seemed to be pulled backward. The wind whistled in my ears oddly, and each step felt far more difficult than it should have. I began to sweat, and soon it was tough to even walk.

Something was very, very wrong. As I continued to move, forcing myself on despite the strange force towing me backward, I began to think I could *feel* the dark thing behind me. I could sense it, twisted and vile, getting closer and closer.

I could barely move. Each. Step. Got. Tougher.

A rope ladder slapped down against the tarmac a short distance in front of me. I cried out and lunged for it, grabbing ahold. My weight must have told those above that I was on board, because the ladder suddenly jerked upward, towing me with it and ripping me free from whatever force had been holding me back. I felt the pressure lighten and glancing down, I let out a relieved breath.

The figure still stood there, indistinct in the fog, only a few feet from where I'd been. It stared up as I was lifted to safety, until the ground and the creature disappeared into the fog.

I let out a sigh of relief, relaxing against the wood and rope. A few minutes later, my ladder and I were pulled free from the fog, bursting out into open air.

I looked up and saw perhaps the most awesome sight I'd ever seen in my entire life.

2

This is the second book of the series. Those of you who have read the first book can skip this introduction and move on. The rest of you, stay put.

I'd like to congratulate you on finding this book. I'm glad you're reading a serious work about real world politics, rather than wasting your time on something silly like a fantasy book about a fictional character like Napoleon. (Either Napoleon, actually. They both have something to do, in their own way, with being Blownapart.)

Now, I do have to admit something. I find it very disturbing that you readers have decided to begin with the *second* book in the series. That's a very bad habit to have – worse, even than wearing mismatched socks. In fact, on the bad-habit scale, it ranks somewhere between chewing with your mouth open and making quacking noises when your friends are trying to study. (Try that one sometime – it's really fun.)

It's because of people like you that we authors have to clog our second books with all kinds of explanations. We have to, essentially, invent the wheel again – or at least renew our patent.

You should already know who I am, and you should understand Oculatory Lenses and Smedry Talents. With all of that knowledge, you could easily understand the events that led me to the point where I hung dangling from a rope ladder, staring up at something awesome that I haven't yet described.

Why don't I just describe it now? Well, by asking that question, you prove that you haven't read the first book. Let me explain by using a brief object lesson.

Do you remember the first chapter of this book? (I certainly hope that you do, since it was only a few pages back.) What did

I promise you there? I promised that I was going to stop using cliff-hangers and other frustrating storytelling practices. Now, what did I do at the end of the very same chapter? I left you with a frustrating cliff-hanger, of course.

That was intended to teach you something: That I'm completely trustworthy and would never dare lie to you. At least not more than, oh, half a dozen times per chapter.

I dangled from the rope ladder, wind whipping at my jacket, heart still pounding from my escape. Flying above me was an enormous glass dragon.

Perhaps you've seen a dragon depicted in art or cinema. I certainly have. However, looking up at the thing above me in the air, I knew that the images I'd seen in films were only approximations. Those movies tended to make dragons – even the threatening ones – seem bulbous, with large stomachs and awkward wingspans.

The reptilian form above me was nothing like that. There was an incredible sleekness to it, snakelike but at the same time powerful. It had three sets of wings running down the length of its body, and they flapped in harmony. I could see six legs as well – all tucked up underneath the slender body – and it had a long glass tail whipping behind it in the air.

Its triangular head twisted about – translucent glass sparkling – and looked at me. It was angular, with sharp lines, like an arrowhead. And there were people standing in its eyeball.

This isn't a creature at all, I realized, hanging desperately to the ladder. *But a vehicle. One crafted completely from glass!*

'Alcatraz!' a voice called from above, barely audible over the sound of the wind.

I glanced up. The ladder led into an open section of the dragon's stomach. A familiar face was poking out of the hole, looking down at me. The same age as I am, Bastille had long, silver hair that whipped in the wind. The last time I'd seen her, she'd gone with two of my cousins into hiding.

Grandpa Smedry had worried that keeping us all together was making us easier to track.

She said something, but it was lost in the wind.

'What?' I yelled.

'I *said*,' she yelled, 'are you going to climb up here, or do you intend to hang there looking stupid for the entire trip?'

That's Bastille for you. She did kind of have a point, though. I climbed up the swinging ladder – which was much harder and much more nerve-racking than you might think.

I forced myself onward. It would have been a pretty stupid end to get lifted to safety at the last moment, then drop off the ladder and squish against the ground below. When I got close enough, Bastille gave me a hand and helped me up into the dragon's belly. She pulled a glass lever on the wall, and the ladder began to retract.

I watched, curious. At that point in my life, I hadn't really seen much silimatic technology, and I still considered it all to be 'magic.' There was no noise as the ladder came up – no clinking of gears or hum of a motor. The ladder just wound around a turning wheel.

A glass plate slid over the open hole in the floor. Around me, glass walls sparkled in the sunlight, completely transparent. The view was amazing – we'd already moved beyond the fog – and I could see the landscape below, extending in all directions. I almost felt as if I were hovering in the sky, alone, in the beautiful serenity of—

'You done gawking yet?' Bastille snapped, arms folded.

I shot her a glance. 'Excuse me,' I said, 'but I'm trying to have a beautiful moment here.'

She snorted. 'What are you going to do? Write a poem? Come on.' With that, she began to walk along the glass hallway inside the dragon, moving toward the head. I smiled wryly to myself. I hadn't seen Bastille in over two months, and neither of us had known if the other would even survive long enough to meet up again.

But, where Bastille is concerned, that was actually a nice reception. She didn't throw anything, or even swear at me. Rather heartwarming.

I rushed to catch up with her. 'What happened to your business suit?'

She looked down. Instead of wearing her stylish jacket and slacks, she was dressed in a much more stiff, militaristic costume. Black with silver buttons, it looked kind of like the dress uniforms that military personnel wear on formal occasions. It even had those little metal things on the shoulders that I can never remember how to spell.

'We're not in the Hushlands anymore, Smedry,' she said. 'Or, at least, we soon won't be. So why wear their clothing?'

'I thought you liked those clothes.'

She shrugged. 'It's my place to wear this now. Besides, I like wearing a glassweave jacket, and this uniform has one.'

I *still* haven't figured out how they make clothing out of glass. It's apparently very expensive but worth the cost. A glassweave jacket could take quite a beating, protecting its wearer almost as well as a suit of armor. Back in the library infiltration we'd done, Bastille had survived a blow that really should have killed her.

'All right,' I said. 'What about this thing we're flying in? I assume it's some sort of vehicle and not really a living creature?'

Bastille gave me one of her barely tolerant looks. I keep telling her she should trademark those. She could sell photos of herself to scare children, turn milk to curds, or frighten terrorists into surrendering.

She doesn't find comments like that very funny.

'Of *course* it's not alive,' she said. 'Alivening things is Dark Oculary, as I believe you've been told.'

'Okay, but why make it in the shape of a dragon?'

'What should we do?' Bastille said. 'Build our aircraft in the shapes of … long tubey contraptions, or whatever it is those airplanes look like? I can't believe they stay in the air. Their wings can't even flap!'

'They don't need to flap. They have jet engines!'

'Oh, and then why do they have wings?'

I paused. 'Something about airlift and physics and stuff like that.'

Bastille snorted again. 'Physics,' she muttered. 'A Librarian scam.'

'Physics isn't a scam, Bastille. It's very logical.'

'Librarian logic.'

'Facts.'

'Oh?' she asked. 'And if they're facts, then why are they so complicated? Shouldn't explanations about the natural world be simple? Why is there all of that needless math and complexity?' She shook her head, turning away from me. 'All of that is just intended to confuse people. If the Hushlanders think that science is too complicated to understand, then they'll be too afraid to ask questions.'

She eyed me, obviously watching to see if I would continue the argument. I did not. There was one thing about hanging around with Bastille – it was teaching me when to hold my tongue. Even if I didn't hold my brain.

How does she know so much about what the Librarians teach in their schools? I thought. *She knows an awful lot about my people.*

Bastille was still an enigma to me. She'd wanted to be an Oculator when she was younger, so she knew quite a bit about Lenses. However, I still couldn't quite figure out why she'd even wanted to be one so badly in the first place. Everyone – or, well, everyone outside the Hushlands – knows that Oculatory powers are hereditary. One can't just 'become' an Oculator in the same way one can choose to become a lawyer, and accountant, or a potted plant.

Either way, I was finding it increasingly disconcerting to be able to see through the floor, particularly when we were so high up. The motions of the giant vehicle didn't help either. Now that I was inside of it, I could see that the dragon was made of glass plates that slid together such that the entire thing could move and twist. Each flap of the wings made the body undulate around me.

We reached the head, which I assumed was the dragon's version of a cockpit. The glass door slid open. I stepped up onto a maroon carpet – thankfully obscuring my view of the ground – and was met by two people.

Neither of them was my grandfather. *Where is he?* I wondered with growing annoyance. Bastille, strangely, took up position next to the doorway, standing with a stiff back and staring straight ahead.

One of the people turned toward me. 'Lord Smedry,' the woman said, standing with arms straight at her sides. She had on a suit of steel plate armor, like what I'd seen in museums. Except this armor seemed a lot better fitting. The pieces bent together in a more flexible manner, and the metal itself was thinner.

The woman bowed her head to me, helmet under her arm, her hair a deep, metallic silver. The face seemed familiar. I glanced at Bastille, then back at the woman.

'You're Bastille's mother?' I asked.

'I am indeed, Lord Smedry,' the woman said, the tone of her voice as stiff as her armor. 'I am—'

'Oh, Alcatraz!' the other person said, interrupting the woman. This girl sat in the chair beside the dash of the cockpit, and she wore a pink tunic with brown trousers. She had the face I'd seen through the Courier's Lenses – long black hair, a little bit curly, with dark skin and slightly plump features.

'I'm so glad you made it,' the girl exclaimed. 'For a while, I thought we'd lost you! Then Bastille saw that light shooting into the air, and we figured it was from you. It seems that we were right!'

'And you are ...?' I asked.

'Australia Smedry!' she said, hopping out of her chair and rushing over to give me a hug. 'Your cousin, silly! Sing's sister.'

'Gak!' I said, nearly being crushed by the powerful hug. Bastille's mother looked on, arms crossed behind her back in a kind of parade-rest sort of pose.

Australia finally let me go. She was probably around sixteen, and she had on a pair of blue Lenses.

'You're an Oculator!' I said.

'Of course I am!' she said. 'How else do you think I contacted you? I'm not really that good with these Lenses. Or ... um, most Lenses, actually. Anyway, it's so wonderful to meet you, finally! I've heard a lot about you. Well, a couple of things really. Okay, so only two letters from Sing, but they were *very* complimentary. Do you really have the Talent of Breaking Things?'

I shrugged. 'That's what they tell me. What's your Talent?'

Australia smiled. 'I can wake up in the morning looking incredibly ugly!'

'Oh … how wonderful.' I still wasn't certain how to respond to Smedry Talents. I usually couldn't ever tell if the Person telling me was excited or disappointed by the power.

Australia, it seemed, was excited by pretty much everything. She nodded perkily. 'I know. It's a fun Talent – nothing like breaking things – but I make it work for me!' She glanced about. 'I wonder where Kaz went. He'll want to meet you too.'

'Another cousin?'

'Your uncle, actually,' Australia said. 'Your father's brother. He was just here … Must have wandered off again.'

I sensed another Talent. 'His Smedry ability is to get lost?'

Australia smiled. 'You've heard of him!'

I shook my head. 'Lucky guess.'

'He'll show up eventually – he always does. Anyway, I'm just *so* excited to meet you!'

I nodded hesitantly.

'Lady Smedry,' Bastille's mother said from behind. 'I do not intend to give offence, but shouldn't you be flying the *Dragonaut*?'

'Gak!' Australia said, hopping back into her seat. She put her hand onto a glowing square on the front of what appeared to be a glass control panel.

I walked up beside her, looking out through the dragon's eye. We were still moving upward and soon would enter the clouds.

'So,' I said, glancing back at Bastille. 'Where's Grandpa?'

Bastille remained silent, staring ahead, back stiff.

'Bastille?'

'You should not address her, Lord Smedry,' Bastille's mother said. 'She's only here acting as my squire, and is currently beneath your notice.'

'That's nonsense! She's my friend.'

Bastille's mother didn't respond to that, though I caught a slight look of disapproval in her eyes. She immediately stiffened, as if having noticed that I was studying her.

'Squire Bastille has been stripped of her rank, Lord Smedry,' Bastille's mother said. 'You should address all of your questions to me, as I will be acting as your Knight of Crystallia from now on.'

Great, I thought.

I should note here that Bastille's mother – Draulin – is by no means as stiff and boring a person as she might at first seem. I have it on good authority that once, about ten years ago, she was heard to laugh, though some still claim it was a particularly nasty sneeze. She has also been known to blink occasionally, though only on her lunch break.

'Squire Bastille has not executed her duty in a manner befitting one who carried the title Knight of Crystallia,' Draulin continued. 'She performed in a sloppy, embarrassing manner that endangered not one, but *both* Oculators under her protection. She allowed herself to be captured. She allowed a member of the Conclave to Kings to be tortured by a Dark Oculator. And, on top of all of that, she lost her bonded Crystin sword.'

I glanced at Bastille, who still stared straight ahead, jaw clenched tightly. I felt anger rise in me.

'None of that was her fault,' I said, looking back at Draulin. 'You can't punish her for it! *I'm* the one who broke her sword.'

'It isn't fault that is punished,' Draulin said, 'but failure. This is the decision of the Crystin leaders, Lord Smedry, and I was sent to deliver it. The judgment will stand. As you know, the Crystin are outside the jurisdiction of any kingdom or royal line.'

Actually, I didn't know that. I didn't know a whole lot about Crystallia in the first place. I'd barely even gotten used to being called 'Lord Smedry.' I had come to understand that Smedries are held in great respect by most Free Kingdomers, and figured that my title was something of a term of affection for them.

There was, of course, a lot more to it than that. But, there always is, isn't there?

I glanced back at Bastille, where she stood at the back of the cockpit, face red. *I need to talk to my grandfather,* I decided. *He can help sort this out.*

I sat down in the chair beside Australia. 'All right, where's my grandfather?'

Australia glanced at me, then blushed. 'We're not exactly sure. We got a note from him this morning – delivered via Transcriber's Lenses. It told us what to do. I can show you the note, if you want.'

'Please,' I said.

Australia fished in her tunic for a moment, searching through pockets. Finally, she found a wrinkled-up piece of paper and handed it over to me.

> Australia, it read.
>
> I don't know if I'll be there at the pickup point. Something has come up that requires my attention. Kindly fetch my grandson for me, as planned, and take him to Nalhalla. I will meet up with you when I can.
>
> Leavenworth Smedry

Outside, we rose into the clouds. The vehicle really seemed to be picking up speed.

'So, we're going to Nalhalla?' I asked, glancing back at Bastille's mother.

'As long as that's what you command,' the woman said. Her tone implied it was really the only choice.

'I guess it is, then,' I said, feeling a slight disappointment, the reason for which I couldn't pin down.

'You should go to your quarters, Lord Smedry,' Draulin said. 'You can rest there; it will take several hours to journey across the ocean to Nalhalla.'

'Very well,' I said, rising.

'I will lead you,' Draulin said.

'Nonsense,' I said, glancing at Bastille. 'Have the squire do it.'

'As you command,' the knight said, nodding her head at Bastille. I walked from the cockpit, Bastille trailing behind, then waited until the door slid closed. Though its glass, I could see Draulin turn and stand, still at parade rest, facing out the eyeball of the dragon.

I turned to Bastille. 'What's *that* all about?'

She flushed. 'Just what she said, Smedry. Come on. I'll take you to your room.'

'Oh, don't get like that with me,' I said, rushing to catch up. 'You lose one sword, and they bust you back to squire? That doesn't make any sense.'

Bastille flushed even more deeply. 'My mother is a very brave and well-respected Knight of Crystallia. She always does what is best for the order and never acts without careful thought.'

'That doesn't answer my question.'

Bastille glanced down. 'Look, I told you when I lost my sword that I would be in trouble. Well, see, I'm in trouble. I'll deal with it. I don't need your pity.'

'It isn't pity! It's annoyance.' I eyed her. 'What aren't you telling me, Bastille?'

Bastille muttered something about Smedries but otherwise gave no response. She stalked through the glass corridors, leading me toward – I assumed – my cabin.

As I walked, however, I grew more and more displeased with events. Grandpa Smedry must have discovered something, otherwise he wouldn't have missed the pickup, and I hated feeling like I was being left out of important things.

Now, this is a stupid way to feel, if you think about it. I was *always* being left out of important things. At that very moment, there were thousands of people doing very important things all across the world – everything from getting married to jumping out windows – and I wasn't a part of any of it. The truth is, even the most important people get left out of most things that happen in the world.

But I was still annoyed. As I walked, I realized I still had on my Courier's Lenses. They were very limited in range, but maybe Grandfather was close by.

I activated the Lenses. *Grandfather?* I thought, focusing. *Grandfather, are you there?*

Nothing. I sighed. It had been a long shot anyway. I didn't really—

A very faint image appeared in front of me. *Alcatraz?* a distant voice said.

Grandfather? I thought, growing excited. *Yes, it's me!*

Flustered Farlands! How did you contact me across such a distance? The voice was so weak that I could barely hear it, even though it was speaking directly into my mind.

Grandfather, where are you?

The voice said something, but was too soft to hear. I focused harder, closing my eyes. *Grandfather!*

Alcatraz! I think I've found your father. He came here. I'm sure of it!

Where, Grandfather? I asked.

The voice was growing even fainter. *The Library . . .*

Grandfather! What Library?

Library . . . of Alexandria . . .

And then he was gone. I concentrated, but the voice didn't come back. Finally, I sighed, opening my eyes.

'You all right, Smedry?' Bastille asked, giving me a strange look.

'The Library of Alexandria,' I said. 'Where is it?'

Bastille eyed me. 'Um, in Alexandria?'

Right. 'Where is that?'

'Egypt.'

'Like, the real Egypt? My Egypt?'

Bastille shrugged. 'Yeah, I think so. Why?'

I glanced back toward the cockpit.

'No,' Bastille said, folding her arms. 'Alcatraz, I know what you're thinking. We're *not* going there.'

'Why not?'

'The Library of Alexandria is extremely dangerous. Even regular Librarians are scared to go into it. Nobody in their right mind ever visits that place.'

'That sounds about right,' I said. 'Because Grandpa Smedry is there right now.'

'How would you know something like that?'

I tapped my Lenses.

'They wouldn't work at such a distance.'

'They did. I just talked to him. He's there, Bastille.' *And ... he thinks my father is too.*

That gave me a twist in my stomach. I'd grown up assuming that both of my parents were dead. Now I was beginning to think that both were actually alive. My mother was a Librarian and worked for the wrong side. I wasn't entirely sure I wanted to know what my father was like.

No. That's wrong. I *really* wanted to know what my father was like. I was just afraid of it at the same time.

I glanced back at Bastille.

'You're sure he's there?' she asked.

I nodded.

'Shattering Glass,' she muttered. 'Last time we tried something like this, you almost got killed, your grandfather got tortured and I lost my sword. Do we *really* want to go through that again?'

'What if he's in trouble?'

'He's *always* in trouble,' Bastille said.

We fell silent. Then, both of us turned and rushed back to the cockpit.

3

I'd like to make something clear. I have been unfair to you. That is to be expected, liar that I am.

In the first book of this series, I made some sweeping generalizations about librarians, many of which are not completely true.

I need to come clean. There are several kinds of librarians. There are the ones that I talked about in my last book – the Librarians, with a capital L. We also call them the Librarians of Biblioden, or the Scrivener's librarians. Most of what I said about that particular group is, indeed, factual.

However, I didn't take the time to explain that they're not the *only* kind of librarians. You may, therefore, have assumed that all librarians are evil cultists who want to take over the world, enslave humanity, and sacrifice people on their altars.

This is completely untrue. Not all librarians are evil cultists. Some librarians are instead vengeful undead who want to suck up your soul.

I'm glad we cleared that up.

'You want to do *what*?' Bastille's mother demanded.

'Fly to the Library of Alexandria,' I said.

'Out of the question, my lord. We can't possibly do that.'

'We have to,' I said.

Australia turned toward me, leaving one hand on the glowing glass square that allowed her, somehow, to pilot the *Dragonaut*. 'Alcatraz, why would you want to go to Alexandria? It's not a very friendly place.'

'Grandpa Smedry is there,' I said. 'That means we need to go too.'

'He didn't say he was going to Egypt,' Australia said, glancing again at the crumpled note that he'd sent.

'The Library of Alexandria is one of the most dangerous places in the Hushlands, Lord Smedry,' Draulin continued. 'Most regular Librarians will only kill or imprison you. The Curators of Alexandria, however, will steal your soul. I cannot, in good conscience, allow you to be placed in such danger.'

The tall, armored woman still stood with her arms behind her back. She kept her silver hair long but in a utilitarian ponytail, and she did not meet my eyes, but instead stared directly forward.

Now, I'd like to point out that what I did next was completely logical. Really. There's a law of the universe – unfamiliar to most people in the Hushlands but quite commonly known to Free Kingdoms scientists. It is the called the Law of Inevitable Occurrence.

In simple layman's terms, this law states that some things just *have* to happen. If there's a red button on a console with the words DON'T PUSH taped above it, someone will push it. If there's a gun hanging conspicuously above Chekhov's fireplace, someone is going to end up shooting it (probably at Nietzsche).

And if there's a stern woman telling you what to do – yet at the same time calling you 'my lord' – you're going to just have to figure out how far you can push her.

'Jump up and down on one foot,' I said, pointing at Draulin.

'Excuse me?' she asked, flushing.

'Do it. That's an order.'

And she did, looking rather annoyed.

'You can stop,' I said.

She did so. 'Would you mind telling me what that was about, Lord Smedry?'

'Well, I wanted to figure out if you'd do what I commanded.'

'Of course I will,' Draulin said. 'As the oldest child of Attica Smedry, you are the heir to the pure Smedry line. You outrank both your cousin and your uncle, which means you are in command of this vessel.'

'Wonderful,' I said. 'So that means I can decide where we go, right?'

Bastille's mother fell silent. 'Well,' she finally said, 'that is technically true, my lord. However, I have been charged with bringing you back to Nalhalla. Asking me to take you to such a dangerous location would be foolhardy, and—'

'Yeah, that's just spiffy,' I said. 'Australia, let's get going. I want to be in Egypt as soon as possible.'

Bastille's mother closed her mouth, growing even more red in the face. Australia just shrugged and reached over to put her hand on another glass square. 'Um, take us to the Library of Alexandria,' she said.

The giant glass dragon shifted slightly, beginning to undulate in a different direction, six wings flapping in succession.

'That's it?' I asked.

Australia nodded. 'It'll still take us a few hours to get there, though. We'll fly up over the pole and down into the Middle East, rather than out toward Nalhalla.'

'Well, good, then,' I said, feeling a little anxious as I realized what I'd done. Only a short time back, I'd been eager to get to safety. Now I was determined to head to a place that everyone else was telling me was insanely, ridiculously dangerous?

What was I doing? What business did I have taking command and giving orders? Feeling self-conscious, I left the cockpit again. Bastille trailed along behind me. 'I'm not sure why I did that,' I confessed as we walked.

'Your grandfather might be in danger.'

'Yeah, but what are *we* going to do about it?'

'We helped him in the last Library infiltration,' she said. 'Saved him from Blackburn.'

I fell silent, walking down the glass corridor. Yes, we had saved Grandpa Smedry ... but ... well, something told me that Grandpa Smedry would have gotten away from Blackburn eventually. The old Smedry had lived for more than a century, and – from what I understood – had managed to wiggle out of plenty of predicaments far worse than that one.

He'd been the one to fight Blackburn with the Lenses – I'd been helpless. True, I'd managed to break the Firebringer's Lens and trick Blackburn in the end. But I hadn't really known what I was doing. My victories seemed more like happenstance than they did anything else. And now I was heading into danger yet again?

Nevertheless, it was done. The *Dragonaut* had changed course, and we were on our way. *We'll look around outside the place,* I thought. *If it looks too dangerous, we don't have to go in.*

I was about to explain this decision to Bastille when a sudden voice spoke from behind us. 'Bastille! We've changed course. What's that all about?'

I turned in shock. A short man, perhaps four feet tall, was walking down the corridor toward us. He most certainly hadn't been there before and I couldn't figure out where he'd come from.

The man wore rugged clothing: a leather jacket, his tunic tucked into sturdy pants, a pair of boots. He had a wide face with a broad chin and dark curly hair.

'A fairy!' I said immediately.

The short man stopped, looking confused. 'That's a new one,' he noted.

'What kind are you?' I asked. 'Leprechaun? Elf?'

The short man raised an eyebrow, then glanced at Bastille. 'Hazelnuts, Bastille,' he swore. 'Who's *this* clown?'

'Kaz, this is your nephew Alcatraz.'

The short man glanced back at me. 'Oh ... I see. He seems a bit more dense than I assumed he'd be.'

I flushed. 'You're ... not a fairy then?'

He shook his head.

'Are you a dwarf? Like in *Lord of the Rings*?'

He shook his head.

'You're just a ... midget?'

He regarded me with a flat stare. 'You realize that *midget* isn't a good term to use, don't you? Even most Hushlanders know that. Midgets are what people used to call my kind when they stuck us in freak shows.'

I paused. 'What should I call you, then?'

'Well, Kaz is preferable. Kazan is my full name, though the blasted Librarians finally named a prison that a while back.'

Bastille nodded. 'In Russia.'

The short man sighed. 'Regardless, if you absolutely *have* to reference my height, I generally think that *short person* works just fine. Anyway, is someone going to explain why we changed course?'

I was still too busy being embarrassed to answer. I hadn't intended to insult my uncle. (Fortunately, I've gotten much better at this over the years. I'm now quite good at insulting people intentionally, and I can even do it in languages you Free Kingdomers don't speak. So there, you dagblad.)

Thankfully, Bastille spoke up and answered Kaz's question. 'We got word that your father is at the Library of Alexandria. We think he might be in trouble.'

'So we're heading there?' Kaz asked.

Bastille nodded.

Kaz perked up. 'Wonderful!' he said. 'Finally, some good news on this trip.'

'Wait,' I said. 'That's *good* news?'

'Of course it is! I've wanted to explore that place for decades. Never could find a good enough excuse. I'll go get preparing!' He took off down the corridor toward the cockpit.

'Kaz?' Bastille called. He stopped, glancing back.

'Your room is that way.' She pointed down a side corridor.

'Coconuts,' he swore under his breath. Then, he headed the way she'd indicated.

'That's right,' I said. 'His Talent. Getting lost.'

Bastille nodded. 'What's worse is that he generally acts as our guide.'

'How does *that* work?'

'Oddly,' she said, continuing down the corridor.

I sighed. 'I don't think he likes me very much.'

'You seem to have that effect on people when they first meet you. I didn't like you very much at first either.' She eyed me. 'Still not sure if that's changed or not.'

'You're so kind.' As we walked down the dragon's snake-like body, I noticed a large glow coming from between the shoulder blades of a pair of wings above. The glass here sparkled and shifted, as if there were a lot of surfaces and delicate parts moving about. At the center of the mass was a deep, steady glow – like a smoldering fire. The light was being shaded by occasional moving pieces of glass that weren't translucent. So, every few seconds, the light would grow darker – then grow brighter again.

I pointed up, 'What's that?'

'The engine,' Bastille said.

There weren't any of the noises I had come to associate with a running motor – no hum, no moving pistons, no burning fire. Not even any steam.

'How does it work?'

Bastille shrugged. 'I'm no silimatic engineer.'

'You're no Oculator, either,' I noted. 'But you know enough about Lenses to surprise most people.'

'That's because I *studied* Lenses. Never did care much about silimatics. Come on. Do you want to get to your room or not?'

I did, and I was tired, so I let her lead me away. Turns out, actually, that silimatic engines aren't really that complex. They're actually a fair bit more easy to understand than regular Hushlander engines.

It all involves a special kind of sand, named brightsand, which gives off a glow when it's heated. That light then causes certain types of glass to do strange things. Some will rise into the air when exposed to silimatic light, others will drop downward when exposed to it. So, all you have to do is control which glass sees the light at which time, and you've got an engine.

I know you Hushlanders probably find that ridiculous. You ask yourselves, 'If sand is that valuable, why is it so commonplace?' You are, of course, the victims of a terrible conspiracy. (Don't you ever get tired of that?)

The Librarians take great pains to make people ignore sand. They have, at great expense, flooded the Hushlands with dullsand – one of the few types of sand that doesn't really do anything at all, even when you melt it. What better way is there to make people ignore something than to make it seem commonplace?

Don't even get me started on the economic value of belly-button lint.

We finally reached my quarters. The body of the dragon-snake was a good twenty feet wide, so there was plenty of room along its length for rooms. I noticed, however, that all of the rooms were translucent.

'Not a lot of privacy here, is there?' I asked.

Bastille rolled her eyes, then placed her hand on a panel on the side of the wall. 'Dark,' she said. The wall immediately grew black. She glanced back at me. 'We had it on translucent so that it would be easier to hide from people.'

'Oh,' I said. 'So, this is technology and not magic?'

'Of course it is. Anyone can do it, after all. Not just Oculators.'

'But Australia is the one flying the dragon.'

'That's not because she's an Oculator, it's because she's a pilot. Look, I've got to get back to the cockpit. My mother's going to be angry at me for taking so long.'

I glanced back at her. It seemed like something was really bothering her. 'I'm sorry I broke your sword,' I said.

She shrugged. 'I didn't ever really deserve it in the first place.'

'Why do you say that?'

'Everyone knows it,' Bastille said, her voice betraying more than a little bitterness. 'Even my mother felt that I should never have been dubbed a full knight. She didn't think that I was ready.'

'She sure is stern.'

'She hates me.'

I looked over at her, shocked. 'Bastille! I'm sure she doesn't hate you. She's your mother.'

'She's ashamed of me,' Bastille said. 'Always has been. But …
I don't know why I'm talking to *you* about this. Go take a nap, Smedry. Leave the important things to people who know what they're doing.'

With that, she stalked away, heading back toward the cockpit. I sighed, but pulled open the glass door and walked into the room. There was no bed, though I did find a rolled-up mattress in the corner. The room, like the rest of the dragon, undulated up and down, each flap of the wings sending a ripple down the entire length of the body.

It had been a bit sickening at first, but I was getting used to it. I sat down, staring out the glass wall of my room. It was still transparent – Bastille had only made the one behind me black.

Clouds spread out below me, extending into the distance, white and lumpy, like the landscape of some alien planet – or perhaps like mashed potatoes that hadn't been whipped quite long enough. The sun, setting in the distance, was a brilliant yellow pat of butter, slowly melting as it disappeared.

As that analogy might have indicated, I was getting a bit hungry.

Still, I was safe. And I was finally free. Out of the Hushlands, ready to begin my journey to the lands where I'd been born. True, we'd stop in Egypt to pick up my grandfather, but I still felt relieved to be moving.

I was on my way. On my way to find my father, perhaps on my way to discover who I really was.

I'd eventually realize I didn't like what I found. But, for the moment, I felt good. And – despite the glass beneath me showing a drop straight down, despite my hunger, despite our destination – I found myself feeling relaxed. I drifted off, curling up on the mattress and falling asleep.

I woke up when a missile exploded a few feet from my head.

4

You think you've figured it out, have you? My logical dilemma? My argumentative lapse? My brain freeze of rationality? My … uh … traffic jam of lucidity?

Let's just forget that last one.

Anyway, there is – as you've probably noticed – a flaw in my logic. I claim to be a liar. Outright, without any guile, and straightforward.

Yet, after declaring myself to be a liar, I have proceeded to write a book about my life. So, therefore, how can you trust the story itself? If it's being told by a liar, won't it all be false? In fact, how can you trust that I'm a liar? If I always lie, then wouldn't I have had to be lying about saying I'm a liar?

Now you see why I mentioned brain freezes, eh? Let me clarify. I *have been* a liar. Most of my life is a sham – the heroics I'm known for, the life I've led, the fame I've enjoyed. Those are lies.

The things I'm telling you here are factual. In this case, I can only prove that I'm a liar by telling the truth, though I will also include some lies – which I will point out – to act as object lessons proving the truth that I'm a liar.

Got that?

I was thrown off the bedroll and rammed against the glass wall as the *Dragonaut* shook, twisting away from the explosion that was still visible in the darkness outside my wall. Our vessel didn't appear to have been damaged, but it had been a close call.

I rubbed my head, coming awake. Then cursed quietly and scrambled out the door. At that moment, the *Dragonaut* lurched again, moving to the right. I was thrown off my feet as a flaring missile just barely missed our ship. It trailed a glow of flaming smoke behind it, then exploded off in the distance.

I righted myself just in time to see something else shoot past the *Dragonaut* – not another missile, but something with roaring engines. It looked alarmingly like an F-15 fighter jet.

'Shattering Glass!' I exclaimed, forcing myself to my feet and pulling out my Oculator's Lenses. I shoved them on and rushed to the cockpit. I arrived, stumbling through the doorway as Bastille pointed. 'Left!' she yelled. 'Bank left!'

I could see sweat on Australia's face as she turned the *Dragonaut* to the side, out of the way of the approaching fighter. I barely managed to stay on my feet as the ship dodged another missile.

I groaned, shaking my head. Kaz stood on a seat, hands leaning against the control dash, looking out the other eyeball. 'Now *this*,' the short man proclaimed, 'is more like it! It's been ages since anyone shot missiles at me!'

Bastille gave him a harsh stare, then glanced to the side as I rushed up, grabbing a chair to steady myself.

Ahead, the fighter launched another missile.

I focused, trying to get my talent to engage at a distance and destroy the jet like it did guns. Nothing happened.

Australia twisted the *Dragonaut* just in time, throwing me to the side, my hands slipping free of the chair. That's one problem with making everything out of glass. Handholds become rather difficult to maintain.

Bastille managed to stay up, but she had on her Warrior's Lenses, which enhanced her physical abilities. Kaz didn't have any Lenses on, but he seemed to have an excellent sense of balance.

I rubbed my head as the missile exploded off in the distance. 'This shouldn't be possible!' I said. 'That jet has so many moving parts, my Talent should have been able to stop it easy.'

Bastille shook her head, glancing at me. 'Glass missiles, Alcatraz.'

'I've never seen *anything* like this,' Australia agreed, glancing over her shoulder, watching the jet's fire trails. 'That ship isn't Hushlander technology – or, well, not completely. It's some kind of fusion. Parts of the jet body look like they're metal, but others look like they're glass.'

Bastille gave me a hand to help me back up to my feet.

'Aw, birchnuts!' Kaz swore, pointing. I squinted, leaning against the chair, watching the jet bank and turn back toward us. It seemed more maneuverable, more precise, than a regular jet. As it turned toward us, its cockpit started to glow.

Not the whole cockpit. Just the glass covering it. I frowned, and my friends seemed equally confused.

The jet's canopy shot forth a beam of glowing white power, directed at us. It hit one of the dragon's wings, spraying out shards of ice and snow. The wing, caught in the grip of the cold, froze in place. Then, as its mechanisms tried to force it to move, the wing shattered into a thousand pieces.

'Frostbringer's Lens!' Bastille shouted as the *Dragonaut* rocked.

'That was no Lens!' Australia said. 'That fired from the canopy glass!'

'Amazing!' Kaz said, holding on to his seat as the ship rocked.

We're going to die, I thought.

It wasn't the first time I'd felt that icy pit of terror, that sense of horrible doom that came from thinking I was going to die. I felt it on the altar when I was about to get sacrificed, I felt it when Blackburn shot me with his Torturer's Lens, and I felt it as I watched the F-15 turn back toward us for another run.

I never got used to that feeling. It's kind of like getting punched in the face by your own mortality.

And mortality has a wicked right hook.

'We need to do something!' I shouted as the *Dragonaut* lurched. Australia, however, had her eyes closed – I'd later learn that she was mentally compensating for the lost wing, keeping us in the air. Ahead of us, the fighter's cockpit began glowing again.

'We *are* doing something,' Bastille said.

'What?'

'Stalling!'

'For what?'

Something thumped up above. I glanced up, apprehensive as I looked through the translucent glass. Bastille's mother, Draulin, stood up on the roof of the *Dragonaut*. A majestic cloak fluttered out behind her, and she wore her steel armor. She carried a Sword of Crystallia.

I'd seen one once before, during the Library infiltration. Bastille had pulled it out to fight against Alivened monsters. I'd thought, maybe, that I'd remembered the sword's ridiculous size wrong – that perhaps it had simply *looked* big next to Bastille.

I was wrong. The sword was enormous, at least five feet long from tip of blade to hilt. It glittered, made completely of the crystal from which the Crystin, and Crystallia itself, get their name.

(The knights aren't terribly original with names. Crystin, Crystallia, crystals. One time when I was allowed into Crystallia, I jokingly dubbed my potato a 'Potatin potato, grown and crafted in the Fields of Potatallia.' The knights were not amused. Maybe I should have used my carrot instead.)

Draulin stepped across the head of our flying dragon, her armored boots clinking against the glass. Somehow, she managed to retain a sure footing despite the wind and the shaking vehicle.

The jet fired a beam from its Frostbringer's glass, aiming for another wing. Bastille's mother jumped, leaping through the air, cloak flapping. She landed on the wing itself, raising her crystal-line sword. The beam of frost hit the sword and disappeared in a puff. Bastille's mother barely even bent beneath the blow. She stood powerfully, her armored visor obscuring her face.

The cockpit fell silent. It seemed impossible to me that Draulin had managed such a feat. Yet, as I waited, the jet fired again, and once again Bastille's mother managed to get in front of the beam and destroy it.

'She's ... standing on *top* of the *Dragonaut*,' I said as I watched through the glass.

'Yes,' Bastille said.

'We appear to be going several hundred miles an hour.'

'About that.'

'She's blocking laser beams fired by a jet airplane.'

'Yes.'

'Using nothing but her sword.'

'She's a Knight of Crystallia,' Bastille said, looking away. 'That's the sort of thing they do.'

I fell silent, watching Bastille's mother run the entire length of the *Dragonaut* in the space of a couple seconds, then block an ice beam fired at us from behind.

Kaz shook his head. 'Those Crystin,' he said. 'They take the fun out of everything.' He smiled toothily.

To this day, I haven't been able to tell if Kaz genuinely has a death wish, or if he just likes to act that way. Either way, he's a loon. But, then, he's a Smedry. That's virtually a synonym for 'insane, foolhardy lunatic.'

I glanced at Bastille. She watched her mother move above, and seemed longing, yet ashamed at the same time.

That's the sort of thing they expect her to be able to do, I thought. *That's why they took her knighthood from her – because they thought she wasn't up to their standards.*

'Um, trouble!' Australia said. She'd opened her eyes, but looked very frazzled as she sat with her hand on the glowing panel. Up ahead, the fighter jet was charging its glass again – and it had just released another missile.

'Grab on!' Bastille said, getting ahold of a chair. I did the same, for all the good it did. I was again tossed to the side as Australia dodged. Up above, Draulin managed to block the Frostbringer's ray, but it looked close.

The missile exploded just a short distance from the body of the *Dragonaut.*

We can't keep doing this, I thought. *Australia looks like she can barely hold on, and Bastille's mother will get tired eventually.*

We're in serious trouble.

I picked myself up, rubbing my arm, blinking away the after-image of the missile explosion. I could feel something as the jet shot past us. A dark twisting in my stomach, just like the feeling I'd felt on the runway. It felt a little like the sense that told me when an Oculator nearby was using one of their Lenses. Yet, this was different. Tainted somehow.

The creature from the airport was in that jet. Before, it had shot the Lens out of my hand. Now it used a jet that could fire on me without exploding. Somehow, it seemed to understand how to use both Free Kingdoms technology and Hushlands technology together.

And that seemed a very, very dangerous combination.

'Do we have any weapons on board the ship?' I asked.

Bastille shrugged. 'I have a dagger.'

'That's it?'

'We've got you, cousin,' Australia said. 'You're an Oculator and a Smedry of the pure line. You're better than any regular weapons.'

Great, I thought. I glanced up at Bastille's mother, who stood on the nose of the dragon. 'How can she stand there like that?'

'Grappler's Glass,' Bastille said. 'It sticks to other kinds of glass, and she's got some plates of it on the bottom of her boots.'

'Do we have any more?'

Bastille paused, then – without questioning me – she rushed over to a side of the cockpit, searching through a glass trunk on the floor. She came up a few moments later with a pair of boots.

'These will do the same thing,' she said, handing them to me. They looked far too large for my feet.

The ship rocked as Australia dodged another missile. I didn't know how many of those the jet had, but it seemed like it could carry far more than it should be able to. I slumped back against the wall as the *Dragonaut* shook, then I pulled the first boot on over my own shoe and tied the laces tight.

'What are you doing?' Bastille asked. 'You're not planning to go up there, are you?'

I pulled on the other boot. My heart was beginning to beat faster.

'What do you expect to do, Alcatraz?' Bastille asked quietly. 'My mother is a full Knight of Crystallia. What help could you possibly be to her?'

I hesitated, and Bastille flushed slightly at how harsh the words had sounded, though it wasn't really in her nature to retract things like that. Besides, she was right.

What *was* I thinking?

Kaz moved over to us. 'This is bad, Bastille.'

'Oh, you finally noticed that, did you?' she snapped.

'Don't get touchy,' he said. 'I may like a good ride, but I hate sudden stops as much as the next Smedry. We need an escape plan.'

Bastille fell silent for a moment. 'How many of us can you use your Talent to transport?'

'Up here, in the sky?' he asked. 'Without any place to flee? I'm not sure, honestly. I doubt I'd be able to get all of us.'

'Take Alcatraz,' Bastille said. 'Go now.'

My stomach twisted. 'No,' I said, standing. My feet immediately locked on to the glass floor of the cockpit. When I tried to take a step, however, my foot came free. When I put it down again, it locked into place.

Nice, I thought, trying not to focus on what I was about to do.

'Chestnuts, kid!' Kaz swore. 'You might not be the brightest torch in the row, but I don't want to see you get killed. I owe your father that much. Come with me – we'll get lost, then head to Nalhalla.'

'And leave the others to die?'

'We'll be just fine,' Bastille said quickly. Too quickly.

The thing is, I paused. It may not seem very heroic, but a large part of me wanted to go with Kaz. My hands were sweating, my heart thumping. The ship rocked as another missile nearly hit us. I saw a spiderweb of cracks appear on the right side of the cockpit.

I could run. Escape. Nobody would blame me. I wanted so badly to do just that.

I didn't. This might look like bravery, but I assure you that I'm a coward at heart. I'll prove that at another time. For now, simply believe that it wasn't bravery that spurred me on, it was pride.

I was the Oculator. Australia had said I was their main weapon. I determined to see what I could do. 'I'm going up,' I said. 'How do I get there?'

'Hatch on the ceiling,' Bastille finally said. 'In the same room where you came up on the rope. Come on, I'll show you.'

Kaz caught her arm as she moved. 'Bastille, you're actually going to let him do this?'

She shrugged. 'If he wants to get himself killed, what business is it of mine? It just means one less person we have to worry about saving.'

I smiled wanly. I knew Bastille well enough to hear the concern in her voice. She was actually worried about me. Or, perhaps, just angry at me. With her, the difference is difficult to judge.

She took off down the corridor, and I followed, quickly getting the rhythm of walking with the boots. As soon as they touched glass, they locked on, making me stable – something I appreciated when the ship rocked from anther blast. I moved a little more slowly than normal in them, but they were worth it.

I caught up to Bastille in the room, and she threw a lever, opening a hatch in the ceiling.

'Why *are* you letting me do this?' I asked. 'Usually you complain when I try to get myself killed.'

'Yeah, well, at least this time *I* won't be the one who looks bad if you die. My mother's the knight in charge of protecting you.'

I raised an eyebrow.

'Plus,' she said. 'Maybe you'll be able to do something. Who knows. You've gotten lucky in the past.'

I smiled, and somehow the vote of confidence – such that it was – bolstered me. I glanced up. 'How do I get out there?'

'Your feet stick to the walls, stupid.'

'Oh, right,' I said. Taking a deep breath, I stepped up onto the side of the wall. It was easier than I'd thought it would be – silimatic technicians say that Grappler's Glass works to hold your entire body in place, not just your feet. Either way, I found it rather easy (if a little disorienting) to walk up the side of the wall and out onto the top of the *Dragonaut*.

Let's talk about air. You see, air is a really nifty thing. It lets us make cool sounds with our mouths, it carries smells from one person to another, and without it nobody would be able to play air guitar. Oh, and there is that other thing it does: It lets us breathe, allowing all animal life to exist on the planet. Great stuff, air.

The thing about air is, you don't really think about it until (a) you don't have enough or (b) you have *way* too much of it. That second one is particularly nasty when you get hit in the face by a bunch of it going somewhere in the neighborhood of three hundred miles an hour.

The wind buffeted me backward, and only the Grappler's Glass on my feet kept me upright. Even with it, I bent backward precariously, like some gravity-defying dancer in a music video. I'd have felt kind of cool about that if I hadn't been terrified for my life.

Bastille must have seen my predicament, for she rushed toward the cockpit. I'm still not sure how she persuaded Australia to slow the ship – by all accounts, that should have been a very stupid thing to do. Still, the wind lessened to a slightly manageable speed, and I was able to clomp my way across the top of the ship toward Draulin.

Massive wings beat beside me, and the dragon's snake body rolled. Each step was sure, though. I passed beneath stars and moon, the cloud cover glowing beneath us. I arrived near the front of the vehicle just as Draulin blocked another blast of Frostbringer's ray. As I grew closer, she spun toward me.

'Lord *Smedry?*' she asked, voice muffled by both wind and her helmet. 'What in the name of the first sands are you doing here?'

'I've come to help!' I yelled above the howl of the wind.

She seemed dumbfounded. The jet shot past in the night sky, rounding for another attack.

'Go back!' she said, waving with an armored hand.

'I'm an Oculator,' I said, pointing to my Lenses. 'I can stop the Frostbringer's ray.'

It was true. An Oculator can use his Oculator's Lenses to counter an enemy's attack. I'd seen my grandfather do it when dueling Blackburn. I'd never tried it myself, but, I figured it couldn't be that hard.

I was completely wrong, of course. It happens to the best of us at times.

Draulin cursed, running across the dragon's back to block another blast. The ship rolled, nearly making me sick, and I was suddenly struck by just how high up I was. I crouched down, holding my stomach, waiting for the world to orient itself again. When it did, Draulin was standing beside me.

'Go back down!' she yelled. 'You can be of no help here!'

'I—'

'Idiot!' she yelled. 'You're going to get us killed!'

I fell silent, the wind tussling my hair. I felt shocked to be treated so, but it was probably no more than I deserved. I turned away, clomping back toward the hatch, embarrassed.

To the side, the jet fired a missile. The glass on its cockpit fired another Frostbringer's ray.

And the *Dragonaut* didn't dodge.

I spun toward the cockpit and could just barely see Australia slumped over her control panel, dazed. Bastille was trying to slap her awake – she's particularly good at anything that requires slapping – and Kaz was furiously trying to make the ship respond.

We lurched, but the wrong way. Draulin cried out, barely slicing her sword through the icy beam as she stumbled. She vaporized it, but the missile continued on, directly toward us.

Directly toward me.

I've talked about the uneasy truce my Talent and I have. Neither of us is really ever in control. I can usually break things if I really want to, but rarely in exactly the way I want. And, my Talent often breaks things when I don't want it to.

What I lack in control, I make up for in power. I watched that missile coming, saw its glass length reflect the starlight, and saw the trail of smoke leading back to the fighter behind.

I stared at my reflection in oncoming death. Then I raised my hand and released my Talent.

The missile shattered, shards of glass spraying from it, twinkling and spinning into the midnight air. Then, those shards exploded, vaporizing to powdered dust, which sprayed around me, missing me by several inches on each side.

The smoke from the missile's engine was still blowing forward, and it licked my fingers. Immediately, the line of smoke quivered. I screamed and a wave of power shot from my chest, pulsing up the line of smoke like water in a tube, moving toward the fighter, which was screaming along in the same path its missile had taken.

The wave of power hit the jet. All was silent for a moment.

Then, the fighter just ... fell apart. It didn't explode, like one might see in an action movie. Its separate pieces simply departed one from another. Screws fell out, panels of metal were thrown free, pieces of glass separated from wing and cockpit. In seconds, the entire machine looked like a box of spare parts that had been carelessly tossed into the air.

The mess shot over the top of the *Dragonaut*, then fell toward the clouds below. As the pieces disbursed, I caught a glimpse of an angry face in the midst of the metal. It was the pilot, twisting among the discarded parts. In an oddly surreal moment, his eyes met mine, and I saw cold hatred in them.

The face was not all human. Half looked normal, the other half was an amalgamation of screws, springs, nuts, and bolts – not unlike the pieces of the jet falling around it. One of his eyes was of the deepest, blackest glass.

He disappeared into the darkness.

I gasped suddenly, feeling incredibly weak. Bastille's mother crouched, one hand steadying herself against the roof, watching me with an expression I couldn't see through her knightly face-plate.

Only then did I notice the cracks in the top of the *Dragonaut*. They spread out from me in a spiral pattern, as if my feet had been the source of some great impact. Looking desperately, I saw that most of the giant flying dragon now bore flaws or cracks of some kind.

My Talent – unpredictable as always – had shattered the glass beneath me as I'd used it to destroy the jet. Slowly, terribly, the massive dragon began to droop. Another of the wings fell free, the glass cracking and breaking. The *Dragonaut* lurched.

I'd saved the ship ... but I'd also destroyed it.

We began to plummet downward.

5

Now, there are several things you should consider doing if you were plummeting to your death atop a glass dragon in the middle of the ocean.

Those things do *not*, mind you, include getting into an extended discussion of classical philosophy.

Leave that to professionals like me.

I want you to think about a ship. No, not a flying dragon ship like the one that was falling apart beneath me as I fell to my death. Focus. I obviously survived the crash, since this book is written in the first person.

I want you to think of a regular ship. The wooden kind, meant for sailing on the ocean. A ship owned by a man named Theseus, a Greek king immortalized by the writer Plutarch.

Plutarch was a silly little Greek historian best known for being born about three centuries too late, for having a great fascination with dead people, and for being *way* too long-winded. (He produced well over 800,000 words' worth of writing. The Honorable Council of Fantasy Writers Whose Books Are Way Too Long – good old THCoFWWBAWTL – is considering making him an honorary member.)

Plutarch wrote a metaphor about the Ship of Theseus. You see, once the great king Theseus died, the people wanted to remember him. They decided to preserve his ship for future generations.

The ship got old, and its planks – as wood obstinately insists on doing – began to rot. After that, other pieces got old, and they replaced those too.

This continued for years. Eventually, every single part on the ship had been replaced. So, Plutarch relates an argument that many philosophers wonder about. Is the ship still the Ship of

Theseus? People call it that. Everyone knows it is. Yet, there's a problem. Not all the pieces are actually from the ship that Theseus used.

Is it the same ship?

I think it isn't. That ship is gone, buried, rotted. The copy everyone then *called* the Ship of Theseus was really just a ... copy. It might have looked the same, but looks can be deceiving.

Now, what does this have to do with my story? Everything. You see, I'm that ship. Don't worry. I'll probably explain it to you eventually.

The *Dragonaut* fell into the clouds. The puffs of white passed around me in a furious maelstrom. Then, we were out of them, and I could see something very dark and very vast beneath me.

The ocean. I had that same feeling as before – the terrible thought that we were all going to die. And this time, it was my fault.

Stupid mortality.

The *Dragonaut* lurched, taking my stomach along with it. The mighty wings continued to beat, reflecting diffuse starlight that shone through the clouds. I'd twisted, looking to the cockpit, and saw Kaz concentrating, hand on the panel. Sweat beaded on his brow, but he managed to keep the ship in the air.

Something cracked. I looked down, realizing that I was standing in the very center of the broken portion of glass.

Uh-oh ...

The glass beneath me shattered, but fortunately the ship twisted at that moment, lurching upward. I was thrown down into the body of the vessel. I hit the glass floor, then had the peace of mind to slam one of my feet against the wall – locking it into place – as the ship writhed.

Kaz was doing an impressive job. The four remaining wings beat furiously, and the ship wasn't falling as quickly. We'd gone from a plummet of doom into a controlled spiral of doom.

I twisted, standing, the Grappler's Glass giving me enough stability to walk back to the cockpit. As I walked, I took off my Lenses and tucked them into their pocket, feeling lucky that I hadn't lost them in the chaos.

Inside, I found Bastille huddled over Australia, who looked very groggy. My cousin was bleeding from a blow to the head – I later learned she'd been thrown sideways into the wall when the ship began to fall.

I knew exactly what that felt like.

Bastille managed to strap poor Australia into a harness of some kind. Kaz was still focused on keeping us in the air. 'Blasted thing,' he said through gritted teeth, 'why do you tall people have to fly up so high?'

I could just barely see land approaching ahead of us, and I felt a thrill of hope. At that moment, the back half of the dragon broke off, taking two more of the wings with it. We staggered in the air again, spinning, and the wall beside me exploded outward from the pressure.

Australia screamed, Kaz swore. I fell down on my back, knees bent, feet still planted on the floor.

And Bastille was sucked out the opening in the wall.

Now, I'll tell you time and time again that I'm not a hero. However, sometimes I *am* a bit quick-witted. As I saw Bastille shoot past me, I knew that I wouldn't be able to grab her in time.

I couldn't grab her, but I *could* kick her. So I did.

I slammed my foot into her side as she passed by, as if to shove her out the hole. Fortunately, she stuck to my foot – for, if you will remember, she was wearing a jacket made with glass fibers.

Bastille whipped out of the *Dragonaut*, her jacket stuck to the Grappler's Glass on the bottom of my foot. She twisted about, surprised, but grabbed my ankle to steady herself. This, of course, pulled me up and toward her – though fortunately my other foot was still planted on the glass floor.

Bastille held on to one foot, as the other stuck to the ship. It was not a pleasant sensation.

I yelled in pain as Kaz managed to angle the broken machine toward the beach. We crashed into the sand – even more glass breaking –and everything became a jumbled mess of bodies and debris.

*

I blinked awake, regaining consciousness a few minutes after the crash. I found myself lying on my back, staring out the broken hole of the ceiling.

There was an open patch in the clouds, and I could see the stars.

'Uh ...,' a voice said. 'Is everyone okay?'

I twisted about, brushing bits of glass from my face – fortunately, the cockpit appeared to be made out of something like Free Kingdoms safety glass. Though it had shattered into shards, the pieces were surprisingly dull, and I hadn't been cut at all.

Australia – the one who had spoken – sat, holding her head where it was still bleeding. She looked about, seeming dazed. The pathetic remains of the *Dragonaut* lay broken around us, like the long-dead carcass on some mythical beast. The eyes had both shattered, and I sat in the skull. One of the wings jutted up a short distance away, pointing into the air.

Bastille groaned beside me, her jacket now laced with a spider-web of lines. It had absorbed some of the shock from the landing for her. My legs, unfortunately, didn't have any such glass, and they ached from being yanked about.

There was a rustling a short distance away, up where the beach turned into trees. Suddenly, Kaz walked out of the forest, looking completely unbruised and unhurt.

'Well!' he said, surveying the beach. 'That was certainly interesting. Anybody dead? Raise your hand if you are.'

'What if you *feel* like you're dead?' Bastille asked, pulling herself free from her jacket.

'Raise a finger, then,' Kaz said, walking down the beach toward us.

I won't say which one she raised.

'Wait,' I said, wobbling a bit as I stood. 'You got thrown all that way, but you're all right?'

'Of course I didn't get thrown that far,' Kaz said with a laugh. 'I got lost right about the time when we crashed, and I just found my way back. Sorry I missed the impact – but it didn't look like a whole lot of fun.'

Smedry Talents. I shook my head, checking my pockets to make certain my Lenses had survived. Fortunately, the padding had protected them. But, as I worked, I realized something. 'Bastille! Your mother!'

Just then, a sheet of glass rattled and was shoved over by something beneath it. Draulin stood up, and I heard a faint moan from inside her helmet. In one hand, she still held her Crystin blade. She reached up, sheathing it into a strap on her back, then pulled the helmet off. A pile of sweaty, silver hair fell around her face. She turned to regard the wreckage.

I was a little surprised to see her in such good shape. Of course, I should have realized that the armor she wore was of silimatic technology. It had worked as an even better cushion than Bastille's jacket.

'Where *are* we?' Bastille asked, picking her way across a field of broken glass, now wearing only a black T-shirt tucked into her militaristic trousers.

It was a good question. The forest looked vaguely junglelike. Waves quietly rolled up and down the starlit beach, grabbing bits of glass and towing them into the ocean.

'Egypt, I guess,' Australia said. She held a bandage to her head, but otherwise seemed to have come out all right. 'I mean, that's where we were heading, right? We were almost there when we crashed.'

'No,' Draulin said, stalking across the beach toward us. 'Lord Kazan was required to take over control of the ship when you lost consciousness, which means ...'

'My Talent came into play,' Kaz said. 'In other words, we're lost.'

'Not *that* lost,' Bastille said. 'Isn't that the Worldspire?'

She pointed out across the ocean. And, just vaguely in the distance, I could see what appeared to be a tower rising from the ocean. Considering the distance, it must have been enormous.

I was later to learn that enormous was a severe under-estimate. The Worldspire is said by the Free Kingdomers to be the exact center of the world. It's a massive glass spike running from the upper atmosphere directly into the center of the planet – which is, of course, made of glass. Isn't everything?

'You're right,' Draulin said. 'That means we're probably somewhere in the Kalmarian Wilds. Well outside the Hushlands.'

'Well, that shouldn't be a problem,' Kaz said.

'You think you can get us to Nalhalla, my lord?' Draulin asked.

'Probably.'

I turned. 'What about the Library of Alexandria?'

'You still want to go *there*?' Draulin asked.

'Of course.'

'I don't know if—'

'Draulin,' I said, 'don't make me force you to hop on one foot again.'

She fell silent.

'I agree with Alcatraz,' Kaz said, walking over to pick through the rubble. 'If my father's in Alexandria, then he's undoubtedly getting into trouble. If he's in trouble, that means I'm missing out on some serious fun. Now, let's see if we can salvage anything ...'

I watched him work, and soon Draulin joined him, picking through the pieces. Bastille walked up beside me.

'Thanks,' she said. 'For saving me when I fell out of the side of the dragon, I mean.'

'Sure. I'll kick you any time you want.'

She snorted softly. 'You're a real friend.'

I smiled. Considering that we'd crashed so soundly, it was remarkable that nobody had been severely hurt. Actually, you may find this annoying. It would have been a better story if someone had died here. An early fatality can really make a book seem much more tense, as it lets people realize how dangerous things can be.

You have to remember, however, that this is not fiction, but a real-life account. I can't help it if all my friends were too selfish to do the narratively proper thing and get themselves killed off to hike up the tension of my memoirs.

I've spoken to them at length about this. If it makes you feel better, Bastille dies by the end of this book.

Oh, you didn't want to hear that? I'm sorry. You'll just have to forget that I wrote it. There are several convenient ways to do that. I hear hitting yourself on the head with a blunt object can be very effective. You should try using one of Brandon Sanderson's fantasy novels. They're big enough, and goodness knows, that's really the only useful thing to do with them.

Bastille – completely unaware that she was condemned – glanced at the half-buried dragon's head. Its broken eyes stared out toward the jungle, its maw opened slightly, teeth cracked. 'It seems such a sad end for the *Dragonaut*,' she said. 'So much powerful glass wasted.'

'Is there any way to ... I don't know, fix it?'

She shrugged. 'The silimatic engine is gone, and that's what gave the glass its power. I supposed if you could get a new engine, it would still work. But, cracked as the ship is, it would probably make more sense to smelt the whole thing down.'

The others came up with a couple of backpacks full of food and supplies. Kaz eventually let out a whoop of joy, then dug out a little bowler of a hat, which he put on. This was joined by a vest he wore under his jacket. It was an odd combination, since the jacket itself – along with his trousers – were made of heavyweight, rugged material. He came across looking like some cross between Indiana Jones and a British gentleman.

'We ready?' he asked.

'Almost,' I said, finally pulling off the boots with the Grappler's Glass on them. 'Any way to turn these off?' I held up the boot, critically eyeing the bottom, which was now stuck with shards of glass and – not surprisingly – sand.

'For most people there is no way,' Draulin said, sitting on a piece of the wreckage, then taking off her armored boots. She pulled out a few pieces of specially shaped glass and slid them into place. 'We simply cover them with plates like these, so the boots stick to those instead.'

I nodded. The plates in question had soles and heels on the bottom, and probably felt just like regular shoes.

'You, however, are an Oculator,' she said.

'What does that have to do with it?'

'Oculators aren't like regular people, Alcatraz,' Australia said, smiling. Her head had stopped bleeding, and she'd tied a bandage to it. A pink one. I had no idea where she had found it.

'Indeed, my lord,' Draulin said. 'You can use the Lenses, but you also have some limited power over silimatic glass, what we call "technology".'

'You mean, like the engine?' I asked, slipping on my Oculator's Lenses.

Draulin nodded. 'Try deactivating the boots like you would Lenses.'

I did so, touching them. Surprisingly, the sand and glass dropped free, the boots becoming inert.

'Those boots had been given a silimatic charge,' Australia explained. 'Kind of like batteries you use in the Hushlands. The boots will run out eventually. Until then, an Oculator can turn them off and on.'

'One of the great mysteries of our age,' Draulin said, her boots replaced. The way she said it indicated that she really didn't care how or why things worked, only that they did.

Me, I was more curious. I'd been told several times about Free Kingdomer technology. It seemed a simple distinction to me. Magic was that sort of thing that only worked for certain people, while technology – often called silimatics – worked for anyone. Australia had been able to fly the *Dragonaut*, but so had Kaz. It was technology.

But what I had just learned seemed to indicate that there was a relationship between this technology of theirs and Oculatory powers. However, the conversation reminded me of something else. I didn't have any idea if we were closer to Alexandria now than we had been before, but it seemed a good idea to try contacting my grandfather again.

I slipped on the Courier's Lenses and concentrated. Unfortunately, I wasn't able to get anything out of them. I left them on just in case, then stuffed the Grappler's Glass boots into one of the packs.

I slung it over my shoulder; however, Bastille took it from me. I shot her a frown.

'Sorry,' she said. 'My mother's orders.'

'You don't need to carry anything, Lord Smedry,' Draulin said, hefting another pack. 'Let Squire Bastille do it.'

'I can carry my own pack, Draulin,' I snapped.

'Oh?' she asked. 'And if we get attacked, do you not need to be ready and agile so that you can use your Lenses to defend us?' She turned away from me. 'Squire Bastille is good at carrying things. Allow her to do this – it will let her be useful and make her feel a sense of accomplishment.'

Bastille flushed. I opened my mouth to argue some more, but Bastille shot me a glance that quieted me.

Fine, I thought. We all looked toward Kaz, ready to go. 'Onward then!' the short man said, taking off across the sand up toward the trees.

6

A dults are not idiots.

    Often, in books such as this one, the opposite impression is given. Adults in these stories will either (a) get captured, (b) disappear conspicuously when there is trouble, or (c) refuse to help.

(I'm not sure what authors have against adults, but everyone seems to hate them to an extent usually reserved for dogs and mothers. Why else make them out to be such idiots? 'Ah, look, the dark lord of evil has come to attack the castle! Annnnd, there's my lunch break. Have fun saving the world on your own, kids! ')

In the real world, adults tend to get involved in everything, whether you want them to or not. They won't disappear when the dark lord appears, though they may try to sue him. This discrepancy is yet another proof that most books are fantasies while this book is utterly true and invaluable. You see, in this book, I will make it completely clear that all adults are *not* idiots.

They are, however, hairy.

Adults are like hairy kids who like to tell others what to do. Despite what other books may claim, they do have their uses. They can reach things on high shelves, for instance. (Though, Kaz would argue that such high shelves shouldn't be necessary. Reference Reason number sixty-three, which will be explained at a later point.)

Regardless, I often wish that the two groups – adults and kids – could find a way to get along better. Some sort of treaty or something. The biggest problem is, the adults have one of the most effective recruitment strategies in the world.

Give them enough time, and they'll turn *any* kid into one of them.

We entered the jungle.

'Everyone remember to *stay in sight* of someone else in the group,' Kaz said. 'There's no telling where we'll leave you if you get separated!'

With that, Kaz pulled out a machete and began to cut his way through the undergrowth. I glanced back at the beach, bidding silent farewell to the translucent dragon, cracked from landing, its body slowly being buried in the sand from the rising tide. One wing still hung up in the air, as if in defiance of its death.

'You were the most majestic thing I'd ever seen,' I whispered. 'Rest well.' A little melodramatic, true, but it felt appropriate. Then I quickly rushed after the others, careful not to lose sight of Draulin, who walked in the rear.

The jungle was thick, and the canopy overhead made the darkness near absolute. Draulin pulled an antiquated-looking lantern from her pack, then tapped it with one finger. It started to glow, the flame coming to life without needing a match. Even with it, however, it felt creepy to be traveling through a dense jungle in the middle of the night.

In order to still my nerves, I moved to walk by Bastille. She, however, didn't want to talk. I eventually worked my way up through the column until I was behind Kaz. I figured that he and I had started off on the wrong foot, and I hoped I could patch things up a bit.

Those of you who recall the events of the first book will realize that this was quite a change in me. For most of my life, I'd been abandoned by family after family. It was tough to blame them, however, since I'd spent my childhood breaking everything in sight. I'd gone on such a rampage that I would have made the proverbial bull in the proverbial china shop look unproverbially good by proverbial comparison. (Personally, I don't even know how he'd fit through the door. Proverbially.)

Regardless, I had grown into the habit of pushing people away as soon as I got to know them – abandoning them before they could abandon me. It had been tough to realize what I was doing, but I was already starting to change.

Kaz was my uncle. My father's brother. For a kid who had spent most of his life thinking that he had no living relatives, having Kaz think I was a fool was a big deal. I wanted desperately to show him I was capable.

Kaz glanced at me as he chopped at the foliage – though he only tended to cut away things up to his own height of four feet, leaving the rest of us to get branches in our faces. 'Well?' he asked.

'I wanted to apologize for that whole midget thing,'

He shrugged.

'It's just that ...,' I said. 'Well, I figured with all of the magic and stuff they have in the Free Kingdoms, they would have been able to cure dwarfism by now.'

'They haven't been able to cure stupidity, either,' he said. 'So I guess we won't be able to help you.'

I blushed. 'I ... didn't mean ...'

Kaz chuckled, slicing off a couple of fronds. 'Look, it's all right. I'm used to this. I just want you to understand that I don't need to be *cured*.'

'But ...,' I said, trying hard to express what I felt without being offensive, 'isn't being short like you a genetic disease?'

'Genetic, yes,' Kaz said. 'But is it disease just because it's different? I mean, you're an Oculator; that's genetic too. Would *you* like to be cured?'

'That's different,' I said.

'Is it?'

I paused to think about it. 'I don't know,' I finally said. 'But don't you get tired of being short?'

'Don't you get tired of being tall?'

'I ...' It was tough to come up with an answer to that one. I really wasn't all that tall – barely five feet, now that I'd launched into my teens. Still, I was tall compared with him.

'Now, personally,' Kaz continued, 'I think you tall people are really missing out. Why the entire world would be a better place if you were all shorter.'

I raised an eyebrow.

'You look doubtful,' Kaz said, smiling. 'Obviously you need to be introduced to The List!'

'The List?'

From behind, I heard Australia sigh. 'Don't encourage him, Alcatraz.'

'Hush, you!' Kaz said, eyeing Australia and eliciting a bit of an *eep* from her. 'The List is a time-tested and scientifically researched collection of facts that *prove* that short people are better off than tall ones.'

He glanced at me. 'Confused?'

I nodded.

'Slowness of thought,' he said. 'A common ailment of tall people. Reason number forty-seven: Tall people's heads are in a thinner atmosphere than those of short people, so the tall people get less oxygen. That makes it so that their brains don't work quite as well.'

With that, he chopped his way through the edge of the forest and walked out into a clearing. I stopped in the path, then glanced at Australia.

'We're not sure if he's serious or not,' she whispered. 'But, he really *does* keep that List of his.'

After getting a glare from Bastille for pausing for so long, I rushed out into the clearing with Kaz. I was surprised to see that the jungle broke just a little further out, giving us a view of ...

'Paris?' I asked in shock. 'That's the Eiffel Tower!'

'Ah, is that what that is?' Kaz asked, scribbling something on a notepad. 'Great! We're back in the Hushlands. Not as badly lost as I thought.'

'But ...,' I said. 'We were on another continent! How did we cross the ocean?'

'We're lost, kid,' Kaz said, as if that explained everything. 'Anyway, I'll get us where we need to be. Always trust the short person to know his way! Reason number twenty-eight: Short people can find things easier and follow trails better because they're closer to the ground.'

I stood, nearly dumbfounded. 'But ... there aren't any jungles near Paris!'

'He gets lost,' Bastille said, walking up to me, 'in some very incredible ways.'

'I think this is the strangest Talent I've ever seen,' I said. 'And that's saying a lot.'

She shrugged. 'Didn't yours break a chicken once?'

'Good point.'

Kaz led us back to the trees, cutting us a half pathway. 'So, your Talent can take you anywhere!' I said to the short man.

He shrugged. 'Why do you think I was on the *Dragonaut*? In case things went wrong, I was to get you and your grandfather out of the Hushlands.'

'Why even send the ship, then? You could have come got me on your own!'

He snorted. 'I have to know what to look for, Al. I have to have a destination. Australia had to come so that we could use Lenses to contact you, and we figured it was a good idea to bring a Knight of Crystallia for protection. Besides, my Talent can be a little ... unpredictable.'

'I think they all can,' I said.

He chuckled. 'Well, that's the truth. Just hope you never have to see Australia after she's just gotten up in the morning. Anyway, we figured that rather than taking a chance on my Talent – which has occasionally gotten me lost for weeks – we should bring the ship.'

'So ... wait,' I said. 'We could be walking like this for weeks?'

'Maybe,' Kaz said, parting some fronds, looking out. I peeked through beside him. What looked like a desert was sprawling out beyond us. He rubbed his chin in thought. 'Walnuts,' he swore. 'We're a bit off track.' He let the fronds fall back into place and we continued walking.

Several weeks. My grandfather could be in danger. In fact, knowing Grandpa Smedry, he most definitely *was* in danger. Yet, I couldn't get to him because I was traipsing through the jungle, occasionally peering out through another clearing at ...

'Dodger Stadium?' I asked. 'I *know* there aren't any jungles there!'

'Must be up past the nosebleed seats,' Kaz said, taking another turn, leading us in a different direction. It was already growing light, and dawn would soon arrive. As we started again, Draulin marched up beside me. 'Lord Alcatraz? Might I have a moment of your time?'

I nodded slowly. Being called 'lord' was still a little unsettling to me. What was required of me? Was I expected to sip tea and behead people? (If so, I certainly hoped I wouldn't need to do both at the same time.)

What did it mean to be called 'lord'? I'll assume you've never had the honor, since I doubt any of you happen to be British royalty. (And, if by chance you are, then let me say, 'Hello, Your Majesty! Welcome to my stupid book. Can I borrow some cash?')

It seemed that the Free Kingdomers had unrealistic expectations of me. I wasn't normally the type to doubt myself, but I'd rarely had a chance to be a leader. The more others started to look to me, the more I began to worry. What if I failed them?

'My lord,' Draulin said. 'I feel the need to apologize. I spoke quite out of turn to you while we were fighting atop the *Dragonaut*.'

'It's all right,' I said, shaking myself out of my moment of self-doubt. 'We were in a tense situation.'

'No, there is no excuse.'

'Really,' I said. 'Anyone could have gotten snappish in a predicament like that.'

'My lord,' she said sternly, 'a Knight of Crystallia isn't just "anyone". More is expected of us – not just in action, but in attitude as well. We don't just respect men of your station, we respect and serve all people. We must *always* strive to be the best, for the reputation of the entire order depends on it.'

Bastille was walking just behind us. For some reason, I got the feeling that Draulin was preaching less to me, and more to her daughter. It seemed backhanded.

'Please,' Draulin continued. 'I would be more at peace if you would chastise me.'

'Uh ... okay,' I said. (How does one scold a Knight of Crystallia some twenty years your senior? 'Bad knight'? 'Go straight to bed without polishing your sword'?)

'Consider yourself chastised,' I said instead.

'Thank you.'

'Aha!' Kaz called.

The line paused. Sunlight was beginning to peek through the canopy of leaves. Ahead, Kaz was looking out through some bushes. He flashed us a smile, then cut the bushes away with a swipe of the machete.

'I knew I'd find my way!' he said, gesturing out. I looked for the first time at the great Library of Alexandria – a place so entrenched in lore and mythology that I'd been taught about it even in Hushlander schools. One of the most dangerous buildings on the planet.

It was a one-room hut.

7

I am a fish.

No, really. I am. I have fins, a tail, scales. I swim about, doing fishy things. This isn't a metaphor or a joke, but a real and honest fact. I am a fish.

More on this later.

'We came all this way for *that*?' I asked, looking at the hut. It stood on an open plain of sandy, scrubby ground. The roof looked like it was about to fall in.

'Yup, that's it,' Kaz said, walking out of the jungle and down the slope toward the hut.

I glanced back at Bastille, who just shrugged. 'I've never been here before.'

'I have,' Bastille's mother said. 'Yes, that is the Library of Alexandria.' She clomped out of the jungle. I shrugged, then followed her, Australia and Bastille joining me. As we walked, I glanced back at the jungle.

It, of course, had vanished. I stopped, but then thought better of asking. After everything that I'd been through in the last few months, a disappearing jungle wasn't really even all that odd.

I hurried to catch up to Kaz. 'You're *sure* this is the place? I kind of expected it to look ... well, a little less like a hut.'

'You would have preferred a yurt?' Kaz asked, walking up to the doorway and peeking in. I followed.

Inside, a large set of stairs was cut into the ground. They led down into the depths of the earth. The dark opening seemed un-naturally black to me – like someone had cut a square in the floor and pulled away the fabric of existence with it.

'The Library,' I said. 'It's underground?'

'Of course,' Kaz said. 'What did you expect? This is the

Hushlands – things like the Library of Alexandria need to keep a low profile.'

Draulin walked up beside us, then pointed for Bastille to check the perimeter. She moved off. Draulin went the other way, scouting the area for danger.

'The Curators of Alexandria aren't like Librarians you've seen before, Al,' Kaz said.

'What do you mean?'

'Well, they're undead wraiths, for one thing,' he said, 'though it's not really nice to be prejudiced against people because of their race.'

I raised an eyebrow.

'Just saying . . . ,' he said with a shrug. 'Anyway, the Curators are older than the Librarians of Biblioden. Actually, the Curators are older than most things in this world. The Library of Alexandria was started back during the days of classical Greece. Alexandria was, after all, founded by Alexander the Great.'

'Wait,' I said. 'He was a real person?'

'Of course he was,' Australia said, joining us. 'Why wouldn't he be?'

I shrugged. 'I don't know. I guess I figured that all the things I'd learned in school were Librarian lies.'

'Not all of them,' Kaz said. 'The Librarian teachings only *really* started to deviate from the truth about five hundred years back – about the time that Biblioden lived.' He paused, scratching his face. 'Of course, I guess they *do* lie about this place. I think they teach that it was destroyed.'

I nodded. 'By the Romans or something.'

'Complete fabrication,' Kaz said. 'The Library outgrew its old location, so the Curators moved it here. Guess they wanted a place where they could hollow out as much ground as they wanted. It's kind of tough to find room inside a big city to store every book ever written.'

'*Every* book?'

'Of course,' Kaz said. 'That's the point of this place. It's a storage of all knowledge ever recorded.'

Suddenly, things started to make sense. 'That's why my father came here and why Grandpa Smedry followed! Don't you see! My father can read texts in the Forgotten Language now; he has a set of Translator's Lenses like mine, forged from the Sands of Rashid.'

'Yes,' Kaz said. 'And?'

'And so he came here,' I said, looking at the stairway leading into the darkness. 'He came for knowledge. Books in the Forgotten Language. He could study them here, learn what the ancient people – the Incarna – knew.'

Australia and Kaz shared a glance.

'That's ... not really all that likely, Alcatraz,' Australia said.

'Why not?'

'The Curators gather the knowledge,' Kaz said, 'but they're not that great at sharing. They'll let you read a book, but they charge a terrible cost.'

I felt a chill. 'What cost?'

'Your soul,' Australia said. 'You can read one book, then you become one of them, to serve in the Library for eternity.'

Great, I thought, glancing at Kaz. The shorter man looked troubled. 'What?' I asked.

'I know your father, Al. We grew up together – he's my brother.'

'And?'

'He's a true Smedry. Just like your grandfather. We don't tend to think things through. Things like charging into danger, like infiltrating Libraries, or ...'

'Like reading a book that will cost you your soul?'

Kaz looked away. 'I don't *think* he'd be that stupid. He'd get the knowledge he wanted, but he'd never be able to share it or use it. Even Attica wouldn't get *that* hungry for answers.'

The comment begged another question. *If he didn't come for a book, then why visit?* I thought.

Draulin and Bastille arrived a few moments later. Now, you might have noticed something important. Look up the name Draulin on your favorite search engine. You won't get many results, and the ones you do get will probably be typos, not prisons.

(Though, the two are related in that they are both things I tend to be affiliated with far too often.) Either way, there's no prison named Draulin, though there is one named Bastille.

(That last bit about the names – that is foreshadowing. So don't say I never give you anything.)

'Perimeter is secure,' Draulin said. 'No guards.'

'There never are,' Kaz said, glancing back at the stairs. 'I've been here half a dozen times – mostly due to getting lost – though I've never gone in. The Curators don't guard the place. They don't need to – anyone who tries to steal even a single book will automatically lose their soul, whether they know about the rules or not.'

I shivered.

'We should camp here,' Draulin said, glancing over at the rising sun. 'Most of us didn't get any sleep last night, and we shouldn't go down into the Library without our wits about us.'

'Probably a good idea,' Kaz said, yawning. 'Plus, we don't really know if we *need* to go in. Al, you said my father visited this place. Did he go in?'

'I don't know,' I said. 'I couldn't tell for certain.'

'Try the Lenses again,' Australia said, nodding encouragingly – sometimes that appeared to be one of her favorite gestures.

I was still wearing the Courier's Lenses; as before, I tried to contact my grandfather. All I received was a low buzz and a kind of wavering fuzz in my vision. 'I'm trying,' I said. 'All I get is a blurry fuzz. Anyone know what that means?'

I glanced at Australia. She shrugged – for an Oculator, she sure didn't seem to know much. Then, I was one too, and I knew even less, so it was a little hard to judge.

'Don't ask me,' Kaz said. 'That ability skipped me, fortunately.'

I looked over at Bastille.

'Don't look at her,' Draulin said. 'Bastille is a squire of Crystallia, not an Oculator.'

I caught Bastille's eyes. She glanced at her mother.

'I command her to speak,' I said.

'It means there's interference of some sort,' Bastille said quickly.

'Courier's Lenses are temperamental, and certain kinds of glass can block them. I'll bet the Library down there has precautions to stop people from grabbing a book, then – before their soul is taken – reading its contents off to someone listening via Lenses.'

'Thanks, Bastille,' I said. 'You know, you're kind of useful to have around sometimes.'

She smiled but then caught sight of Draulin looking at her with displeasure, and stiffened.

'So, do we camp?' Kaz asked.

I realized everyone was looking at me. 'Uh, sure.'

Draulin nodded, then moved over to some kind of fern-type plant and began to cut off fronds to make some shelter. It was already getting warm, but I guess that was to be expected, what with us being in Egypt and all.

I went to help Australia rifle through the packs, getting out some foodstuffs. My stomach growled as we worked; I hadn't eaten since the stale chips in the airport. 'So,' I said. 'You're an Oculator?'

Australia flushed. 'Well, not a very good one, you know. I can never really figure out how the Lenses are supposed to work.'

I chuckled. 'I can't either.'

That only seemed to make her more embarrassed.

'What?' I asked.

She smiled in her perky way. 'Nothing. I just, well. You're a natural, Alcatraz. I've tried to use Courier's Lenses a dozen times before, and you saw how poorly I managed when contacting you at the airport.'

'I think you did all right,' I said. 'Saved *my* skin.'

'I suppose,' she said, looking down.

'Don't you have any Oculator's Lenses?' I asked, noticing for the first time that she wasn't wearing any Lenses. I had put back on my Oculator's Lenses after trying to contact Grandpa Smedry.

She flushed, then rifled through her pocket, eventually pulling out a pair with far more stylish frames than mine. She slid them on. 'I ... don't really like how they look.'

'They're great,' I said. 'Look, Grandpa Smedry told me that I have to wear mine a lot to get used to them. Maybe you just need more practice.'

'I've had, like, ten years.'

'And how much of that did you spend wearing the Lenses?'

She thought for a moment. 'Not much, I guess. Anyway, since you're here, I guess my being an Oculator isn't all that important.' She smiled, but I could sense something else. She seemed good at hiding things beneath her bubbly exterior.

'I don't know about that,' I said, cutting slices of bread. *'I'm* certainly glad there's another Oculator with us – especially if we have to go down in that Library.'

'Why?' she said. 'You're far better with Lenses than I am.'

'And if we get separated?' I asked. 'You could use the Courier's Lenses to contact me. Having two Oculators is never a bad thing, I've found.'

'But … the Courier's Lenses won't work down there,' she said. 'That's what we just discovered.'

She's right, I realized, flushing. Then, something occurred to me. I reached into one of my pockets, pulling out a pair of Lenses. 'Here, try these,' I said. They were yellow tinted.

She took them hesitantly, then tried them on. She blinked. 'Hey!' she said. 'I can see footprints.'

'Tracker's Lenses,' I said. 'Grandpa Smedry loaned them to me. With these, you can retrace your steps back to the entrance if you get lost – or even find me by following my footprints.'

Australia smiled broadly. 'I've never tried a pair of these before. I can't believe they work so well!'

I didn't mention that Grandpa Smedry had said they were among the most simple of Lenses to use. 'That's great,' I said. 'Maybe you've just always tried the wrong types of Lenses. Best to begin with the ones that work. You can borrow those.'

'Thanks!' She gave me an unexpected hug, then hopped to her feet to go fetch the other pack. Smiling, I watched her go.

'You're good at that,' a voice said.

I turned to find Bastille standing a short distance away. She'd cut down several long branches and was in the process of dragging them back to her mother.

'What?' I asked.

'You're good,' she said. 'With people, I mean.'

I shrugged. 'It's nothing.'

'No,' Bastille said. 'You really made her feel better. Something had been bothering her since you arrived, but now she seems back to her old self. You kind of have a leader's flair about you, Smedry.'

It makes sense, if you think about it. I had spent my entire childhood learning how to shove people away from me. I'd learned just the right buttons to push, just the right things to break, to make them hate me. Now, those same skills were coming in handy helping people feel good, rather than making them hate me.

I should have realized the trouble I was getting myself into. There's nothing worse than having people look up to you – because the more they expect, the worse you feel when you fail them. Take my advice. You don't want to be the one in charge. Becoming a leader is, in a way, like falling off a cliff. It feels like a lot of fun at first.

Then it stops being fun. Really, really fast.

Bastille hauled the branches over to her mother, who was making a lean-to. Then, Bastille sat down beside me and took out one of our water bottles to get a drink. The water level in it didn't seem to go down at all as she gulped.

Neat, I thought.

'There's something I've been meaning to ask you,' I said.

She wiped her brow. 'What?'

'That jet that was chasing us,' I said. 'It fired a Frostbringer's Lens. I thought only Oculators could activate things like that.'

She shrugged.

'Bastille,' I said, eyeing her.

'You saw my mother,' she grumbled. 'I'm not supposed to talk about things like that.'

'Why?'

'Because I'm not an Oculator.'

'I'm not a pigeon either,' I said. 'But I can talk about feathers if I want.'

She eyed me. 'That's a really bad metaphor, Smedry.'

'I'm good at those kind.'

Feathers. Much less comfortable than scales. Glad I'm a fish instead of a bird. (You haven't forgotten about that, have you?)

'Look,' I said. 'What you know could be important. I ... I think the thing that flew that jet is still alive.'

'It fell from the sky!' she said.

'So did we.'

'It didn't have a dragon to glide on.'

'No, but it did have a face half-made from metal screws and springs.'

She froze, bottle halfway to her lips.

'Ha!' I said. 'You *do* know something.'

'Metal face,' she said. 'Was it wearing a mask?'

I shook my head. 'The face was *made* out of bits of metal. I saw the creature before, on the airfield. When I ran away, I felt ... pulled backward. It was hard to move.'

'Voidstormer's Lenses,' she said absently. 'The opposite of those Windstormer's Lenses you have.'

I patted the Windstormer's Lenses in my pocket. I'd almost forgotten about those. With my last Firebringer's Lens now broken, the Windstormer's Lenses were my only real offensive Lenses. Besides them, I only had my Oculator's Lenses, my Courier's Lenses, and – of course – my Translator's Lenses.

'So, what has a metal face, flies jets, and can use Lenses?' I asked. 'Sounds like a riddle.'

'An easy one,' Bastille said, kneeling down, speaking quietly. 'Look, don't tell my mother you got this from me, but I think we're in serious trouble.'

'When are we not?'

'More so now,' she said. 'You remember that Oculator you fought in the Library?'

'Blackburn? Sure.'

'Well,' she said, 'he belonged to a sect of Librarians known as the Dark Oculators. There are other sects, though – four, I think – and they don't get along very well. Each sect wants to be in charge of the whole organization.'

'And this guy chasing me …?'

'One of the Scrivener's Bones,' she said. 'It's the smallest sect. Other Librarians tend to avoid the Scrivener's Bones, except when they need them, because they have … odd habits.'

'Like?'

'Like ripping off parts of their bodies, then replacing them with Alivened materials.'

I stared at her for a moment. We fish do that sometimes. We can't blink, after all. 'They do *what*?'

'Just what I said,' Bastille whispered. 'They're part Alivened. Twisted half human, half monsters.'

I shivered. We'd fought a couple of Alivened in the downtown library. Those were made of paper, but they'd been far more dangerous than that could possibly sound. It was fighting them that lost Bastille her sword.

Alivening things – bringing inanimate objects to life with Oculatory power – is a very evil art. It requires the Oculator to give up some of his or her own humanity.

'The Scrivener's Bones usually work on commission,' Bastille said. 'So, another Librarian hired it.'

My mother, was my immediate thought. *She's the one who hired him.* I avoided thinking about her, since doing so tended to make me sick, and there's no use being sick unless you can get out of school for it.

'He used Lenses,' I said. 'So this Scrivener's Bone is an Oculator?'

'Not likely,' Bastille said.

'Then how?'

'There's a way to make a Lens that anyone can use,' she whispered very quietly.

'There is?' I asked. 'Well, why in the world don't we have more of *those*?'

Bastille glanced to the side. 'Because, idiot,' she hissed. 'You have to sacrifice an Oculator and use his blood to forge one.'

'Oh,' I said.

'He was probably using a blood-forged Lens,' she said, 'hooked somehow into the cockpit glass so that it could fire out at us. That sounds like something the Scrivener's Bones would do. They like mixing Oculatory powers with Hushlander technology.'

This talk of blood-forged Lenses should mean something to you. Finally, you may understand why I end up finding my way to an altar, about to get sacrificed. What Bastille neglected to mention was that the power of the Oculator who was killed had a direct effect on how powerful the blood-forged Lens was. The more powerful the Oculator, the more awesome the Lens.

And I, as you might have realized, was very, very powerful.

Bastille left to cut down more branches. I sat quietly. It was probably just in my head, but I thought I could feel something off in the distance. That same dark sense I'd felt escaping from the airfield and fighting the jet.

That's silly, I told myself, shivering. *We've traveled hundreds of miles using Kaz's Talent. Even if that Scrivener's Bone did survive, it would take him days to get here.*

So I assumed.

A short time later I lay beneath a canopy of fronds, my black sneakers off and wrapped in my jacket to form a pillow. The others dozed, and I tried to do likewise. Yet, I couldn't stop thinking about what I'd been told.

It seemed like it all must be related somehow. The way the Lenses worked. Smedry Talents. The fact that the blood of an Oculator could make a Lens that worked for anyone. The connection between silimatic energy and Oculatory energy.

All connected. But, it was too much for me to figure out, considering the fact that I was just a fish. So, I went to sleep.

Which is pretty hard to do when you don't have eyelids.

8

All right, so I'm not a fish. I admit it. What? Figured that out on your own, did you? You're so clever. What gave it away? The fact that I'm writing books, the fact that I don't have fins, or the fact that I'm a downright, despicable liar?

Anyway, there *was* a purpose in that little exercise – one beyond my standard purpose. (Which is, of course, to annoy you.) I wanted to prove something. In the last chapter, I told you that I was a fish – but I also mentioned that I had black sneakers. Do you remember?

Here's the thing. That was a lie; I didn't have black sneakers. I have never owned a pair of black shoes. I was wearing white shoes; I told you about them back in Chapter One.

Why does it matter? Let's talk about something called misdirection.

In the last chapter, I told a big lie, then made you focus on it so much that you ignored the smaller lie. I said I was a fish. Then, I mentioned my black shoes in passing, so you didn't pay attention to them.

People use this strategy all the time. They drive fancy cars to distract others from their having a small house. They wear bright clothing to distract from their being – unfortunately – rather bland people. They talk really loudly to distract you from their having nothing to say.

This is what has happened to me. Everywhere I go in the Free Kingdoms, people are always excited to congratulate me, praise me, or ask for my blessing. They're all looking at the fish. There are so focused on the big thing – that I supposedly saved the world from the Librarians – that they completely ignore the facts. They don't see who I am, or what my presumed heroism cost.

So, that's why I'm writing my autobiography. I want to teach you to ignore the fish and pay attention to the shoes. Fish and shoes. Remember that.

'Alcatraz!' a voice called, waking me up. I opened bleary eyes, then sat up.

I'd been dreaming. About a wolf. A metal wolf, running, charging, getting closer.

He's coming, I thought. *The hunter. The Scrivener's Bone. He's not dead.*

'Alcatraz!' I looked toward the sound and was met by a stunning sight. My grandfather was standing just a short distance away.

'Grandpa Smedry!' I said, climbing to my feet. Indeed, it was the old man, with his bushy white mustache and tuft of white hair running around the back of his head.

'Grandpa!' I said, rushing forward. 'Where have you been?!'

Grandpa Smedry looked confused, then glanced over his shoulder. He cocked his head at me. 'What?'

I slowed. Why was he wearing Tracker's Lenses instead of his Oculator's Lenses? In fact, looking more closely, I saw that he had on some very odd clothing. A pink tunic and brown trousers.

'Alcatraz?' Grandpa Smedry asked. 'What are you talking about?' His voice was far too feminine. In fact it sounded just like . . .

'Australia?' I asked, stupefied.

'Oops!' he/she suddenly said, eyes opening wide. The doppelganger scrambled over to the pack and pulled out a mirror, then groaned and sat down. 'Oh, Shattering Glass!'

Back under the tent, Kaz was waking up, blinking. He sat up, then began to chuckle.

'What?' I asked, looking back at him.

'My Talent,' Australia said, sounding morose. 'I warned you, didn't I? Sometimes, I look *really* ugly when I wake up.'

'What are you saying about my grandfather?' I said, growing amused.

Australia – still looking like Grandpa – blushed. 'I'm sorry,' She said. 'I didn't mean to say *he* was ugly. Just, well, this is ugly for me.'

I held up a hand. 'I understand.'

'It's worse when I fall asleep thinking about someone,' she said. 'I was worried about him, and I guess the Talent took over. It should begin to wear off in a little bit.'

I smiled, then found myself laughing at Australia's expression. I'd seen several very strange Talents in my short time with the Smedries, but until that moment, I had never run into one that I thought was more embarrassing than my own.

I would like to point out that it's not very kind to take amusement in someone else's pain. Doing so is a very bad habit – almost as bad as reading the second book in a series without having read the first.

However, it's quite different when your female cousin goes to sleep, then wakes up looking like an old man with a bushy mustache. Then it's okay to make fun of her. That happens to be one of the very few exclusions covered by the Law of Things That Are So Funny You Can't Be Blamed for Laughing at Them, No Matter What.

(Other exceptions include getting bitten by a giant penguin, falling off a giant cheese sculpture carved to look like a nose, and getting named after a prison by your parents. I have a petition in the courts to revoke that third one.)

Kaz joined me in the laughter, and eventually, even Australia was chuckling. That's the way we Smedries are. If you can't laugh at your Talent, you tend to end up very grumpy.

'So, what did you want to talk to me about?' I asked Australia.

'Huh?' she asked, poking at her mustache with her finger.

'You woke me up.'

Australia looked up, shocked. 'Oh! Right! Um, I think I found something interesting!'

I raised an eyebrow, and she stood, rushing over to the other side of the Library's hut. She pointed at the ground. 'See!' she said.

'Dirt?' I asked.

'No, no, the footprints!'

There were no footprints in the dirt – of course, Australia

was wearing the Tracker's Lenses. I reached up and tapped her Lenses.

'Oh, right!' she said, pulling off the Lenses and handing them to me.

In all fairness, you shouldn't judge Australia too harshly. She's not stupid. She just gets distracted. By, you know, breathing.

I slipped on the Lenses. There, burning on the ground, were a set of fiery white footprints. I recognized them immediately – each person leaves distinctive prints.

These belonged to my grandfather, Leavenworth Smedry. Australia herself trailed a set of puffy pink prints. Kaz's were the blue footprints, mixing with my own whitish ones, glowing in front of the hut where we'd inspected the day before. I could also see Bastille's red ones crossing the area several times, and since I hadn't known Draulin very long – and she wasn't related to me – there were only a few of her gray ones, as they disappeared rather quickly.

'See?' Australia asked again, nodding quickly. As she did so, her mustache began to fall free. 'None of us gives off prints like those – though yours are close.'

Kaz had joined us. 'They belong to your father,' I said to him.

He nodded. 'Where do they lead?'

I began to walk, following the prints. Kaz and Australia followed as I made my way around the outside of the hut. Grandpa had inspected the place, just like we had. I peeked inside and noted that the prints led to one corner of the hut, then turned and walked down the stairs into the darkness.

'He went in,' I said.

Kaz sighed. 'So they're both down there.'

I nodded. 'Although, my father must have come this way too long ago for his prints to have remained. We should have thought of using the Tracker's Lenses earlier! I feel like an idiot.'

Kaz shrugged. 'We've found the prints. That's what's important.'

'So, I did something good, right?' Australia asked.

I glanced at her. Her head had begun to sprout her normal dark hair, and her face looked like some kind of hybrid between hers and Grandpa Smedry's. While seeing her before had been amusing, now she was downright creepy.

'Um, yeah,' I said. 'You did a great job. I can follow these prints, and we'll find my grandfather. Then, at least, we'll know where *one* of them is.'

Australia nodded. Even between the times I'd glanced at her, she'd grown to look more like herself, though she seemed sad.

What? I thought. *She made a great discovery. Without her, we wouldn't have . . .*

Australia had made the discovery because she'd had the Tracker's Lenses. Now I'd taken them back and was ready to charge off after Grandfather. I took off the Tracker's Lenses. 'Why don't you keep these, Australia?'

'Really?' she said, perking up.

'Sure,' I said. 'You can lead us to Grandpa Smedry just as well as I can.'

She smiled eagerly, taking them back. 'Thank you so much!' She rushed outside, following the prints back the way they had come, apparently to see if Grandpa Smedry had visited any other places.

Kaz regarded me. 'I may have misjudged you, kid.'

I shrugged. 'She hasn't had much luck being an Oculator. I figured I shouldn't take away the only pair of Lenses that she's been able to use effectively.'

Kaz smiled, nodding in approval. 'You've got a good heart. A Smedry heart. Of course, not as good as a *short person's* heart, but that's to be expected.'

I raised an eyebrow.

'Reason number one hundred and twenty-seven. Short people have smaller bodies, but regular-size hearts. That gives us a larger ratio of heart to flesh – making us, of course, far more compassionate than big people.' He winked, then sauntered out of the room.

I shook my head, moving to follow, then stopped. I glanced at the corner, where the footprints had lead, then walked over and fished around in the dirt.

There, covered by small leaves and placed in a little hollow in the ground, was a small velvet pouch. I pulled it open and to my surprise found a pair of Lenses inside, along with the note.

Alcatraz! it read.

I was too late to stop your father from going down into the Library. I fear for the worst! He's always been the curious type and might be foolish enough to exchange his soul for information. I'm only a few days behind him, but the Library of Alexandria is a terrible maze of passages and corridors. I'm hoping that I'll be able to find him and stop him before he does anything foolish.

I'm sorry I couldn't meet you in the airport. This seemed more important. Besides, I have the feeling you can handle things on your own.

If you're reading this, then you didn't go to Nalhalla like you should have. Ha! I knew you wouldn't. You're a Smedry! I've left you a pair of Discerner's Lenses, which should be of use to you. They'll let you tell how old something is, just by looking at it.

Try not to break anything too valuable if you come down below. The Curators can be a rather unpleasant bunch. Comes from being dead, I suppose. Don't let them trick you into taking one of their books.

Love,

Grandpa Smedry

P.S. If that crazy son of mine Kazan is there, smack him on the head for me.

I lowered the note, then pulled out the Lenses. I quickly swapped them on, then glanced about the hut. They put a glow about anything I focused on – a kind of whitish shine, like you might get from sunlight reflecting off of something very pale. Except the shine was different for different objects. Most of the boards in the hut were actually downright dull, while the velvet pouch in my hand was rather bright.

Age, I thought. *They tell me how old something is – the boards were created and put there long ago. The pouch was made recently.*

I frowned to myself. Why couldn't he have left me another pair of Firebringer's Lenses? True, I'd broken the first pair – but that sort of thing tended to happen a lot around me.

The thing is, Grandpa Smedry tended to place little value on offensive Lenses. He thought information was a far better weapon.

Personally, I felt that being able to shoot superheated beams of light from your eyes was far more useful than being able to tell how old something was. But, I figured I would take what I was given.

I left the hut, walking over to the others, who were talking about Australia's discovery. They looked up as I approached, waiting for me again, like they had before.

Waiting for leadership.

Why look to me? I thought with annoyance. *I don't know what I'm doing. I don't even want to be in charge.*

'Lord Smedry,' Draulin said, 'should we wait for your grandfather, or should we go in after him?'

I glanced down at the pouch and was annoyed to find that the strings had unraveled as I was walking. My Talent, acting up again. 'I don't know,' I said.

The others looked at one another. That hadn't been the response they'd been expecting.

Grandpa Smedry obviously wanted me to lead the group into the Library. But what if I gave the order to go down below, and something went wrong? What if someone got hurt or got captured? Wouldn't that be my fault?

But, what if my father and Grandpa Smedry really needed help?

That's the problem with being a leader. It's all about choices – and choices are *never* very much fun. If someone gives you a candy bar, you're excited. But, if someone offers you two *different* candy bars and tells you that you can have only one, what then? Whichever one you take, you'll feel that you missed out on the other one.

And I *like* candy bars. What about when you have to choose between two terrible things? Did I wait, or lead my group down into danger? That was like having to choose to either eat a tarantula or a bunch of tacks. Neither option is very appealing – both make you sick to your stomach, and both are tough to choke down without catsup.

Personally, I like it much better when someone else does the decision making. That way you have legitimate grounds to whine and complain. I tend to find both whining and complaining quite interesting and amusing, though sometimes – unfortunately – it's hard to choose which one of the two I want to do.

Sigh. Life can be so tough sometimes.

'I don't want to make that decision,' I complained. 'Why are you all looking at me?'

'You're the lead Oculator, Lord Smedry,' Draulin said.

'Yeah, but I've only known about Oculators for three months!'

'Ah, but you're a Smedry,' Kaz said.

'Yes, but ...' I trailed off. Something was wrong. The others looked at me, but I ignored them, focusing on what I was feeling.

'What's he doing?' Australia whispered. By now, she'd gone back to looking just like her old self, though her hair was a bit messy from sleep.

'I don't know,' Kaz whispered back.

'Do you think that last comment was him swearing, do you?' she whispered. 'Hushlanders like to talk about our posteriors ...'

He was coming.

I could feel it. Oculators can sense when other Oculators are using Lenses nearby. It's something built in to us, just like our ability to activate Lenses.

The sense of wrongness I felt, it was like that of someone activating a Lens. But, it was twisted and dark. Frightening.

It meant someone was activating a Lens nearby that had been created in a terrible way. The hunter had found us. I spun, searching out the source of the feeling, causing the others to jump.

There he was. Standing atop a hill a short distance away, one arm too long for his body, staring down at us with his twisted face. All was silent for a moment.

Then he began to run.

Draulin cursed, whipping out her sword.

'No!' I said, running toward the hut. 'We're going in!'

Draulin didn't question. She'd just nodded, waiting for the others to go first. We dashed across the ground, Kaz pulling out a pair of Warrior's Lenses and slipping them on. His speed immediately increased, and he was able to keep up with us despite his short legs.

I reached the hut, waving Kaz and Australia inside. Bastille had taken a detour and was in the process of grabbing one of the packs.

'Bastille!' I yelled. 'There isn't time!'

Draulin was backing toward us; she glanced at Bastille, then at the Scrivener's Bone. He had crossed half the distance to us, and I saw something flash in his hand. A line of whitish blue frost shot from it toward me.

I yelped, ducking into the hut. The structure shook as the burst of cold hit it, and one wall started to freeze.

Bastille skidded in a second later. 'Alcatraz,' she said, puffing. 'I don't like this.'

'What?' I asked. 'Leaving your mom out there?'

'No, she can care for herself. I mean going down into the Library in a rush, without planning.'

Something hit the frozen wall, and it shattered. Bastille cursed and I cried out, falling backward.

Through the opening I could see the hunter dashing toward me. After freezing the wall, he'd thrown a rock to break it.

Draulin burst in through the half-broken door. 'Down!' she said, waving her sword toward the stairs, then bringing it back up to block a ray from the Frostbringer's Lens.

I glanced at Bastille.

'I've heard terrible things about this place, Alcatraz,' she said.

'No time for that now,' I decided, scrambling to my feet, heart thumping. I gritted my teeth, then charged down the steps toward the darkness, Bastille and Draulin following close behind.

All went black. It was like I had passed through a gateway beyond which light could not penetrate. I felt a sudden dizziness, and I fell to my knees.

'Bastille?' I called into the darkness.

No response.

'Kaz! Australia! Draulin!'

My voice didn't even echo back to me.

I'll take one chocolate bar and a handful of tacks, please. Anyone got any catsup?

9

I would like to try an experiment. Get out some paper and write a 0 on it. Then I want you to go down a line and put a 0 there. You see, the 0 is a magic number, as it is – well – 0. You can't get better than that! Now, on the next one, 0 isn't enough. 7 is the number to put here. Why isn't the 0 good enough here? 0 is not magical now. Once great, the 0 had been reduced to being nonsense. Now, take your paper and throw it away, then turn this book sideways.

Look closely at the paragraph above this one. (Or, uh, I guess since you turned the book sideways it's the paragraph *beside* this one.) Regardless, you might be able to see a face in the numbers in the paragraph – 0s form the eyes, the 7 is a nose, and a line of 0s form the mouth. It's smiling at you because you're holding your book sideways, and – as everyone knows – that's not the way to read books. In fact, how are you reading this paragraph, anyway? Turn the book around. You look silly.

Oh, very clever. Now you've got it upside down.

There. That's better. Anyway, I believe I talked in my last book about how first impressions are often wrong. You may have had the impression that I was done talking about first impressions. You were wrong. Imagine that.

There's so much more to be learned here. It's not just people's *first* impressions that are often wrong. Many of the ideas we have thought and believed for a long time are, in fact, dead wrong. For instance, I believed for years that Librarians were my friends. Some people believe that asparagus tastes good. Others don't buy this book because they think it won't be interesting.

Wrong, wrong, and so wrong. In my experience, I've found it best not to judge what I *think* I'm seeing until I've had enough time to study and learn. Something that appears to make no sense may, actually, be brilliant. (Like my art in paragraph one.)

Remember that. It might be important somewhere else in this book.

I forced myself to my feet in the complete darkness. I looked about, but of course that did no good. I called out again. No response.

I shivered in the darkness. Now, it wasn't just dark down there. It was *dark*. Dark like I'd been swallowed by a whale, then that whale had been eaten by a bigger whale, then that bigger whale had gotten lost in a deep cave, which had then been thrown into a black hole.

It was so dark I began to fear that I'd been struck blind. I was therefore overjoyed when I caught a glimmer of light. I turned toward it, relieved.

'Thank the first sands,' I exclaimed. 'It's—'

I choked off. The light was coming from the flames burning in the sockets of a bloodred skull.

I cried out, stumbling away, and my back hit a rough, dusty wall. I moved along it, scrambling in the darkness, but ran forehead first into another wall at the corner. Trapped, I spun around, watching the skull grow closer. The fires in its eyes soon illuminated the creature's robe-like cloak and thin skeleton arms. The whole body – skull, cloak, even the flames – seemed faintly translucent.

I had met my first Curator of Alexandria. I fumbled, reaching into my jacket, remembering for the first time that I was carrying Lenses.

Unfortunately, in the darkness, I couldn't tell which pocket was which, and I was too nervous to count properly.

I pulled out a random pair of spectacles, hoping I'd grabbed the Windstormer's Lenses. I shoved them on.

The Curator glowed with a whitish light. *Great*, I thought. *I know how old it is. Maybe I can bake it a birthday cake.*

The Curator said something to me, but it was in a strange, raspy language that I didn't understand.

'Uh ... I missed that ...,' I said, fumbling for a different pair of Lenses. 'Could you repeat yourself ... ?'

It spoke again, getting closer. I whipped out another pair of Lenses and put them on, focusing on the creature and hoping to blow it backward with a gust of wind. I was pretty sure I'd gotten the right pocket this time.

I was wrong, of course.

'... visitor to the great Library of Alexandria,' the thing hissed, 'you must pay the price of entry.'

The Lenses of Rashid – Translator's Lenses. Now, not only did I know how old it was, I could understand its demonic voice as it sucked out my soul. I made a mental note to speak sternly with my grandfather about the kinds of Lenses he gave me.

'The price,' the creature said, stepping up to me.

'Uh ... I seem to have left my wallet outside ...,' I said, fumbling in my jacket for another pair of Lenses.

'Cash does not interest us,' another voice whispered.

I glanced to the side, where another Curator – with burning eyes and a red skull – was floating toward me. With the extra light, I could see that neither creature had legs. Their cloaks just kind of trailed off into nothingness at the bottoms.

'Then, what do you want?' I asked, gulping.

'We want ... your paper.'

I blinked. 'Excuse me?'

'Anything you have written down,' a third creature said, approaching. 'All who enter the Library of Alexandria must give up their books, their notes, and their writings so that we may copy them and add them to our collection.'

'Okay ... ,' I said. 'That sounds fair enough.'

My heart continued to race, as if it refused to believe that a bunch of undead monsters with flames for eyes weren't going to kill me. I pulled out everything I had – which only included the note from Grandpa Smedry, a gum wrapper, and a few American dollars.

They took it all, plucking them from me and leaving my hands feeling icy and cold. Curators, it might be noted, give off a freezing chill. Because of this, they never need ice for their drinks. Unfortunately, since they're undead spirits, they can't really drink soda. It's one of the great ironies of our world.

'That's all I have,' I said, shrugging.

'Liar,' one hissed.

That isn't the type of thing one likes to hear from undead spirits. 'No,' I said honestly. 'That's it!'

I felt the freezing hands on my body, and I cried out. Despite looking translucent, the things had quite firm grips. They spun me about, then ripped the tag from my shirt and from my jeans.

Then, they just backed away. 'You want *those*?' I asked.

'All writing must be surrendered,' one of the creatures said. 'The purpose of the Library is to collect all knowledge ever written down.'

'Well, you won't get there very fast by copying down the tags off T-shirts,' I grumbled.

'Do not question our methods, mortal.'

I shivered, realizing it probably wasn't a good idea to sass the soul-sucking monster with a burning skull for a head. In that way, soul-sucking monsters with burning skulls are a lot like teachers. (I understand your confusion; I get them mixed up too.)

With that, the three spirits began to drift away.

'Wait,' I said, anxious not to return to the darkness. 'What about my friends? Where are they?'

One of the spirits turned back. 'They have been separated from you. All must be alone when they enter the Library.' It drifted closer. 'Have you come seeking knowledge? We can provide it for you. Anything you wish. Any book, any volume, any tome. Anything that has been written, we can provide. You need but ask ...'

The robed body and burning skull drifted around me, voice subtle and inviting as it whispered. 'You can know anything. Including, perhaps, where your father is.'

I spun toward the creature. 'You know that?'

'We can provide some information,' it said. 'You need but ask to check out the volume.'

'And the cost?'

The skull seemed to smile, if that was possible. 'Cheap.'

'My soul?'

The smile deepened.

'No, thank you,' I said, shuddering.

'Very well,' the Curator said, drifting away.

Suddenly, lamps on the walls flickered to life, lighting the room. The lamps were little oil-filled containers that looked like the kind you'd expect a genie to hold in an old Arabian story. I didn't really care; I was just glad for the light. By it, I could see that I stood in a dusty room with old brick walls. There were several hallways leading away from the room, and there were no doors in the doorways.

Great, I thought. *Of all the times to give away my Tracker's Lenses . . .*

I picked a door at random and walked out into the hallway, immediately struck by how vast it was. It seemed to extend forever. Lamps hung from pillars that – extending into the distance – looked like a flickering, haunting runway on a deserted airfield. To my right and to my left were shelves filled with scrolls.

There were thousands upon thousands of them, all with the same dusty, catacomb-like feel. I felt a little bit daunted. Even my own footsteps sounded too loud as they echoed in the vast chamber.

I continued for a time, stepping softly, studying the rows and rows of cobwebbed scrolls. It was as if I were in a massive crypt – except, instead of bodies, this was the place where manuscripts were placed to die.

'They seem endless,' I whispered to myself, looking up. The pockets of scrolls reached all the way up the walls to the ceiling some twenty feet above. 'I wonder how many there are.'

'You could know, if you wanted,' a voice whispered. I spun to find a Curator hovering behind me. How long had it been there?

'We have a list,' it whispered, floating closer, its skull face looking more shadowed now that there was external light. 'You could read it, if you want. Check it out from the Library.'

'No, thank you,' I said, backing away.

The Curator remained where it was. It didn't make any threatening moves, so I continued onward, occasionally glancing over my shoulder.

You may be wondering how the Curators can claim to have every book ever written. I have it on good authority that they have many means of locating books and adding them to their collection. For instance, they have a tenuous deal with the Librarians who control the Hushlands.

In the United States alone, there are thousands upon thousands of books published every year. Most of these are either 'literature,' books about people who don't do anything, or they are silly fiction works about dreadfully dull topics, such as dieting.

(There *is* a purpose to all of these useless books produced in America. They are, of course, intended to make people self-conscious about themselves so that the Librarians can better control them. The quickest way I've found to feel bad about yourself is to read a self-help book, and the second quickest is to read a depressing literary work intended to make you feel terrible about humanity in general.)

Anyway, the point is that the Librarians publish hundreds of thousands of books each year. What happens to all of these books? Logically, we should all be overwhelmed by them. Buried in a tsunami of texts, gasping for breath as we drown in an endless sea of stories about girls with eating disorders.

The answer is the Library of Alexandria. The Librarians ship their excess books there in exchange for the promise that the Curators won't go out into the Hushlands and seek the volumes themselves. It's really a shame. After all, the Curators – being skeletons – could probably teach us a few things about dieting.

I continued to wander the musty halls of the Library, feeling rather small and insignificant compared with the massive pillars and rows and rows and rows and rows and rows and rows and rows and rows and rows and rows and rows and rows of books.

Occasionally, I passed other hallways that branched off the first. They looked identical to the one I was walking in, and I soon realized that I had no idea which way I was going. I glanced back-ward, and was disappointed to realize that the only place in the Library that seemed clean of dust was the floor. There would be no footprints to guide me back the way I had come, and I had no bread crumbs to leave as a trail. I considered using belly-button lint, but decided that would not only be gross, but wasteful as well. (Do you have any idea how much that stuff is worth?)

Besides, there wouldn't be much point in leaving a trail in the first place. I didn't know where I was going, true, but I also didn't know where I'd been. I sighed. 'I don't suppose there's a map of this place anywhere?' I asked, turning back to the Curator who followed a short distance behind.

'Of course there is,' he said in a phantom voice.

'Really? Where is it?'

'I can fetch it for you.' The skull smiled. 'You'll have to check it out, though.'

'Great,' I said flatly. 'I can give you my soul to discover the way out, then not be able to use the way out because you'd own my soul.'

'Some have done so before,' the ghost said. 'Traveling the library stacks can be maddening. To many, it is worth the cost of their soul to finally see the solution.'

I turned away. The Curator, however, continued talking. 'In fact, you'd be surprised the people who come here, searching for the solutions to simple puzzles.' The creature's voice grew louder as it spoke, and it floated closer to me. 'Some old women grow very attached to a modern diversion known as the "Crossword Puzzle." We've had several come here, looking for answers. We have their souls now.'

I frowned, eyeing the thing.

'Many would rather give up what remains of their lives than live in ignorance,' it said. 'This is only one of the many ways that we gain souls. In truth, some do not care which book they get, for once they become one of us, they can read other books in the Library. By then, of course, their soul is bound here, and they can never leave or share that knowledge. However, the endless knowledge appeals to them.'

Why was it talking so loudly? It seemed to be pushing up against me a bit, its coldness prodding me on. As if it were trying to force me to walk faster.

In a moment I realized what was going on. The Curator was a fish. If that were the case, what were the shoes? (Metaphorically speaking, of course. Read back a few chapters if you've forgotten.)

I closed my eyes, focusing. There, I heard it. A quiet voice, calling for help. It sounded like Bastille.

I snapped my eyes open and ran down a side hallway. The ghost cursed in an obscure language – my Translator's Lenses kindly let me know the meaning of the word, and I will be equally kind here in not repeating it, since it involved eggbeaters – and followed me.

I found her hanging from the ceiling between two pillars in the hallway, letting out a few curses of her own. She was tangled up in a strange network of ropes; some of them twisted around her legs, others held her arms. It seemed that her struggles were only making things worse.

'Bastille?' I asked.

She stopped struggling, silver hair hanging down around her face. 'Smedry?'

'How did you get up there?' I asked, noticing a Curator hanging in the air upside down beside her. Its robe didn't seem to respond to gravity – but, then, that's rather common for ghosts, I would think.

'Does it matter?' Bastille snapped, flailing about, apparently trying to shake herself free.

'Stop struggling. You're only making it worse.'

She huffed, but stopped.

'Are you going to tell me what happened?' I asked.

'Trap,' she said, twisting about a bit. 'I triggered a trip wire, and the next moment I was hanging up here. If that wasn't bad enough, the burning-eyed freak here keeps whispering to me that he can give me a book that will show me how to escape. It'll just cost my soul!'

'Where's your dagger?' I asked.

'In my pack.'

I saw it on the floor a short distance away. I walked over, watching out for trip wires. Inside, I found her crystalline dagger, along with some foodstuffs and – I was surprised to remember – the boots with Grappler's Glass on the bottoms. I smiled.

'I'll be right there,' I said, putting the boots on and activating the glass. Then, I proceeded to try walking up the side of the wall.

If you've never attempted this, I heartily recommend it. There's a very nice rush of wind, accompanied by an inviting feeling of vertigo, as you fall backward and hit the ground. You also look something like an idiot – but for most of us, that's nothing new.

'What are you *doing?*' Bastille asked.

'Trying to walk up to you,' I said, sitting up and rubbing my head.

'Grappler's Glass, Smedry. It only sticks to other pieces of glass.'

Ah, right, I thought. Now this might have seemed like a very stupid thing to forget, but you can't blame me. I was suffering from having fallen to the ground and a hit to the head, after all.

'Well, how am I going to get up to you, then?'

'You could just throw me the dagger.'

I looked up skeptically. The ropes seemed wound pretty tightly around her. They, however, were connected to the pillars.

'Hang on,' I said, walking up to one of the pillars.

'Alcatraz ...,' she said, sounding uncertain. 'What are you doing?'

I laid my hand against the pillar, then closed my eyes. I'd destroyed the jet by just touching the smoke ... could I do something like that here too? Guide my Talent up the pillar to the ropes?

'Alcatraz!' Bastille said. 'I don't want to get squished by a bunch of falling pillars. Don't ...'

I released a burst of breaking power.

'Gak!'

She said this last part as her ropes – which were connected to the pillars – frayed and fell to pieces. I opened my eyes in time to see her grab the one remaining whole piece of rope and swing down to the ground, landing beside me, puffing slightly.

She looked up. The pillar didn't fall on us. I removed my hand.

She cocked her head, then regarded me. 'Huh.'

'Not bad, eh?'

She shrugged. 'A real man would have climbed up and cut me down with the dagger. Come on. We've got to find the others.'

I rolled my eyes, but took her thank-you for what it was worth. I walked over as she stuffed the boots and dagger back in her pack, then threw it over her shoulder. We walked down the hallway for a moment, then spun as we heard a crashing sound.

The pillar had finally decided to topple over, throwing up broken chips of stone as it hit the ground. The entire hallway shook from the impact.

A wave of dust from the rubble puffed over us. Bastille gave me a suffering look, then sighed and continued walking.

10

You may wonder why I hate fantasy novels so much. Or, maybe you don't. That doesn't really matter, because I'm going to tell you anyway.

(Of course, if you want to know how the book ends, you could just skip to the last page – but I wouldn't recommend that. It will prove very disturbing to your psyche.)

Anyway, let's talk about fantasy novels. First, you have to understand that when I say 'fantasy novels' I mean books about dieting or literature or people living during the Great Depression. Fantasy novels, then, are books that don't include things like glass dragons, ghostly Curators, or magical Lenses.

I hate fantasy novels. Well, that's not true. I don't actually really *hate* them. I just get annoyed by what they've done to the Hushlands.

People don't read anymore. And, when they do, they don't read books like this one, but instead read books that depress them, because those books are seen as important. Somehow, the Librarians have successfully managed to convince most people in the Hushlands that they shouldn't read anything that isn't boring.

It comes down to Biblioden the Scrivener's great vision for the world – a vision in which people never do anything abnormal, never dream, and never experience anything strange. His minions teach people to stop reading fun books, and instead focus on fantasy novels. That's what I call them, because those books keep people trapped. Keep them inside the nice little fantasy that they consider to be the 'real' world. A fantasy that tells them they don't need to try something new.

After all, trying new things can be difficult.

'We need a plan,' Bastille said as we walked the corridors of the Library. 'We can't just keep wandering around in here.'

'We need to find Grandpa Smedry,' I said, 'or my father.'

'We also need to find Kaz and Australia, not to mention my mother.' She grimaced a bit at that last part.

And ... that's not everything either, I thought. *My father came in here for a reason. He came searching for something.*

Something very important.

I'd found a communication from him several months back – it had come with the package that had contained the Sands of Rashid. My father had sounded tense in his letter. He'd been excited, but worried too.

He'd discovered something dangerous. The Sands of Rashid – the Translator's Lenses – had only been the beginning. They were a step toward uncovering something much greater. Something that had frightened my father.

He'd spent thirteen years searching for whatever the something was. That trail had ended here, at the Library of Alexandria. Could he really have come because he'd grown frustrated? Had he traded his soul for the answers he sought, just so that he could finally stop searching?

I shivered, glancing at the Curators, who floated behind us. 'Bastille,' I said. 'You said that one of them spoke to you?'

'Yeah,' she said. 'Kept trying to get me to borrow a book.'

'It spoke to you in English?'

'Well, Nalhallan,' she said. 'But it's pretty much the same thing. Why?'

'Mine spoke to me in a language I didn't understand.'

'Mine did that at first too,' she said. 'Several of them surrounded me and searched through my possessions. They grabbed the supply list and several of the labels off of the foodstuffs. Then, they left – all except for that one behind us. It continued to jabber at me in that infuriating language. It was only after I'd been caught that it started speaking Nalhallan.'

I glanced again at the Curators. *They use traps*, I thought.

But not ones that kill – ones that keep people tangled up. They separate everyone who comes in, then they make each one wander the hallways, lost. They talk to us in a language they know we don't understand when they could easily speak in English instead.

This whole place is all about annoying people. The Curators are trying to make us frustrated. All so that we'll give up and take one of the books they're offering.

'So,' Bastille said. 'What's our plan?'

I shrugged. 'Why ask me?'

'Because you're in charge, Alcatraz,' she said, sighing. 'What's your problem, anyway? Half the time you seem ready to give orders and charge about. The other half of the time, you complain that you don't want to be the one who has to make the decisions.'

I didn't answer. To be honest, I hadn't really figured out my feelings either.

'Well?' she asked.

'First, we find Kaz, Australia, and your mother.'

'Why would you need to find me?' Kaz asked. 'I mean, I'm right here.'

We both jumped. And, of course, there he was. Wearing his bowler and rugged jacket, hands in his pockets, smiling at us impishly.

'Kaz!' I said. 'You found us!'

'You were lost,' he said, shrugging. 'If I'm lost, it's easier for me to find someone else who is lost – since abstractly, we're both in the same place.'

I frowned, trying to make sense of that. Kaz looked around, eyeing the pillars and their archways. 'Not at all like I imagined it.'

'Really?' Bastille asked. 'It looks pretty much like I figured it would.'

'I expected them to take better care of their scrolls and books,' Kaz said.

'Kaz,' I said. 'You found us, right?'

'Uh, what did I just say, kid?'

'Can you find Australia too?'

He shrugged. 'I can try. But, we'll have to be careful. Quite nearly got myself caught in a trap a little ways back. I tripped a wire, and a large hoop swung out of the wall and tried to grab me.'

'What happened?' Bastille said.

He laughed. 'It went right over my head. Reason number fifteen, Bastille: Short people make smaller targets!'

I just shook my head.

'I'll scout ahead,' Bastille said. 'Looking for trip wires. Then the two of you can follow. Kaz will engage his Talent at each intersection and pick the next way to go. Hopefully, his Talent will lead us to Australia.'

'Sounds like a good enough plan for now,' I said.

Bastille put on her Warrior's Lenses, then took off, moving very carefully down the hallway. Kaz and I were left standing there with nothing to do.

Something occurred to me. 'Kaz,' I said. 'How long did it take you to learn to use your Talent?'

'Ha!' he said. 'You make it sound like I *have* learned to use it, kid.'

'But, you're better with yours than I am with mine.' I glanced back at the rubbled pillar, which was still visible in the distance behind us.

'Talents are tough, I'll admit,' he said, following my gaze. 'You do that?'

I nodded.

'You know, it was the sound of that pillar falling that let me know I was close to you. Sometimes, what looks like a mistake turns out to be kind of useful.'

'I know that, but I still have trouble. Every time I think I've got my Talent figured out, I break something I didn't intend to.'

The shorter man leaned against a pillar on the side of the hallway. 'I know what you mean, Al. I spent most of my youth getting lost. I couldn't be trusted to go to the bathroom on my own because I'd end up in Mexico. Once, I stranded your father and myself on an island alone for two weeks because I couldn't figure out how to make the blasted Talent work.'

He shook his head. 'The thing is, the more powerful a Talent is, the harder it is to control. You and I – like your father and grandfather – have prime Talents. Right on the Incarnate Wheel, fairly pure. They're bound to give us lots of trouble.'

I cocked my head. 'Incarnate Wheel?'

He seemed surprised. 'Nobody's explained it to you?'

'The only one I've really talked to about Talents is my grandfather.'

'Yeah, but what about in school?'

'Ah ... no,' I said. 'I went to Librarian school, Kaz. I did hear a lot about the Great Depression, though.'

Kaz snorted. 'Fantasy books. Those Librarians ...'

He sighed, squatting down by the floor and pulling out a stick. He grabbed a handful of dust from the corner, threw it out on the floor, then drew a circle in it.

'There have been a *lot* of Smedries over the centuries,' he said, 'and a lot of Talents. Many of them tend to be similar, in the long run. There are four kinds: Talents that affect space, time, knowledge, and the physical world.' He drew a circle in the dust, then split it into four pieces.

'Take my Talent, for instance,' he continued. 'I change things in space. I can get lost, then get found again.'

'What about Grandpa Smedry?'

'Time,' Kaz said. 'He arrives late to things. Australia, however, has a Talent that can change the physical world – in this case, her own shape.' He wrote her name in the dust on the wheel. 'Her Talent is fairly specific, and not as broad as your grandfather's. For instance, there was a Smedry a couple of centuries back who could look ugly *any* time he wanted, not just when he woke up in the morning. Others have been able to change anyone's appearance, not just their own. Understand?'

I shrugged. 'I guess so.'

'The closer the Talent gets to its purest form, the more powerful it is,' Kaz said. 'Your grandfather's Talent is very pure – he can manipulate time in a lot of different circumstances. Your father and I have very similar Talents – I can get lost and Attica can lose things – and both are flexible. Siblings often have similar powers.'

'What about Sing?' I asked.

'Tripping. That's what we call a knowledge Talent – he knows how to do something normal with extraordinary ability. Like Australia, though, his power isn't very flexible. In that case, we put them at the edge of the wheel near the rim. Talents like my father's, which are more powerful, we place closer to the center.'

I nodded slowly. 'So ... what does this have to do with me?'

Bastille had returned, and was watching with interest.

'Well, it's hard to say,' Kaz said. 'You're getting into some deep philosophy now, kid. There are those who argue that the Breaking Talent is simply a physical-world Talent, but one that is very versatile and very powerful.'

He met my eyes, then poked his stick into the very center of the circle. 'There are others who argue that the Breaking Talent is much more. It seems to be able to do things that affect all four areas. Legends say that one of your ancestors – one of only two others to have this Talent – broke time and space together forming a little bubble where nothing aged.

'Other records speak of breakings equally marvelous. Breakings that change people's memory or their abilities. What is it to "break" something? What can you change? How far can the Talent go?'

He raised his stick, pointing at me. 'Either way, kid, *that's* why it's so hard for you to control. To be honest, even after centuries of studying them, we really don't understand the Talents. I don't know that we ever will, though your father was very keen on trying.'

Kaz stood up, dusting off his hands. 'And that's why he came here, I guess.'

'How do you know so much?' I asked.

Kaz raised an eyebrow. 'What? You think I spend all my time making up witty lists and getting lost on my way to the bathroom? I have a job, kid.'

'Lord Kazan's a scholar,' Bastille said. 'Focusing on arcane theory.'

'Great,' I said, rolling my eyes. 'Another professor.' After Grandpa Smedry, Sing, and Quentin, I was half convinced that everyone who lived in the Free Kingdoms was one kind of academic or another.

Kaz shrugged. 'It's a Smedry trait, kid. We tend to be very interested in information. Either way, your father was the real genius – I'm just a humble philosopher. Bastille, how's the pathway up ahead look?'

'Clean,' she said. 'No trip wires that I found.'

'Great,' he said.

'You actually seem a bit disappointed.'

Kaz shrugged. 'Traps are interesting. They're always a surprise, kind of like presents on your birthday.'

'Except these presents might decapitate you,' Bastille said flatly.

'All part of the fun, Bastille.'

She sighed, shooting me a glance over her sunglasses. *Smedries*, it seemed to say. *All the same.*

I smiled at her, and nodded for us to get moving. Kaz took the lead. As we walked, I noticed that a couple of Curators were busy copying down Kaz's drawing. I turned away, then jumped as I found a Curator hanging beside me.

'The Incarna knew about Smedry Talents,' the thing whispered. 'We have a book here, one of theirs, written millennia ago. It explains exactly where the Talents first came from. We have one of only two copies that still exist.'

It hovered closer.

'You can have it,' the creature whispered. 'Check it out, if you wish.'

I snorted. 'I'm not *that* curious. I'd be a fool to give you my soul for information I could never use.'

'Ah, but maybe you *could* use it,' the Curator said. 'What could you accomplish if you understood your Talent, young Smedry? Would you, perhaps, have enough skill to gain your freedom from us? Get your soul back? *Break* out of our prison ...'

This gave me pause. It made a twisted, frightening sense. Maybe I *could* trade my soul away, then learn how to free myself using the book I gained. 'It's possible, then?' I asked. 'Someone could break free after having been turned into a Curator?'

'Anything is possible,' the creature whispered, focusing its burning sockets on me. 'Why don't you try? You could learn so much. Things people haven't known for millennia ...'

It is a testament to the subtle trickery of the Curators that I actually thought, for just a moment, about trading my soul for a book on arcane theory.

And then I came to my senses. I couldn't even control my Talent as it was. What made me think that I, of all people, would be able to use it to outsmart a group as ancient and powerful as the Curators of Alexandria?

I chuckled and shook my head, causing the Curator to back away in obvious displeasure. I hurried my pace, catching up with the others. Kaz walked in front, leading us as he had before, letting his Talent lose us and carry us toward Australia. Theoretically.

Indeed, as I walked, I swore that I could see the stacks of scrolls changing around us. It wasn't that they transformed or anything – yet, if I glanced at a stack, then turned away, then glanced back, I couldn't tell if it was actually the same one or not. Kaz's Talent was carrying us through the corridors without our being able to feel the change.

Something occurred to me. 'Kaz?'

The short man looked back, raising an eyebrow.

'So ... your Talent has lost us, right?'

'Yup,' he said.

'As we walk, we're moving through the Library hopping to different points, even though we feel like we're just walking down a corridor.'

'You've got it, kid. I've got to tell you – you're smarter than you look.'

I frowned. 'So, what exactly was the purpose of having Bastille scout ahead? Didn't we leave that corridor behind the moment you turned on your Talent?'

Kaz froze.

At that moment, I heard something click beneath me. I looked down with shock to see that I'd stepped directly onto a trip wire.

'Ah, wing nuts,' Kaz swore.

11

I must apologize for the beginning of that last chapter. My goal is to write a completely frivolous book, for if I actually say anything important, I run the risk of making people worship or respect me even more. Therefore, I should ask that you will do me a favor. Get out some scissors, and cut out the next few paragraphs in this chapter. Paste them over the beginning of the last chapter, hiding it away so that you never have to read its pretentious editorializing again.

Ready? Go.

Once there was a bunny. This bunny had a birthday party. It was the bestest birthday party ever. Because that was the day the bunny got a bazooka.

The bunny loved his bazooka. He blew up all sorts of things on the farm. He blew up the stable of Henrietta the Horse. He blew up the pen of Pugsly the Pig. He blew up the coop of Chuck the Chicken.

'I have the bestest bazooka ever,' the bunny said. Then the farm friends proceeded to beat him senseless and steal his bazooka. It was the happiest day of his life.

The end.

Epilogue: Pugsly the pig, now without a pen, was quite annoyed. When none of the others were looking, he stole the bazooka. He tied a bandana on his head and swore vengeance for what had been done to him.

'From this day on,' he whispered, raising the bazooka, 'I shall be known as *Hambo*.'

There. I feel much better. Now we can return to the story, refreshed and confident that you're reading the right kind of book.

I cringed, tense, looking down at my foot on the trip wire. 'So,' I said, glancing at Bastille, 'is it going to do any—

'Gak!'

At that moment, panels on the ceiling fell away dumping what seemed like a thousand buckets full of dark, sticky sludge on us. I tried to move out of the way, but I was far too slow. Even Bastille, with her enhanced Crystin speed, couldn't dodge fast enough.

It hit, covering us in a tarlike substance. I tried to yell, but the sound came out in a gurgle as the thick, black material got into my mouth. It had a rather unpleasant flavor. Kind of like a cross between bananas and tar, heavy on the tar.

I struggled and was frustrated to feel the goop suddenly harden. I was frozen in place, one eye open, the other closed, my mouth filled with hard tar, my nose – fortunately – unplugged.

'Great,' Bastille said. I could just barely see her, covered in hardened sludge a short distance away, stuck in a running posture. She'd had the sense to shade her face, so her eyes and mouth were uncovered – but her arm was glued to her forehead. 'Kaz, you stuck too?'

'Yeah,' said a muffled voice. 'I tried to lose myself, but it didn't work. We were already lost.'

'Alcatraz?' Bastille asked.

I made a grumbling noise through my nose.

'He looks all right,' Kaz said. 'He isn't going to be waxing eloquent anytime soon, though.'

'As if he ever does,' Bastille said, struggling.

Enough of this, I thought in annoyance, releasing my Talent into the goop. Nothing happened. There are, unfortunately, plenty of things that are resistant to Smedry Talents.

Several Curators glided across the floor to us, looking quite pleased with themselves. 'We can provide a book for you that will explain how to get out,' one said.

'You will find it very interesting,' said another.

'Shatter yourselves,' Bastille snapped, grunting again as she tried to get free. Nothing moved but her chin.

'What kind of offer is that?' Kaz demanded. 'We wouldn't be able to read the book like this!'

'We'd be happy to read it to you,' one of the others said. 'So that you would understand how to escape in the moments before your soul was taken.'

'Plus,' another whispered, 'you would have all of eternity to study. Surely that must appeal to you, a scholar. An eternity with the knowledge of the Library. All at your fingertips.'

'Never able to leave,' Kaz said. 'Trapped forever in this pit, forced to entice others into the trap.'

'Your brother thought the trade worthwhile,' one of them whispered.

What! I thought. *Father!*

'You lie,' Kaz said. 'Attica would never fall for one of your tricks!'

'We didn't have to trick him,' another whispered, floating close to me. 'He came quite willingly. All for a book. A single, special book.'

'What book?' Bastille asked.

The Curators fell silent, skull heads smiling. 'Will you trade your soul for that knowledge?'

Bastille began to swear, struggling harder. The Curators moved around her, speaking in a language that my Lenses told me was classical Greek.

If I could just get to my Windstormer's Lenses, I thought. *Perhaps I could blow some of this goop away.*

I couldn't even wiggle my fingers, though, let alone reach into my jacket.

If only my Talent would work! I focused, drawing forth all of the power I could, and released it into the goop. Yet, it refused to break or yield.

Something occurred to me. The goop was resistant, but what about the floor beneath me? I gathered my Talent again, then released it downward.

I strained, feeling the pulsings of energy run through my body and out my feet. I felt my shoes unravel, the rubber slipping free, the canvas falling apart. I felt the rock beneath my heels crumble.

But, that was ultimately useless, since my body was still held tightly by the goop. The ground fell away beneath me, but I didn't fall with it.

The Curator closest to me turned. 'Are you certain you don't want that book on Talents, young Oculator? Perhaps it would help you free yourself.'

Focus, I thought as the rest of the Curators continued to torment Bastille. *They said that there's a book on how to escape this goop. Well, that means there's a way out.*

I continued struggling, but that was obviously useless. If it was possible to break free with just muscles, then Bastille would manage to long before I did.

So, instead, I focused on the goop itself. What could I determine about it? The stuff in my mouth seemed slightly softer than the stuff around the outside of my body. Was there a reason for that? Spit, perhaps? Maybe the goop didn't harden when it was wet.

I began to drool out some saliva, trying to get it on the goop. Spit began to seep out of the top of my mouth, and down the front of the glob of goop on my face.

'Uh ... Alcatraz?' Bastille asked. 'You all right?'

I tried to grunt in a reassuring way. But, then, I've found that it's very hard to grunt eloquently when you're spitting.

After several minutes, I came to the unpleasant conclusion that the goop didn't dissolve in saliva. Unfortunately, now I was not only being held tightly by a sheet of hardened black tar, I'd also drooled all over the front of my shirt.

'Getting frustrated?' a Curator asked, hovering around me in a circle. 'How long will you struggle? You need not be able to speak. Simply blink three times if you want to trade your soul for the way out.'

I kept my eyes wide open. They began to dry out, which was appropriately ironic, considering the state of my shirt.

The Curator looked disappointed, but continued to hover. *Why bother with all of the cajoling?* I wondered. *We're in their power. Why not kill us? Why not just take our souls from us by force?*

That thought made me pause. If they hadn't done that already, then it probably meant that they *couldn't*. Which seemed to imply that they were bound by some kind of laws or a code or something.

My jaw was getting tired. It seemed an odd thing to think of. I was being held tightly in all places, and I was worried about my jaw? Was that because it wasn't being held as tightly as the rest? But, I'd already determined that. The goop in my mouth wasn't as hard.

So, uncertain what else to do, I bit down. Hard. Surprisingly, my teeth cut through the stuff, and the chunk of goop came off in my mouth. Suddenly, the entire blanket of it – the stuff covering me, Bastille, Kaz, and the floor – shuddered.

What? I thought. The stuff I'd bitten off immediately became liquid again, and I nearly choked as I was forced to swallow it. The piece in front of my face withdrew slightly after the bite, and I could still see it wiggling. Almost as if ... the entire blob were alive.

I shivered. Yet, I didn't have many options. Wiggling my head a bit – it was looser now that the stuff had retreated from my face – I snapped forward and took another bite out of the stuff. It shook and pulled farther away. I leaned over, and – spitting out the chunk of tarry-bananaish stuff – I took another bite.

The blanket of goop pulled back from me completely, like a shy dog that had been kicked. The metaphor seemed apt, and so I kicked it.

The blob shook, then retreated off of Bastille and Kaz, fleeing away down the corridor. I spit a few times, grimacing at the taste. Then I eyed the Curators. 'Perhaps you should train your traps a little better.'

They did not look pleased. Kaz, on the other hand, was smiling widely. 'Kid, I'm almost tempted to make you an official short person!'

'Thanks,' I said.

'Course, we'd have to cut your legs off at the knees,' Kaz said. 'But that would be a small price to pay!' He winked at me. I'm pretty sure that was a joke.

I shook my head, stepping out of the rubbled pocket I'd made in the floor with my Talent. My shoes barely hung to my feet, and I kicked them off, forced to walk barefoot.

Still, I'd gotten us free. I turned, smiling, to Bastille. 'Well, I believe that makes two traps I've saved you from.'

'Oh?' she said. 'And are we going to start a count of the ones you got me *into*, as well? Who was it who stepped on that trip wire again?'

I flushed.

'Any one of us could have tripped it, Bastille,' Kaz said, walking up to us. 'As fun as that was, I'm starting to think it might be a good idea if we didn't hit any more of those. We need to go more carefully.'

'You think?' Bastille asked flatly. 'The trick is, I can't scout ahead. Not if you're leading us with your Talent.'

'We'll just have to be more cautious, then,' Kaz said. I looked down at the trip wire, thinking about the danger. We couldn't afford to stumble into every one of those we came across. Who knew if we'd even be able to think of a way out of the next one?

'Kaz, Bastille, wait a second.' I reached into a pocket, pulling out my Lenses. I left the Windstormer's Lenses alone and put on the Discerner's Lenses – the ones that Grandpa Smedry had left for me up above.

Immediately, everything around me began to give off a faint glow, indicating how old it was. I looked down. Sure enough, the trip wire glowed far lighter than the stones or the scrolls around it. It was newer than the original construction of the building. I looked up, smiling. 'I think I've found a way around the problem.'

'Are those Discerner's Lenses?' Bastille asked.

I nodded.

'Where in the sands did you get a pair of those?'

'Grandpa Smedry left them for me,' I said. 'Outside, along with a note.' I frowned, glancing at the Curators. 'Speaking of which, didn't you say you'd return the writings you took from me?'

The creatures glanced at one another. Then, one of them approached, betraying a sullen look. The apparition bent down and set some things on the ground: copies of my tags, the wrapper that had been taken from me, and Grandpa Smedry's note. There were also copies of the money I'd given them – they were perfect replicas, except that they were colorless.

Great, I thought. *But I probably didn't need that anymore anyway.* I stooped down to gather the things, which all glowed brightly, since they all had been created brand new. Bastille took the note, looked it over with a frown, then handed it to Kaz.

'So, your father really is down here somewhere,' she said.

'Looks like it.'

'And ... the Curators claim he already gave up his soul.'

I fell silent. *They gave back my papers when I asked*, I thought, *and they keep trying to get us to agree to give away our souls, but don't take them by force. They're bound by rules.*

I should have realized this earlier. You see, everything is bound by rules. Society has laws, as does nature, as do people. Many of society's rules have to do with expectations – which I'll talk about later – and therefore can be bent. A lot of nature's laws, however are hard-set.

There are many more of these than you might expect. In fact, there are even natural laws relating to this book, my favorite of which is known as the Law of Pure Awesomeness. This law, of course, simply states that any book I write is awesome. I'm sorry, but it's a fact.

Who am I to argue with science?

'You,' I said, looking toward a Curator. 'Your kind have laws, don't they?'

The Curator paused. 'Yes,' it finally said. 'Do you want to read them? I can give you a book that explains them in detail.'

'No,' I said. 'No, I don't want to read about them. I want to hear about them. From you.'

The Curator frowned.

'You have to tell me, don't you?' I said, smiling.

'It is my privilege to do so,' the creature said. Then, it began to smile. 'Of course, I am going to have to tell them to you in their original language.'

'We are impressed that you speak ancient Greek,' another said. 'You are one who came to us prepared. There are few that do that, these days.'

'But,' another whispered, 'we doubt that you know how to speak Elder Faxdarian.'

Speak ancient Greek ... , I thought, confused. Then it occurred to me. *They don't know about my Translator's Lenses! They think that because I understood them back at the beginning, I must have known the language.*

'Oh, I don't know about that,' I said casually, swapping my Discerner's Lenses back for my Translator's Lenses. 'Try me.'

'Ha,' one of them said in a very odd, strange language – it consisted mostly of spitting sounds. Like always, the Translator's Lenses let me hear the words in English. 'The fool thinks he knows our language.'

'Give him the rules, then,' another hissed.

'First rule,' said the one in front of me. 'If anyone enters our domain bearing writing, we may separate them from their group and demand the writing be given to us. If they resist, we may take the writing, but we must return copies. We may hold these back for one hour but, unless the items are requested, can keep them from then on.

'Second rule, we may take the souls of those who enter, but we can do so only if the souls are offered freely and lawfully. Souls may be coerced, but not forced.

'Third rule, we may accept or reject a person's request for a soul contract. Once the contract is signed, we must provide the specific book requested, then refrain from taking their soul for the time specified in the contract. This time may not be longer than ten hours. If a person takes a book off its shelf without a contract, we may take their soul after ten seconds.'

I shivered. Ten seconds or ten hours, it didn't seem to matter much. You still lost your soul. Of course, in my experience, there's really only one book in all of the world that is worth your soul to read – and you're holding it right now.

I accept credit cards.

'Fourth rule,' the Curator continued. 'We cannot directly harm those who enter.'

Hence the traps, I thought. *Technically, when we trip those, we harm ourselves.* I continued to stare blankly ahead, acting as if I didn't understand a word they were saying.

'Fifth rule, when a person gives up their soul and becomes a Curator, we must deliver up their possessions to their kin, should a member of the family come to the Library and request such possessions.

'Sixth rule, and most important of them all. We are the protectors of knowledge and truth. We cannot lie, if asked a direct question.'

The Curator fell silent.

'That it?' I asked.

If you've never seen a group of undead Curators with flaming eyes jump into the air with surprise ... okay, I'm going to assume that you've never seen a group of undead Curators with flaming eyes jump into the air with surprise. Suffice it to say that the experience was quite amusing, in a creepy sort of way.

'He speaks our language!' one hissed.

'Impossible,' another said. 'Nobody outside the Library knows it.'

'Could he be Tharandes?'

'He would have died millennia ago!'

Bastille and Kaz were watching me. I winked at them.

'Translator's Lenses,' one of the Curators suddenly hissed. 'See!'

'Impossible,' another said. 'Nobody could have gathered the Sands of Rashid.'

'But he has ... ,' said a third. 'Yes, they must be Lenses of Rashid!'

The three ghosts looked even more amazed than they had before.

'What's happening?' Bastille whispered.

'I'll tell you in a minute.'

Based on the Curators' own rules, there was one way to discover if my father really had come to the Library of Alexandria and given up his soul. 'I am the son of Attica Smedry,' I said to the group of creatures. 'I've come here for his personal effects. Your own laws say you must provide them to me.'

There was a moment of silence.

'We cannot,' one of the Curators finally said.

I sighed in relief. If my father had come to the Library, then he hadn't given up his soul. The Curators didn't have his personal items.

'We cannot,' the Curator continued, skull teeth beginning to twist upward in an evil smile. 'Because we have already given them away!'

I felt a stab of shock. *No. It can't be*! 'I don't believe you,' I whispered.

'We cannot lie,' another said. 'Your father came to us, and he sold his soul to us. He only wanted three minutes to read the book, and then he was taken to become one of us. His personal items have already been claimed – someone did so this very day.'

'Who?' I demanded. 'Who claimed them? My grandfather?'

'No,' the Curator said, smile deepening. 'They were claimed by Shasta Smedry. Your mother.'

12

I would like to apologize for the introduction to the last chapter. It occurs to me that this book, while random at times, really shouldn't waste its time on anarchist farm animals, whether or not they have bazookas. It's just plain silly, and since I abhor silliness, I would like to ask you to do me a favor.

Flip back two chapters, where the introduction should now contain the bunny paragraphs (since you cut them out of chapter Eleven and pasted them in chapter Ten instead). Cut those paragraphs out again, then go find a book by Jane Austen and paste them in there instead. The paragraphs will be much happier there, as Jane was quite fond of bunnies and bazookas, or so I'm told. It has to do with being a proper young lady living in the nineteenth century. But that's another story entirely.

I walked, head bowed, watching the ground in front of us for trip wires. I wore the Discerner's Lenses again, the Translator's Lenses stowed carefully in their pocket.

I was beginning to accept that my father – a man I'd never met, but whom I'd traveled halfway across the world to find – might be dead. Or worse than dead. If the Curators were telling the truth, Attica's soul had been ripped away from him, then used to fuel the creation of another twisted Curator of Alexandria. I would never know him, never meet him. My father was no more.

Equally disturbing was the knowledge that my mother was somewhere in these catacombs. Though I'd always known her as Ms. Fletcher, her actual name was Shasta. (Like many Librarians, she was named after a mountain.)

Ms. Fletcher – or Shasta, or whatever her name was – had worked as my personal caseworker during my years as a foster child in the Hushlands. She'd always treated me harshly, never giving me a hint that she was, in truth, my blood mother. Did she have something to do with the twisted, half-human Scrivener's Bone that was hunting me? How had she known about my father's trip to Alexandria? And what would she do if she found me here?

Something glowed on the ground in front of us, slightly brighter than the stones around it.

'Stop,' I said, causing Bastille and Kaz to freeze. 'Trip wire, right there.'

Bastille knelt down. 'So there is,' she said, sounding impressed.

We carefully made our way over it, then continued on. During our last hour of walking, we'd left hallways filled with scrolls behind. More and more frequently, we were passing hallways filled with bookshelves. These books were still and musty, with cracking leather-bound covers, but they were obviously newer than the scrolls.

Every book ever written. Was there, somewhere in here, a room filled with paperback romance novels? The thought was amusing to me, but I wasn't sure why. The curators claimed to collect knowledge. It didn't matter to them what kinds of stories or facts the books contained – they would gather it all, store it, and keep it safe. Until someone wanted to trade their soul for it.

I felt very sorry for the person who was tricked into giving up their soul for a trashy romance novel.

We kept moving. Theoretically Kaz's Talent was leading us toward Australia, but it seemed to me like we were just walking aimlessly. Considering the nature of his Talent, that was probably a good sign.

'Kaz,' I said. 'Did you know my mother?'

The short man eyed me. 'Sure did. She was ... well, is ... my sister-in-law.'

'They never divorced?'

Kaz shook his head. 'I'm not sure what happened – they had a falling-out, obviously. Your father gave you away to be cared for in foster homes, and your mother took up position watching over you.' He paused, then shook his head. 'We were all there at your naming, Al. That was the day when your father pronounced the

Sands of Rashid upon you as your inheritance. We're still not sure how he got them to you at the right time, in the right place.'

'Oracle's Lenses' I said.

'He has a pair of *those*?'

I nodded.

'Walnuts! The prophets in Ventat are supposed to have the only pair in existence. I wonder where Attica found some.'

I shrugged. 'He mentioned them in the letter he sent me.'

Kaz nodded thoughtfully. 'Well, your father disappeared just a few days after pronouncing your blessing, so I guess there just wasn't time for a divorce. Your mother could ask for one, but she really has no motivation to do so. After all, she'd lose her Talent.'

'*What?*'

'Her Talent, Al,' Kaz said. 'She's a Smedry now.'

'Only by marriage.'

'Doesn't matter,' Kaz said. 'The spouse of a Smedry gains their husband's or wife's same Talent as soon as the marriage is official.'

I'd assumed that Talents were genetic – that they were passed on from parents to children, kind of the same way that skin color or hair color was. But this meant they were something different. That seemed important.

That does make some things make more sense, I thought. *Grandpa Smedry said he'd worried that my mother had only married my father for his Talent.* I'd assumed that she'd been enthralled with the Talent, much as someone might marry a rock star for his guitar skills. However, that didn't sound like my mother.

She'd wanted a Talent. 'So, my mother's Talent is ...'

'Losing things,' Kaz said. 'Just like your father's.' He smiled, eyes twinkling. 'I don't think she's ever figured out how to use it properly. She's a Librarian – she believes in order, lists, and catalogues. To use a Talent, you just have to be able to let yourself be out of control for a while.'

- I nodded. 'What did you think? When he married her, I mean.'

'I thought he was an idiot,' Kaz said. 'And I told him so, as is the solemn duty of younger brothers. He married her anyway, the stubborn hazelnut.'

About what I expected, I thought.

'But, Attica seemed to love her,' Kaz continued with a sigh. 'And, to be perfectly honest, she wasn't as bad as many Librarians. For a while, it seemed like they might actually make things work. Then … it fell apart. Right around the time you were born.'

I frowned. 'But, she was a Librarian agent all along, right? She just wanted to get Father's Talent.'

'Some still think that's the case. She really did seem to care for him, though. I … well, I just don't know.'

'She *had* to be faking,' I said stubbornly.

'If you say so,' Kaz said. 'I think you may be letting your preconceptions cloud your thinking.'

I shook my head. 'No. I don't do that.'

'Oh, you don't?' Kaz said, amused. 'Well then, let's try something. Why don't you tell me about your grandfather; pretend I don't know anything about him, and you want to describe him to me.'

'Okay,' I said slowly. 'Grandpa Smedry is a brilliant Oculator who is a little bit zany, but who is one of the Free Kingdom's most important figures. He has the Talent to arrive late to things.'

'Great,' Kaz said. 'Now tell me about Bastille.'

I eyed her, and she shot me a threatening glance. 'Uh, Bastille is a Crystin. I think that's about all I can say without her throwing something at me.'

'Good enough. Australia?'

I shrugged. 'She seems a bit scatterbrained, but is a good person. She's an Oculator and has a Smedry Talent.'

'Okay,' Kaz said. 'Now talk about me.'

'Well, you're a short person who—'

'Stop,' Kaz said.

I did so, shooting him a questioning glance.

'Why is it,' Kaz said, 'that with the others, the first thing you described about them was their job or their personality? Yet, with me, the first thing you mentioned was my height?'

'I … uh …'

Kaz laughed. 'I'm not trying to trap you, kid. But, maybe you see why I get so annoyed sometimes. The trouble with being different is that people start defining you by *what* you are instead of by *who* you are.'

I fell silent.

'Your mother is a Librarian,' Kaz said. 'Because of that, we tend to think of her as a Librarian first, and a person second. Our knowledge of her as a Librarian clouds everything else.'

'She's not a good person, Kaz,' I said. 'She offered to sell me to a Dark Oculator.'

'Did she?' Kaz asked. 'What exactly did she say?'

I thought back to the time when Bastille, Sing, and I had been hiding in the library, listening to Ms. Fletcher speak with Blackburn. 'Actually,' I said, 'she didn't say anything. It was the Dark Oculator who said something like, "You'd sell the boy too, wouldn't you? You impress me." And she just shrugged or nodded or something.'

'So,' Kaz said, 'she *didn't* offer to sell you out.'

'She didn't contradict Blackburn.'

Kaz shook his head. 'Shasta has her own agenda, kid. I don't think any of us can presume to understand exactly what she's up to. Your father saw something in her. I still think he's a fool for marrying her, but for a Librarian, she wasn't too bad.'

I wasn't convinced. My bias against Librarians wasn't the *only* thing making me distrust Shasta. She had consistently berated me as a child, saying I was worthless. (I now know she had been trying to get me to stop using my Talent, for fear it would expose me to those who were searching for the Sands.) Either way, she'd been my mother all that time, and she hadn't ever given me even a hint of confirmation.

Though ... she *had* stayed with me, always, watching over me.

I pushed that thought aside. She didn't deserve credit for that – she'd just been hoping for the chance to grab the sands of Rashid. The very day they arrived, she showed up and swiped them.

'... don't know, Kaz,' Bastille was saying. '*I* think that the main reason people think of your height first is because of that ridiculous List of yours.'

'My List is *not* ridiculous,' Kaz said with a huff. 'It's very scientific.'

'Oh?' Bastille asked. 'Didn't you claim that "short people are better because it takes them longer to walk places, therefore they get more exercise"?'

'That one has been clinically proven.' Kaz said, pointing at her.

'It does seem a bit of a stretch,' I said, smiling.

'You forget Reason number one,' he said. '"Don't argue with the short person." He's always right.'

Bastille snorted. 'It's a good thing you don't claim short people are more humble.'

Kaz fell silent. 'That's Reason two thirty-six,' he muttered quietly. 'I just haven't mentioned that one yet.'

Bastille shot me a glance through her sunglasses, and I could tell she was rolling her eyes. However, even though I didn't believe Kaz about my mother, I thought his comments about how to treat people were valid.

Who we are – meaning, the person we become by doing things – which – incidentally – is actually a function of who we are – for example, I've become an Oculator – which is quite fun – by doing things that relate to Oculators – not who we can be – is more important – actually – than what we look like.

For instance, the fact that I use lots of dashes in my writing is part of what makes me, me. I'd rather be known by this – since it's cool – than by the fact that I have a big nose. Which I don't. Why are you looking at me like that?

'Wait!' I said, holding out a hand.

Bastille froze.

'Trip wire,' I said, heart pounding. Her foot hovered just a few inches from it.

She backed away, and Kaz squatted down. 'Well done, kid. It's a good thing you have those Lenses.'

'Yeah,' I said, taking them off and cleaning them. 'I guess.' I still wished I had a weapon instead of another pair of Lenses that showed me random stuff. Wouldn't a sword have been equally useful?

Of course, I might think that just because I really like swords. Give me the chance, and I'd probably cut my wedding cake with one.

I did have to admit, though, that I'd made pretty good use of the Discerner's Lenses. Maybe I'd discounted them too quickly at first. I cleaned my Lenses, feeling an odd sensation from inside. It was slight, a little like indigestion, but less foody.

I shook my head and put the Discerner's Lenses back on, then guided the other two over the trip wire. As I did, I noticed something interesting. 'There's a second trip wire just a few feet ahead.'

'They're getting more clever,' Bastille said. 'They figured we'd see this one, but hoped we'd feel safe once we passed it – then go right on and trip the second.'

I nodded, glancing at the Curators floating behind. I noticed that the odd sensation was getting stronger. It was hard to explain. It wasn't really a sick feeling. More like a slight itch on my emotions.

'We need to find Australia quickly, Kaz,' Bastille said. 'Is it supposed to take this long?'

'Never can tell, with the Talent,' Kaz said. 'Australia might not actually be lost. If that's the case, it will take me a lot longer to find her than it took me to find you. Like I mentioned earlier, if I don't know where to go, then my Talent can't really take me there.'

Bastille didn't seem pleased to hear this. 'Maybe we should start looking for the Old Smedry instead.'

'If I know my father, he's not lost,' Kaz said, rubbing his chin. 'He'll be even more difficult to find.'

I was barely paying attention to them. The itch was still there. It wasn't the same feeling that I got from the hunter that was chasing me, but it was similar.... .

'So, do we just keep going?' Bastille asked.

'I guess so,' Kaz said.

'No,' I said suddenly, looking at them. 'Kaz, turn off your Talent.'

Bastille looked at me, frowning. 'What is it?'

'Someone's using a Lens nearby.'

'The Scrivener's Bone chasing us?'

I shook my head. 'This is a regular Lens, not a twisted one like he uses. It means there is an Oculator close to us.' I paused, then pointed. 'That way.'

Bastille shared a look with Kaz. 'Let's go check it out,' she said.

13

I have to apologize for the introduction to that last chapter. It was far too apologetic. There's been too much apologizing going on in this book. I'm sorry. I want to prove to you that I'm a liar, not a wimp.

The thing is, you never know who is going to be reading your books. I've tried to write this one for members of both the Hushlands and the Free Kingdoms, and that's tough enough. However, even within the Hushlands, the variety of people who could pick this book up is incredible.

You could be a young boy, wanting to read an adventure story. You could be a young girl, wanting to investigate the truth of the Librarian Conspiracy. You might be a mother, reading this book because you've heard that so many of your kids are reading it. Or you could be a serial killer who specializes in reading books, then seeking out the authors and murdering them in horrible ways.

(If you happen to fall into that last category, you should know that my name isn't really Alcatraz Smedry, nor is it Brandon Sanderson. My name is really Garth Nix, and you can find me in Australia. Oh, and I insulted your mother once. What're you going to do about it, huh?)

Anyway it's very difficult to relate this story to everyone who might be reading my book. So, I've decided not to try. Instead, I'll just say something that makes no sense to anyone: Flagwat the happy beansprout.

Confusion, after all, is the *true* universal language.

'The feeling is coming from that direction,' I said, pointing. Unfortunately, 'that direction' happened to be straight through a wall full of books.

'So ... one of the books is an Oculator?' Kaz asked.

I rolled my eyes.

He chuckled. 'I understood what you meant. Stop acting like Bastille. Obviously we have to find a way around. There must be another hallway on the other side.'

I nodded, but ... the Lens felt *close*. We'd walked down a few rows already, coming to this point, and I felt like it was just on the other side of the wall.

I took off my Discerner's Lenses, putting on my Oculator's Lenses instead. One of their main functions was to reveal Oculatory power, and they made the entire wall glow with a bright white light. I stumbled back, shocked by the powerful illumination.

'Glowing, eh?' Bastille asked, walking up to me.

I nodded.

'That's strange,' she said. 'It takes time for an area to charge with Oculatory power. The Lens you sensed must have been here for a while if it has started making things around it glow.'

'What are you implying?' I asked.

She shook her head. 'I'm not sure. When you first spoke, I assumed we were close to Grandpa Smedry, since he's the only other Oculator we know to be down here. Except for, well, your father, and he ...'

I didn't want to think about that. 'It's probably not Grandpa. He came down here only a little while before we did.'

'What, then?' Bastille asked.

I took off my Oculator's Lenses, then put on my Discerner's Lenses again. I walked carefully along the wall full of books, inspecting the brickwork.

I didn't have to look far before I discovered that one section of the wall was much older than all of the others. 'Something is back there,' I said. 'I think there might be a secret passage or something.'

'How do we trigger it?' Bastille asked. 'Pull one of the books?'

'I guess.'

One of the ever-present Curators floated closer. 'Yes,' it said. 'Pull one of the books. Take it.'

I paused, hand halfway up to the shelf. 'I'm not going to take it; I'll just shake it a bit.'

'Try it,' the Curator whispered. 'Whether you pick up a book, or whether it falls off accidentally, it does not matter. Move even one of the books a few inches off its shelf, and your soul is ours.'

I lowered my hand. The Curator seemed too eager to scare me away from trying to move one of the books. *It seems like they don't want me to find out what is behind there.*

I inspected the bookshelf. There was enough space to the side of it – between it and the next bookshelf over – that I could reach through and touch the back wall. I took a deep breath, leaning up against the bookcase, careful to keep from touching any of the books.

'Alcatraz . . . ,' Bastille said with concern.

I nodded, careful as I pressed my hand against the back wall. *If I break this, and the bookshelf falls over, it will cost me my soul.*

My Discerner's Lenses told me that this portion of the brick wall behind the bookshelf was older than even the rest of the walls and floor. Whatever was behind that wall had been there even before the Curators moved into the area.

I released my power.

The wall crumbled, bricks breaking free of their mortar. I anxiously tried to hold the bookcase steady as the wall collapsed behind it. Kaz rushed forward, grabbing it on the other side, and Bastille pressed her hands against the books that were teetering slightly on their shelves. Apparently, none of this was enough to give the Curators leave to take our souls, because they watched with an air of petulance as not a single book slid out.

I wiped my brow. The entire wall had fallen away, and there *was* some kind of room back there.

'That was rash, Alcatraz,' Bastille said, folding her arms.

'He's a true Smedry!' Kaz said, laughing.

I glanced at the two of them, suddenly embarrassed. 'Someone had to break down that wall. It's the only way we were going to get through.'

Bastille shrugged. 'You complain about having to make decisions, then you make one like that without even asking. Do you want to be in charge or not?'

'Uh … Well … I, that is …'

'Brilliant,' she said, peeking into the hole between the bookcases. 'Very inspiring. Kaz, do you think we can get through?'

Kaz was prying a lamp off the wall. 'Sure we can. Though we may have to move that bookcase.'

Bastille eyed it and then, sighing, helped me ease the bookcase back from the wall just a few inches. We didn't, fortunately, lose any books – or any souls – in the process. Once finished, Kaz was able to slip through the opening.

'Wow!' he said.

Bastille, standing on that side of the bookcase, went next. I, therefore, had to go last – which I found rather unfair, considering that I'd been the one to discover the place. However, all feelings of annoyance vanished as I stepped into the chamber.

It was a tomb.

I'd seen enough movies about wisecracking archaeologists to know what an Egyptian pharaoh's tomb looked like. A massive sarcophagus sat in the center, and there were delicate golden pillars spaced around it. Mounds of wealth were heaped in the corners – coins, lamps, statues of animals. The floor itself seemed to be of pure gold.

So, I did what anyone would do if he'd discovered an ancient Egyptian tomb. I yelped for joy, then rushed directly over to the nearest pile of gold and reached for a handful.

'Alcatraz, wait!' Bastille said, grabbing my arm with a burst of Crystin speed.

'What?' I asked in annoyance. 'You're not going to give me some kind of nonsense about grave robbing or curses, are you?'

'Shattering Glass, no,' Bastille said. 'But look – those coins have words on them.'

I glanced to the side and noticed that she was right. Each coin was stamped with a foreign kind of character that wasn't Egyptian, as far as I could tell. 'So?' I asked. 'What does it matter if …'

I trailed off, then glanced at the three Curators, who floated in through the wall in a fittingly ghostly manner.

'Curators,' I said. 'Do these coins count as books?'

'They are written,' one said. 'Paper, cloth, or metal, it matters not.'

'You can check one out, if you wish,' another whispered, floating up to me.

I shivered, then glanced at Bastille. 'You just saved my life,' I said, feeling numb.

She shrugged. 'I'm a Crystin. That's what we do.' However, she did seem to walk a little bit more confidently as she joined Kaz, who was inspecting the sarcophagus.

You should have realized that I wouldn't be able to have any of the coins. That's what happens in stories like this. Characters in books find heaps of gold or hidden treasure all over the place – but then, of course, they never get to spend a penny of it. Instead, they either

1) Lose it in an earthquake or natural disaster.
II) Put it in a backpack that then breaks at a climactic moment, dropping all of the treasure as the heroes flee.
c) Use it to rescue their orphanage from foreclosure.

Stupid orphanages.

Anyway, it is very common for authors to do things like this to the people in their stories. Why? Well, we will *claim* it's because we want to teach the reader that the real wealth is friendship, or caring, or something stupid like that. In reality we're just mean people. We like to torment our readers, and that translates to tormenting our characters. After all, there is only one thing more frustrating than finding a pile of gold, then having it snatched away from you.

And that's being told that at least you learned something from the experience.

I sighed, leaving the coins behind.

'Oh, don't mope, Alcatraz,' Bastille said, waving indifferently toward another corner of the room. 'Just take some of those gold bars, instead. They don't seem to have anything written on them.'

I turned and smacked my forehead, suddenly realizing that I *wasn't* in a fictional story. This was an autobiography and was completely real – which meant that the 'lesson' I could learn from it all is that grave robbing is way cool.

'Good idea!' I said. 'Curators, do those bars count as books?'

The ghosts floated sullenly, one shooting an angry glare at Bastille. 'No,' it finally said.

I smiled, then proceeded to stuff a few bars in my pocket, then a few more in Bastille's pack. In case you were wondering, yes. Gold really is as heavy as they say. And it's totally worth carrying anyway.

'Don't you guys want any of this?' I asked, putting another bar in my jacket pocket.

Kaz shrugged. 'You and I are Smedries, Alcatraz. We're friends to kings, counselors to emperors, defenders of the Free Kingdoms. Our family is incredibly wealthy, and we can pretty much have anything we want. I mean, that silimatic dragon we crashed was probably worth more money than most people would ever be able to spend in a lifetime.'

'Oh,' I said.

'And I kind of took a vow of poverty,' Bastille said, grimacing.

That was new. 'Really?'

She nodded. 'If I brought some of that gold, it would just end up going to the Knights of Crystallia – and I'm a little annoyed with them right now.'

I stuffed a few bars in my pocket for her anyway.

'Alcatraz, come look at this,' Kaz said.

I reluctantly left the rest of the gold behind, clinking my way over to the other two. They stood a distance away from the sarco-phagus, not approaching. 'What's wrong?'

'Look closely,' Kaz said, pointing.

I did, squinting in the light of the single lamp. With effort, I saw what he was talking about. Dust. Hanging in the air, motionless.

'What's that?' I asked.

'I don't know,' Kaz said. 'But, if you look, there's a bubble of clean ground around the sarcophagus. No dust.'

There was a large circle on the ground, running around the casket, where either the dust had been cleaned away, or it had never fallen. Now that I thought to notice, I realized that the rest of this room was far more dusty than the Library. It hadn't been disturbed in some time.

'There's something odd about this place,' Bastille said, hands on hips.

'Yeah,' I said, frowning. 'Those hieroglyphics don't quite look like any I've seen before.'

'Seen a lot?' she asked, raising a skeptical eyebrow.

I flushed. 'I mean, they don't look the way Egyptian ones should.'

It was hard to explain. As one might expect, the walls were covered with small pictures, drawn as if to be words. Yet, instead of people with cattle or eagle heads, there were pictures of dragons and serpents. Instead of scarabs, there were odd geometric shapes, like runes. Above the doorway where we had come in, there was ...

'Kaz!' I said, pointing.

He turned, then his eyes opened wide. There, inscribed over the door, was a circle split into four sections, with symbols written in each of the four pieces. Just like the diagram Kaz had drawn for me on the ground, the one about the different kinds of Talents. The Incarnate wheel.

This one also had a small circle in the center with its own symbol, along with a ring around the outside, split into two sections, each with another character in them.

'It could just be a coincidence,' Kaz said slowly. 'I mean, it's just a circle split into four pieces. It isn't *necessarily* the same diagram.'

'It is,' I said. 'It feels right.'

'Well, maybe the Curators put it there,' Kaz said. 'They saw me draw it on the ground, and copied it down. Maybe they have placed it here for us to find, so it would confuse us.'

I shook my head. 'I've still got my Discerner's Lenses on. That inscription is as old as the rest of the tomb.'

'What does it say?' Bastille asked. 'Won't that tell us what it is?'

Why didn't I think of that? I thought, embarrassed again. Bastille certainly was quick on her feet. Or maybe I was slow. Let's not discuss that possibility any further. Forget I mentioned it.

'Can I read that text without losing my soul?' I asked.

We looked at the Curators. One reluctantly spoke. 'You can,' it said. 'You lose your soul when you check out or move a book. A symbol on the wall can be read without being checked out.'

It made sense. If it were that easy to get souls, the Curators could just have posted signs, then taken the souls of any who read them.

With that, I pulled off my Discerner's Lenses and put on my Translator's Lenses. They immediately interpreted the strange symbols.

'The inner squares say the things you taught, Kaz,' I said. 'Time, Space, Matter, Knowledge.'

Kaz whistled. 'Walnuts! That means whoever built this place knew an awful lot about Smedry Talents and arcane theory. What about that symbol in the middle of the circle? What does it say?'

'It says Breaking,' I said quietly.

My Talent.

'Interesting,' Kaz said. 'They give it its own circle on the diagram. What is that outer circle?'

The ring was split into two pieces. 'One says Identity,' I said. 'The other says Possibility.'

Kaz looked thoughtful. 'Classical philosophy,' he said. 'Metaphysics. It appears that our dead friend there was a philosopher of some kind. Makes sense, considering that we're near Alexandria.'

I wasn't paying much attention to that. Instead, I turned, hesitant, to read the words on the walls. My Translator's Lenses instantly changed them to English for me.

I immediately wished that I hadn't read them.

14

Time for a history lesson.

Stop complaining. This isn't an adventure story; it's a factual autobiography. The purpose isn't to entertain you, but to teach you. If you want to be entertained, go to school and listen to the imaginary facts your teachers make up.

The Incarna. I talked about them in my last book, I believe. They're the ones who developed the Forgotten Language. In the Free Kingdoms, everyone is a little annoyed at them. After all, the Incarna supposedly had this fantastic understanding of both technology and magic. But, instead of sharing their wisdom with the rest of the world, they developed the Forgotten Language and then – somehow – managed to change all of their texts and writings so that they were written in this language.

No, the Forgotten Language *wasn't* their original method of writing. Everybody knows that. They *transformed* all of their books into it. Kind of like … applying an encrypting program to a computer document. Except, it affected all forms of writing, whether on paper, in metal, or in stone.

Nobody knows how they managed this. They were a race of mega-evolved, highly intelligent superbeings. I doubt it was all that tough for them. They could probably turn lead into gold, grant immortality, and make a mean dish of cold fusion too. Doesn't really matter. Nobody can read what they left behind.

Except me. With my Translator's Lenses.

Perhaps now you can see why the Librarians would hire a twisted, half-human assassin to hunt me down and retrieve them, eh?

'Alcatraz?' Bastille said, apparently noticing how white my face had become. 'What's wrong?'

I stared at the wall with its strange words, trying to sort through what I was reading. She shook my arm.

'Alcatraz?' she asked again, then glanced at the wall. 'What does it say?'

I read the words again.

Beware all ye who visit this place of rest. Know that The Dark Talent has been released upon the world. We have failed to keep it contained.

Our desires have brought us low. We sought to touch the powers of eternity, then draw them down upon ourselves. But we brought with them something we did not intend.

Be careful of it. Guard it well, and beware its use. Do not rely upon it. We have seen the possibilities of the future and the ultimate end. It could destroy so much, if given the chance.

The Bane of Incarna. That which twists, that which corrupts, and that which destroys. The Dark Talent.

The Talent of Breaking.

'This place is important,' I whispered. 'This place is really, *really* important.'

'Why?' Bastille said. 'Shattering Glass, Smedry. When are you going to tell me what that says?'

'Get out your pen and paper,' I said, kneeling. 'I need to write this down.'

Bastille sighed, but did as I asked, fetching a pen and paper from her pack. Kaz wandered over, watching with interest as I transcribed the writing on the wall.

'What language is that, anyway?' I asked. 'It mentions the Incarna, but it's not the Forgotten Language.'

'That's old Nalhallan,' Kaz said. 'I can't read it, but we have a few scholars back in the capital who can. When the Incarna fell, its few survivors ended up in Nalhalla to live.'

I finished the translation. Then, immediately, the three Curators surrounded me.

'You must give up all writings to the Library when you enter,' one hissed. 'A copy will be returned to you once we have completed it. If a copy cannot be made in one hour's time, we will return the original instead.'

I rolled my eyes. 'Oh, for heaven's sake!' However, I let them pull the sheet away and vanish with it.

Bastille was frowning – she'd read the translation as I wrote it. 'That inscription makes it seem like your Talent is dangerous.'

'It is,' I said. 'Do you know how many times I've nearly been beaten up for breaking something at the wrong time?'

'But—' She cut off, however, obviously sensing that I didn't want to talk about it further.

To be honest, I didn't know what to think. It was strange enough to find ancient writings that dealt with Smedry Talents. To have them give a caution about mine specifically … well, it was a little disturbing.

That was the first time I really got any hint of the troubles that were coming. You Free Kingdomers call me a savior. Can I really be considered a savior if I *caused* the very problem I helped fix?

'Wait a moment,' Bastille said. 'Didn't we get drawn here by an Oculatory Lens? Whatever happened to that?'

'That's right,' I said, standing. I could still sense it working, though I'd been distracted by everything else in the tomb.

I swapped my Translator's Lenses for my Oculator's Lenses, then had to turn down their power because of how blinding the room was. Once I'd done so, I could see the Lens that had drawn me here. It was set into the lid of the sarcophagus.

'It's there,' I said, pointing. 'On the top of the sarcophagus.'

'I don't trust that thing,' Kaz said. 'That circle around it is strange. We should leave, gather a research team, then come back and study this place in detail.'

I nodded absently. Then, I walked toward the sarcophagus.

'Alcatraz!' Bastille said. 'Are you going to do something stupid and brash again?'

I turned. 'Yeah.'

She blinked. 'Oh. Well, then, you probably shouldn't. Consider me opposed to it. Whatever it is.'

'Objection noted,' I said.

'I—' Bastille said. She stopped as I stepped into the circle of clean ground around the sarcophagus.

Everything immediately changed. Dust began to fall around me, sparkling like very fine powdered metal. Lamps burned with bright flames set to the top of the pillars around the sarcophagus. It was like I'd entered a small column of golden light. Somehow I'd moved from a long-dead tomb to someplace alive with motion.

There was still a sense of reverence to the area. I turned, noticing Bastille and Kaz standing outside the ring of light. They seemed frozen in place, mouths open as if to speak.

I turned back to the sarcophagus, the dust falling very faintly in the air, sprinkling over everything. I held up a hand. It was indeed metallic, and it glittered with a yellow sheen. Gold dust.

Why had I stepped blindly into the circle like that?

It's hard to explain. Imagine you have the hiccups. In fact, you not only have the hiccups, you have *The* Hiccups. These are the hiccups to end all hiccups. You've hiccupped all of your life, without a moment of freedom. You've hiccupped so much that you've lost friends, made everyone annoyed at you, and grown pretty down on yourself.

And then, amazingly, you discover a group of people who have similar problems. Some of them burp all the time, others sniffle all the time, and still others have really bad gas. They all make annoying noises, but they come from a land where that's really cool. They're all impressed with your hiccupping.

You hang out with these people for a time, and start to grow proud of your hiccups. Then, you pass a billboard that mentions – for the first time – that your hiccups will probably end up destroying the world.

You might, then, feel a little like I did. Confused, betrayed, unsettled. Willing to step into a strange ring of power to confront, hopefully, the person who made the billboard.

Even if he did happen to be dead.

I pushed aside the top of the sarcophagus. It was heavier than I'd expected, and I had to heave. It clattered to the floor, scattering gold dust.

There was a man's body inside, and he wasn't even a bit decomposed. In fact, he looked so lifelike that I jumped backward.

The man in the sarcophagus didn't move. I edged closer, eyeing him. He looked to be in his fifties, and was wearing an ancient set of clothing – a kind of skirtlike wrap around the lower legs, then a flowing cloaklike shirt on his back that left his bare chest exposed. He had a golden headband around his forehead.

I hesitantly poked his face. (Don't pretend you wouldn't have done the same.)

The man didn't move. So, carefully, cringing, I checked for a pulse. Nothing.

I stepped back. Now, perhaps you've seen a dead body before. I sincerely hope that you haven't, but let's be realistic. People die sometimes. They have to – if they didn't, funeral homes and graveyards would go out of business.

Dead bodies don't look like they were ever alive. Corpses tend to look like they're made from wax – they don't seem like people at all, but mannequins.

This body didn't look that way. The cheeks were still flush, the face surreal in the way it seemed ready to take a breath at any moment.

I glanced back at Bastille and Kaz. They were still frozen, as if time weren't moving for them. I looked back at the body, and suddenly began to catch a hint of what might be going on.

I put on my Translator's Lenses, then walked over to the discarded lid of the sarcophagus. There, printed in ornate letters, was a name:

Allekatrase the Lens-wielder, first Bearer of the Dark Talent.

Intrinsically, my Translator's Lenses let me know that the word *Lens-wielder* when spoken in ancient Nalhallan would sound different to my ears. The ancient Nalhallan word for 'Lens' was *smaed* and their word for 'person who uses' was *dary*.

Allekatrase the Lens-wielder. Allekatrase Smaed-dary.

Alcatraz Smedry the First.

Golden dust fell around me, sprinkling my hair. 'You broke

time, didn't you?' I asked. 'Kaz mentioned that there were legends of you having done so. You created for yourself a tomb where time would not pass, where you could rest without decomposing.'

It was the ultimate method of embalming. I personally suspect that the Egyptian custom of making mummies of their kings came from the story of Alcatraz Smedry the First.

'I have your Talent,' I said, stepping up beside the sarcophagus, looking at the man inside. 'What am I supposed to do with it? Can I control it? Or will it always control me?'

The body was silent. They're like that. Completely lacking in social graces, those corpses.

'Did it destroy you?' I asked. 'Is that what the warning is for?'

The body was so serene. Gold dust was beginning to gather on its face. Finally, I just sighed, kneeling down to look at the Lens in the lid of the sarcophagus. It was completely clear, with no color to indicate what it did. Yet, I knew it was powerful because it had drawn me here.

I reached out and tried to pry it free. It was stuck on the lid very soundly, but I wasn't about to leave a Lens that powerful sitting in a forgotten tomb.

I touched the lid and released my Talent into it. Immediately, the Lens popped free, flipping up into the air. I was caught so off guard that I barely managed to grab it before it fell and shattered.

As soon as I touched the Lens, it stopped giving off power. The bubble of strange time-shift continued to be in force, however, so the Lens hadn't been behind that.

I moved to stand up, but then noticed something. In the place where the Lens had been affixed, there was an inscription. It would have been hidden beneath the glass of the Lens, which had a small black paper backing to keep the text from being seen until the Lens was removed.

It was in ancient Nalhallan. With my Translator's Lenses, I could read it with ease.

To my descendant, the tiny inscription read.
If you have released this Lens, then I know you have the

Dark Talent. Part of me rejoices, for this means it is still being protected and borne by our family, as is our curse.

Yet, I am also worried, for it means you haven't found a way to banish it. As long as the corrupting Talent remains, it is a danger.

This Lens is the most precious of my collection. I have given others to my son. His lesser Talent, though corrupted, is not to be feared. Only when the Talent can Break is it dangerous. In all others, it simply taints what they have done.

Use the Lens. Pass on this Knowledge, if it has been forgotten.

And care well for the burden, blessing and curse you have been given.

I sat back, trying to decide what I thought of the words. I wished that I had something I could write with, but then decided that it was better that I didn't copy the text. The Curators would take what I wrote, and if they didn't already know of the inscription, I didn't want them to.

I stood up. With some effort, I managed to get the lid of the sarcophagus back on. Then, I lay my hand on the inscription and somehow Broke it. The text of the letters scrambled, becoming gibberish, even to my Translator's Lenses.

I pulled my hand back, surprised. I'd never done anything like that before. I stood silently, then solemnly bowed my head to the sarcophagus, which had been carved to match the face of the man who rested inside.

'I'll do my best,' I said. Then I stepped from the circle.

The light faded. The room became musty and old again, and Bastille and Kaz began moving.

'—don't think this is a good idea,' Bastille said.

'Objection noted again,' I said, dusting the gold powder from my shoulders, where it had gathered like King Midas's dandruff.

'Alcatraz?' Kaz asked. 'What just happened?'

'Time moves differently in there,' I said, looking back at the sarcophagus. It seemed unchanged, the dust hanging in the air, the lamps extinguished. The Lens on the lid, however, was gone. I still had it in my hand.

'I think stepping into that circle takes you back in time to the moment he died,' I said. 'Something like that. I'm not exactly sure.'

'That's ... very odd,' Kaz said. 'Did you find out who he was?'

I nodded, looking down at the Lens. 'Alcatraz the First.'

The other two were silent.

'That's impossible, Al,' Kaz said. 'I've seen the tomb of Alcatraz the First. It's down in the Nalhallan royal catacombs. It's one of the city's greatest tourist attractions.'

'It's a fake,' Bastille said.

We both looked at her sharply.

'The royal family made it a thousand years back or so,' she said, glancing away. 'As a symbol of Nalhalla's founding. It bothered the royals that they didn't know where Alcatraz the First was buried, so they came up with a fake historical site to commemorate him.'

Kaz whistled softly. 'I guess you'd know, Bastille. That's some cover-up. But, why is he here, in the Library of Alexandria, of all places?'

'This room is older than the parts around it,' I said. 'I'd say that the Curators moved their Library here on purpose. Weren't you the one who told me that it changed locations in favor of a place with more room?'

'True,' Kaz said. 'What's that Lens?'

I held it up. 'I'm not sure; I found it on the sarcophagus. Bastille, do you recognize it?'

She shook her head. 'It's not tinted. It could do anything.'

'Maybe I should just activate it.'

Bastille shrugged, and Kaz seemed to have no objections. So, hesitantly, I tried it. Nothing happened. I looked through the Lens, but couldn't see anything different about the room.

'Nothing?' Bastille asked.

I shook my head, frowning. *He called this his most powerful of Lenses. So, what does it do?*

'It makes sense, I guess,' Kaz said. 'It was active before – it's what drew you here. Maybe all it does is send out a signal to other Oculators.'

'Maybe' I said, unconvinced. I slipped it into the single-Lens pocket in my jacket that had once held my Firebringer's Lens.

'We should probably just show it to my father,' Kaz said. 'He'll be able to ...'

He kept talking, but I stopped paying attention. Bastille was acting oddly. She'd suddenly perked up, growing tense. She glanced out the broken wall.

'Bastille?' I asked, cutting Kaz off.

'Shattering Glass!' she said, then took off in a dash out of the room.

Kaz and I stood, dumbfounded.

'What do we do?' Kaz asked.

'Follow her!' I said, slipping out of the room – careful not to tip over the bookcase outside. Kaz followed, grabbing Bastille's pack and pulling out a pair of Warrior's Lenses. As I took off at a dash down the hallway after Bastille, he managed to keep up by virtue of the enhancements the Lenses granted.

I quickly began to realize why characters in books tend to lose their gold before the end of the story. That stuff was *heavy*. Reluctantly, I tossed most of the gold to the side, keeping only a couple of bars in my pocket.

Even without the gold, however, neither of us was fast enough to follow a Crystin.

'Bastille!' I yelled, watching her disappear into the distance.

There was no response. Soon, Kaz and I reached an intersection and paused, puffing. We'd moved into yet another part of the Library. Here, instead of rows of scrolls or bookcases, we were in a section that looked like a dungeon. There were lots of intermixing hallways and small rooms, lamps flickering softly on the walls.

To make things more confusing, some of the doorways – even some of the hallways – had bars set across them, blocking the way forward. My suspicion is that this part of the Library was intended to be a maze – another means of frustrating people.

Bastille suddenly rushed back toward us, running out of a side corridor.

'Bastille?' I asked.

She cursed and passed us, going down another of the side hallways. I glanced at Kaz, who just shrugged. So, we took off after her again.

As we ran, I noticed something. A feeling. I froze, causing Kaz to pull up short beside me.

'What?' he asked.

'He's near,' I said.

'Who?'

'The hunter. The one chasing us.'

'National Union of Teachers!' Kaz swore. 'You're sure?'

I nodded. Ahead, I could hear Bastille yelling. We moved, passing a set of bars on our right. Through them, I could see another hallway. It would be very easy to get lost in this section of the Library.

But, then, we were already lost. So, it didn't really seem to matter. Bastille came running back, and this time I managed to grab her arm as she ran by. She jerked to a halt, brow sweating, looking wild-eyed.

'Bastille!' I said. 'What is going on?'

'My mother,' Bastille said. 'She's near, and she's in pain. I can't get to her because every one of these shattering passages is a dead end!'

Draulin? I thought. *Here?* I opened my mouth to ask how Bastille could possibly know that, and then I felt something. That dark, oppressive force. The twisted, unnatural feeling given off by a Lens that had been forged with Oculator blood. It was near. Very near.

I looked down a side hallway. Lamps flickered along its sides, and at the very end, I saw a massive iron grate covering the way forward.

Beyond the grate stood a shadowed figure, one arm unnaturally long, the face misshapen.

And it held Draulin's Crystin sword in its hands.

15

It's my fault.

I'll admit the truth; I did it. You've undoubtedly noticed it by now, if you've been reading closely. I apologize. Of all the dirty tricks I've used, this is undoubtedly the nastiest of them all. I realize it might have ruined the book for you up until now but I couldn't help myself.

You see, doing something like this consistently, over fourteen chapters, was quite challenging. And I'm always up for a challenge. When you noticed it, you probably realized how clever I was, even as you blushed. I know this is supposed to be a book for kids, and I thought it was well enough hidden that it wouldn't come out. I guess I was too obvious.

I'd have taken it out, but it's just so clever. Most people won't be able to find it, even though it's there in every chapter, on every page.

The most brilliant literary joke I've ever made.

My apologies.

I stood, facing down the silhouetted creature, still holding on to Bastille's arm. I slowly came to understand something.

I had been wrong to run from the creature – that had caused my group to get split up. Now the hunter could take us one at a time, grabbing us from the catacombs as we ran about in confusion.

We couldn't continue to run. It was time to confront it. I gulped, beginning to sweat. This is one of the reasons why I'm no hero – because even though I walked down that corridor toward the creature, I pulled Bastille along with me. I figured two targets were better than one.

As we moved forward, Kaz trailing behind, Bastille lost a bit of her frenzied look. She pulled her dagger from its sheath, the crystalline blade sparkling in the flickering lamplight.

At the end of the corridor was a small room, split in half by the large iron grate. The Scrivener's Bone was on the other side of the bars. He smiled as I approached – one side of his face curling up, lips leering. The other side of his face mimicked the motion, though it was made of bits of metal that twisted and clicked, like a clock mechanism that had been compressed tenfold until all of the gears and pins were smushed together.

'Smedry,' the thing said, voice ragged, as if the sounds themselves had been flayed.

'Who are you?' I asked.

The creature met my eyes. The entire left half of its body had been replaced by the bits of metal, held together by a force I didn't understand. One of its eyes was human. The other was a pit of dark glass. Alivener's Glass.

'I am Kilimanjaro,' the creature said. 'I have been sent to retrieve something from you.'

I was still wearing the Lenses of Rashid. I raised my fingers to them, and Kiliman nodded.

'Where did you get that sword?' I asked, trying to hide my nervousness.

'I have the woman,' the creature said. 'I took it from her.'

'She's here, Alcatraz,' Bastille said. 'I can feel her Fleshstone.'

Fleshstone? I thought. *What in the name of the first sands is that?*

'You mean this?' Kiliman asked, voice deep and crackling. He held up something before him. It looked like a crystal shard, about the size of two fingers put together. It was bloody.

Bastille gasped. 'No!' she said, rushing toward the bars; I grabbed her arm and barely managed to hang on.

'Bastille!' I said. 'He's goading you!'

'How could you?' she screamed at the creature. 'You'll kill her!'

Kiliman lowered the crystal, placing it in a pouch at his belt. He still held the sword in front of him. 'Death is immaterial, Crystin. I must retrieve what I seek. You have it, and I have the woman. We will trade.'

Bastille fell to her knees, and at first I thought she was weeping. Then I could see that she was simply shaking, white faced. I didn't know it at the time, but pulling the Fleshstone from the body of a Crystin is an unspeakably vulgar and gruesome act. To Bastille, it was like Kiliman had shown her Draulin's heart, still beating in his hand.

'You think I'd bargain with *you*?' I asked.

'Yes,' Kiliman said simply. He didn't have the flair of evil that Blackburn had shown – no flaunted arrogance, no sharp clothing, or laughing voice. Yet, the quiet danger this creature expressed was somehow even more haunting.

I shivered.

'Careful, Al,' Kaz said quietly. 'Those creatures are dangerous. *Very* dangerous.'

Kiliman smiled, then dropped the sword and flipped a hand forward. I cried out as I saw a Lens in his hand. It flashed, shooting out a beam of frosty light.

Bastille came up, her dagger held clawlike in her hand. She took the beam straight on the crystalline blade, then stumbled backward. She held it, but just barely.

I growled, throwing off the Translator's Lenses and pulling out my Windstormer's Lenses. He wanted to fight? Well, I'd show him.

I snapped the Lenses on, then focused on the Scrivener's Bone, sending forth a wave of powerful wind. My ears popped, and Kaz cried out from the sudden increase in pressure. The blast of wind hit Kiliman, throwing him backward, spraying bits of metal from his body.

Kiliman growled, and his Frostbringer's Lens turned off. To my side, Bastille fell to her knees again; I could see that her hand looked blue and was crusted with ice. Her little dagger's blade was cracked in several places. Like the Crystin swords, it could deflect Oculatory powers, but it obviously wasn't meant to handle much punishment.

Kiliman righted himself, and I could see the bits of metal that had fallen off of him spring up little spiderlike legs. The nuts, screws, and gears scuttled across the floor, climbing up his body and rejoining with the entire pulsing, undulating heap of metal scraps.

He met my eyes and growled, bringing up his other hand. I focused again, blasting him with another wave of wind, but the creature stayed on his feet. Suddenly, I felt myself being pulled forward. His other hand held the Lens that Bastille had called a Voidstormer's Lens, the one that sucked in air.

The Lens was pulling me toward the bars, even though I was pushing Kiliman away with my own Lenses. I slipped on the ground, stumbling, growing panicked.

Suddenly, hands grabbed me from behind, steadying me. 'What did I tell you, kid?' Kaz called over the sound of the wind. 'That thing is part Alivened! You can't kill him with regular means! And those are blood-forged Lenses he's using. They'll be more powerful than yours!'

He was right. Even with Kaz holding on to me, I could feel myself being pulled toward Kiliman. I turned my Windstormer's Lenses away from him, then focused them on the wall, pushing myself back.

Kiliman turned his Lens off.

I was shaken by the force of the wind blowing from my face. I stumbled, knocking Kaz over, and I nearly lost my footing as I turned my Lenses off.

In that moment, Kiliman focused *his* Lens directly at the pair of Translator's Lenses in my other hand. Apparently, the Voidstormer's Lens – just like my Windstormer's Lenses – could focus on a single object. The Translator's Lenses were pried free from my fingers and sucked across the room.

I yelled, shocked, but Bastille snatched the Lenses from the air as they passed her. She stood up, dagger in one hand, Lenses in the other. I stepped up beside her, readying my Windstormer's Lenses, trying not to look at the frosty wounds on Bastille's hand.

Kiliman stood up, but did not raise his Lenses. 'I still hold the knight,' he whispered, picking up the fallen Crystin sword. 'She will die, for you don't know where to find her. Only I can replace her Fleshstone.'

The room fell silent. Suddenly, Kiliman's face began to disintegrate, the tiny bits of metal all springing legs and crawling down his body. Half of his head, then his shoulder, and finally one arm all transformed to tiny, metal spiders, which crawled across the bars separating us, swarming like bees in a hive.

'She will die,' the Scrivener's Bone said, somehow speaking despite the fact that half of his face was now missing. 'I do not lie, Smedry. You know I do not lie.'

I stared him down, but felt an increasing sense of dread. Do you remember what I said about choices? It seems to me that no matter what you choose, you end up losing something. In this case, it was either the Lenses or Draulin's life.

'I will trade her to you for the Lenses,' Kiliman said. 'I was sent to hunt those, not you. Once I have them, I will leave.'

The metal spiders were crawling into the room, crossing the floor, but they stayed away from Bastille and me. Kaz groaned, finally getting to his feet from where I'd inadvertently pushed him.

I closed my eyes. Bastille's mother, or the Lenses? I wished that I could do something to fight. But, the Windstormer's Lenses couldn't hurt this thing – even if they blew him back, he could simply flee and wait for Draulin to die. Australia was still lost somewhere in the Library. Would she be next?

'I will trade,' I said quietly.

Kiliman smiled – or, at least, the remaining half of his face smiled. Then, to the side, I saw several of his spiders climb up on something.

A trip wire in the room where I was standing.

The floor fell away beneath Bastille and me as the spiders tripped the wire. Bastille cried out, reaching for the edge of the floor, but she just barely missed grabbing it.

'Rocky Mountain Oysters!' Kaz swore in shock, though the pit opened a few feet away from him. I caught one last glimpse of his panicked face as I tumbled into the hole.

We plummeted some thirty feet and landed with a thud on a

patch of too-soft ground. I hit on my stomach, but Bastille – who twisted herself to protect the Translator's Lenses she still clutched – scraped against the wall, then hit the ground in a much more awkward position. She grunted in pain.

I shook my head, trying to clear it. Then, I crawled over to Bastille. She groaned, looking even more dazed than I felt, but she seemed all right. Finally, I glanced up the dark shaft toward the light above. A concerned Kaz stuck his head out over the opening.

'Alcatraz!' he yelled. 'You two all right?'

'Yeah,' I called up. 'I think we are.' I poked at the ground, trying to decide why it had broken our fall. It appeared to be made of some kind of cushioned cloth.

'The ground is padded,' I called up to Kaz. 'Probably to keep us from breaking our necks.' It was another Curator trap, meant to frustrate us, but not kill us.

'What was the point of that?' I heard Kaz bellow at Kiliman. 'They just agreed to trade with you!'

'Yes, he did.' I could faintly hear Kiliman's voice. 'But the Librarians of my order have a saying: Never trust a Smedry.'

'Well, he's not going to be able to trade with you while he's trapped in a pit!' Kaz yelled.

'True,' Kiliman said. 'But you can trade. Have him pass you the Translator's Lenses, then meet me at the center of the Library. You are the one who has the power to Travel places, are you not?'

Kaz fell silent.

This creature knows a lot about us, I thought with frustration.

'You are a Smedry,' Kiliman said to Kaz. 'But not an Oculator. I will deal with you instead of the boy. Bring me the Lenses, and I will return the woman – with her Fleshstone – to you. Be quick. She will die within the hour.'

There was silence, broken only by Bastille's groan as she sat up. She still had the Translator's Lenses in her hand. Eventually, Kaz's head popped out above the pit.

'Alcatraz?' he called. 'You there?'

'Yeah,' I said.

'Where else would we be?' Bastille grumbled.

'It's too dark to see you,' Kaz said. 'Anyway, the Scrivener's Bone has left, and I can't get through the bars to follow him. What should we do? Do you want me to try to find some rope?'

I sat, trying – with all of my capacity – to think of a way out of the predicament. Bastille's mother was dying because a piece of crystal had been ripped from her body. Kiliman had her and would trade her only for the Translator's Lenses. I was trapped in a pit with Bastille, who had taken a much harder hit falling than I had, and we had no rope.

I was stuck, looking for a solution where there wasn't one. Sometimes, there just isn't a way out, and thinking won't help, no matter how clever you are. In a way, that's kind of like what I wrote at the beginning of this chapter. You remember, the secret 'thing' I claimed to have done in this book? The shameful, clever trick? Did you go looking for it? Well, whatever you found, that wasn't what I was intending – because there is no trick. No hidden message. No clever twist I put into the first fourteen chapters.

I don't know how hard you searched, but it couldn't have been harder than I searched for a way to both save Draulin and keep my Lenses. I was quickly running out of time, and I knew it. I had to make a decision. Right then. Right there.

I chose to take the Lenses from Bastille and throw them up to Kaz. He caught them, just barely.

'Can your Talent take you to the center of the Library?' I asked.

He nodded. 'I think so. Now that I have a location to search for.'

'Go,' I said. 'Trade the Lenses for Draulin's life. We'll worry about getting them back later.'

Kaz nodded. 'All right. You wait here – I'll find a rope or some-thing and come back for you once Bastille's mother is safe.'

He disappeared for a moment, then returned, head sticking back out over the opening. 'Before I go, do you want this?' He held out Bastille's pack.

The Grappler's Glass boots were inside. I felt a stab of hope, but quickly dismissed it. The sides of the shaft were stone.

Besides, even if I did get free, I'd still have to trade the Lenses for Draulin. I'd just have to do it in person. Still, there was food in the pack. No telling how long we'd be in the pit. 'Sure,' I called up to him, 'drop it.'

He did so, and I stepped to the side, letting it hit the soft ground. By now, Bastille was on her feet, though she leaned woozily against the side of the pit.

This was why I shouldn't ever have been made a leader. This is why nobody should ever look to me. Even then, I made the wrong decisions. A leader has to be hard, capable of making the right choice.

You think I *did* make the right one? Well, then, you'd be as poor a leader as I was. You see, saving Draulin was the *wrong* choice. By trading the Translator's Lenses, I may have saved one life, but at a terrible cost.

The Librarians would gain access to the knowledge of the Incarna people. Sure, Draulin would live – but how many would die as the war turned against the Free Kingdoms? With ancient technology at their disposal, the Librarians would become a force that could no longer be held back.

I'd saved one life, but doomed so many more. That's not the sort of weakness a leader can afford. I suspect that Kaz knew the truth of that. He hesitated, then asked, 'You sure you want to do this, kid?'

'Yes,' I said. At the time, I didn't think about things like protecting the future of the Free Kingdoms or the like. I just knew one thing: I couldn't be the one responsible for Draulin's death.

'All right,' Kaz said. 'I'll be back for you. Don't worry.'

'Good luck, Kaz.'

And he was gone.

16

Writers – particularly storytellers like myself – write about people. That is ironic, since we actually know nothing about them.

Think about it. Why does someone become a writer? Is it because they *like* people? Of course not. Why else would we seek out a job where we get to spend all day, every day, cooped up in our basement with no company besides paper, a pencil, and our imaginary friends?

Writers hate people. If you've ever met a writer, you know that they're generally awkward, slovenly individuals who live beneath stairwells, hiss at those who pass, and forget to bathe for weeklong periods. And those are the socially competent ones.

I looked up at the sides of our pit.

Bastille sat on the floor, obviously trying to pretend she was a patient person. It worked about as well as a watermelon trying to pretend it was a golf ball. (Though not as messy and half as much fun.)

'Come on, Bastille,' I said, glancing at her. 'I know you're as frustrated as I am. What are you thinking? Could I break these walls somehow? Make a slope we can climb up?'

'And risk the sides of the wall toppling down on us?' she asked flatly.

She had a point. 'What if we tried to climb up without using the Talent?'

'These walls are slick and polished, Smedry,' she snapped. 'Not even a Crystin can climb that.'

'But if we shimmied up, feet on one wall, back against the other one ...'

'The hole is *way* too wide for that.'

I fell silent.

'What?' she asked. 'No other brilliant ideas? What about *jumping up*? You should try that a few times.' She turned away from me, looking at the side of our pit, then sighed.

I frowned. 'Bastille, this isn't like you.'

'Oh?' she asked. 'How do you know what's "like me" and what isn't? You've known me for what, a couple of months? During which time we've spent all of three or four days together?'

'Yes, but ... well, I mean ...'

'It's over, Smedry,' she said. 'We're beaten. Kaz has probably already arrived at the center of the Library and given up those Lenses. Chances are, Kiliman will just take him captive and let my mother die.'

'Maybe we can still find a way out. And go help.'

Bastille didn't seem to be listening. She simply sat down, arms folded across her knees, staring at the wall. 'They really are right about me,' she whispered. 'I never deserved to be a knight.'

'What?' I asked, squatting down beside her. 'Bastille, that's nonsense.'

'I've only done two real operations. This one and the infiltration back in your hometown. Both times I ended up trapped, unable to do anything. I'm useless.'

'We *all* got trapped,' I said. 'Your mother didn't fare much better.'

She ignored this, still shaking her head. 'Useless. You had to save me from those ropes, and then you had to save me *again* when we were covered in tar. That's not even counting the time you saved me from falling out the side of the *Dragonaut*.'

'You saved me too,' I said. 'Remember the coins? If it wasn't for you, I'd be floating around with burning eyes, offering illicit books to people as if I were a drug dealer looking for a new victim.'

(Hey, kids? Want a taste of Dickens? It's awesome, man. Come on. First chapters of *Hard Times* are free. I know you'll be back for *Tale of Two Cities* later.)

'That was different,' Bastille said.

'No, it wasn't. Look, you saved my life – not only that, but without you, I wouldn't know what half these Lenses are supposed to do.'

She looked up at me, brow furled. 'You're doing it again.'

'What?'

'Encouraging people. Like you did with Australia, like you've done with all of us this entire trip. What is it about you, Smedry? You don't want to make any decisions, but you take it upon yourself to encourage us all anyway?'

I fell silent. How had that happened? This conversation had been about her, and suddenly she'd thrown it back in my face. (I've found that throwing things in people's faces – words, conversations, knives – is one of Bastille's specialties.)

I looked toward the light flickering faintly in the room above. It seemed haunting and inviting, and as I watched it, I realized something about myself. While I hated being trapped because I worried about what might happen to Kaz and Draulin, there was a larger cause of my frustration.

I wanted to be helping. I didn't want to be left out. I wanted to be in charge. Leaving things to others was tough for me.

'I *do* want to be a leader, Bastille,' I whispered.

She rustled, turning to look at me.

'I think all people, in their hearts, want to be heroes,' I continued. 'But, the ones who want it most are the outcasts. The boys who sit in the backs of rooms, always laughed at because they're different, because they stand out, because ... they break things.'

I wondered if Kaz understood that there were more ways than one to be abnormal. Everyone was strange in some way – everyone had weaknesses that could be mocked. I *did* know how he felt. I'd felt it too.

I didn't want to go back.

'Yes, I want to be a hero,' I said. 'Yes, I want to be the one leader. I used to sit and dream of being the one that people looked to. Of being the one who could *fix* things, rather than break them.'

'Well, you have it,' she said. 'You're the heir to the Smedry line. You're in charge.'

'I know. And that terrifies me.'

She regarded me. She'd taken off her Warrior's Lenses, and I could see the light from above reflecting in her solemn eyes.

I sat down, shaking my head. 'I don't know what to do, Bastille. Being the kid who's always in trouble didn't exactly prepare me for this. How do I decide whether or not to trade my most powerful weapon to save someone's life? I feel like ... like I'm drowning. Like I'm swimming in water over my head and can't ever reach the top.

'I guess that's why I keep saying I don't want to lead. Because I know if people pay *too* much attention to me, they'll realize that I'm doing a terrible job.' I grimaced. 'Just like I am now. You and I captured, your mother dying, Kaz walking into danger, and Australia – who *knows* where she is.'

I fell silent, feeling even more foolish now that I'd explained it. Yet, oddly, Bastille didn't laugh at me.

'I don't think you're doing a terrible job, Alcatraz,' she said. 'Being in charge is hard. If everything goes well, then nobody pays attention. Yet, if something goes wrong, you're always to blame. I think you've done fine. You just need to be a little bit more sure of yourself.'

I shrugged. 'Maybe. What do you know of it, anyway?'

'I ...'

I glanced at her, the tone in her voice making me curious. Some things about Bastille had never added up, in my estimation. She seemed to *know* too much. True, she'd said that she'd wanted to be an Oculator, but that didn't give me enough of an explanation. There was more.

'You *do* know about it,' I said.

Now it was her turn to shrug. 'A little bit.'

I cocked my head.

'Haven't you noticed?' she asked, looking at me. 'My mother doesn't have a prison name.'

'So?'

'So, I do.'

I scratched my head.

'You really *don't* know anything, do you?' she asked.

I snorted. 'Well, excuse me for being raised on a completely different continent from you people. What are you talking about?'

'You are named Alcatraz after Alcatraz the First,' Bastille said. 'The Smedries use names like that a lot, names from their heritage. The Librarians, then, have tried to discredit those names by using them for prisons.'

'You're not a Smedry,' I said, 'but you have a prison name too.'

'Yes, but my family is also ... traditional. They tend to use famous names over and over again, just like your family does. That's not something that common people do.'

I blinked.

Bastille rolled her eyes. 'My father's a nobleman, Smedry,' she said. 'That's what I'm trying to tell you. I have a traditional name because I'm his daughter. My full name is Bastille Vianitelle the Ninth.'

'Ah, right.' It's sort of like what rich people, kings, and popes do in the Hushlands – they reuse old names, then just add a number.

'I grew up with everyone expecting me to be a leader,' she said. 'Only, I'm not very well suited to it. Not like you.'

'I'm not well suited to it!'

She snorted. 'You are good with people, Smedry. Me, I don't *want* to lead people. They kind of annoy me.'

'You should have become a novelist.'

'Don't like the hours,' she said. 'Anyway, I can tell you that growing up learning how to lead doesn't make any difference. A lifetime of training only makes you understand just how inadequate you are.'

We fell silent.

'So ... what happened?' I asked. 'How did you end up as a Crystin?'

'My mother,' Bastille said. 'She's not noble, but she *is* a Crystin. She always pushed me to become a Knight of Crystallia, saying that my father didn't need another useless daughter hanging about. I tried to prove her wrong, but I'm too well-bred to do something simple, like become a baker or a carpenter.'

'So you tried to become an Oculator.'

She nodded. 'I didn't tell anyone. I'd heard that Oculatory power was genetic, of course, but I intended to prove everyone wrong. I'd be the first Oculator in my line, then my mother and father would be impressed.

'Well, you know how that turned out. So, I just joined the Crystin, like my mother had always said I should. I had to give up my title and my money. Now I'm realizing just how foolish that decision was. I make an even worse Crystin than I did an Oculator.'

She sighed, folding her arms again. 'The thing is, I thought – for a while – that I *would* be good at it. I made knight faster than anyone ever had. Then, I was immediately sent out to protect the Old Smedry – which was one of the most dangerous, difficult assignments the knights had. I *still* don't know why they picked that as my first job. It's never made sense.'

'It's almost like they were setting you up to fail.'

She sat for a moment. 'I never thought about it that way. Why would anyone do such a thing?'

I shrugged. 'I don't know. But, you have to admit, it does sound suspicious. Maybe someone in charge of giving the assignments was jealous of how quickly you made it to knight, and wanted to see you fall.'

'At the cost, maybe, of the Old Smedry's life?'

I shrugged. 'People do strange things sometimes, Bastille.'

'I still find it hard to believe,' she said. 'Besides, my mother was part of the group that makes those assignments.'

'She seems like a hard one to please.'

Bastille snorted. 'That's an understatement. I made knight, and all she could say was, "Make certain you live up to the honor." I think she was *expecting* me to bungle my first job – maybe that's why she came to get me herself.'

I didn't reply, but somehow I knew we were thinking the same thing. Bastille's own *mother* couldn't have been the one to set her up to fail, could she? That seemed a stretch. Of course, my mother had stolen my inheritance, then sold me out to the Librarians. So, maybe Bastille and I were a well-matched pair.

I sat with my back against the wall, looking up, and my mind turned away from Bastille's problems and back to what I'd said earlier. It had felt good to get the thoughts out. It had helped me, finally, sort out how I felt. A few months back, I would have settled for simply being normal. Now I knew that being a Smedry meant something. The more time I spent filling that role, the more I wanted to do it well. To justify the name I bore, and live up to what my grandfather and the others expected of me.

Perhaps you find that ironic. There I was, deciding bravely that I would take upon myself the mantle that had been quite randomly thrust upon me. Now, here I am, writing my memoirs, trying as hard as I can to throw off that very same mantle.

I *wanted* to be famous. That should, in itself, be enough to make you worried. Never trust a man who wants to be a hero. We'll talk about this more in the next book.

'We're quite the pair, aren't we?' Bastille asked, smiling for the first time I'd seen since we fell down the shaft.

I smiled back. 'Yeah. Why is it that my best soul-searching moments always come when I'm trapped?'

'Sounds like you should be imprisoned more often.'

I nodded. Then, I jumped as something floated out of the wall next to me. 'Gak!' I said before I realized it was just a Curator.

'Here,' it said, dropping a leaf of paper to the ground.

'What's this?' I asked, picking it up.

'Your book.'

It was the paper I'd written in the tomb, the inscription about the Dark Talent. That meant we'd been trapped for nearly an hour. Bastille was right. Kaz had probably already reached the center of the Library.

The Curator floated away.

'Your mother,' I said, folding up the paper. 'If she gets that crystal thing back, she'll be all right?'

Bastille nodded.

'So, since we're trapped here with no hope of rescue, do you mind telling me what that crystal was? You know, to help pass the time?'

Bastille snorted, then stood up and pulled the silvery hair up off the back of her neck. She turned around, and I could see a sparkling blue crystal set into the skin on the back of her neck. I could see it easily, as she still only wore the tight black T-shirt tucked into the trousers of her militaristic uniform.

'Wow,' I said.

'Three kinds of crystals grow in Crystallia,' she said, letting her hair back down. 'The first we turn into swords and daggers. The second become Fleshstones, which are what really make us into Crystin.'

'What does it do?' I asked.

Bastille paused. 'Things,' she finally replied.

'How wonderfully specific.'

She flushed. 'It's kind of personal, Alcatraz. It's because of the Fleshstone that I can run so quickly. Stuff like that.'

'Okay,' I said. 'And the third type of crystal?'

'Also personal.'

Great, I thought.

'It's not really important,' she said. As she moved to sit down, I noticed something. Her hand – the one that had been holding the dagger that had blocked the Frostbringer's Lens – had red and cracking skin.

'You okay?' I asked, nodding to her hand.

'I'll be fine,' she said. 'Our daggers are made from immature swordstones – they aren't meant to hold out against powerful Lenses for long. A little of the ice got around and hit my fingers, but it's nothing that won't heal.'

I wasn't as convinced. 'Maybe you should—'

'Hush!' Bastille said suddenly, climbing to her feet.

I did so, frowning. I followed Bastille's gaze up toward the top of our hole.

'What?' I asked.

'I thought I heard something,' she replied.

We waited tensely. Finally, we saw shadows moving above. Bastille slowly pulled her dagger from its sheath, and even in the darkness, I could see that it was laced with cracks. What she expected to do at such a distance was beyond me.

Finally, a head leaned out over the hole.

'Hello?' Australia asked. 'Anybody down there?'

17

I hope you didn't find the last line of that previous chapter to be exciting. It was simply a convenient place to end.

You see, chapter breaks are, in a way, like Smedry Talents. They defy time and space. (This, alone, should be enough to prove to you that traditional Hushlander physics is just a load of unwashed underpants.)

Think about it. By putting in a chapter break, I make the book longer. It takes extra spaces, extra pages. Yet, because of those chapter breaks, the book becomes shorter as well. You read it more quickly. Even an unexciting hook, like Australia's showing up, encourages you to quickly turn the page and keep going.

Space becomes distorted when you read a book. Time has less relevance. In fact, if you look closely, you might be able to see golden dust floating down around you right now. (And if you can't see it, you're just not trying hard enough. Maybe you need to hit yourself on the head with another big thick fantasy novel.)

'We're down here!' I yelled up to Australia. Beside me, Bastille looked relieved and slipped her dagger back into its sheath.

'Alcatraz?' Australia asked. 'Uh … what are you doing down there?'

'Having a tea party,' I yelled back. 'What do you think? We're trapped!'

'Silly,' she said. 'Why'd you go and get trapped?'

I glanced at Bastille. She just rolled her eyes. That's Australia for you.

'We didn't exactly have a choice,' I called back.

'I climbed a tree once and couldn't get back down,' Australia said. 'I guess it's kind of the same, right?'

'Sure,' I said. 'Look, I need you to find some rope.'

'Uh,' she said. 'Where exactly am I going to find something like that?'

'I don't know!'

'All right then.' She sighed loudly and disappeared.

'She's hopeless,' Bastille said.

'I'm realizing that. At least she's still got her soul. I was half afraid that she'd end up in serious trouble.'

'Like getting captured by a member of the Scrivener's Bones, or perhaps falling down a pit?'

'Something like that,' I said, kneeling down. I wasn't about to count on Australia to get us out. I'd already been around her long enough to realize that she probably wasn't going to be of much help.

(Which, incidentally, was why you shouldn't have been all that excited to see her show up. You still turned the page, didn't you?)

I opened Bastille's pack and pulled out the boots with the Grappler's Glass on the bottom. I activated the glass, then stuck a boot to the side of the wall. As expected, it didn't stick. They only worked on glass.

'So ... maybe we *should* have you try to break the walls down,' Bastille said speculatively. 'You'll probably bury us in stone, but that would be better than sitting around talking about our feelings and that nonsense.'

I glanced over, smiling.

'What?' she asked.

'Nothing,' I said. 'Just good to have you back.'

She snorted. 'Well? Breaking? Can you do it?'

'I can try,' I said speculatively. 'But, well, it seems like a long shot.'

'We've never had to depend on one of those before,' she said.

'Good point.' I rested my hands against the wall.

The Dark Talent ... beware it.... .

The words from the tomb wall returned to my mind. The paper with the inscription sat in my pocket, but I tried not to think about it. Now that I'd begun to understand what my Talent was, it didn't seem a good time to start second-guessing its nature.

There would be time enough for that later.

I tentatively sent a wave of breaking power into the wall. Cracks twisted away from my palms, moving through the stone. Bits of dust and chips began to fall in on us, but I kept going. The wall groaned.

'Alcatraz!' Bastille said, grabbing my arm and pulling me back.

I stumbled back, dazed, away from the wall as a large chunk of stone toppled inward and hit the floor where I had been standing. The soft, springy ground gave way beneath the stone. Kind of like my head would have, had it been in the way. Only that would have involved a lot more blood and a lot more screaming.

I stared at the chunk of stone. Then, I glanced, up at the wall. It was cracked and broken, and other bits of it seemed ready to fall off too.

'Okay, that was expected,' Bastille said, 'but still kind of dumb of us, eh?'

I nodded, stooping over to pick up a Grappler's boot. If only I could get it to work. I put it up against the wall again, but it refused to stick.

'That's not going to do anything, Smedry,' Bastille said.

'There's silicon in the rock. That's the same thing as glass.'

'True,' Bastille said. 'But there isn't enough to make the Grappler's Glass stick.'

I tried anyway. I focused on the glass, closing my eyes, treating it like it was a pair of Lenses.

During the months Grandpa Smedry had been training me, I'd learned how to activate stubborn Lenses. There was a trick to it. You had to give them energy. Pour part of yourself into them to make them function.

Come on! I thought to the boot, pressing it to the wall. *There's glass in the wall. Little bits of it. You can stick. You have to stick.*

I'd contacted Grandpa Smedry at a much greater distance than I was supposed to be able to. I'd done that by focusing hard on my Courier's Lenses, somehow giving them an extra boost of power. Could I somehow do the same to this boot?

I thought I felt something. The boot, pulling slightly toward the wall. I focused harder, straining, feeling myself grow tired. Yet, I didn't give up. I continued to push, opening my eyes and staring intently.

The glass on the bottom of the boot began to glow softly. Bastille looked over, shocked.

Come on, I thought again. I felt the boot drawing something from me, taking it out, feeding on it.

When I carefully pulled my hand away, the boot stayed where it was.

'Impossible,' Bastille whispered, walking over.

I wiped my brow, smiling triumphantly.

Bastille reached out with a careful touch, poking the boot. Then, she easily pulled it off the wall.

'Hey!' I said. 'Did you see what I had to go through to get that to stick?'

She snorted. 'It came off easily, Smedry. Do you honestly expect that you'd be able to walk up the wall with it?'

I felt my sense of triumph deflate. She was right. If I had to work *that* hard to get one boot to stay in one place, there was no way I'd be able to summon enough effort to get all the way to the top.

'Still,' Bastille said. 'That's pretty amazing. How did you do it?'

I shrugged. 'I just shoved a little extra power into the glass.'

Bastille didn't reply. She stared at the boot, then looked at me. 'This is silimatic,' she said. 'Technology, not magic. You shouldn't be able to push it like that. Technology has limits.'

'I think your technology and your magic are more related than people believe, Bastille,' I said.

She nodded slowly. Then, she moved quickly, putting the boot back into the pack and zipping it up. 'You still have those Windstormer's Lenses?' she asked.

'Yeah,' I said. 'Why?'

She looked up, meeting my eyes. 'I have an idea.'

'Should I be frightened?' I asked.

'Probably,' she said. 'The idea's a little bit strange. Like one you might have come up with, actually.'

I raised an eyebrow.

'Get out those Lenses,' she said, throwing her pack over her shoulder.

I did so.

'Now, break the frames.'

I paused, eyeing her.

'Just do it,' she said.

I shrugged, then activated my Talent. The frames fell apart easily.

'Double up the Lenses,' she said.

'Okay,' I said, sliding one over the other.

'Can you do to those Lenses what you did to the boots? Put extra power through them?'

'I should be able to,' I said. 'But . . .'

I trailed off, suddenly coming to understand. If I blew a huge blast of air out of the Lenses, then I would be forced upward – like a fighter jet, with the Lenses being my engine. I looked up at Bastille. 'Bastille! That's absolutely insane.'

'I know,' she said, grimacing. 'I've been spending way too much time with you Smedries. But my mother is probably only a few minutes away from death. Are you willing to give it a try?'

I smiled. 'Of course I am! It sounds awesome!'

Inclined toward leadership or not, thoughtful or not, uncertain of myself or not, I was still a teenage boy. And, you have to admit, it really did sound awesome.

Bastille stepped up close to me, putting one arm around my waist, then holding on to my shoulder with the other. 'Then I'm going with you,' she said. 'Hang on to my waist.'

I nodded, feeling a bit distracted having her so close. For the first time in my life, I realized something.

Girls smell weird.

I started to feel nervous. If I blew with the Lenses too softly we'd just fall back down into the pit. If I blasted too hard, we'd end up smashing into the ceiling. It seemed like a very fine balance.

I lowered my arm, pointing the Lenses down straight by my

side, my other arm held tentatively around Bastille's waist. I took a breath, preparing myself.

'Smedry,' Bastille said, her face just inches from mine.

I blinked. Having her right there was suddenly really, *really* distracting. Plus, she was hanging on rather tightly, with the grip of a person whose strength has been enhanced by a Crystin Fleshstone.

I fumbled for a response, my mind fuzzy. (Girls, you might have noticed, can do things like this to guys. It's a result of their powerful pheromones. They evolved that way, gaining the ability to make us men fuzzy-headed, so that it would be easier for them to hit us on the heads with hardback fantasy novels and steal our cheese sticks.)

'You okay?' she asked.

'Uh ... yeah,' I managed to get out. 'What did you want?'

'I just wanted to say thanks.'

'For what?'

'For provoking me,' she said. 'For making me think that some-one had set me up to fail on purpose. It's probably not true, but it's what I needed. If there's a chance that someone stuck me in that situation intentionally, then I want to figure out who it was and why they did it. It's a challenge.'

I nodded. That's Bastille for you. Tell her that she's wonderful, and she'd just sit there and sulk. But, hint that she might have a hidden enemy somewhere, and she'd jump to her feet, full of energy.

'You ready?' I asked.

'Ready as I'll ever be.'

I focused on the Lenses – trying to ignore how close Bastille was – and built up Oculatory energy.

Then, holding my breath, I released the power.

We shot upward in a lurching burst of wind. Dust and chips of stone blew out beneath us, puffing up the sides of the shaft. We blasted upward, wind tussling my hair, the opening to the pit approaching far too quickly. I cried out, deactivating the Lenses, but we had too much momentum.

We passed the lip of the hole and continued on. I threw up my hands in front of my face as we approached the ceiling. With the Lenses no longer jetting, gravity slowed us. We crested the blast a few inches from the ceiling, then began to plummet downward again.

'Now, kick!' Bastille said, twisting and putting both of her feet against my chest.

'Wha—' I began, but Bastille kicked, throwing me to the side and pushing herself the other direction.

We hit the ground on either side of the pit. I rolled, then came to a rest, staring upward. The room spun around me.

We were free. I sat up, holding my head. Across the pit, Bastille was smiling as she jumped to her feet. 'I can't believe that actually worked!'

'You kicked me!' I said with a groan.

'Well, I owed it to you,' she said. 'Remember, you kicked me back in the *Dragonaut*. I didn't want you to feel like I didn't return the feeling.'

I grimaced. This, by the way, is a pretty good metaphor for my entire relationship with Bastille. I'm thinking of writing a book on the concept. *Kicking Your Friends for Fun and Profit.*

Suddenly, something occurred to me. 'My Lenses!' They lay in shattered pieces on the ground beside the pit. I'd dropped them as I hit. I stood up and rushed over, but it was no use. There wasn't enough of them left to use.

'Gather up the pieces,' Bastille said. 'They can be reforged.'

I sighed. 'Yeah, I suppose. This means we're going to have to face Kiliman without them.'

Bastille fell silent.

I don't have any offensive Lenses, and Bastille's only got a close-to-broken dagger. How are we going to fight that creature?

I brushed the pieces of glass into a pouch, then put it into one of my Lens pockets.

'We're free,' Bastille said, 'but we still don't really know what to do. In fact, we don't even know how to get to Kiliman.'

'We'll find a way,' I said, standing up.

She looked at me, then – surprisingly – nodded. 'All right, then, what do we do?'

'We—'

Suddenly, Australia rushed back into the room. She was puffing from exertion. 'All right, I found your rope!'

She held up an empty hand.

'Uh, thanks,' I said. 'Is the rope imaginary, then?'

'No, silly,' she said, laughing. She picked something up between two fingers. 'Look!'

'Trip wire,' Bastille said.

'Is that what it is?' Australia said. 'I just found it on the ground over there.'

'And how exactly were you going to use that to get us out of the pit?' I asked. 'I doubt it's long enough, and even if it is, it would never have held our weight.'

Australia cocked her head. '*That's* why you wanted rope?'

'Sure,' I said. 'So that we could climb out of the pit.'

'But, you're already out of the pit.'

'We are now,' I said with exasperation. 'But we weren't at the time. I wanted you to find rope so that we could climb it.'

'Oh!' Australia said. 'Well, you should have said so, then!'

I stood, stupefied. 'You know what, never mind,' I said, taking the length of trip wire. I was about to stuff it in my pocket, then paused, looking at it.

'What?' Bastille asked.

I smiled.

'You have an idea?'

I nodded.

'What is it?'

'Tell you in a minute,' I said. 'First, we have to figure out how to get to the center of the Library.'

We all looked at one another.

'I've been wandering through the hallways all day,' Australia said. 'With those ghost things offering me books at every turn. I keep explaining that I *hate* reading, but they don't listen. If I hadn't run across your footprints, Alcatraz, I'd still be lost!'

'Footprints!' I said. 'Australia, can you see Kaz's footprints?'

'Of course.' She tapped the yellow Lenses, my Tracker's Lenses, which she was still wearing.

'Follow them!'

She nodded, then led us from the room. Only a few feet down the hallway, however, she stopped.

'What?' I asked.

'They end here.'

His Talent, I realized. *It's jumping him about the Library, leading him to the center. We'll never be able to track him.*

'That's it, then,' Bastille said, beginning to sound depressed again. 'We'll never get there in time.'

'No,' I said. 'If I'm in charge, then we're not going to give up.'

She looked taken aback. Then, she nodded. 'All right. What do we do?'

I stood for a moment, thinking. There had to be a way. *Information, lad*, Grandpa Smedry's voice seemed to return to me. *More powerful than any sword or gun ...*

I looked up sharply. 'Australia, can you follow my footprints back the way I originally came, before I entered that room with the pit?'

'Sure,' she said.

'Do it, then.'

She led us through cagelike chambers and corridors. In a few minutes, we left the dungeon section of the Library and entered the section with the bookshelves. The gold bars I'd discarded on the ground proved that we were back where we'd started. I, of course, piled the bars into Bastille's pack.

No, not because of some great plan to use them. I just figured that if I survived all this, I'd want some gold. (I don't know if you realize this, but you can totally buy stuff with it.)

'Great,' Bastille said. 'We're back here. I don't mean to question you, O Great Leader, but we were lost when we were *here* too. We still don't know which way to go.'

I reached into a pocket, then pulled out the Discerner's Lenses. I put them on, then looked at the bookshelves. I smiled.

'What?' Bastille asked.

'They hold every book ever written, right?'

'That's what the Curators claim.'

'So, they would have gathered them chronologically. When a new book comes out, the Curators get a copy, then put it on their shelves.'

'So?'

'That means,' I said, 'that the newer books are going to be at the outer edges of the Library. The older the books get, the closer we'll get to the center. That's the place where they would have put their first books.'

Bastille opened her mouth slightly, then her eyes widened as she understood. 'Alcatraz, that's brilliant!'

'Must have been that bump to the head,' I said, then pointed down the hallway. 'That way. The books get older as they move down the row that direction.'

Bastille and Australia nodded, and we were off.

18

We're almost at the end of the second book. Hopefully, you've enjoyed the ride. I'm certain you know more about the world now than you did when you began.

In fact, you've probably learned all you need to. You know about the Librarian conspiracy, and you know that I'm a liar. Everything I wanted to do has been accomplished. I suppose I can just end the book right here.

Thanks for reading.

The end.

Oh, so that's not good enough for you, eh? Demanding today, are we?

All right, fine. I'll finish it for you. But, not because I'm a nice guy. I'll do it because I can't wait to see the look on your face when Bastille dies. (You didn't forget about that part, did you? I'll bet you think I'm lying. However, I promise you that I'm not. She really dies. You'll see.)

Bastille, Australia, and I raced through the Library hallways. We'd passed through the rooms with books and were up to the ones with scrolls. These too were arranged by age. We were close. I could feel it.

That worried me. Bastille's mother was dying, and Kaz was likely in serious danger. We had little hope in fighting Kiliman. We were outmatched and outmaneuvered, and we were charging right into the enemy's hands.

However, I figured that it wasn't a good idea to explain to the others how bad things seemed. I was determined to keep a 'stiff upper lip', even if I didn't really understand what that meant. (Though it does sound vaguely uncomfortable.)

'All right,' I said. 'We have to beat this guy. What are our resources?' That sounded like the kind of thing a leader would say.

'One cracked dagger,' Bastille said. 'Probably won't survive another hit from those Frostbringer's Lenses.'

'We've got that string,' Australia added, poking through Bastille's pack as we ran. 'And ... it looks like a couple of muffins. Oh, and one pair of boots.'

Great, I thought. 'Well, I'm down to three pairs of Lenses. We've got my Oculator's Lenses – which won't be much good, since Grandpa Smedry *still* hasn't bothered to teach me how to use them defensively. We've got the Discerner's Lenses, which will get us to the center. And we've got Australia's Tracker's Lenses.'

'Plus that Lens you found in the tomb,' Bastille noted.

'Which, unfortunately, we can't seem to use.'

Bastille nodded. 'Though, we've also got two Smedries – and two Talents.'

'That's right,' I said. 'Australia, do you have to fall asleep for yours to work?'

'Of course I do, silly,' she said. 'I can't wake up looking ugly if I don't fall asleep!'

I sighed.

'I'm *really* good at falling asleep,' she said.

'Well, that's something at least,' I grumbled. Then, I cursed myself. 'I mean, bravely onward we must go, troops!'

Bastille shot me a grimace.

'Little too much?'

'Just a smidge,' she said drily, 'I—'

She cut off as I held up a hand. We skidded to a halt in the musty hallway. To the sides, ancient lamps flickered, and a trio of Curators floated around us, ever present, watching for an opportunity to offer us books.

'What?' Bastille asked.

'I can feel the creature,' I said. 'At least, his Lenses.'

'Then he can feel us?'

I shook my head. 'Scrivener's Bones aren't Oculators. Those blood-forged Lenses might make him tough, but we hold the edge in information. We . . .'

I trailed off as I noticed something.

'Alcatraz?' Bastille asked, but I wasn't paying attention.

There, on the wall directly above the archway leading onward, was a set of scribbles. Like those made by a child too young to even draw pictures. To my eyes, they seemed to glow with a pure white color.

That aura came from the Discerner's Lenses. The scribbles were fairly fresh – no older than a couple of days. Compared with the ancient stones and scrolls in the hallway, the scribbles seemed a pure white.

'*Alcatraz*,' Bastille hissed. 'What's going on?'

'That's the Forgotten Language,' I said, pointing to the scribbles.

'What?'

To her eyes, the scribbles would be almost invisible – only the Discerner's Lenses had let me see them so starkly.

'Look closer,' I said.

Eventually, she nodded. 'Okay, so I think I see some lines up there. What of it?'

'They're new,' I said. 'Written within the last few days. So, if that really *is* the Forgotten Language, then only someone wearing Translator's Lenses could have written it.'

Finally, she seemed to understand. 'And that means ...'

'My father was here.' I looked back up at the marks. 'And I can't read the message he left for me because I gave my Lenses away.'

Our group fell silent.

My father has Lenses that let him glimpse the future. Could he have left me a message to help me fight Kiliman?

I felt frustrated. There was no way to read the inscription. If my father *had* seen into the future, wouldn't he have realized I wouldn't have my Lenses?

No – Grandpa Smedry had said that Oracle's Lenses were very unreliable and gave inconsistent information. My father very well *could* have seen that I'd be fighting Kiliman, but not known that I'd be without my Translator's Lenses.

Just to be certain, I tried the Lens I'd found in the tomb of Alcatraz the First. But, it wasn't a Translator's Lens, so it didn't let me read the inscription. Sighing, I put it away.

Information. I didn't have it. Finally, I began to grasp what Grandpa Smedry kept saying. The person who won the battle wasn't necessarily the one with the biggest army or the best weapons – it was the one who understood the most about the situation.

'Alcatraz,' Bastille said. 'Please. My mother ...'

I glanced at her. Bastille is strong. Her toughness isn't just an act, like it is with some people. Yet, I've seen her really, truly worried on a number of occasions. It's always when someone she loves is in danger.

I wasn't sure if Draulin deserved that loyalty, but I wasn't going to question a girl's love for her mother.

'Right,' I said. 'Sorry. We'll come back for this later.'

Bastille nodded. 'You want me to go scout?'

'Yeah. Be careful. I can feel Kiliman just ahead.'

She needed no further warning. I turned toward Australia. 'How quickly can you fall asleep?'

'Oh, in about five minutes.'

'Get to it, then,' I said.

'Who should I think about?' she asked. 'That'll be the person I look like when I wake up.' She grimaced at that concept.

'It depends,' I said. 'How flexible *is* your Talent? What kinds of things can you become, if you try?'

'I once dreamed about a hot day and I woke up as a Popsicle.'

Well, I thought, *that's one thing she's got on me.* Either way, it meant that the Talent was pretty darn flexible – more so than Kaz had given it credit.

Bastille was back a few seconds later. 'He's there,' she whispered. 'Talking into a Courier's Lens, but not making much progress because of the Library's interference. I think he's seeking direction about what to do with you.'

'Your mother?'

'Tied up on the side of the room,' Bastille said. 'They're in a large, circular chamber with scroll cases running along the outside. Alcatraz ... he's got Kaz too, tied up with my mother. Kaz can't use his Talent if he can't move.'

'Your mother?' I asked. 'How's she look?'

Bastille's expression grew dark. 'It was hard to tell from the distance, but I could see that she hasn't been healed yet. Kiliman must still have her Fleshstone.' She pulled her dagger from its sheath.

I grimaced, then glanced at Australia.

'So, who am I supposed to look like again?' she asked, yawning. To her credit, she already looked drowsy.

'Put away that dagger, Bastille,' I said. 'We're not going to need it.'

'It's the only weapon we have!' she protested.

'Actually, it's not. We've got something far, far better ...'

*

Are you sure I can't stop the book here? I mean, this next part isn't really all that important. Really.

All right, fine.

Bastille and I dashed into the room. It was just like she had described – wide and circular, with a domed roof and racks of scrolls around the outside. I didn't need the Discerner's Lenses to tell that these scrolls were *old*. It was a wonder they hadn't fallen apart.

A smattering of ghostly Curators moved through the chamber, several of them whispering tempting words to Kaz and Draulin. The captives lay on the ground – Kaz looking furious, Draulin looking sickly and dazed – directly opposite from the doorway Bastille and I came in through.

Kiliman stood near the captives, Crystin sword on an ancient reading table beside him. He looked up when we entered, seeming completely shocked. Even if he'd anticipated trouble, he obviously hadn't been expecting me to charge into the room head-on.

To be honest, I was a little surprised myself.

Kaz began to struggle even harder, and a Curator floated toward him, looming menacingly. Kiliman smiled, flesh lips rising on one side of his twisted face, metal ones rising on the other side. Gears, bolts, and screws shifted around his single, beady glass eye. The Scrivener's Bone immediately grabbed Draulin's crystal sword in one hand, then he pulled out a Lens with the other.

'Thank you, Smedry,' he said, 'for saving me the trouble of having to go and fetch you.'

We charged. To this day, that is probably one of the very most ridiculous sights in which I've ever participated. Two kids, barely into our teens, carrying no visible weapons, charging directly at a seven-foot-tall half-human Librarian with a massive crystalline sword.

We reached him at the same time – Bastille had paced herself to keep from outrunning me – and I felt my heart begin to flutter with anxiety.

What was I doing?

Kiliman swung. At me, of course. I threw myself into a roll, feeling the sword whoosh over my head. At that moment – while Kiliman was distracted – Bastille whipped a boot out of her pack and threw it directly at Kiliman's head.

It hit, sole first. The Grappler's Glass immediately locked onto the glass of Kiliman's left eye. The front tip of the boot extended over the bridge of his nose, jutting out past the side of his face, almost completely obscuring the view out his flesh eye as well.

The Librarian stood for a moment, seeming completely dumbfounded. That was probably the proper reaction for one who had just gotten hit in the face by a large, magical boot. Then he cursed, reaching up awkwardly, trying to pull the boot off of his face.

I scrambled to my feet. Bastille whipped out the second boot, then threw it – her aim dead on – at the pouch on Kiliman's belt. The boot stuck to the glass inside, and Bastille yanked hard on the trip wire in her hands – which was, of course, tied to the boot.

The pouch ripped free, and Bastille pulled the whole lot – wire, boot, and pouch – back into her hands, like some strange fisherman without enough money to afford a pole. She grinned at me, then pulled open the pouch, triumphantly revealing the crystal inside, stuck to the boot.

She tossed it all to me. I caught the boot, then turned off its glass. The pouch fell into my hand. Inside it, I found the Fleshstone – which I tossed to Bastille – and something else. A Lens.

I pulled it out eagerly. It wasn't, however, my Translator's Lenses. It was just the Tracker's Lens that Kiliman had been using to follow us.

We'll have to worry about the Translator's Lenses later, I thought. *No time right now.*

Kiliman bellowed, finally getting one hand inside the boot, then pulling it free by making as if he were taking a step with the hand. The Grappler's Glass let go, and Kiliman tossed the boot aside.

I gulped. He wasn't supposed to have figured that out so quickly.

'Nice trick,' he said, swinging the sword at me again. I scrambled away, dashing back toward the exit. Kiliman, however, just raised his Frostbringer's Lens, getting ready to fire it square into my back.

'Hey, Kiliman!' a voice suddenly yelled. 'I'm free and I'm making a face at you!'

Kiliman spun with shock to find Kaz, standing free from his bonds and smiling broadly. A Curator hovered next to him – but this Curator had grown legs and was starting to look more and more like Australia as her Talent wore off. We'd sent her in first, looking like one of the ghosts, to untie the captives.

Kiliman had another moment of dumbfounded shock, which Bastille took advantage of by tossing her mother's Fleshstone to Kaz. The short man caught it, then grabbed one of Draulin's ropes – she was still tied up – while Australia grabbed the other one. Together, they towed the knight behind them, running away.

Kiliman screamed in rage. It was a terrible, half-metallic sound. He spun his Frostbringer's Lens around. The glass was already glowing, and a beam of bluish light shot out.

But Kaz and the other two were already gone, lost by Kaz's Talent, into the netherspaces of the Library.

'Smedry!' Kiliman said, turning back toward me as I reached the doorway. 'I will hunt you. Even if you escape me today, I will follow. You will *never* be free of me!'

I paused. Bastille should have already run for freedom. Yet, she still stood in the center of the room, from where she'd tossed the Fleshstone to Kaz.

She was staring at Kiliman. Slowly, he became aware of her presence, and he turned.

Run, Bastille! I thought.

She did. Directly *at* Kiliman.

'No!' I yelled.

Later when I had time to think about it, I would realize why Bastille did what she did. She knew that Kiliman wasn't lying. He intended to chase us, and he was an expert hunter. He'd probably find us again before we even got out of the Library.

There was only one way to be rid of him. And that was to face him. Now.

I wasn't aware of this reasoning at the time. I just thought she was being stupid. Yet, I did something even more stupid.

I charged back into the room.

19

L ife is not fair.

If you are the discriminating reader that I think you are (you picked up this book, after all), then you should have figured this out. There are very few aspects about life that are, in any way, fair.

It isn't fair that some people are rich and others are poor. It isn't fair that I'm rambling like this, instead of continuing the climax of the story. It isn't fair that I'm so outrageously handsome, while most people are simply ordinary. It isn't fair that *diphthong* gets to be such an awesome-sounding word, yet has to mean something relatively unawesome.

No, life is not fair. It is, however, funny.

The only thing you can do is laugh at it. Some days, you have to sit in your boring chair sipping warm cocoa. Other days, you get to blast your way out of a pit in the ground, and then run off to fight a half-metal monster who is holding your friend's mother captive. Other days, you need to dress like a green hamster and dance around in circles while people throw pomegranates at you.

Don't ask.

There are two lessons I think one should learn from this book. The second one I'll blather on about in the next chapter, but the first one – and perhaps more interesting one – is this: Please remember to laugh. It's good for you. (Plus, while you're laughing, it's easier for me to hit you with the pomegranate.)

Laugh when good things happen. Laugh when bad things happen. Laugh when life is so plain boring that you can't find anything amusing about it beyond the fact that it's so utterly unamusing.

Laugh when books come to a close, even if the endings aren't happy.

This isn't part of the plan, I thought desperately as I dashed back into the room. *What's the point of having a plan if people don't follow it?*

Kiliman activated the Frostbringer's Lens, blasting it toward Bastille. She dropped her pack and whipped up her dagger, slicing it directly through the icy beam. The dagger shattered, and her hand turned blue. But, she blocked the ray long enough to get inside Kiliman's reach, and she delivered a solid blow to his stomach with her other hand.

Kiliman let out an *oof* of pain and stumbled backward. Angered, he slammed his sword down toward Bastille. Somehow, she got out of the way, and the sword hit the ground with a harsh sound.

She's so quick! I thought. She was already around to Kiliman's side and delivered a powerful kick to his ribs. Although he didn't look like he enjoyed the blow, he didn't react as much as I would have thought a regular person would. He was part Alivened; regular weapons couldn't kill this creature. That was a job for an Oculator.

As I grew close, Kiliman spun, slamming his shoulder into Bastille's chest. The blow threw her backward to the ground, and Kiliman laughed, then raised the Frostbringer's Lens, pointing it directly at her.

'No!' I yelled. The only thing I had, however, was the Grappler's Glass boot. So, I threw it.

The Lens began to glow. For once in my life, however, my aim was true – and the boot hit the Lens square on and locked into place. When the Lens went off, ice formed in a large block around the shoe, weighing it down, but also filling the boot itself, making it impossible to reach inside and turn it off.

Kiliman cursed, shaking his hand. As he did so, I realized that I still had ahold of the trip wire tied to the boot. Thinking that I'd be able to pull the Frostbringer's Lens to myself, I yanked on the wire.

I hadn't stopped to think that Kiliman might yank back. And he was a *lot* stronger than I was. His pull caused the wire to bite into my hands as it yanked me off my feet. I cried out, hitting the ground, and my Talent proactively broke the wire before Kiliman could pull me any farther toward him. I looked up, dazed, ten feet of wire still wrapped around my hands.

Kiliman freed his hand from the frozen Lens-boot combination, and he tossed both aside. Bastille was climbing to her feet. Without her jacket – which had broken when the *Dragonaut* crashed – she couldn't take much more punishment than a regular person, and Kiliman had hit her square on with a metal shoulder. It was a wonder she could even walk.

Kiliman hefted the Crystin blade in two hands, then smiled at us. He didn't seem to be at all threatened; that attitude, however, seemed to make Bastille even more determined. Despite my yelled warning, she charged the monster again.

And she calls us Smedries crazy! I thought with frustration, pushing myself to my feet. As Kiliman raised his weapon to swing at Bastille, I slammed my hand to the ground and released the Breaking Talent.

The floor cracked. There was an awesome, deafening sound as rocks shattered and sections of floor became rubble. Kiliman idly stepped to the side, raising a metallic eyebrow at the rift that appeared behind him.

'What, exactly, was that supposed to do?' it asked, glancing at me.

'It was supposed to make you stumble,' I said. 'But, it'll work as a distraction too.'

At that moment, Bastille tackled him.

Kiliman yelled, falling to the ground, the Crystin blade sliding from his grip. As he hit, something fell from one of his pockets and skidded across the floor.

My Translator's Lenses.

I cried out, dashing toward them. From behind, I could hear Bastille grunting as she snatched the Crystin blade. Kiliman, how- ever, was just too strong. He grabbed her foot with a metal-bolt hand, then threw her to the side, causing her to drop the sword.

She hit the wall with a terrible thud. I spun in alarm.

Bastille slid to the ground. She looked dazed. Her forehead was bleeding from a cut, and one of her hands was still blue from the blast of frost. She favored her side and grimaced as she tried – then failed – to stand. She seemed to be in *really* bad shape.

Kiliman stood up, then recovered the Crystin blade. He shook his head, as if to clear it, and with his flesh hand he pulled out another Lens. The Voidstormer's Lens: the one that sucked things toward him.

He pointed the Lens toward Bastille. She groaned as she began to slide across the floor toward him, unable to even stand. Kiliman raised the sword.

I dived for the Translator's Lenses, which had skidded across the floor to rest beside one of the scroll-covered walls. I knelt beside the Lenses, hurriedly grabbing them.

'Ha!' Kiliman said. 'You'd fetch those Lenses even as I kill your friend. I thought that Smedries were supposed to be bold and honorable. We can see what happens to your grand ideals once real danger is near!'

I knelt there for a moment, my back to Kiliman, Translator's Lenses in my fingers. I knew I couldn't let him have them. Not even to save my life or Bastille's …

I glanced over my shoulder. Bastille came to a rest in front of Kiliman. She had her eyes closed, and barely seemed to be breathing. He raised her mother's sword to kill her.

This is the part I've been warning you about. The part I know you're not going to like. I'm sorry.

I dashed away, making for the exit of the room.

Kiliman laughed even more loudly. 'I knew it!'

At that moment, in my haste, I tripped. I stumbled on the uneven ground and fell facedown, the Translator's Lenses sliding from my fingers and hitting the stone floor. They tumbled away. 'No!' I yelled.

'Aha!' Kiliman said, then spun his Voidstormer's Lens toward the fallen Translator's Lenses. They whipped off the floor and flew toward him. I watched the Lenses go, meeting Kiliman's eyes – one human, one glass – as he exulted in his victory.

Then I smiled. I think it was about that moment when he

noticed the trip wire tied around the frame of the Translator's Lenses, which flew through the air toward him.

A thin wire, nearly invisible. It stretched from the spectacles to a place across the room. The place where I'd been kneeling by the wall a moment before.

The place where I'd tied the other end of the trip wire to one of the scrolls.

Kiliman caught the Lenses. The trip wire pulled taut. The scroll popped off of its shelf, falling to the ground.

The Librarian monster's eyes opened wide, and his mouth gaped in shock. The Translator's Lenses fell to the ground in front of him.

Immediately, the Curators surrounded Kiliman. 'You have taken a book!' one cried.

'No!' Kiliman said, stepping back. 'It was an accident!'

'You signed no contract,' another said, skull face smiling. 'Yet you took a book.'

'Your soul is ours.'

'NO!'

I shuddered at the pain in that voice. Kiliman reached toward me, furious, but it was too late. A fire grew from nothing at his feet. It burned around him, and he screamed again.

'You will fall, Smedry! The Librarians will have your blood! It will be spilt on an altar to make the very Lenses we'll use to destroy your kingdoms, break that which you love, and enslave those who follow you. You may have beaten me, but *you will fall!*'

I shivered. The fires consumed Kiliman, and I had to shield my eyes against the bright light.

And then, it was gone. I blinked, clearing the after-image from my eyes, and saw a new Curator – one with only half of a skull – hovering where Kiliman had stood. A group of discarded nuts, bolts, gears, and springs were scattered on the ground.

The half-skull Curator hovered over to the side of the room, carefully replacing the scroll that had been pulled free. I ignored it; there were more important things to worry about.

'Bastille!' I said, rushing over to her. There was blood on her lips, and she seemed so bruised and battered. I knelt beside her.

She groaned softly. I gulped.

'Nice trick,' she whispered. 'With the trip wire.'

'Thanks.'

She coughed, then spit up some blood.

By the first sands, I thought with a sudden stab of fear. *No. This can't be happening!*

'Bastille, I …' I suddenly found tears in my eyes. 'I wasn't fast enough or smart enough. I'm sorry.'

'What are you blathering about?'

I blinked. 'Well, you look kind of bad, and …'

'Shut up and help me to my feet,' she said, stumbling to her knees.

I stared at her.

'What?' she said. 'It's not like I'm dying or anything. I just broke a few ribs and bit my tongue. Shattering Glass, Smedry, do you have to be so melodramatic all the time?'

With that, she stretched, grimaced, and stumbled over to pick up the fallen Crystin sword.

I got to my feet, feeling relieved and a little foolish. I went over and carefully untied the Translator's Lenses from the trip wire, then slid them into their pocket, where they belonged. To the side, I could see Kaz peek into the room, apparently having returned from depositing Draulin and Australia somewhere safe. He smiled broadly when he saw me and Bastille, then rushed into the room.

'Alcatraz, kid, I can't believe you're still alive!'

'I know,' I said. 'I thought for sure one of us was going to die. You know, if I ever write my memoirs, this section is going to seem really boring because nobody was narratively dynamic enough to get themselves killed.'

Bastille snorted, joining us, holding one of her arms close to her side. 'That's real inspiring, Smedry.'

'You're the one who stopped following the plan,' I said.

'What? Kiliman was faster than you. How exactly were you planning to keep him from chasing you down as you ran?'

'I'm ... not sure,' I admitted.

Kaz just laughed. 'What happened to Kiliman anyway?'

I pointed toward the Curator with half of a skull. 'He's doing a little bit of soul-searching,' I said. 'You could say that watching over these books is his *soul* responsibility now. He'll probably enjoy the *soul*-itary lifestyle.'

'Can I hit him?' Bastille asked flatly.

I smiled, then noticed something on the ground. I picked it up – a single, yellow Lens.

'What's that?'

'Tracker's Lens,' I said. 'Kiliman's. It had been in the pouch with Draulin's Fleshstone.'

'My mother,' Bastille said. 'How is she?'

'I'm fine,' Draulin's voice said. We spun to find her standing beside a sheepish Australia in the doorway.

'Fine' was a stretch – Draulin still looked pale, like someone who had been sick for far too long. Yet, her step was steady as she walked into the room and joined us.

'Lord Smedry,' she said, going down on one knee. 'I've failed you.'

'Nonsense,' I said.

'The Librarian of the Scrivener's Bones captured me,' she said. 'I was caught in a trap, tied up, and he was able to take me without any trouble. I have shamed my order.'

I rolled my eyes. 'The rest of us got caught in Curator traps too. We were just lucky enough to wiggle out of them before Kiliman found us.'

Draulin still bowed her head. On the back of her neck, I caught sight of a sparkling crystal – her Fleshstone, replaced.

'Get up and stop apologizing,' I said. 'I'm serious. You did well. You forced a confrontation with Kiliman, and we won that confrontation. So, consider yourself part of our victory.'

Draulin stood up, though she didn't appear appeased. She fell into her traditional parade-rest stance, looking straight ahead. 'As you wish, Lord Smedry.'

'Mother,' Bastille said.

Draulin looked down.

'Here,' Bastille said, holding up the Crystin blade.

I blinked in shock. For some reason, I'd been expecting Bastille to keep that.

Draulin hesitated for a moment, then took the sword.

'Thank you,' she said, then sheathed it on her back. 'What are your plans now, Lord Smedry?'

'I'm . . . not sure yet,' I said.

'Then I will set up a perimeter around this room.' Draulin bowed to me, then walked over to the entrance and took up a guard position. Bastille moved toward the other entrance, but I grabbed her arm.

'That woman should be begging for your forgiveness.'

'Why?' Bastille asked.

'You're in so much trouble because you lost your sword,' I said. 'Well, Draulin didn't do much better now, did she?'

'But she got hers back.'

'So?'

'So, she didn't break it.'

'Only because of us.'

'No,' Bastille said, 'because of *you*, Alcatraz. Kiliman defeated me just like the Alivened in the downtown Library did. You had to save me both times.'

'I . . .'

Bastille carefully removed my hand from her arm. 'I appreciate it, Smedry. I really do. I'd be dead several times over if it wasn't for you.'

With that, she walked away. Never before had a thank-you seemed so despondent to my ears.

Things aren't going to get fixed that easily, I thought. *Bastille still considers herself a failure.*

We're going to have to do something about that.

'You going to destroy that, kid?' Kaz asked.

I glanced down, realizing that I still had Kiliman's Tracker's Lens in my fingers.

'It's *very* Dark Oculary,' Kaz said, rubbing his chin. 'Blood-forged Lenses are bad business.'

'We *should* destroy it, then,' I said. 'At least turn it over to someone who knows what to do with it. I ...'

I trailed off. (Obviously.)

'What?' Kaz asked.

I didn't answer. I'd caught something through the Tracker's Lens. I held it up to my eye and was surprised to see footprints on the ground. There were lots of them, of course. Mine, Bastille's, even Kiliman's – though those were fading quickly, since I didn't know him well. More important, however, I saw three sets of footprints that were very distinct. All led toward a small, inconspicuous door on the far side of the room.

One set of footprints was Grandpa Smedry's. Another set of yellowish black ones belonged to my mother. The final set, a blazing red-white, was undoubtedly that of my father. All went through the doorway, but there were no sets leading back out.

'Hey,' I said, turning to the nearest Curator. 'What's through that door?'

'That's where we keep the possessions of those who have been turned into Curators,' the creature said in a raspy voice. Indeed, I saw several Curators cleaning up the remnants of Kiliman's transformation – the bits of metal and the clothing he had been wearing.

I lowered the Tracker's Lens. 'Come on,' I said to the others. 'We almost forgot the reason why we came here in the first place.'

'And what was that reason again?' Kaz asked.

I pointed at the door. 'To find out what's on the other side of that.'

20

Hangook Mal Malha GiMa Ship Shio.
Expectations. They are among the most important things in all of existence. (Which is amusing, because, being abstract concepts, you could argue that they don't even 'exist' at all.)

Everything we do, everything we experience and everything we say is clouded by our expectations. We go to school or work in the mornings because we expect that it will be rewarding. (Or, at least, we expect that if we don't, we'll get in trouble.)

We build friendships based on expectations. We expect our friends to act in a certain way, and then we act as they expect us to. Indeed, the very fact that we get up in the mornings shows that we expect the sun to rise, the world to keep spinning, and our shoes to fit, just like they all did the day before.

People have real trouble when you upset their expectations. For instance, you likely didn't expect me to begin this chapter writing in Korean. Though, after the bunny-bazooka story, one begins to wonder how you can possibly maintain any expectations about this book at all.

And that, my friends, is the point.

Half of you reading this book live in the Hushlands. I was a Hushlander myself, once, and I am not so naïve as to assume that you all believe my story is true. You probably read my first book, thought it was fun. You're reading this one not because you believe its text, but because you *expected* another fun story.

Expectations. We rely on them. That's why so many Hushlanders have trouble believing the Free Kingdoms and the Librarian conspiracy. You don't *expect* to wake up and discover that everything you know about history, geography, and politics is wrong.

So, perhaps you can begin to see why I've included some of

the things I have. Bunnies with bazookas, ships that get repaired (more on that later), faces made of numbers, editorials from short people about how we regard the world, and a lesson on shoes and fish. All of these examples try to prove that you need to have an open mind. Because not everything you believe is true, and not everything you expect to happen will.

Maybe this book will mean nothing to you. Maybe my tale of demonic Curators and magical Lenses will pass you by as pure silliness, to be read but then forgotten. Perhaps because this story deals with people who are far away – and, perhaps, not even real at all – you will assume it doesn't relate to you.

I hope not. Because, you see, I have expectations too, and they whisper to me that you'll understand.

We found a long hallway on the other side of the door. At the end of that hallway was another door, and on the other side of that door was a small chamber.

It had one occupant. He sat on a dusty crate, staring down at the ground in front of him. He was not locked in. He simply seemed to have been sitting there, thinking.

And crying.

'Grandpa Smedry?' I asked.

Leavenworth Smedry, Oculator Dramatus, friend of kings and potentates, looked up. It had only been a few days since I'd last seen him, but it felt like so much longer. He smiled at me, eyes sorrowful.

'Alcatraz, lad,' he said. 'Huddling Hales, you *did* follow me!'

I rushed forward, grabbing him in an embrace. Kaz and Australia followed me in, Bastille and Draulin taking up positions by the door.

'Hey, Pop,' Kaz said, raising a hand.

'Kazan!' Grandpa Smedry said. 'Well, well. Been corrupting your nephew, I assume?'

Kaz shrugged. 'Somebody needs to.'

Grandpa Smedry smiled, but there was something ... sorrowful about even that expression. He wasn't his usual lively self. Even the little tufts of hair behind his ears seemed less perky.

'Grandpa, what is it?' I asked.

'Oh, nothing, lad,' Grandpa Smedry said, hand on my shoulder. 'I ... really should have been done grieving by now. I mean, your father has been gone for thirteen years! I still kept hope, all that time. I thought for sure we'd find him here. I arrived too late, it seems.'

'What do you mean?' I asked.

'Oh, I didn't show you, did I?' He handed something out to me. A note. 'I found this in the room. Your mother had already been here, it seems, and collected Attica's belongings. Clever one, that Shasta. Always a step ahead of me, even without my Talent interfering. She was in and out of the Library before we even arrived. Yet, she left this behind. I wonder why.'

I looked down, reading the note.

Old man, it said.

I assume you got my letter telling you that Attica was coming to the Library of Alexandria. By now you probably realize that we were both too late to stop him from doing something foolish. He always was an idiot.

I've confirmed that he gave up his soul, but for what purpose, I cannot fathom. Those blasted Curators won't tell me anything useful. I've taken his possessions. It's my right, whatever you may claim, as his wife.

I know you don't care for me. I return the sentiment. I am sad to see Attica finally gone, though. He shouldn't have had to die in such a silly way.

The Librarians now have the tools we need to defeat you. It's a shame we couldn't come to an agreement. I don't care if you believe me about Attica or not. I thought I should leave this note. I owe him that much.

Shasta Smedry

I looked up from the note, frustrated.

There were still tears in Grandpa Smedry's eyes, and he wasn't looking at me. He just stared at the wall, eyes unfocused. 'Yes,

I should have grieved long ago. I'm late to that, it appears. Late indeed ...'

Kaz read over my shoulder. 'Nutmeg!' he swore, pointing at the note. 'We don't believe this, do we? Shasta's a lying Librarian rat!'

'She's not lying, Kazan,' Grandpa Smedry said. 'At least not about your brother. The Curators confirmed it, and they cannot lie. Attica has become one of them.'

Nobody objected to Grandpa Smedry's assertion. It was the truth. I could feel it. With the Tracker's Lens, I could even see the place where my father's tracks ended. My mother's tracks, however, left by a different door.

The ground at my feet began to crack, my Talent sensing my frustration, and I felt like pounding on something. We'd come all this way, just to be turned away at the end. Why? Why had my father done something so foolish?

'He always was too curious for his own good,' Kaz said softly, laying a hand on Grandpa Smedry's shoulder. 'I told him it would lead him to a bad end.'

Grandpa Smedry nodded. 'Well, he has the knowledge he always wanted. He can read book upon book, learn anything he wants.'

With that, he stood. We joined him, making our way out of the hallway. We walked through the central room and out into the stacks beyond, trailed by a couple of Curators who were – undoubtedly – hoping we'd make one last-minute mistake and lose our souls.

I sighed, then turned and gave one final glance at the place where my father had ended his life. There, above the doorway, I saw the scribbles. The ones scratched into the stone. I frowned, then pulled out the Translator's Lenses and put them on. The message was simple, only one sentence long.

I am not an idiot.

I blinked. Grandpa Smedry and Kaz were speaking softly about my father and his foolishness.

I am not an idiot.

What would prompt a person to give up his soul? Was unlimited knowledge really worth that? Knowledge that you couldn't use? Couldn't share? Unless …

I froze, causing the others to stop. I looked right at a Curator. 'What happens when you write something down while you're in the Library?'

The creature seemed confused. 'We take the writing from you and copy it. Then, we return the copy to you an hour later.'

'And if you were to write something right before you gave up your soul?' I asked. 'What if you were a Curator by the time the copy came back?'

The Curator glanced away.

'You cannot lie!' I said, pointing.

'I can choose not to speak.'

'Not if property must be returned,' I said, still pointing. 'If my father wrote something before he was taken, then you wouldn't have had to give it to my mother unless she knew to ask for it. You *do* have to return it if I demand it. And I do. Give it to me.'

The Curator hissed. Then, all of those standing around us hissed. I hissed back at them.

I'm … uh, not sure why I did that.

Finally, a Curator floated forward, carrying a slip of paper in its translucent hand. 'This doesn't count as taking one of your books, does it?' I asked hesitantly.

'This is not ours,' the Curator said, throwing the paper at my feet.

As the others stood around me, confused, I snatched up the paper and read it. It wasn't what I'd been expecting.

It's so simple, the paper read.

The Curators are, like most things in this world, bound by laws. They are strange laws, but they are strong laws.

The trick is to not own your own soul when you sign the contract. So, I bequeath my soul to my son, Alcatraz Smedry. I sign it away to him. He is its true owner.

I looked up.

'What is it, lad?' Grandpa Smedry asked.

'What would you do, Grandpa?' I asked. 'If you were going to give up your soul not for a specific book, but because you wanted access to the Library's entire contents. What book would you ask for?'

Grandpa Smedry shrugged. 'Vague Volskies, lad, I don't know! If you're just giving up your soul so that you can read the other books in the Library, it wouldn't matter which book you picked as the first, would it?'

'Actually, it would,' I whispered. 'The Library contains all the knowledge humans have ever known.'

'So?' Bastille asked.

'So, it contains the solutions to every problem. I know what I'd ask for.' I looked straight at the Curators. 'I'd ask for the book that explained how to get my soul back after I'd given it to the Curators!'

There was a moment of stunned silence. The Curators suddenly began floating away from us.

'Curators!' I yelled. 'This note bequeaths the soul of Attica Smedry to me! You have taken it unlawfully, and I demand it back!'

The creatures froze, then they began to scream in a howling, despairing cry.

One of them suddenly spun and threw back its hood, the fires in its eyes puffing out, replaced by human eyeballs. The skull bulged, growing the flesh of a hawk-faced, noble-looking man.

He tossed aside his robe, wearing a tuxedo underneath. 'Aha!' he said. 'I *knew* you'd figure it out, son!' The man turned, pointing at the hovering Curators. 'Thank you kindly for the time you let me spend rummaging through your books, you old spooks! I beat you. I told you I would!'

'Oh, dear,' Grandpa Smedry said, smiling. 'We'll never shut him up now. He's gone and come back from the dead.'

'It's him, then?' I asked. 'My ... father?'

'Indeed,' Grandpa Smedry said. 'Attica Smedry, in the flesh.

Ha! I should have known. If ever there were a man to lose his soul and then find it again, it would be Attica!'

'Father, Kaz!' Attica said, walking over, putting an arm around each one. 'We have work to do! The Free Kingdoms are in deep danger! Did you retrieve my possessions?'

'Actually,' I said. 'Your wife did that.'

Attica froze, looking back at me. Even though he'd addressed me earlier, it seemed that now he was seeing me for the first time. 'Ah,' he said. 'She has my Translator's Lenses, then?'

'We assume so, son,' Grandpa Smedry said.

'Well then, that means we have even *more* work to do!' And with that, my father strode down the hallway, walking as if he expected everyone to hop quickly and follow.

I stood, staring after him. Bastille and Kaz paused, looking at me.

'Not what you were expecting?' Bastille asked.

I shrugged. This was the first time I'd met my father, and he had barely glanced at me.

'He's just distracted, I'm sure,' Bastille said. 'A little addled from having spent so long as a ghost.'

'Yeah,' I said. 'I'm sure that's it.'

Kaz slapped me on the shoulder. 'Don't get down, Al. This is a time for rejoicing!'

I smiled, his enthusiasm contagious. 'I suppose you're right.' We began to walk, my step growing a bit more springy. Kaz was right. True, everything wasn't perfect, but we *had* managed to save my father. Coming down into the Library had proven to be the best choice, in the end.

I might have been a bit inexperienced, but I'd made the right decision. I found myself feeling rather good as we walked.

'Thanks, Kaz,' I said.

'For what?'

'For the encouragement.'

He shrugged. 'We short people are like that. Remember what I said about being more compassionate.'

I laughed. 'Perhaps. I do have to say, though – I've thought of at least *one* reason why it's better to be a tall person.'

Kaz raised an eyebrow.

'Lightbulbs,' I said. 'If everyone were short like you, Kaz, then who'd change them?'

He laughed. 'You're forgetting Reason number sixty-three, kid!'

'Which is?'

'If everyone were short, we could build lower ceilings! Think of how much we'd save on building costs!'

I laughed, shaking my head as we caught up to the others and made our way out of the Library.

EPILOGUE

There you go. Book two of my memoirs. It's not the end, of course. You didn't think it would be, did you? We haven't even gotten to the part where I end up tied to that altar, about to be sacrificed! Besides, these things always come in trilogies, at least. Otherwise they're not epic!

This volume contained an important section of my life. My first meeting – humble though it was – with the famous Attica Smedry. My first real taste of leadership. My first chance to use Windstormer's lenses like a jet engine. (I never get tired of that one.)

Before we part, I owe you one more explanation. It has to do with a boat: the Ship of Theseus. do you remember? Every plank in it had been replaced, until it *looked* like the same ship, but wasn't.

I told you that I was that ship. Perhaps now, after reading this book, you can see why.

You should now know the young me pretty well. You've read two books about him and have seen his progress as a person. You've even seen him do some heroic things, like climb on top of a glass dragon, face down a member of the Scrivener's Bones, and save his father from the clutches of the Curators of Alexandria.

You may wonder why I've started my autobiography so far back, when I still showed hints that I might be a good person. Well, I'm the Ship of Theseus. I was once that boy, full of hope, full of potential. That's not who I am anymore. I'm a copy. A fake.

I'm the person that young boy grew into, but I'm not him. I'm not the hero that everyone says – even though I look like I should be.

The purpose of this series is to show the changes I went

through. To let you see the pieces of me slowly getting replaced until nothing is left of the original.

I'm a sad, pathetic person, writing his life story in the basement of a lavish castle he really doesn't deserve. I'm not a hero. Heroes don't let the people they love die.

I'm not proud of what I've become, but I intend to make certain that everyone knows the truth. It's time for the lies to end; time for people to realize that their Ship of Theseus is just a copy.

If the real one ever existed in the first place.

was not my place to say so.

'Bastille!' I screamed, holding her bloody body in my arms. 'Why?'

She didn't respond. She just stared into the air, eyes glazed over, her spirit already gone. I shivered, pulling her close, but the body was growing cold.

'You can't die, you can't!' I said. 'Please.'

It was no use. Bastille was dead. Really dead. Deader than a battery left all night with the high beams on. So dead, she was twice as dead as anyone I'd ever seen dead. She was *that* dead.

'This is all my fault,' I said. 'I shouldn't have brought you in to fight Kiliman!'

I felt at her pulse, just in case. There was nothing. Because, you know, she was dead.

'Oh, cruel world,' I said, sobbing.

I put a mirror up to her face to see if she was breathing. Of course, there was no mist on the mirror. Seeing as how Bastille was totally and completely dead.

'You were so young,' I said. 'Too young to be taken from us. Why did it have to happen to you, of all people, when you are so young? Too young to die, I mean.'

I pricked her finger to make sure she wasn't just faking, but she didn't even flinch. I pinched her, then slapped her face. Nothing worked.

How many times do I have to explain that she was dead? I looked down at her body, her face turning blue from death, and I wept some more.

She was so dead that I didn't even realize that this section is in the book for two reasons. First, so that I could have Bastille die somewhere, just like I promised. (See, I wasn't lying about this! Ha!)

The second reason is, of course, so that if anyone skips forward to the end to read the last page – one of the most putrid and unholy things any reader can do – they will be shocked and annoyed to read that Bastille is dead.

The rest of you can ignore these pages. (Did I mention that Bastille is dead?)

The end.

ALCATRAZ VERSUS THE KNIGHTS OF CRYSTALLIA

For Jane, who does her best to keep me looking fashionable, and does it in such an endearing way that I can't even convince myself to wear mismatched socks anymore (except on Thursdays)

AUTHOR'S FOREWORD

I am awesome.

No, really. I'm the most amazing person you've ever read about. Or that you ever *will* read about. There's nobody like me out there. I'm Alcatraz Smedry, the unbelievably incredible.

If you've read the previous two volumes of my autobiography (and I hope that you have, for if you haven't, I will make fun of you later on), you might be surprised to hear me being so positive. I worked hard in the other books to make you hate me. I told you quite bluntly in the first book that I was not a nice person, then proceeded to show you that I was a liar in the second.

I was wrong. I'm an amazing, stupendous person. I might be a little selfish at times, but I'm still rather incredible. I just wanted you to know that.

You might remember from the other two books (assuming you weren't too distracted by how awesome I am) that this series is being published simultaneously in the Free Kingdoms and in the Hushlands. Those in the Free Kingdoms – Mokia, Nalhalla, and the like – can read it for what it really is, an autobiographical work that explains the truth behind my rise to fame. In the Hushlands – places like the United States, Mexico, and Australia – this will be published as a fantasy novel to disguise it from Librarian Agents.

Both lands need this book. Both lands need to understand that I am no hero. The best way to explain this, I have now decided, is to talk repeatedly about how awesome, incredible, and amazing I am.

You'll understand eventually.

1

So there I was, hanging upside down underneath a gigantic glass bird, speeding along at a hundred miles an hour above the ocean, in no danger whatsoever.

That's right. I wasn't in any danger. I was more safe at that moment than I'd ever been in my entire life, despite a plummet of several hundred feet looming below me. (Or, well, *above* me, since I was upside down.)

I took a few cautious steps. The oversized boots on my feet had a special type of glass on the bottom, called Grappler's Glass, which let them stick to other things made of glass. That kept me from falling off. (At which point *up* would quickly become *down* as I fell to my death. Gravity is such a punk.)

If you'd seen me, with the wind howling around me and the sea churning below you may not have agreed that I was safe. But these things – like which direction is up – are relative. You see, I'd grown up as a foster child in the Hushlands: lands controlled by the evil Librarians. They'd carefully watched over me during my childhood, anticipating the day when I'd receive a very special bag of sand from my father.

I'd received the bag. They'd stolen the bag. I'd gotten the bag back. Now I was stuck to the bottom of a giant glass bird. Simple, really. If it doesn't make sense to you, then might I recommend picking up the first two books of a series before you try to read the third one?

Unfortunately, I know that some of you Hushlanders have trouble counting to three. (The Librarian-controlled schools don't want you to be able to manage complex mathematics.) So I've prepared this helpful guide.

Definition of 'book one': The best place to start a series. You can identify 'book one' by the fact that it has a little '1' on the spine. Smedrys do a happy dance when you read book one first. Entropy shakes its angry fist at you for being clever enough to organize the world.

Definition of 'book two': The book you read *after* book one. If you start with book two, I will make fun of you. (Okay, so I'll make fun of you either way. But honestly, do you want to give me more ammunition?)

Definition of 'book three': The worst place, currently, to start a series. If you start here, I will throw things at you.

Definition of 'book four': And … how'd you manage to start with that one? I haven't even written it yet. (You sneaky time travelers.)

Anyway, if you haven't read book two, you missed out on some very important events. Those include: a trip into the fabled Library of Alexandria, sludge that tastes faintly of bananas, ghostly Librarians that want to suck your soul, giant glass dragons, the tomb of Alcatraz the First, and – most important – a lengthy discussion about belly button lint. By not reading book two, you *also* just forced a large number of people to waste an entire minute reading that recap. I hope you're satisfied.

I clomped along, making my way toward a solitary figure standing near the chest of the bird. Enormous glass wings beat on either side of me, and I passed thick glass bird legs that were curled up and tucked back. Wind howled and slammed against me. The bird – called the *Hawkwind* – wasn't quite as majestic as our previous vehicle, a glass dragon called the *Dragonaut*. Still, it had a nice group of compartments inside where one could travel in luxury.

My grandfather, of course, couldn't be bothered with something as normal as waiting *inside* a vehicle. No, he had to cling to the bottom and stare out over the ocean. I fought against the wind as I approached him – and then, suddenly, the wind vanished. I froze in shock, one of my boots locking into place on the bird's glass underside.

Grandpa Smedry jumped, turning. 'Rotating Rothfusses!' he exclaimed. 'You surprised me, lad!'

'Sorry,' I said, walking forward, my boots making a clinking sound each time I unlocked one, took a step, then locked back onto the glass. As always, my grandfather wore a sharp black tuxedo – he thought it made him blend in better in the Hushlands. He was bald except for a tuft of white hair that ran around the back of his head, and he sported an impressively bushy white mustache.

'What happened to the wind?' I asked.

'Hum? Oh, that.' My grandfather reached up, tapping the green-specked spectacles he wore. They were Oculatory Lenses, a type of magical glasses that – when activated by an Oculator like Grandpa Smedry or myself – could do some very interesting things. (Those things don't, unfortunately, include forcing lazy readers to go and reread the first couple of books, thereby removing the need for me to explain all of this stuff over and over again.)

'Windstormer's Lenses?' I asked. 'I didn't know you could use them like this.' I'd had a pair of Windstormer's Lenses, and I'd used them to shoot out jets of wind.

'It takes quite a bit of practice, my boy,' Grandpa Smedry said in his boisterous way. 'I'm creating a bubble of wind that is shooting out from me in exactly the *opposite* direction of the wind that's pushing against me, thereby negating it all.'

'But ... shouldn't that blow *me* backward as well?'

'What? No, of course not! What makes you think that it would?'

'Uh ... physics?' I said. (Which you might agree is a rather strange thing to be mentioning while hanging upside down through the use of magical glass boots.)

Grandpa Smedry laughed. 'Excellent joke, lad. Excellent.' He clasped me on the shoulder. Free Kingdomers like my grandfather tend to be very amused by Librarian concepts like physics, which they find to be utter nonsense. I think that the Free Kingdomers don't give the Librarians enough credit. Physics isn't nonsense – it's just incomplete.

Free Kingdomer magic and technology have their own kind of logic. Take the glass bird. It was driven by something called a silimatic engine, which used different types of sands and glass to propel it. Smedry Talents and Oculator powers were called 'magic' in the Free Kingdoms, since only special people could use them. Something that could be used by anyone – such as the silimatic engine or the boots on my feet – was called technology.

The longer I spent with people from the Free Kingdoms, the less I bought that distinction. 'Grandfather,' I said, 'did I ever tell you that I managed to power a pair of Grappler's Glass boots just by touching them?'

'Hum?' Grandpa Smedry said. 'What's that?'

'I gave a pair of these boots an extra boost of power,' I said. 'Just by touching them … as if I could act like some kind of battery or energy source.'

My grandfather was silent.

'What if that's what we do with the Lenses?' I said, tapping the spectacles on my face. 'What if being an Oculator isn't as limited as we think it is? What if we can affect all kinds of glass?'

'You sound like your father, lad,' Grandpa Smedry said. 'He has a theory relating to exactly what you're talking about.'

My father. I glanced upward. Then, eventually, I turned back to Grandpa Smedry. He wore his pair of Windstormer's Lenses, keeping the wind at bay.

'Windstormer's Lenses,' I said. 'I … broke the other pair you gave me.'

'Ha!' Grandpa Smedry said. 'That's not surprising at all, lad. Your Talent is quite powerful.'

My Talent – my Smedry Talent – was the magical ability to break things. Every Smedry has a Talent, even those who are only Smedrys by marriage. My grandfather's Talent was the ability to arrive late to appointments.

The Talents were both blessings and curses. My grandfather's Talent, for instance, was quite useful when he arrived late to things like bullets or tax day. But he'd also arrived too late to stop the Librarians from stealing my inheritance.

Grandpa Smedry fell uncharacteristically silent as he stared out over the ocean, which seemed to hang above us. West. Toward Nalhalla, my homeland, though I'd never once set foot upon its soil.

'What's wrong?' I asked.

'Hum? Wrong? Nothing's wrong! Why, we rescued your father from the Curators of Alexandria themselves! You showed a very Smedry-like keenness of mind, I must say. Very well done! We've been victorious!'

'Except for the fact that my mother now has a pair of Translator's Lenses,' I said.

'Ah, yes. There *is* that.'

The Sands of Rashid, which had started this entire mess, had been forged into Lenses that could translate any language. My father had somehow collected the Sands of Rashid, then he'd split them and sent half to me, enough to forge a single pair of spectacles. He'd kept the other pair for himself. After the fiasco at the Library of Alexandria, my mother had managed to steal his pair. (I still had mine, fortunately.)

Her theft meant that, if she had access to an Oculator she could read the Forgotten Language and understand the secrets of the ancient Incarna people. She could read about their technological and magical marvels, discovering advanced weapons. This was a problem. You see, my mother was a Librarian.

'What are we going to do?' I asked.

'I'm not sure,' Grandpa Smedry said. 'But I intend to speak with the Council of Kings. They should have something to say on this, yes indeed.' He perked up. 'Anyway, there's no use worrying about it at the moment! Surely you didn't come all the way down here just because you wanted to hear doom and gloom from your favorite grandfather!'

I almost replied that he was my *only* grandfather. Then I thought for a moment about what having only one grandfather would imply. Ew.

'Actually,' I said, looking up toward the *Hawkwind*, 'I wanted to ask you about my father.'

'What about him, lad?'

'Has he always been so ...'

'Distracted?'

I nodded.

Grandpa Smedry sighed. 'Your father is a very driven man, Alatraz. You know that I disapprove of the way he left you to be raised in the Hushlands ... but, well, he *has* accomplished some great things in his life. Scholars have been trying to crack the Forgotten Language for millennia! I was convinced that it couldn't be done. Beyond that, I don't think any Smedry has mastered their Talent as well as he has.'

Through the glass above, I could see shadows and shapes – our companions. My father was there, a man I'd spent my entire childhood wondering about. I'd expected him to be a little more ... well, excited to see me.

Even if he *had* abandoned me in the first place.

Grandpa Smedry rested his hand on my shoulder. 'Ah, don't look so glum. Amazing Abrahams, lad! You're about to visit Nalhalla for the first time! We'll work this all out eventually. Sit back and rest for a bit. You've had a busy few months.'

'How close are we anyway?' I asked. We'd been flying for the better part of the morning. That was after we'd spent two weeks camped outside the Library of Alexandria, waiting for my uncle Kaz to make his way to Nalhalla and send a ship back to pick us up. (He and Grandpa Smedry had agreed that it would be faster for Kaz to go by himself. Like the rest of us, Kaz's Talent – which is the ability to get lost in very spectacular ways – can be unpredictable.)

'Not too far, I'd say,' Grandpa Smedry said, pointing. 'Not far at all ...'

I turned to look across the waters, and there it was. A distant continent, just coming into view. I took a step forward, squinting from my upside-down vantage. There was a city built along the coast of the continent, rising boldly in the early light.

'Castles,' I whispered as we approached. 'It's filled with castles?'

There were dozens of them, perhaps hundreds. The entire *city* was made of castles, reaching toward the sky, lofty towers and delicate spires. Flags flapping from the very tips. Each castle had a different design and shape, and a majestic city wall surrounded them all.

Three structures dominated the rest. One was a powerful black castle on the far south side of the city. Its sides were sheer and tall, and it had a powerful feel to it, like a mountain. Or a really big stone bodybuilder. In the middle of the city, there was a strange white castle that looked something like a pyramid with towers and parapets. It flew an enormous, brilliant red flag that I could make out even from a distance.

On the far north side of the city, to my right, was the oddest structure of all. It appeared to be a gigantic crystalline mushroom. It was at least a hundred feet tall and twice as wide. It sprouted from the city, its bell top throwing a huge shadow over a bunch of smaller castles. Atop the mushroom sat a more traditional-looking castle that sparkled in the sunlight, as if constructed entirely from glass.

'Crystallia?' I asked, pointing.

'Yes indeed!' Grandpa Smedry said.

Crystallia, home of the Knights of Crystallia, sworn protectors of the Smedry clan and the royalty of the Free Kingdoms. I glanced back up at the *Hawkwind*. Bastille waited inside, still under condemnation for having lost her sword back in the Hushlands. Her homecoming would not be as pleasant as mine would be.

But ... well, I couldn't focus on that at the moment. I was coming *home*. I wish I could explain to you how it felt to finally see Nalhalla. It wasn't a crazy sense of excitement or glee – it was far more peaceful. Imagine what it's like to wake up in the morning, refreshed and alert after a remarkably good sleep.

It felt *right*. Serene.

That, of course, meant it was time for something to explode.

2

I hate explosions. Not only are they generally bad for one's health but they're just so demanding. Whenever one comes along, you have to pay attention to it instead of whatever else you were doing. In fact, explosions are suspiciously like baby sisters in that regard.

Fortunately, I'm not going to talk about the *Hawkwind* exploding right now. Instead, I'm going to talk about something completely unrelated: fish sticks. (Get used to it. I do this sort of thing all the time.)

Fish sticks are, without a doubt, the most disgusting things ever created. Regular fish is bad enough, but fish sticks ... well, they raise disgustingness to an entirely new level. It's like they exist *just* to make us writers come up with new words to describe them, since the old words just aren't horrible enough. I'm thinking of using *crapaflapnasti*.

Definition of 'crapaflapnasti': 'Adj. Used to describe an item that is as disgusting as fish sticks.' (Note: This word can only be used to describe fish sticks themselves, as nothing has yet been found that is equally *crapaflapnasti*. Though the unclean, moldy, cluttered space under Brandon Sanderson's bed comes close.)

Why am I telling you about fish sticks? Well, because in addition to being an unwholesome blight upon the land, they're all pretty much the same. If you don't like one brand, chances are very good you won't like any of them.

The thing is, I've noticed that people tend to treat books like fish sticks. People try one, and they figure they've tried them all.

Books are not fish sticks. While they're not all as awesome as the one you are now holding, there's so much variety to them that it can be unsettling. Even within the same genre, two books can be totally different.

We'll talk more about this later. For now just try not to treat books like fish sticks. (And if you are forced to eat one of the two, go with the books. Trust me.)

The right side of the *Hawkwind* exploded.

The vehicle pitched in the air, chunks of glass sparkling as they blew free. To the side of me, the glass bird's leg broke off and the world lurched, spun, and distorted – like I was riding a madman's version of a merry-go-round.

At that moment, my panicked mind realized that the section of glass under my feet – the one my boots were still stuck to – had broken away from the *Hawkwind*. The vehicle was still managing to fly. I, however, was not. Unless you count plummeting to your doom at a hundred miles an hour 'flying.'

Everything was a blur. The large piece of glass I was stuck to was flipping end over end, the wind tossing it about like a sheet of paper. I didn't have much time.

Break! I thought, sending a shock of my Talent through my legs, shattering my boots and the sheet beneath them. Shards of glass exploded around me, but I stopped spinning. I twisted, looking down at the waves. I didn't have any Lenses that could save me – all I was carrying were the Translator's Lenses and my Oculator's Lenses. All my other pairs had been broken, given away, or returned to Grandpa Smedry.

That only left my Talent. The wind whistled about me, and I extended my arms. I always wondered just what my Talent could break, if given the chance. Could I, perhaps ... I closed my eyes, gathering my power.

BREAK! I thought, shooting the power out of my arms and into the air.

Nothing happened.

I opened my eyes, terrified, as the waves rushed up at me. And rushed up at me. And rushed up at me. And ... rushed up at me some more.

It sure is taking a long time for me to plunge to my death, I thought. I *felt* as if I were falling, yet the nearby waves didn't actually seem to be getting any closer.

I turned, looking upward. There, falling toward me, was Grandpa Smedry, his tuxedo jacket flapping, a look of intense concentration on his face as he held his hand toward me, fingers extended.

He's making me arrive late to my fall! I thought. On occasion, I'd been able to make my Talent work at a distance, but it was difficult and unpredictable.

'Grandpa!' I yelled in excitement.

Right about that moment, he plowed into me face-first, and both of us crashed into the ocean. The water was cold, and my exclamation of surprise quickly turned into a gurgle.

I burst free from the water, sputtering. Fortunately, the water was calm – if frigid – and the waves weren't bad. I straightened my Lenses – which, remarkably, had remained on my face – and looked around for my grandfather, who came up a few seconds later, his mustache drooping and his wisps of white hair plastered to his otherwise bald head.

'Wasted Westerfields!' he exclaimed. 'That was exciting, eh, lad?'

I shivered in response.

'All right, prepare yourself,' Grandpa Smedry said. He looked surprisingly fatigued.

'For what?' I asked.

'I'm letting us arrive late to some of that fall, lad,' Grandpa Smedry said. 'But I can't make it go away entirely. And I don't think I can bear it for long!'

'So, you mean that—' I cut off as it hit me. It was as if I'd landed in the water again, the air getting knocked out of my lungs. I slipped beneath the ocean waters, disoriented and freezing, then forced myself to struggle back up toward the sparkling light. I burst into the air and took a gasping breath.

Then it hit me again. Grandpa Smedry had broken our plummet into small steps, but even those small steps were dangerous. As I sank again, I barely caught sight of my grandfather trying to stay afloat. He wasn't doing any better than I was.

I felt useless – I should have been able to do something with my Talent. Everyone always told me that my ability to break things was powerful – and, indeed, I'd done some amazing things with it. But I still didn't have the control that I envied in Grandpa Smedry or my cousins.

True, I'd only even been aware of my place as a Smedry for about four months. But it's hard to not be down on yourself when you're in the middle of drowning. So I did the sensible thing and went ahead and passed out.

When I awoke, I was – fortunately – not dead, though part of me wished that I was. I hurt pretty much all over, as if I'd been stuffed inside a punching bag, which had then been put through a blender. I groaned, opening my eyes. A slender young woman knelt beside me. She had long silver hair and wore a militaristic uniform.

She looked angry. In other words, she looked just about like she always did. 'You did that on *purpose*,' Bastille accused.

I sat up, raising a hand to my head. 'Yes, Bastille. I keep trying to get killed because it's inconvenient for you.'

She eyed me. I could tell that a little piece of her did believe that we Smedrys got ourselves into trouble just to make her life difficult.

My jeans and shirt were still wet, and I lay in a puddle of salty seawater, so it probably hadn't been very long since the fall. The sky was open above me, and to my right, the *Hawkwind* stood on its one remaining leg, perched on the side of a wall. I blinked, realizing that I was on top of some kind of castle tower.

'Australia managed to get the *Hawkwind* down to grab you two out of the water,' Bastille said, answering my unasked question as she stood up. 'We aren't sure what caused the explosion. It came from one of the rooms, that's all we know.'

I forced myself to my feet, looking over at the silimatic vehicle. The entire right side had blown out, exposing the rooms inside. One of the wings was laced with cracks, and – as I'd so vividly discovered – a large chunk of the bird's chest had fallen free.

My grandfather was sitting beside the tower's railing, and he waved weakly as I looked over. The others were slowly trying to climb out of the *Hawkwind*. The explosion had destroyed the boarding steps.

'I'll go get help,' Bastille said. 'Check on your grandfather, and *try* not to fall off the tower's edge or anything while I'm gone.' With that, she dashed down a set of steps into the tower.

I walked over to my grandfather. 'You all right?'

'Course I am, lad, of course I am.' Grandpa Smedry smiled through a sodden mustache. I'd seen him this tired only once before, just after our battle with Blackburn.

'Thanks for saving me,' I said, sitting down next to him.

'Just returning the favor,' Grandpa Smedry said with a wink. 'I believe *you* saved *me* back in that library infiltration.'

That had mostly been a matter of luck. I glanced at the *Hawkwind*, where our companions were still trying to find a way down. 'I wish I could use my Talent like you use yours.'

'What? Alcatraz, you're very good with your Talent. I saw you shatter that glass you were stuck to. I'd never have gotten a line of sight on you in time if you hadn't done that! Your quick thinking saved your life.'

'I tried to do more,' I said. 'But it didn't work.'

'More?'

I blushed. It now seemed silly. 'I figured ... well, I thought if I could break gravity, then I could fly.'

Grandpa Smedry chuckled quietly. 'Break gravity, eh? Very bold of you, very bold. A very Smedry-like attempt! But a little bit beyond the scope of even *your* power, I'd say. Imagine the chaos if gravity stopped working all across the entire world!'

I don't have to imagine it. I've lived it. But, then, we'll get to that. Eventually.

There was a scrambling sound, and a figure finally managed to leap from the broken side of the *Hawkwind* and land on the tower top. Draulin, Bastille's mother, was an austere woman in silvery armor. A full Knight of Crystallia – a title Bastille had recently lost – Draulin was very effective at the things she did. Those included: protecting Smedrys, being displeased by things, and making the rest of us feel like slackers.

Once on the ground, she was able to assist the vehicle's other two occupants. Australia Smedry, my cousin, was a plump, sixteen-year-old Mokian girl. She wore a colorful, single-piece dress that looked something like a sheet and – like her brother – had tan skin and dark hair. (Mokians are relatives of the Hushlands' Polynesian people.) As she hit the floor, she rushed over to Grandpa Smedry and me.

'Oh, Alcatraz!' she said. 'Are you all right? I didn't see you fall, I was too busy with the explosion. Did you see it?'

'Um, yes, Australia,' I said. 'It kind of blew me off of the *Hawkwind*.'

'Oh, right,' she said, bouncing slightly up and down on her heels. 'If Bastille hadn't been watching, we'd have never seen where you hit! It didn't hurt too much when I dropped you on the top of the tower here, did it? I had to scoop you up in the *Hawkwind*'s leg and set you down here so that I could land. It's missing a leg now. I don't know if you noticed.'

'Yeah,' I said tiredly. 'Explosion, remember?'

'Of course I remember, silly!'

That's Australia. She's not dim-witted, she just has trouble remembering to be smart.

The last person off the *Hawkwind* was my father, Attica Smedry. He was a tall man with messy hair, and he wore a pair of red-tinted Oculator's Lenses. Somehow, on him, they didn't look pinkish and silly like I always felt they did on me.

He walked over to Grandpa Smedry and me. 'Ah, well,' he said. 'Everyone's all right, I see. That's great.'

We watched each other awkwardly for a moment. My father didn't seem to know what else to say, as if made uncomfortable by the need to act parental. He seemed relieved when Bastille charged back up the steps, a veritable fleet of servants following behind, wearing the tunics and trousers that were standard Free Kingdomer garb.

'Ah,' my father said. 'Excellent! I'm sure the servants will know what to do. Glad you're not hurt, son.' He walked quickly toward the stairwell.

'Lord Attica!' one of the servants said. 'It's been so long.'

'Yes, well, I have returned,' my father replied. 'I shall require my rooms made up immediately and a bath drawn. Inform the Council of Kings that I will soon be addressing them in regards to a very important matter. Also, let the newspapers know that I'm available for interviews.' He hesitated. 'Oh, and see to my son. He will need, er, clothing and things like that.'

He disappeared down the steps, a pack of servants following him like puppies. 'Wait a sec,' I said, standing and turning to Australia. 'Why are they so quick to obey?'

'They're his servants, silly. That's what they do.'

'His servants?' I asked, stepping over to the side of the tower to get a better look at the building below. 'Where are we?'

'Keep Smedry, of course,' Australia said. 'Um ... where else would we be?'

I looked out over the city, realizing that we had landed the *Hawkwind* on one of the towers of the stout black castle I'd seen earlier. Keep Smedry. 'We have our own *castle*?' I asked with shock, turning to my grandfather.

A few minutes of rest had done him some good, and the twinkle was back in his eyes as he stood up, dusting off his soggy tuxedo. 'Of course we do, lad! We're Smedrys!'

Smedrys. I still didn't really understand what that meant. For your information, it meant ... well, I'll explain it in the next chapter. I'm feeling too lazy right now.

One of the servants, a doctor of some sort, began to prod at Grandpa Smedry, looking into his eyes, asking him to count backward. Grandpa looked as if he wanted to escape the treatment, but then noticed Bastille and Draulin standing side by side, arms folded, similarly determined expressions on their faces. Their postures indicated that my grandfather and I *would* be checked over, even if our knights had to string us up by our heels to make it happen.

I sighed, leaning back against the rim of the tower. 'Hey, Bastille,' I said as some servants brought me and Grandpa Smedry towels.

'What?' she asked, walking over.

'How'd you get down?' I said, nodding to the broken *Hawkwind*. 'Everyone else was trapped inside when I woke up.'

'I ...'

'She jumped free!' Australia exclaimed. 'Draulin said the glass was precarious and that we should test it, but Bastille jumped right on out!'

Bastille shot Australia a glare, but the Mokian girl kept on talking, oblivious. 'She must have been really worried about you, Alcatraz. She ran right over to your side. I—'

Bastille tried, subtly, to stomp on Australia's foot.

'Oh!' Australia said. 'We squishing ants?'

Remarkably, Bastille blushed. Was she embarrassed for disobeying her mother? Bastille tried so hard to please the woman, but I was certain that pleasing Draulin was pretty much impossible. I mean, it couldn't have been concern for *me* that made her jump out of the vehicle. I was well aware of how infuriating she found me.

But ... what if she *was* worried about me? What did that mean? Suddenly, I found myself blushing too.

And now I am going to do everything in my power to distract you from that last paragraph. I really shouldn't have written it. I should have been smart enough to clam up. I should have flexed my mental muscles and stopped thinking at a snail's pace.

Have I mentioned how shellfish I can be sometimes?

At that moment, Sing burst up the stairs, saving Bastille and me from our awkward moment. Sing Sing Smedry, my cousin and Australia's older brother, was an enormous titan of a man. Well over six feet tall, he was rather full-figured. (Which is a nice way of saying he was kinda fat.) The Mokian man had the Smedry Talent for tripping and falling to the ground – which he did the moment he reached the top of the tower.

I swear, I felt the stones themselves shake. Every one of us ducked, looking for danger. Sing's Talent tends to activate when something is about to hurt him. That moment, however, no danger appeared. Sing looked around, then climbed to his feet and rushed over to grab me out of my nervous crouch and give me a suffocating hug.

'Alcatraz!' he exclaimed. He reached out an arm and grabbed Australia, giving her a hug as well. 'You guys *have* to read the paper I wrote about Hushlander bartering techniques and advertising methodology! It's so exciting!'

Sing, you see, was an anthropologist. His expertise was Hushland cultures and weaponry, though, fortunately, this time he didn't appear to have any guns strapped to his body. The sad thing is, most people I've met in the Free Kingdoms – particularly my family – *would* consider reading an anthropological study to be exciting. Somebody really needs to introduce them to video games.

Sing finally released us, then turned to Grandpa Smedry and gave a quick bow. 'Lord Smedry,' he said. 'We need to talk. There has been trouble in your absence.'

'There's always trouble in my absence,' Grandpa Smedry said. 'And a fair lot of it when I'm here too. What's it this time?'

'The Librarians have sent an ambassador to the Council of Kings,' Sing explained.

'Well,' Grandpa Smedry said lightly, 'I hope the ambassador's posterior didn't get hurt *too* much when Brig tossed him out of the city.'

'The High King didn't banish the ambassador, my lord,' Sing said softly. 'In fact, I think they're going to sign a treaty.'

'That's impossible!' Bastille cut in. 'The High King would never ally with the Librarians!'

'Squire Bastille,' Draulin snapped, standing stiffly with her hands behind her back. 'Hold your place and do *not* contradict your betters.'

Bastille blushed, looking down.

'Sing,' Grandpa Smedry said urgently. 'This treaty, what does it say about the fighting in Mokia?'

Sing glanced aside. 'I ... well, the treaty would hand Mokia over to the Librarians in exchange for an end to the war.'

'Debating Dashners!' Grandpa Smedry exclaimed. 'We're late!

We need to do something!' He immediately dashed across the rooftop and scrambled down the stairwell.

The rest of us glanced at one another.

'We'll have to act with daring recklessness and an intense vibrato!' Grandpa Smedry's voice echoed out of the stairwell. 'But that's the Smedry way!'

'We should probably follow him,' I said.

'Yeah,' Sing said, glancing about. 'He just gets so excited. Where's Lord Kazan?'

'Isn't he here?' Australia said. 'He sent the *Hawkwind* back for us.'

Sing shook his head. 'Kaz left a few days ago, claiming he'd meet back up with you.'

'His Talent must have lost him,' Australia said, sighing. 'There's no telling where he might be.'

'Uh, hello?' Grandpa Smedry's head popped out of the stairwell. 'Jabbering Joneses, people! We've got a disaster to avert! Let's get moving!'

'Yes, Lord Smedry,' Sing said, waddling over. 'But where are we going?'

'Send for a crawly!' the elderly Oculator said. 'We need to get to the Council of Kings!'

'But ... they're in session!'

'All the better,' Grandpa Smedry said, raising a hand dramatically. 'Our entrance will be much more interesting that way!'

3

Having royal blood is a really big pain. Trust me, I have some *very* good sources on this. They all agree: Being a king stinks. Royally.

First off, there are the hours. Kings work all of them. If there's an emergency at night, be ready to get up, because you're king. Inconvenient war starting in the middle of the play-offs? Tough. Kings don't get to have vacations, potty breaks, or weekends.

Instead, they get something else: responsibility.

Of all the things in the world that come close to being crapaflapnasti, responsibility is the most terrible. It makes people eat salads instead of candy bars, and makes them go to bed early of their own free choice. When you're about to launch yourself into the air strapped to the back of a rocket-propelled penguin, it's that blasted responsibility that warns you that the flight might not be good for your insurance premiums.

I'm convinced that responsibility is some kind of psychological disease. What else but a brain malfunction would cause someone to go jogging? The problem is, kings need to have responsibility like nothing else. Kings are like deep, never-ending wells of responsibility – and if you don't watch out, you may get tainted by them.

The Smedry clan, fortunately, realized this a number of years back. And so they did something about it.

'We did *what*?' I asked.

'Gave up our kingdom,' Grandpa Smedry said happily. 'Poof. Gone. Abdicated.'

'Why did we do that?'

'For the good of candy bars everywhere,' Grandpa Smedry said, eyes twinkling. 'They need to be eaten, you see.'

'Huh?' I asked. We stood on a large castle balcony, waiting for a 'crawly,' whatever that was. Sing was with us, along with Bastille and her mother. Australia had stayed behind to run an errand for Grandpa Smedry, and my father had disappeared into his rooms. Apparently, he couldn't be bothered by something as simple as the impending fall of Mokia as a sovereign kingdom.

'Well, let me explain it this way,' Grandpa Smedry said, hands behind his back as he looked out over the city. 'A number of centuries ago, the people realized that there were just too many kingdoms. Most were only the size of a city, and you could barely go for an afternoon stroll without passing through three or four of them!'

'I hear it was a real pain,' Sing agreed. 'Every kingdom had its own rules, its own culture, its own laws.'

'Then the Librarians started conquering,' Grandpa Smedry explained. 'The kings realized that they were too easy to pick off. So they began to band together, joining their kingdoms into one, making alliances.'

'Often, that involved weddings of one sort or another,' Sing added.

'That was during the time of our ancestor King Leavenworth Smedry the Sixth,' Grandpa continued. 'He decided that it would be better to combine our small kingdom of Smedrious with that of Nalhalla, leaving the Smedrys free of all that bothersome reigning so that we could focus on things that were more important, like fighting the Librarians.'

I wasn't sure how to react to that. I was the heir of the line. That meant if our ancestor *hadn't* given up the kingdom, I'd have been directly in line for the throne. It was a little bit like discovering that your lottery ticket was one number away from winning.

'We gave it away,' I said. 'All of it?'

'Well, not *all* of it,' Grandpa Smedry said. 'Just the boring parts! We retained a seat on the Council of Kings so that we could still have a hand in politics, and as you can see, we have a nice castle and a large fortune to keep us busy. Plus, we're still nobility.'

'So what does that get us?'

'Oh, a number of perks,' Grandpa Smedry said. 'Call-ahead seating at restaurants, access to the royal stables and the royal silimatic carrier fleet – I believe we've managed to wreck two of those in the last month. We're also peerage – which is a fancy way of saying we can speak in civil disputes, perform marriage ceremonies, arrest criminals, that sort of thing.'

'Wait,' I said. 'I can *marry* people?'

'Sure,' Grandpa Smedry said.

'But I'm only thirteen!'

'Well, you couldn't marry *yourself* to anyone. But if somebody else asked you, you could perform the ceremony. It wouldn't do for the king to have to do all of that himself, you know! Ah, here we are.'

I glanced to the side, then jumped as I saw an enormous reptile crawling along the sides of the buildings toward us. Like a spider crawling across the front of a fence.

'Dragon!' I yelled, pointing.

'Brilliant observation, Smedry,' Bastille noted from beside me.

I was too alarmed to make an amazing comeback. Fortunately, I'm the author of this book, so I can rewrite history as I feel necessary. Let's try that again.

Ahem.

I glanced to the side, whereupon I noticed a dangerous scaly lizard slithering its way along the sides of the buildings, obviously bent on devouring us all.

'Behold!' I bellowed. ''Tis a foul beast of the netherhells. Stand behind me and I shall slay it!'

'Oh, Alcatraz,' Bastille breathed. 'Thou art awesomish and manlyish.'

'Lo, let it be such,' I said.

'Don't be alarmed, lad,' Grandpa Smedry said, glancing at the reptile. 'That's our ride.'

I could see that the wingless, horned creature had a contraption on its back, a little like a gondola. The massive beast defied gravity, clinging to the stone faces of the buildings, kind of like a lizard clinging to a cliff – only this lizard was large enough to swallow a bus. The dragon reached Keep Smedry, then climbed up to our balcony, its claws gripping the stones. I took an involuntary step backward as its enormous serpentine head crested the balcony and looked at us.

'Smedry,' it said in a deep voice.

'Hello, Tzoctinatin,' Grandpa Smedry said. 'We need a ride to the palace, quickly.'

'So I have been told. Climb in.'

'Wait,' I said. 'We use dragons as taxis?'

The dragon eyed me, and in that eye I saw a vastness. A deep, swirling depth, colors upon colors, folds upon folds. It made me feel small and meaningless.

'I do not do this of my own will, young Smedry,' the beast rumbled.

'How long left on your sentence?' Grandpa Smedry asked.

'Three hundred years,' the creature said, turning away. 'Three hundred years before they will return my wings so that I may fly again.' With that, the creature climbed up the side of the wall a little farther, bringing the gondola basket into view. A walkway unfolded from it, and the others began to climb in.

'What'd he do?' I whispered to Grandpa Smedry.

'Hum? Oh, first-degree maiden munching, I believe. It happened some four centuries back. Tragic story. Watch that first step.'

I followed the others into the gondola. There was a well-furnished room inside, complete with comfortable-looking couches. Draulin was the last one in, and she closed the door. Immediately, the dragon began to move – I could tell by looking out the window. However, I couldn't feel the motion. It appeared that no matter which direction the dragon turned or which way was 'up,' the gondola occupants always had gravity point the same way.

(I was later to learn that this, like many things in the Free Kingdoms, was due to a type of glass – Orientation Glass – that allows one to set a direction that is 'down' when you forge it into a box. Therefore, anything inside the box is pulled in that direction, no matter which way the box turns.)

I stood for a long time, watching out the window, which glowed faintly to my eyes because of my Oculator's Lenses. After the chaos of the explosion and my near death, I hadn't really had a chance to contemplate the city. It was amazing. As I'd seen, the entire city was filled with castles. Not just simple brick and stone buildings, but actual *castles*, with high walls and towers, each one different.

Some had a fairy-tale feel, with archways and slender peaks. Others were brutish and no-nonsense, the type of castles you might imagine were ruled over by evil, blood-thirsty warlords. (It should be noted that the Honorable Guild of Evil Warlords has worked very hard to counter the negative stereotype of its members. After several dozen bake sales and charity auctions, someone suggested that they remove the word *evil* from the title of their organization. The suggestion was eventually rejected on account of Gurstak the Ruthless having just ordered a full box of embossed business cards.)

The castles lined the streets like skyscrapers might in a large Hushlander city. I could see people moving on the road below – some in horse-drawn carriages – but our dragon continued to crawl lizardlike across the sides of buildings. The castles were close enough that when he came to a gap between buildings, he could simply stretch across.

'Amazing, isn't it?' Bastille asked. I turned, not having realized that she'd joined me at the window.

'It is,' I said.

'It always feels good to get back,' Bastille said. 'I love how clean everything is. The sparkling glass, the stonework and the carvings.'

'I would have thought that coming back would be rough this time,' I said. 'I mean, you left as a knight, but have to come back as a squire.'

She grimaced. 'You really have a way with women, Smedry. Anyone ever told you that?'

I blushed. 'I just … uh …' Dang. You know, when I write my memoirs, I'm *totally* going to put a better line right there.

(Too bad I forgot to do that. I really need to pay better attention to my notes.)

'Yeah, whatever,' Bastille said, leaning against the window and looking down. 'I guess I'm resigned to my punishment.'

Not this again, I thought, worried. After losing her sword and being reprimanded by her mother, Bastille had gone through a serious funk. The worst part was that it was my fault. She'd lost her sword because *I'd* broken it while trying to fight off some sentient romance novels. Her mother seemed determined to prove that one mistake made Bastille completely unworthy to be a knight.

'Oh, don't look at me like that,' Bastille snapped. 'Shattering Glass! Just because I'm resigned to my punishment doesn't mean I'm giving up completely. I still intend to find out who set me up like this.'

'You're sure someone did?'

She nodded, eyes narrowing as she grew decidedly vengeful. I was happy that, for once, her wrath didn't seem directed at me.

'The more I've thought about it,' she said, 'the more the things you said the other week make sense. Why did they assign a freshly knighted girl – on such a dangerous mission? Somebody in Crystallia *wanted* me to fail – someone was jealous of how fast I'd achieved knighthood, or wanted to embarrass my mother, or simply wanted to prove that I couldn't succeed.'

'That doesn't sound very honorable,' I noted. 'A Knight of Crystallia wouldn't do something like that, would they?'

'I ... don't know,' Bastille said, glancing toward her mother.

'I find it hard to believe,' I said, though I didn't completely believe that. You see, jealousy is an awful lot like farting. Neither is something you like to imagine a brave knight being involved in, but the truth is, knights are just people. They get jealous, they make mistakes, and – yes – they break wind. (Though, of course, knights never use the term 'break wind.' They prefer the term 'bang the cymbals.' Guess that's what they get for wearing so much armor.)

Draulin stood at the back of the room, and – for once – wasn't standing in a stiff 'parade rest' stance. Instead, she was polishing her enormous crystal sword. Bastille suspected her mother had been the one to set her up, as Draulin was one of the knights who gave out assignments. But why would she send her own daughter on a mission that was obviously too hard for her?

'Something is wrong,' Bastille said.

'You mean, aside from the fact that our flying hawk mysteriously exploded?'

She waved an indifferent hand. 'The Librarians did that.'

'They did?'

'Of course,' Bastille said. 'They have an ambassador in town and we're going to stop them from taking over Mokia. Hence, they tried to kill us. Once the Librarians try to blow you up a few dozen times, you get used to it.'

'Are we sure it was them?' I asked. 'One of the rooms exploded, you said. Whose?'

'My mother's,' Bastille replied. 'We think it might have been from some Detonator's Glass slipped into her pack before she left Nalhalla. She carried that pack all the way through the Library of Alexandria, and it was set to go off when she got back in range of the city.'

'Wow. Elaborate.'

'That's the Librarians. Anyway, something is bothering my mother. I can tell.'

'Maybe she's feeling bad for punishing you so harshly.'

Bastille snorted. 'Not likely. This is something else, something about the sword ...'

She trailed off and didn't seem to have anything else to add. A few moments later, Grandpa Smedry waved me toward him. 'Alcatraz!' he said. 'Come listen to this!'

My grandfather was sitting with Sing on the couches. I walked over and sat down next to my grandfather, noting how comfortable the couch was. I hadn't seen any other dragons like this one crawling across the walls of the city, so I assumed that the ride was a special privilege.

'Sing, tell my grandson what you've been telling me,' Grandpa Smedry said.

'Well, here's the thing,' Sing said, leaning forward. 'This ambassador sent by the Librarians, she's from the Wardens of the Standard.'

'Who?' I asked.

'It's one of the Librarian sects,' Sing explained. 'Blackburn was from the Order of the Dark Oculators, while the assassin you faced in the Library of Alexandria was from the Order of the Scrivener's Bones. The Wardens of the Standard have always claimed to be the most kindly of the Librarians.'

'Kindly Librarians? That seems like an oxymoron.'

'It's also an act,' Grandpa Smedry said. 'The whole order is founded on the idea of *looking* innocent; they're really the deadliest snakes in the lot. The Wardens maintain most of the Hushlander libraries. They pretend that because they're only a bunch of bureaucrats, they're not dangerous like the Dark Oculators or the Order of the Shattered Lens.'

'Well, act or not,' Sing replied, 'they're the only Librarians who have ever made any kind of effort to work *with* the Free Kingdoms, rather than just trying to conquer us. This ambassador has convinced the Council of Kings that she is serious.'

I listened, interested, but not quite sure why my grandfather wanted me to know this. I'm a rather awesome person (have I mentioned that?) but I'm really not that great at politics. It's one of the three things I've no experience whatsoever doing, the other two being writing books and atmospheric rocket-propelled penguin riding. (Stupid responsibility.)

'So ... what does this have to do with me?' I asked.

'Everything, lad, everything!' Grandpa Smedry pointed at me. 'We're Smedrys. When we gave up our kingdom, we took an oath to watch over *all* of the Free Kingdoms. We're the guardians of civilization!'

'But wouldn't it be good if the kings make peace with the Librarians?'

Sing looked pained. 'Alcatraz, to do so, they would give up *Mokia*, my homeland! It would get folded into the Hushlands, and a generation or two from now, the Mokians wouldn't even *remember* being free. My people can't continue to fight the Librarians without the support of the other Free Kingdoms. We're too small on our own.'

'The Librarians won't keep their promise of peace,' Grandpa Smedry said. 'They've wanted Mokia badly for years now – I still don't know why they're so focused on it, as opposed to other kingdoms. Either way, taking over Mokia will put them one step closer to controlling the entire world. Manhandling Moons! Do you really think we can just give away an entire kingdom like that?'

I looked at Sing. The oversized anthropologist and his sister had become very dear to me over the last few months. They were earnest and fiercely loyal, and Sing had believed in me even when I'd tried to push him away. And for that, I wanted to do whatever I could to help him.

'No,' I said. 'You're right, we can't let that happen. We've *got* to stop it.'

Grandpa Smedry smiled, laying a hand on my shoulder. It might not seem like much, but this was a drastic turning point for me. It was the first time I really decided that I was in. I'd entered the Library of Alexandria only because I'd been chased by a monster. I'd only gone into Blackburn's lair because Grandpa Smedry had urged me on.

This was different. I understood then why my grandfather had called me over. He wanted me to be part of this – not just a kid who tags along, but a full participant.

Something tells me I'd have been much better off hiding in my room. Responsibility. It's the opposite of selfishness. I wish I'd known where it would get me. But this was before my betrayal and before I went blind.

Through one of the windows, I could see that the dragon had begun to descend. A moment later, the gondola settled against the ground.

We had arrived.

4

All right, I understand. you're confused. Don't feel ashamed; it happens to everyone once in a while. (Except me, of course.)

Having read the previous two books of my autobiography (as I'm *sure* by now you have), you know that I'm generally down on myself. I've told you that I'm a liar, a sadist, and a terrible person. And yet now in this volume, I've started talking about my awesomeness. Have I really changed my mind? Have I actually decided that I am a hero? Am I wearing kitty-cat socks right now?

No. (The socks have dolphins on them.)

I've realized something. By being so hard on myself in the previous books, I *sounded* like I was being humble. Readers assumed that because I said I was a terrible person, I must – indeed – be a saint.

Honestly, are you people determined to drive me insane? Why can't you just *listen* to what I tell you?

Anyway, I've come to the conclusion that the only way to convince you readers that I'm a terrible person is to show you how arrogant and self-centered I am. I'll do this by talking about my virtues. Incessantly. All the time. Until you're completely sick of hearing about my superiority.

Maybe then you'll understand.

The royal palace of Nalhalla turned out to be the white, pyramid-like castle at the center of the city. I stepped from the gondola, trying not to gawk as I gazed up at the magnificent building. The stonework was carved up as high as I could see.

'Forward!' Grandpa Smedry said, rushing up the steps like a general running into battle. He's remarkably spry for a person who is always late to everything.

I glanced at Bastille, who looked kind of sick. 'I think I'll wait outside,' she said.

'You're going in,' Draulin snapped, walking up the steps, her armor clinking.

I frowned. Usually, Draulin was very keen on making Bastille wait outside, since a mere 'squire' shouldn't be involved in important issues. Why insist that she enter the palace? I shot Bastille a questioning glance, but she just grimaced. So I rushed to catch up to my grandfather and Sing.

' . . . afraid I can't tell you much more, Lord Smedry,' Sing was saying. 'Folsom is the one who has been keeping track of the Council of Kings in your absence.'

'Ah, yes,' Grandpa Smedry said. 'He'll be here, I assume?'

'He should be!' Sing said.

'Another cousin?' I asked.

Grandpa Smedry nodded. 'Quentin's elder brother, son of my daughter, Pattywagon. Folsom's a fine lad! Brig had his eye on the boy for quite some time to marry one of his daughters, I believe.'

'Brig?' I asked.

'King Dartmoor,' Sing said.

Dartmoor. 'Wait,' I said. 'That's a prison, isn't it? Dartmoor?' (I know my prisons, as you might guess.)

'Indeed, lad,' Grandpa Smedry said.

'Doesn't that mean he's related to us?'

It was a stupid question. Fortunately I knew I'd be writing my memoirs and understood that a lot of people might be confused about this point. Therefore, using my powers of awsomosity, I asked this stupid-*sounding* question in order to lay the groundwork for my book series.

I hope you appreciate the sacrifice.

'No,' Grandpa Smedry said. 'A prison name doesn't necessarily mean that someone is a Smedry. The king's family is traditional, like ours, and they tend to use names of famed historical people over and over. The Librarians then named prisons after those same famous historical people to discredit them.'

'Oh, right,' I said.

Something about that thought bothered me, but I couldn't quite put my finger on it. Probably because the thought was inside my head, and so 'putting my finger on it' would have required sticking said finger through my skull, which sounds kind of painful.

Besides, the beauty of the hallway beyond those doors stopped me flat and cast all thoughts from my mind.

I'm no poet. Anytime I try to write poetry, it comes out as insults. I probably should have been a rapper, or at least a politician. Regardless, I sometimes find it hard to express beauty through words.

Suffice it to say that the enormous hallway stunned me, even after seeing a city full of castles, even after being carried on a dragon's back. The hallway was big. It was white. It was lined with what appeared to be pictures, but there was nothing in the frames. Other than glass.

Different kinds of glass, I realized as we walked down the magnificent hallway. *Here, the glass is the art!* Indeed, each framed piece of glass was a different color. Plaques at the top listed the types of glass. I recognized some, and most of them glowed faintly. I was wearing my Oculator's Lenses, which allowed me to see auras of powerful glass.

In a Hushlander palace, the kings showed off their gold and their silver. Here, the kings showed off their rare and expensive pieces of glass.

I watched in wonder, wishing Sing and Grandpa Smedry weren't rushing so quickly. We eventually turned through a set of doors and entered a long rectangular chamber filled with elevated seats on both the right and the left. Most of these were filled with people who quietly watched the proceedings below.

In the center of the room sat a broad table at which were seated about two dozen men and women wearing rich clothing of many exotic designs. I spotted King Dartmoor immediately. He was sitting on an elevated chair at the end of the table. Clothed in regal blue-and-gold robes, he wore a full red beard, and my Oculator's Lenses – which sometimes enhanced the images of people and places I looked at – made him seem slightly *taller* than he really was. More noble, larger than life.

I stopped in the doorway. I'd never been in the presence of royalty before, and—

'Leavenworth *Smedry*!' a vivacious feminine voice squealed. 'You rascal! You're back!'

The entire room seemed to turn as one, looking at a full-figured (remember what that means?) woman who leaped from her chair and barreled toward my grandfather. She had short blond hair and an excited expression.

I believe that's the first time I ever saw a hint of fear in my grandfather's eyes. The woman proceeded to grab the diminutive Oculator in a hug. Then she saw me.

'Is this Alcatraz?' she demanded. 'Shattering Glass, boy, does your mouth always hang open like that?'

I shut my mouth.

'Lad,' Grandpa Smedry said as the woman finally released him. 'This is your aunt, Pattywagon Smedry. My daughter, Quentin's mother.'

'Excuse me,' a voice called from the floor below. I blushed, realizing that the monarchs were watching us. 'Lady Smedry,' King Dartmoor said in a booming voice, 'is it *requisite* that you disrupt these proceedings?'

'Sorry, Your Majesty,' she called down. 'But these fellows are a lot more exciting than you are!'

Grandpa Smedry sighed, then whispered to me, 'Do you want to take a guess at her Smedry Talent?'

'Causing disruptions?' I whispered back.

'Close,' Grandpa Smedry said. 'She can say inappropriate things at awkward moments.'

That seemed to fit.

'Oh, don't give me that look,' she said, wagging her finger at the king. 'You can't tell me you're not excited to see them back too.'

The king sighed. 'We will take a recess of one hour for family reunions. Lord Smedry, did you return with your long-lost grandson, as reports indicated you might?'

'Indeed I did!' Grandpa Smedry proclaimed. 'Not only that but we also brought a pair of the fabled Translator's Lenses, smelted from the Sands of Rashid themselves!'

This prompted a reaction in the crowd, and murmuring began immediately. One small contingent of men and women sitting directly across from us did not seem pleased to see Grandpa Smedry. Instead of tunics or robes, the members of this group wore suits – the men with bow ties, the women with shawls. Many wore glasses, which had horned rims.

Librarians.

The room grew chaotic as the audience members began to stand, producing an excited buzz, almost like a thousand hornets had suddenly been released. My aunt Patty began to speak animatedly with her father, demanding the details of his time in the Hushlands. Her voice managed to carry out over the noise of the crowd, though she didn't appear to be yelling. That's just how she was.

'Alcatraz?'

I glanced to the side, where Bastille stood shuffling uncomfortably. 'Yeah?' I said.

'This ... might be an appropriate place to mention something.'

'Wait,' I said, growing nervous. 'Look, the king's coming up this way!'

'Of course he is,' Bastille said. 'He wants to see his family.'

'Of course. He wants to ... Wait, *what*?'

At that moment, King Dartmoor stepped up to us. Grandpa Smedry and the others bowed to him – even Patty – so I did the same. Then the king kissed Draulin.

That's right. He *kissed* her. I watched with shock, and not just because I'd never imagined that anyone would want to kiss Draulin. (Seemed a little like kissing an alligator.)

And if Draulin was the king's wife, that meant ...

'You're a princess!' I said, pointing an accusing finger at Bastille.

She grimaced. 'Yeah, kind of.'

'How can you "kind of" be a princess?'

'Well, I can't inherit the throne,' she said. 'I renounced claim on it when I joined the Knights of Crystallia. Vow of poverty and all that.'

The crowd milled about us, some exiting the room, others stopping – oddly – to gawk at my grandfather and me.

I should have realized that Bastille was royalty. Prison names. She has one, but her mother doesn't. That was an easy indication that her father's family was of an important breed. Besides, stories such as this one *always* have at least one hidden member of royalty among the core cast. It's, like, some kind of union mandate or something.

I had several options at this point. Fortunately, I chose the one that didn't make me look like a total dork.

'That's *awesome!*' I exclaimed.

Bastille blinked. 'You're not mad at me for hiding it?'

I shrugged. 'Bastille, I'm some kind of freaky noble thing myself. Why should it matter if you are too? Besides, it's not like you were lying or anything. You just don't like to talk about yourself.'

Brace yourselves. Something very, very strange is about to happen. Stranger than talking dinosaurs. Stranger than glass birds. Stranger, even, than my analogies to fish sticks.

Bastille got teary eyed. Then she hugged me.

Girls, might I make a suggestion at this point? Don't go around hugging people without warning. To many of us (a number somewhere near half), this is akin to pouring an entire bottle of seventeen-alarm hot sauce in our mouths.

I believe that at this point in the story, I made several very interesting and incoherent noises, followed – perhaps – by a blank expression and then some numb-faced drooling.

Someone was talking. '... I cannot interfere with the rules of Crystallia, Bastille.'

I fuzzed back into consciousness. Bastille had released me from her unprovoked, unregistered hug and moved on to speak with her father. The room had cleared out considerably, though there was still a number of people standing at the perimeter of the room, curiously watching our little group.

'I know, Father,' Bastille said. 'I must face their reprimand, as is my duty to the order.'

'That's my girl,' the king said, laying a hand on her shoulder. 'But don't take what they say *too* harshly. The world is far less intense a place than the knights sometimes make it out to be.'

Draulin raised her eyebrow at this. Looking at them – the king in his blue-and-gold robes, Draulin in her silvery armor – they actually seemed to *fit* together.

I still felt sorry for Bastille. *No wonder she's so uptight,* I thought. *Royalty on one side, hard-line knight on the other.* That would be like trying to grow up pressed between two boulders.

'Brig,' Grandpa Smedry said. 'We need to speak about what the Council is planning to do.'

The king turned. 'You're too late, I'm afraid, Leavenworth. Our minds are all but made up. You'll have your vote, but I doubt it will make a difference.'

'How could you even consider giving up Mokia?' Grandpa Smedry asked.

'To save lives, my friend.' The king spoke the words in a wearied voice, and I could almost *see* the burdens he was carrying. 'It is not a pleasant choice to make, but if it stops the war ...'

'You can't honestly expect them to keep their promises. Highlighting Heinleins, man! This is insanity.'

The king shook his head. 'I will not be the king who was offered peace and who passed it by, Leavenworth. I will not be a warmonger. If there is a chance at reconciliation ... But we should speak of this someplace outside the public eye. Let us retire to my sitting room.'

My grandfather nodded curtly, then stepped to the side and waved me over. 'What do you think?' he asked quietly as I approached.

I shrugged. 'He seems sincere.'

'Brig is nothing if not sincere,' Grandpa Smedry whispered. 'He is a passionate man; those Librarians must have done some clever talking to bring him to this point. Still, he's not the only vote on the Council.'

'But he's the king, isn't he?'

'He's the High King,' Grandpa Smedry said, raising a finger. 'He is our foremost leader but Nalhalla isn't the only kingdom in our coalition. There are thirteen kings, queens, and dignitaries like myself who sit on that Council. If we can persuade enough of them to vote against this treaty, then we might be able to kill it.'

I nodded. 'What can I do to help?' Mokia *couldn't* fall. I would see that it didn't.

'I'll speak with Brig,' Grandpa Smedry said. 'You go see if you can track down your cousin Folsom. I put him in charge of Smedry affairs here in Nalhalla. He might have some insight about this whole mess.'

'Okay.'

Grandpa Smedry fished in one of the pockets of his tuxedo jacket. 'Here, you might want this back.' He held out a single Lens with no coloring or tint to it. It glowed radiantly to my Oculator's eyes, more powerfully than any I'd ever seen except for the Translator's Lenses.

I'd almost forgotten about it. I'd discovered the Lens in the Library of Alexandria at the tomb of Alcatraz the First, but hadn't been able to determine what it did. I'd given it over to my grandfather for inspection.

'Did you figure out what it does?' I asked, taking it from him.

He nodded eagerly. 'There were lots of tests I had to do. I meant to tell you yesterday but, well ...'

'You're late.'

'Exactly!' Grandpa Smedry said. 'Anyway, this is a very useful Lens. Useful indeed. Almost mythical. Couldn't believe it myself, had to test the thing three times before I was convinced.'

I grew excited, imagining the Lens summoning the spirits of the dead to fight at my side. Or, instead, perhaps it would make people explode in a wave of red smoke if I focused it on them. Red smoke rocks.

'So what does it do?'

'It allows you to see when someone is telling the truth.'

That wasn't exactly what I'd been expecting.

'Yes,' Grandpa Smedry said. 'A Truthfinder's Lens. I never thought I'd hold one myself. Quite remarkable!'

'I ... don't suppose it makes people explode when they tell lies?'

'Afraid not, lad.'

'No red smoke?'

'No red smoke.'

I sighed and tucked the Lens away anyway. It did seem useful, though after discovering it hidden in the tomb, I'd really been hoping for some kind of weapon.

'Don't look so glum, lad,' Grandpa Smedry said. 'I don't think you understand the gem you hold in your pocket. That Lens could prove extremely useful to you over the next few days. Keep it close.'

I nodded. 'I don't suppose you have another pair of Firebringer's Lenses you could loan me?'

He chuckled. 'Didn't do enough damage with the last pair, eh? I don't have any more of those, but ... here, let me see.' He fished around inside his tuxedo jacket again. 'Ah!' he said, whipping out a pair of Lenses. They glowed with a modest light and had a violet tint.

That's right, violet. I wondered if the people who forge Oculatory Lenses *try* to make us all look like pansies, or if that was just accidental.

'What are they?' I asked.

'Disguiser's Lenses,' Grandpa Smedry said. 'Put them on, focus on the image of someone in your head, and the Lenses will disguise you to look like that person.'

It seemed pretty cool. I took the Lenses appreciatively. 'Can they make me look like other things? Like, say, a rock?'

'I guess,' Grandpa Smedry said. 'Though that rock would have to be wearing glasses. The Lenses appear in any disguise you use.'

That made them less powerful, but I figured I'd come up with a way to use them. 'Thanks,' I said.

'I might have some other offensive Lenses I can dig up later when I get back to the keep,' Grandpa Smedry said. ' I suspect that we'll deliberate here for another two or three hours before adjourning until the vote this evening. It's about ten right now; let's meet back at Keep Smedry in three hours to share information, all right?'

'All right.'

Grandpa Smedry winked at me. 'See you this afternoon, then. If you break anything important, be sure to blame it on Draulin! It'll be good for her.'

I nodded, and we parted ways.

5

It's time for me to talk about someone other than myself. Please don't be too heartbroken; once in a while, we need to discuss somebody who is not quite as charming, intelligent, or impressive as I am.

That's right, it's time to talk about you.

Occasionally, while infiltrating the Hushlands, I run across enterprising young people who want to resist Librarian control of their country. You ask me what you can do to fight. Well, I have three answers for you.

First, make sure you buy lots and lots and lots of copies of my books. There are plenty of uses for them (I'll discuss this in a bit) and for every one you buy, we donate money to the Alcatraz Smedry Wildlife Fund for Buying Alcatraz Smedry Cool Stuff.

The second thing you can do isn't quite as awesome, but it's still good. You can *read*.

Librarians control their world via information. Grandpa Smedry says that information is a far better weapon than any sword or Oculatory Lens, and I'm beginning to think he might be right. (Though the kitten chain saw I discussed in book two is a close second.)

The best way to fight the Librarians is to read a lot of books. Everything you can get your hands on. Then do the third thing I'm going to tell you about.

Buy lots of copies of my books.

Oh, wait. Did I already mention that? Well, then, there are *four* things you can do. But this intro is already too long. I'll tell you about the last one later. Know, however, that it involves popcorn.

'Okay,' I said, turning to Bastille. 'How do I find this Folsom guy?'

'I don't know,' she said flatly, pointing. 'Maybe ask his *mom*, who is standing right there?'

Oh, right, I thought. *Quentin's brother, that makes Pattywagon his mother.*

She was talking animatedly (which is how she always talks) with Sing. I waved to Bastille, but she hesitated.

'What?' I asked.

'My mission is officially over,' she said, grimacing and glancing toward Draulin. 'I need to report at Crystallia.' Draulin had made her way toward the exit of the room, and she was regarding Bastille in that way of hers that was somehow both insistent and patient.

'What about your father?' I said, glancing in the direction he and Grandpa Smedry had disappeared. 'He barely got time to see you two.'

'The kingdom takes precedence over everything else.'

That sounded like a rehearsed line to me. Probably something Bastille had heard a lot when growing up.

'Okay,' I said. 'Well, uh, I'll see you, then.'

'Yeah.'

I braced myself for another hug (known in the industry as a 'teenage boy forced reboot') but she just stood there, then cursed under her breath and hurried out after her mother. I was left trying to figure out just when things between us had grown so awkward.

(I was tempted to think back on all the good times we had spent together. Bastille smacking me in the face with her handbag. Bastille kicking me in the chest. Bastille making fun of something dumb I'd said. I would probably have a good case for abuse if I hadn't also (1) broken her sword, (2) kicked her first, and (3) been so awesome.)

Feeling strangely abandoned, I stepped up to my aunt Patty.

'You done being affectionate with the young knight there?' she asked me. 'Cute thing, isn't she?'

'What's this?' Sing said. 'Did I miss something?'

'Urk!' I said, blushing. 'No, nothing!'

'I'm sure,' Patty said, winking at me.

'Look, I need to find your son Folsom!'

'Hum. Whatcha need him for?'

'Important Smedry business.'

'Well, it's a good thing I'm an important Smedry, then, isn't it!'

She had me there. 'Grandpa wants me to ask about what the Librarians have been doing in town since he left.'

'Well, why didn't you say so?' Patty said.

'Because ... well, I ...'

'Slowness of thought,' Patty said consolingly. 'It's okay, hon. Your father isn't all that bright either. Well, let's go find Folsom, then! See ya, Sing!'

I reached for Sing, hoping he wouldn't abandon me to this awful woman, but he had already turned to go with some other people, and Patty had me by the arm.

I should stop and note here that in the years since that day, I've grown rather fond of Aunt Pattywagon. This statement has nothing at all to do with the fact that she threatened to toss me out a window if I didn't include it.

The mountainous woman pulled me from the room and down the hallway. Soon we were standing in the sunlight on the front steps outside as Patty sent one of the serving men to fetch transportation.

'You know,' I said, 'if you tell me where Folsom is, I could just go find him on my own. No need to—'

'He's out and about on very important business,' Patty said. 'I'll have to lead you. I can't tell you. You see, as a Librarian expert, he's been put in charge of a recent defection.'

'Defection?'

'Yes,' she said. 'You know, a foreign agent who decides to join the other side? A Librarian fled her homeland and joined the Free Kingdoms. My son is in charge of helping her grow accustomed to life here. Ah, here's our ride!'

I turned, half expecting another dragon, but apparently we two didn't warrant a full-size dragon this time. Instead, a coachman rode up with an open-topped carriage pulled by rather mundane horses.

'Horses?' I said.

'Of course,' Patty said, climbing into the carriage. 'What were you expecting? A ... what is it you call them? A pottlemobile?'

'Automobile,' I said, joining her. 'No, I wasn't expecting one of those. Horses just seem so ... rustic.'

'Rustic?' she said as the coachman urged his beasts into motion. 'Why, they're far more advanced than those bottlemobiles you Hushlanders use!'

It's a common belief in the Free Kingdoms that everything they have is more advanced than what we backward Hushlanders use. For instance, they like to say that swords are more advanced than guns. This may sound ridiculous until you realize their swords are magical and are, indeed, more advanced than guns – the kinds of early guns the Free Kingdomers had before they switched to silimatic technology.

Horses, though ... I've never bought that one.

'Okay, look,' I said. 'Horses are *not* more advanced than cars.'

'Sure they are,' Patty said.

'Why?'

'Simple. Poop.'

I blinked. 'Poop?'

'Yup. What do those slobomobiles make? Foul-smelling gas. What do horses make?'

'Poop?'

'Poop,' she said. 'Fertilizer. You get to go somewhere, *and* you get a useful by-product.'

I sat back, feeling a little bit disturbed. Not because of what Patty said – I was used to Free Kingdomer rationalizations. No, I was disturbed because I'd somehow managed to talk about both excrement and flatulence in the course of two chapters.

If I could somehow work in barfing, then I'd have a complete potty humor trifecta.

Riding in the carriage allowed me a good look at the city's people, buildings, and shops. Oddly, I was just surprised by how ... well, normal everyone seemed. Yes, there were castles. Yes, the people wore tunics and robes instead of slacks and blouses.

But the expressions on their faces – the laughter, the frustration, even the boredom – were just like those back home.

Actually, riding down that busy road – with the castle peaks rising like jagged mountains into the sky – felt an awful lot like riding in a taxi through New York City. People are people. Wherever they come from or whatever they look like, they're the same. As the philosopher Garnglegoot the Confused once said: 'I'll have a banana and crayon sandwich, please.' (Garnglegoot always did have trouble staying on topic.)

'So where do all of these people live?' I asked, then cringed, expecting Bastille to shoot back something like 'In their homes, stupid.' It took me a second to remember that Bastille wasn't there to make fun of me. That made me sad, though I should have been happy to avoid the mockery.

'Oh, most of them are from Nalhalla City here,' Patty said. 'Though a fair number of them probably traveled in today via Transporter's Glass.'

'Transporter's Glass? '

Aunt Patty nodded her blond-haired head. 'It's some very interesting technology, just developed by the Kuanalu Institute over in Halaiki using sands your father discovered a number of years ago. It lets people cross great distances in an instant, using a feasibly economic expenditure of brightsand. I've read some very exciting research on the subject.'

I blinked. I believe I've mentioned how unreasonably scholarly the Smedry clan is. A remarkable number of them are professors, researchers, or scientists. We're like an unholy mix of the Brady Bunch and the UCLA honors department.

'You're a professor, aren't you?' I accused.

'Why, yes, dear!' Aunt Patty said.

'Silimatics?'

'That's right; how'd you guess?'

'Just lucky,' I said. 'Have you ever heard of a theory that says Oculators can power technological types of glass in addition to their Lenses?'

She harrumphed. 'Been speaking with your father, I see.'

'My father?'

'I'm well aware of that paper he wrote,' Aunt Patty continued, 'but I don't buy it. Claiming that Oculators were somehow brightsand in human form. Doesn't that seem silly to you? How can sand be human in form?'

'I—'

'I'll admit that there *are* some discrepancies,' she continued, ignoring my attempt to interject. 'However, your father is jumping to conclusions. This will require *far* more research than he's put into it! Research by people who are more practiced at true silimatics than that scoundrel. Oh, looks like you're getting a zit on your nose, by the way. Too bad that man in the carriage next to us just took a picture of you.'

I jumped, glancing to the side where another carriage had pulled up. The man there was holding up squares of glass about a foot on each side, pointing them toward us, then tapping them. I was still new to all this, but I was pretty sure he was doing something very similar to taking pictures with a camera. When he noticed my attention, he lowered his panes of glass, tipped his cap toward me, and his carriage pulled away.

'What was that all about?' I asked.

'Well, hon, you *are* the heir of the Smedry line – not to mention an Oculator raised inside the Hushlands. That kind of thing interests people.'

'People *know* about me?' I asked, surprised. I knew I'd been born in Nalhalla, but I'd just assumed that the people in the Free Kingdoms had forgotten.

'Of course they do! You're a celebrity, Alcatraz – the Smedry who disappeared mysteriously as a child! There have been *hundreds* of books written on you. When it came out a few years back that you were being raised in the Hushlands, that only made things more interesting. You think all those people over there are staring because of me?'

I'd never been in Nalhalla before (duh) so I hadn't thought it strange that there were people standing along the streets, watching the road. Now, however I noticed how many of them were pointing toward our carriage.

'Shattering Glass,' I whispered. 'I'm *Elvis*.'

You Free Kingdomers may not know that name. Elvis was a powerful monarch from Hushlander past, known for his impassioned speeches to inmates, for his odd footwear, and for looking less like himself than the people who dress like him. He vanished mysteriously as the result of a Librarian cover-up.

'I don't know who that is, hon,' Aunt Patty said. 'But whoever he is, he's probably a lot less well known than you are.'

I sat back, stunned. Grandpa Smedry and the others had *tried* to explain how important our family was, but I'd never really understood. We had a castle as large as the king's palace. We controlled incredible wealth. We had magical powers that others envied. There had been volumes and volumes of books written about us.

That was the moment, riding in that carriage, when it all finally hit me. I understood. *I'm famous*, I thought, a smile growing on my face.

This was a very important point in my life. It's where I started to realize just how much power I had. I didn't find fame intimidating. I found it exciting. Instead of hiding from the people with their silimatic cameras, I started waving to them. They began to point even more excitedly, and the attention made me feel good. Warm, like I'd suddenly been bathed in sunlight.

Some say that fame is a fleeting thing. Well, it has clung to me tenaciously, like gum stuck to the sidewalk, blackened from being stepped on a thousand times. I haven't been able to shake it, no matter what.

Some also say fame is shallow. That's easy to say when you haven't spent your childhood being passed from family to family, scorned and discarded because of a curse that made you break whatever you touched.

Fame is like a cheeseburger. It might not be the best or most healthy thing to have, but it will still fill you up. You don't really care how healthy something is when you've been without for so long. Like a cheeseburger, fame fills a need, and it tastes so good going down.

It isn't until years later that you realize what it has done to your heart.

'Here we are!' Aunt Patty said as the carriage slowed. I was surprised. After hearing that my cousin Folsom was in charge of guarding former Librarians, I'd expected to be taken to some sort of police station or secret service hideout. Instead, we'd come to a shopping district with little stores set into the fronts of the castles. Aunt Patty paid our driver with some glass coins, then climbed down.

'I thought you said he was guarding a Librarian spy,' I said, getting out.

'He is, hon.'

'And where does one do that?'

Aunt Patty pointed toward a store that looked suspiciously like an ice cream parlor. 'Where else?'

6

Once, when I was very young, I was being driven to the public swimming pool by my foster mother. This was a long time ago, so far distant in my memory I can barely remember it. I must have been three or four years old.

I recall an image: a group of strangely shaped buildings beside the road. I'd seen them before, and I'd always wondered what they were. They looked like small white domes, three or four of them, the size of houses.

As we passed, I turned to my foster mother. 'Mom, what are those?'

'That is where the crazy people go,' she said.

I hadn't realized there was a mental institution in my town. But it was nice to know where it was. For years after that, when the topic of mental illness came up, I'd explain where the hospital was. I was proud, as a child, to know where they took the crazy people when they went ... well, crazy.

When I was twelve or so, I remember being driven past that place again with a different foster family. By then, I could read. (I was quite advanced for my age, you know.) I noticed the sign hanging on the domelike buildings.

It didn't say the buildings were a mental institution. It said that they were a church.

Suddenly, I understood. 'That's where all the crazy people go' meant something completely different to my foster mother than it had to me. I spent all those years proudly telling people where the asylum was, all the while ignorant of the fact that I'd been completely wrong.

This will all relate.

I stepped into the ice cream shop, trying to be ready for anything.

I had seen coolers that turned out to hide banquet rooms. I had seen libraries that hid a dark hideout for cultists. I figured that a place that looked like an ice cream shop was probably something entirely different, like an explosive crayon testing facility. (Ha! That's what you get for writing on the walls, Jimmy!)

If, indeed, the ice cream parlor was fake, it was doing a really good job of that fakery. It looked exactly like something from the fifties, including colorful pastels, stools by the tables, and waitresses in striped red-and-white skirts. Though said waitresses *were* serving banana splits and chocolate shakes to a bunch of people dressed in medieval clothing.

A sign on the wall proudly proclaimed the place to be an AUTHENTIC HUSHLANDER RESTAURANT! When Aunt Patty and I entered, the place grew still. Outside, others were clustering around the windows, looking in at me.

'It's all right, folks,' Aunt Patty proclaimed. 'He's really not all that interesting. Actually, he kind of smells, so you probably want to keep your distance.'

I blushed deeply.

'Notice how I keep them from fawning over you?' she said, patting me on the shoulder. 'You can thank me later, hon. I'll go fetch Folsom!' Aunt Patty pushed her way through the busy room. As soon as she was gone, Free Kingdomers began to approach me, ignoring her warning. They were hesitant, though; even the middle-aged men seemed as timid as children.

'Um ... can I help you?' I asked as I was surrounded.

'You're him, aren't you?' one of them asked. 'Alcatraz the Lost.'

'Well, I don't feel that lost,' I said, growing uncomfortable. To have them so close and so in awe ... well, I didn't quite know how to react. What was the proper protocol for a long-lost celebrity when first revealing himself to the world?

A young fan, maybe seven years old, solved the problem. He stepped up, holding a square piece of glass five or six inches across. It was clear and flat, as if it had been cut right out of a windowpane. He offered the glass to me with a shaking hand.

Okay, I thought, *that's weird*. I reached out and took the glass.

As soon as I touched it, the glass began to glow. The boy pulled it back eagerly, and I could see that my thumb and fingers had left glowing prints. Apparently, this was the Free Kingdomer version of getting an autograph.

The others began to press forward. Some had squares of glass. Others wanted to shake my hand, get their pictures taken with me, or have me use my Talent to break something of theirs as a memento. The bustle might have annoyed someone else, but after a childhood of being alternately mocked (for breaking things) and feared (for breaking things), I was ready for a little bit of adulation.

After all, didn't I deserve it? I'd stopped the Librarians from getting the Sands of Rashid. I'd defeated Blackburn. I'd saved my father from the horrors of the Library of Alexandria.

Grandpa Smedry was right; it was time to relax and enjoy myself. I made thumbprints, posed for pictures, shook hands, and answered questions. By the time Aunt Patty returned, I had launched into a dramatic telling of my first infiltration with Grandpa Smedry. That day in the ice cream parlor was the day I realized that I might make a good writer. I seemed to have a flair for storytelling. I teased the audience with information about what was coming, never quite revealing the ending but hinting at it.

By the way, did you know that later that day, someone was going to try to assassinate King Dartmoor?

'All right, all right,' Aunt Patty said, shoving aside some of my fans. 'Give the boy some room.' She grabbed me by the arm. 'Don't worry, hon, I'll rescue you.'

'But—!'

'No need to thank me,' Aunt Patty said. Then, in a louder voice, she proclaimed, 'Everyone, stay back! Alcatraz has been in the Hushlands! You won't want to catch any of his crazy-strange Librarian diseases!'

I saw numerous people's faces pale, and the crowd backed away. Aunt Patty then led me to a table occupied by two people. One, a young man in his twenties with black hair and a hawk-ish face, looked vaguely familiar. I realized this must be Folsom

Smedry; he looked a lot like his brother, Quentin. The young woman seated across from him wore a maroon skirt and white blouse. She had dark skin and her spectacles had a chain.

To be honest, I hadn't expected the Librarian to be so pretty, or so young. Certainly, none of the ones I'd met so far had been pretty. Granted, most of those had been trying to kill me at the time, so perhaps I was a little biased.

Folsom stood up. 'Alcatraz!' he said, holding out a hand. 'I'm Folsom, your cousin.'

'Nice to meet you,' I said. 'What's your Talent?' (I'd learned by now to ask Smedrys that as soon as I met them. Sitting down to eat with a Smedry without knowing their Talent was a little like accepting a grenade without knowing if the pin had been pulled or not.)

Folsom smiled modestly as we shook hands. 'It's not really all that important a Talent. You see, I can dance really poorly.'

'Ah,' I said. 'How impressive.'

I tried to sound sincere. I had trouble. It's just so hard to compliment someone for being a bad dancer.

Folsom smiled happily, releasing my hand and gesturing for me to sit. 'Great to finally meet you,' he said. 'Oh, and I'd give that handshake a four out of six.'

I sat down. 'Excuse me?'

'Four out of six,' he said, sitting. 'Reasonable firmness with good eye contact, but you held on a little bit long. Anyway, may I present Himalaya Rockies, formerly of the Hushlands?'

I glanced over at the Librarian, then hesitantly held out my hand. I half expected her to pull out a gun and shoot me. (Or at least to chastise me for my overdue books.)

'Pleased to meet you,' she said, taking my hand without even trying to stab me. 'I hear you grew up in America like I did.'

I nodded. She had a Boston accent. I'd only been away from the United States for a couple of weeks, and I had been very eager to escape, but it still felt good to hear someone from my homeland.

'So, er, you're a Librarian?' I asked.

'A *recovering* Librarian,' she said quickly.

'Himalaya defected six months ago,' Folsom said. 'She brought lots of great information for us.'

Six months, eh? I thought, eyeing Folsom. He didn't give any indication, but if it had been six months, I found it odd that we were still keeping track of Himalaya. Folsom and the king, I figured, must still worry that she was secretly a spy for the Librarians.

The booths around us filled quickly, and the parlor enjoyed quite a boost in business from my patronage. The owner must have noticed this, for he soon visited our table. 'The famous Alcatraz Smedry, in my humble establishment!' he said. The pudgy man wore a pair of bright red-and-white-striped pants. He waved to one of his waitresses, who rushed over with a bowl filled with whipped cream. 'Please have a bandana split on the house!'

'*Bandana?*' I asked, cocking my head.

'They get a few things wrong here,' Himalaya whispered, 'but it's still the closest you'll get to American food while in Nalhalla.'

I nodded thankfully to the owner, who smiled with pleasure. He left a handful of mints on the table, though I don't quite know why, then went back to serving customers. I glanced at the dessert he'd provided. It was, indeed, a large bandana filled with ice cream. I tasted it hesitantly but it actually was kind of good, in an odd way. I couldn't quite place the flavor.

That probably should have worried me.

'Alcatraz Smedry,' Folsom said, as if taking the name for a test drive. 'I have to admit, your latest book was a disappointment. One and a half stars out of five.'

I had a moment of panic, thinking he referred to the second book of my autobiography. However, I soon realized that was silly, since it not only hadn't been written yet but I didn't even know that I *would* write it. I promptly stopped that line of thinking before I caused a temporal rift and ended up doing something silly, like killing a butterfly or interfering with mankind's first warp jump.

'I have no idea what you're talking about,' I said, taking another bite of ice cream.

'Oh, I have it here somewhere,' Folsom said, rifling in his shoulder bag.

'I didn't think it was so bad,' Himalaya said. 'Of course, my tastes *are* tainted by ten years as a Librarian.'

'Ten years?' I asked. She didn't look much older than twenty-five to me.

'I started young,' she explained, playing idly with the mints on the table. 'I apprenticed to a master Librarian after I'd proven my ability to use the reverse lighthouse system.'

'The what?'

'That's when you arrange a group of books alphabetically based on the third letter of the author's mother's maiden name. Anyway, once I got in, the Librarians let me live the high life for a time – buttering me up with advanced reader copies of books and the occasional bagel in the break room. When I was eighteen, they began introducing me into the cult.'

She shivered, as if remembering the horrors of those early days. I wasn't buying it, though. As pleasant as she was, I was still suspicious of her motives.

'Ah,' Folsom said, pulling something out of his pack. 'Here it is.' He set a book on the table – one that appeared to have a painting of *me* on the cover. Me riding an enormous vacuum cleaner while wearing a sombrero. I held a flintlock rifle in one hand and what appeared to be a glowing, magical credit card in the other.

Alcatraz Smedry and the Mechanic's Wrench, it read.

'Oh, dear,' Aunt Patty said. 'Folsom, don't tell me you read those dreadful fantasy novels!'

'They're fun, Mother,' he said. 'Meaningless, really, but as a diversion I give the genre three out of four marks. This one here was terrible, though. It had all the elements of a great story – a mystical weapon, a boy on a journey, quirky sidekicks. But it ended up ruining itself by trying to say something important, rather than just being amusing.'

'That's me!' I said, pointing at the cover.

If Bastille were there, she'd have said something pithy, such as

'Glad you can recognize your own face, Smedry. Be careful not to wear a mustache, though. Might confuse yourself.'

Unfortunately, Bastille wasn't there. Once again, I found myself annoyed, and once again, I found myself annoyed at myself for being annoyed, which probably annoys you. I know it annoys my editor.

'It's a fictionalized account, of course,' Folsom said about the book. 'Most scholars know that you didn't do any of these things. However, you're such a part of the cultural unconsciousness that stories about you are quite popular.'

The cultural what? I thought, bemused. People were writing books about me! Or, at least, books with me as the hero. That seemed pretty darn cool, even if the facts were sketchy.

'That's the kind of thing they think happens in the Hushlands,' Himalaya said, smiling at me, still playing idly with the mints. 'Epic battles with the Librarians using strange Hushlander technology. It's all very romanticized and exaggerated.'

'Fantasy novels,' Aunt Patty said, shaking her head. 'Ah, well. Rot your brain if you want. You're old enough that I can't tell you what to do, though I'm glad you kicked that bed-wetting habit before you moved out!'

'Thanks, Mother,' Folsom said, blushing. 'That's ... well, that's really nice. We should—' He cut off, glancing at Himalaya. 'Um, you're doing it again.'

The former Librarian froze, then looked down at the mints in front of her. 'Oh, bother!'

'What?' I asked.

'She was classifying them,' Folsom said, pointing at the mints. 'Organizing them by shape, size, and ... it appears, color as well.'

The mints sat in a neat little row, color coordinated and arranged by size. 'It's just so hard to kick the habit,' Himalaya said with frustration. 'Yesterday, I found myself cataloging the tiles on my bathroom floor, counting the number of each color and the number of chipped ones. I can't seem to stop!'

'You'll beat it eventually,' Folsom said.

'I hope so,' she said with a sigh.

'Well,' Aunt Patty said, standing. 'I've got to get back to the court discussion. Folsom should be able to give you the information you want, Alcatraz.'

We bid farewell, and Aunt Patty made her way from the room – though not before pointing out to the owner that he *really* ought to do something about his bad haircut.

'What information is it you wanted?' Folsom asked.

I eyed Himalaya, trying to decide just what I wanted to say in front of her.

'Don't worry,' Folsom said. 'She's completely trustworthy.'

If that's the case, then why does she need a guard to watch over her? I didn't buy that Folsom was needed to accustom her to life in the Free Kingdoms – not after six months. Unfortunately, there didn't seem to be any getting around talking with her there, so I decided to explain. I didn't think I'd be revealing anything *too* sensitive.

'My grandfather and I would like a report on Librarian activities here in the city,' I said. 'I understand you're the one to come to about that sort of thing.'

'Well, I *do* have a good time keeping an eye on Librarians,' Folsom said with a smile. 'What do you want to know?'

I didn't honestly know, as I was still kind of unused to this hero stuff. Whatever the Librarians had been up to lately probably had something to with their current attempt to conquer Mokia, but I didn't know what specifically to look for.

'Anything that seems suspicious,' I said, trying to sound suave for my fans, in case any of them were eavesdropping. (Being awesome is hard work.)

'Well, let's see,' Folsom said. 'This treaty mess started about six months back, when a contingent from the Wardens of the Standard showed up in the city, claiming they wanted to set up an embassy. The king was suspicious, but after years of trying hard to get the Librarians to engage in peace talks, he couldn't really turn them down.'

'Six months?' I asked. That would be a little bit after Grandpa Smedry left for the Hushlands to check in on me. It was also about the length of time a frozen burrito would stay in the freezer without turning totally nasty. (I know this because it's very heroic and manly.)

'That's right,' Himalaya said. 'I was one of the Librarians who came to staff the embassy. That's how I escaped.'

I actually hadn't made that connection, but I nodded, as if that were exactly what I'd been thinking, as opposed to comparing my manliness to a frozen food.

'Anyway,' Folsom continued, 'the Librarians announced they were going to offer us a treaty. Then they started going to parties and socializing with the city's elite.'

That sounded like the kind of information my grandfather wanted. I wondered if I should just grab Folsom and take him back.

But, well, Grandfather wouldn't be back to the castle for hours yet. Besides, I was no errand boy. I hadn't simply come to fetch Folsom and then sit around and wait. Alcatraz Smedry, brave vacuum cleaner rider and wearer of the awesome sombrero, didn't stand for things like that. He was a man of action!

'I want to meet with some of these Librarians,' I found myself saying. 'Where can we find them?'

Folsom looked concerned. 'Well, I guess we could head to the embassy.'

'Isn't there somewhere else we could find them? Someplace a little more neutral?'

'There will probably be some at the prince's lunch party.' Himalaya said.

'Yeah,' Folsom said. 'But how will we get into *that*? You have to RSVP months in advance.'

I stood up, making a decision. 'Let's go. Don't worry about getting us in – I'll handle that.'

7

Okay, go back and reread the introductions to chapters two, five, and six. Don't worry, I can wait. I'll go make some popcorn.

Pop. Pop-pop. Pop-pop-pop. Pop. POP!

What, done already? You must not have read very carefully. Go back and do it again.

Munch. Munch-munch. Munch-munch-munch. Munch. Crunch.

Okay, that's better. You should have read about:

1) Fish sticks

2) Several things you can do to fight the Librarians

3) Mental hospitals that are really churches

The connection between these three things should be readily obvious to you:

Socrates.

Socrates was a funny little Greek man best known for forgetting to write things down and for screaming, 'Look, I'm a philosopher!' in the middle of a No Philosophy zone. (He was later forced to eat his words. Along with some poison.)

Socrates was the inventor of something very important: the question. That's right, before Socrates, languages had no ability to ask questions. Conversations went like this:

Blurg: 'Gee, I wish there were a way I could speak to Grug and see if he's feeling all right.'

Grug: 'By the tone of your voice, I can tell that you are curious about my health. Since I just dropped this rock on my foot, I would like to request your help.'

Blurg: 'Alas, though our language has developed the imperative form, we have yet to discover a method of using the interrogative.

If only there were a simple way to ease communication between us.'

Grug: 'I see that a Pteroydeactyl has begun to chew on your head.'

Blurg: 'Yes, you are quite right. Ouch.'

Fortunately, Socrates eventually came along and invented the question, allowing people like Blurg and Grug to speak in a way that wasn't quite so awkward.

All right, I'm lying. Socrates didn't invent the question. But he *did* popularize it through something we call the Socratic method. In addition, he taught people to ask questions about everything. To take nothing for granted.

Ask. Wonder. Think.

And that's the final thing you can do to help fight the evil Librarians. That, and buy lots of my books. (Or did I mention that one already?)

'So, who's this prince that's throwing the party?' I asked as Folsom, Himalaya, and I traveled by carriage.

'The High King's son,' Folsom said. 'Rikers Dartmoor. Out of seven crowns, I'd give him five and a half. He's likable and friendly, but he doesn't have his father's brilliance.'

I'd been trying for a while to figure out why Folsom rated everything like that. So I asked: 'Why do you rate everything all the time like that?' (Thanks, Socrates!)

'Hum?' Folsom asked. 'Oh, well, I *am* a critic.'

'You are?'

He nodded proudly. 'Head literary critic for the *Nalhallan Daily*, and a staff writer for plays as well!'

I should have known. Like I said, all of the Smedrys seemed to be involved in one academic field or another. This was the worst yet. I looked away, suddenly feeling self-conscious.

'Shattering Glass!' Folsom said. 'Why do people always get like that when they find out?'

'Get like what?' I asked, trying to act like I wasn't trying to act like anything at all.

'Everyone grows worried when they're around a critic,' Folsom complained. 'Don't they understand that we can't properly evaluate them if they're not acting *normal*?'

'Evaluate?' I squeaked. 'You're evaluating me?'

'Well, sure,' Folsom said. 'Everybody evaluates. We critics are just trained to talk about it.'

That didn't help. In fact, that made me even more uncomfortable. I glanced down at the copy of *Alcatraz Smedry and the Mechanic's Wrench*. Was Folsom judging how much I acted like the hero in the book?

'Oh, don't let that thing annoy you,' Himalaya said. She was sitting next to me on the seat, uncomfortably close, considering how little I trusted her. Her voice sounded so friendly: Was that a trick?

'What do you mean?' I asked.

'The book,' she said, pointing. 'I know it's probably bothering you how trite and ridiculous it is.'

I looked down at the cover again. 'Oh, I don't know, it's not *that* bad ...'

'Alcatraz, you're riding a *vacuum cleaner*.'

'And a noble steed he was. Or, er, well, he appears to be one ...' Somewhere deep – hidden far within me, next to the nachos I'd had for dinner a few weeks back – a piece of me acknowledged that she was right. The story did seem rather silly.

'It's a good thing that copy is Folsom's,' Himalaya continued. 'Otherwise we'd have to listen to that dreadful theme music every time you opened the book. Folsom removes the music plate before he reads the books.'

'Why'd he do that?' I asked, disappointed. *I have theme music?*

'Ah,' Folsom said. 'Here we are!'

I looked up as the carriage pulled to a halt outside a very tall, red-colored castle. It had a wide green lawn (the type that was randomly adorned with statues of people who were missing body parts) and numerous carriages parked in front. Our driver brought us right up to the front gates, where several men in white uniforms stood about looking very butler-y.

One stepped up to our carriage. 'Invitation?' he asked.

'We don't have one,' Folsom said, blushing.

'Ah, well, then,' the butler said, pointing. 'You can pull around that direction to leave, then—'

'We don't need an invitation,' I said, gathering my confidence. 'I'm Alcatraz Smedry.'

The butler gave me a droll glance. 'I'm sure you are. Now, you go that way to leave—'

'No,' I said, standing up. 'Really, I'm him. Look.' I held up the book cover.

'You forgot your sombrero,' the butler said flatly.

'But it does look like me.'

'I'll admit that you are a good look-alike, but I *hardly* think that a mythical legend has suddenly appeared just so that he can go to a lunch party.'

I blinked. It was the first time in my life someone had refused to believe that *I* was *me*.

'Surely you recognize me,' Folsom said, stepping up beside me. 'Folsom Smedry.'

'The critic,' the butler said.

'Er, yes,' Folsom replied.

'The one who panned His Highness's latest book.'

'Just … well, trying to offer some constructive advice,' Folsom said, blushing again.

'You should be ashamed of trying to use an Alcatraz imposter to insult His Highness at his own party. Now, if you'll just pull along in that direction …'

This was getting annoying. So I did the first thing that came to mind. I broke the butler's clothing.

It wasn't that hard. My Talent is very powerful, if a little tough to control. I simply reached out and touched the butler's sleeve, then sent a burst of breaking power into his shirt. Once, this would have simply made it fall off – but I was learning to control my abilities. So, first I made the white uniform turn pink, *then* I made it fall off.

The butler stood in his underwear, pointing into the distance with a naked arm, pink clothing around his feet. 'Oh,' he finally said. 'Welcome, then, Lord Smedry. Let me lead you to the party.'

'Thank you,' I replied, hopping down from the carriage.

'That was easy,' Himalaya said, joining Folsom and me. The butler led the way, still wearing only his underwear, but walking in a dignified manner regardless.

'The breaking Talent,' Folsom said, smiling. 'I forgot about it! It's extremely rare, and there's only one person alive – mythical legend or not – who has it. Alcatraz, that was a five out of five point five maneuver.'

'Thanks,' I said. 'But what book of the prince's did you give such a bad review to?'

'Er, well,' Folsom said. 'Did you ever look at the *author* of the book you're carrying?'

I glanced down with surprise. The fantasy novel bore a name on the front that – in the delight of looking at my own name – I'd completely missed. Rikers Dartmoor.

'The prince is a *novelist*?' I asked.

'His father was terribly disappointed to hear about the hobby,' Folsom said. 'You know what terrible people authors tend to be.'

'They're mostly social miscreants,' Himalaya agreed.

'Fortunately, the prince has mostly avoided the worst habits of authors,' Folsom said. 'Probably because writing is only a hobby for him. Anyway, he's fascinated with the Hushlands and with mythological things like motorcycles and eggbeaters.'

Great, I thought as we walked through the castle doorway. The corridors inside held framed classic-era movie posters from the Hushlands. Cowboys, *Gone with the Wind*, B movies with slime monsters. I began to understand where the prince got his strange ideas about life in the United States.

We entered a large ballroom. It was filled with people in fancy clothing, holding drinks and chatting. A group of musicians played music by rubbing their fingers on crystal cups.

'Uh-oh,' Himalaya said, grabbing Folsom as he started to jerk erratically. Himalaya pulled him out of the room.

'What?' I asked, turning with shock, prepared for an attack.

'It's nothing,' she said, stuffing cotton balls into Folsom's ears.

I didn't have time to comment on the strange behavior as the mostly naked butler cleared his throat. He pointed at me and proclaimed with a loud voice, 'Lord Alcatraz Smedry and guests.' Then he turned around and walked away.

I stood awkwardly a t the doorway suddenly aware of my bland clothing: T-shirt and jeans, with a green jacket. The people before me didn't seem to be dressed in any one style – some were wearing medieval gowns or hose, others had what looked to be antiquated vests and suits. All were better dressed than I was.

A figure suddenly pushed to the front of the crowd. The thirty-something man was wearing lavish robes of blue and silver, and had a short red beard. He also wore a bright red baseball cap on his head. This was undoubtedly Rikers Dartmoor, novelist, prince, fashion mistake.

'You're here!' the prince said, grabbing and shaking my hand. 'I can barely contain myself! Alcatraz Smedry, in the flesh! I hear you exploded upon landing in the city!'

'Yes, well,' I said. 'It wasn't that bad an explosion, all things considered.'

'Your life is so exciting!' Rikers said. 'Just like I imagined it. And now you're at *my* party! And who is this with you?' His face fell as he recognized Folsom, whose ears were now stuffed with cotton. 'Oh, the critic,' the prince said. Then, more softly, 'Well, I guess we can't help who we're related to, can we?' He winked at me. 'Please, come in! Let me introduce you to everyone!'

And he meant *everyone*.

When I first wrote this next section of the book, I tried to be very accurate and detailed. Then I realized that's just plain boring. This is a story about evil Librarians, Teleporting Glass, and sword fights. It's not a book about dumb parties. So, instead, I'm just going to summarize what happened next:

Person one: 'Alcatraz, you're so awesome!'

Me: 'Yes, I know I am.'

The prince: 'I always knew he was. Have you read my latest book?'

Person two: 'Alcatraz, you are more awesome even than your-self.'

Me: 'Thank you. I think.'

The prince: 'He's my buddy, you know. I write books about him.'

This went on for the better part of an hour or so. Only, it wasn't boring for me at the time. I enjoyed it immensely. People were paying attention to me, telling me about how wonderful I was. I actually started to believe I was the Alcatraz from Rikers's stories. It became a little hard to focus on why I'd come to the party in the first place. Mokia could wait, right? It was important that I get to know people, right?

Eventually, Prince Rikers brought me to the lounge, chatting about how they'd managed to make his books play music. In the lounge, people sat in comfortable chairs, making small talk while they sipped exotic drinks. We passed a large group of party-goers laughing together, and they seemed focused on someone I couldn't see.

Another celebrity, I thought. *I should be gracious to them – I wouldn't want them to get jealous of how much more popular I am than they are.*

We approached the group. Prince Rikers said, 'And, of course, you already know this next person.'

'I do?' I asked, surprised. The figure in the middle of the crowd of people turned toward me.

It was my father.

I stopped in place. The two of us looked at each other. My father had a large group of people doting on him, and most of them – I noticed – were attractive young women. The types who wore gowns that were missing large chunks of cloth on the back or on the sides.

'Attica!' the prince said. 'I must say, your son is proving to be quite a popular addition to the party!'

'Of course he is,' my father said, taking a sip of his drink. 'He's *my* son, after all.'

The way he said it bothered me. It was as if he implied that all of my fame and notoriety were simply because of him. He smiled at me – one of those fake smiles you see on TV – then turned away and said something witty. The women twittered adoringly.

That completely ruined my morning. When the prince tried to pull me away to meet some more of his friends, I complained of a headache and asked if I could sit down. I soon found myself in a dim corner of the lounge, sitting in a plush chair. The soft, whisperlike sounds of the crystal music floated over the buzz of chattering people. I sipped some fruit juice.

What right did my father have to act so dismissive of me? Hadn't *I* been the one to save his life? I'd grown up inside the Hushlands, oppressed by the Librarians, all because *he* wasn't responsible enough to take care of me.

Of all the people in the room, shouldn't he be the one who was most proud of me?

I should probably say something to lighten the tone here, but I find it hard. The truth was that I didn't feel like laughing, and I don't really think *you* should either. (If you must, you can imagine the butler in his underpants again.)

'Alcatraz?' a voice asked. 'Can we join you?'

I looked up to find Folsom and Himalaya being held back by the servant left to guard me. I waved for him to let them pass, and they took seats near me.

'Nice party,' Folsom said in an overly loud voice. 'I give it four out of five wineglasses, though the finger food only rates a one and a half.'

I made no comment.

'Did you find what you were looking for?' Folsom asked in a loud voice. His ears were still stuffed with cotton for some reason.

Had I found what I was looking for? What had I been looking for? *Librarians*, I thought. *That's right.* 'I didn't see any Librarians around.'

'What do you mean?' Himalaya said. 'They're all over the place.'

They were? 'Er … I mean, I didn't see them doing anything nefarious.'

'They're up to something,' Himalaya said. 'I bet you anything.

There are a *lot* of them here. Look, I made a list.'

I looked over with surprise and embarrassment as she handed me a sheet of paper.

'They're listed by their Librarian sect,' she said, somewhat apologetically. 'Then by age. Then, uh, by height.' She glanced at Folsom. 'Then by blood type. Sorry. Couldn't help it.'

'What?' he asked, having trouble hearing.

I scanned the list. There were some forty people on it. I really *had* been distracted. I didn't recognize any of the names, but –

I cut off as I read a name near the bottom of the list. *Fletcher*.

'Who is this?' I demanded, pointing at the name.

'Hum?' Himalaya asked. 'Oh. I only saw her once. I don't know which of the orders she belongs to.'

'Show me,' I said, standing.

Himalaya and Folsom rose and led me through the ballroom.

'Hey, Alcatraz!' a voice called as we walked.

I turned to see a richly dressed group of young men waving at me. One of those at their lead, a man named Rodrayo, was a minor nobleman the prince had introduced me to. Everyone seemed so eager to be my friend; it was difficult not to join them. However, the name on that list – Fletcher – was too intimidating. I waved apologetically to Rodrayo, then continued with Himalaya.

A few moments later, she laid a hand on my shoulder. 'There,' she said, pointing at a figure who was making her way out the front doors. The woman had dyed her hair dark brown since I'd last seen her, and she wore a Free Kingdomer gown instead of her typical business suit.

But it was her: my mother. Ms. Fletcher was an alias. I felt a sudden sense of shame for getting so wrapped up in the party. If my mother was in the city, it meant something. She was too businesslike for simple socializing; she was always plotting.

And she had my father's Translator's Lenses.

'Come on,' I said to Folsom and Himalaya. 'We're following her.'

8

Once there was a boy named Alcatraz. He did some stuff that was kind of interesting. Then one day, he betrayed those who depended on him, doomed the world, and murdered someone who loved him.

The end.

Some people have asked me why I need multiple volumes to explain my story. After all, the core of my argument is very simple. I just told it to you in one paragraph.

Why not leave it at that?

Two words: Summarizing sucks.

Summarizing is when you take a story that is complicated and interesting, then stick it in a microwave until it shrivels up into a tiny piece of black crunchy tarlike stuff. A wise man once said, 'Any story, no matter how good, will sound really, really dumb when you shorten it to a few sentences.'

For example, take this story: 'Once there was a furry-footed British guy who has to go throw his uncle's ring into a hole in the ground.' Sounds dumb, doesn't it?

I don't intend to do that. I intend to make you experience each and every painful moment of my life. I intend to prove how dreadful I am by talking about how awesome I am. I intend to make you read through a whole series before explaining the scene in which I started the first book.

You remember that one, right? The one where I lay tied to an altar made from encyclopedias, about to get sacrificed by the Librarians? That's when my betrayal happened. You may be wondering when I'm finally going to get to that most important point in my life.

Book five. So there.

'So who is this person we're following?' Folsom asked, pulling the cotton from his ears as we left the prince's castle.

'My mother,' I said curtly, glancing about. A carriage was leaving, and I caught a glance of my mother's face in it. 'There. Let's go.'

'Wait,' Folsom said. 'That's *Shasta Smedry*?'

I nodded.

He whistled. 'This could get dangerous.'

'There's more,' Himalaya said, catching up to us. 'If what I heard in there is true, then *She Who Cannot Be Named* is going to be arriving in the city soon.'

'Wait, who?' I asked.

'I just told you,' Himalaya said. 'She Who Cannot Be Named. The Librarians aren't satisfied with how the treaty negotiations are proceeding, so they decided to bring in a heavy hitter.'

'That's bad,' Folsom said.

'She Who Cannot Be Named?' I asked. 'Why can't we say her name? Because it might draw the attention of evil powers? Because we're afraid of her? Because her name has become a curse upon the world?'

'Don't be silly,' Himalaya said. 'We don't say her name because nobody can pronounce it.'

'Kangech . . .' Folsom tried. Kangenchenug . . . Kagenchachsa . . .

'She Who Cannot Be Named,' Himalaya finished. 'It's easier.'

'Either way,' Folsom said, 'We should report back to Lord Smedry – this is going to get very dangerous, very quickly.'

I snorted. 'It's no more dangerous than when I testified against the Acrophobic English Teachers of Poughkeepsie!'

'Uh, you didn't actually do that, Alcatraz,' he pointed out. 'That was in one of the books Rikers wrote.'

I froze. That's right. I'd been talking about it with the prince, but that didn't change the fact that it hadn't ever actually happened.

It *also* didn't change the fact that Shasta's carriage was quickly disappearing. 'Look,' I said, pointing. 'My grandfather put you in charge of watching the Librarians in the city. Now you're going to let one of the most infamous ones get away without following?'

'Hum,' he said. 'Good point.'

We rushed down the steps and toward the carriages. I picked a likely one, then hopped up into it. 'I'm commandeering this vehicle!' I said.

'Very well, Lord Smedry,' said the driver.

I hadn't expected it to be that easy. You should remember that we Smedrys are legal officers of the government in Nalhalla. We're able to commandeer pretty much anything we want. (Only doughnuts are outside our reach, as per the Doughnut Exemption act of the eighth century. Fortunately, doughnuts don't exist in the Free Kingdoms, so the law doesn't get used much.)

Folsom and Himalaya climbed into the carriage after me, and I pointed at Shasta's disappearing vehicle. 'Follow that carriage!' I said in a dramatic voice.

And so, the driver did. Now, I don't know if you've ever been in a city carriage before, but they travel at, like, two miles an hour – particularly during afternoon traffic. After my rather dramatic and heroic (if I do say so myself) proclamation, things took a decidedly *slow* turn as our driver guided the horses out onto the street, then clopped along behind Shasta's vehicle. I felt more like I was out on a casual evening drive than part of a high-speed chase.

I sat down. 'Not very exciting, is it?'

'I'll admit, I was expecting more,' Folsom said.

At that moment, we passed a street performer playing a lute on the side of the road. Himalaya reached for Folsom, but it was too late. My cousin stood up in a quick motion, then jumped up onto the back of the carriage and began doing expert kung fu moves.

'Gak!' I said, diving for the floor as a karate chop narrowly missed my head. 'Folsom, what are you doing?'

'It's his Talent,' Himalaya said, scrambling down beside me. 'He's a bad dancer! The moment he hears music, he gets like this. It—'

We passed the street performer and Folsom froze mid-swing, his foot mere inches from my face. 'Oh,' he said, 'terribly sorry about that, Alcatraz. My Talent can be a bit difficult at times.'

'A bit difficult' is an understatement. Folsom once wandered into a ballroom dance competition. He not only managed to trip every single person in the room but he also ended up stuffing one of the judges in a tuba. If you're wondering, yes, that's why Himalaya had filled Folsom's ears with cotton before letting him enter the party room. It's also why Folsom had removed the theme music glass from his copy of *Alcatraz Smedry and the Mechanic's Wrench*.

'Alcatraz!' Himalaya said, pointing as we seated ourselves again.

I spun, realizing that my mother's carriage had stopped at an intersection, and our carriage was pulling up right beside hers. 'Gak!' I said. 'Driver, what are you doing?'

The driver turned, confused. 'Following that carriage, like you said.'

'Well, don't let them *know* that we're following them!' I said. 'Haven't you ever seen any superspy movies?'

'What's a movie?' the driver asked, followed by, 'And ... what's a superspy?'

I didn't have time to explain. I waved for Himalaya and Folsom to duck. However, there just wasn't enough room – one of us would have to sit up. Would my mother recognize Folsom, a famous Smedry? What about Himalaya, a rebel Librarian? We were all conspicuous.

'Can't you two do something to hide us?' Himalaya hissed. 'You know, magic powers and all that.'

'I could beat up her horse, if we had music,' Folsom said thoughtfully.

Himalaya glanced at me, worried, and it wasn't until that moment that I remembered that I was an Oculator.

Oculator. Lens-wielder. I had magic glasses, including the ones my grandfather had given me earlier. I cursed, pulling out the purple ones he'd called Disguiser's Lenses. He'd told me to think of something, then look at someone, and I would appear to be that thing. I slid the Lenses on and focused.

Himalaya yelped. 'You look like an old man!'

'Lord Smedry?' Folsom asked, confused.

That wouldn't do. Shasta would recognize Grandpa Smedry for sure. I threw myself up into the seat and thought of someone else. My sixth-grade teacher, Mr. Mann. I remembered, at the last minute, to picture him wearing a tunic like he was from the Free Kingdoms. Then I looked over at my mother, sitting in the next carriage.

She glanced at me. My heart thumped in my chest. (Hearts tend to do that. Unless you're a zombie. More on those later.)

My mother's eyes passed over me without showing any signs of recognition. I breathed a sigh of relief as the carriages started again.

Using the Disguiser's Lenses was more difficult than any others I'd used before. I got a jolt if my shape changed forms, and that happened whenever I let my mind wander. I had to remain focused to maintain the illusion.

As we continued, I felt embarrassed at taking so long to re-member the Disguiser's Lenses. Bastille often chastised me for forgetting that I was an Oculator, and she was right. I still wasn't that used to my powers, as you will see later.

(You'll notice that I often mention ideas I'm going to explain later in the book. Sometimes I do this because it makes nice foreshadowing. Other times, I'm just trying to annoy you. I'll let you decide which is which.)

'Do either of you recognize where we are?' I asked as the car-riage 'chase' continued.

'We're approaching the king's palace, I think,' Folsom said. 'Look, you can see the tips of the towers.'

I followed his gesture and saw the white peaks of the palace. On the other side of the street, we passed an enormous rect-angular building that read in big letters ROYAL ARCHIVES (NOT A LIBRARY!) on the front. We turned, then rolled past a line of castles on the back side of the street. My mother's carriage turned as if to round the block again. Something seemed wrong.

'Driver, catch up to the carriage up there,' I said.

'Indecisive today, aren't we?' the driver asked with a sigh. At the next intersection, we rolled up beside the carriage, and I looked over at my mother.

Only, she wasn't there. The carriage held someone who *looked* a little like her, but wasn't the same woman. 'Shattering Glass!' I cursed.

'What?' Folsom asked, peeking up over the lip of the carriage.

'She gave us the slip,' I said.

'Are you sure that's not her?' Folsom asked.

'Um, yeah. Trust me.' I might not have known she was my mother at the time, but 'Ms. Fletcher' had watched over me for most of my childhood.

'Maybe she's using Lenses, like you,' Himalaya said.

'She's not an Oculator,' I replied. 'I don't know if she knew she was being followed, but she somehow got out of that carriage when we weren't looking.'

The other two got up off the floor, sitting again. I eyed Himalaya. Had she somehow tipped off my mother that we were following?

'Shasta Smedry,' Himalaya said. 'Is she a relative of yours, then?'

'Alcatraz's mother,' Folsom said, nodding.

'Really?' Himalaya said. 'Your mother is a recovering Librarian?'

'Not so much on the "recovering" part,' I said. The carriage bearing the look-alike stopped and let her off at a restaurant. I ordered our driver to wait so we could watch, but I knew we wouldn't learn anything new.

'She and his father broke up soon after he was born,' Folsom said. 'Shasta went back to the Librarians.'

'Which order is she part of?'

I shook my head. 'I don't know. She ... doesn't quite fit with the others. She's something different.' My grandfather had once said that her motivations were confusing, even to other Librarians.

She had the Lenses of Rashid; if she found an Oculator to help her she could read the Forgotten Language. That made her very, very dangerous. Why had she been at that party? Had she spoken with my father? Had she been trying to do something to the prince?

'Let's get back to the castle,' I said. Perhaps Grandpa Smedry would be able to help.

9

Chapter breaks are very useful. They let you skip a lot of boring parts of stories. For instance, after tailing – then losing – my mother, we had a pleasant drive back to Keep Smedry. The most exciting thing that happened was when we stopped so that Folsom could use the restroom.

Characters in books, you may have noticed, rarely have to go potty. There are several reasons for this. Many books – unlike this one – simply aren't real, and everyone knows fictional characters can 'hold it' as long as they need to. They just wait until the end of the book before using the restroom.

In books like this one, which *are* real, we have more problems. After all, we're not fictional characters, so we have to wait until chapter breaks, when nobody is looking. It can get hard for longer chapters, but we're quite self-sacrificing. (I really feel sorry for the people in Terry Pratchett's novels, though.)

Our carriage pulled up to the dark, stone Keep Smedry, and I was surprised to see a small crowd gathered in front.

'Not this again,' Himalaya said with a sigh as some of the people began to wave pieces of glass in my direction, taking images of me in the strange Free Kingdoms way.

'Sorry,' Folsom said with a grimace. 'We can send them away, if you want.'

'Why would we do that?' I asked. After the disappointment of losing Shasta, it felt good to see people eager to praise me again.

Folsom and Himalaya exchanged a look. 'We'll be inside, then,' Folsom said, helping Himalaya down. I jumped out, then went to meet with my adoring fans.

The first ones to rush up to me carried pads of paper and quills. They all talked over one another, so I tried to quiet them down by raising my hands. That didn't work; they all just kept talking, trying to get my attention.

So I broke the sound barrier.

I'd never done it before, but my Talent can do some really wacky things. I was standing there, frustrated, hands in the air, wishing I could get them to be quiet. Then my Talent engaged, and there were twin CRACK sounds in the air, like a pair of whips snapping.

The people fell silent. I started, surprised by the tiny sonic booms I'd made.

'Er, yes,' I said. 'What do you want? And before you start arguing, let's start with you on the end.'

'Interview,' the man said. He wore a hat like Robin Hood. 'I represent the Eastern Criers Guild. We want to do a piece on you.'

'Oh,' I said. That sounded cool. 'Yeah, we can do that. But not right now. Maybe later tonight?'

'Before or after the vote?' the man asked.

Vote? I thought. *Oh, right. The vote about the treaty with the Librarians.* 'Uh, after the vote.'

The others began to talk, so I raised my hands threateningly and quieted them down. All were reporters, wanting interviews. I made appointments with each one, and they went on their way.

The next group of people approached. These didn't appear to be reporters of any sort, which was good. Reporters, it might be noted, are a lot like little brothers. They're talkative, annoying, and they tend to come in groups. Plus, if you yell at them, they get even in very unsettling ways.

'Lord Smedry,' a stout man said. 'I was wondering … My daughter is getting married this upcoming weekend. Would you perform the ceremony?'

'Uh, sure,' I said. I'd been warned about this, but it was still something of a surprise.

He beamed, then told me where the wedding was. The next woman in line wanted me to represent her son in a trial and speak on his behalf. I wasn't sure what to do about that one, so I said I'd get back to her. The next man wanted me to seek out – then punish – a miscreant who had stolen some galfalgos from his garden. I made a mental note to ask someone what the heck galfalgos were, and told him I'd look into it.

There were some two dozen people with questions or requests like those. The more that was asked of me, the more uncomfortable I grew. What did I really know about any of this stuff? I finally cleared through that group, making vague promises to most of them.

There was one more group of people waiting for me. They were well-dressed younger men and women, in their late teens or early twenties. I recognized them from the party.

'Rodrayo?' I asked, to the guy at their lead.

'Hey,' he said.

'And ... what is it you want of me?' I asked.

A couple of them shrugged.

'Just thought being around you would be fun,' Rodrayo said. 'Mind if we party with you a little bit?'

'Oh,' I said. 'Well, sure, I guess.'

I led the group through some hallways in Keep Smedry, getting lost, and trying to act like I knew where everything was. The hallways of Keep Smedry were appropriately medieval, though the castle was far more warm and homey than one might have expected. There were hundreds of rooms – the building was of mansion-sized proportions – and I really didn't know where I was going.

Eventually, I found some servants and had them take us to a denlike room, which had couches and a hearth. I wasn't certain what 'partying with me' meant to Rodrayo and the others. Fortunately, they took the lead, sending the servants to get some food, then lounging around on the couches and chairs, chatting. I wasn't sure why they needed me there, or even who most of them were, but they'd read my books and thought my adventures were very impressive. That made them model citizens in my opinion.

I had just finished telling them about my fight with the paper monsters when I realized that I'd never checked in with Grandpa

Smedry. It had been about five hours since we'd split up, and I was tempted to just let it slide until he came looking for me. But we needed more hooberstackers, and the servants had vanished, so I decided to leave my new friends and go looking for the servants to ask for a resupply. Maybe they'd know where my grandfather was.

However, finding servants proved more difficult than I'd assumed. I felt uncharacteristically fatigued as I wandered the hallways, even though I hadn't really done that much during the last couple of hours. Just sit around and be adored.

Eventually, I spotted a crack of light down one brickwalled corridor. It turned out to be coming from a half-open door, so I peeked inside. There, I found my father sitting at a desk, scribbling on a piece of parchment. An ancient-looking lamp gave off a flickering light, only faintly illuminating the room. I could see rich-looking furniture and sparkling bits of glass – Lenses and other Oculatory wonders, which seemed to have a glow about them because of my Oculator's Lenses. On his desk was a half-empty wineglass, and he still wore the antiquated suit he'd had on at the party, though he'd undone the ruffled tie. His shoulder-length hair was wavy and disheveled. He looked a lot like a Hushlands rock star after an evening performance.

As a child, I'd often dreamed about what my father would be like. The only facts I'd had to go on were that he'd named me after a prison and that he'd abandoned me. One would think that I would have imagined a terrible person.

And yet, I'd secretly *wished* for there to be more. A good reason why he'd given me up. Something impressive and mysterious. I had wondered if, perhaps, he'd been involved in some dangerous line of work, and had sent me away to protect me.

Grandpa Smedry's arrival, and the discovery that my father was both alive and working to save the Free Kingdoms, fulfilled a lot of these secret wishes. Finally, I gained a picture of who my father might be. A dashing, heroic figure who hadn't *wanted* to get rid of me, but had been betrayed by his wife, then forced to give me up for the greater good.

That father in my dreams would have been excited to reunite

with his son. I'd been hoping for enthusiasm, not indifference. I'd imagined someone a little more like Indiana Jones, and a little less like Mick Jagger.

'Mother was there,' I said, stepping into the doorway more fully.

My father didn't look up from his document. 'Where?' he asked, not even jumping or looking surprised at the intrusion.

'At the party this afternoon. Did you see her?'

'Can't say that I did,' my father said.

'I was surprised to see you there.'

My father didn't respond; he just scribbled something on his parchment. I couldn't figure him out – at the party, he had seemed completely involved in being a superstar. Now, at his desk, he was absorbed in his work.

'What are you working on?' I asked.

He sighed, finally looking up at me. 'I understand that children sometimes need distractions. Is there something I can have the servants bring you? Entertainment? Just speak it, and I shall see it done.'

'That's all right,' I said. 'Thanks.'

He nodded and turned back to his work. The room fell still; the only sound was that of his quill scratching against parchment.

I left and didn't feel like searching out servants or my grand-father anymore. I just felt sick. Like I'd eaten three whole bags of Halloween candy, then been punched in the stomach. I wandered, vaguely making my way in the direction of where I'd left my new friends. When I arrived back at the den where I'd left them, however, I was surprised to see them being entertained by an unlikely figure.

'Grandpa?' I asked, looking in.

'Ah, Alcatraz, my boy,' Grandpa Smedry said, perched atop a tall-legged chair. 'Excellent to see you! I was just explaining to these fine young fellows that you'd be back very soon, and that they shouldn't worry about you.'

They didn't seem all that worried, though they *had* found some more snacks somewhere – popcorn and hooberstackers. I stood at the doorway. For some reason, the idea of talking to my groupies in front of Grandpa Smedry made me feel even more sick.

'Not looking too well, my boy,' Grandpa Smedry said, rising. 'Maybe we should get you something for that.'

'I ... I think that would be nice,' I said.

'We'll be back in a snap!' Grandpa Smedry said to the others, hopping off his chair. I followed him down the hallway until he stopped at a darkened stone intersection, turning to me. 'I've got the perfect solution, lad! Just the thing to make you feel better in a jiffy.'

'Great,' I said. 'What is it?'

He smacked me across the face.

I blinked in surprise. It hadn't really hurt, but it *had* been un-expected. 'What was that?' I asked.

'I smacked you,' said Grandpa Smedry. Then, in a slightly lower tone, he added, 'It's an old family remedy.'

'For what?'

'Being a nigglenut,' said Grandpa Smedry. He sighed, sitting down on the hallway carpeting. 'Sit down, lad.'

Still a little stunned, I did so.

'I just got done speaking with Folsom and his lovely friend Himalaya,' Grandpa Smedry said, pleasantly smiling, as if he hadn't just smacked me in the face. 'It seems that they think you are reckless!'

'That's a problem?'

'Velcroed Verns, of course not! I was quite proud to hear that. Recklessness and boldness, great Smedry traits. Thing is, they said some other things about you – things they'd only admit after I pushed them on it.'

'What things?'

'That you're self-centered. That you think you're better than regular people, and that all you talk about is yourself. Now, this didn't sound like the Alcatraz I knew. Not at all. So I came back here to investigate – and what did I find? A pile of Attica's syco-phants lounging about my castle, just like the old days.'

'My *father*'s sycophants?' I asked, glancing at the room a little down the hallway. 'But they're fans of mine! Not my father's.'

'Is that so?'

'Yeah, they've read my books. They talk about them all the time.'

'Alcatraz, lad,' Grandpa Smedry said. 'Have *you* read those books?'

'Well, no.'

'Then how the blazes do you know what's in them?'

'Well, I . . .' This was frustrating. Didn't I deserve to finally have someone looking up to me, respecting me? Praising me?

'This is my fault,' Grandpa Smedry said with a sigh. 'Should have prepared you better for the kinds of people you'd find here. But, well, I thought you'd use the Truthfinder's Lens.'

The Truthfinder's Lens. I'd almost forgotten about it – it could tell me when people were lying. I pulled it free from my pocket, then glanced at Grandpa Smedry. He nodded back down the hallway, so hesitantly I stood up and took off my Oculator's Lenses, walking down the hallway to the room.

I looked in, holding the Truthfinder's Lens in front of my eye.

'Alcatraz!' Rodrayo said. 'We've missed you!' As he spoke, he seemed to spit mouthfuls of black beetles from his mouth. They squirmed and writhed, and I jumped backward, removing the Lens. The beetles vanished when I did so. I hesitantly replaced the Lens.

'Alcatraz?' Rodrayo asked. 'What's wrong? Come in, we want to hear more about your adventures.'

More beetles. I could only assume that meant he was lying.

'Hey,' said Jasson, 'yeah. Those stories are fun!'

Lying.

'There's the greatest man in the city!' another said, pointing at me.

Lying.

I stumbled away from the room, then fled back down the hallway. Grandpa Smedry waited for me, still sitting on the floor. 'So,' I said, sitting down next to him. 'It's all lies. Nobody really looks up to me.'

'Lad, lad,' Grandpa Smedry said, laying a hand on my shoulder. 'They don't *know* you. They only know the stories and the legends!

Even that lot in there, useless though they tend to be, have their good points. But everyone is going to assume that because they've heard so much about you, they *know* you.'

They were wise words. Prophetic, in a way. Ever since I left the Hushlands, I've felt like every person who looked at me saw someone different, and I wasn't any of them. My reputation only grew more daunting after the events at the Library of Congress and the Spire of the World.

'It's not easy to be famous,' Grandpa Smedry said. 'We all deal with it differently. Your father gluts himself on his fame, then flees from it. I tried for years to teach him to keep his ego in check, but I fear I have failed.'

'I thought ...' I said, looking down. 'I thought if he heard people talking about how wonderful I was, he might actually *look* at me once in a while.'

Grandpa Smedry fell silent. 'Ah, lad,' he finally said. 'Your father is ... well, he is what he is. We just have to do our best to love him. But I worry that the fame will do to *you* what it's done to him. That's why I was so excited that you found that Truthfinder's Lens.'

'I thought it was for me to use on the Librarians.'

'Ha!' Grandpa Smedry said. 'Well, it could be of *some* use against them – but a clever Librarian agent will know not to say any direct lies, lest they get caught in them.'

'Oh,' I said, putting the Truthfinder's Lens away.

'Anyway, you look better, lad! Did the old family remedy work? We can try again if you want ...'

'No, I feel much better,' I said, holding up my hands. 'Thanks, I guess. Though it *was* nice to feel like I had friends.'

'You do have friends! Even if you are kind of ignoring them at the moment.'

'Ignoring them?' I said. 'I haven't been ignoring anyone.'

'Oh? And where's Bastille?'

'She ran off on me,' I said. 'To be with the other knights.'

Grandpa Smedry snorted. 'To go on trial, you mean.'

'An unfair trial,' I spat. 'She didn't break her sword – it was *my* fault.'

'Hum, yes,' Grandpa Smedry said. 'If only there were someone willing to speak on her behalf.'

'Wait,' I said. 'I can *do* that?'

'What did I tell you about being a Smedry, lad?'

'That we could marry people,' I said, 'and arrest people, and ...' And that we could demand a right to testify in legal cases.

I stood up, shocked. 'I've been an idiot!'

'I prefer the term "nigglenut",' Grandpa Smedry said. 'Though that's probably because I just made it up and feel a certain paternal sense toward it.' He smiled, winking.

'Is there still time?' I asked. 'Before her trial, I mean?'

'It's been going on all afternoon,' Grandpa Smedry said, pulling out an hourglass. 'And they're probably almost ready to render judgment. Getting there in time will be tricky. Limping Lowrys, if *only* we could teleport there via use of a magical glass box sitting in the basement of this very castle!'

He paused. 'Oh, wait, we can!' He leaped to his feet. 'Let's go! We're late!'

10

There's a dreadful form of torture in the Hushlands, devised by the Librarians. Though this is supposed to be a book for all ages, I feel that it's time to confront this disturbing and cruel practice. Somebody has to be brave enough to shine a light on it.

That's right. It's time to talk about after-school specials.

After-school specials are a type of television programming that the Librarians put on right when children get home from school. The specials are usually about some kid who is struggling with a nonsensical problem like bullying, peer pressure, or gerbil snorting. We see the kid's life, his struggles, his problems – and then the show provides a nice, simple solution to tie everything up by the end.

The point of these programs, of course, is to be so blatantly awful and painful to watch that the children wish they were back in school. That way, when they have to get up the next morning and do long division, they'll think: *Well, at least I'm not at home watching that terrible after-school special.*

I include this explanation here for all of you in the Free Kingdoms so that you'll understand what I'm about to say. It's very important for you to understand that I don't want this book to sound like an after-school special.

I let my fame go to my head. The point of this book isn't to show how that's bad, it's to show the truth about me as a person. To show what I'm capable of. That first day in Nalhalla, I think, says a lot about who I am.

I don't even *like* hooberstackers.

Deep within the innards of Keep Smedry, we approached a room with six guards standing out front. They saluted Grandpa

Smedry; he responded by wiggling his fingers at them. (He's like that sometimes.)

Inside, we discovered a group of people in black robes who were polishing a large metal box.

'That's quite the box,' I said.

'Isn't it, though?' Grandpa Smedry said, smiling.

'Shouldn't we be summoning a dragon or something to take us to Crystallia?'

'This will be faster,' Grandpa Smedry said, waving over one of the people in robes. (Black robes are the Free Kingdoms' equivalent of a white lab coat. Black makes way more sense – this way, when the scientists blow themselves up, at least the robes have a chance of being salvageable.)

'Lord Smedry,' the woman said. 'We've applied for a Swap Time with Crystallia. Everything will be ready for you in about five minutes.'

'Excellent, excellent!' Grandpa Smedry said. Then his face fell.

'What?' I asked, alarmed.

'Well, it's just that … we're *early*. I'm not sure what to think about that. You must be having a bad influence on me, my boy!'

'Sorry,' I said. It was hard to contain my anxiety. Why hadn't I thought of going to help Bastille? Would I arrive in time to make a difference? If a train left Nalhalla traveling at 3.14 miles an hour and a train left Bermuda at 45 MHz, what time does the soup have pancakes?

'Grandfather,' I said as we waited. 'I saw my mother today.'

'Folsom mentioned that. You showed great initiative in following her.'

'She's *got* to be up to something.'

'Of course she is, lad. Problem is, what?'

'You think it might be related to the treaty?'

Grandpa Smedry shook his head. 'Maybe. Shasta's a tricky one. I don't see her working with the Wardens of the Standard on one of their projects unless it were helping her own goals. Whatever those are.'

That seemed to trouble him. I turned back to the robed men

and women. They were focused on large chunks of glass that were affixed to the corners of the metal box.

'What is that thing?' I asked.

'Hum? Oh. Transporter's Glass, lad! Or, well, that's Transporter's Glass at the corners of the box. When the right time arrives – the one we've scheduled with the engineers at a similar box up in Crystallia – both groups will shine brightsand on those bits of glass. Then the box will be swapped with the one over in Crystallia.'

'Swapped?' I said. 'You mean we'll get teleported there?'

'Indeed! Fascinating technology. Your father helped develop it, you know.'

'He did?'

'Well, he was the first to discover what the sand did,' Grandpa Smedry said. 'We'd known that the sand had Oculatory distortions; we didn't know what it *did*. Your father spent a number of years researching it and discovered that this new sand could teleport things. But it only worked if *two* sets of Transporter's Glass were exposed to brightsand at the same time, and if they were transporting two items that were exactly the same size.'

Brightsand. It was the fuel of silimatic technology. When you expose other sands to brightsand's glowing light, they do interesting things. Some, for instance, start to float. Others grow very heavy.

I could see enormous canisters in the corners of the room, likely filled with brightsand. The sides of the containers could be pulled back, letting the light shine on the Transporter's Glass.

'So,' I said. 'You had to send ahead to Crystallia and tell them what time we were coming so that they could activate *their* Transporter's Glass at the same time.'

'Precisely!'

'What if someone else activated *their* brightsand at exactly the same time that we do? Could we get teleported there by accident?'

'I suppose,' Grandpa Smedry said. 'But they'd have to be sending a box *exactly* the same size as this one. Don't worry, lad. It would be virtually impossible for that kind of error to happen!'

Virtually impossible. The moment you read that, you probably assumed that the error would – of course – happen by the end of this book. You assumed this because you've read far too many novels. You make it very difficult for us writers to spring proper surprises on you because—

LOOK OVER THERE!

See, didn't work, did it?

'All right,' one of the black-robed people said. 'Step into the box and we'll begin!'

Still a little worried about a disaster that was 'virtually' impossible, I followed Grandpa Smedry into the box. It felt a little like stepping into a large elevator. The doors shut, then immediately opened again.

'Is something wrong?' I asked.

'Wrong?' Grandpa Smedry said. 'Why if something had gone wrong, we'd have been shredded to little pieces and turned into piles of sludge!'

'*What?*'

'Oh, did I forget to mention that part?' Grandpa Smedry said. 'Like I said, virtually impossible. Come on, my boy, we have to keep moving! We're late!'

He scuttled out of the box, and I followed more cautiously. We had, indeed, been teleported somewhere else. It had been so quick I hadn't even felt the change.

This new room we entered was made completely of glass. In fact, the entire *building* around me seemed to be made of glass. I remembered the enormous glass mushroom I'd seen when flying into the city, with the crystalline castle built atop of it. It was a safe bet I was in Crystallia. Of course, there was *also* a pair of knights holding massive swords made entirely from crystal standing at the doorway. They were kind of a clue too.

The knights nodded to Grandpa Smedry, and he bustled out of the room, and I followed hastily. 'We're really there?' I asked. 'Atop the mushroom?'

'Yes indeed,' Grandpa Smedry said. 'It's a rare privilege to be allowed into these halls. Crystallia is forbidden to outsiders.'

'Really?'

Grandpa Smedry nodded. 'Like Smedrious, Crystallia used to be a sovereign kingdom. During the early days of Nalhalla, Crystallia's queen married their king and swore her knights as protectors of their noble line. It's actually a rather romantic and dramatic story – one I would eagerly tell you, except for the fact that I recently forgot it based on its being far too long and having not enough decapitations.'

'A just reason for forgetting any story.'

'I know,' Grandpa Smedry said. 'Anyway, the treaty that merged Nalhalla and Crystallia stipulated that the land atop the mushroom become home to the knights, and is off-limits to common citizens. The order of knights also retained the right to discipline and train its members, once recruited, without interference from the outside.'

'But aren't we here to interfere?'

'Of course we are!' Grandpa Smedry said, raising a hand. 'That's the Smedry way! We interfere with all kinds of stuff! But we're also Nalhallan nobility, which the knights are sworn to protect and – most important – not kill for trespassing.'

'That's not a very comforting rationale for why we might be safe here.'

'Don't worry,' Grandpa Smedry said happily. 'I've tested this. Just enjoy the view!'

It was tough. Not that the view wasn't spectacular – we were walking down a hallway constructed entirely from glass blocks. It was late afternoon outside, and the translucent walls refracted the light of the sun, making the floor sparkle. I could see shadows of people moving through distant hallways, distorting the light further. It was as if the castle were alive, and I could see the pulsing of its organs within the walls around me.

It was quite breathtaking. However, I was still dealing with the fact that I'd betrayed Bastille, that I'd just risked being turned into a pile of goo, and that the only thing keeping me from being cut apart by a bunch of territorial knights was my last name.

Beyond that, there was the sound. It was a quiet ringing, like a crystal vibrating in the distance. It was soft, but it was also one of those things that was very hard to un-notice once you spotted it.

Grandpa Smedry obviously knew his way around Crystallia, and soon we arrived at a chamber being guarded by two knights. The crystal doors were closed, but I could vaguely make out the shapes of people on the other side.

Grandpa Smedry walked over to open the door, but one of the knights raised his hand. 'You are too late, Lord Smedry,' the man said. 'The judgment has begun.'

'What?' Grandpa Smedry declared. 'I was told it wouldn't happen for an hour yet!'

'It is happening now,' the knight said. As much as I like the knights, they can be ... well, blunt. And stubborn. And really bad at taking jokes. (Which is why I feel I need to mention page 40 again, just to annoy them.)

'Surely you can let us in,' Grandpa Smedry said. 'We're important witnesses in the case!'

'Sorry,' the knight said.

'We are also close personal friends of the knight involved.'

'Sorry.'

'We also have very good teeth,' Grandpa Smedry said, then smiled.

This seemed to confuse the knight. (Grandpa Smedry has that effect on people.) However, once again, the knight simply shook his head and said, 'Sorry.'

Grandpa Smedry stepped back, annoyed, and I felt a twist of despair. I'd failed to help Bastille after all she'd gone through for me. She should have known that she shouldn't rely on me.

'How are you feeling, lad?' Grandpa Smedry asked.

I shrugged.

'Annoyed?' he prompted.

'Yeah.'

'Frustrated?'

'A bit.'

'Bitter?'

'You're not helping.'

'I know I'm not. Angry?'

I didn't answer. The truth was, I *did* feel angry. At myself, mostly. For partying with Rodrayo and his friends while Bastille was in trouble. For forgetting about Mokia and its problems. For letting my grandfather down. It hadn't been that long ago that I'd always assumed that I'd let everyone down. I'd pushed people away before they could abandon me.

But working with Grandpa Smedry and the others had made me begin to feel that I *could* lead a normal life. Maybe I *didn't* have to alienate everyone. Maybe I *was* capable of having friendships, of having family, of . . .

There was a slight cracking sound.

'Oops!' Grandpa Smedry said in a loud voice. 'Looks like you've gone and upset the boy!'

I started, looking down, realizing that I'd let my Talent crack the glass beneath my feet. Twin spiderwebs of lines crept from my shoes, marring the otherwise perfect crystal. I blushed, embarrassed.

The knights had grown pale. 'Impossible!' one said.

'This crystal is supposed to be unbreakable!' the other said.

'My grandson,' Grandpa Smedry said proudly. 'He has the breaking Talent you know. Upset him too much, and the entire floor could shatter. Actually, the entire castle could—'

'Get him out, then,' one of the knights said, shooing me away like one might treat an unwanted puppy.

'What?' Grandpa Smedry said. 'Antagonize him by throwing him out, and you could destroy the castle itself! We'll just have to see if he calms down. His Talent can be very unpredictable when he's emotional.'

I could see what Grandpa Smedry was doing. I hesitated, then focused my power, trying to further crack the glass at my feet. It was an extremely foolhardy thing to do. That's what made it *exactly* the sort of plan Grandpa Smedry would come up with.

The spiderwebs at my feet grew larger. I steadied myself by touching the wall, and immediately created a ring of cracks around my hand.

'Wait!' one of the knights exclaimed. 'I'll go in and ask if you can enter!'

Grandpa Smedry beamed. 'What a nice fellow,' he said, taking my arm, stopping me from breaking more. The knight opened the door, stepping inside.

'Did we really just *blackmail* a Knight of Crystallia?' I asked under my breath.

'Two of them, I believe,' Grandpa Smedry said. 'And it was really more "intimidation" than it was "blackmail." Maybe with a twist of "extortion." It's always best to use the proper terminology!'

The knight returned, then – with a sigh – gestured for us to enter the chamber. We walked in eagerly.

And then Grandpa Smedry exploded.

11

Okay, so he didn't really explode. I just wanted you to turn the page really fast.

You see, if you turn the pages quickly, you might rip one of them. If you do that, then – obviously – you'll want to go buy another copy of the book. Who wants one with a ripped page? Not you. You have refined tastes.

In fact, think of all the wonderful ways you can use this book. It will make an excellent coaster. You could also use it as building material. Or you could frame the pages as art. (After all, each page is a perfect work of art. Look at 56. Exquisite.)

Obviously, you need *lots* of copies. One isn't enough. Go buy more. Have you forgotten that you need to fight the Librarians?

Anyway, after getting done *not* exploding, Grandpa Smedry went into the chamber. I followed, expecting to find a courtroom. I was surprised to find only a simple wooden table with three knights sitting behind it. Bastille stood by the far wall, at attention, hands at her sides, staring straight ahead. The three knights at the table weren't even looking at her as they decided her punishment.

One of the knights was a masculine, burly man with an enormous chin. He was dangerous in an 'I'm a knight, and I could totally kill you' sort of way.

Next to him was Bastille's mother, Draulin, who was dangerous in an 'I'm Bastille's mother, and I could also kill you' sort of way.

The third one was an elderly, bearded knight who was dangerous in a 'Stop playing your rap music so loud, you darn kids! Plus, I could kill you too' sort of way.

Judging by their expressions, they were not happy to see my grandfather and me. 'Lord Smedry,' the man with the chin said,

'Why have you interrupted these proceedings? You know you have no authority here.'

'If I let that stop me, I'd never have any fun!' Grandpa Smedry said.

'This is *not* about fun, Lord Smedry,' Bastille's mother said. 'It's about justice.'

'Oh, and since when has it been "just" to punish someone for things that were not their fault?'

'We are not looking at fault,' said the aged knight. 'If a knight is incapable of protecting his or her charges, then that knight must be removed from his or her station. It is not young Bastille's fault if we promoted her too quickly and—'

'You didn't promote her too quickly,' I snapped. 'Bastille is the most amazing knight in your ranks.'

'And you know much about the knights in our ranks, young Smedry?' the aged knight asked.

He was right. I felt a little foolish – but then when has *that* ever stopped a Smedry?

'No,' I admitted. 'But I do know that Bastille has done a fantastic job of protecting my grandfather and me. She's an excellent soldier – I saw her go head-to-head with one of the Scrivener's Bones and hold her own with only a dagger. I've seen her take down two Librarian thugs before I could even finish blinking.'

'She lost her sword,' Draulin said.

'So?' I demanded.

'It's the symbol of a Knight of Crystallia,' Big Chin said.

'Well, get her another sword, then!' I snapped.

'It's not that easy,' the old knight explained. 'The fact that a knight is not capable of caring for her sword is very disturbing. We need to maintain quality in the order for the good of all nobility.'

I stepped forward. 'Did she tell you how the sword broke?'

'She was fighting Alivened,' Draulin said. 'She rammed it in one of their chests, then she was hit and knocked aside. When the Alivened was killed by falling through the floor, the sword was lost.'

I glanced back at Bastille. She didn't meet my eyes.

'No,' I said, looking back at them. 'That's what happened, yes, but it's not what *happened*. It wasn't the fall, or even the death of the Alivened, and the sword wasn't just lost. It was destroyed. By me. My Talent.'

The big-chinned knight gave a chuckle at that. 'Lord Smedry,' he said, 'I understand that you are loyal and care for your friends, and I respect you for it. Good man! But you shouldn't make such wild exaggerations. Everyone knows that full Crystin shards are impervious to things like Oculator's Lenses and Smedry Talents!'

I stepped forward to the table. 'Hand me your sword, then.'

The knight started. 'What?'

'Give it to me,' I said, holding out a hand. 'Let's see if it's impervious.'

There was silence in the small glass chamber for a moment. The knight seemed incredulous. (Crystin don't let others hold their swords. Asking Big Chin to give me his was a little like asking the president to loan me his nuclear missile launching codes for the weekend.)

Still, backing down would make Big Chin look like he believed my claim. I could see the indecision in his eyes, his hand hovering toward the hilt of his weapon, as if to hand it over.

'Be careful, Archedis,' Grandpa Smedry said quietly. 'My grandson's Talent is not to be underestimated. The breaking Talent, by my estimation, hasn't been manifest this powerfully for centuries. Perhaps millennia.'

The knight moved his hand away from the sword. 'The breaking Talent,' he said. 'Well, perhaps it *is* possible for that to affect a Crystin sword.'

Draulin pursed her lips, and I could tell that she wanted to object.

'Um,' I said, glancing at my grandfather. He indicated that I should keep talking. 'Anyway, I've come to speak at this trial, as is my right as a member of the Smedry clan.'

'I believe you have been doing that already,' Draulin said flatly. (Sometimes I can see where Bastille gets her snark.)

'Yes, well,' I continued, 'I want to vouch for Bastille's skill and cleverness. Without her intervention, both Grandpa Smedry and I would be dead. *You* probably would be too, Draulin. Let's not forget that you were captured by the very Librarian that Bastille defeated.'

'I saw *you* defeat that Librarian, Lord Smedry,' Draulin said. 'Not my daughter.'

'We did it together,' I said. 'As part of a plan we came up with as a team. You got your sword back only because Bastille and I retrieved it for you.'

'Yes,' said the elderly knight. 'But then, that is part of the problem.'

'It is?' I said. 'Wounding Draulin's pride caused that much trouble?'

Draulin blushed – I felt pleased, though a little ashamed, for getting such a reaction out of her.

'It's more than that,' Big Chin – Archedis – said. 'Bastille held her mother's sword.'

'She didn't have much choice,' I said. 'She was trying to save my life, and that of her mother – not to mention my father's life by association. Besides, she only picked it up for a short time.'

'Regardless,' Archedis said. 'Bastille's use of the sword . . . interfered with it. It is more than tradition that keeps us from letting others hold our weapons.'

'Wait,' I said. 'Does this have to do with those crystals in your necks?'

The three knights shared a look.

'We don't discuss these kinds of things with outsiders,' the elderly knight said.

'I'm not an outsider,' I said. 'I'm a Smedry. Besides, I know most of it already.' There were three kinds of Crystin shards – the ones that they made into swords, the ones they implanted in Crystin necks, and a third one Bastille hadn't wanted to talk about.

'You bond to those neck crystals,' I said, pointing. 'You bond to the swords too, don't you? Is that what this is all about? When Bastille picked up her mother's sword to fight Kilimanjaro, it interfered with the bond?'

'That's not *all* this is about,' the oldest knight said. 'This is much bigger than that. What Bastille did in fighting with her mother's sword showed recklessness – just like losing her own sword did.'

'So?' I demanded.

'So?' Draulin asked. 'Young Lord Smedry, we are an order *founded* on the principle of keeping people like yourself alive. The kings, nobility, and particularly *Smedrys* of the Free Kingdoms seem to seek their own deaths with regularity. In order to protect them, the Knights of Crystallia must be constant and coolheaded.'

'With all due respect, young Lord Smedry,' the aged knight said, 'it is our job to counteract your foolhardy nature, not encourage it. Bastille is not yet right for knighthood.'

'Look,' I said. 'Somebody decided that she was worthy of being a knight. Maybe we should talk to them?'

'We *are* them,' Archedis said. 'We three elevated Bastille to knighthood six months ago, and are also the ones who chose her first assignment. That is why we are the ones who must face the sad task of stripping her knighthood from her. I believe it is time for us to vote.'

'But—'

'Lord Smedry,' Draulin said curtly. 'You have had your say, and we suffered you. Have you anything more to say that will *productively* add to this argument?'

They all regarded me. 'Would calling them idiots be productive?' I asked, turning toward my grandfather.

'Doubtful,' he said, smiling. 'You could try "nigglenut," since I bet they don't know the meaning. That probably wouldn't help much either.'

'Then I'm done,' I said, feeling even more annoyed than when I'd first entered the room.

'Draulin, your vote?' the aged knight – obviously in charge – said.

'I vote to strip knighthood from her,' Draulin said. 'And sever her from the Mindstone for one week to remove her taint from Crystin blades that do not belong to her.'

'Archedis?' the elderly knight asked.

'The young Smedry's speech has moved me,' the large-chinned knight said. 'Perhaps we have been hasty. I vote to suspend knighthood, but not remove it. Bastille's taint of another's sword must be cleansed, but I believe one week to be too harsh. One day should suffice.'

I didn't really know what that last part meant, but the big knight earned a few points in my book for his kindness.

'Then it is up to me,' the aged knight said. 'I will take the middle road. Bastille, we strip your knighthood from you, but will have another hearing in one week to re-evaluate. You are to be severed from the Mindstone for two days. Both punishments are effective immediately. Report to the chamber of the Mindstone.'

I glanced back at Bastille. Somehow I felt that decision wasn't in our favor. Bastille continued to stare straight ahead, but I could see lines of tension – even fear – in her face.

I won't let this happen! I thought, enraged. I gathered my Talent. They couldn't take her. I could stop them. I'd show them what it was like when my Talent broke their swords and –

'Alcatraz, lad,' Grandpa Smedry said softly. 'Privileges, such as our ability to visit Crystallia, are retained when they are not abused. I believe we have pushed our friends as far as they will go.'

I glanced at him. Sometimes there was a surprising depth of wisdom in those eyes of his.

'Let it go, Alcatraz,' he said. 'We'll find another way to fight this.'

The knights had stood and were making their way from the room, likely eager to get away from my grandfather and me. I watched, helpless, as Bastille followed them. She shot me a glance as she left and whispered a single word. 'Thanks.'

Thanks, I thought. *Thanks for what? For failing?*

I was, of course, feeling guilty. Guilt, you may know, is a rare emotion that is much like an elevator made of Jell-O. (Both will let you down quite abruptly.)

'Come, lad,' Grandpa Smedry said, taking my arm.

'We failed,' I said.

'Hardly! They were ready to strip her knighthood completely. At least we've got a chance for her to get it back. You did well.'

'A chance to get it back,' I said, frowning. 'But if the same people are going to vote again in a week, then what good have we done? They'll just vote to strip her knighthood completely.'

'Unless we show them she deserves it,' Grandpa said. 'By, say, stopping the Librarians from getting that treaty signed and taking over Mokia?'

Mokia was important. But even if we *could* do what he said, and even if we *could* get Bastille involved, how was fighting a political battle going to prove anything to do with knighthood?

'What's a Mindstone?' I asked as we walked back to the Transporter chamber.

'Well,' Grandpa Smedry said, 'You're not supposed to know about that. Which, of course, makes it all the more fun to tell you. There are three kinds of Crystin shards.'

'I know,' I interjected. 'They make swords from one type.'

'Right,' Grandpa Smedry said. 'Those are special in that they're very resilient to Oculatory powers and things like Smedry Talents, which lets the Knights of Crystallia fight Dark Oculators. The second type of shards are the ones in their necks – the Fleshstones, they call them.'

'Those give them powers,' I said. 'Make them better soldiers. But what's the third one?'

'The Mindstone,' Grandpa Smedry said. 'It is said to be a shard from the Worldspire itself, a single crystal that connects all the other Crystin shards. Even I don't know for certain what it does, but I think it connects all Crystin together, letting them draw upon the strength of other knights.'

'And they're going to cut Bastille off from it,' I said. 'Maybe that will be a good thing. She'll be more her own person.'

Grandpa Smedry eyed me. 'The Mindstone doesn't make the knights all have a single mind, lad. It lets them share skills. If one of them knows how to do something, they all get a fraction of a tad of an iota better at that same thing.'

We entered the room with the box, then stepped inside it; apparently, Grandpa Smedry had left instructions for the boxes to be swapped every ten minutes until we returned.

'Grandfather,' I said. 'My Talent. Is it as dangerous as you said back there?'

He didn't reply.

'In the tomb of Alcatraz the First,' I said as the doors to our box closed, 'the writing on the walls spoke of the breaking Talent. The writing ... called it the "Dark Talent" and implied it had caused the fall of the entire Incarna civilization.'

'Others have held the breaking Talent, lad,' Grandpa Smedry said. 'None of them caused any civilizations to fall! Though they did knock down a wall or two.'

His attempt at mirth seemed forced. I opened my mouth to ask more, but the doors to the box opened. Standing directly outside was Folsom Smedry in his red robes, Himalaya at his side.

'Lord Smedry!' Folsom said, looking relieved. 'Finally!'

'What?' Grandpa Smedry said.

'You're late,' Folsom said.

'Of course I am,' Grandpa said. 'Get on with it!'

'She's here.'

'Who?'

'*Her*,' Folsom said. 'She Who Cannot Be Named. She's in the keep, and she wants to talk to you.'

12

Right now, you should be asking yourself some questions. Questions like: 'How is it possible that this book can be *so* awesome?' and 'Why did the Librarian slip and fall down?' and 'What exactly was it that exploded and made the *Hawkwind* crash in Chapter Two?'

Did you think I'd forgotten that last one? No, not at all. (The crash nearly killed me, after all.) I figured that the Librarians might be behind it, as everyone else assumed. But *why* had they done it? And, more important, *how*?

There just hadn't been time to ask those questions, important though they were. Too much was going on. We'll get to it, though.

(Also, the answer to the second question in the first paragraph is obvious. She fell because she was looking through the library's nonfriction section.)

We approached Keep Smedry's audience lounge, where Sing – with his hefty Mokian girth – stood guard. It was time to confront She Who Cannot Be Named – the most dangerous Librarian in all of the Order of the Wardens of the Standard. I'd fought Blackburn, Dark Oculator, and felt the pain of his Torturer's Lens. I'd fought Kilimanjaro, of the Scrivener's Bones, with his blood-forged Lenses and terrible half-metal smile. Librarian hierarchs were not to be trifled with.

I tensed, entering the medium-sized castle chamber with Grandpa Smedry and Folsom, ready for anything. The Librarian, however, wasn't there. The only person in the room was a little old grandmother wearing a shawl and carrying an orange handbag.

'It's a trap!' I said. 'They sent a grandmother as a decoy! Quickly, old lady. You're in great danger! Run for safety while we secure the area!'

The old lady met Grandpa Smedry's eyes. 'Ah, Leavenworth. Your family is always such a delight!'

'Kangchenjunga Sarektjåkkå,' Grandpa Smedry said, his voice uncharacteristically subdued. Almost cold.

'You always *were* the only one out here who could pronounce that correctly!' said Kagechech ... Kachenjuaha ... She Who Cannot Be Named. Her voice had a decidedly kindly tone to it. *This?* This was She Who Cannot Be Named? The most dangerous Librarian of all? I felt a little bit let down.

'Such a dear you are, Leavenworth,' she continued.

Grandpa Smedry raised an eyebrow. 'I can't say it's good to see you, Kangchenjunga, so instead – perhaps – I will say that it's *interesting* to see you.'

'Does it have to be that way?' she asked. 'Why, we're old friends!'

'Hardly. Why have you come here?'

The old grandmother sighed, then walked forward on shaky legs, back bowed with age, using a cane to walk. The room was carpeted with a large maroon rug, the walls bearing similar tapestries, along with several formal-looking couches for meeting with dignitaries. She didn't sit in one of these, however, she just walked up to my grandfather.

'You never *have* forgiven me for that little incident, have you?' the Librarian asked, fiddling in her handbag.

'Incident?' Grandpa Smedry said. 'Kangchenjunga, I believe you left me dangling from a frozen mountain cliff, my foot tied to a slowly melting block of ice, my body strapped with bacon and stuck with a sign that read "Free Wolf-chow."'

She smiled wistfully. 'Ah, now *that* was a trap. Kids these days don't know how to do it correctly.' She reached into her handbag. I tensed, and then she pulled out what appeared to be a plate of chocolate chip cookies, wrapped in plastic wrap. She handed these to me, then patted me on the head. 'What a pleasant lad,' she said, then turned to my grandfather.

'You asked why I had come, Leavenworth,' she said. 'Well, we want the kings to know that we are serious about this treaty, and so I have come to speak before the final vote this evening.'

I stared down at the cookies, expecting them to explode or something. Grandpa Smedry didn't seem worried – he kept his eyes focused directly on the Librarian.

'We won't let this treaty happen,' Grandpa said.

The Librarian tsked quietly, shaking her head as she shuffled out of the room. 'So unforgiving, you Smedrys. What can we do to show that we're sincere? What possible solution is there to all of this?'

She hesitated by the door, then turned and winked at us. 'Oh, and *don't* get in my way. If you do, I'll have to rip out your entrails, dice them into little bits, then feed them to my goldfish. Toodles!'

I stared in shock. Everything about her screamed 'kindly grandmother.' She even smiled in a cute old-lady sort of way when she mentioned our entrails, as if discussing a favored knitting project. She exited, and a couple of keep guards followed her.

Grandpa Smedry sat down on one of the couches, exhaling deeply, Folsom sitting next to him. Sing still stood by the door, looking disturbed.

'Well, then,' Grandpa said. 'My, my.'

'Grandfather,' I said, looking down at the cookies. 'What should we do with these?'

'We probably shouldn't eat them,' he said.

'Poison?' I asked.

'No. They'll spoil our dinner.' He stopped, then shrugged. 'But that's the Smedry way!' He slipped a cookie out and took a bite. 'Ah, yes. As good as I remember. One of the nice things about facing off against Kangchenjunga is the treats. She's an excellent baker.'

I noticed a motion to the side, and turned as Himalaya entered the room. 'Is she gone?' the dark-haired former Librarian asked.

'Yes,' Folsom said, standing up immediately.

'That woman is *dreadful*,' Himalaya said, sitting down.

'Ten out of ten points for evilness,' Folsom agreed.

I remained suspicious of Himalaya. She had stayed outside because she didn't want to face a former colleague. But that had left her unsupervised. What had she been doing? Planting a bomb, like the one that blew up the *Hawkwind*? (See, I told you I hadn't forgotten about that.)

'We need a plan,' Grandpa Smedry said. 'We only have a few hours until the treaty vote. There *has* to be a way to stop this!'

'Lord Smedry, I've been talking to the other nobility,' Sing said. 'It ... doesn't look good. They're all so tired of war. They want it to end.'

'I'll agree the war is terrible,' Grandpa Smedry said. 'But, Clustering Campbells, surrendering Mokia isn't the answer! We need to show them that.'

Nobody responded. The five of us sat in the room for a time, thinking. Grandpa Smedry, Sing, and Folsom enjoyed the cookies, but I held off. Himalaya wasn't eating them either. If they *were* poisoned, then she would know.

A short time later, a servant entered. 'Lord Smedry,' the young boy said, 'Crystallia is requesting a Swap Time.'

'Approved,' Grandpa Smedry said.

Himalaya took a cookie and finally ate one. *So much for that theory*, I thought with a sigh. A short time later, Bastille walked in.

I stood up, shocked. 'Bastille! you're here!'

She appeared dazed, like she'd just suffered a repeated beating to the face. She looked at me and seemed to have trouble focusing. 'I ...' she said. 'Yes, I am.'

That gave me chills. Whatever they'd done to her in Crystallia must have been horrible if it left her unable to make sarcastic responses to my dumb comments. Sing rushed to pull over a chair for her. Bastille sat, hands in her lap. She was no longer wearing the uniform of a squire of Crystallia – she had on a generic brown tunic and trousers, like a lot of the people I'd seen in the city.

'Child,' Grandpa Smedry said, 'how do you feel?'

'Cold,' she whispered.

'We're trying to think of a way to stop the Librarians from conquering Mokia, Bastille,' I said. 'Maybe ... maybe you can help.'

She nodded absently. How were we going to involve her in helping expose the Librarian plot – and thereby get her knighthood back – if she could barely talk?

Grandpa Smedry glanced at me. 'What do you think?'

'I think I'm going to go break some crystal swords,' I snapped.

'Not about Bastille, lad,' Grandpa said. 'I can assure you, we're all in agreement about how she's been treated. We've got larger problems right now.'

I shrugged. 'Grandpa, I don't know anything about politics back in the *Hushlands*, let alone the politics here in Nalhalla! I have no idea what to do.'

'We can't just sit here!' Sing said. 'My people are dying as we speak. If the other Free Kingdoms remove their support, Mokia won't have the supplies to keep fighting.'

'Maybe ... maybe I could look at the treaty?' Himalaya said. 'If I read it over, perhaps I would see something that you Nalhallans haven't. Some trick the Librarians are pulling that we could show to the monarchs?'

'Excellent!' Grandpa Smedry said. 'Folsom?'

'I'll take her to the palace,' he said. 'There's a public copy there we can read.'

'Lord Smedry,' Sing said, 'I think that you should speak to the kings again.'

'I've tried that, Sing!'

'Yes,' the Mokian said, 'but maybe you could address them formally in session. Maybe ... I don't know maybe that will embarrass them in front of the crowds.'

Grandpa Smedry frowned. 'Well, yes. I'd rather do a daring infiltration, though! '

'There ... aren't many places to infiltrate,' Sing said. 'The entire city is friendly toward us.'

'Except that Librarian embassy,' Grandpa Smedry said, eyes twinkling.

We sat for a moment, then glanced at Bastille. She was supposed to be the voice of reason, telling us to avoid doing things that were ... well, stupid.

She just stared forward, though, stunned from what had been done to her.

'Blast,' Grandpa Smedry said. 'Somebody tell me that infiltrating the embassy is a terrible idea!'

'It's a terrible idea,' I said. 'I don't know why, though.'

'Because there's not likely to be anything of use there!' Grandpa Smedry said. 'They're too clever for that. If anything, they have a secret base somewhere in the city. That's where we'd need to infiltrate, but we don't have time to find it! Somebody tell me that I should just go speak to the kings again.'

'Uh,' Sing said, 'didn't I just do that?'

'I need to hear it again, Sing.' Grandpa Smedry said. 'I'm old and stubborn!'

'Then, really, you should speak to the kings.'

'Spoilsport,' Grandpa Smedry muttered under his breath.

I sat back, thinking. Grandpa Smedry was right – there probably *was* a secret Librarian lair in the city. My bet was that we'd find it somewhere near where my mother vanished when I was trailing her.

'What are the Royal Archives?' I asked.

'They're not a library,' Folsom said quickly.

'Yes, the sign said that,' I replied. 'But if they aren't a library, what are they?' (I mean, telling me what something *isn't* really wasn't all that useful. I could put out a blorgadet and hang a sign on it that said 'Most certainly *not* a hippopotamus' and it wouldn't help. I'd also be lying, since 'blorgadet' is actually Mokian for hippopotamus.)

Grandpa Smedry turned toward me. 'The Royal Archives—'

'*Not* a library,' Sing added.

'—are a repository for the kingdom's most important texts and scrolls.'

'That, uh, sounds an *awful* lot like a library,' I said.

'But it's not,' Folsom said. 'Didn't you hear?'

'Right …' I said. 'Well, a repository for books—'

'Which is in no way a library,' Grandpa Smedry said.

'—sounds like exactly the sort of place the Librarians would be interested in.' I frowned in thought. 'Are there books in the Forgotten Language in there?'

'I'd guess some,' Grandpa Smedry said. 'Never been in there myself.'

'You haven't?' I asked, shocked.

'Too much like a library,' Grandpa Smedry said. 'Even if it isn't one.'

You Hushlanders may be confused by statements like this. After all, Grandpa Smedry, Sing, and Folsom have all been presented as very literate fellows. They're academics – quite knowledgeable about what they do. How, then, have they avoided libraries and reading?

The answer is that they *haven't* avoided reading. They love books. However, to them, books are a little like teenage boys: Whenever they start congregating, they make trouble.

'The Royal Archives,' I said, then quickly added, 'and I know it's *not* a library. Whatever it is, that's where my mother was going. I'm sure of it. She has the Translator's Lenses; she's trying to find something in there. Something important.'

'Alcatraz, the place is *very* well guarded,' Grandpa Smedry said. 'I doubt even Shasta would be able to sneak in unseen.'

'I still think we should visit,' I said. 'We can look and see if there's anything suspicious going on.'

'All right,' Grandpa Smedry said. 'You take Bastille and Sing and go. I'll compose a stirring speech to give at the final proceedings this evening! Maybe if I'm lucky, someone will try to assassinate me during the speech. That would make it at least ten times more dramatic!'

'Grandpa,' I said.

'Yes?'

'You're crazy.'

'Thank you! All right, let's get moving! We have an entire continent to save!'

13

People tend to believe what other people tell them. This is particularly true if the people who are telling the people the thing that they're telling them are people who have a college degree in the thing about which they are telling people. (Telling, isn't it?)

College degrees are very important. Without college degrees, we wouldn't know who was an expert and who wasn't. And if we didn't know who was an expert, we wouldn't know whose opinion was the most important to listen to.

Or at least that's what the experts want us to believe. Those who have listened to Socrates know that they're supposed to ask questions. Questions like 'If all people are equal, then why is my opinion worth less than that of the expert?' or 'If I like reading this book, then why should I let someone else tell me that I *shouldn't* like reading it?'

That isn't to say that I don't like critics. My cousin is one, and – as you have seen – he's a very nice fellow. All I'm saying is that you should question what others tell you, even if they have a college degree. There are a lot of people who might try to stop you from reading this book. They'll come up to you and say things like 'Why are you reading that trash?' or 'You should be doing your homework,' or 'Help me, I'm on fire!'

Don't let them distract you. It's of vital importance that you keep reading. This book is very, very important.

After all, it's about *me*.

'The Royal Archives,' I said, looking up at the vast building in front of me.

'Not a library,' Sing added.

'Thanks, Sing,' I said dryly. 'I'd almost forgotten.'

'Glad to help!' he said as we walked up the steps. Bastille followed; she was still barely responsive. She'd come to us because she'd been kicked out of Crystallia. Getting cut off from the knights' magic rock also required a period of exile from their giant glass mushroom.

(Those of you in the Hushlands, I *dare* you to work that last sentence into a conversation. 'By the way, Sally, did you know that getting cut off from the knights' magic rock also requires a period of exile from their giant glass mushroom?')

A dragon crawled along the sides of the castles above me, growling quietly to itself. The Royal Archives (not a library) looked a lot like a building out of Greek history, with its magnificent white pillars and marble steps. The only difference was that it had castlelike towers. In Nalhalla, *everything* has castle towers. Even the outhouses. (You know, in case someone tries to seize the throne.)

'It's been a long time since I've been here,' Sing said, happily waddling beside me. It was good to spend time with the pleasant anthropologist again.

'You've been here before?' I asked.

Sing nodded. 'During my undergraduate days, I had to do research on ancient weapons. This place has books you can't find anywhere else. I'm actually a little sad to be back.'

'This place is that bad?' I asked as we entered the cavernous main room of the Royal Archives. I didn't see any books – it looked mostly empty.

'This place?' Sing asked. 'Oh, I didn't mean the Royal Archives, which is not a library. I was talking about Nalhalla. I didn't get to do as much research in the Hushlands as I wanted! I was deeply engaged in a study on Hushlander transportation when your grandfather got me and we started our infiltration.'

'It's really not that interesting there,' I said.

'You just say that because you are accustomed to it!' Sing said. 'Each day, something new and exciting happened! Right before we left, I finally managed to meet a real *cabdriver*! I had him drive me around the block, and while I was disappointed that we didn't get into a car wreck, I'm sure after a few more days I could have experienced one.'

'Those are kind of dangerous, Sing.'

'Oh, I was ready for danger,' he said. 'I made sure to wear safety goggles!'

I sighed, but made no other comment. Trying to curb Sing's love of the Hushlands was like … well, like kicking a puppy. A six-foot-eight, three-hundred-fifty-pound Hawaiian puppy. Who liked to carry guns.

'This place doesn't look all that impressive,' I said, glancing about at the majestic pillars and enormous hallways. 'Where are the books?'

'Oh, this isn't the archives,' Sing said, pointing toward a doorway. 'The archives are in there.'

I raised an eyebrow and walked to the door, then pulled it open. Inside, I found an army.

There were a good fifty or sixty soldiers, all standing at attention in ranks, their metal helmets glistening in the lamplight. At the back of the room, there was a set of stairs leading down.

'Wow,' I said.

'Why, young Lord Smedry!' a voice boomed. I turned and was surprised to see Archedis – the big-chinned Knight of Crystallia from Bastille's trial – walking toward me. 'How surprising to see you here!'

'Sir Archedis,' I said. 'I could say the same of you, I guess.'

'There are always two full knights on guard at the Royal Archives,' Archedis said.

'Not a library,' one of the soldiers added.

'I was just here overseeing a shift change,' Archedis said, stepping up to me.

He was a lot more intimidating when standing. Silvery armor, rectangular face, a chin that could destroy small countries if it fell into the wrong hands. Sir Archedis was the type of knight that people stuck on recruitment posters.

'Well,' I said. 'We came to investigate the Royal Archives—'

'Not a library,' Sir Archedis said.

'—because we think the Librarians might be interested in them.'

'They're quite well protected,' Archedis said in his deep voice. 'A half platoon of soldiers and two Crystin! But I suppose it couldn't hurt to have an Oculator around too, particularly when there are Librarians in town!'

He glanced over my shoulder. 'I see that you've brought young Bastille with you,' he added. 'Good job – keep her moving about and not wallowing in her punishment!'

I glanced back at Bastille. She'd focused on Sir Archedis, and I thought I was beginning to see some emotion return to her. Likely she was thinking about how much she'd like to ram something long and pointy into his chest.

'I'm sorry we had to meet under such poor circumstances, Lord Smedry,' Archedis said to me. 'I've been following your exploits.'

'Oh,' I said, flushing. 'You mean the books?'

Archedis laughed. 'No, no, your *real* exploits! The battle against Blackburn was reportedly quite impressive, and I would have liked to see that fight with the Alivened. I hear that you handled yourself quite well.'

'Oh,' I said, smiling. 'Well, thanks.'

'But tell me,' he said, leaning down. 'Did you *really* break a Crystin sword with that Talent of yours?'

I nodded. 'Hilt came right off in my hand. I didn't realize it, but the problem was my emotion. I was so nervous that the Talent activated with a lot of power.'

'Well, I guess I just have to take your word!' Archedis said. 'Would you like a knight as guard for your person during this investigation?'

'No,' I said. 'I think we'll be fine.'

'Very well, then,' he said, slapping me on the back. (Side note: Getting slapped – even affectionately – on the back by someone wearing gauntlets is *not* comfortable.) 'Carry on, and best of luck.' He turned to the soldiers. 'Let them pass and follow their orders! This is the heir of House Smedry!'

The soldiers, en masse, saluted. With that, Archedis marched out the door, armor clinking.

'I *like* that guy,' I said after he was gone.

'Everyone does,' Sing said. 'Sir Archedis is one of the most influential knights in the order.'

'Oh, I don't think *everyone* likes him,' I said, glancing at Bastille. She was watching the doorway.

'He's amazing,' she whispered, surprising me. 'He's one of the reasons I decided to join.'

'But he was one of the ones who voted to have you stripped of your rank!'

'He was the least harsh on me,' Bastille said.

'Only because *I* convinced him to be.'

She regarded me with an odd expression; it seemed that she was coming out of her funk a little bit. 'I thought you liked him.'

'Well, I do,' I said.

Or at least I *had* liked him – right up until the point that Bastille had started talking about how wonderful he was. Now, quite suddenly, I became convinced that Sir Archedis was plain and dull-witted. I prepared to explain this to Bastille, but was interrupted as the soldiers began to make way for us to pass.

'Ah, nice,' Sing said, walking forward. 'Last time, I had to spend an hour appeasing their security requirements.'

Bastille followed. She obviously hadn't recovered completely, even if she was a little more animated. We entered the stairwell, and for a brief moment I was reminded of the Library of Alexandria, with its wraithlike Librarians and endless rows of dusty tomes and scrolls. It had been beneath the ground too.

The similarity soon ended. Not only was the Royal Archives *not* a library, but the stairwell didn't end in a strange teleporting darkness. Instead, it stretched on for a distance, dusty and dry. When we finally reached the bottom, we found the two Knights of Crystallia standing guard at another set of doors. They saluted, apparently recognizing Sing and me.

'How long will you need access, my lord?' one of the knights asked.

'Oh,' I said. 'Um, I'm not really sure.'

'Check back with us in an hour, if you don't mind,' said the other knight – a stout woman with blond hair.

'All right,' I said.

With that, the two knights pushed open the doors, letting me, Sing, and Bastille into the archives. 'Wow,' I said. That just didn't seem to cover it. '*Wow*,' I repeated, this time with emphasis.

You're probably expecting a grand description here. Something impressive to depict the majestic collection of tomes that made up the archives.

That's because you misinterpreted my 'wow.' You see, like all alphabetically late palindromic exclamations, 'wow' can be interpreted a lot of different ways. It's what we call 'versatile,' which is just another way of saying that it's a dumb thing to say.

After all, 'wow' could mean 'That's great!' Or it could mean 'That's disturbing.' It could also mean 'Oh, hey, look, a dinosaur is about to eat me!' Or it could even mean 'I just won the lottery, though I don't know what I'll do with all that money, seeing as how I'm in the stomach of a dinosaur.'

(As a side note to this side note: As we found in book one, it is true that most dinosaurs are fine folk and not at all man-eaters. However, there are some notable exceptions, such as the Quesadilla and the infamous Brontësister.)

In my case, 'wow' didn't mean any of these things. It meant something closer to: 'This place is a total mess!'

'This place is a total mess!' I exclaimed.

'No need to repeat yourself,' Bastille grumbled. (Bastille speaks fluent woweeze.)

Books were heaped like piles of scrap in an old, rundown junkyard. There were mountains of them, discarded, abused, and in total disarray. The cavern seemed to extend forever, and the piles of books formed mounds and hills, like sand dunes made from pages and letters and words.

I glanced back at the knights guarding the doorway. 'Is there some kind of organization to all of this?' I asked hopefully.

The knight paled in the face. 'Organization? Like … a cataloging system?'

'Yeah,' I said. 'You know, so that we can find stuff easily?'

'That's what Librarians do!' the blond knight said.

'Great,' I said. 'Just great. Thanks anyway.' I sighed, stepping away from the door, which the knights closed behind me. I grabbed a lamp off the wall. 'Well, let's go investigate,' I said to the others. 'See if we can find anything suspicious.'

We wandered the room, and I tried not to let my annoyance get the better of me. The Librarians had done some horrible things to the Free Kingdoms; it made sense that the Nalhallans would have an irrational fear of Librarian ways. However, I found it amazing that a people who loved learning so much could treat books in such a horrible manner. From the way the tomes were strewn, it seemed to me that their method of 'archiving' books was to toss them into the storage chamber and forget about them.

The piles grew larger and more mountainous near the back of the chamber, as if they'd been systematically pushed there by some infernal, literacy-hating bulldozer. I stopped, hands on my hips. I had expected a museum, or at least a den filled with bookshelves. Instead, I'd gotten a teenage boy's bedroom.

'How could they tell if anything was missing?' I asked.

'They can't,' Sing said. 'They figure if nobody can get in to steal books, then they don't have to keep them counted or organized.'

'That's stupid,' I said, holding up my light. The chamber was longer than it was wide, so I could see the walls on either side of me. The place wasn't infinite, like the Library of Alexandria had seemed. It was essentially just one very big room filled with thousands and thousands of books.

I walked back down the pathway between the mounds. How could you tell if anything was suspicious about a place you'd never visited before? I was about to give up when I heard it. A sound.

'I don't know, Alcatraz,' Sing was saying. 'Maybe we—'

I held up a hand, quieting him. 'Do you hear that?'

'Hear what?'

I closed my eyes, listening. Had I imagined it?

'Over there,' Bastille said. I opened my eyes to find her pointing toward one of the walls. 'Scraping sounds, like ...'

'Like digging,' I said, scrambling over a stack of books.

I climbed up the pile, slipping on what appeared to be several volumes of the royal tax code, until I reached the top and could touch the wall. It was, of course, made of glass. I pressed an ear against it.

'Yeah,' I said. 'There are *definitely* digging sounds coming from the other side. My mother didn't sneak in here, she snuck into a nearby building! They're tunneling into the Royal Archives!'

'Not—' Sing began.

'Yes,' I said, 'it's *not a library*. I get it.'

'Actually,' he said, 'I was going to say "Not to disagree, Alcatraz, but it's impossible to break into this place."'

'What?' I said, sliding back down the pile of books. 'Why?'

'Because it's built out of Enforcer's Glass,' Bastille said. She was looking better, but still somewhat dazed. 'You can't break that, not even with Smedry Talents.'

I looked back at the wall. 'I've seen impossible things happen. My mother has Translator's Lenses; there's no telling what she's learned from the Forgotten Language so far. Maybe they know a way to get through that glass.'

'Possible,' Sing said, scratching his chin. 'Though, to be honest, if I were them, I'd just tunnel into the stairwell out there, then come through the door.'

I glanced at the wall. That *did* seem likely. 'Come on,' I said, rushing over and pulling open the door. The two knights outside glanced in.

'Yes, Lord Smedry?' one asked.

'Someone may be trying to dig into the stairwell,' I said. 'Librarians. Get some more troops down here.'

The knights looked surprised, but they obeyed my orders, one rushing up the stairs to do as commanded.

I looked back at Bastille and Sing, who still stood in the room. Soldiers weren't going to be enough – I wasn't just going to sit and wait to see what plot the Librarians were going to be putting into effect. Mokia was in trouble, and *I* had to help. That meant blocking what my mother and the others were doing, perhaps even exposing their double-dealing to the monarchs.

'We need to figure out what it is in here that my mother wants,' I said, 'then take it first.'

Bastille and Sing looked at each other, then glanced back at the ridiculous number of books. I could read their thoughts in their expressions.

Find the thing my mother wanted? Out of this mess? How could anyone find *anything* in here?

It was then that I said something I never thought I'd hear myself say, no matter how old I grew.

'We need a Librarian,' I declared. *'Fast.'*

14

Yes, you heard that right. I – Alcatraz Smedry – needed a Librarian.

Now, you may have gotten the impression that there are absolutely no uses for Librarians. I'm sorry if I implied that. Librarians are *very* useful. For instance, they are useful if you are fishing for sharks and need some bait. They're also useful for throwing out windows to test the effects of concrete impact on horn-rimmed glasses. If you have enough Librarians, you can build bridges out of them. (Just like witches.)

And, unfortunately, they are *also* useful for organizing things.

I hurried up the stairs with Sing and Bastille. We had to push our way past the soldiers who now lined the steps; the men and women held their swords, looking concerned. I'd sent a soldier with a message for my grandfather and another for my father, warning them of what we'd discovered. I'd also ordered one of the knights to send a contingent to search nearby buildings – maybe they'd be able to find the librarian base and the other end of the tunnel. I wasn't counting on that happening, though. My mother wouldn't be caught so easily.

'We need to go *fast*,' I said. 'There's no telling when my mother will break into that chamber.'

I still felt a little bit sick for needing the help of a Librarian. It was frustrating. Terribly frustrating. In fact, I don't think I can accurately – through text – show you just *how* frustrating it was.

But because I love you, I'm going to try anyway. Let's start by randomly capitalizing letters.

'We cAn SenD fOr a draGOn to cArry us,' SinG saId As we burst oUt oF the stAirWeLL and ruSHED tHrough ThE roOm aBovE.

'ThAT wILl taKe tOO Long,' BaStiLlE saiD.

'We'Ll haVe To graB a VeHiCle oFf thE STrEet,' I sAid.

(You know what, that's not nearly frustrating enough. I'm going to have to start adding in random punctuation marks too.)

We c!RoS-Sed thrOu?gH t%he Gra##ND e`nt<Ry>WaY at 'A' de-aD Ru)n. OnC$e oUts/iDE, I Co*Uld sEe T^haT the suN wa+S nEar to s=Ett=ING – it w.O.u.l.d Onl>y bE a co@uPle of HoU[rs unTi^L the tR}e}atY RATi~FiCATiON ha,pPenEd. We nEeDeD!! To bE QuicK?.?

UnFOrTu()nAtelY, tHE!re weRe no C?arriA-ges on tHe rOa^D for U/s to cOmMan><dEer. Not a ON~e~. THerE w+eRe pe/\Ople wa|lK|Ing aBoUt, BU?t no caRr#iaGes.

(Okay, you know what? That's not frustrating enough either. Let's start replacing some random vowels with the letter Q.)

I lqOk-eD abO!qT, dE#sPqrA#te, fRq?sTr/Ated (like you, hopefully), anD aNn\qYeD. Jq!St eaR&lIer, tHqr^E hq.d BeeN DoZen!S of cq?RriqgEs on The rQA!d! No-W tHqRe wA=Sn't a SqnGl+e oN^q.

'ThE_rQ!' I eXclai$mqd, poIntIng. Mqv=Ing do~Wn th_e RqaD! a shoRt diStq++nCe aWay <wAs> a sTrAngq gLaSs cqnTrAPtion. I waSN't CqrTain What it <\wAs>, bUt It w!qs MoV?ing – aND s%qmewhat quIc:=}Kly. 'LeT's G_q gRA?b iT!'

(Okay, you know how frustrated you are trying to read that? Well, that's about *half* as frustrated as I was at having to go get a Librarian to help me. Aren't you happy I let you experience what I was feeling? That's the sign of excellent storytelling: writing that makes the reader have the same emotions as the characters. You can thank me later.)

We rushed up to the thing walking down the road. It was a glass animal of some sort, a little like the *Hawkwind* or the *Dragonaut*, except instead of flying, it was walking. As we rounded it, I got a better view.

I froze in place on the street. 'A *pig*?'

Sing shrugged. Bastille, however, rushed toward the pig in a determined run. She looked less dazed, though she still had a very … worn-out cast to her. Her eyes were dark and puffy, her face haggard and exhausted. I jogged after her. As we approached the enormous pig, a section of glass on its backside slid away, revealing someone standing inside.

I feel the need to pause and explain that I don't approve of potty humor in the least. There has already been far too much of it in this book, and – trifecta or not – it's just not appropriate. Potty humor is the literary equivalent of potato chips and soda. Appealing, perhaps, but at the same time, dreadful and in poor taste. I will have you know that I don't stand for such things and – as in the previous volumes of my narrative – intend to hold this story to rigorous quality standards.

'Farting barf-faced poop!' a voice exclaimed from inside the pig's butt.

(Sigh. Sorry. At least that's another great paragraph to try working into a random conversation.)

The man standing in the pig's posterior was none other than Prince Rikers Dartmoor, Bastille's brother, son of the king. He still wore his royal blue robes, his red baseball cap topping a head of red hair.

'Excuse me?' I said, stopping short outside the pig. 'What was that you said, Your Highness?'

'I hear that Hushlanders like to use synonyms for excrement as curses!' the prince said. 'I was trying to make you feel at home, Alcatraz! What in the world are you doing in the middle of the street?'

'We need a ride, Rikers,' Bastille said. '*Fast.*'

'Explosive diarrhea!' the prince exclaimed.

'And for the last time, *stop* trying to talk like a Hushlander. It makes you sound like an idiot.' She jumped up into the pig, then extended a hand to help me up.

I smiled, taking her hand.

'What?' she asked.

'Nice to see you're feeling better.'

'I feel terrible,' she snapped, sliding on her dark sunglasseslike Warrior's Lenses. 'I can barely concentrate, and I've got this horrible buzzing in my ears. Now shut up and climb in the pig's butt.'

I did as ordered, letting her pull me up. Doing so was harder for her than it would have been previously – being disconnected from the Mindstone must have taken away some of her abilities – but she was still far stronger than any thirteen-year-old girl had a right to be. The Warrior's Lenses probably helped; they're one of the few types of Lenses that anyone can wear.

Bastille helped Sing up next as the prince rushed through the glass pig – which had a very nice, lush interior – calling for his driver to turn around.

'Uh, where are we going on our amazing adventure?' the prince called.

Amazing adventure? I thought. 'To the palace,' I called. 'We need to find my cousin Folsom.'

'The palace?' the prince said, obviously disappointed – for him, at least, that was a fairly mundane location. He called out the order anyway.

The pig started to move again, tromping down the street. The pedestrians apparently knew to stay out of its way, and despite its large size, it made very good time. I sat down on one of the regal red couches, and Bastille sat next to me, exhaling and closing her eyes.

'Does it hurt?' I asked.

She shrugged. She's good at the tough-girl act, but I could tell that the severing still bothered her deeply.

'Why do we need Folsom?' she asked, eyes still closed, obviously trying to distract me from asking after her.

'He'll be with Himalaya,' I said, then realized that Bastille had never met the Librarian. 'She's a Librarian who supposedly defected to our side six months back. I don't think she's to be trusted, though.'

'Why?'

'Folsom stays suspiciously close to her,' I said. 'He rarely lets her out of his sight – she's really a Librarian spy.'

'Great,' Bastille said. 'And we're going to ask *her* for help?'

'She's our best bet,' I said. 'She is a fully trained Librarian – if anyone can sort through that mess in the Royal Archives—'

'Not a library!' Rikers called distantly from the front of the pig.

'—it will be a Librarian. Besides, maybe if she *is* a spy, she'll know what the Librarians are looking for and we can force it out of her.'

'So, your brilliant plan is to go to someone you suspect of being our enemy, then bring her into the very place that the Librarians are trying to break into.'

'Er ... yes.'

'Wonderful. Why do I feel that I'm going to end this ridiculous fiasco wishing I'd just given up my knighthood and become an accountant instead?'

I smiled. It felt *good* to have Bastille back. It was hard for me to feel too impressed by my own fame with her there pointing out the holes in my plans.

'You don't really mean that, do you?' I asked. 'About quitting the knighthood?'

She sighed, opening her eyes. 'No. As much as I hate to admit it, my mother was right. I'm not only good at this, but I enjoy it.' She looked at me, meeting my eyes. 'Somebody set me up, Alcatraz. I'm convinced of it. They *wanted* me to fail.'

'Your ... mother was the one who voted most harshly against your reinstatement.'

Bastille nodded, and I could see that she was thinking the same thing that I was.

'We have quite the parents, don't we?' I asked. 'My father ignores me; my mother married him just to get his Talent.'

Marry a Smedry, and you got a Talent. Apparently, it didn't matter if you were a Smedry by blood or by marriage: A Smedry was a Smedry. The only difference was that in the case of a marriage, the spouse got their husband's or wife's same Talent.

'My parents aren't like that,' Bastille said fiercely. 'They're good people. My father is one of the most respected and popular kings Nalhalla has ever known.'

'Even if he is giving up on Mokia,' Sing said quietly from his seat across from us.

'He *thinks* he's doing the best thing,' Bastille said. 'How would you like to have to decide whether to end a war – and save thousands of lives – or keep fighting? He sees a chance for peace, and the people *want* peace.'

'My people want peace,' Sing said. 'But we want freedom more.'

Bastille fell silent. 'Anyway,' she finally said, 'assuming my mother *was* the one to set me up, I can see exactly why she'd do it. She worries about showing favoritism toward me. She feels she needs to be extra hard on me, which is why she'd send me on such a difficult mission. To see if I failed, and therefore needed to go back into training. But she *does* care for me. She just has strange ways of showing it.'

I sat back, thinking about my own parents. Perhaps Bastille could come up with good motives for hers, but they were a noble king and a brave knight. What did I have? An egotistical rock-star scientist and an evil Librarian who even other *Librarians* didn't seem to like very much.

Attica and Shasta Smedry were not like Bastille's parents. My mother didn't care about me – she'd married only to get the Talent. And my father obviously didn't want to spend any time with me.

No wonder I turned out like I did. There is a saying in the Free Kingdoms: 'A cub's roar is an echo of the bear.' It's a little bit like one we use in the Hushlands: 'The apple doesn't fall far from the tree.' (It figures that the Librarian version would use apples instead of something cool, like bears.)

I'm not sure if I ever had a chance to be anything *but* the selfish jerk I became. Despite Grandpa Smedry's chastisement, I still longed for the fleeting satisfaction of fame. It had been really nice to hear people talk about how great I was.

My taste of fame sat in me like a corrupt seed, blackened and putrid, waiting to sprout forth slimy dark vines.

'Alcatraz?' Bastille asked, elbowing me.

I blinked, realizing that I'd zoned out. 'Sorry,' I mumbled.

She nodded to the side. Prince Rikers was approaching. 'I called ahead, and Folsom isn't at the palace,' he said.

'He isn't?' I asked, surprised.

'No, the servants said that he and a woman looked over the

treaty, then left. But never fear! We can continue our quest, for the servant said that we could find Folsom in the Royal Gardens—'

'*Not* a park,' Sing said. 'Or, er, never mind.'

'—across the street.'

'All right,' I said. 'What's he doing in the gardens?'

'Something terribly exciting and important, I'd guess,' Rikers said. 'Eldon, take notes!'

A servant in a scribe's robes appeared from a nearby room, as if from nowhere, with a notepad. 'Yes, my lord,' the man said, scribbling.

'This will make an excellent book,' Rikers said, sitting down.

Bastille just rolled her eyes.

'So, wait,' I said. 'You called ahead? How'd you do that?'

'Communicator's Glass,' Rikers said. 'Lets you talk with some-one across a distance.'

Communicator's Glass. However, something about that bothered me. I reached into my pocket, pulling out my Lenses. I'd once had a pair of Lenses that let *me* communicate across a distance. I didn't have them anymore – I'd given them back to Grandpa Smedry. I did have the new set of Disguiser's Lenses, though. What about the power they gave me? If I was thinking about someone, I could make myself look like them …

(By the way, yes, this *is* foreshadowing. However, you'll need to have read the previous two books in the series to figure out what's going on. So if you haven't read them, then too bad for you!)

'Wait,' Bastille said, pointing at the Truthfinder's Lens in my hand. 'Is that the one you found in the Library of Alexandria?'

'Yeah. Grandpa figured out that it's a Truthfinder's Lens.'

She perked up. '*Really*? Do you know how rare those are?'

'Well … to be honest, I kind of wish that it could blow things up.'

Bastille rolled her eyes. 'You wouldn't know a useful Lens if you cut your finger on it, Smedry.'

She had a point. 'You know a lot more about Lenses than I do, Bastille,' I admitted. 'But I think there's something odd about all of this. Smedry Talents, the Oculator's Lenses, brightsand … it's all connected.'

She eyed me. 'What are you talking about?'

'Here, let me show you.' I tucked my Lenses away, standing up and scanning the chamber, looking for a likely candidate. On one wall, there was a small shelf with some glass equipment on it. 'Your Highness, what's that?'

Prince Rikers turned. 'Ah! My new silimatic phonograph! Haven't hooked it up yet, though.'

'Perfect,' I said, walking over and picking up the glass box; it was about the size of a briefcase.

'That won't work, Alcatraz,' the prince said. 'It needs a silimatic power plate or some brightsand to—'

I channeled power into the glass. Not breaking power from my Talent, but the same 'power' I used to activate Lenses. Early on, I had simply needed to touch Lenses to power them; now I was learning to control myself so that I didn't activate them unintentionally.

Either way, the box started playing music – a peppy little symphony. It's a good thing Folsom wasn't there, otherwise he would have begun to 'dance.'

'Hey, how'd you do that?' Prince Rikers asked. 'Amazing!'

Bastille regarded me quizzically. I set the music box down, and it continued to play for a time, powered by the charge I'd given it.

'I'm starting to think that Oculatory Lenses and regular technological glass might just be the same thing.'

'That's impossible,' she said. 'If that were so, then you could power Oculator's Lenses with brightsand.'

'You can't?'

She shook her head.

'Maybe it's not concentrated enough,' I said. 'You *can* power the Lenses with Smedry blood, if you forge them using it.'

'Ick,' she noted. 'It's true. But ick anyway.'

'Ah, here we are!' Rikers said suddenly, standing up as the pig slowed.

I shot Bastille a look. She shrugged; we'd discuss this more later. We stood and joined Rikers, looking out the window (or, well, the *wall*) at the approaching gardens. My sense of urgency returned. We needed to grab Himalaya and get back to the Royal, nonlibrary Archives.

Rikers pulled a lever, and the back of the pig unfolded, forming steps. Bastille and I rushed out, Sing hustling along behind. The Royal Gardens were a large, open field of grass dotted occasionally by beds of flowers. I scanned the green, trying to locate my cousin. Of course, Bastille found him first.

'There,' she said, pointing. Squinting, I could see that Folsom and Himalaya were sitting on a blanket, enjoying what appeared to be a picnic.

'Wait here!' I called to Sing and Rikers as Bastille and I crossed the springy grass, passing families enjoying the afternoon and kids playing.

'What in the world are those two doing?' I asked, looking at Folsom and Himalaya.

'Uh, I think that's called a picnic, Smedry,' Bastille said flatly.

'I know, but why would Folsom take an enemy spy on a picnic? Perhaps he's trying to get her to relax so he can mine her for information.'

Bastille regarded the two of them, who sat on the blanket enjoying their meal. 'So, wait,' she said as we rushed forward. 'They're always together?'

'Yeah,' I said. 'He's been watching her like a hawk. He's always looking at her.'

'You'd say he's been spending a lot of time with her?'

'A *suspicious* amount of time.'

'Hanging out at restaurants?'

'Ice cream parlors,' I said. 'He claims to be showing her around so that she'd get used to Nalhallan customs.'

'And you think he's doing this because he suspects her of being a spy,' Bastille said, voice almost amused.

'Well, why else would he—'

I froze, stopping on the grass. Just ahead, Himalaya laid her hand on Folsom's shoulder, laughing at something he'd said. He regarded her, seeming transfixed by her face. He seemed to be enjoying himself, as if ...

'Oh,' I said.

'Boys are such idiots," Bastille said under her breath, moving on.

'How was I supposed to know they were in love!" I snapped, rushing up to her.

'Idiot,' she repeated.

'Look, she *could* still be a spy. Why, maybe she's seducing Folsom to get at his secrets!'

'Seductions don't look so cutesy,' Bastille said as we approached their blanket. 'Anyway, there's a simple method to find out. Pull out that Truthfinder's Lens.'

Hey, that's a good idea, I thought. I fumbled, pulling out the Lens and looking through it toward the Librarian.

Bastille marched right up to the blanket. 'You're Himalaya?' she asked.

'Why, yes,' the Librarian said. As I looked through the Lens, her breath seemed to glow like a white cloud. I assumed that meant she was telling the truth.

'Are you a Librarian spy?' Bastille asked. (She's like that, blunter than a rock and twice as ornery.)

'What?' Himalaya said. 'No, of course not!'

Her breath was white.

I turned to Bastille. 'Grandpa Smedry warned that Librarians were good at saying half-truths, which might get them around my Truthfinder's Lens.'

'Are you saying half-truths?' Bastille said. 'Are you trying to fool that Lens, trick us, seduce this man, or do anything like that?'

'No, no, no,' Himalaya said, blushing.

Bastille looked at me.

'Her breath is white,' I said. 'If she's lying, she's doing a really great job of it.'

'Good enough for me,' Bastille said, pointing. 'You two, get in the pig. We're on a tight schedule.'

They jumped to their feet, not even asking questions.

When Bastille gets that tone in her voice, you do what she says. For the first time, I realized where Bastille's ability to order people about might have come from. She was a princess – she'd probably spent her entire childhood giving commands.

By the First Sands, I thought. *She's a* princess.

'All right,' Bastille said. 'We've got your Librarian, Smedry. Let's hope she can actually help.'

We headed back to the pig, and I eyed the setting sun. Not much time left. This next part was going to have to go quickly. (I suggest you take a deep breath.)

15

Humans are funny things. From what I've seen, the more we agree with someone, the more we like listening to them. I've come up with a theory. I call it the macaroni and cheese philosophy of discourse.

I love macaroni and cheese. It's amazing. If they serve food in heaven, I'm certain mac and cheese graces each and every table. If someone wants to sit and talk to me about how good mac and cheese is, I'll talk to them for hours. However, if they want to talk about fish sticks, I generally stuff them in a cannon and launch them in the general direction of Norway.

That's the wrong reaction. I *know* what mac and cheese tastes like. Wouldn't it be more useful for me to talk to someone who likes something else? Maybe understanding what other people like about fish sticks could help me understand how they think.

A lot of the world doesn't think this way. In fact, a lot of people think that if they like mac and cheese rather than fish sticks, the best thing to do is *ban* fish sticks.

That would be a tragedy. If we let people do things like this, eventually we'd end up with only one thing to eat. And it probably wouldn't be mac and cheese or fish sticks. It'd probably be something that *none* of us likes to eat.

You want to be a better person? Go listen to someone you disagree with. Don't argue with them, just *listen*. It's remarkable what interesting things people will say if you take the time to not be a jerk.

We dashed from the giant glass pig like deployed soldiers, then stormed up the steps to the Royal Archives. (Go ahead, say it with me. I know you want to.)

Not a library.

Bastille in her Warrior's Lenses was the fastest, of course, but Folsom and Himalaya kept up. Sing was in the rear, right beside ...

'Prince *Rikers*?' I said, freezing in place. I'd assumed that the prince would remain with his vehicle.

'Yes, what?' the prince said, stopping beside me, turning and looking back.

'Why are you here?' I said.

'I finally have a chance to see the famous Alcatraz Smedry in action! I'm not going to miss it.'

'Your Highness,' I said, 'this might be dangerous.'

'You really think so?' he asked excitedly.

'What's going on?' Bastille said, rushing back down the steps. 'I thought we were in a hurry.'

'He wants to come,' I said, gesturing.

She shrugged. 'We can't really stop him – he's the crown prince. That kind of means he can do what he wants.'

'But what if he gets killed?' I asked.

'Then they'll have to pick a new crown prince,' Bastille snapped. 'Are we going or not?'

I sighed, glancing at the red-haired prince. He was smiling in self-satisfaction.

'Great,' I muttered, but continued up the stairs. The prince rushed beside me. 'By the way,' I said. 'Why a *pig*?'

'Why,' he said, surprised, 'I heard that in the Hushlands, it is common for tough guys to ride hogs.'

I groaned. 'Prince Rikers, "hog" is another word for a motorcycle.'

'Motorcycles look like pigs?' he asked. 'I never knew that!'

'You know what, never mind,' I said. We rushed into the room with the soldiers; it looked like the knights had sent for reinforcements. There were a lot of them on the stairs too. I felt good knowing they were there in case the Librarians *did* break into the Royal Archives.

'Not a library,' Sing added.

'What?' I asked.

'Just thought you might be thinking about it,' Sing said, 'and figured I should remind you.'

We reached the bottom. The two knights had taken up guard positions inside the room, and they saluted the prince as we entered.

'Any Librarians?' I asked.

'No,' the blond knight said, 'but we can still hear the scrapings. We have two platoons on command here, and two more searching nearby buildings. So far, we've not discovered anything – but we'll be ready for them if they break into the stairwell!'

'Excellent,' I said. 'You should wait outside, just in case.' I didn't want them to see what was about to happen. It was embarrassing.

They left and closed the door. I turned to Himalaya. 'All right,' I said. 'Let's do it.'

She looked confused. 'Do what?'

Oh, right, I thought. We'd never actually explained why we needed her. 'Somewhere in this room are some books the Librarians really want,' I said. 'Your former friends are tunneling in here right now. I need you to ...'

I could see Bastille, Folsom, and Sing cringe as I prepared to say it.

'... I need you to *organize* the books in here.'

Himalaya paled. 'What?'

'You heard me right.'

She glanced at Folsom. He looked away.

'You're testing me,' she said, forming fists. 'Don't worry, I can resist it. You don't need to do this.'

'No, really,' I said, exasperated. 'I'm not testing you. I just need these books to have some kind of order.'

She sat down on a pile. 'But ... but I'm recovering! I've been clean for months now! You can't ask me to go back, you *can't*.'

'Himalaya,' I said, kneeling beside her. 'We really, really need you to do this.'

She started trembling, which made me hesitate.

'I—'

She stood and fled the room, tears in her eyes. Folsom rushed after her and I was left kneeling, feeling horrible. Like I'd just told a little girl that her kitten was dead. Because I'd run it over. And that I'd also eaten it.

And that it had tasted really bad.

'Well, that's that, then,' Bastille said. She sat down on a pile of books. She was starting to look haggard again. We'd kept her distracted for a time, but the severing was still weighing on her.

I could still hear the scraping sounds, and they were getting louder. 'All right, then,' I said, taking a deep breath. 'We're going to have to destroy them.'

'What?' Sing asked. 'The books?'

I nodded. 'We *can't* let my mother get what she wants. Whatever it is, I'll bet it involves Mokia. This is the only thing I can think of – I doubt we can move these books out in time.' I looked toward the mounds. 'We're going to have to burn them.'

'We don't have the authority for that,' Bastille said tiredly.

'Yes,' I said, turning toward Prince Rikers. 'But I'll bet that he does.'

The prince looked up – he'd been poking through a pile of books, probably looking for fantasy novels. 'What's this?' he asked. 'I have to say, this adventure hasn't been very exciting. Where are the explosions, the rampaging wombats, the space stations?'

'This is what a real adventure is like, Prince Rikers,' I said. 'We need to burn these books so the Librarians don't get them. Can you authorize that?'

'Yes, I suppose,' he said. 'A bonfire might be exciting.'

I walked over and grabbed one of the lamps off the walls. Bastille and Sing joined me, looking at the books as I prepared to begin the fire.

'This feels wrong,' Sing said.

'I know,' I said. 'But what does anyone care about these books? They just stuffed them in here. I'll bet people rarely even come look at them.'

'I did,' Sing said. 'Years back. I can't be the only one. Besides, they're *books*. Knowledge. Who knows what we might lose? There are books in here that are so old, they might be the only copies in existence outside of the ones at the Library of Alexandria.'

I stood with the fire in my hand. Now, I hadn't meant this to be a metaphor for anything – I'm simply relating what happened. It *did* seem like the right thing to do. And yet, it also felt like the *wrong* thing too. Was it better to burn the books and let nobody have the knowledge, or take the chance that the Librarians would get them?

I knelt and put the lamp toward a stack of books, its flame flickering.

'Wait,' Bastille said, kneeling beside me. 'You have to turn it to "burn".'

'But it's already burning,' I said, confused.

'Not that argument again,' she said, sighing. (Go read book one.) 'Here.' She touched the glass of the lamp, and the flame seemed to pulse. 'It's ready now.'

I took a deep breath, then – hand trembling – lit the first book on fire.

'Wait!' a voice called. 'Don't do it!' I spun to see Himalaya standing in the doorway, Folsom at her side. I looked back at the books desperately; the flame was already spreading.

Then, fortunately, Sing tripped. His enormous Mokian bulk smashed onto the pile of books, his gut completely extinguishing the flames. A little trickle of smoke curled out from underneath him.

'Whoops,' he said.

'No,' Himalaya said, striding forward. 'You did the right thing, Sing. I'll do it. I'll organize them. Just ... just don't hurt them. Please.'

I stepped back as Folsom helped Sing to his feet. Himalaya knelt by the pile that had almost gone up in flames. She touched one of the books lovingly, picking it up with her delicate fingers.

'So ... uh,' she said, 'What order do you want? Reverse time-share, where the books are organized by the minute when they were published? Marksman elite, where we organize them by the number of times the word "the" is used in the first fifty pages?'

'I think a simple organization by topic will do,' I said. 'We need to find the ones about Oculators or Smedrys or anything suspicious like that.'

Himalaya caressed the book, feeling its cover, reading the spine. She carefully placed it next to her, then picked up another. She placed that one in another pile.

This is going to take forever, I thought with despair.

Himalaya grabbed another book. This time, she barely glanced at the spine before setting it aside. She grabbed another, then another, then another, moving more quickly with each volume.

She stopped, taking a deep breath. Then she burst into motion, her hands moving more quickly than I could track. She seemed to be able to identify a book simply by touching it, and knew exactly where to place it. In mere seconds, a small wall of books was rising around her.

'A little help, please!' she called. 'Start moving the stacks over, but don't let them get out of order!'

Sing, Folsom, Bastille, and I hurried forward to help. Even the prince went to work. We rushed back and forth, moving books where Himalaya told us, struggling to keep up with the Librarian.

She was almost superhuman in her ability to organize – a machine of identification and order. Dirty, unkempt piles disappeared beneath her touch, transformed into neat stacks, the dust and grime cleaned from them in a single motion of her hand.

Soon Folsom got the idea to recruit some of the soldiers to help. Himalaya sat in the center of the room like some multi-armed Hindu goddess, her hands a blur. We brought her stacks of books and she organized them in the blink of an eye, leaving them grouped by subject. She had a serene smile on her face. It was the smile my grandfather had when he spoke of an exciting infiltration, or the way Sing looked when he spoke of his cherished antique weapons collection. It was the look of someone doing work they perfectly and truly enjoyed.

I rushed forward with another stack of books. Himalaya snatched them without looking at me, then threw them into piles like a dealer dealing cards.

Impressive! I thought.

'All right, I have to say it,' Himalaya said as she worked. Soldiers clinked in their armor, rushing back and forth, delivering stacks of unorganized books to her feet, then taking away the neatly organized ones she placed behind her.

'What is wrong with you Free Kingdomers?' she demanded, ranting as if to nobody in particular. 'I mean, I left the Hushlands because I disagreed with the way the Librarians were keeping information from the people.

'But why is it bad to organize? Why do you have to treat books like this? What's wrong with having a little order? You Free Kingdomers claim to like things loose and free, but if there are never any rules, there is chaos. Organization is *important*.'

I set down my stack of books, then rushed back.

'Who knows what treasures you could have lost here?' she snapped, arms flying. 'Mold can destroy books. Mice can chew them to bits. They need to be cared for, *treasured*. Somebody needs to keep track of what you have so that you can appreciate your own collection!'

Folsom stepped up beside me, his brow dripping with sweat. He watched Himalaya with adoring eyes, smiling broadly.

'Why did I have to give up who I was?' the Librarian ranted. 'Why can't I be me, but also be on your side? I don't want to stifle information, but I do want to organize it! I don't want to rule the world, but I do want to bring it order! I don't want everything to be the same, but I *do* want to understand!'

She stopped for a moment. 'I am a *good* Librarian!' she declared in a triumphant voice, grabbing a huge stack of unorganized books. She shook them once, like one might a pepper shaker, and somehow the books all aligned in order by subject, size, and author.

'*Wow*,' Folsom breathed.

'You really *do* love her,' I said.

Folsom blushed, looking at me. 'Is it that obvious?'

It hadn't been to me. But I smiled anyway.

'These last six months have been amazing,' he said, getting that dreamy, disgusting tone to his voice that lovesick people often use. 'I started out just watching to see if she was a spy, but after I determined that she was safe … well, I wanted to keep spending time with her. So I offered to coach her on Nalhallan customs.'

'Have you told her?' I asked, soldiers bustling around me, carrying stacks of books.

'Oh, I couldn't do that,' Folsom said. 'I mean, look at her. She's amazing! I'm just a regular guy.'

'A regular guy?' I asked. 'Folsom, you're a Smedry. You're nobility!'

'Yeah,' he said, looking down. 'But I mean, that's just a name. I'm a boring person, when you get down to it. Who thinks a critic is interesting?'

I resisted pointing out that Librarians weren't exactly known for being the most exciting people either.

'Look,' I said. 'I don't know a lot about things like this, but it seems to me that if you love her, you should say so. I—'

At that moment, Prince Rikers walked up. 'Hey, look!' he said, proffering a book. 'They have one of my novels in here! Preserved for all of posterity. The music even still works. See!'

He opened the cover.

And so, of course, Folsom punched me in the face.

16

Now, I would like to make it clear that violence is rarely the best solution to problems.

For instance, the next time you get attacked by a group of angry ninjas, one solution would be to kick the lead ninja, steal his katana, and proceed to slay the rest of the group in an awesome display of authorial fury. While this might be fulfilling – and a little bit fun – it would also be rather messy, and would earn you the ire of an entire ninja clan. They'd send assassins after you for the rest of your life. (Having to fight off a ninja in the middle of a date can be quite embarrassing.)

So instead of fighting, you could bribe the ninjas with soy sauce, and then send them to attack your siblings instead. That way, you can get rid of some unwanted soy sauce. See how easy it is to avoid violence?

Now, there *are* some occasions when violence is appropriate. Usually, those are occasions when you want to beat the tar out of somebody. Unfortunately, 'somebody' at this moment happened to be me. Folsom's punch was completely unexpected, and it hit me full in the face.

Right then, I realized something quite interesting: That was the first time I'd ever been punched. It was a special moment for me. I'd say it was a little like being kicked, only with more knuckles and a hint of lemon.

Maybe the lemon part was just my brain short-circuiting as I was tossed backward onto the chamber's glass floor. The blow left me dazed, and by the time I finally shook myself out of it, the scene in front of me was one of total chaos.

The soldiers were trying to subdue Folsom. They didn't want to hurt him, as he was a nobleman; they were forced to try to grab him and hold him down. It wasn't working very well. Folsom fought with a strange mixture of terrified lack of control and calculated precision. He was like a puppet being controlled by a kung fu master. Or maybe vice versa. A trite melody played in the background – my theme music, apparently.

Folsom moved among the soldiers in a blur of awkward (yet somehow well-placed) kicks, punches, and head-butts. He'd already knocked down a good ten soldiers, and the other ten weren't doing much better.

'It's so exciting!' the prince said. 'I hope somebody is taking notes! Why didn't I bring any of my scribes? I should send for some!' Rikers stood a short distance from the center of the fight.

Please punch him, I thought, standing up on shaky knees. *Just a little bit.*

But it wasn't to be – Folsom was focused on the soldiers. Himalaya was calling for the soldiers to try to get their hands over Folsom's ears. Where was Bastille? She should have come running at the sounds of the fight.

'The Alcatraz Smedry Theme' continued to play its peppy little melody, coming from somewhere near the prince. 'Prince Rikers!' I yelled. 'The book! Where is it? We have to close it!'

'Oh, what?' He turned. 'Um, I think I dropped it when the fight started.'

He was standing near a pile of unsorted books. I cursed, scrambling toward the pile. If we could stop the music, Folsom would stop dancing.

At that moment the battle shifted in my direction. Folsom – his eyes wide with worry and displaying a distinct lack of control – spun through a group of soldiers, throwing four of them into the air.

I stood facing him. I didn't *think* he'd do me any serious harm. I mean, Smedry Talents are unpredictable, but they rarely hurt people too badly.

Except ... hadn't I used my own Talent to break some arms and cause monsters to topple to their deaths?

Crud, I thought. Folsom raised his fist and prepared to punch directly at my face.

And my Talent engaged.

One of the odd things about Smedry Talents, mine in particular, is how they sometimes act proactively. Mine breaks weapons at a distance if someone tries to kill me.

In this case, something dark and wild seemed to rip from me. I couldn't see it, but I could feel it snapping toward Folsom. His eyes opened wide, and he tripped, his graceful martial-arts power failing him for a brief moment. It was as if he'd suddenly *lost* his Talent.

He toppled to the ground before me. At that moment, a book in the pile beside me exploded, throwing up scraps of paper and glass. The music stopped.

Folsom groaned. The trip left him kneeling right in front of me, confettilike scraps of paper falling around us. The beast within me quieted, pulling back inside, and all fell still.

When I'd been young, I'd thought of my Talent as a curse. Now I'd begun thinking of it as a kind of wild super-power. This was the first time, however, that I thought of it as something foreign inside of me.

Something alive.

'That was incredible!' said one of the soldiers. I looked up and saw the soldiers regarding me with awe. Himalaya seemed stunned. The prince stood with his arms folded, smiling in contentment at finally getting to witness a battle.

'I saw it,' one of the soldiers whispered, 'like a wave of power, pulsing out of you, Lord Smedry. It stopped even another Talent.'

It felt *good* to be admired. It made me feel like a leader. Like a hero. 'See to your friends,' I said, pointing to the fallen soldiers. 'Give me a report on the wounded.' I reached down, helping Folsom to his feet.

He looked down in shame, as Himalaya walked over to comfort him. 'Well, I give myself nine out of ten points for being an idiot,' he said. 'I can't believe I let that happen. I should be able to *control* it!'

'I know how hard it is,' I said. 'Trust me. It wasn't your fault.'

Prince Rikers walked over to join us, his blue robes swishing. 'That was wonderful,' he said. 'Though it's kind of sad how the book turned out.'

'I'm heartbroken,' I said flatly, glancing about for Bastille. Where *was* she?

'Oh, it's all right,' Rikers said, reaching into his pocket. 'They have the sequel here too!' He pulled out a book and moved to open the cover.

'Don't you *dare!*' I snapped, grabbing his arm.

'Oh,' he said. 'Yeah, probably a bad idea.' He glanced at my grip on his arm. 'You know, you remind me a lot of my sister. I thought you'd be a little less uptight.'

'I'm not uptight,' I snapped. 'I'm annoyed. There's a difference. Himalaya, how's the sorting going?'

'Uh, maybe halfway done,' she said. Indeed, the mountains of books were quickly becoming large stacks, like walls. A much smaller stack was particularly interesting to me – it contained books in the Forgotten Language.

There were only four so far, but it was amazing to me that we'd even managed to find them among all the other books. I walked over to the stack, fishing in my jacket pocket for my pair of Translator's Lenses.

I swapped them for my Oculator's Lenses. I almost forgot that I was wearing those. They were starting to feel natural to me, I guess. With the Translator's Lenses on, I could read the titles of the books.

One appeared to be some kind of philosophical work on the nature of laws and justice. Interesting, but I couldn't see it being important enough for my mother to risk so much in order to get.

The other three books were unimpressive. A manual on building chariots, a ledger talking about the number of chickens a particular merchant traded in Athens, and a cookbook. (Hey, I guess even ancient, all-powerful lost societies needed help baking cookies.)

I checked with the soldiers and was relieved to find that none of them was seriously wounded. Folsom had knocked out no fewer than six of them, and some others had broken several limbs. The wounded left for the infirmary and the others returned to helping Himalaya. None of them had seen Bastille.

I wandered through what was quickly becoming a maze of enormous book stacks. Maybe Bastille was looking for signs of the diggers breaking into the room. The scraping sounds had been coming from the southeast corner, but when I neared, I couldn't hear them anymore. Had my mother realized we were on to her? With that sound gone, I could hear something else.

Whispering.

Curious, and a little creeped out, I walked in the direction of the sound. I turned a corner around a wall-like stack of books, and found a little dead-end hollow in the maze.

Bastille lay there, curled up on the cold glass floor whispering to herself and shivering. I cursed, rushing over to kneel beside her. 'Bastille?'

She curled up a little bit further. Her Warrior's Lenses were off, clutched in her hand. I could see a haunted cast to her eyes. A sense of loss, of sorrow, of having had something deep and tender ripped from her, never to be returned.

I felt powerless. Had she been hurt? She shivered and moved, then looked up at me, eyes focusing. She seemed to realize for the first time that I was there.

She immediately pushed away from me and sat up. Then she sighed and wrapped her arms around her knees, bowing her head between them. 'Why is it that you always see me like this?' she asked quietly. 'I'm strong, I really am.'

'I know you are,' I said, feeling awkward and embarrassed.

We remained like that for a time, Bastille unresponsive, me feeling like a complete idiot, even though I wasn't sure what I'd done wrong. (Note to all the young men reading this: Get used to that.)

'So ...' I said. 'Er ... you're still having trouble with that severing thing?'

She looked up, eyes red like they'd been scratched with sandpaper. 'It's like ...' she said in a quiet voice. 'It's like I used to have memories. Fond ones, of places I loved, of people I knew. Only now they're gone. I can *feel* the place where they were, and it's a hole, ripped open inside of me.'

'The Mindstone is that important?' I asked. It was a dumb thing to say, but I felt I should say *something*.

'It connects all of the Knights of Crystallia,' she whispered. 'It strengthens us, gives us comfort. By it, we all share a measure of who we are.'

'I should have shattered the swords of those idiots who did this to you,' I growled.

Bastille shivered, holding her arms close. 'I'll get reconnected eventually, so I should probably tell you not to be so angry. They're good people and don't deserve your scorn. But honestly, I'm having trouble feeling sympathy for them right now.' She smiled wanly.

I tried to smile back, but it was hard. 'Someone *wanted* this to happen to you, Bastille. They set you up.'

'Maybe,' Bastille said, sighing. It appeared that her episode was over, though it had left her weakened even further.

'Maybe?' I repeated.

'I don't know, Smedry,' she said. 'Maybe nobody set me up. Maybe I really did just get promoted too quickly, and really did just fail on my own. Maybe ... maybe there is no grand conspiracy against me.'

'I guess you could be right,' I said.

You, of course, don't believe that. I mean, when is there *not* some grand conspiracy? This entire series is about a *secret cult of evil Librarians who rule the world*, for Sands' sake.

'Alcatraz?' a voice called. Sing wandered around the corner a moment later. 'Himalaya found another book in the Forgotten Language. Figured you would want to look at it.'

I glanced at Bastille; she waved me away. 'What, you think I need to be babied?' she snapped. 'Go. I'll be there in a moment.'

I hesitated, but followed Sing around a few walls of books to the center of the room. The prince sat, looking bored, on what appeared to be a throne made of books. (I'm still not sure who he got to make it for him.) Folsom was directing the moving of stacks; Himalaya was still sorting, with no sign of slowing down.

Sing handed me the book. Like all of the others in the Forgotten Language, the text on it looked like crazy scribbles. Before he had died, Alcatraz the First – my ultimate ancestor – had used the Talent to break the language of his people so that nobody could read it.

Nobody, except for someone with a pair of Translator's Lenses. I put mine on and flipped to the first page, hoping it wasn't another cookbook.

Observations on the Talents of the Smedry people, the title page read, *and an explanation of what led up to their fate. As written by Fenilious K. Wandersnag, scribe to His Majesty, Alcatraz Smedry.*

I blinked, then read the words again.

'Guys?' I said, turning. 'Guys!'

The group of soldiers hesitated, and Himalaya glanced toward me. I held the book up.

'I think we just found what we've been looking for.'

17

Things are about to go very wrong.

Oh, didn't you know that already? I should think that it would be obvious. We're almost to the end of the book, and we just had a very encouraging victory. Everything looks good. So, of course, it's all going to go wrong. You should pay better attention to plot archetypes.

I'd like to promise you that everything will turn out all right, but I think there's something you should understand. This is the middle book of the series. And, as everyone knows, the heroes *always* lose in the middle book. It makes the series more tense.

Sorry. But hey, at least my books have awesome endings, right?

I dismissed the soldiers, ordering them to return to their posts. Sing and Folsom joined me, looking at the book, even though they couldn't read it. I suspected that my mother must have an Oculator with her to read the book – to her alone, the Lenses would be useless.

'You're sure this is what we're after?' Sing asked, turning the book over in his fingers.

'It's a history of the fall of Incarna,' I said, 'told by Alcatraz the First's personal scribe.'

Sing whistled. 'Wow. What are the chances?'

'Pretty good, I'd say,' Bastille said, rounding the corner and joining us. She still looked quite the worse for wear, but at least she was standing. I gave her what I hoped was an encouraging smile.

'Nice leer,' she said to me. 'Anyway, this is the Royal Archives—'

'*Not* a—' Folsom began to say.

'—don't interrupt,' Bastille snapped. She appeared to be in rare form – but then, having a piece of your soul cut out tends to do that to people.

'This is the Royal Archives,' Bastille continued. 'A lot of these books have passed down through the royal Nalhallan line for centuries – and the collection has been added to by the Smedrys, the Knights of Crystallia, and the other noble lines who have joined with us.'

'Yes indeed,' Prince Rikers said, taking the book from Sing, looking it over. 'People don't just throw away books in the Forgotten Language. A lot of these have been archived here for years and years. They're copies of copies.'

'You can copy these scribbles?' I asked with surprise.

'Scribes can be quite meticulous,' Sing said. 'They're almost as bad as Librarians.'

'Excuse me?' Himalaya huffed, walking up to us. She'd finished giving orders to the last couple of soldiers, who were arranging the books she'd just organized. The room looked kind of strange, with the back half of it still dominated by gargantuan piles of books, the front half filled with neatly organized stacks.

'Oh,' Sing said. 'Um, I didn't mean *you*, Himalaya. I meant Librarians who aren't recovering.'

'I'm not either,' she said, folding her arms, adopting a very deliberate stance as she stood in her Hushlander skirt and blouse. 'I meant what I said earlier. I intend to prove that you can be a Librarian without being evil. There *has* to be a way.'

'If you say so ...' Sing said.

I still kind of agreed with Sing. Librarians were ... well, Librarians. They'd oppressed me since my childhood. They were trying to conquer Mokia.

'I think you did wonderfully,' Folsom said to Himalaya. 'Ten out of ten on a scale of pure, majestic effectiveness.'

Prince Rikers sniffed at that. 'Excuse me,' he said, then handed me the Forgotten Language book and walked away.

'What was that about?' Himalaya asked.

'I think Folsom just reminded the prince that he was a book critic,' Bastille said.

Folsom sighed. 'I don't want to make people mad. I just ... well, how can people get better if you don't tell them what you honestly think?'

'I don't think everyone wants to hear what you honestly think, Folsom,' Himalaya said, laying a hand on his arm.

'Maybe I could go talk to him,' Folsom said. 'You know, explain myself.'

I didn't think the prince would listen, but I didn't say anything as Folsom walked after Rikers. Himalaya was watching after the determined critic with fondness.

'You're in love with him, aren't you?' I asked her.

Himalaya turned, blushing. Bastille immediately punched me in the arm.

'Ow!' I said. (My Talent never seemed to work when Bastille is doing the punching. Perhaps it thought I deserved the punishment.) 'Why'd you do that?'

Bastille rolled her eyes. 'You don't need to be so blunt, Smedry.'

'You're blunt all the time!' I complained. 'Why's it wrong when I do it?'

'Because you're *bad* at it, that's why. Now apologize for embarrassing the young woman.'

'It's all right,' Himalaya said, still blushing. 'But, please, don't say such a thing. Folsom is just being kind to me because he knows I feel so lost in Free Kingdoms society. I don't want to burden him with my silliness.'

'But, he said – gak!'

'He said "Gak"?' Himalaya asked, confused. She obviously hadn't seen Bastille step forcefully on my toe in the middle of my sentence.

'Excuse us,' Bastille said, smiling at Himalaya, then towing me away. Once we were at a safe distance, she pointed at my face and said, 'Don't get involved.'

'Why?' I demanded.

'Because they'll work it out on their own, and they don't need you messing things up.'

'But I talked to Folsom and he likes her too! I should tell her about it so they can stop acting like lovesick crocodiles.'

'Crocodiles?'

'What?' I said defensively. 'Crocodiles fall in love. Baby crocodiles come from *somewhere*. Anyway, that's beside the point. We should talk to those two and settle this misunderstanding so they can get on with things.'

Bastille rolled her eyes. 'How can you be so clever sometimes, Smedry, but such an *idiot* other times?'

'That's unfair, and you—' I stopped. 'Wait, you think I'm clever?'

'I said you're clever *sometimes*,' she snapped. 'Unfortunately, you're annoying *all the time*. If you mess this up, I'll … I don't know. I'll cut off your thumbs and send them to the crocodiles as a wedding present.'

I crinkled my brow. 'Wait. What?'

She just stalked away. I watched her go, smiling.

She thought I was clever.

I stood in a happy stupor for a few minutes. Finally, I wandered back over to Sing and Himalaya.

'… think about it,' Himalaya was saying. 'It's not the *Librarian* part that's a problem, it's the *evil* part. I could start a self-help program. World-dominating Cultists Anonymous or something like that.'

'I dunno,' Sing said, rubbing his chin. 'Sounds like you have an uphill battle.'

'You Free Kingdomers need to be educated about this as much as the Librarians do!' She smiled at me as I arrived. 'Anyway, I feel that we should organize the rest of these books. You know, for consistency's sake.'

I looked down at the book in my hands. 'Do what you want,' I said. 'I intend to take this someplace safe. We've probably wasted too much time as it is.'

'But what if there are other books in here that are important?' Himalaya asked. 'Maybe that's *not* the one your mother wants.'

'It is,' I said. Somehow I *knew*.

'But how would she even know it was in here?' Himalaya asked. 'We didn't.'

'My mother's resourceful,' I said. 'I'll bet she—'

At that moment, Sing tripped.

'Oh, dear!' Himalaya said. 'Are you all right – gak!'

She said this last part as I grabbed her by the arm and dived for cover behind a stack of books. To the side, I could see Bastille doing the same with the prince and Folsom. Sing himself rolled over to my hiding place, then got to his knees, looking nervous.

'What are you all *doing*?' Himalaya asked.

I put a finger to my lips, waiting tensely. Sing's Talent, like all of them, couldn't be trusted implicitly – however, he had a good track record of tripping right before dangerous events. His foresight – or, well, his clumsiness – had saved my life back in the Hushlands.

I almost thought that this one was a false alarm. And then I heard it. Voices.

The door to the room opened, and my mother walked in.

Oh, wait. You're still here? I thought that last line was going to end the chapter. It seemed like a nice, dramatic place.

Chapter isn't long enough yet? Really? Hum. Well, guess we'll move on, then. Ahem.

I stared in shock. That really was my mother, Shasta Smedry. She'd ditched the wig she'd been wearing at the party and wore her usual blond hair up in a bun, along with standard-issue horn-rimmed glasses. Her face was so hard. Emotionless. Even more so than what I'd seen from other Librarians.

My heart twisted. Other than the faint glimpses of her I'd caught earlier in the day, this was the first time I'd seen her since the library in my hometown. The first time I'd seen her since … learning that she was my mother.

Shasta was accompanied by a dangerously large group of Librarian thugs – oversized, muscle-bound types that wore bow ties and glasses. (Kind of like a genetic mutant created by mixing nerd DNA with linebacker DNA. I'll bet they spend their free time giving themselves wedgies, then stuffing themselves in lockers.)

Also with her was a young, freckled man about twenty years old. He wore a sweater-vest and slacks (Librarian-type clothing) and had on glasses. Tinted ones.

A *Dark Oculator* I thought. *So I was right.* He would be there to use the Translator's Lenses for her but this guy didn't seem *nearly* as dangerous as Blackburn had been. Of course, my mother more than made up for the difference.

But how had they gotten by the soldiers on the stairs? It looked like Sing had been right, and they'd been tunneling into the stairwell. Shouldn't we have heard sounds of fighting? What of the two knights on duty? I itched to rush out and see what had happened.

The group of Librarians stopped at the front of the room. I remained hidden behind my wall of books. Bastille had successfully pulled the prince and Folsom behind another wall of books, and I could just barely see her peeking around the corner. She and I met each other's eyes, and I could see the questions in her face.

Something very odd was going on. Why hadn't we heard any sounds of fighting from the stairwell?

'Something very odd is going on here,' my mother said, her voice echoing in the quiet room. 'Why are all of these books stacked like this?'

The freckled Oculator adjusted his spectacles. Fortunately, they weren't red-tinted Oculator's Lenses – which would have let him notice me – but were instead tinted with orange-and-blue stripes. I didn't recognize that type.

'The scholars I interviewed said the place was messy, Shasta,' he said in a kind of nasal voice, 'but who knows what they consider clean or messy? These stacks look like they were arranged and organized by a buffoon!'

Himalaya huffed in outrage, and Sing had to grab her by the arm to keep her from marching out to defend her cataloging abilities.

'All right,' Shasta said. 'I don't know how long it will be before someone notices what we've done. I want to find that book and get out of here as soon as possible.'

I frowned. That made it seem like they had gotten into the room by stealth. It was a good plan; if a book disappeared from the Royal-Archives-Not-a-Library™, then it would probably be centuries before anyone realized it was gone. If they even realized it at all.

But that meant my mother and a group of about thirty Librarians had managed to *sneak* past the archives' defenses. That seemed impossible.

Either way, we were in trouble. I didn't have any offensive Lenses, and Bastille's severing had her on the brink of collapse. That left us with Folsom. I'd just seen him do some serious damage, but I hated trusting a Smedry Talent as unpredictable as his.

It seemed a far, far better idea to get out and grab our army, then come back for a fight. I liked that idea a whole lot, particularly since we'd probably be able to send to the palace for Grandpa Smedry. (And maybe the Free Kingdomer version of a Sherman tank or two.)

But how to get out? The Librarians were beginning to move through the stacks. We were near the middle of the room, our position shadowed by a lack of lamplight, but we obviously couldn't remain hidden for long.

'All right,' I whispered to Sing and Himalaya, 'we need to get out of here! Any ideas?'

'Maybe we could sneak around the outside of the room,' Himalaya said, pointing at the mazelike corridors.

I didn't like the idea of risking running into one of those thugs. I shook my head.

'We could hide in the back,' Sing whispered. 'Hope they get frustrated and leave ...'

'Sing, this is a whole *group* of Librarians,' I said. 'They'll all be able to do what Himalaya did. They'll sort through this room in minutes!'

Himalaya snorted quietly. 'I doubt it,' she said. 'I was one of the Wardens of the Standard – the best sorters in all the world. Most of those are just basic acolytes. They'll barely be able to alphabetize, let alone sort based on the Sticky Hamstring methodology.'

'Either way,' I whispered, 'I doubt they're going to leave without *this*.' I glanced down at the volume I still carried, then looked across the central aisle to Bastille. She looked tense, poised. She was getting ready to fight – which tended to be her solution to a lot of things.

Great, I thought. *This is not going to end well.*

'If only my sister were here,' Sing said. 'She could make herself look like one of those thugs and slip away.'

I froze. Sing's sister, Australia, would be back with the Mokian contingent trying to lobby the Council of Kings to make the right decision. She had the Talent to go to sleep, then wake up looking really ugly. That usually meant looking like someone else for a short time. We didn't have her but we did have the Disguiser's Lenses. I hurriedly pulled them out. They could get me out – but what about the others?

I looked across the corridor. Bastille met my eyes, then saw the Lenses in my hands. I could tell she recognized them. She met my eyes, then nodded.

Go, the look said. *Take that book to safety. Don't worry about us.*

If you've read through my series this far, then you know that at that age I considered myself too noble to abandon my friends. I was starting to change, however. My nibble of fame – one I still secretly longed to taste again – had begun to work inside me.

I put on the Lenses and focused, imagining the image of a Librarian thug. Himalaya gasped quietly as I changed, and Sing raised an eyebrow. I glanced at them.

'Be ready to run,' I said. I looked at Bastille and held up one finger to indicate that she should wait. Then I pointed at the door. She seemed to get my meaning.

I took a deep breath, then stepped out. The center of the room was poorly lit, since we'd obscured a lot of the lamps with book walls. Those lamps were hung back in their places on the walls, even the one I'd tried to use to burn the place down.

I walked forward, holding my breath, expecting the Librarians to raise an alarm against me, but they were too busy searching. Nobody even turned. I walked right up to my mother. She glanced at me, the woman I'd always known as Ms. Fletcher the woman who had spent years berating me as a child.

'Well, what is it?' she snapped, and I realized I'd just been standing there, staring.

I held up the book, the one she was searching for. Her eyes opened wide with anticipation.

And so, I handed the book to her.

Is this a good place? Can I stop here now? Okay, finally. About time.

18

I'd like to apologize. Way back in my first book of this series, near the end, I made fun of the fact that readers sometimes stay up *way* too late reading books. I know how it is. You get involved in a story and you don't want to stop. Then the author does very unfair things, like confront his mother face-to-face at the end of the chapter, forcing you to turn to the next page and read what happens next.

This sort of thing is terribly unfair, and I shouldn't be engaging in such activities. After all, there is one thing that every good book should have in it: That, of course, is a potty break.

Sure, we characters can go between chapters, but what about you? You have to wait until there's a portion of the book that is slow and boring. And since those don't *exist* in my books, I force you to wait until the story is done. That's just not fair. And so, get ready, here's your chance. It's time for the slow, boring part.

The furry panda is a noble creature, known for its excellent chess-playing skills. Pandas often play chess in exchange for lederhosen, which make up a large chunk of their preferred diet. They also make a fortune off their licensing deals, in which they shrink and stuff members of their clan and sell them as plush toys for young children. It is often theorized that one day all of these plush pandas will decide to rise up and rule the world. And that will be fun, because pandas rock.

Okay, done doing your business? Great. Now maybe we can finally get on with this story. (It's really annoying to have to wait for you like that, so you should thank me for my patience.)

My mother took the book from me and waved eagerly to the freckled Dark Oculator. 'Fitzroy, get over here.'

'Yes, yes, Shasta,' he said a little too eagerly. He regarded her adoringly. 'What is it?'

'Read this,' she said, handing him the book and the Translator's Lenses.

The young man grabbed the book and the Lenses; it disgusted me how eager he was to please my mother. I inched away, raising my hand toward the nearby wall.

'Hum, yes ...' Fitzroy said. 'Shasta, this is it! The very book we wanted!'

'Excellent,' my mother said, reaching for the book.

At that moment, I touched the glass wall and released a powerful blast of breaking power into it. Now, I knew I couldn't break the glass – I was counting on that. In previous circumstances, I'd been able to use things like walls, tables, even smoke trails as a conduit. Like a wire carried electricity, an object could carry my breaking power within it, shattering something on the other end.

It was a risk, but I wasn't going to leave my allies alone in a room full of Librarians. Particularly not when one of those allies was the official Alcatraz Smedry novelist. I had my legacy to think about.

Fortunately, it worked. The breaking power moved through the wall like ripples on a lake. The lamps on the walls shattered.

And everything plunged into darkness.

I leaped forward and snatched the book, which was being passed between Shasta and Fitzroy. Voices called out in shock and surprise, and I distinctly heard my mother curse. I rushed for the doorway, bursting out into the lit hallway beyond and quickly taking off my Disguiser's lenses.

There was a sudden crash from inside the room. Then a face appeared from the darkness. It was a Librarian thug. I cringed, preparing for a fight, but the man suddenly grimaced in pain and fell to the ground. Bastille jumped over him as he groaned and grabbed his leg; her brother, the prince, ran along behind her.

I ushered Rikers through the door, relieved that Bastille had understood my hand gestures. (Though I used the universal signal for 'Wait here for a sec, then run for the door,' that signal also happens to be the universal hand sign for 'I need a milk shake; I think I'll find one in that direction.')

'Where's Folsom—' I began, but the critic soon appeared, carrying Rikers's novel in his hand, prepared to open the cover and start dancing at a moment's notice. He puffed, coming through the door as Bastille knocked aside another thug who was clever enough to make for the light. Only a few seconds had passed, but I began to worry. Where were Sing and Himalaya?

'I give this escape a three and a half out of seven and six-eighths, Alcatraz,' Folsom said nervously. 'Clever in concept, but rather nerve-wracking in execution.'

'Noted,' I said tensely, glancing about. Where *were* those soldiers of ours? They were supposed to be out in the stairwell here, but it was empty. In fact, something seemed odd about the stairwell.

'Guys?' Rikers said. 'I think—'

'There!' Bastille said, pointing as Sing and Himalaya appeared from the shadows of the room. The two rushed through the door, and I slammed it closed, using my breaking power to jam the lock. 'What was that crash?' I asked.

'I tripped into a couple rows of books,' Sing said, 'throwing them down on the Librarians to keep them distracted.'

'Smart,' I said. 'Let's get out of here.'

We began to rush up the stairwell, the wooden steps creaking beneath our feet. 'That was risky, Smedry,' Bastille said.

'You expected less of me?'

'Of course not,' she snapped. 'But why hand the book over to the Librarian?'

'I got it back,' I said, holding it up. 'Plus, now we know for sure that *this* is the volume they wanted.'

Bastille cocked her head. 'Huh. You *are* clever sometimes.'

I smiled. Unfortunately, the truth is, *none* of us was being very clever at that moment. None of us but Rikers, of course – and we'd chosen to ignore him. That's usually a safe move.

Except, of course, when you're rushing up the wrong stairwell. It finally dawned on me, and I froze in place, causing the others to stumble to a halt.

'What is it, Alcatraz?' Sing asked.

'The stairs,' I said. 'They're wooden.'

'So?'

'They were stone before.'

'That's what I've been trying to say!' Prince Rikers exclaimed. 'I wonder how they turned the steps to a different material.'

I suddenly felt a sense of horror. The door was just above us. I walked up nervously and pushed on it.

It opened into a medieval-looking castle chamber completely different from the one that had held our soldiers. This room had red carpeting, library stacks in the distance, and was filled with a good *two hundred* Librarian soldiers.

'Shattering Glass!' Bastille cursed, slamming the door in front of me. 'What's going on?'

I ignored her for the moment, rushing back down the steps. The Librarians locked inside the archives room were pounding on the door, trying to break it down. Now that I paused to consider, the landing right in front of the door looked very different from the way it had before. It was far larger, and it had a door at the left side.

As the others piled down the steps after me, I threw open the door to my left. I stepped into an enormous chamber filled with wires, panes of glass, and scientists in white lab coats. There were large containers on the sides of the room. Containers that I'm sure were filled with brightsand.

'What in the *Sands* is going on?' Folsom demanded, peeking in behind me.

I stood, stunned. 'We're not in the same building anymore, Folsom.'

'What?'

'They swapped us! The archive filled with books – the *entire glass room* – they swapped it for another room using Transporter's Glass! They weren't digging a tunnel to get in, they were digging to the corners so they could affix glass there and teleport the room away!'

It was brilliant. The glass was unbreakable, the stairwell

guarded. But what if you could take the whole room away and replace it with another one? You could search out the book you needed, then swap the rooms back, and nobody would be the wiser.

The door behind us broke open, and I turned to see a group of muscular Librarians force their way into the stairwell. I could just barely make out Bastille tensing for combat, and Folsom moved to open the novel with the music.

'No,' I said to them. 'We're beaten. Don't waste your energy fighting.'

Part of me found it strange that they listened to me. Even Bastille obeyed my command. I would have expected the prince to preempt me and take charge, but he seemed perfectly content to stand and watch. He even seemed excited.

'Wonderful!' he whispered to me. 'We've been captured!'

Great, I thought as my mother pushed her way out through the broken door. She saw me and smiled – a rare expression for her. It was the smile of a cat who'd just found a mouse to play with.

'Alcatraz,' she said.

'Mother,' I replied coldly.

She raised an eyebrow. 'Tie them up,' she said to her thugs. 'And fetch that book for me.'

The thugs pulled out swords and herded us into the room with the scientists.

'Why'd you stop me?' Bastille hissed.

'Because it wouldn't have done any good,' I whispered back. 'We don't even know where we are – we could be back in the Hushlands, for all we know. We have to get back to the Royal Archives.'

I waited for it, but nobody said the inevitable 'not a library.' I realized that nobody else could hear us – which, indeed, is kind of the point of whispering in the first place. (That, and sounding more mysterious.)

'How do we get back, then?' Bastille asked.

I glanced at the equipment around us. We had to activate the silimatic machines and swap the rooms again. But how?

Before I could ask Bastille about this, the thugs pulled us all apart and bound us with ropes. This wasn't too big a deal – my Talent could snap ropes in a heartbeat, and if the thugs assumed that we were tied up, then maybe they'd get lax and give us a better chance for escaping.

The Librarians began to rifle through our pockets, depositing our possessions – including all of my Lenses – on a low table. Then they forced us to the ground, which was sterile and white. The room itself bustled with activity as Librarians and scientists checked monitors, wires, and panes of glass.

My mother flipped through the book on Smedry history, though – of course – she couldn't read it. Her lackey, Fitzroy, was more interested in my Lenses. 'The other pair of Translator's Lenses,' he said, picking them up. 'These will be very nice to have.'

He slid them into his pocket, continuing on to the others. 'Oculator's Lenses,' he said, 'boring.' He set those aside. 'A single, untinted Lens,' he said, looking over the Truthfinder's Lens. 'It's probably worthless.' He handed the Lens to a scientist, who snapped it into a spectacle frame.

'Ah!' Fitzroy continued. 'Are those Disguiser's Lenses? Now *these* are valuable!'

The scientist returned the spectacles with the single Truthfinder's Lens in them, but Fitzroy set this aside, picking up the violet Disguiser's Lenses and putting them on. He immediately shifted shapes, melding to look like a much more muscular and handsome version of himself. 'Hum, very nice,' he said, inspecting his arms.

Why didn't I think of that? I thought.

'Oh, I almost forgot,' Shasta said, pulling something out of her purse. She tossed a few glass rings to her Librarian thugs. 'Put those on that one, that one, and that one.' She pointed at me, Folsom, and Sing.

The three Smedrys. That seemed ominous. Perhaps it was time to try an escape. But … we were surrounded and we still didn't know how to use the machines to get us back. Before I could make up my mind, one of the thugs snapped a ring on my arm and locked it.

I didn't feel any different.

'What you aren't feeling,' my mother said offhandedly, 'is the loss of your Talent. That's Inhibitor's Glass.'

'Inhibitor's Glass is a myth!' Sing said, aghast.

'Not according to the Incarna people,' my mother said, smiling. 'You'd be amazed what we're learning from these Forgotten Language books.' She snapped the book in her hands closed. I could see a smug satisfaction in her smile as she pulled open a drawer beneath the table and dropped the book in it. She closed the drawer, then – oddly – she picked up one of the rings of Inhibitor's Glass and snapped it onto her own arm.

'Handy things, these rings,' she said. 'Smedry Talents are far more useful when you can determine exactly when they are to activate.' My mother had my father's same Talent – losing things – which she'd gained by marriage. My grandfather said he thought she'd never learned to control it, so I could guess why she'd want to wear Inhibitor's Glass.

'You people,' Sing said, struggling as the thugs snapped a ring on his arm. 'All you want to do is control. You want everything to be normal and boring, no freedom or uncertainty.'

'I couldn't have said it better myself,' my mother said, putting her hands behind her back.

This was getting bad. I cursed myself. I should have let Bastille fight, then tried to find a way to activate the swap during the confusion. Without our Talents, we were in serious trouble. I tested my Talent anyway, but got nothing. It was a very odd feeling. Like trying to start your car, but only getting a pitiful grinding sound.

I wiggled my arm, trying to see if I could get the ring of Inhibitor's Glass off, but it was on tight. I ground my teeth. Maybe I could use the Lenses on the table somehow.

Unfortunately, the only Lenses left were my basic Oculator's Lenses and the single Truthfinder's Lens. *Great*, I thought, wishing – not for the first time – that Grandpa Smedry had given me some Lenses that I could use in a fight.

Still, I had to work with what I had. I stretched my neck, wiggling to the side, and finally managed to touch the side of the Truthfinder's spectacles with my cheek. I could activate them as long as I was touching the frames.

'You are a monster,' Sing said, still talking to my mother.

'A monster?' Shasta asked. 'Because I like order? I think you'll agree with our way, once you see what we can do for the Free Kingdoms. Aren't you Sing Sing Smedry the anthropologist? I hear that you're fascinated by the Hushlands. Why speak such harsh words about Librarians if you are so fascinated by our lands?'

Sing fell silent.

'Yes,' Shasta said. 'Everything will be better when the Librarians rule.'

I froze. I could just barely see her through the side of the Lens by my head on the table. And those words she'd just spoken – they weren't completely true. When she'd said them, to my eyes she'd released a patch of air that was muddied and gray. It was as if my mother herself weren't sure that she was telling the truth.

'Lady Fletcher,' one of the Librarian thugs said, approaching. 'I have informed my superiors of our captives.'

Shasta frowned. 'I . . . see.'

'You will, of course, deliver them to us,' the Librarian soldier said. 'I believe that is Prince Rikers Dartmoor – he could prove to be a very valuable captive.'

'These are *my* captives, Captain.' Shasta said. 'I'll decide what to do with them.'

'Oh? This equipment and these scientists belong to the Scrivener's Bones. All you were promised was the book. You said we could have anything else in the room we wanted. Well, these people are what we demand.'

Scrivener's Bones, I thought. *That explains all the wires*. The Scrivener's Bones were the Librarian sect who liked to mix Free Kingdoms technology and Hushlander technology. That was probably why there were wires leading from the brightsand containers. Rather than just opening the containers and bathing the glass in light, the Librarians used wires and switches.

That could be a big help. It meant there might be a way to use the machinery to activate the swap.

'We are very insistent,' the leader of the Librarian soldiers said. 'You can have the book and the Lenses. We will take the captives.'

'Very well,' my mother snapped. 'You can have them. But I want half of my payment back as compensation.'

I felt a stab inside my chest. So she *would* sell me. As if I were nothing.

'But, Shasta,' the young Librarian Oculator said, stepping up to her. 'You'll give them up? Even the boy?'

'He means nothing to me.'

I froze.

It was a lie.

I could see it plain and clear through the corner of the Lens. When she spoke the words, black sludge fell from her lips.

'Shasta Smedry,' the soldier said, smiling. 'The woman who would marry just to get a Talent, and who would spawn a child just to sell him to the highest bidder!'

'Why should I feel anything for the son of a Nalhallan? Take the boy. I don't care.'

Another lie.

'Let's just get on with this,' she finished. Her manner was so controlled, so calm. You'd never have known that she was lying through her teeth.

But ... what did it *mean*? She couldn't care for me. She was a terrible, vile person. Monsters like her didn't have feelings.

She *couldn't* care about me. I didn't want her to. It was so much more simple to assume that she was heartless.

'What about Father?' I found myself whispering. 'Do you hate him too?'

She turned toward me, meeting my eyes. She parted her lips to speak, and I thought I caught a trail of black smoke begin to slip out and pour toward the ground.

Then it stopped. 'What's he doing?' she snapped, pointing. 'Fitzroy, I thought I told you to keep those Lenses secured!'

The Oculator jumped in shock, rushing over and grabbing the

Truthfinder's Lens and pocketing it. 'Sorry,' he said. He took the other Lenses and placed them in another pocket of his coat.

I leaned back, feeling frustrated. What now?

I was the brave and brilliant Alcatraz Smedry. Books had been written about me. Rikers was smiling, as if this were all a big adventure. And I could guess why. He didn't feel threatened. He had me to save him.

It was then that I understood what Grandpa Smedry had been trying to tell me. Fame itself wasn't a bad thing. Praise wasn't a bad thing. The danger was assuming that you really *were* what everyone imagined you to be.

I'd come into this all presuming that my Talent could get us out. Well, now it *couldn't*. I'd brought us into danger because I'd let my self-confidence make me overconfident.

And you all are to blame for this, in part. This is what your adoration does. You create for yourselves heroes using our names, but those fabrications are so incredible, so elevated that the real thing can never live up to them. You destroy us, consume us.

And I am what's left over when you're done.

19

O h, wasn't that how you expected me to end that last chapter? Was it kind of a downer? Made you feel bad about yourself? Well, good.

We're getting near the end, and I'm tired of putting on a show for you. I've tried to prove that I'm arrogant and selfish, but I just don't think you're buying it. So, maybe if I make the book a depressing pile of slop, you'll leave me alone.

'Alcatraz?' Bastille whispered.

I mean, why is it that you readers always assume that you're never to blame for anything? You just sit there, comfortable on your couch while we suffer. You can *enjoy* our pain and our misery because *you're* safe.

Well, this is real to me. It's real. It still affects me. Ruins me.

'Alcatraz?' Bastille repeated.

I am not a god. I am not a hero. I can't be what you want me to be. I can't save people, or protect them, because I can't even save myself!

I am a murderer. Do you understand? *I KILLED HIM*.

'Alcatraz!' Bastille hissed.

I looked up from my bonds. A good half hour had passed. We were still captive, and I'd tried dozens of times to summon my Talent. It was unresponsive. Like a sleeping beast that refused to awaken. I was powerless.

My mother chatted with the other Librarians, who had sent in teams to rifle through the books and determine if there was anything else of value inside the archives. From what I'd heard when I cared enough to pay attention, they were planning on swapping the rooms back soon.

Sing had tried to crawl away at one point. He had earned

himself a boot to the face – he was already beginning to get a black eye. Himalaya sniffled quietly, leaning against Folsom. Prince Rikers continued to sit happily, as if this were all a big exciting amusement-park ride.

'We need to escape,' Bastille said. 'We need to get out. The treaty will be ratified in a matter of minutes!'

'I've failed, Bastille,' I whispered. 'I can't get us out.'

'Alcatraz …' she said. She sounded so exhausted. I glanced at her and saw the haunted fatigue from before, but it seemed even worse.

'I can barely keep myself awake,' she whispered. 'This hole inside … it seems to be chewing on my mind, sucking out everything I think and feel. I can't do this without you. You've *got* to lead us. I love my brother but he's useless.'

'That's the problem,' I said, leaning back. 'I am too.'

The Librarians were approaching. I stiffened, but they didn't come for me. Instead, they grabbed Himalaya.

She cried out, struggling.

'Let go of her!' Folsom bellowed. 'What are you doing?'

He tried to jump after them, but his hands and legs were tied, and all he managed to do was lurch forward onto his face. The Librarian thugs smiled, shoving him to the side, where he caused the table beside us to topple over. It scattered our possessions – some keys, a couple of coin pouches, one book – to the floor.

The book was the volume of *Alcatraz Smedry and the Mechanic's Wrench* that Folsom had been carrying earlier and it fell open to the front page. My theme music began to play, and I tensed, hoping for Folsom to attack.

But, of course, he didn't. He wore the Inhibitor's Glass on his arm. The little melody continued to sound; it was supposed to be brave and triumphant, but now it seemed a cruel parody.

My theme music played while I failed.

'What are you doing to her?' Folsom repeated, struggling uselessly as a Librarian stood with his boot on Folsom's back.

The young Oculator Fitzroy approached; he still wore my Disguiser's Lenses, which gave him an illusionary body that made him look handsome and strong. 'We've had a request,' he said. 'From She Who Cannot Be Named.'

'You're in contact with *her*?' Sing demanded.

'Of course we are,' Fitzroy said. 'We Librarian sects get along far better than you all would like to think. Now, Ms. Snorgan ... Sorgavag ... She Who Cannot Be Named was *not* pleased to discover that Shasta's team had planned to steal the Royal Archives – *definitely* a library – on the very day of the treaty ratification. However, when she heard about a very special captive we'd obtained, she was a little more forgiving.'

'You shall never get away with this, foul monster!' Prince Rikers suddenly exclaimed. 'You may hurt me, but you shall never wound me!'

We all stared at him.

'How was that?' he asked me. 'I think it was a good line. Maybe I should do it over. You know, get more baritone into it. When the villain talks about me, I should respond, right?'

'I wasn't talking about you,' Fitzroy said, shaking Himalaya. 'I'm talking about She Who Cannot Be Named's former assistant. I think it's time to show you all what happens when someone betrays the Librarians.'

I had sudden flashbacks to being tortured by Blackburn. The Dark Oculators seemed to delight in pain and suffering.

It didn't seem that Fitzroy was even going to bother with the torture part. The thugs held Himalaya back, and Fitzroy produced a knife. He held it to her neck. Sing began to cry out, requiring several guards to hold him down. Folsom was bellowing in rage. Librarian scientists just continued monitoring their equipment in the background.

This is what it came down to. Me, too weak to help. I was nothing without my Talent or my Lenses.

'Alcatraz,' Bastille whispered. Somehow I heard her over all the other noise. 'I believe in you.'

It was virtually the same thing others had been telling me since I'd arrived in Nalhalla. But those things had all been lies. They hadn't known me.

But Bastille did. And she believed in me.

From her, that *meant* something.

I turned with desperation, looking at Himalaya, who was held captive, weeping. Fitzroy seemed to be enjoying the pain he was causing the rest of us by holding that knife to her throat. I knew, at that moment, that he really intended to kill her. He would murder her in front of the man who loved her.

Who *loved* her.

My Lenses were gone. My Talent was gone. I only had one thing left.

I was a Smedry.

'Folsom!' I screamed. 'Do you love her?'

'What?' he asked.

'Do you love Himalaya?'

'Of course I do! Please, don't let him kill her!'

'Himalaya,' I demanded, 'do you love him?'

She nodded as the knife began to cut. It was enough.

'Then I pronounce you married,' I said.

Everyone froze for a moment. A short distance away, my mother turned and looked at us, suddenly alarmed. Fitzroy raised an eyebrow, his knife slightly bloodied. My theme music played faintly from the little book on the floor.

'Well, that's touching,' Fitzroy said. 'Now you can die as a married woman! I—'

At that moment, Himalaya's fist took him in the face.

The ropes that bound her fell to the ground, snapped and broken, as she leaped into the air and kicked the two thugs beside her. The men went down, unconscious, and Himalaya spun like a dancer toward the group standing behind. She cleared them all with a sweeping kick, delivered precisely, despite the fact that she seemed to have no idea what she was doing.

Her face was determined, her eyes wide with rage; a little trickle of blood ran down her throat. She twisted and spun, fighting with a beautiful, uncoordinated rage, fully under the control of her brand-new Talent.

She was now Himalaya Smedry. And, as everyone knows (and

I believe I've pointed out to you), when you marry a Smedry, you get their Talent.

I rolled to where Fitzroy had fallen. More important, where his knife had fallen. I kicked it across the floor to Bastille, who – being Bastille – caught it even though her hands (literally) were tied behind her back. In a second, she'd cut herself free. In another second, both Sing and I were free.

Fitzroy sat up, holding his cheek, dazed. I grabbed the Disguiser's Lenses off his face, and he immediately shrank back to being spindly and freckled. 'Sing, grab him and make for the archives room!'

The hefty Mokian didn't need to hear that again. He easily tucked the squirming Fitzroy under his arm while Bastille attacked the thugs who were holding Folsom down, defeating them both. But then she wavered nauseously.

'Get to the room, everyone!' I yelled as Himalaya kept the thugs at bay. Bastille nodded, wobbling as she helped the prince to his feet. Shasta watched from the side, yelling for the thugs to attack – but they were wary of engaging a Smedry Talent.

After struggling for a second to get that band of glass off my arm – it wouldn't budge – I pulled open the drawer of the table and snatched the book my mother had stowed there.

That left us with one major problem. We were right back where we'd been when I'd made us surrender. Retreating into the archives room wouldn't help if we remained surrounded by Librarians. We had to activate the swap. Unfortunately, there was no *way* I'd be able to reach those terminals. I figured I only had one chance.

Folsom rushed past, grabbing the still-playing music book off the ground and snapping it closed so Himalaya could come out of her super-kung-fu-Librarian-chick trance. She froze midkick, looking dazed. She had dropped all the thugs around her. Folsom grabbed her by the shoulder and spun her into a kiss. Then he pulled her after the others.

That only left me. I looked across the room at my mother, who met my eyes. She seemed rather self-confident, considering what had happened, and I figured that *she* figured that I couldn't escape. Go figure.

I grabbed the pile of electrical cords off the ground and – pulling as hard as I could – yanked them out of their sockets in the machinery. Then I raced after my friends.

Bastille waited at the door that led into the archives room. 'What's that?' she said, pointing at the cords.

'Our only chance,' I replied, ducking into the room. She followed, then slammed the door – or, at least, what was left of it. It was pitch dark inside. I'd broken the lamps.

I heard the breathing of my little group, shallow, worried.

'What now?' Sing whispered.

I held the cords in my hands. I touched the tips with my fingers, then closed my eyes. This was a big gamble. Sure, I'd been able to make the music box work, but this was something completely different.

I didn't have time to doubt myself. The Librarians would be upon us in a few moments. I held those cords, held my breath, and activated them like I would a pair of Oculator's Lenses.

Immediately, something drained from me. My strength was sapped away, and I felt a shock of exhaustion – as if my body had decided to run a marathon when I wasn't looking. I dropped the cords, wobbling, and reached out to steady myself against Sing.

'You're all dead, you know,' Fitzroy sputtered in the darkness; he was still held – I assumed – under Sing's arm. 'They'll burst in here in a second and then you're dead. What did you think? You're trapped! Sandless idiots!'

I took a deep breath, righting myself. Then I pushed the door open.

The blond Knight of Crystallia standing guard was still outside. 'You all right?' she asked, peeking in. 'What happened?' Behind her, I could see the stone stairwell of the Royal Archives, still packed with soldiers.

'We're back!' Sing said. 'How ... ?'

'You powered the glass,' Bastille said, looking at me. 'Like you did with Rikers's silimatic music box. You initiated a swap!'

I nodded. At my feet, the cords to the Librarian machinery lay cut at the ends. Our swap had severed them where they'd poked through the door.

'Shattering Glass, Smedry!' Bastille said. 'How in the name of the first Sands did you do that?'

'I don't know,' I said, rushing out the doorway. 'We can worry about it later. Right now, we've got to save Mokia.'

20

Questions.

We're at the end, and you probably have a few of them. If you've been paying attention closely, you probably have more than just 'a few'.

You should probably have more than you do.

I've tried to be honest, as honest as I can be. I haven't lied about anything important.

But some of the people in the story ... well, they're lying for certain.

No matter how much you think you know, there is always more to learn. It all has to do with Librarians, knights, and, of course, fish sticks. Enjoy this next part. I'll see you in the Epilogue.

'Aha!' I said, pulling not one but *two* pairs of Translator's Lenses from Fitzroy's jacket. The Dark Oculator himself lay tied up on the floor as we rode in the prince's giant glass pig. I'd told my soldiers to get some sort of equipment and dig to the corner of the archives room and remove the glass there, so that the Librarians couldn't swap the room back and steal any of the other books.

'I still don't understand what happened,' Sing said, sitting nervously as our vehicle plodded toward the palace.

'Oculators can power glass,' I said. 'Like Lenses.'

'Lenses are magic,' Sing said. 'That Transporter's Glass was technology.'

'The two are more similar than you think, Sing. In fact, I think *all* of these powers are connected. Do you remember what you said when you and I were hiding down there a few moments ago? The thing about your sister?'

'Sure,' Sing said. 'I mentioned that I wished she'd been there, because she could have imitated one of the Librarians.'

'Which I could do with these,' I said, holding up the pair of Disguiser's Lenses, which we'd retrieved from Fitzroy. 'Sing, these work *just* like Australia's Talent does. If she falls asleep thinking about somebody, she wakes up looking just like them. Well, if I wear these and concentrate, I can do the same thing.'

'What are you saying, Alcatraz?' Folsom asked.

'I'm not sure,' I admitted. 'It just seems suspicious to me. I mean, look at your Talent. It makes you a better warrior when you hear music, right?'

He nodded.

'Well, what do Bastille's Warrior's Lenses do?' I said. 'They make her a better fighter. My uncle Kaz's Talent lets him transport people across great distances, which sounds an awful lot like what that Transporter's Glass did.'

'Yes,' Sing said. 'But what about your grandfather's Talent? It lets him arrive late to things, and there aren't Lenses that do *that*.'

'There are lots of types of glass we don't know about,' I said. I picked up one of the rings of Inhibitor's Glass, which we'd managed to get off our arms using a set of keys in Fitzroy's pocket. 'You thought these were mythical.'

Sing fell silent, and I turned, watching through the translucent walls as we approached the palace. 'I think this is all related,' I said more softly. 'The Smedry Talents, silimatic technology, Oculators ... and whatever it is my mother is trying to accomplish. It's all connected.'

She didn't believe what she said about the Librarians ruling every-thing. She wasn't certain.

She has different goals from the other Librarians. But what are they?

I sighed, shaking my head, reaching over to pick up the book we'd brought from the archives. At least we had it, as well as both pairs of Translator's Lenses. I slipped the Lenses on, then glanced at the first page.

Soups for everyone, it read. *A guide to the best Greek and Incarna cooking.*

I froze. I flipped through the book anxiously, then took off the Lenses and tried the other pair. Both showed the same thing.

This wasn't the same book.

'What?' Sing asked. 'Alcatraz, what is it?'

'She switched books on us!' I said, frustrated. 'This isn't the book on Incarna history – it's the cookbook!' I'd seen her work with deft fingers before, when she'd snatched the Sands of Rashid right out from under my nose back in my room in the Hushlands. Plus, she had access to my father's Talent of losing things. It might be of help in hiding stuff.

I slammed the book back down on the table. Around me, the rich, red-furnished room shook as the glass pig continued on its way.

'That's not important right now,' Bastille said in an exhausted voice. She sat on the couch beside Folsom and Himalaya, and she looked like she'd gotten even worse since we'd left the Librarians. Her eyes were unfocused, as if she'd been drugged, and she kept rubbing her temples.

'We need to stop the treaty first,' she said. 'Your mother can't do anything with that book as long as *you* have both pairs of Translator's Lenses.'

She was right. Mokia had to be our focus now. As the pig pulled up to the palace, I took a deep breath. 'All right,' I said. 'You all know what to do?'

Sing, Folsom, Himalaya, and Prince Rikers each nodded. We'd discussed our plan during the chapter break. (Neener, neener.)

'The Librarians aren't likely to let this go smoothly,' I said, 'but I doubt there will be much they can do with all of the soldiers and knights guarding the palace. However, they're Librarians, so be ready for anything.'

They nodded again. We prepared to go, and the door on the pig's butt opened. (I think that undermined our dramatic exit.) Bastille stood to go with us, wobbling on unsteady feet.

'Uh, Bastille,' I said. 'I think you should wait here.'

She gave me a stiff glance – the kind that made me feel like I'd just been smacked across the face with a broom. I took that as her answer.

'All right,' I said with a sigh. 'Let's go, then.'

We marched out of the pig and up the steps. Prince Rikers called for guards immediately – I think he just liked the drama of having a full troop of soldiers with us. Indeed, our entrance into the hallway with the wall-hanging panes of glass was rather intimidating.

The Knights of Crystallia standing at attention in the hallway saluted us as we passed, and I felt significantly more safe, knowing they were there.

'Do you think your mother will have warned the others of what happened?' Sing whispered.

'I doubt it,' I said. 'Mother's allies contacted She Who Cannot Be Named to gloat over having captured some valuable prisoners. You don't call to gloat over having lost those same prisoners. I think we'll surprise them.'

'I hope so,' Sing said as we approached the doors to the council room. We nodded to the pair of knights, and then I stepped aside.

'Time for your big entrance, your Highness,' I said, gesturing for Prince Rikers.

'Really?' he said. 'I get to do it?'

'Go ahead,' I said.

The prince dusted himself off. He smiled broadly, then strode through the doors into the chamber and bellowed in a loud voice, 'In the name of all that is just, I demand these proceedings to be halted!'

Down below, the monarchs sat around their table, a large document set out before them. King Dartmoor held a quill in his hand, poised to sign. We'd arrived just in the nick of time. (What the heck is a nick anyway?)

The monarchs' table sat in the open area in the center of the room, between the two raised sets of bleacherlike seats that were filled with patrons. Knights of Crystallia stood in a ring around the bottom of the floor, between the people and the rulers. They were most concentrated, I noticed, near where the Librarians sat.

She Who Cannot Be Named sat at the front of the Librarian group, pleasantly knitting an afghan.

'What is this?' King Dartmoor asked as the rest of my team piled into the room.

'The Librarians are lying to You, Father!' Rikers declared. 'They tried to kidnap me!'

'Why, that's the most distressing thing I've ever heard,' said She Who Cannot Be Named. (You know what? That name is really too hard to type all the time. From here on, I'm going to call her Swcbn.)

My companions looked at me. I wore the Truthfinder's spectacles, one eye closed to look through the single Lens. Unfortunately, Swcbn hadn't said anything that was false – she'd avoided doing so deliberately, I'm sure.

'Father,' Prince Rikers said, 'We can provide proof of what happened!' He waved behind him, and the two knights we'd brought with us entered, carrying the tied and gagged Fitzroy. 'This is a Librarian of the order of the Dark Oculators! He was involved in a plot to steal books from the Royal Archives—'

'Mumf mu mumfmumf,' Fitzroy added.

'—which turned into a plot to kidnap me, the royal heir!' Rikers continued.

Rikers certainly did know how to get into a part. He didn't seem as much a buffoon now that he was in his element of the court.

'Lady Librarian,' King Dartmoor said, turning to Swcbn.

'I'm … not sure what is happening,' she said. Another half-truth that didn't come out as a lie.

'She does, Your Majesty,' I declared, stepping up. 'She ordered the death of Himalaya, who is now a member of the Smedry clan.'

That caused a stir.

'Lady Librarian,' the king said, red-bearded face growing very stern. 'Is what he says true, or is it false?'

'I'm not sure if you should be asking me, dear. It's quite—'

'Answer the question!' the king bellowed. 'Have Librarians been plotting to steal and kidnap from us while these very treaty hearings have been occurring?'

The grandmotherly Librarian looked at me, and I could tell that she knew she was caught. 'I think,' she said, 'that my team and I should be granted a short recess to discuss.'

'No recess!' the king said. 'Either you answer as asked, or I'm tearing this treaty in half this instant.'

The elderly Librarian pursed her lips, then finally set down her knitting. 'I will admit,' she said, 'that some *other* branches of the Librarians have been pursuing their own ends in the city. However, this is one of the main reasons we are signing this treaty – so that you can give *my* sect the authority it needs to stop the other sects from continuing this needless war!'

'And the execution of my beloved?' Folsom demanded.

'In my eyes, young man,' Swcbn said, 'that one is a traitor and a turncoat. How would your own laws treat someone who committed treason?'

The room fell still. Where was my grandfather? His seat at the table was noticeably empty.

'Considering this information,' said King Dartmoor, 'how many of you *now* vote against signing the treaty?'

Five of the twelve monarchs raised their hands.

'And I assume Smedry would still vote against the signing,' Dartmoor said, 'assuming he hadn't stormed out in anger. That leaves six against six. I am the deciding vote.'

'Father,' the prince called. 'What would a hero do?'

The king hesitated. Then, embarrassingly, he looked up at me. He stared me in the eyes. Then he ripped the treaty in two.

'I find it telling,' he declared to Swcbn, 'that you cannot control your own people despite the importance of these talks! I find it disturbing that you would be willing to execute one of your own for joining a kingdom with which you *claim* you want to be friends. And, most of all, I find it disgusting what I nearly did. I want you Librarians out of my kingdom by midnight. These talks are at an end.'

The room exploded with sound. There were quite a number of cheers – many of these coming from the section where the Mokians, Australia included, were sitting. There were some boos, but mostly there was just a lot of excited chatter. Draulin approached from the ranks of knights, laying a hand on the king's shoulder and – in a rare moment of emotion – nodded. She actually thought that ripping up the treaty was a good idea.

Maybe that meant she'd see Bastille's help in this entire mess as validation for restoring her daughter's knighthood. I glanced about for Bastille, but she wasn't to be found. Sing tapped my arm and pointed behind. I could see Bastille in the hallway, sitting in a chair, arms wrapped around herself, shivering. She'd lost her Warrior's Lenses back when we'd been captured, and I could see that her eyes were red and puffy.

My first instinct was to go to her, but something made me hesitate. Swcbn didn't seem particularly disturbed by these events. She'd turned back to her knitting. That bothered me.

'Socrates,' I whispered.

'What's that, Alcatraz?' Sing asked.

'This guy I learned about in school,' I said. 'He was one of those annoying types who always asked questions.'

'Okay …' Sing said.

Something was wrong. I began asking questions that should have bothered me long before this.

Why was the most powerful Librarian in all of the Hushlands here to negotiate a treaty that the monarchs had already decided to sign?

Why wasn't she worried at being surrounded by her enemies, capable of being captured and imprisoned at a moment's notice?

Why did I feel so unsettled, as if we hadn't really won after all?

At that moment, Draulin screamed. She collapsed to the ground, holding her head. Then every Knight of Crystallia in the room dropped to the ground, crying out in pain.

'Hello, everyone!' a voice suddenly cried. I spun to find my grandfather standing behind us. 'I'm back! Did I miss anything important?'

21

At that moment, a lot of things happened at once.

The common people in the crowd began to scream in fear and confusion. A group of Librarian thugs pushed their way down to the floor around Swcbn, who continued to sit and knit.

King Dartmoor unsheathed his sword and turned to face the thugs. Grandpa Smedry and I tried to rush down the stairs to get to the monarchs, but were blocked by the crowds, who were trying to flee.

'Hiccupping Huffs!' Grandpa Smedry cursed.

'Follow me, Lord Smedry!' Sing said, muscling up to the top of the stairs beside us. Then he tripped.

Now, I don't know how *you'd* react if a three-hundred-pound Mokian tripped and began to roll down the stairs toward you, but I safely say that I'd either:

1) Scream like a girl and jump out of the way.
2) Scream like a gerbil and jump out of the way.
3) Scream like a Smedry and jump out of the way.

The people on the steps chose to scream like a bunch of people on some steps, but they *did* get out of the way.

Grandpa Smedry, Folsom, Himalaya, and I charged down the stairs behind the Mokian. Prince Rikers stayed behind, looking confused. 'This part actually looks dangerous,' he called. 'Maybe I should stay here. You know, and guard the exit.'

Whatever, I thought. His father, at least, proved to have a spine. King Dartmoor stood over the body of his fallen wife, facing down the group of Librarian thugs, sword held before him. The other monarchs were in the processes of scattering away.

It looked as if the Librarians would easily cut down the king before we could reach him.

'Hey!' a voice yelled suddenly. I recognized my aunt Patty standing in the audience, pointing. As always, her voice managed to carry over any and every bit of competition. 'I don't mean to be rude,' she bellowed, 'but is that *toilet paper* stuck to your leg?'

The Librarian thug at the front immediately looked down, then blushed, realizing that he did indeed have toilet paper stuck to him. He bent down to pull it off, causing the others to bunch up behind him awkwardly.

That distraction gave us just enough time to cover the distance to the king. Grandpa Smedry whipped out a pair of Lenses. I recognized the green specks in the glass, marking them as Windstormer's Lenses. Sure enough, the Lenses released a blast of air, knocking back the Librarians as they tried to rush the king.

'What happened to the knights?' the king yelled, desperate.

'Librarians must have corrupted the Mindstone, Brig,' Grandpa Smedry said.

That's the problem with having a magic rock that connects the minds of all of your best soldiers. Take down the stone, and you take down your soldiers. Kind of like how taking out one cell phone tower can knock out the texting ability of an entire school's worth of teenage girls.

Grandpa Smedry focused on blasting the Librarians with his Lenses, but they got smart quickly. They spread out, forcing their way around the perimeter of the floor, trying to get at the king. Grandpa Smedry couldn't focus on all the different groups; there were too many.

The room was a chaotic mess. People screaming, Librarians pulling out swords, wind blowing. The monarchs were trying to escape, but the stairs were clogged again. Sing sat dazed from his roll down the stairs. He wouldn't be able to help again anytime soon.

'Alcatraz, get those monarchs out!' Grandpa Smedry said, pointing toward the wall. 'Folsom, if you'd help me ...'

And with that, Grandpa Smedry began to sing.

I stared at him, dumbfounded, until I realized this gave Folsom the music he needed to dance. Both Folsom and Himalaya spun toward the Librarians, knocking down those who had tried to push around the outsides of the room.

I turned and dashed up a section of bleacherlike seats. 'Monarchs, up here!' I said. The seats here were empty, their occupants all trying to crowd out the other door.

Several of the monarchs turned toward me as I reached the far wall. I placed two hands against it and blasted it with breaking power. The entire wall fell away as if it had been shoved by the hand of a giant.

Monarchs rushed up the steps, wearing a variety of costumes and crowns: A man with dark skin in red African-style clothing. The Mokian king in his islander wrap. A king and queen in standard crowns and European robes. I counted them off, but didn't see Bastille's father.

That was, apparently, because he was still down below. I could see that he was trying to pull Draulin to safety – unfortunately, she weighed like a bazillion pounds with all that armor on, not to mention the awkward sword strapped to her back. The king must have come to the same conclusion, as he pulled free her sword and tossed it aside, then began to work off the armor.

I moved to go help, but the crowds had seen my new exit and were swarming around me. I had to fight against them, and it really slowed me down.

'Grandpa!' I yelled, pointing.

Below, my grandfather turned toward the king, then cursed. Folsom and Himalaya were holding off the Librarians pretty well, so Grandpa Smedry rushed over to help the High King. I tried to do likewise, but it was slow going with the crowd in my way. Fortunately, it looked like I wouldn't be needed.

People escaped out of the broken hole in the wall. Folsom and Himalaya handled the Librarians. My grandfather helped the High King pick up Draulin. Everything seemed good.

Swcbn continued to knit quietly.

Questions. They still itched at me.

How exactly, I wondered, *did the Librarians get to the Crystin Mindstone? That thing must be freakishly well guarded.*

Why was Swcbn acting so content? Who *had* blown up the *Hawkwind*? It had to have been someone who would have been able to get Detonator's Glass into Draulin's pack. Hers was the room that had exploded.

I glanced at Himalaya, who fought beside her new husband, knocking down enemy after enemy as my grandfather sang opera. It occurred to me that perhaps we'd overlooked something. And at that moment, I asked the most important question of all.

If there could be such a thing as a good Librarian, might there also be such a thing as an evil Knight of Crystallia? A knight who could get to the Mindstone and corrupt it? A knight who could slip a bomb into Draulin's pack? A knight who had been involved in sending Bastille out to fail?

A knight whom I had personally seen hanging around the Royal Archives within a few hours of the swap?

'Oh, no . . .' I whispered.

At that moment, one of the 'unconscious' knights near Grandpa Smedry began to move. He lifted his head, and I could see a deadly smile on it.

Archedis, otherwise known as Mr. Big Chin, supposedly the most accomplished of all the Knights of Crystallia.

I should have listened more to Socrates.

'Grandfather!' I screamed, trying to fight the crowd and run forward, but they were so frightened that I barely got a few steps before being pushed back again.

Grandpa Smedry turned, still singing, looking up at me and smiling. In a flash, Archedis rose, pulling free his crystalline sword. He slammed the pommel against Grandpa Smedry's head.

The old man went cross-eyed – his Talent unable to protect him from the power of a Crystin blade – and he fell to the side. With his singing gone, Himalaya and Folsom immediately stopped fighting and froze in place.

The Librarians tackled them.

I struggled against the flow of people again, trying desperately to get down. The seats on the north side were now completely empty, save for Swcbn. The grandmotherly woman looked up at me, smiling. She held up the afghan she'd been knitting.

It depicted a bloody skull. Archedis turned toward King Dartmoor.

'No!' I screamed.

The corrupted knight raised his sword. Then he froze as a small, quiet figure stepped between him and the king.

Bastille. She hadn't been affected by the fall of the Mindstone ... because the knights themselves had cut her off from it.

Bastille raised her mother's sword. I don't know where she'd gotten it – I don't even know how she'd gotten into the room. She had found a pair of Warrior's Lenses, but I could see from her profile that she was still exhausted. She looked tiny before the figure of the enormous knight, with his silvery armor and heroic smile.

'Come now,' Archedis said. 'You can't stand against me.'

Bastille didn't reply.

'I maneuvered you into obtaining knighthood,' Archedis said. 'You never really deserved it. That was all a ploy to kill the old Smedry.'

Kill the old Smedry ... Of course. Bastille and I had assumed that someone had been setting *her* up to fail so that she or her mother would be disgraced. We'd completely missed that Bastille had been acting as Grandpa Smedry's bodyguard.

It hadn't been a plot against her at all. It had been a plot against my grandfather. (And, if you're wondering, no – I couldn't actually hear what they were saying down there. But someone repeated it to me later, so give me a break.) I continued to fight against the crowd, trying to get down to her. It was all happening so quickly – though pages have passed in this narrative, it had only been moments since Archedis had stood up.

I was forced to watch as Bastille raised her mother's sword. She seemed so tired, her shoulders slumping, her stance uncertain.

'I'm the best there's ever been,' Archedis said. 'You think you can fight me?'

Bastille looked up, and I saw something showing through her fatigue, her pain, and her sorrow. Strength.

She attacked. Crystal met crystal with a sound that was somehow more melodic than that of steel against steel. Archedis pushed Bastille back with his superior strength, laughing.

She came at him again.

Their swords met, pinging again and again. As before, Archedis rebuffed Bastille.

And she attacked again.

And again.

And again.

Each time, her sword swung a little faster. Each time, the ringing of blades was a little louder. Each time, her posture was a little more firm. She fought, refusing to be beaten down.

Archedis stopped laughing. His face grew solemn, then angry. Bastille threw herself at him repeatedly, her sword becoming a flurry of motion, the crystalline blade flashing with iridescence as it shattered light from the windows, throwing out sparkling colors.

And then Bastille actually started to push Archedis back.

Few people outside of Crystallia have seen two Crystin fight in earnest. The fleeing crowd slowed, its members turning back. Librarian thugs stopped beating on Himalaya and Folsom. Even I hesitated. We all grew still, as if in reverence, and the once chaotic room became as quiet as a concert hall.

We were an audience, watching a duet. A duet in which the violinists tried to ram their violins down each other's throats.

The massive knight and the spindly girl circled, their swords beating against each other as if in a prescribed rhythm. The weapons seemed things of beauty, the way they reflected the light. Two people trying to kill each other with rainbows.

Bastille should have lost. She was smaller, weaker, and exhausted. Yet each time Archedis threw her down, she scrambled back to her feet and attacked with even more fury and determination. To the side, her father, the king, watched in awe. To my surprise, I even saw her mother stir. The woman looked dazed and sick, but she seemed to have regained enough consciousness to open her eyes.

Archedis made a mistake. He tripped slightly against a fallen Librarian thug. It was the first error I'd seen him make, but that didn't matter. Bastille was on him in a heartbeat, pounding her sword against his, forcing him backward from his precarious position.

Looking dumbfounded, Archedis tripped backward and fell onto his armored butt. Bastille's sword froze at his neck, a hair's width from slicing his head free.

'I ... yield,' Archedis said, sounding utterly shocked.

I finally managed to shove my way through the crowd, which had been stunned by the beautiful fight. I skidded to a stop beside my grandfather. He was breathing, though unconscious. He appeared to be humming to himself in his sleep.

'Alcatraz,' Bastille said.

I looked over at her. She still had her sword at Archedis's neck.

'I have something for you to do,' she said, nodding to Archedis.

I smiled, then walked over to the fallen knight.

'Look, hey,' he said, smiling. 'I'm a double agent, really. I was just trying to infiltrate them. I ... uh, is it true that you have a Truthfinder's Lens?'

I nodded.

'Oh,' he said, knowing that I'd been able to see that he was lying.

'Do it,' Bastille said, nodding toward the ground.

'Gladly,' I said, reaching down to touch Archedis's blade. With a magnificent crackling sound, it shattered beneath the power of my Talent.

Swcbn finally put down her knitting. 'You,' she said, 'are very *bad* children. No cookies for you.'

And with that, she vanished – replaced with an exact statue of herself sitting in that very position.

ROYAL EPILOGUE (*NOT* A CHAPTER)

There comes a time in every book when a single, important question must be asked: 'Where's my lunch?'

That time isn't right now. However, it is time to ask another question, almost as important: 'So, what's the point?'

It's an excellent question. We should ask it about everything we read. The problem is, I have no idea how to answer it.

The point of this book is really up to you. My point in writing it was to look at my life, to expose it, to illuminate it. As Socrates once said, 'the unexamined life is not worth living.'

He died for teaching that to people. I feel I should have died years ago. Instead, I proved myself to be a coward. You'll see what I mean, eventually.

This book means whatever you make of it. For some, it will be about the dangers of fame. For others, it will be about turning your flaws into talents. For many, it will simply be entertainment, which is really quite all right. Yet for others, it will be about learning to question everything, even that which you believe.

For, you see, the most important truths can always withstand a little examination.

One week after the defeat of Archedis and the Librarians, I sat in the Chamber of Kings. Grandpa Smedry sat to my left, dressed in his finest tuxedo. Bastille sat to my right, wearing the plate armor of a full Knight of Crystallia. (Yes, of course she got her knighthood back. As if the knights could refuse after watching her defeat Archedis while they lay on the ground drooling.)

I still wasn't clear on what Archedis had done. From what I gather, the Mindstone was cut from the Spire of the World itself. Like the Spire, the Mindstone has the power to radiate energy and knowledge to everyone connected to it. Archedis had been able to resist the Sundering as he'd cut himself off from the Mindstone earlier.

Either way, with both Bastille and Archedis being cut off – and with both wearing Warrior's Lenses – their speed and strength had been equalized. And Bastille had beaten him. She'd won because of her skill and her tenacity, which I'd say are the more important indicators of knighthood. She'd worn her silvery armor virtually nonstop since it had been given back to her. A crystal sword hung from her back, newly bonded to Bastille.

'Can't we get on with this?' she snapped. 'Shattering Glass, Smedry. Your father is such a drama hog.'

I smiled. That was another sign she was feeling better – she was back to her usual charming self.

'What's wrong with you?' she said, eyeing me. 'Stop staring at me.'

'I'm not staring at you,' I said. 'I'm having an internal monologue to catch the readers up on what has happened since the last chapter. It's called a denouement.'

She rolled her eyes. 'Then we can't actually be having this conversation; it's something you just inserted into the text while writing the book years later. It's a literary device – the conversation didn't exist.'

'Oh, right,' I said.

'You're such a freak.'

Freak or not, I was happy. Yes, my mother escaped with the book. Yes, Swcbn escaped as well. But we caught Archedis, saved Mokia, and got back my father's pair of Translator's Lenses.

I'd shown them to him. He'd been surprised, had taken them back, then had returned to whatever important 'work' it was he'd been doing this whole time. We were supposed to find out about it today; he was going to present his findings before the monarchs. Apparently, he always revealed his discoveries this way.

So – of course – the place was a circus. No, literally. There was a circus outside the front of the palace to entertain the kids while their parents came in to listen to my father's grand speech.

The place was almost as packed as it had been during the treaty ratification.

Hopefully, this time there would be fewer Librarian hijinks. (those wacky Librarians and their hijinks.)

There was a large number of reporter types waiting in the reaches of the room, anticipating my father's announcement. As I'd come to learn, anything involving the Smedry family was news to the Free Kingdomers. This news, however, was even more important.

The last time my father had held a session like this, he'd announced that he had discovered a way to collect the Sands of Rashid. The time before that, he'd explained that he'd broken the secret of Transporter's Glass. People were expecting a lot from this speech.

I couldn't help but feel that it was all just a little ... bad for my father's ego. I mean, a *circus*? who gets a circus thrown for them?

I glanced at Bastille. 'You dealt with this kind of stuff most of your childhood, didn't you?'

'This kind of stuff?' she asked.

'Fame. Notoriety. People paying attention to everything you do.' She nodded.

'So how did you deal with it?' I asked. 'And not let it ruin you?'

'How do you know it *didn't* ruin me?' she asked. 'Aren't princesses supposed to be nice and sweet and stuff like that? Wear pink dresses and tiaras?'

'Well ...'

'Pink dresses,' Bastille said, her eyes narrowing. 'Someone gave me a pink dress once. I burned it.'

Ah, I thought. *That's right; I forgot. Bastille got around fame's touch by being a freaking psychopath.*

'You'll learn, lad,' Grandpa Smedry said from behind me. 'It might take some time, but you'll figure it out.'

'My father never did,' I said.

Grandpa Smedry hesitated. 'Oh, well, I don't know about that. I think he did, for a while. Back around the time he got married. I just think he forgot.'

Around the time he got married. The words made me think of Folsom and Himalaya. We'd saved them seats, but they were late. As I looked around, I caught a glance of them working their way through the crowd. Grandpa Smedry waved enthusiastically, though they'd obviously already seen us.

But then, that's Grandpa.

'Sorry,' Folsom said as he and his new wife seated themselves. 'Getting some last-minute packing done.'

'You still determined to go through with this?' Grandpa Smedry asked.

Himalaya nodded. 'We're moving to the Hushlands. I think … Well, there isn't much I can do for my fellow Librarians here.'

'We'll start an underground resistance for good Librarians,' Folsom said.

'Lybrarians,' Himalaya said. 'I've already begun working on a pamphlet!'

She pulled out a sheet of paper. *Ten steps to being less evil*, it read. *A helpful guide for those who want to take the 'Lie' out of 'Liebrarian.'*

'That's … just great,' I said. I wasn't certain how else to respond. Fortunately for me, my father chose that moment to make his entrance – which was particularly good, since this scene was starting to feel a little long anyway.

The monarchs sat behind a long table facing a raised podium. We all grew quiet as my father approached, wearing dark robes to mark him as a scientist. The crowd hushed.

'As you may have heard,' he said, his voice carrying through the room, 'I have recently returned from the Library of Alexandria. I spent some time as a Curator, escaping their clutches with my soul intact by the means of some clever planning.'

'Yeah,' Bastille muttered, 'Clever planning, and some undeserved help.' Sing, who sat in front of us, gave her a disapproving look.

'The purpose of all this,' my father continued, 'was to gain access to the fabled texts collected and controlled by the Curators of Alexandria. Having managed to create a pair of Translator's Lenses from the sands of Rashid—'

This caused a ripple of discussion in the crowd.

'—I was able to read texts in the Forgotten Language,' my father continued. 'I was taken by the Curators and transformed into one of them, but still retained enough free will to sneak the Lenses from my possessions and use them to read. This allowed me to spend weeks studying the most valuable contents of the Library.'

He stopped, leaning forward on the podium, smiling winningly. He certainly did have a charm about him, when he wanted to impress people.

In that moment, looking at that smile, I could swear that I'd seen him somewhere, long before my visit to the Library of Alexandria.

'What I did,' my father continued, 'was dangerous; some may even call it brash. I couldn't know that I'd have enough freedom as a Curator to study the texts, nor could I count on the fact that I'd be able to use my lenses to read the Forgotten Language.'

He paused for dramatic effect. 'But I did it anyway. For that is the Smedry way.'

'He stole that line from me, by the way,' Grandpa Smedry whispered to us.

My father continued. 'I've spent the last two weeks writing down the things I memorized while I was a Curator. Secrets lost in time, mysteries known only to the Incarna. I've analyzed them, and am the only man to read and understand their works for over two millennia.'

He looked over the crowd. 'Through this,' he said, 'I have discovered the method by which the Smedry Talents were created and given to my family.'

What? I thought, shocked.

'Impossible,' Bastille said, and the crowd around us began to speak animatedly.

I glanced at my grandfather. Though the old man is usually wackier than a penguin-wrangling expedition to Florida, occasionally I catch a hint of wisdom in his face. He has a depth that he doesn't often show.

He turned toward me, meeting my eyes, and I could tell that he was worried. *Very* worried.

'I anticipate great things from this,' my father said, hushing the crowd. 'With a little more research, I believe I can discover how to give Talents to ordinary people. I imagine a world, not so distant in the future, where *everyone* has a Smedry Talent.'

And then he was done. He retreated from the podium, stepping down to speak with the monarchs. The room, of course, grew loud with discussions. I found myself standing, pushing my way down to the floor of the room. I approached the monarchs, and the knights standing guard there let me pass.

'... need access to the Royal Archives,' my father was saying to the monarchs.

'Not a library,' I found myself whispering.

My father didn't notice me. 'There are some books there I believe would be of use to my investigations, now that I've recovered my Translator's Lenses. One volume, in particular, was conspicuously missing from the Library of Alexandria – the Curators claimed their copy had been burned in a very strange accident. Fortunately, I believe there may be another one here.'

'It's gone,' I said, my voice soft in the room's buzzing voices.

Attica turned to me, as did several of the monarchs. 'What is that, son?' my father asked.

'Didn't you pay attention at *all* to what happened last week?' I demanded. 'Mother has the book. The one you want. She stole it from the archives.'

My father hesitated, then nodded to the monarchs. 'Excuse us.' He pulled me aside. 'Now, what is this?'

'She stole it,' I said. 'The book you want, the one written by the scribe of Alcatraz the First. She took it from the archives. That's what the entire mess last week was about!'

'I thought that was an assassination attempt on the monarchs,' he said.

'That was only part of it. I sent you a message in the middle of it, asking you to come help us protect the archives, but you completely ignored it!'

He waved an indifferent hand. 'I was occupied with greater things. You must be mistaken – I'll look through the archives and—'

'I looked already,' I said. 'I've looked at the title of every single book in there that was written in the Forgotten Language. They're all cookbooks or ledgers or things. Except that one my mother took.'

'And you let her steal it?' my father demanded indignantly.

Let her. I took a deep breath. (And, next time you think *your* parents are frustrating, might I invite you to read this passage through one more time?)

'I believe,' a new voice said, 'that young Alcatraz did everything he could to stop the aforementioned theft.'

My father turned to see King Dartmoor, wearing his crown and blue-gold robes, standing behind him. The king nodded to me. 'Prince Rikers has spoken at length of the event, Attica. I believe there will be a novel forthcoming.'

Wonderful, I thought.

'Well,' my father said, 'I guess ... well, this changes every-thing...'

'What is this about giving everyone Talents, Attica?' the king asked. 'Is that really wise? From what I hear, Smedry Talents can be very unpredictable.'

'We can control them,' my father said, waving another indiffer-ent hand. 'You know how the people dream of having our powers. Well, I will be the one to make those dreams become a reality.'

So that was what it was about. My father, sealing his legacy. Being the hero who made everyone capable of having a Talent.

But if everyone had a Smedry Talent ... Then, well, what would that mean for us? We wouldn't be the only ones with Talents anymore. That made me feel a little sick.

Yes, I know it is selfish, but that's how I felt. I think this is – perhaps – the capstone of this book. After all I'd been through, after all the fighting to help the Free Kingdoms, I was still selfish enough to want to keep the Talents for myself.

Because the Talents were what made us special, weren't they?

'I will have to think on this more,' my father said. 'It appears that we'll have to search out that book. Even if it means confronting ... her.'

He nodded to the kings, then walked away. He put on a smiling face when he met with the press, but I could tell that he was bothered. The disappearance of that book had fouled up his plans.

Well, I thought, *he should have paid better attention!*

I knew it was silly, but I couldn't help feeling that I'd let him down. That this was my fault. I tried to shake myself out of it and walked back to my grandfather and the others.

Had my parents been like Folsom and Himalaya once? Bright, loving, full of excitement? If so, what had gone wrong? Himalaya was a Librarian and Folsom was a Smedry. Were they doomed to the same fate as my parents?

And Smedry Talents for everyone. My mind drifted back to the words I'd read on the wall of the tomb of Alcatraz the First.

Our desires have brought us low. We sought to touch the powers of eternity, then draw them down upon ourselves. But we brought with them something we did not intend ...

The Bane of Incarna. That which twists, that which corrupts, and that which destroys.

The Dark Talent.

Wherever my father went on his quest to discover how to 'make' Smedry Talents, I determined that I would follow after him. I would watch, and make certain he didn't do anything *too* rash.

I had to be ready to stop him, if need be.

THE LAST PAGES

Alcatraz walks onto the stage. He smiles at the audience, looking right into the camera.

'Hello,' he says. 'And welcome to the after-book special. I'm your host, Alcatraz Smedry.'

'And I'm Bastille Dartmoor,' Bastille says, joining Alcatraz on the stage.

Alcatraz nods. 'We're here to talk to you about a pernicious evil that is plaguing today's youth. A terrible, awful habit that is destroying them from the inside out.'

Bastille looks at the camera. 'He's talking, of course, about skipping to the ends of books and reading the last pages first.'

'We call it "Last-Paging"' Alcatraz says. 'You may think it doesn't involve you or your friends, but studies show that there has been a 4,000.024 percent increase in Last-Paging during the past seven minutes alone.'

'That's right, Alcatraz,' Bastille says. 'And did you know that Last-Paging is the largest cause of cancer in domesticated fruit bats?'

'Really?'

'Yes indeed. Also, Last-Paging makes you lose sleep, grow hair in funny places, and can decrease your ability to play Halo by forty-five percent.'

'Wow,' Alcatraz says. 'Why would anyone do it?'

'We're not certain. We only know that it happens, and that this terrible disease isn't fully understood. Fortunately, we've taken actions to combat it.'

'Such as putting terrible after-book specials at the backs of books to make people feel sick?' Alcatraz asks helpfully.

'That's right,' Bastille says. 'Stay away from Last-Paging, kids! Remember, the more you know ...'

'... The more you can forget tomorrow!' Alcatraz says. 'Good night, folks. And be sure to join us for next week's after-book special, where we expose the dangers of gerbil snorting!'

AUTHOR'S AFTERWORD

No, we're not done yet. Be patient. We've only had three endings so far; we can stand another one. Both of my other books had afterwords, so this one will too. (And if we need to send someone to Valinor to justify this last ending, let me know. I'm not going to marry Rosie, though.)

Anyway, there you have it. My first visit to Nalhalla, my first experience with fame. You've seen the actions of a hero and the actions of a fool – and you know that both hero and fool are the same person.

I know I said that this was the book where you'd see me fail – and, in a way, I did fail. I let my mother escape with the Incarna text. However, I realize this wasn't as big a failure as you might have been expecting.

You should have known. I won't warn you when my big failure is about to arrive. It will hurt far more when it's a surprise.

You'll see.

ALCATRAZ
VERSUS THE
SHATTERED LENS

For Peter Ahlstrom
   Who is not only a good friend and great man,
   But one who has been reading my books since the days when they were terrible,
   And who strives very hard to keep them from being that way again.
      Insoluble, Incalculable, Indefinable.
         Indispensible.

AUTHOR'S FOREWORD

I am an idiot.

You should know this already, if you've read the previous three volumes of my autobiography. If, by chance, you haven't read them, then don't worry. you'll get the idea. After all, nothing in this book will make any kind of sense to you. You'll be confused at the difference between the Free Kingdoms and the Hushlands. You'll wonder why I keep pretending that my glasses are magical. You'll be baffled by all these insane characters.

(Actually, you'll probably wonder all of those same things if you start from the beginning too. These books don't really make a lot of sense, you see. Try living through one of them sometime. Then you'll know what it *really* means to be confused.)

Anyway, as I was saying, if you haven't read the other three books, then don't bother. That will make this book even more confusing to you, and that's exactly what I want. By way of introduction, just let me say this. My name is Alcatraz Smedry, my talent is breaking things, and I'm stoopid. Really, really stoopid. So stoopid, I don't know how to spell the word stupid.

This is my story. Or, well, part four of it. Otherwise known as 'The part where everything goes wrong, and then Alcatraz has a cheese sandwich.'

Enjoy.

2

So there I was, holding a pink teddy bear in my hand. It had a red bow and an inviting, cute, bearlike smile. Also, it was ticking.

'Now what?' I asked.

'Now you throw it, idiot!' Bastille said urgently.

I frowned, then tossed the bear to the side, through the open window, into the small room filled with sand. A second later, an explosion blasted back through the window and tossed me into the air. I was propelled backward, then slammed into the far wall.

With an *urk* of pain, I slid down and fell onto my back. I blinked, my vision fuzzy. Little flakes of plaster – the kind they put on ceilings just so they can break off and fall to the ground dramatically in an explosion – broke off the ceiling and fell dramatically to the ground. One hit me on the forehead.

'Ow,' I said. I lay there, staring upward, breathing in and out. 'Bastille, did that teddy bear just explode?'

'Yes,' she said, walking over and looking down at me. She had on a gray-blue militaristic uniform, and wore her straight, silver hair long. On her belt was a small sheath that had a large hilt sticking out of it. That hid her Crystin blade; though the sheath was only about a foot long, if she drew the weapon out it would be the length of a regular sword.

'Okay. Right. *Why* did that teddy bear just explode?'

'Because you pulled out the pin, stupid. What else did you expect it to do?'

I groaned, sitting up. The room around us – inside the Nalhallan Royal Weapons Testing Facility – was white and featureless. The wall where we'd been standing had an open window looking into the blast range, which was filled with sand. There were no other windows or furniture, save for a set of cabinets on our right.

'What did I expect it to do?' I said. 'Maybe play some music? Say "mama"? Where I come from, exploding is not a normal bear habit.'

'Where you come from, a lot of things are backward,' Bastille said. 'I'll bet your poodles don't explode either.'

'No, they don't.'

'Pity.'

'Actually, exploding poodles *would* be awesome. But exploding teddy bears? That's dangerous!'

'Duh.'

'But Bastille, they're for *children!*'

'Exactly. So that they can defend themselves, obviously.' She rolled her eyes and walked back over to the window that looked into the sand-filled room. She didn't ask if I was hurt. She could see that I was still breathing, and that was generally good enough for her.

Also, you may have noticed that this is Chapter Two. You may be wondering where Chapter One went. It turns out that I – being stoopid – lost it. Don't worry, it was kind of boring anyway. Well, except for the talking llamas.

I climbed to my feet. 'In case you were wondering—'

'I wasn't.'

'—I'm fine.'

'Great.'

I frowned, walking up to Bastille. 'Is something bothering you, Bastille?'

'Other than you?'

'I *always* bother you,' I said. 'And you're always a little grouchy. But today you've been downright *mean.*'

She glanced at me, arms folded. Then I saw her expression soften faintly. 'Yeah.'

I raised an eyebrow.

'I just don't like losing.'

'Losing?' I said. 'Bastille, you recovered your place in the knights, exposed – and defeated – a traitor to your order, and stopped the Librarians from kidnapping or killing the Council of Kings. If that's "losing," you've got a really funny definition of the word.'

'Funnier than your face?'

'Bastille,' I said firmly.

She sighed, leaning down, crossing her arms on the windowsill. 'She Who Cannot Be Named got away, your mother escaped with a pair of Translator's Lenses, and – now that they're not hiding behind the ruse of a treaty – the Librarians are throwing everything they've got at Mokia.'

'You've done what you could. *I've* done what I could. It's time to let others handle things.'

She didn't look happy about that. 'Fine. Let's get back to your explosives training.' She wanted me well prepared in case the war came to Nalhalla. It wasn't likely to happen, but my ignorance of proper things – like exploding teddy bears – has always been a point of frustration to Bastille.

Now, I realize that many of you are just as ignorant as I am. That's why I prepared a handy guide that explains everything you need to know and remember about my autobiography in order to not be confused by this book. I put the guide back in Chapter One. If you ever have trouble, you can reference it. I'm such a nice guy. Dumb, but nice.

Bastille opened one of the cabinets on the side wall and pulled out another small, pink teddy bear. She handed it to me as I walked up to her. It had a little tag on the side that said *Pull me!* in adorable lettering.

I took it nervously. 'Tell me honestly. Why do you build grenades that look like teddy bears? It's not about protecting children.'

'Well, how do you feel when you look at that?'

I shrugged. 'It's cute. In a deadly, destructive way.' *Kind of like Bastille, actually*, I thought. 'It makes me want to smile. Then it makes me want to run away screaming, since I know it's really *a grenade*.'

'Exactly,' Bastille said, taking the bear from me and pulling the tag – the pin – out. She tossed it out the window. 'If you build weapons that *look* like weapons, then everyone will know to run away from them! This way, the Librarians are confused.'

'That's sick,' I said. 'Shouldn't I be ducking or something?'

'You'll be fine,' she said.

Ah, I thought. *This one must be some kind of dud or fake.*

At that second, the grenade outside the window exploded. Another blast threw me backward. I hit the wall with a grunt, and another piece of plaster fell on my head. This time, though, I managed to land on my knees.

Oddly, I felt remarkably unharmed, considering I'd just been blown backward by the explosion. In fact, neither explosion seemed to have hurt me very badly at all.

'The pink ones,' Bastille said, 'are blast-wave grenades. They throw people and things away from them, but they don't actually hurt anyone.'

'Really?' I said, walking up to her. 'How does *that* work?'

'Do I look like an explosives expert?'

I hesitated. With those fiery eyes and dangerous expression …

'The answer is no, Smedry,' she said flatly, folding her arms. 'I don't know how these things work. I'm just a soldier.'

She picked up a blue teddy bear and pulled the tag off, then tossed it out the window. I braced myself, grabbing the window-sill, preparing for a blast. This time, however, the bear grenade made a muted thumping sound. The sand in the next room began to pile up in a strange way, and I was suddenly yanked *through* the window into the next room.

I yelped, tumbling through the air, then hit the mound of sand face-first.

'That,' Bastille said from behind, 'is a *suction-wave* grenade. It explodes in reverse, pulling everything toward it instead of push-ing it away.'

'Mur murr mur mur murrr,' I said, since my head was buried in the sand. Sand, it should be noted, does *not* taste very good. Even with ketchup.

I pulled my head free, leaning back against the pile of sand, straightening my Oculator's Lenses and looking back at the window, where Bastille was leaning with arms crossed, smiling faintly. There's nothing like seeing a Smedry get sucked through a window to improve her mood.

'That should be impossible!' I protested. 'A grenade that explodes *backward*?'

She rolled her eyes again. 'You've been in Nalhalla for months now, Smedry. Isn't it time to stop pretending that everything shocks or confuses you?'

'I ... er ...' I wasn't pretending. I'd been raised in the Hushlands, trained by Librarians to reject things that seemed too ... well, too strange. But Nalhalla – city of castles – was nothing *but* strangeness. It was hard not to get overwhelmed by it all.

'I still think a grenade shouldn't be able to explode *inward*,' I said, shaking sand off my clothing as I walked up to the window. 'I mean, how would you even make that work?'

'Maybe you take the same stuff you put in a regular grenade, then put it in backward?'

'I ... don't think it works that way, Bastille.'

She shrugged, getting out another bear. This one was purple. She moved to pull the tag.

'Wait!' I said, scrambling through the window. I took the bear grenade from her. 'This time you're going to tell me what it does first.'

'That's no fun.'

I raised a sceptical eyebrow at her.

'This one is harmless,' she said. 'A stuff-eater grenade. It vaporizes everything nearby that *isn't* alive. Rocks, dead wood, fibers, glass, metal. All gone. But living plants, animals, people – perfectly safe. Works wonders against Alivened.'

I looked down at the little purple bear. Alivened were objects brought to life through Dark Oculatory magic. I'd once fought some created from romance novels. 'This could be useful.'

'Yeah,' she said. 'Works well against Librarians too. If a group is charging at you with those guns of theirs, you can vaporize the weapons but leave the Librarians unharmed.'

'And their clothing?' I asked.

'Gone.'

I hefted the bear, contemplating a little payback for being sucked through the window. 'So you're saying that if I threw this at you, and it went off, you'd be left—'

'Kicking you in the face?' Bastille asked coolly. 'Yes. Then I'd staple you to the outside to a tall castle and paint "dragon food" over your head.'

'Right,' I said. 'Er . . . why don't we just put this one away?'

'Yeah, good idea.' She took it from me and stuffed it back into the cabinet.

'So . . . I noticed that none of those grenades are, well, actually *deadly*.'

'Of course they aren't,' Bastille said. 'What do you take us for? Barbarians?'

'Of course not. But you *are* at war.'

'War's no excuse for *hurting* people.'

I scratched my head. 'I thought war was all *about* hurting people.'

'That's Librarian thinking,' Bastille said, folding her arms and narrowing her eyes. 'Uncivilized.' She hesitated. 'Well, actually, even the *Librarians* use many nonlethal weapons in war these days. You'll see, if the war ever comes here.'

'All right . . . but you don't have any objections to hurting *me* on occasion.'

'You're a Smedry,' she said. 'That's different. Now do you want to learn the rest of these grenades or not?'

'That depends. What are they going to do to me?'

She eyed me, then grumbled something and turned away.

I blinked. I'd gotten used to Bastille's moods by now, but this seemed irregular even for her. 'Bastille?'

She walked over to the far side of the room, tapping a section of glass, making the wall turn translucent. The Royal Weapons Testing Facility was a tall, multitowered castle on the far side of Nalhalla City. Our vantage point gave us a great view of the capital.

'Bastille?' I asked again, walking up to her.

She said, arms folded, 'I shouldn't be berating you like this.'

'How *should* you be berating me, then?'

'Not at all. I'm sorry, Alcatraz.'

I blinked. An apology. From *Bastille*? 'The war really is bothering you, isn't it? Mokia?'

'Yeah. I just wish there were more to do. More that *we* could do.'

I nodded, understanding. My escape from the Hushlands had snowballed into the rescue of my father from the Library of Alexandria, and following that we'd gotten sucked into stopping Nalhalla from signing a treaty with the Librarians. Now, finally, things had settled down. And not surprisingly, other people – people with more experience than Bastille and me – had taken over doing the most important tasks. I was a Smedry and she a full Knight of Crystallia, but we were both only thirteen. Even in the Free Kingdoms – where people didn't pay as much attention to age – that meant something.

Bastille had been rushed through training during her childhood and had obtained knighthood at a very young age. The others of her order expected her to do a lot of practice and training to make up for earlier lapses. She spent half of every day seeing to her duties in Crystallia.

Generally, I spent my days in Nalhalla learning. Fortunately, this was a *whole* lot more interesting than school had been back home. I was trained in things like using Oculatory Lenses, conducting negotiations, and using Free Kingdomer weapons. Being a Smedry – I was coming to learn – was like being a mix of secret agent, special forces commando, diplomat, general, and cheese taster.

I won't lie. It was shatteringly cool. Instead of sitting around all day writing biology papers or listening to Mr Layton from algebra class extol the virtues of complex factoring, I got to throw teddy bear grenades and jump off buildings. It was really fun at the start.

Okay, it was really fun the WHOLE TIME.

But there was something missing. Before, though I'd been

stumbling along without knowing what I was doing, we'd been involved in important events. Now we were just ... well, kids. And that was annoying.

'Something needs to happen,' I said. 'Something exciting.' We looked out the window expectantly.

A bluebird flew by. It didn't, however, explode. Nor did it turn out to be a secret Librarian ninja bird. In fact, despite my dramatic proclamation, nothing at all interesting happened. And nothing interesting will happen for the next three chapters.

Sorry. I'm afraid this is going to be a rather boring book. Take a deep breath. The worst part is coming next.

6

Whew! Those were some *boring* chapters, weren't they? I know you really didn't want to hear – in intricate detail – about the workings of the Nalhallan sewer systems. Nor did you care to get a scholarly explanation of the original Nalhallan alphabet and how the letters are based on logographic representations of ancient Cabafloo. And, of course, that vibrant, excruciatingly specific description of what it's like to get your stomach pumped probably made you feel sick.

Don't worry, though. These scenes are extremely important to Chapter Thirty-Seven of the novel. Without Chapters Three, Four and Five, you would be *completely* lost when we get to a later point in the book. It's for your own good that I included them. You'll thank me later.

'Wait,' I said, pointing out through the clear glass wall of the grenade testing room. 'I recognize that bird.'

Not the bluebird. The giant glass bird rising from the city a short distance away. It was called the *Hawkwind*, and it had carried me on my first trip to Nalhalla. It was about the size of a small airplane and was constructed completely of beautiful translucent glass.

Now, some of you Hushlanders might wonder how I could recognize that particular vessel among all of those that were flying in and out of Nalhalla. That's because in the Hushlands, the Librarians make sure all vehicles look the same. All airplanes of a certain size look identical. Most cars pretty much look the same: trucks look like every other truck, sedans look like very other sedan. They let you change the color. Whoopee.

The Librarians claim it has to be this way, giving some gobbledygook about manufacturing costs or assembly lines. Those, of course, are lies. The real reason everything looks the same has to be with one simple concept: underpants.

I'll explain later.

The Free Kingdoms don't follow Hushlander ways of thinking. When they build something, they like to make it distinctive and original. Even an idiot, like me, could tell the difference between any two vehicles from a distance.

'The *Hawkwind*,' Bastille said, nodding as the glass bird flapped its way into the sky, turning westward. 'Isn't that the ship your father was outfitting for his secret mission?'

'Yes,' I said.

'Do you think . . .'

'He just left without saying good-bye?' I watched the *Hawkwind* streak away into the distance. 'Yes.'

'To my father and son,' Grandpa Smedry read, adjusting his Oculator's Lenses as he examined the note. 'I am bad at saying good-bye. Good-bye.' He lowered the paper, shrugging.

'That's *it*?' Bastille exclaimed. 'That's all he left?'

'Er, yes,' Grandpa Smedry said, holding up two small orange pieces of paper. 'That and what appears to be two coupons for half off a scoop of koala-flavored ice cream.'

'That's terrible!' Bastille said.

'Actually, it's my favorite flavor,' Grandpa replied, tucking the coupons away. 'Quite considerate of him.'

'I meant the note,' she said, standing with arms folded. We were back in Keep Smedry, an enormous black stone castle nestled on the far south side of Nalhalla City. Fireglass crackled on a hearth at the side of the room. Yes, in the Free Kingdoms there is a kind of glass that can burn. Don't ask.

'Ah yes,' Grandpa said, rereading the note. 'Yes, yes, yes. You have to admit, though, he *is* very bad at good-byes. This note makes a very good argument for that. I mean, he even spelled *good-bye* wrong. Bad at it indeed!'

I sat in an overstuffed red chair beside the hearth. It was the chair on which we'd found the note. Apparently my father hadn't told anyone outside his inner circle that he was leaving. He'd gathered his group of soldiers, assistants, and explorers and then taken off.

We were the only three in the black-walled room. Bastille eyed me. 'I'm sorry, Alcatraz,' she said. 'This has to be the *worst* thing he could have done to you.'

'I don't know,' Grandpa said. 'The coupons could have been for Rocky Road instead.' He cringed. 'Dreadful stuff. Who puts a *road* in ice cream? I mean really.'

Bastille regarded him evenly. 'You're not helping.'

'I wasn't really trying to,' Grandpa said, scratching his head. He was bald save for a tuft of white hair running around the back of his head and sticking out behind his ears – like someone had stapled a cloud to his scalp – and he had a large white mustache. 'But I suppose I should. Ragged Resnicks, lad! Don't look so glum. He's a horrible father anyway, right? At least he's gone now!'

'You're terrible at this,' Bastille said.

'Well, at least I didn't spell anything wrong.'

I smirked. I could see a twinkle in my grandfather's eyes. He was just trying to cheer me up. He walked over, sitting down on the chair beside me. 'Your father doesn't know what to make of you, lad. He didn't have a chance to grow into being a parent. I think he's scared of you.'

Bastille sniffed in disdain. 'So Alcatraz is just supposed to sit here in Nalhalla waiting for him to come back? Last time Attica Smedry vanished, it took him *thirteen years* to reappear. Who knows what he's even planning to do!'

'He's going after my mother,' I said softly.

Bastille turned toward me, frowning.

'She has the book he wants,' I said. 'The one that has secrets on how to give everyone Smedry Talents.'

'That's a specter your father has been chasing for many, many years, Alcatraz,' Grandpa Smedry said. 'Giving everyone Smedry Talents? I don't think it's possible.'

'People said that about finding the Translator's Lenses too,' Kaz noted. 'But Attica managed that.'

'True, true,' Grandpa said. 'But this is different.'

'I guess,' I said. 'But—'

I froze, then turned to the side. My uncle, Kazan Smedry, sat in the third chair beside the fireplace. He was about four feet tall and, like most people, hated being called a midget. He wore sunglasses, a brown leather jacket, and a tunic underneath that he tucked into a pair of rugged trousers. He was covered in a black, sootlike dust.

'Kaz!' I exclaimed. 'You're back!'

'Finally!' he said, coughing.

'What . . .' I asked, indicating the soot.

'Got lost in the fireplace,' Kaz said, shrugging. 'Been in the blasted thing for a good two weeks now.'

Every Smedry has a Talent. The Talent can be powerful, it can be unpredictable, and it can be disastrous. But it's always interesting. You could get one by being born a Smedry or by marrying a Smedry. My father wanted everyone to get a Talent.

And I was beginning to suspect that this is what my mother had been seeking all along. The Sands of Rashid, the years of searching, the theft from the Royal Archives (not a library) in Nalhalla – all of this was focused on finding a way to bestow Smedry Talents on people who didn't normally have them. I suspected that my father did it because he wanted to share our powers with everyone. I suspected that my mother, however, wanted to create an invincible, Talent-wielding Librarian army.

Now, I'm not too bright, but I figured that this was a bad thing. I mean, if Librarians had my Talent – breaking things? Here's a handy list of things I figure they'd probably break if they could:

1) **Your lunch.** Every day, when you'd open your lunch – no matter what you brought – you'd find it had been changed into a pickle-and-orange-slug sandwich. And there would be NO SALT.
2) **Dance.** You don't want to see any break-dancing Librarians. Really. Trust me.
3) **Recess.** That's right. They'd break recess and turn it into

a session of advanced algebra instead. (Note: The same thing happens when you go to middle school or junior high. Sorry.)

4) **Wind.** No explanation needed.

As you can see, it would be a disaster.

'Kazan!' Grandpa said, smiling toward his son.

'Hey, Pop.'

'Still getting in trouble, I presume?'

'Always.'

'Good lad. Trained you well!'

'Kaz,' I said. 'It's been months! What took you so long?'

Kaz grimaced. 'The Talent.'

In case you've forgotten, my grandfather had the Talent of arriving late to things, while Kaz had the Talent to get lost in rather amazing ways. (I don't know why I'm repeating this, since I clearly explained it all in Chapter One. Ah well.)

'Isn't that a long time to get lost, even for you?' Bastille asked, frowning.

'Yeah,' Kaz said. 'I haven't been *this* lost for years.'

'Ah yes,' Grandpa Smedry said. 'Why, I remember your mother and I once spending upward of two months frantically searching for you when you were two, only to have you appear back in your crib one night!'

Kaz looked wistful. 'I was an … interesting child to raise.'

'All Smedrys are,' Grandpa added.

'Oh?' Bastille said, finally sitting down in the fourth and final chair beside the hearth. 'You mean there are Smedrys who eventually grow up? Can I get assigned to one of them sometime? It would be a nice change.'

I chuckled, but Kaz just shook his head, looking distracted by something. 'I've got my Talent under control again,' he said. 'Finally. But it took far too long. It's like … the Talent went haywire for a while. I haven't had to wrestle with it like this for years.' He scratched his chin. 'I'll have to write a *paper* about it.'

Most members of my family, it should be noted, are some

kind of professor, teacher, or researcher. It may seem odd to you that a bunch of dedicated miscreants like us are also a bunch of scholars. If you think that, it means you haven't known enough professors in your time. What better way is there to avoid growing up for the rest of your life than to spend it perpetually in school?

'Pelicans!' Kaz swore suddenly, standing up. 'I don't have time for a paper right now! I nearly forgot. Pop, while I was wandering around lost, I passed through Mokia. Tuki Tuki itself is besieged!'

'We know,' Bastille said, her arms folded.

'We do?' Kaz said, scratching at his head.

'We've sent troops to help Mokia,' Bastille said. 'But the Librarians have begun to raid our nearby coasts. We can't give any more support to Mokia without leaving Nalhalla undefended.'

'It's more than that, I'm afraid,' Grandpa Smedry said. 'There are ... elements in the Council of Kings who are dragging their feet.'

'What?' Kaz exclaimed.

'You missed the whole thing with the treaty, son,' Grandpa said. 'I fear some of the kings have made alliances with the Librarians. They nearly got a motion through the Council to abandon Mokia entirely. That was defeated, but only by one vote. Those who were in favor of the motion are still working to deny support to Mokia. They have a lot of influence in the Council.'

'But the Librarians tried to kill them!' I exclaimed. 'What about the assassination attempt?'

As a side note, I hate assassination. It looks way too much like a dirty word. Either that or the name of a country populated entirely by two donkeys.

Grandpa just shrugged. 'Bureaucrats, lad! They can be denser than your uncle Kaz's bean soup.'

'Hey!' Kaz said. 'I like that soup!'

'I do too,' Grandpa said. 'Makes wonderful glue.'

'We need to do something,' Kaz said.

'I'm *trying* to,' Grandpa said. 'You should hear the speeches I'm giving!'

'Talk,' Kaz said. 'Tuki Tuki is close to falling, Pop! If the capital falls, the kingdom will fall with it.'

'What about the knights?' I said. 'Bastille, didn't you say most of the Knights of Crystallia are still here, in the city? Why aren't they on the battlefield?'

'The Crystin can't be used for that kind of purpose, lad,' Grandpa said, shaking his head. 'They're forbidden from taking sides in political conflicts.'

'But this isn't a political conflict!' I said. 'This is against the *Librarians*. They infiltrated the Crystin; they corrupted the Mindstone! If they win, they'll undoubtedly disband the knights anyway!'

Bastille grimaced. 'You see why I'm on edge? We *know* all of this, but our oaths forbid us from taking part unless we're defending a Smedry or one of the kings.'

'Well, one of the kings is in danger,' I said. 'Kaz just said so!'

'King Talakimallo isn't in the palace at Tuki Tuki,' Grandpa said, shaking his head. 'The knights got him away to a safe location soon after the palace came under siege The queen is leading the defense.'

'The queen of Mokia . . .' I said. 'Bastille, isn't that . . .'

'My sister,' she said, nodding. 'Angola Dartmoor.'

'The knights won't protect her?' I asked.

'She's not heir to a line,' Bastille said, shaking her head. 'They probably left one guard to protect her, but maybe not. The knights in the area probably all went with the king or with the heir, Princess Kamali.'

'Tuki Tuki is a *hugely* important tactical position,' Kaz said. 'We can't lose it!'

'The knights *want* to help, but we can't,' Bastille complained. 'It's forbidden. Besides, most of us have to be here in Nalhalla City to defend the Council of Kings and the Smedrys.'

'Though the Council no longer trusts the Crystin like they once did,' Grandpa added, shaking his head. 'And they forbid the knights' entrance to most important meetings.'

'So we just end up *sitting around*,' Bastille said, frustratedly knocking her head back against the backrest of her chair, 'going through endless training sessions and throwing the occasional grenade at someone who deserves it.' She eyed me.

'Baking Browns, what a mess!' Grandpa said. 'Maybe we need some snacks. I work better with a good broccoli yogurt pop to chew on.'

'First,' I said 'ew. Grandpa, that's almost crapaflapnasti. Second ...' I hesitated for a moment, an idea occurring to me. 'You're saying the knights have to protect important people.'

Bastille gave me one of her trademarked 'Well, duh, Alcatraz, you idiot'™ looks. I ignored it.

'And the Mokian palace is besieged, about to fall?' I continued.

'That's what it looked like to me,' Kaz said.

'So what if we sent someone really important off to Mokia?' I asked. 'The knights would have to follow, right? And if we had that someone take up residence in the Mokian palace, then the knights would *have* to defend the place, right?'

At that moment, something incredible happened. Something amazing, something incredible, something unbelievable.

Bastille smiled.

It was a deep, knowing smile. An eager smile. Almost a *wicked* smile. Like the smile on a jack-o'-lantern carved by a psychopathic kitten. (Oh, wait. *All* kittens are psychopathic. If you've forgotten, read book one again. In fact, read book one again either way. Someone told me once that it was really funny. What? You believed me in the foreword when I told you not to read them? What, you think you can trust *me*?)

Bastille's smile shocked me, pleased me, and made me nervous at the same time. 'I think,' she said, 'that is just about the *most brilliant* thing you've ever said, Alcatraz.'

Granted, the statement didn't have much competition for the title.

'It's certainly bold,' Grandpa said. 'Smedry-like for certain!'

'Who would we send?' Kaz said, growing eager. 'Could you go, Pop? They'd be *certain* to send knights to defend you.'

Grandpa hesitated, then shook his head. 'If I did that, I'd leave the king without an ally on the Council of Kings. He needs my vote.'

'But we'd need a direct heir,' Kaz said. 'I could go – I *will* go – but I've never been important enough to warrant more than a single knight. I'm not the direct heir. We could send Attica.'

'He's gone,' Bastille said. 'Fled the city. It's what we were talking about when you arrived.'

Grandpa nodded. 'We'd need to put someone in danger who is so valuable the knights *have* to respond. But this person also has to be *uncompromisingly* stoopid. It's idiocy on a grand scale to send oneself directly to a palace on the brink of destruction, surrounded by Librarians, in a doomed kingdom! Why, they'd have to be stoopid on a colossal degree. Of the likes previously unseen to all of humankind!'

And suddenly, for some reason, all eyes in the room turned toward me.

π

Okay, so maybe I exaggerated that last conversation just a little bit. Grandpa *might* have actually said something along the lines of 'We'd need someone really, really brave.' I felt that it's all right to make this swap, however, since bravery and stoopidity are practically one and the same.

Actually, there's a mathematical formula for it: STU ≥ BVE. That reads, quite simply, 'A person's stoopidity is greater than or equal to their bravery.' Simple, eh?

Oh, you want proof? You actually expect me to *justify* my ridiculous assertions? Well, all right. Just this once.

Look at it this way. If a man stumbled accidentally into a trap set by a group of Librarian agents, we'd think him stoopid. Right? However, if he charges valiantly into that same trap knowing it's there, he'd be called *brave*. Think about that for a moment. Which sounds dumber? Accidentally falling into the trap or *choosing* to fall into it?

There are plenty of ways to be stoopid that don't involve being brave. However, bravery is – by definition – always stoopid. Therefore, your stoopidity is *at least* equal to your level of bravery. Probably greater.

After all, reading that ridiculous explanation probably made you feel dumber just by association. (Reading this book sure is brave of you.)

I burst into the small meeting chamber. The monarchs sat in thrones arranged in a half circle, listening to one of their members – in this case, a woman in an ancient-looking suit of bamboo armor – stand before them and argue her point. The walls depicted murals of beautiful mountain scenes, and a little indoor stream gurgled its way along the far wall.

All of the monarchs turned toward me, eyes aghast at being interrupted.

'Ah, young Smedry!' said one of them, a regal-looking man with a square red beard and a set of kingly robes to match it. Brig Dartmoor, Bastille's father, was king of Nalhalla and generally considered foremost among the monarchs. He stood up from his chair. 'How ... unusual to see you.'

The others looked panicked. I realized that the *last* time I'd barged in on them like this, I'd come to warn them about a Librarian plot and had ended up nearly getting them all assassinated. (The non-donkey kind.)

I took a deep breath. 'I can't take it any longer!' I exclaimed. 'I hate being cooped up in this city! I need a vacation!'

The monarchs glanced at one another, relaxing slightly. I hadn't come to warn them of impending disaster; this was just the usual Smedry drama.

'Well, that's fine, I guess ...' King Dartmoor said. Anyone else would probably have demanded to know why this 'vacation' was so important as to interrupt the Council of Kings. But Dartmoor was quite accustomed to handling Smedrys. I was only just beginning to understand what a reputation for oddness my family had – and this was compared with everyone around them, who lived in a city filled with castles, dragons that climbed on walls, grenades that look like teddy bears, and the occasional talking dinosaur in a vest. Being odd compared with all of them took *quite* a bit of effort. (My family is a bunch of overachievers when it comes to freakish behavior.)

'Perhaps you'd like to visit the countryside,' said one of the kings. 'The firelizard trees are in bloom.'

'I hear the lightning caverns are electrifying this time of year,' another added.

'You could always try skydiving off the Worldspire,' said the woman in the Asian-style bamboo armor. 'Drop through the Bottomless Chasm for a few hours? It's rather relaxing, with a waterfall on all sides, falling through the air.'

'Wow,' I said, losing a bit of my momentum. 'Those *do* sound interesting. Maybe I—' Bastille elbowed me from behind at that point, making me exclaim a surprised 'Gak!'

'Protect your straw!' one of the monarchs cried, taking off his large straw hat. He looked around urgently. 'Oh, false alarm.'

I cleared my throat, glancing over my shoulder. Bastille and Grandpa Smedry had entered the room after me but had left the door open so that the knights guarding outside could hear what I was saying. Bastille's stern mother, Draulin, stood with folded arms, eyeing us suspiciously. She obviously expected some kind of shenanigan.

Very clever of her.

'No!' I declared to the kings. 'None of that will do. They're not exciting enough.' I held up my finger. 'I'm going to Tuki Tuki. I hear that the royal mud baths there are *extremely* intense.'

'Wait,' King Dartmoor said. 'You think *skydiving* through a *bottomless pit* in the ocean isn't exciting enough, so instead you want to go visit the Mokian palace spa?'

'Er, yes,' I said. 'I have a fondness for mud baths. Exfoliating my homeopathic algotherapy and all that.'

The monarchs glanced at one another.

'But,' one of them said, 'the palace is *kind of* besieged right now, and—'

'I will not be dissuaded!' I exclaimed with forced bravado. 'I am a Smedry, and we do ridiculous, unexpected, eccentric things like this all the time! Ha-ha!'

'Oh dear,' Grandpa Smedry said in an exaggerated voice. 'He really does seem determined. My poor grandson will be killed because of his awesome, Smedry-like impulsiveness. If only there were a group of people dedicated to protecting him!'

With that, we turned and dashed away from the chamber, leaving the kings and knights dumbfounded. Bastille, Grandpa, and I entered the main palace hallway, which was lined with frames containing rare and exotic types of glass. They glowed faintly to my eyes, as I was still wearing my Oculator's Lenses.

'Do you think they'll buy it?' I asked.

'Wait,' Bastille said, frowning. 'Buy it? Did you try to sell them something?'

'Er, no. It's a figure of speech.'

'The figure giving a speech?' Bastille said. 'If you're *that* interested in her figure, you should be ashamed. Queen Kamiko is a married woman and *as least* forty years older than you are!'

I sighed. 'Do you think,' I rephrased, 'they'll believe the act? It seemed a little exaggerated to me.'

'Exaggerated?' Bastille said. 'What part?'

'The part about me going to Mokia – into a war zone – just to take a vacation. It's kind of ridiculous.'

'Sounds like a Smedry activity to me,' Bastille grumbled.

'They'll buy it, lad,' Grandpa said, jogging along beside us. 'The knights in particular tend to be very ... literal people. They'll assume the worst, and that worst – in this case – is that you are going to blunder off into a war zone because you feel that your pores are clogged. I don't think we'll have any trouble getting them to—'

A clanking sound came from behind us. I glanced over my shoulder.

No fewer than *fifty* Knights of Crystallia were rushing down the hallway in our direction.

'Gak!' I cried.

'Alcatraz, would you stop saying—' Bastille looked over her shoulder. 'GAK!'

'Scribbling Scalzis!' Grandpa exclaimed, noticing the fleet of knights charging in our direction. Most wore full plate, the silvery metal clanking as their amored feet hit the floor. It sounded like someone had opened a closet filled with pots and then dumped them all onto the ground at once.

We redoubled our efforts, running in front of the storm of knights with all we had. But they were faster. They had Warrior's Lenses, not to mention Crystin enhancements. They'd catch us for sure.

'Alcatraz, lad,' Grandpa Smedry said in a confiding tone as we ran down the wide hallway. 'I believe I may have discovered a slight flaw in your clever plan.'

'You think?'

'I knew this would happen!' Bastille said from my other side. 'I'm such an *idiot*. Alcatraz, if they can catch you before you leave, they can take you into protective care for your own good!'

'Protective care?' I asked.

'Usually involves a locked door,' Grandpa said. 'Padded cell. Bread and water. Oh, and a jail. Can't forget that.'

'They'll throw us in *jail*?' I exclaimed.

'Hmm, yes,' Grandpa Smedry said. 'The knights are bodyguards, lad. They have the right to determine when someone under their charge is going to be put into too much danger. They only have power to do it while we're inside Nalhalla.' He smiled. 'They rarely invoke the privilege. We must *really* have them worried! Good job, lad! You should feel proud.'

This is a very exciting scene, isn't it? You're not too tired, are you? From all that exciting running?

Wait, you're *not running*? Why am I doing all the work? Don't you realize that you're supposed to be acting out these scenes as I describe them? Don't you know how to read books? I mean honestly, what are the Librarians teaching people these days?

Let me explain it to you. Everyone always talks about the magic of books being able to take you to other places, to let you see exotic worlds, to make you experience new and interesting things. Well, do you think words alone can do this? Of course not!

If you've ever thought that books are boring, it's because you don't know how to read them correctly. From now on, when you read a book, I want you to scream the words of the novel out loud while reading them, then do exactly what the characters are doing in the story.

Trust me, it will make books *way* more exciting. Even dictionaries. *Particularly* dictionaries. So go ahead and try it out with this next part of this book. If you do it right, you'll win the bonus prize.

'Come on!' I yelled, ducking into a side room. I figured that the knights would have trouble following through smaller chambers, since there were so many of them. The room was filled with furniture, however, and I was forced to leap up on top of a couch and hurl myself behind it.

'What do we do?' Bastille asked, looking over her shoulder. The knights were rushing into the room behind us.

'I'm not sure!' I said, picking my nose.

We burst out of the room into a hallway, where I hopped up and down on one foot three times, then punched myself (softly) in the forehead. After that, we pranced down the hallway flapping our arms like chickens. Then we twirled around, smacking our brother if he happened to be near. Then we stuck our feet in our mouths before dumping pudding on our heads while singing 'Hambo the Great' in Dutch.

Now see, didn't I *tell* you it would be more exciting this way? You should act out all books you read. (And by the way, the bonus prize is getting to smack your brother and blame it on me.)

'Why are we doing this?' Bastille cried.

'It's not really helping, is it?' I replied.

'I don't mean to be depressing,' Grandpa noted, 'but I do think they're gaining on us.'

It was an understatement. They were *right* behind us. I yelped, bolting down a side hallway, Bastille easily keeping up. She had Warrior's Lenses on and could outrun Grandpa and me, but she hung back.

'Only one thing for me to do!' Grandpa Smedry said, raising a finger.

'What's that?' I asked.

'Switch sides!' he replied. And then he stopped running, letting the knights catch up to him. 'Come on, let's get him!' Grandpa cried, pointing at me.

I froze, looking at him, shocked. Bastille tugged me forward, and I stumbled into motion, running again. The knights didn't take Grandpa into protective care. One did pick him up and carry him, however, so he didn't slow them down. In seconds, we were being chased not only by an entire force of Knights of Crystallia but my moustachioed grandfather as well.

'What's he doing?' I demanded.

'Burn him at the stake!' Grandpa yelled from just behind.

'Well,' Bastille said, 'he never *was* going to go with us. Remember? When we acted in front of the kings, his part was to claim that he didn't want you to go and couldn't stop you.'

'Dice him up and feed him to the fishes!' Grandpa yelled, voice softer.

'Why did we decide that again?' I sputtered.

'Pull his insides out through his nose and paint him with eyeliner!' Grandpa Smedry yelled distantly.

'Because we didn't want him to get into trouble for what you're doing!' Bastille said.

'Make him watch old *Little House on the Prairie* reruns!' Grandpa Smedry bellowed, voice dwindling.

'Well, does he have to get into the part so enthusiastically?' I said. 'He's making me ... Wait, *voice dwindling?*' I glanced over my shoulder.

The knights and my grandfather had fallen back. I frowned, confused. The knights seemed to be running as hard as ever. In fact, they seemed to be running even *harder* than before. And yet they were still losing ground.

'What?' I said.

'He's making them late!' Bastille said. 'Using his Talent! By joining their side, then trying to chase after us, he's making them all too slow to catch us!'

I gawked, amazed. My grandfather's skill with using his Talent was incredible. I wondered, not for the first time, what I could manage with my *own* Talent if I were as trained as he was. Mostly, these last few months in Nalhalla, I'd spent my time learning to *avoid* using my Talent. I had it almost completely under control. I hadn't broken anything unexpected in weeks.

I was beginning to think that I might be able to live a normal life. But sometimes, when my grandfather did incredible things with his Talent, it made me envious.

That was stoopid. (And trust me, I'm an expert on stoopid.) I'd spent my entire childhood ruled and dominated by my Talent. Accomplishing something like Grandpa just did was incredible, but also unpredictable. Even the best of Smedrys couldn't make events like this work all the time.

I wanted to be rid of my Talent. Free. Didn't I?

'Gee, what a nice moment of reflection,' Bastille said, stepping up to me.

'Yeah,' I said, watching the troop of frustrated knights, who seemed to be all but running in place, barely inching forward.

'Do you want another moment or two to, you know, be all philosophical and crud? Or do you want to get your *shattering* legs moving so we can escape!'

'Oh, right,' I said. Grandpa wouldn't be able to hold them back forever. In fact, they already looked like they were moving more quickly, regaining some momentum.

I turned with Bastille and continued running. We needed to get out of the city, and *fast*.

4½

It's undoubtedly becoming obvious to you that my stoopidity in this book is pretty shatteringly spectacular. Not only am I planning to charge off into a war zone with nothing to protect me but a couple of bits of glass but I just managed to alienate and anger an entire order of knights in the process. I just spent the three previous volumes of my autobiography trying to *escape* the Librarians. Now that I had finally found peace and safety in Nalhalla, I'd decided to run off and put myself into the middle of the war?

Stoopid.

Actually, no, it's *not* stoopid. *Stoopid* just isn't specific enough. Fortunately, since I'm an expert on stoopidity – and an expert on making up stuff – I'm going to give you a set of *new* definitions to use for things that are really stoopid. For example, what I was about to go do can be referred to as *stoopidalicious*, which is defined as 'about as stoopid as a porcupine-catching contest during a swimsuit competition.'

Bastille and I dashed up a set of stairs onto the upper level of the palace. Once there, I slammed a hand down on the top step and engaged my Talent. A shock of power ran down my arm, hitting the stairs and making them crumble away behind us. Stone blocks crashed to the ground and the banister fell sideways. An enormous puff of dust erupted into the air, like the noxious breath of a belching giant. As it cleared, I could see a group of annoyed knights standing below. They'd finally gotten smart and broken into two groups. Grandpa Smedry could keep only one group late, so the other group was free to chase Bastille and me.

Now they were trapped below. But there were other ways up

to our floor. 'I don't think we can keep staying ahead of them like this,' I said. 'We need to get out of the city.'

'You just said that at the end of the last chapter!' Bastille complained.

'Well, it's still true!' I snapped. Below, the knights split again, some running off to find another way up. A few remained behind and began giving one another leg-ups or jumping. They got surprisingly close to reaching the upper floor.

I yelped and hurried away from the hole, Bastille following.

'Sorry about the stairs,' I said. 'Your father won't be mad at me for that, will he?'

'We have Smedrys over to the palace for dinner frequently,' she said. 'Things like broken staircases are routine for us. However, I *will* point out that you just trapped us on the upper floor of the palace. I'll bet my mother and the other knights will have the stairwells all blocked off shortly.'

'Do you have a Transporter's Glass station?'

'Yeah. In the basement.'

'It's guarded anyway,' Kaz added.

I cursed. 'You've got to have some kind of secret exit from the building, right, Bastille? Tunnels? Passages hidden in the walls? A fireplace that rotates around and reveals your secret crime-fighting lair?'

'Nope,' Kaz said.

Bastille nodded. 'My father feels that sort of thing is too easy for enemies to use against him.'

'No secret passages at all?' I exclaimed. 'What kind of castle *is* this?'

'The non-stoopidalicious kind!' Bastille said. 'Who puts passages *inside* the walls? Isn't that a little ridiculous?'

'Not when you need to sneak out!'

'Why would I need to sneak out of my own home?'

'Because Knights of Crystallia are chasing you!'

'This sort of thing doesn't happen to me very often!' Bastille snapped. 'In fact, it *only* seems to happen when you're involved!'

'I can't help the fact that people like to chase me. We need to—'

I froze in the middle of the hallway. 'Kaz!' I exclaimed, pointing at him.

'Me!' he exclaimed back.

'Idiots!' Bastille said, pointing at both of us.

'When did you get here?' I demanded of my short uncle.

'A few moments ago,' he said. 'Everything's packed back at Keep Smedry, ready for takeoff. I borrowed a vehicle from the Mokian embassy, as I didn't want to alert the king of what we were doing.'

'We have a pilot?' I asked.

'Sure do,' he replied. 'Aydee Ecks.'

'Who?'

'Your cousin,' he said. 'Sister to Sing and Australia. She was delivering a message to the embassy from Mokia.'

'Sounds good,' I said. It was always nice to have another Smedry along on a mission. Well, nice and catastrophic at the same time. But when you're a Smedry, you learn to make the catastrophes work for you.

A distant clanking preceded a group of knights, who stormed out of a side hallway a moment later. They spotted us and began running in our direction.

'Kaz!' I said. 'Get us out of here!'

'Are you sure?' he said. 'My Talent has been—'

'Now, Kaz!' I said.

'All right,' he said with a sigh, walking over and pulling open a door. We'd used Kaz's Talent of getting lost to transport us before. Like all Smedry Talents, it was unpredictable – but it was fairly safe to use across short distances.

Besides, we didn't have time to try anything else. I raced through the doorway, Bastille behind me. Kaz pulled the door closed behind us.

The room smelled musty and wet inside, like mold or fungus, but it was too dark to see anything.

'Activate your Talent!' I told Kaz.

'I already did,' he replied.

There was a scraping noise. Like something very large being pulled across the stone floor. I blinked as Bastille unsheathed her sword, the crystalline weapon shedding a cool, blue light across our surroundings. We were in a cave. And standing before us, looking very confused, was an enormous black dragon. It cocked its head at us, smoke trailing from its nostrils.

'Well,' I said, relieved. 'It's just a dragon. For a moment, I was frightened!' We'd met a dragon before, and it had quite nicely *not* eaten us. In fact, it had carried us on its back.

The dragon inhaled deeply.

'Kaz!' Bastille said, panicked.

'Put away that light!' he said. 'It's hard to get lost if I can see where I'm going!'

I frowned at the others. 'It's just a dragon.'

'Just a free baledragon,' Bastille said with alarm, 'who – unlike Tzoctinatin – is not serving a prison sentence, and who is perfectly free to roast us because we're invading his den and violating the draco-human treaty!' She slammed her sword back in its sheath, plunging us into darkness.

'Oh,' I said.

A light appeared in front of us, illuminating the inside of the dragon's mouth as fire gathered in its throat and began to blast toward us.

'Reason number two hundred and fifty-seven why it's better to be a short person that a tall person!' Kaz exclaimed. 'Standing next to a tall person gives you a really great shield for dragon's breath!'

Bastille grabbed me by the collar and yanked me hard after her, and everything spun. I felt a strange *force* around me, a lurching feeling as Kaz activated his Talent, getting us lost. The dragon's flames vanished.

I recognized that force – the force of the Talent – immediately, though I'd never experienced it before when Kaz had used his Talent. It was hard to explain. It felt like I could see the warping of the air, could tell what was going on as Kaz saved us.

It almost seemed familiar. Like Kaz wasn't just getting us lost, like he was … well, like he was *breaking* the way that motion worked. Deconstructing the natural, linear progression of the world and rebuilding it so that we could move in directions we shouldn't have been able to.

In that moment, I thought I saw something. An enormous, magnificent stone disk, full of carvings and etchings, divided into four different quadrants. And at the very center, a patch of black rock. There was something crouching there in the center, invisible because of how dark it was. A patch of midnight itself. And it reached tentacles out to the other quadrants, like black vines growing over a wall.

The Bane of Incarna. That which twists ... that which corrupts ... that which destroys ...

The Dark Talent. Of which all others are shadows.

The vision vanished, gone so quickly that I wasn't certain I'd even seen it. Everything was dark again, and I stumbled, tripping. When I hit the ground, I hit something wet, soft, and squishy.

'Ew!' I said, trying to push myself to my feet. The floor undulated beneath me, pulsing, quivering. It was like I'd fallen onto a massive trampoline covered with slick grease. And the stench was *terrible*. Like someone had pelted a skunk with rotten eggs.

Bastille made a gagging noise, pulling her sword from its sheath to give us light. The three of us were crowded together inside of a pink room, the walls and ceiling all made of the same soft, quivering material. It was like we were trapped in some kind of sack. There wasn't even room enough to sit up, and we were coated with a slick, goolike substance.

'Aw, sparrows,' Kaz swore.

'I think I'm going to be sick!' Bastille said. 'Are we ...?'

'My Talent transported us into the dragon's stomach, it appears,' Kaz said, scratching his head, trying to stand up on the fleshy surface. 'Whoops.'

'Whoops?' I cried, realizing that the liquidy stuff had to be some kind of bile or phlegm. 'That's all you can say? Whoops?'

'Ew!' Bastille said.

'Well, if we're going to be eaten by a dragon,' he noted, 'this is the way to do it. Bypassing the teeth and all.'

'I'd rather not be eaten at all!'

'Ew!' Bastille repeated.

'Hide the sword,' Kaz said, finally getting to his feet. He was short enough to stand upright. 'I'll get us out of here.'

'Great,' I said, the light winking out. 'Maybe you could get us a bath too, and – gruble-garb-burgle!'

I was suddenly underwater.

I thrashed about in the dark, terrified, suffocating. The water was horribly cold, and my skin grew numb in a few heartbeats. I opened my mouth to cry out—

Which, mind you, was a pretty stoopidalicious thing to do.

And then I washed out into open air, water rushing around me as I fell through an open doorway. Kaz stood to the side, gasping, holding the door open. He'd managed to get us to Keep Smedry; a familiar black stone hallway led in either direction.

I sat up, holding my head, my clothing wet. We appeared to have fallen out of the cleaning closet, and the floor of the hallway was now soaked with salty seawater. A few small, white-eyed fish flopped around on the stones. Bastille lay in front of me, hair a soggy silver mass. She groaned and sat up, flipping her hair back.

'Where were we?' I asked.

'Bottom of the ocean,' Kaz said, taking off his soaked leather jacket and eyeing it appraisingly.

'The pressure should have killed us!'

'Nah,' Kaz said, wringing out his jacket, 'we surprised her. We were gone before she realized we were there.'

'Her?' I asked.

'The ocean,' Kaz said. 'She never expects Smedry Talents.'

'Who does?' Bastille said, her voice flat.

'Well, you *did* say you wanted a bath,' Kaz said. 'Come on. We should get moving before those knights think to send someone to Keep Smedry.'

I sighed, climbing to my feet, and the three of us jogged down the hallway – our clothing making squishing noises – and entered a stairwell. We climbed to the top of one of the keep's towers and ran out onto the landing pad. There we found an enormous glass butterfly lethargically flapping its wings. It reflected the sunlight, throwing out colourful sparkles of light in all directions.

I froze. 'Wait. *This* is our escape vehicle?'

'Sure,' Kaz said. 'The *Colorfly*. Something wrong?'

'Well, it's not particularly ... manly.'

'So?' Bastille said, hands on hips.

'Er ... I mean ... Well, I was hoping to be able to escape in something a little more impressive.'

'So if it's not manly, it's not impressive?' Bastille said, folding her arms.

'I ... er ...'

'Now would be a good time to shut up, Al,' Kaz said, chuckling. 'You see, if your mouth is closed, that will prevent you from saying anything else. And that will prevent you from getting a foot in your mouth – either yours placed there or hers kicking you.'

It seemed like good advice. I shut my mouth and trotted after Kaz, making my way to the gangplank up to the glass butterfly.

To this day, however, I'm bothered by that departure. I was going on what was, in many ways, my first real mission. Before, I'd stumbled into things accidentally. But now I'd actively decided to go out and help.

It seemed that I should be able to make my triumphant departure inside something cooler than a butterfly. In heroic journey terms, that's like being sent to college driving a pale yellow '76 Pacer. (Ask your parents.)

But, as I believe I've proven to you in the past, life is not fair. If life were fair, ice cream would be calorie free, kittens would come with warning labels stamped on their foreheads, and James Joyce's 'The Dead' would totally be about zombies. (And don't get me started on Faulkner's *As I Lay Dying*.)

'Hey, cousin!' a voice exclaimed. A head popped out of the bottom of the butterfly. It had short, black hair with dark tan skin. A hand followed, waving at me. Both belonged to a young Mokian girl. If she were from the Hushlands, she'd have been described as Hawaiian or Samoan. She was wearing a colourful red-and-blue sarong and had a flower pinned in her hair.

'Who are you?' I asked, walking under the glass vehicle.

'I'm your cousin Aydee! Kaz says you need me to fly you to Mokia.' There was an exuberance about her that reminded me of her sister, Australia. Only Australia was much older. This girl couldn't be more than eight years old.

'*You're* our pilot? But you're just a kid!'

'I know! Ain't it great?' She smirked, then pulled back into the butterfly, a glass plate sliding into place where she'd been hanging.

'Best not to challenge her, Al,' Kaz said, walking up and laying a hand on my arm.

'But we're going into a war zone!' I said, looking at Kaz. 'We shouldn't bring a kid into that.'

'Oh, so perhaps I should leave *you* behind?' Kaz said. 'The Hushlanders would call you a kid too.'

'That's different,' I said lamely.

'Her homeland is being attacked,' Bastille said, climbing up the gangplank. 'She has a right to help. Nobody sends children into battle, but they can help in other ways. Like flying us to Mokia. Come on! Have you forgotten that we're being chased?'

'It seems like I'm *always* being chased,' I said, climbing up the gangplank. 'Come on. Let's get going.'

Kaz followed me up, and the gangplank swung closed. The butterfly lurched into the air and swooped

... well, fluttered ...

away from the city in a dramatic

... well, leisurely ...

flight toward Mokia, with a dangerous

... well, mostly just a *cute* ...

determination to see the kingdom protected and defended!

Either that or we'd just spend our time drinking nectar from flowers. You know, whatever ended up working.

42

Change.

It's important to change. I, for instance, change my underwear every day. Hopefully you do too. If you don't, please stay downwind.

Change is frightening. Few of us ever want things to change. (Well, things other than underwear.) But change is also fascinating – in fact, it's necessary. Just ask Heraclitus.

Heraclitus was a funny little Greek man best known for letting his brother do all of the hard work, for calling people odd names, and for writing lyrics for Disney songs about two thousand years too early for them to be sung. He was quite an expert on change, even going so far as to change from *alive* to *dead* after smearing cow dung on his face. (Er, yes, that last part is true, I'm afraid.)

Heraclitus is the first person we know of to ever gripe about how often things change. In fact, he went so far as to guess that you can never touch the same object twice – because everything and everybody changes so quickly, any object you touch will change into something else before you touch it again.

I suppose that this is true. We're all made of cells, and those are bouncing around, breaking off, drying, changing. If nothing could change, then we wouldn't be able to think, grow, or even breathe. What would be the point? We'd all be about as dynamic as a pile of rocks. (Though, as I think about it, even that pile of rocks is changing moment by moment, as the winds blow and break off atoms.)

So ... I guess what Heraclitus was saying is that your underpants are always changing, and *technically* you now have on a different pair than you did when you began reading this chapter. So I guess you *don't* have to change them every day.

Sweet! Thanks, philosophy!

I whistled in amazement, hanging upside down from the tree. 'Wow! That was *quite* the trip! Aydee, you're a fantastic pilot.'

'Thanks!' Aydee said, hanging nearby.

'I mean, I thought thirty-seven chapters' worth of flying would be boring,' I said. 'But that was probably the most exciting thing I've been a part of since Grandpa showed up on my doorstep six months ago!'

'I particularly enjoyed the fight with the giant half squid, half wombat,' Bastille said.

'You really showed him something!' I said.

'Thanks! I didn't realize he'd be so interested in my stamp collection.'

'Yeah, I didn't realize you'd taken so many pictures of people's faces you'd stamped on!'

'Personally,' Kaz said, untangling himself from the bushes below, 'I preferred the part where we flew up into space.'

'We should have done that in book two,' Bastille said. 'Then that cover would have made sense.'

'There were so many exciting things on this trip,' I said, still swinging in the vines. 'It's tough to pick just one as my favorite.'

Kaz dusted himself off, looking up at me. 'Reason number eighty-two why it's better to be a short person: When you plummet to your doom, you don't fall as far as tall people.'

'What?' I said. 'Of course you do!'

'Nonsense,' Kaz said. 'Maybe our *feet* fall as far as yours, but our heads have less distance to fall. So it's less dangerous for us on average.'

'I don't think it works that way,' Bastille said.

Kaz shrugged. 'Anyway, Al, if you ever write your autobiography, you're going to have a real tough time writing out that trip here. I mean ... words just won't be able to describe how perfectly *awesome* it was.'

'I'm sure I'll think of something,' I said, letting Bastille help me untangle myself from the vines. I dropped awkwardly to the ground beside Kaz, and then Bastille went to help Aydee get down.

'Where are we?' I asked.

'Just outside of Tuki Tuki, by my guess,' Kaz said. 'I'm certain that rock that knocked down the *Colorfly* was thrown by a Librarian machine. I'll go scout for a moment. Wait here.'

Kaz moved off into the bushes, pulling out his machete. He didn't – thankfully – engage his Talent. I made sure to keep an eye on him as he walked out toward the sunlit ridge in the near distance. We were in a dense, tropical jungle arrayed with a large number of flowers hanging from vines, sprouting from trees, and blooming at our feet. Insects buzzed around, moving from flower to flower, and didn't seem to have any interest in me or the others.

The flight had taken a long time, but it had seemed to pass remarkably quickly, considering how busy we'd been with wombats, outer space, and stamp collections. It seemed like just a few moments ago that we'd left Nalhalla, yet now here we were, hours of flying later, in Mokia. In fact, those chapters were so fast, so quick, so exciting, it almost feel like I skipped writing them.

Good thing I didn't, though. That would have been pretty stoopid of me, eh?

Aydee sighed as Bastille helped her down. 'I'm going to miss that ship.'

'You know,' I said, 'that's the third time I've been up in one of those glass ships, and it's *also* the third time I've crash-landed. I'm beginning to think that they aren't very safe.'

'Of course there *couldn't* be another explanation,' Bastille said dryly.

'What do you mean?'

'I've flown in them hundreds of times,' Bastille said. 'And the only three times *I've* crash-landed, I've been flying with you.'

'Oh,' I said, scratching my head.

'I'm going to have to travel with you more often, cousin!' Aydee said. 'I *never* get shot down when I fly on my own!'

It appeared that Aydee had inherited the characteristic Smedry sense of adventure. I eyed my diminutive cousin. We hadn't had much of a chance to talk, despite the lengthy flight – we'd had to spend too much time dodging war koalas while building a new lighthouse for underprivileged children. (You might want to reread Chapters Five through Forty-One to relive the adventure of it all.)

I reached out to her. 'I don't believe I've properly introduced myself. I'm Alcatraz.'

'Aydee Ecks,' she said energetically. 'Is it true you have the Breaking Talent?'

'The one and only,' I said. 'It's not everything it's cracked up to be.'

'No,' Bastille added, *'everything else* is what it cracks up.'

'What's your Talent?' I asked Aydee, shooting a dry look at Bastille.

'I'm really bad at math!' she proclaimed.

By now I was getting used to Smedry Talents. I'd met family members who were magically bad at dancing, others who were great at looking ugly in the morning. Being bad at math … well, that just seemed to fit right in. 'Congratulations,' I said. 'That sounds useful.'

Aydee beamed.

Kaz came traipsing back a few moments later, his pack slung on his shoulder. 'Yup,' he said, 'we're here. The capital city is just a short hike down that direction, but there's a full Librarian blockade set up around the place.'

'Great,' I said.

The others looked at me, expecting me to take the lead. Partially because of my lineage, but also because I'd organized this trip. It was still odd to be in charge, but I'd taken the lead a number of times now. Though it had originally bothered me, I was getting used to it. (Kind of how listening to really loud music a lot will slowly make your hearing worse.)

'All right,' I said, kneeling down. 'Let's go over our resources. Bastille, what do you have?'

'Sword,' she said, patting the sheath at her side. 'Dagger. Warrior's Lenses. Glassweave outfit.' Her militaristic trousers and jacket were made of a special kind of defensive glass; they could take a pounding and leave her unharmed. She pulled her stylish sunglasses out of her pocket and put them on. They'd enhance her physical abilities.

'Kaz?'

'I've got a pair of Warrior's Lenses too,' he said. He patted his pack. 'I've got my sling to throw rocks, and some standard gear. Rope, a couple of throwing knives, a grappling hook, flares and snacks.'

'Snacks?'

'Pop taught me never to rescue a near-doomed allied kingdom on an empty stomach.'

'Wise man, my grandfather,' I said. 'Aydee, what do you have?'

'A bubbly, infectious personality!' she said. 'And a cute flower in my hair.'

'Excellent.' I fished around in my pocket. 'I've got my standard Oculator's Lenses,' I said, 'along with my Translator's Lenses and one Truthfinder's Lens.' The former had been given to me by my father; the latter I'd discovered in the tomb of Alcatraz the First. Neither were very powerful in battle, but they could be useful in other ways.

As I fished in the pockets of my jacket, I was shocked to discover something else. A pouch that hadn't been there before, at least not in the morning when I'd gotten dressed. I pulled it out, frowning, then undid the laces at the top.

Inside were two pairs of Lenses. They glowed powerfully to my eyes, as I was wearing my Oculator's Lenses.

I took the new Lenses out. One had a baby blue tint to them. I'd used these before; they were called Courier's Lenses. The other Lenses had a green-and-purple tint.

'Wow,' Bastille said, snatching the second pair from my hand, holding them up. 'Alcatraz, where did you get *these*?'

'I have no idea,' I said, looking inside the pouch. There appeared to be a little note tucked into it. 'What are they?'

'Bestower's Lenses,' she said, sounding just a bit awed. 'They're very powerful.'

I got the note out, unfolding it. *You called me once with a set of*

Courier's Lenses when you weren't supposed to be able to, the note said. *Give it a try again.*

It was signed Grandpa Smedry.

I hesitated, then pulled off my Oculator's Lenses and put on the Courier's Lenses. They were supposed to be able to work over only short distances, but I was discovering that there were a lot of things about Lenses and silimatic glass that didn't work the way everyone said they did.

I concentrated, doing something I'd only recently learned to do, giving extra *power* to the Lenses. Static fuzzed in my ears. And then, an image of Grandpa Smedry's face appeared in front of me, hovering in the air. It was faintly translucent.

Ha! Grandpa's voice said in my ears. *Alcatraz, my boy, you really can do it!*

'Yeah,' I said. The others gave me odd looks, but I tapped the glasses.

You found the Lenses, I presume? Grandpa asked.

'I did,' I replied. 'How'd you get them into my pocket?'

Oh, I've been known to practice a little sleight of hand in my day, my boy, he said. *I'd been meaning to give you those Lenses for some time. Make good use of them. I'm sure dear Bastille can tell you how to use them. Ha! The lass seems to know more about my Lenses sometimes than I do! Are you in Mokia yet?*

'We've arrived at Tuki Tuki,' I said. 'I've got Kaz with me, and my cousin Aydee.'

Excellent, lad, excellent. I'm working on the knights. I've almost got them in agreement to come with me to 'rescue' you. But they're not convinced that you're in danger. They think that you tricked them and didn't really fly to Mokia – you just acted like it to try to get them to go join the war.

'Wow,' I said. 'As I think about it, that might have been a pretty good idea.'

Except for the fact that we'll need to prove to them where you are, Grandpa said. *Your cousin Aydee was in town dropping off a bit of Communicator's Glass. The other piece is in the palace, with Bastille's sister, the queen. If you can contact the Mokian embassy* in Nalhalla through it, that will prove that you're there in Mokia. They won't take my word on it with the Courier's Lenses, but if you contact the embassy, the knights will have no choice but to come defend you.

'All right,' I said.

This will be dangerous, lad, Grandpa said. I don't want you getting hurt.

'But that's the Smedry way!' I said, imitating him.

Ha! Well, so it is. But surviving is also the Smedry way. Get in, contact the embassy, and then lay low. Don't go fight on the battlefield yourself. Understand?

'Clear as glass,' I said.

What kind of glass? Grandpa asked.

'The transparent kind,' I said. 'I'll let you know once we're inside.'

Good lad.

His face vanished, and I felt an overwhelming fatigue. I stumbled over to a moss-covered stone and sat down, exhausted.

'Alcatraz,' Bastille said, 'was your grandfather still in Nalhalla?'

I nodded.

'But ... you shouldn't be able to ...'

'I know, Bastille,' I said. 'That's probably why I'm so tired. Impossible things are really rough to do, you know.'

She looked troubled.

'Hey!' Kaz exclaimed suddenly, looking through his pack. 'I forgot that I stuffed these in here.' He pulled out some colored teddy bears.

'Oh!' Aydee said, squealing and running over to snatch them up.

'Aydee!' I said, standing. 'Wait! Those are grenades!'

'I know,' she said enthusiastically.' 'I love grenades!'

Yes, she's a Smedry all right.

'How many do you have?' I asked.

'One of each of the main three kinds,' Kaz said.

'So, six?' Aydee said.

'Uh,' I said. 'Actually, one plus one plus one is ...' I trailed off as, suddenly, Aydee was holding not three, but six bears.

'One plus one plus one,' she proclaimed. 'Six, right?'

I blinked. *She's bad at math* ... Her Talent, it appears, had *forced* the world to match her powers of addition.

'Don't correct her, Al,' Kaz said, chuckling. 'At least not when her bad math is in our favor. Nice work, Aydee.'

'But what did I do?' she said, confused, handing back the exploding bears.

'Nothing,' Kaz said, tucking the bears in his pack.

Aydee was young enough that she hadn't learned to control her Talent yet – and I couldn't really blame her for that, since I barely had mine under control myself. Her Talent would be hard to control anyway, since she could only make mathematical miracles when she legitimately calculated wrong in her head.

'Alcatraz, are you all right?' Bastille asked.

I nodded, still feeling tired but forcing myself to my feet. 'Come on. I want to see what we're up against.'

Kaz led the way over to the ridge. We walked up to it, looking out of the jungle over a daunting sight.

Beneath us, the forest had been trampled to the ground. The black tents of an enormous army were pitched amid the stumps of trees, and the smoke of a hundred fires rose into the sky. The army encircled a small hilltop city made entirely of wooden huts, with a wooden-stake wall around the outside. It looked small and fragile, but it had some kind of shield around it – a bubble of glass, like a translucent dome. That glass was cracked and broken in several places.

The army was bad enough. However, the things that stood behind it were even more daunting – three enormous robots dressed like Librarians, holding enormous swords on their shoulders.

'Giant robots,' I said. 'They have *giant robots*.'

'Er, yes,' Kaz said. 'That's what threw the rock at us.'

'Why didn't anyone shattering *tell* me they had giant robots!'

The others shrugged.

'Maybe we're fighting for the wrong side,' I said.

'We're fighting for what is right,' Kaz said.

'Yeah, *without* giant robots.'

'They're not so tough,' Bastille said, eyes narrowed. 'They're nearly useless in battle. Always tripping over things.'

'But they're great at throwing rocks,' Kaz added.

'All right,' I said, taking a deep breath. 'Grandpa needs us to sneak into the palace and call from inside, using the queen's Communicator's Glass. Any ideas?'

'Well,' Kaz said, 'I could use my Talent to—'

'No!' Bastille and I both said at the same time. I *still* hadn't gotten all of the dragon stomach snot out of my hair.

'You tall people,' Kaz said with a sigh. 'Always so paranoid.'

'We could steal one of those six robots,' Aydee said, thoughtful. 'I might be able to pilot one. My training includes Librarian technology.'

'That's an idea,' I said. 'Maybe ... Wait, *six* robots?'

I looked again, and indeed, where three of the enormous machines had stood, there were now six. A group of Librarians stood around the robot's feet, looking up, seeming confused at where the extra three had come from.

Aydee's Talent, it appeared, could be a hindrance.

'Great,' I said flatly. 'Let's ignore the robots for now.'

'How are we going to get in, then?' Kaz asked.

I bit my lip in thought. At that point, something deeply profound occurred to me. A majestic plan of beauty and power, a plan that would save us all and Mokia as well.

But, being stoopid, I forgot it immediately. So we did something ridiculous instead.

144

For my plan to work, we had to wait until it grew dark. It was a cold night, chill, and I stood a lone sentry atop a stone shelf, lost inside my mind. The ghosts of my past seemed, in that caliginous night, to crawl up from the bowels of the earth and whisper to me. At their forefront was the image that I'd once had of my father, my dreams of what he would be when I finally discovered him. A brave man, a man forced to abandon me because of circumstances, not lack of affection. A person I'd be proud to have as my sire.

That man was just illusion. Dead. Killed by the truth that was Attica Smedry. But the ghost whispered at me for vengeance. Whispered at me to . . .

. . . stop being so pretentious.

The above paragraphs are what we authors like to call literary allusion. That's what we do when we don't know what else to write, so we go and read some other story, looking for great ideas we can steal. However, to avoid *looking* like we're stealing, we leave just enough clues so that someone who is curious can discover the original source. That way, instead of looking like thieves, we instead appear very clever because of the secret meaning we've hidden in our text.

Authors are the only people who get in trouble if they steal from others and try to hide it but get *praised* for stealing when they do it in the open. Remember that. It'll help you a lot in college.

So, to repeat the previous phrase without the literary allusion: I sat on a rock, waiting for it to get dark, thinking about my stoopid father and how he didn't live up to my expectations. It wasn't actually cold out – Mokia is in the tropics, unlike Denmark. My stomach rumbled; the others were eating some bread and cheese that Kaz had brought, but I didn't feel like eating.

A rustling sound came from behind, and Bastille walked up to my rock, Warrior's Lenses tucked into her jacket pocket. Below, the besieging army was getting ready to camp for the night. I was wearing my Oculator's Lenses – which were also called 'Primary Lenses,' I'd come to learn. They had a reddish tint, and allowed an Oculator to do some very basic things: See auras around types of glass and fight off other Oculators. Sometimes they let you see other kinds of auras as well, little hints about the world. I wasn't good at using them for that sort of thing yet, though.

Right now, they showed me that the dome around Tuki Tuki was made of a very powerful type of glass. It was in even worse shape than it looked; my Lenses let me see that the aura was wavering. It pulsed with an almost sickly glow. Whatever the Librarians were doing to break down the dome, it was working.

'Hey,' Bastille said, sitting down. 'What's reflecting?'

'Huh?'

'Free Kingdoms phrase,' Bastille said. 'It just means "What are you thinking about?"'

I shrugged.

'It's your parents, isn't it?' Bastille asked. 'You always get the same look in your eyes when you think about them.'

I shrugged again.

'You're wondering what the point was in rescuing your father, since he didn't end up spending any time with you.'

I shrugged, my stomach rumbling again.

Bastille hesitated. 'I'm not sure I understood that one. My shrug-ese is kind of rusty.'

'I don't know, Bastille,' I said, still looking at the city. 'It's just that … well, I've lost them both again. For a few moments, we were all there, in the same city. And now I'm alone again.'

'You're *not* alone,' she said, sitting down on the rock next to me.

'Even when I was with my father, I wasn't *with* him,' I said. 'He practically ignored me. Every time I tried to talk to him, he acted like I was a bother. He kept sending me off to enjoy myself, offering to give me money, as if the only thing he had to do as a father was provide for me.

'And now, they're both gone. And I don't know what any of it was about. They were in love once. When we were captured a few months ago, I watched my mother talk about me to the other Librarians. She said she didn't care about me, but the Truth-finder's Lens said that she was lying.'

'Huh,' Bastille said. 'Well, that's good, right? It means she cares.'

'It's not good,' I said. 'It's confusing. It would be so much easier if I could just believe that she hates me. Why did they break up? Why did they think a Librarian and a Smedry could marry in the first place? And what made them change their minds? Whose fault was it? They were together until I was born ...'

'Alcatraz,' Bastille said. 'It's *not* your fault.'

I didn't respond.

'Alcatraz ...'

'I know it's not,' I said, mostly to get her to stop prodding me. Bastille fell silent, though I could tell she didn't believe me. She shouldn't have.

I continued staring out into the night. *What is it you're really after, Mother?* I thought. *What is in that book you stole? And why did you lie to the other Librarians about me?*

I'm sorry. Did that last part make you a little depressed? Some-one needs to say something funny. How about this: By the end of this book, you'll see me realize that everything I thought I knew about my life was a lie, and I'll be left even more alone than before.

Oh? That wasn't very funny, you say? That's because you didn't hear the joke. I hid it in the sentence, but you have to read it backward to get it.

Did you get it? You might have to read it out loud to sound it out right, if you want to see the joke. Give it a try. Sound out every word.

How was that? What? Oh, that wasn't supposed to make *you* laugh – it was supposed to make everyone around you laugh at how silly you sounded. Did it work? (If you'll look above, I said, 'Someone needs to say something funny,' but I didn't say it would be me ...)

'So,' Bastille said. 'Do you want to know about those Lenses your grandfather gave you?'

'Sure,' I said, glad for the change in topic. I pulled out the pair of Bestower's Lenses, with their purple-and-green tint. When I wore my Primary Oculator's Lenses, the ones in my hand glowed with a strong aura; they were very powerful.

'These are supposed to be tough to use,' Bastille said, taking the Bestower's Lenses and inspecting them. 'Essentially, they let you give something of yourself to someone else.'

'Something?' I asked. 'What something?'

She shrugged. 'It depends. Like I said, they're hard to use, and nobody seems to understand them perfectly. You put them on, you look at someone and focus on them, then you *send* them something. Some of your strength, something you're feeling, something you can do that they can't. There are reports of some strange events tied to this kind of Lens. An Oculator who had hives from a troll allergy once took a set of these and *gave* the hives to his political opponent when she was giving a speech.'

'Huh,' I said, taking the Lenses back, looking them over.

'Yeah, and since his opponent was a troll herself, it was kind of weird. Anyway, the Lenses are powerful – and dangerous. I'm kind of surprised that your grandfather gave them to you.'

'He trusts me more than he should,' I said, slipping off my Primary Lenses and putting on the Bestower's Lenses. As always, the tint to the glass was invisible to me once I put the Lenses on.

Bastille jumped as I turned toward her. 'Don't point those at me, Smedry!'

'I haven't activated them,' I said, stomach rumbling. 'I'd need to eat before—

Suddenly, I felt full. I cocked my head as Bastille's stomach rumbled.

'Great,' she said. 'You gave me your hunger. Thanks a lot, Smedry. And I just *ate*.'

I felt embarrassed, but Bastille was the one who blushed. I'd given her my embarrassment.

Hurriedly, I pulled the Lenses off. Immediately, the effect wore off – I was hungry and embarrassed again. 'Wow.'

'I *warned* you,' Bastille said. 'Shattering Glass! You Smedrys never listen.' She stormed off, leaving me to sheepishly tuck the Lenses back into my pocket.

Still, they *did* seem like they would be very useful.

I joined the others at our impromptu camp set back from the ridge. 'All right,' I said, squatting down beside them. 'I think it's dark enough. Let's go.'

'Sounds good,' Kaz said. 'What does this plan of yours entail?'

'It's dark,' I said.

'And?'

'And so we sneak past the guards and run to the city,' I said.

The other three blinked at me. '*That's* your plan?' Kaz said.

'Sure,' I replied. 'What did you think it was?'

'Something not lame,' Aydee said with a frown.

Kaz nodded. 'You said you had a plan, and then told us to wait for dark. I figured ... well, that you'd have something a little more original.'

'We could try knocking out guards,' I said, 'and taking their uniforms.'

'I said *more* original,' Kaz said.

'What does originality have to do with it?' I asked.

'Everything!' Kaz said, glancing at Aydee, who nodded vigorously. 'We're Smedrys! We can't do things the way everyone else does.'

'Okay then ...' I said slowly. 'We'll sneak past the guards in the dark, and we'll do it *while quoting Hamlet*.'

'Now that's more like it!' Kaz said.

'Never seen anything like it,' Aydee added. 'It just might be crazy enough to work.' She paused. 'What's a hamlet?'

'It's a small village,' Kaz said.

Bastille rolled her eyes. 'I'll go first,' she said, slipping on her Warrior's Lenses despite the dark night. 'Follow me to the rim of the camp, but don't come any closer until I give the signal.'

'Right,' I said. 'What's the signal?'

'A quote from a hamlet,' Kaz said. 'Obviously.'

'Are you sure a hamlet isn't a very small pig?' Aydee said.

'Nah,' Kaz said. 'That's a hammer.'

Bastille sighed, then hurried off, her dark uniform making her blend into the night. The rest of us followed more slowly, Kaz putting on a pair of rugged, aviator-style sunglasses that were obviously Warrior's Lenses. Aydee got out her own, though hers had yellow rims with flowers painted on them. Uncertain what else to do, I put the Bestower's Lenses back on, though I made certain not to look directly at Kaz or Aydee.

We climbed down from the rim, moving along a game trail through the dense jungle. The Librarian army didn't seem to be anticipating any danger from outside, and most of their attention was focused on Tuki Tuki. Still, guard posts were spaced around the perimeter, each lit by a bonfire. We followed Bastille – who was amazingly quiet as she moved through the underbrush – as she rounded the camp, obviously looking for a place that we could sneak through without causing too much of a disturbance.

She eventually stopped, hiding in the shadows just outside the camp near a watch fire that had been allowed to burn low. It was mostly just coals now, a couple of tired-looking Librarian guards standing watch. They were beefy men, the type with square jaws and stoopid names like 'Biff,' or 'Chad,' or 'Brandon.' They had on white shirts with pocket protectors and pink bow ties but had enormously strong bodies. Like someone had combined a math nerd and a football player into one unholy hybrid.

Bastille took a deep breath, then dashed across the trampled ground with blurring speed. The Librarians barely had time to stand up straight, squinting into the darkness before she was upon them.

Now, in case you somehow slept through the other three books, let me explain something. Bastille is *fast*. Like, cheetah on a sugar buzz fast. She not only has those Warrior's Lenses but she's also a Crystin. Every Knight of Crystallia has a little crystal grown into the skin at the back of their neck – that crystal comes from the Worldspire itself and connects every Crystin to all of the others.

They all share a little of their skills and abilities with the other knights.

This, in turn, turns every shattering one of them into crazy insane supersoldiers, even the thirteen-year-old girls. *Especially* the thirteen-year-old girls. (Every teenage girl has a crazy insane supersoldier inside of them, waiting to get out. If you don't believe me, it probably means you don't have any teenage sisters. Particularly not two who both want to wear the same necklace to the prom.)

Bastille didn't even need to get out her sword. She made the first guard double over with a punch to the stomach, then grabbed his shoulder and used it to steady herself as she spun, kicking the other guard in the neck, dropping him to the ground. She followed this by punching the first guard square in the forehead.

Both men fell to the ground, silent. Bastille glanced back toward where we were hiding. 'I think we ought to get our roads cobbled!' she whispered. Then – I could see her sighing visibly – she added, 'Oink oink oink.'

I smiled as the three of us trotted up to the watch fire. Kaz had out his sling, but hadn't needed it. The two guards were out cold. Bastille waited, tense, glancing toward the two nearest watch fires – one in the distance to either side of us. The guards at them didn't seem to have noticed us.

'Nice work, Bastille,' Kaz said, inspecting the guards, setting aside their futuristic rifles. Like most Free Kingdomers, he didn't find guns and other 'primitive' weapons to be very useful.

I, on the other hand, had watched enough action movies to know that if you're going to sneak through the middle of an enemy army, a gun can be a pretty cool thing to have. So I reached down and picked up one of the rifles.

'Alcatraz!' Bastille said. 'Put that down! Your Talent!'

'Don't worry,' I said. 'I've learned to control it. Look, the gun isn't even falling apart.'

Indeed, it remained in one perfect piece. Bastille relaxed as I lifted the gun, placing it against my shoulder, barrel toward the air.

And – as if to prove me wrong – I felt a little jolt as my Talent was engaged. The gun didn't fall apart, however.

It just fired. Shooting directly into the air with an extremely loud cracking noise, blasting a glowing ball of light into the sky.

Shocked, I dropped the gun. It hit the ground, going off again, shooting another glowing ball out into the forest.

The black night was completely still for a moment. And then, a loud blaring alarm noise began to echo through the camp.

'Frailty,' Bastille said with a sigh, 'thy name is Alcatraz.'

Act V, Scene III

The following chapter introduction is an except from Alcatraz Smedry's bestselling book, *How to Sound Really Smart in Three Easy Steps.*

STEP ONE: Find an old book that everyone has heard of but nobody has read.

The clever writers know that literary allusions are useful for lots of reasons other than giving you stuff to write when you run out of ideas. They can also make you look *way* more important. What better way to seem intelligent than to include an obscure phrase in your story? It screams, 'Look how smart I am. I've read lots of old books.'

STEP TWO: Skim through that old play or document until you find a section that makes no sense whatsoever.

Shakespeare is great for this for one simple reason: *None* of what he wrote makes any sense at all. Using confusing old phrases is important because it makes you look mysterious. Plus, if nobody knows what the original author meant, then they can't complain that you used the phrase wrong. (Shakespeare, it should be noted, was paid by other authors to write gibberish. That way, when they wanted to quote something that didn't make sense, they just had to reach for one of his plays.)

STEP THREE: Include a quote from that play or old document in an obvious place, where people will think they're smart for spotting it.

Note that you get bonus points for changing a few of the words to make a clichéd turn of phrase, as it will stick in people's minds that way. Reference the last sentence of the previous chapter for an example.

Note that if you aren't familiar with Shakespeare, you can

always use Greek philosophers instead. Nobody knows what the heck *they* were talking about, so talking about them in your books is a great way to pretend to be smart.

Everybody wins!

'O horrible, O horrible, most horrible!' Kaz cried as the alarm went off.

'Why,' Aydee said. 'What should be thy fear?'

'More matter,' Bastille said, pointing at the glass dome of the city, then pulling out her sword. 'With *less art.*'

'Bid the players make haste!' I cried, dashing away from the fallen gun. We took off at a run toward Tuki Tuki.

All around us, the camp was coming alert. Fortunately, they didn't know what the disturbance was or what had caused it. Many of the Librarians seemed to assume that the shot had come from the besieged city, and they were forming up battle lines facing the dome. Others were running toward the place where the shot I'd fired had entered the jungle.

'If there be any good thing to be done ...' Bastille said, looking about, worried.

The scrambling soldiers gave me an idea. Up ahead, I saw a gun rack where a bunch of rifles leaned, waiting to be picked up by Librarians for battle. I waved to the others, racing toward the rack. I ran past it, fingers brushing the weapons and engaging my Talent. They all fired, shooting glowing shots up into the air, arcing over the camp and furthering the chaos.

'What a piece of work is a man!' Kaz called, giving me a thumbs-up.

Librarian soldiers ran this way and that, confused. Amid them were men and women dressed in all black – stark black uniforms for the men, with black shirts and ties, and black skirts with black blouses for the women. Some of these noticed my group running through camp and began to cry out, pointing at us.

Aydee yelped suddenly, pointing ahead of us. 'Something is rotten in the state of Denmark!'

Indeed, a group of soldiers had noticed us and – spurred by the Librarians in black – was sprinting for us.

There wasn't much time to think. Bastille charged them at the head, of course. She wouldn't be able to take them all, though. There were too many.

Kaz raised his sling, whipping a rock at a Librarian. The man dropped like Polonius in Act III, Scene iv, but there were still a good ten Librarians to fight. Kaz kept slinging rocks as Bastille surged into the middle of them, sword out and raised before her. Aydee hid behind some barrels at a command from Kaz.

And me. What could I do? I stood there in the chaotic night, trying to decide. I was the leader of this expedition. I needed to help *somehow*!

A Librarian soldier came rushing at me, crying, 'Let me be cruel, not unnatural!' He carried a sword; obviously, these men were ready to deal with Smedrys, just in case. A gun would have been useless against my Talent.

I stepped back nervously. What could I do? Break the ground beneath him? That might as easily toss me into the hole, as well as the others. I couldn't hurt myself in order to . . .

Something occurred to me.

Without bothering to think if it were a good idea, I focused on the men, activating my Lenses. Then, I punched myself in the head.

Now, under normal circumstances, this kind of activity should be frowned upon. In fact, punching yourself in the head is most definitely what we call stoopiderific (defined as 'the level of stoopidity required to go slip-'n'-sliding at the Grand Canyon'). However, in this case, it was slightly less stoopiderific.

The Bestower's Lenses transferred the punch from me to the Librarian. He was suddenly knocked sideways, looking more shocked than hurt.

He stumbled to his feet. 'O, what a rogue and peasant slave am I.'

'There is nothing either good or bad,' I noted, smiling. 'But *thinking* makes it so.' I punched myself in the stomach as hard as I could.

The Librarian grunted, stumbling again. I went at it over and over, until he was groaning and in no shape to get back up. I looked up, scanning the chaotic grounds of the fight. People were running everywhere. Kaz was standing atop the barrels that Aydee was hiding behind, and she'd pulled out a few of the teddy bear grenades. I just managed to dodge to the side as she pulled the tag on a blue one and tossed it at some nearby Librarians, causing them to reverse explode toward each other in a lump.

I picked another Librarian running by and began to pound on him by pounding on myself. However, I wasn't avoiding damage entirely. In fact, when I stopped focusing on Librarians I'd pummeled, the pains started to come back to me. I needed a different method.

'Thou wretched, rash, intruding fool, farewell!' a Librarian cried, dashing toward me.

I spun, focusing on him, and did the first thing I could think of. I pretended that I was crazy. *I'm insane, I'm insane, I'm insane!* I thought.

The man hesitated, lowering his sword. He cocked his head, then wandered away. 'Do you see yonder cloud that's almost in shape of a camel?' he asked, glancing at the sky.

Bastille was in the center of a furious battle. She tried not to hurt people too much, but there was no helping it here. She'd had to stab several of the Librarians, and they lay on the ground holding leg wounds or arm wounds. One man, shockingly, had been stabbed in the mouth. He clutched something in his hand, and as I ran past him, he mumbled, 'But break, my heart, for I must hold my tongue ...'

'O, woe is me,' I said, squeezing my eyes shut, 'to have seen what I have seen, see what I see!'

I couldn't leave my eyes closed for long, though. I opened them, trying to get close to Bastille to help. She seemed to be holding out well. One Librarian came up behind her, trying to attack her from the side. He jumped at her, joined by a group of friends, grabbing her arm and knocking her large, crystal sword out of her hand.

'O, what a noble mind is here o'erthrown!' I yelled, pointing.

Kaz glanced toward us and nodded, grabbing a pink bear from Aydee and tossing it in our direction. It hit, blowing all of us backward. I hit the ground in a roll, but like before, the grenade didn't actually hurt any of us.

That explosion was enough to get Bastille free from her grapplers, but her sword had been knocked far away. I scrambled to get it for her as she pulled her dagger free from her belt, facing down a Librarian.

'Is this a dagger which I see before me?' the Librarian said, holding up a larger, much more imposing sword. He swung.

Bastille just smiled, blocking his sword with her dagger, then stepping unexpectedly forward and kicking him in the crotch with a booted foot.

'Get thee to a nunnery,' she said as he squeaked and fell to the ground.

Bastille *hates* it when people quote from the wrong play.

I grabbed Bastille's sword, then dashed toward her, tossing it into her hands as I passed. 'Neither a borrower nor a lender be: For loan oft loses both itself and friend.'

'Beggar that I am, I am even poor in thanks,' she said with an appreciative nod.

I looked about for more enemies. Shockingly, most of the Librarians in this group were down.

'Will you two help to hasten them?' Kaz yelled, running past us, Aydee at his side. 'Rich gifts wax poor when givers prove unkind!'

I nodded in agreement, bolting toward the far side of the camp. Oddly, as we ran, we passed heaped-up piles of what appeared to be glass. Cups, mirrors, windows – all broken, many broken so badly that they were nearly unrecognizable. I didn't have much energy to ponder on the oddity, though. Using the Bestower's Lenses had taken a lot out of me – my stomach hurt from being punched so often, and the Lenses had sapped away a lot of my strength.

Fortunately, the Librarians were confused enough by the night-time attack that we were able to run the rest of the distance without being stopped again. We burst out of the camp and ran up the hillside toward the glass-domed city above. Behind, Librarians shouted, some pointing at us. A rank of riflemen set up to shoot us down, but they made the mistake of pointing at not one but *three* Smedrys. Three of the riflemen got lost while trying to raise their guns, five miscounted and didn't put any bullets in their guns, and the rest of the weapons fell apart as their owners tried to use them.

Sometimes it's good to have a Talent.

Unfortunately, I hadn't considered how we were going to get *into* the city once we reached it. The glass dome ran all the way down to the ground, and although there appeared to be a place where hinges made a glass door, that was guarded by a group of Mokian soldiers. The stout, well-muscled men were bare-chested, their faces painted with black swirling lines and patterns like Maori war paint. They carried spears made from a black wood, and some of the spearheads were on fire.

Despite the fearsome display, the soldiers themselves looked like they'd had a hard time of it in the fighting. Most of them wore bandages or slings, and they looked at me and my group with suspicion.

'Our purpose may hold there!' one of the men said through a small slit in the glass. 'Who comes here?' They didn't open the door for us.

I stepped forward. 'Sir, my good friend. I do commend me to you.'

Bastille stepped forward, showing her Crystin blade, the symbol of a Knight of Crystallia. 'Swear by my sword,' she proclaimed.

A Crystin seemed enough proof for the Mokians that we were good guys. They opened the small glass doorway, waving us in. We let Kaz and Aydee go first while I looked back at the camp. We'd done it! I puffed in fatigue, but smiled at our victory.

Beside me, Bastille seemed less enthusiastic.

'How is it that the clouds still hang on you?' I asked her.

She shrugged, regarding the chaotic Librarian ranks, particularly the place where we'd been forced to fight. 'My soul is full of discord and dismay.'

'The lady doth protest too much, methinks.'

Bastille looked at me. I could tell from her expression that she blamed me for upsetting everything. That was probably fair, since I'd not only been the one to suggest the plan but the one to ruin it by picking up the Librarian's gun.

'How absolute the knave is,' Bastille said, tapping me on the chest.

'This above all,' I said, shrugging and smiling wryly, 'to thine own self be true.'

And with that, we entered Tuki Tuki.

A+

Aaaaaaaaaaaaaaaaaaaaaaaaaaaaaaaaaaaaaaaaaaaaaaaaaaaaaaaaaaaa
aaaaaaaaaaaaaaaaaaaaaaaaaaaaaaaaaaaaaaaaaaaaaaaaaaaaaaaaaaaa
aaaaaaaaaaaaaaaaaaaaaaaaaaaaaaaaaaaaaaaaaaaaaaaaaaaaaaaaaaaa
aaaaaaaa!!!!!!!!!!!!!!

. . .

Aaaaaaaaaaaaaaaaaaaaaaaaaaaaaaa!!!!!!!!!!!!!!

The Mokian soldiers ushered us through the glass doorway, several of them keeping watchful guard at the army behind. Inside the glass shield, a ten-foot-high wooden wall surrounded the city. The wall was battered and broken, burned in places, and looked like it had seen a lot of fighting before the glass shell had been put in place.

As soon as we were through the door, several soldiers slammed it shut. One of the soldiers called up toward the wall. 'Smedrys have arrived! A Crystin is with them! Lady Aydee has returned!'

Others picked up the shouts, passing them along the line of ragged defenders standing atop the wall. The men around me lost their suspicion and began to look hopeful.

'Lord Smedry,' one of them said. 'You are an advance force? How many troops is Nalhalla sending us?'

'Are there any others with you?' another asked hopefully.

'Are the Knights of Crystallia mobilized?' yet another asked. 'When will they arrive?'

'Er,' I said, taking off my Bestower's Lenses as more questions swarmed me.

'We're alone,' Bastille said curtly. 'We didn't bring any more help, the knights aren't mobilized, and we really don't have time to talk about it.'

Everyone fell silent. Bastille has a talent for killing conversations.

Basically, Bastille has a talent for killing anything.

'What she means,' I said, shooting a glare in her direction, 'is that we're here to help, and we hope more will follow. But we're it for now.'

The soldiers seemed crestfallen.

'I'm sorry we didn't let you in more quickly, Lord Smedry,' said one of the men. 'It seemed like you had young Aydee captive there, and we weren't sure what was going on.'

Oh, right, I thought. *It probably would have made sense to have her approach first, since she's from the city.* Ah well. You can't expect me to think of everything, particularly considering how stoopid I am.

You haven't forgotten that, have you? Don't make me start spelling things wrong to prove it to you.

In the distance, a gate opened in the wooden wall and a contingent of Mokians came out carrying spears that were alight with fire in the night. The soldiers around us made way for the newcomers, and I could tell they respected the man at their lead. He was tall, with long black hair pulled into a ponytail and tied with a beaded string. His face was painted with black lines. He had a powerful, muscular chest and – like most of the other Mokians – wore a simple wrap around his waist, colored red and blue. For some reason, he looked vaguely familiar to me.

'So it is true,' he said, stopping before us, burning spear held to the side. 'Welcome, Lord Alcatraz Smedry, to our doomed city. You have picked an interesting time to visit us. Lady Bastille, your sister will be pleased to see you, though I doubt the circumstances will make her happy. Lord Kazan, you are welcome – as always – in Tuki Tuki.'

'Do I know you?' Kaz said, narrowing his eyes.

'I'm general of the city guard in Tuki Tuki,' the man said. He had a commanding, deep voice. 'I have seen you many times, though I doubt I was worth your notice. Likely, you have seen my face, but we have never been introduced.' He looked to Aydee and nodded to her. 'Child, your brave mission does you honor. We are already in communication with the embassy in Nalhalla.'

Aydee blushed. 'Thank you, Your … er … General Mallo.'

'We had not expected you to return, however,' he said sternly. 'You should have remained in Nalhalla, where it is safe.'

Her blush deepened. 'But my cousin needed a pilot! He had to come to Mokia!'

'Yes,' Mallo said flatly. 'I've received a report from the embassy regarding the urgent departure. A vacation to visit the mud baths? That is ridiculous, even for a Smedry.'

Now it was my turn to blush. 'General,' I said, 'there are other reasons for our visit. I need to speak to the queen as soon as possible – and after that, I'll need a little time with your Communicator's Glass. I might be able to get you some help for this siege.'

The soldiers nearby perked up, and the general gave me an appraising look. 'Very well. The Smedry clan has long been friends, and sometimes family, of the Mokian royalty. You are always welcome.' He gathered some soldiers, then led us to the city gate.

'I feel I should give you some kind of grand introduction, Lord Smedry,' General Mallo said as we entered Tuki Tuki. 'But these are not days for joyful tours. So instead, just let me say this. Welcome to the City of Flowers.' He raised a hand as I stepped through the gate.

We were at the bottom of the gentle hillside. I looked up along the main road that ran all the way to the palace. Flowers grew on virtually everything. The hutlike buildings were overgrown with vines that intertwined with the reeds that made up their walls, and these sprouted colorful, hibiscuslike blossoms. Flower beds ran alongside the road, with exotic bird-of-paradise blooms perching atop them. A line of enormous trees ran behind the buildings, their limbs extending out over the rooftops. These grew heaps of purple flowers that hung down over the road, collected in batches like bunches of grapes. It was gorgeous.

'Wow,' I said. 'Glad I'm not allergic!'

General Mallo grunted, gesturing with his flaming spear, leading us forward. Carrying that spear around struck me as a little bit dangerous, but who was I to speak? After all, I was the one walking around with a weapons-grade Smedry Talent stuffed inside me.

'Fortunately, Lord Smedry,' Mallo said as we walked, 'our flowers are all nonallergenic.'

'How did you get them that way?' I asked.

'We asked them very nicely,' Mallo said.

'Er, okay.'

'It was much more difficult than it sounds, Alcatraz.' Aydee added. 'Do you know how many different species of flower there are in the city? Six thousand! Our floralinguists had to learn each and every language.'

'Floralinguists?' I said.

'They talk to flowers!' Aydee said excitedly.

'I kind of figured that,' I said. 'What kinds of things do they say?'

'Oh,' Mallo said, 'they tend to ramble a lot and use big words, but there isn't often much substance to what they say, despite the beauty and ornamentation of the language.'

'So ... er ...' I said.

'Yeah,' Mallo said. 'Their speech is quite flowery.'

I walked right into that one like a bird hitting a glass sliding door at seventy miles an hour. Beside me, Bastille rolled her eyes.

Kaz whistled, watching the city. 'There are more things in heaven and earth ... er, sorry. I'm having trouble getting over that last chapter. Anyway, I've always loved visiting Tuki Tuki. There's no place like it; I always forget how beautiful it is.'

'Perhaps it was a pleasure to visit in the past,' Mallo said, his face growing even more solemn, 'but the siege has been difficult for all of us. See how our regal daftdonias droop? The Shielder's Glass lets in light, but the plants can feel that they are enclosed. The entire city wilts beneath the Librarian oppression.'

Indeed, many of the flowers lining the street did seem to be drooping. As the wonder of my first sight of Tuki Tuki began to wear off, I saw many other signs of the siege. Open yards where people were up despite the late hour, cutting bandages and boiling them in enormous vats. The sounds of blacksmiths working on weapons rang in the air. Most of the men we passed – and even many of the women – wore bandages and carried weapons. Spears with long, shark-tooth-like ridges down the sides, or swords and axes of wood, also made with shark-tooth sides.

If you're wondering where the Mokians get all of those shark teeth, by the way, it involves using children as bait – specifically children who skip to the ends of books to read the last page first. I'm sure that *you* would never do something like that. That would be downright stoopiderific.

Many of those passing waved hello to Aydee, and she waved back. Her family, the Mokian Smedrys, were well known. Eventually, we approached the palace. It looked like a very large hut, constructed using thick reeds for the walls. It had a crown of red flowers blanketing its thatch roof.

Now, you're probably thinking what I am. Huts? Aren't the Mokians supposed to be one of the most learned, scientifically minded people in the Free Kingdoms? What were they doing living in huts?

I assumed that, obviously, there was a good explanation. 'So, these buildings,' I said. 'They're made of special, reinforced magical reeds, I assume. They *look* like huts, but they're as strong as castles, right?'

'No,' Mallo said. 'They're just huts.'

I frowned.

'We like huts,' Mallo said, shrugging. 'Sure, we could build skyscrapers or castles. But why? To cut ourselves off from the sky with walls of stone and steel?'

'It makes sense,' Bastille added. 'Huts *are* more advanced than the buildings you have in the Hushlands, Smedry. Automatic air-conditioning, for one thing, and—'

'No,' Mallo said. 'With all respect, young knight, we must learn to stop saying things like this. We like to pretend that what *we* have is better than what the Librarians have. But comparisons like those, and the jealousy they inspire, began this war in the first place.'

He looked forward, toward the palace. 'We choose this life in

Mokia. Not because it is "primitive" or "advanced," but because it is what we like. The more complex the things surrounding your life become – the homes, the vehicles, the things you put in your homes and your vehicles – the more time you must spend on them. And the less time you have for thought and study.'

I blinked, shocked to hear those words coming from the mouth of the enormous, spear-wielding, war-painted Mokian. To the side, Bastille folded her arms, brooding. Her assertions that everything in the Free Kingdoms was better than things in the Hushlands had shocked me the first day we met. I had assumed that that was the way that all Free Kingdomers thought, but I was coming to realize that Bastille just has a ... particular way of seeing the world.

(That means that she's bonkers. But I can't *write* that she's bonkers, because if I do, she'll punch me. So, uh, perhaps we should forget I wrote this part, eh?)

We reached the steps up to the palace, where a woman waited for us. She looked familiar too, though this time I could pinpoint why. She looked a lot like her sister, Bastille. Tall and slender, Angola Dartmoor was about ten years older than Bastille and wore a Mokian wrap of yellow and black with a matching flower in her hair. She carried a royal scepter of ornately carved wood.

She was absolutely beautiful. She had long blond hair, kind of the shade of a bowl of mac and cheese. She was smiling a wide, genuine smile – which was rather the shape of a macaroni and cheese noodle. She seemed to radiate light, much like a bowl of mac and cheese might if you stuffed a lightbulb into it. Her skin was soft and squishy, like—

Okay. Maybe I'm too hungry to be writing right now. Either way, though, Angola was *gorgeous*. Definitely one of the most beautiful women I'd ever seen.

Bastille stepped on my foot.

'Ow!' I complained. 'What was that for?'

'Stop gawking at my sister,' Bastille grumbled.

'I wasn't gawking! I was *appreciating*!'

'Well, appreciate her a little less, then. And stop drooling.'

'I'm not—' I cut off as Angola breezed down the steps grace-fully, coming up to us. 'I'm not drooling,' I hissed more softly, then bowed. 'Your Majesty.'

'Lord Smedry!' she said. 'I've heard so much about you!'

'Er ... you have?'

She didn't reply, instead laying her hands gracefully on her sister's shoulders. 'And Bastille. After all these months of writing you and asking you to come visit, now you finally come? During a siege? I should have known that only danger would lure you. Sometimes, I wonder if you're not as attracted to it as those you protect!'

Bastille blushed.

'Come,' Angola said. 'You are welcome to what comforts Mokia can provide you. We will take morning repast and discuss the news you bring. The Aumakua bless that it be of good report, as we have seen too little of that as of late.'

Now, as an aside, you might be shocked to hear such a distinct reference to religion from Angola. After all, I haven't talked much about religion in these books.

This is intentional, mostly from a self-preservation standpoint. I've discovered that talking about religion has a lot in common with wearing a catcher's mask: Both give people liberty to throw things at you. (And in the case of religion, sometimes the 'things' are lightning bolts.)

Unfortunately, in the later years of my life I've developed a very rare affliction known as chronic smart-aleckiness. (It's kind of like dyslexia, only easier to spell. Particularly if you don't have dyslexia.) Because of this tragic, terminal disease, I'm unable to read or write about things without making stoopid wisecracks about them.

Due to my affliction, I've wisely left the topic of religion alone – because if I were to talk about it, I'd have to make fun of it. And that might be offensive, as people take their religions very seriously. Better not to talk about it at all.

Therefore, I will most certainly *not* tell you what religion has in common with explosive vomiting. (Whew. Glad I didn't say anything like that. It could have been *really* offensive.)

Angola nodded to Kaz and Aydee in welcome, giving each a smile, then glided back up the steps, expecting us to follow her in.

'Wow,' I said. 'Is she always so ...'

'Nauseatingly regal?' Bastille asked softly. 'Yeah, even before she was married.'

'Well, I can see why the king married her. Too bad I won't be able to meet him.'

Bastille's eyes flickered toward Mallo. It was only for a moment, but I caught it. Frowning, I turned to study the general, trying to find out what had drawn Bastille's attention. Once again, he looked familiar to me. In fact ...

'You're the king!' I exclaimed, pointing at him.

'What?' Mallo said, voice stiff. 'No I'm not. The king was taken to safety by the Knights of Crystallia weeks ago.'

He was a terrible liar.

'Hey,' Kaz said. 'Yeah, I *thought* I recognized you. Your Majesty! We had dinner once a few years back. Remember? My father spilled cranberry juice on your tapa.'

The man looked embarrassed. 'Perhaps we should go inside,' he said. 'I see there are some things I need to explain.'

(Also, if you're wondering, it's because both often make you fall to your knees.)

No!

I try very hard to be deep, poignant, and meaningful at the beginning of each chapter. Most of the content of these books is basically silliness. (Granted, these events are real silliness that actually *happened* to me, but that doesn't stop them from being silly.) In the introductions, therefore, I feel it's important to explain meaningful and important concepts so that your time reading won't be completely wasted.

I suggest you scrutinize these introductions, searching for their hidden meanings. My thoughts will bring you enlightenment and wisdom. If you are confused by something I say, rest assured that I'll eventually explain myself.

For instance, in reading the introduction to the previous chapter, you might have understood my screams to be an expression of the existential angst felt by modern teens when thrust into a world they were ill-prepared to receive – a world that has changed so drastically from the one their parents knew (thanks for nothing, Heraclitus!). Or you might have seen it as the scream of one realizing that nobody can offer him help or succor.

(Actually, I wrote *that* introduction to express the existential crisis I felt when an enormous spider crawled up my leg while I was typing. But you get the idea.)

We stepped into the palace. It smelled of reeds and thatch, and the wide, open windows let in a cool breeze. The rug was made of long, woven leaves, and the furniture constructed of tied bundles of reeds. Quite cozy, assuming you weren't enraged, confused, and feeling betrayed like I was.

'You knew,' I said, pointing at Bastille.

'I recognized His Majesty immediately,' she admitted. 'But he seemed to want to keep his identity secret. So I played along.'

'I did too,' Aydee said. 'I ... er, just didn't do a very good job of it. Sorry.'

'It's all right,' said Mallo, also known as King Talakimallo of Mokia. His wife stepped up beside him, and the guards watched the doorway into the palace.

'But why hide from me?' I asked.

'And me!' Kaz said, folding his arms, stepping up beside me.

'It wasn't just from you,' the king said. 'It was from all outsiders. You see, we sort of ... well, tricked the knights.'

Bastille raised an eyebrow.

'They insisted that I be protected,' Mallo said, voice fervent. 'They *would not* stop pestering me. I worried they'd kidnap me and take me from the city for my own good.'

'The city is close to falling, Your Majesty,' Bastille said. 'Mokia can't afford for the entire royal family to be taken by the Librarians. What of the rest of the kingdom? It will need leadership.'

'There *is* no "rest of the kingdom," child,' Mallo said. 'Mokia stands here. We've been beaten down by Librarian forces for decades now; if Tuki Tuki falls, it will spell the end for my people. We will become just another Librarian province, slowly assimilated into the Hushlands, our people brainwashed until we forget our past.'

The queen laid a hand on her husband's arm. 'We are not ignorant of the importance of preserving the royal lineage, fair sister – if only so that a proper resistance can be mounted to reclaim Mokia, should that become our fate.'

Before you ask, *yes*, she actually talks like that. I once asked her to pass the butter and she said, 'It pleases me to bequeath this condiment unto you, young Alcatraz.' Really. No kidding.

'But wait,' I said, scratching my head. Being stoopid, I do that a lot. 'You're here, but the knights think that you're safe somewhere else?'

'Our daughter imitated me,' Mallo said. 'She is an Oculator and has a pair of Disguiser's Lenses. The knights shepherded her away to a hidden location while she used her Lenses to appear as if she were me.'

'The lineage is safe,' Angola said.

'And I can stay to fight with my people, as is right.' Mallo looked grim. 'Rather, I can fall with my people. I'm afraid that several Smedrys and a single knight will not be enough to win this siege. Our Defender's Glass is nearly broken, and most of my warriors have fallen to comas in battle. Those who remain have taken many wounds. My silimatic scientists think that one more day of fighting will shatter the dome. We are faced by superior numbers and superior firepower. In the moments before you arrived, I had made the difficult decision to surrender. I was on my way to the wall to announce it to the Librarians.'

The words hung in the air like a foul stench – the kind that everyone notices but doesn't want to point out, for fear of being named the one who caused it.

Well, guess we came here for nothing, I thought. *We should probably turn around and get out of here.*

'I'm here to help, Your Majesty,' I said instead. 'And I can bring others. If you will resist a little longer, I will not let Mokia fall.'

I'm not sure where the brave words came from. Perhaps a smarter man would have known not to say them. Even as they came out of my mouth, I was shocked by my stoopidity. Remember what I said about bravery?

Ridiculous though the proclamation was, the king did not laugh. 'I have found that the word of a Smedry is like gold, young Alcatraz,' King Mallo said appraisingly. 'Of great value, but sometimes easy to bend. Are you certain you can bring aid to my people?'

No.

'Yes,' I said.

The king studied me, then glanced at his wife.

'If we surrender, our people retain their lives,' Angola said, 'but lose their *selves*. If there remains but a slim chance ...'

He nodded in agreement. 'You said you needed to use our Communicator's Glass, Alcatraz. Let us see what you can do with it, and then I will judge.'

*

'Are you certain this is the right thing to do?' Bastille hissed to me.

We sat on a wicker bench, waiting as the king and his wife fetched the Communicator's Glass. Aydee was talking to one of the soldiers, getting news about her family. (Sing, Australia, and their parents had been sent to provide leadership at the other main battlefront in the Mokian war – though I suspect that the king really sent them away to prevent them from being captured when the city fell.) Kaz stood nearby, arms folded as he leaned against the wall, wearing his brown leather jacket and aviator sunglasses.

'I don't know if this is right,' I admitted to Bastille. 'But we can't just let them give up.'

'If they fight, people will get hurt,' Bastille said, leaning in close to me. 'Can we really offer them enough hope to justify that? Now that I've seen how bad it is, I don't even know if the full force of the Knights of Crystallia would be enough to turn this war around.'

'I ...' I trailed off, growing befuddled. I did that frequently when Bastille sat really close to me, particularly when I could smell the scent of the shampoo in her hair. Shouldn't girls smell like flowers or something like that? Bastille just smelled like soap.

It was strangely intoxicating anyway. Obviously she gives off some kind of brain-clouding radiation. That's the only explanation.

'Shattering Glass, what am I saying?' she said, pulling back. 'Of *course* it's better for them to fight! I'm sorry. I've just grown so used to contradicting you on principle that I'm shocked when you do something smart.'

'Duurrr ...' I said.

She narrowed her eyes at me. 'You aren't still mooning over my sister, are you?' Her voice was quite threatening.

I shook out of my stupor. 'What? No. Don't be stoopid.'

'Did you just call me stoopid?'

'No, I told you not to be stoopid. What is it with you and your sister anyway?'

'Nothing! I love my sister. We're like two shattering flowers in a field of shattering daisies.'

'What does that even mean?'

'I don't know! It was supposed to sound sisterly or something.'

I snorted in derision.

'So what's *that* supposed to mean?' Bastille demanded. 'I'm *very* affectionate with my sister!'

'So much so that you've never visited her in Mokia?'

'It's a long way away, and I was busy training to become a knight. So that I could keep idiots like *you* out of trouble!'

'Wait. You get mad when I *imply* that you might be stoopid, but it's all right for you to call me an idiot?'

'Because you're a Smedry!'

'That's always your excuse,' I said. 'I don't buy it. Besides, this time you said you agreed with what I was doing!'

'So!'

'So!'

'So?'

'So maybe we should, like, go catch a movie together or something,' I said, standing up. 'Sometime when we're not being chased by Librarians or being eaten by dragons or things like that!'

Bastille paused, cocking her head, frowning. 'Wait. What?'

I found myself blushing. Why had I said *that*? I mean, I'd been thinking about it for a while, but ...

Brain-clouding radiation. Obviously.

'It was nothing,' I said, panicking. 'I just, uh, got confused, and—'

'What's a "movie"?' she asked. 'And why would we need to catch it? Did one escape?'

'Er, yes. They're these big, monstrous creatures that the Librarians let loose in the Hushlands. To terrorize people ... and, you know, and steal their time, and make them cringe at bad acting, and then make them sit through long boring award shows that give statues of little gold men to people you've never heard of.'

She frowned even further. 'You're an idiot sometimes, Smedry,' she said, then glanced at Kaz, as if asking for an explanation from him.

'I'm not *touching* this one,' he said, smiling. 'In fact, I'm staying so far away from it, I might as well be in the next kingdom over!'

'Whatever,' Bastille said, turning her narrowed eyes back on me – as if she suspected that I was making fun of her in some way she couldn't figure out. I just continued to blush, right up until the point where Mallo and Angola returned. The queen carried a small hand mirror. She crossed the woven rug and handed it to me.

I hesitated, looking down at the mirror. Half of the glass was missing. 'This is it?'

'Communicator's Glass is best if portable,' Mallo said. 'We broke this piece in half and sent it to Nalhalla; it will allow us to communicate for some weeks through the two pieces, until the power fades. Then the glass must be reforged and broken again. It's not the easiest way to talk across a distance, but we were desperate, particularly after sending away our last Oculator to maintain my disguise.'

'Librarian agents destroyed our other means of communication,' one of the soldiers added. 'The Transporter's Glass station, the soundrunners, even the city's stockpile of Messenger's Glass.'

I frowned. 'How'd they do that?'

'They continue to dig tunnels into the city,' Mallo said with a sigh. 'And send strike teams up to harry us. We just caught one earlier today. We captured them before they could do any permanent damage, then collapsed the tunnel. There will be more, however.'

I nodded, raising the hand mirror. They all looked at me expectantly, as if they figured that – being an Oculator – I'd immediately know how to use the glass. 'Um,' I said, turning it sideways. 'Er. Mirror, mirror, in my hand, my food is tasty, but often bland.'

'Alcatraz?' Kaz asked. 'What are you doing? You just have to touch the glass to make it work.'

'Oh,' I said, tapping the mirror. It shimmered, like I'd disturbed the surface of a crystal-clear pool of water. A moment later, the image changed from a reflection of my face to show an image of a stone room. One of the castles in Nalhalla.

A small Mokian boy sat in front of the mirror. He grew alert the moment the image changed, then ran off, yelling. 'Lord Smedry, Lord Smedry!'

Within seconds, my grandfather was there. He looked somewhat frazzled, his hair sticking out at odd angles, his bow tie on sideways. 'Ah, Alcatraz, my lad! You did it!'

'I'm here, Grandpa,' I said, nodding. 'Inside Tuki Tuki. But things are bad here.'

'Of course they are!' Grandpa said. 'That's why we sent you in the first place, eh? Stay there for a moment. I need to get some knights!'

He rushed away. It looked like their half of the mirror had been hung on the wall in some kind of entryway or foyer.

I stood awkwardly for some time. The others crowded around me, looking through the mirror, waiting. Finally, Grandpa returned with several people dressed in full plate armor. One was Draulin, Bastille's mother. The other two were older-looking men.

'Alcatraz, tell them where you are,' Grandpa Smedry said from somewhere to the side.

'I'm in Tuki Tuki,' I said.

'You should leave there immediately,' Draulin said sternly. 'It is not safe, Lord Smedry.'

'Yes, I know,' I said. 'But you know us Smedrys. Crazy, without any regard for our own safety!'

One of the knights frowned. 'This does indeed offer the proof the elder Lord Smedry promised,' he said.

'I sense we are being manipulated,' the other said, shaking his head. 'I do not like the feel of it.'

Draulin remained quiet during the conversation. She seemed to be studying me carefully with those dark eyes of hers.

A thought occurred to me. They needed motivation to come help. Making a snap judgment, I turned the hand mirror around, shining it on Mallo. 'Guess who's here with me?' I said to the knights.

Mallo looked shocked. 'Alcatraz! What are you doing?'

'Trust me,' I said.

'It's a Mokian warrior,' one of the knights said. 'I feel for his plight, but the rules of our order are—'

'Wait,' Draulin's voice said suddenly. There was a silence, followed by her saying, 'Your ... Majesty?'

Mallo sighed visibly, shooting me a glare. 'Yes, it is I.'

'You are supposed to be safe!'

'I will not abandon my people,' Mallo said.

I spun the mirror around. 'So, it's not just a couple of foolish Smedrys, but the Mokian royal line who are in danger here. You should ...'

The image of the glass started to grow turbulent, ripples moving through it. I frowned, shaking the mirror.

'... can't ... what ... doing ...' Draulin's voice said. 'What ... ?'

'I can't see you either,' I said to them.

The others in the room crowded around. I lowered the mirror so all could see.

'That doesn't look good,' Kaz said, rubbing his chin.

'This was supposed to last at least twenty days,' Mallo said. 'We—'

'General Mallo!' a voice cried. We turned as a young Mokian girl ran up the front steps to the palace and entered the main chamber.

'What is it?' Mallo asked, turning sharply.

'The Librarian army,' the girl said. 'They're doing something, something big. You should come see.'

1010

Okay, I can't help myself. I've written three and a half books. I held my tongue. (Figuratively, unlike that guy back in Act V.) But I'm about to burst.

It is time to talk about religion in the Hushlands.

You Free Kingdomers may be confused by Hushlander religions. After all, they are all so very different, and their followers are all so very good at yelling at one another loudly that it's hard to tell what any of them are saying. However, should you infiltrate Librarian nations and need to imitate a Hushlander, you'll probably need to join one of their religions to blend in. Therefore, I've prepared this handy guide.

Religions, in the Hushlands, are basically about food.

That's right, food. In following one religion or another, you end up boycotting certain foods. If you become Hindu, for instance, you give up beef. Mormons give up alcohol and coffee. Catholics can eat pretty much whatever they want, but have to give up the stuff they like the most for one month a year, while Muslims give up *all* food during the daytime hours of Ramadan.

So which religion is the best? Well, it depends. In my cultivated opinion, I'd suggest Judaism.

But that's because I prefer the path of yeast resistance.

We stood atop the wooden palisade wall of Tuki Tuki watching the gigantic Librarian robots drive large, glowing rods into the ground. They shone blue in the night and were as tall as buildings. They illuminated the Librarian war camp, which was far more active now. Men and women had been awakened and were collecting their weapons and forming up battle lines.

'What are they?' Angola asked.

'They look like some kind of glass device,' Aydee said.

'No,' Kaz said. He stood atop a step stool and looked out at the Librarian camp, rubbing his chin. 'This war is being led by the Order of the Shattered Lens.'

'Who?' I asked.

Bastille rolled her eyes at my ignorance.

'The Shattered Lens is a Librarian sect, Al,' Kaz said. He was a scholar of Talents, Oculatory Distortions, and – by extension – Librarians. 'You've met the Dark Oculators, the Scrivener's Bones, and the Wardens of the Standard. Well, the Shattered Lens is the last of them. And probably the largest. The other orders accept, even use, silimatic technology and Oculatory Lenses. These guys, though . . .'

'They don't?' I asked.

'They *hate* all forms of glass.' Kaz said. 'They take Biblioden's teaching very literally. He didn't like anything "strange" like magic or silimatics. Most of the orders interpret his teachings as meaning "Lenses and glasses need to be controlled *very* carefully, so only the important can use them." Those Librarians hide the truth from most Hushlanders, but have no qualms about using Free Kingdomer technology and ideas when they can benefit from them.

'The Order of the Shattered Lens is different. *Very* different. They feel that Lenses and silimatic glasses should *never* be used, not even by Librarians. They think Free Kingdom technology is evil and disgusting.'

I nodded slowly. 'So those piles of glass we passed while running into the city?'

'They hold glass-breakings,' Angola said softly. 'They gather together in groups and smash pieces of glass. Even regular glass, with no kind of Oculatory or silimatic abilities. It's symbolic to them.'

'The other Librarians let them run the wars,' Kaz added. 'Partially, I suspect, to keep them away. There will be trouble within the Librarian ranks if the Free Kingdoms ever *do* fall. The Order of the Shattered Lens works with the Dark Oculators and the Scrivener's Bones for now. There's a bigger enemy to fight.

But once we're gone, there will likely be civil war as the orders struggle for dominance.'

'Civil war across the entire world,' Bastille said softly, nodding. 'The four Librarian sects using people as their pawns. The Shattered Lens trying to hunt down and kill Dark Oculators, the Wardens of the Standard trying to manipulate things with cool-headed politics, the Scrivener's Bones working for whomever will pay them the most ...'

We fell silent. That army outside was large; I glanced back at the city. There didn't seem to be many Mokian soldiers. Perhaps five or six thousand, both men and women. The Librarians had easily four times that number, and they are armed with futuristic guns. The enormous robots continued their work, planting the rods in the ground. They were making a ring of them, encircling the city.

Faced by such daunting numbers, I finally began to realize what I'd gotten myself into. And that's when I invented the term *stoopidanated*, meaning 'about as stoopid as Alcatraz Smedry, the day he snuck into Tuki Tuki just in time to be there when it got overwhelmed by Librarians.'

It's a very specific word, I know. Odd how many times I've been able to use it in my life.

'So the rods aren't glass,' I said. 'What are they, then?'

'Plastic,' Bastille guessed. 'Some sort of glass-disrupting technology? That might be what's making the Communicator's Glass stop working.'

'Might just be for light, though,' Aydee said. 'Look. Those rods are bright enough that the Librarians can move about as if it were day. They look like they're getting ready to attack.' She shrank down a little bit on her stool, as if to hide behind the wall.

Something occurred to me. I pulled the Courier's Lenses out of my pocket and slid them on.

Now, it might seem odd to you Hushlanders that we had so many different ways of talking to one another over a distance. But if you think about it, this makes sense. How many different ways do we have in the Hushlands? Telephone, fax, telegraph, VoIP, e-mail, regular mail, radio, shouting really loud, bottles with notes in them, texting, blimps with advertisements on them, skywriting, voodoo boards, smoke signals, etc.

Communicating with one another is a basic human need. And communicating with people far away is an even *more* basic human need, because that way we can make fun of people and they can't kick us in the face.

By the way, have I mentioned how ugly that shirt is? Yeah. Next time, please try to dress up a little bit when you read my books. Someone might see you, and I have a reputation to maintain.

I concentrated, feeding power into my Lenses, questing out for my grandfather. His face appeared in front of me, but it was fuzzy and indistinct.

Alcatraz, lad! Grandpa said. *I was hoping you'd use the Courier's Lenses. What's happening? Why doesn't the Communicator's Glass work?*

'I don't know,' I replied. 'The Librarians are doing something outside the city – planting these glowing rods in the ground. That might have something to do with it.'

Even as I spoke, one of the robots placed another of the rods. When it did, my grandfather's form fuzzed even more.

'Grandpa,' I said urgently. 'Did we convince the knights?'

Think … enough … help … Grandpa said, his voice cutting in and out. *They know … king still … save His Majesty …*

'I can't understand you!' I said. Another robot raised a rod into the air, preparing to place it.

I raised my hands to the side of the glasses, focusing everything I had into the Lenses. I strained, teeth gritted. Shockingly, the glass started to glow, forcing me to close my eyes as they blazed alight. My grandfather's voice, once weak, surged back, audible again.

… Luring Lovecrafts, what a mess! I said I've nearly got them persuaded. I'll bring them, lad, and anyone else I can get to come. We'll be there. Hold out until morning! Can you hear me, Alcatraz? Morning's first light. Er. Well, no, I'll be late. And that's been done before. But morning's second light, for certain. By third light at the latest, I promise!

The robot planted the rod. My grandfather's voice fuzzed again, and I tried another surge of power, but I'd pushed it too far. My Talent slipped through, mixing with my Oculatory power. I had trouble keeping the two separate; they were like two brightly different colors of paint, mixing and churning inside of me. Use one, and some of the other always wanted to come along.

The Talent surged through my hands before I realized what I was doing, and the frames of the Lenses shattered, dropping the bits of glass off my eyes. I caught them clumsily. Unfortunately, after feeling that resistance, I knew that they wouldn't work again – not as long as those Librarian rods were interfering. I reluctantly slipped the Lenses back in my pocket.

'What did he say?' Aydee asked, anxious.

'He's coming,' I replied. 'With the Knights of Crystallia.'

'When?' Bastille asked.

'Well ... he wasn't really that specific ...' I grimaced. 'He said dawn. Probably.'

'Probably?' Mallo said. 'Young Smedry, I'm not certain I can stake the lives of my people on a "probably."'

'My grandfather is reliable,' I said. 'He's never let me down.'

'Except when he arrived too late to get the Sands of Rashid before the Librarians,' Bastille added. 'Or ... well, when he arrived too late to stop your mother from stealing the Translator's Lenses from the Library of Alexandria. Or when he was too late to—'

'Thanks, Bastille,' I said flatly. 'Real helpful.'

'I think we're all aware of my father's Talent,' Kaz said, stepping up beside me. 'But I know Leavenworth Smedry better than anyone else, now that Mom's dead. If my pop says he'll be here with help, you can count on him. He might be a tad late, but he'll make up for it with style.'

'Style will not protect my people from Librarian weapons,' Mallo said, shaking his head. 'Your help is appreciated, but your promises are flimsy.'

'Please,' I said. 'Your Majesty, you've *got* to give us a chance. At least give it until morning. What do you have to lose by sleeping on it?'

'There will be no sleeping,' Mallo said nodding. 'Look.'

I followed the gesture. Outside the walls, the large robots had finished planting the rods into the ground. Now they were walking over to a large pile of boulders that sat just outside of the camp.

'Our period of rest has ended,' Mallo said grimly. 'They demanded our surrender, and since I've sent back no word, it seems they are going to resume their assaults. I had assumed they would wait until it was light to do so, but you know what they say about assumptions.'

'If you're going to make a donkey joke,' I noted, 'I did that already.'

Mallo frowned at me. 'No, I was going to quote an ancient Mokian proverb, revered and honored by our people over six centuries of use.'

'Oh,' I said, embarrassed. 'Um, sorry. How does it go?'

'"Don't make assumptions, idiot,"' Mallo quoted with a reverent voice.

'Nice proverb.'

'Mokian philosophers like to get to the point,' Mallo said.

'Either way, if we are going to surrender, we need to do it now. Those terrible machines of theirs will be throwing rocks soon, and the Defender's Glass will not last much longer against the assault.'

'If you give up,' Bastille said, 'that is the end of Mokia.'

'Please,' I said. 'Give us more *time*. Wait just a little longer!'

'Husband,' Angola said, laying a hand on his arm, 'most of our people would rather die than be taken by the Librarians.'

'Yes,' Mallo said, 'but sometimes you need to protect people even when they do not wish it. Our warriors think only of honor. But I must consider the future, and what is best for all of our people.'

King Mallo's face adopted a thoughtful expression. He folded a pair of beefy arms, one of his soldiers holding his spear for him. He stared out over the top of the wooden wall, looking at the Librarian forces.

Now, perhaps some of you reading might be thinking of Mallo

as a coward for even *considering* surrender. That's great. Next time you're in charge of the lives of thousands of people, you can make decisions quickly if you want. But Mallo wanted to think.

It all comes back to change. Nothing stays the same, not even kingdoms. Sometimes you have to accept that.

Sometimes, though, things change too quickly for you to even think about it. What happened next is still a blur in my mind. We were standing on the wall, waiting for Mallo to make his decision. And then Librarians were there.

Apparently, they came up through a tunnel they dug that opened just inside the wall. I didn't see that. I just saw a group of bow-tied figures, charging at us along the wall, wielding guns that shot balls of light.

Kaz vanished, his Talent making him get lost.

In the blink of an eye, three Mokian soldiers were standing in front of Aydee where there had been only two, her Talent instantly bringing a man from across the wall forward to defend her.

My Talent broke a few guns, though several of the Librarians had bows, and they fired those. Bastille, moving in a blur, had her sword out in a heartbeat and was cutting arrows from the air.

Seriously. She cut them *out of the air*. Never play baseball against a Crystin.

The Mokian soldiers began to fight, leveling their spears, which also shot out glowing bursts of light.

It was all over in a few seconds. I was the only one who didn't move. I had no training with real combat or war – I was just a stoopid kid who had gotten himself in over his head. By the time I thought to yelp in fear and duck, the skirmish was over, the assassins defeated.

Smoke rose in the air. Men fell still.

I glanced down, checking to make certain all of my important limbs were still attached. 'Wow,' I said.

Bastille stood in front of me, sword out, eyes narrow. She'd probably just saved my life.

'You see, Your Majesty,' I said. 'You can't trust the Librarians! If you give up, they will just ...'

I trailed off, only then noticing something. Mallo wasn't standing beside me, where he had been before. I searched around desperately, and found the king lying on the wall, his body covering that of his wife, whom he'd jumped to protect. Neither of them was moving.

Warriors called out in shock, moving their king and queen. Others called for help. In a daze, I turned, seeing the bodies of the Librarian assassins.

This was *actually* war. People were *actually* dying. Suddenly all of this didn't seem very funny any longer. Unfortunately, fate had a pretty good joke waiting for me in the very near future.

'They're alive,' Bastille said, kneeling with the soldiers beside the king and queen. 'They're still breathing. They don't look to have been hurt, even.'

'The Librarian weapons,' one of the Mokians said, 'will often knock people unconscious. They're trying to conquer Mokia but don't want to exterminate us. They want to rule over us. So they use guns that put us into comas.'

Another of the men nodded. 'We know of no cure – our stunner blasts work differently and have their own antidote. Those wounded can only be awakened by the Librarians, once the war is over. They'll wake us up in small, controllable batches, and brainwash us to forget our freedom.'

'I've heard of this,' Kaz said, kneeling down beside the king. When had Kaz come back? 'They did it when conquering other kingdoms too. Brutally effective tactic – if they knock us into comas, we still have to feed and care for those wounded, which drains our resources. Makes it easier to crack us. Far more effective than just killing.'

One of the soldiers nodded. 'We have thousands of wounded who are sleeping like this. Of course, many of the Librarians lie comatose from our stun-spears as well. The antidote for one does not work on victims of the other.'

We stood back as a Mokian doctor approached. Surprisingly, he was dressed in a white lab coat and spectacles. He carried a large piece of glass, which he held up, using it to inspect the king and queen. 'No internal wounds. Just Librarian Sleep.'

'I would have expected a witch doctor,' I said quietly to Kaz.

'Why?' Kaz said. 'The king's not a witch, and neither's the queen.'

'Take them to their chambers,' the doctor said, standing. 'And place double guards on them! If the Librarians know they're down, they'll want to kidnap them.'

Several soldiers nodded. Others, however, stood up, looking around with confusion. Outside, the Librarian robots began to hurl their boulders. One smashed against the glass covering, making the entire city seem to shake.

'Who is in charge now?' I asked, looking around.

'The captain of the watch fell earlier today,' one of the soldiers said. 'And the last remaining field general before him.'

'The princess rules,' another said.

'But she's outside the city.'

'The Council of Kings will need to ratify a succession,' another said. 'There's no official king until then. Acting king would be the highest person of peerage in the city.'

The group fell silent.

'Which means?' I asked.

'By the Spire itself,' Bastille whispered, eyes opening wide. 'It can't be. No ...'

All eyes turned toward me.

'Wait,' I said, nervous. 'What?'

'The Smedry Clan is peerage,' Bastille said, 'accepted as lords and ladies in all nations belonging to the Council of Kings. Your family gained that right when they abdicated; all recognized that the Smedry Talents could have led you to conquer the Free Kingdoms. But because of that, a direct heir to the Smedry line ranks equal with a duke in most kingdoms. Including Nalhalla and Mokia.'

'And a duke is ...?' I asked.

'Just under a prince,' Aydee said.

The warriors all fell to one knee before me. 'What are your wishes, Your Majesty?' one of them said.

'Aw, *pelicans*,' Kaz swore.

24601

Many of you in the Free Kingdoms have heard about the day I was crowned king of Mokia. It's become quite the legend. And legends have a habit of being exaggerated.

In a way, a legend is like an organism – a virus or a bacteria. It begins as a fledgling story, incubating in just a couple of people. It grows as it is passed to others, and they give it strength. Mutating it. Enlarging it. It grows grander and grander, infecting more and more of the population, until it becomes an epidemic.

The only cure for a legend is pure, antiseptic truth. That's partially why I began writing these books. How did I end up leading Mokia? Well, I was never really king – just 'acting monarch' as they put it. I was the highest-ranked person in the town, but only because most everyone else had either fallen or been sent away.

So no, I didn't heroically take up the king's sword in the middle of battle, as the legend says. My ascent to the throne was not announced by angelic voices. Very little heroism was involved.

But there *was* a whole lot of confusion.

'*What?*' I demanded. 'I can't be king! I'm only thirteen years old!'

'You're not our king, my lord,' one of the Mokians said. 'Just our acting monarch.'

Another rock boomed against the city's dome. Spiderweb cracks formed up the side of the glass.

'Well, what do I do?' I asked, glancing at Kaz, Aydee, and Bastille for support.

'Someone has to make the decision for us, my lord,' said one of the Mokian soldiers. 'The king was about to surrender. Do we go through with it, or do we fight?'

'You're going to make *me* decide?'

They just kept kneeling around me, waiting.

I looked over my shoulder, toward the Librarian camp. The sky was black, but the area around the city was lit as if by floodlights. I could see several places where the Librarians were digging tunnels, using some kind of strange, rodlike devices that appeared to vibrate the dirt and make it move away. The robots kept throwing rocks against the dome.

BOOM! BOOM! BOOM!

Just moments before, I'd been incredulous that the king would even consider surrender. But now the same question fell on me, and it terrified me. I had just seen people die. Librarian soldiers who had come to kill – or at least incapacitate – the king. Could I send the Mokian warriors to perhaps suffer the same fate?

Talk of bravery and freedom was one thing. But it felt different to actually be the one who made the decision. If I gave the order, the men and women who got hurt, killed, or knocked out would be *my* responsibility. That was a lot to heap on the shoulders of a thirteen-year-old kid who hadn't even *known* about Mokia six months ago. And people wonder why I'm so screwed up.

'We fight,' I said quietly.

This seemed to be the answer the soldiers were waiting for. They yelped in excitement, raising their spears – which, as I'd just learned, doubled as flamethrowers and could also shoot a stunning blast like the Librarian guns.

'You,' I said, picking the Mokian who'd been doing the talking. He was a lanky fellow with a lot of war paint and his black hair in a buzz cut. 'What's your name?'

'Aluki,' he said proudly. 'Sergeant of the wall guard.'

'Well, you're now acting as my second in command.' I glanced at the sky, cringing as another rock hit the dome. Above, the moon shone full and bright. The same moon that shone on the Hushlands. 'What time is it? How long until dawn?'

'It's not even eleven yet,' Kaz said, checking his pocket watch. 'Seven hours, maybe?'

'Spread the word,' I said to the soldiers on the wall around me. 'We have to survive for only *seven hours*. Help will come after that.'

They nodded, running off to pass the word. Aluki stayed with me. I turned to the side; Bastille was regarding me with folded arms. I cringed, waiting for her to scour me with condemnations for being so arrogant as to let the Mokians make me king.

'We'll need to do something about those tunnels,' she said. 'We won't hold out for long if teams keep slipping into the city like that.'

'Huh?' I asked.

'Don't forget the robots,' Kaz said as a rock hit above. 'Woodpeckers! That glass is close to cracking. If the dome falls, the tunnels will be our *last* concern.'

'True,' Bastille said. 'Maybe we could do something about the fallen troops, the ones in comas. If we could get them to wake up somehow ...'

'Wait!' I said, looking back and forth between the two. 'Aren't you going to state the obvious?'

'What?' Bastille said. 'That the Shattered Lens has far better technology than we thought?' She narrowed her eyes in a very Bastille-like way, glancing at the enormous machines that were tossing rocks toward the city. She seemed to have a particular dislike for them, along the lines of her hatred of walls. (Read book one.)

'No,' I said, exasperated. 'That I have no business being king! I can barely lead myself to the bathroom in the morning, let alone command an entire army.'

'Too late to change that now, Al,' Kaz said with a shrug.

'I think you'll do a great job,' Aydee added. 'Being king isn't that tough, from what I hear. Use a lot of phrases like "you please the crown" or "we are not amused" and occasionally make up a holiday.'

'Yeah,' I said flatly. 'Sounds as easy as one plus one.'

'Seven?' Aydee asked, cocking her head.

I looked at Bastille. She still had her arms folded. 'Kaz, Aydee,' she said, 'why don't you go get a count and see how many troops we have? Also, Alcatraz will need to know what kind of shape the command structure is in.'

The two Smedrys nodded, hurrying off to do as requested.

'Wait!' Bastille said, turning with a sudden shock. 'Kaz, *you* do the counting, Aydee, you stay away from anything of the sort.'

'Good call,' Kaz said.

'Right!' Aydee called. 'I'll give moral support.'

And they left. That, unfortunately, left me alone on the wall with Bastille. I gulped, backing away as she walked toward me. My back eventually hit the wall behind; if I backed up any farther, I'd topple over and fall to my death on the ground outside the city.

I considered it anyway.

Bastille reached me, placing a finger against my chest. 'You,' she said, 'are *not* going to fail these people.'

'But—'

'I'm tired of you wavering back and forth Alcatraz,' she said. 'Shattering Glass! Half the time, you act like you're panicked by the idea of being in charge, then the other half the time you just take control!'

'I ... er .... well ...'

'And the other half the time you babble incoherently!'

'I like babbling!' I exclaimed. (I'm not sure why.) 'Besides, that sounds like some Aydee math. Three halves?'

She eyed me.

'Yes, you're right about me,' I said. 'Sometimes, this all feels like a game. It twists my head in knots to think of the things I've been through, the things that have become part of my life. I get carried away with it all, with what everyone expects of me just because of my name.

'But I've already decided I want to lead. I decided it months ago. I want to be a hero; I want to be a leader. But that doesn't mean I want to be a *king*! When I actually stop to think about it, I realize how insane it is.'

'Then don't stop to think,' Bastille said. 'I don't see why it should be so hard. Not thinking seems to be one of your specialties.'

I grimaced. 'The things you say to me don't help either, Bastille. Every time I think that I'm starting to do well, I get a faceful of insults from you. And I can never tell if I deserve them or not!'

She narrowed her eyes further, finger pressed against my sternum. I cringed, preparing for the storm.

'I like you,' she said.

I blinked, righting myself. 'What?'

'I. Like. You. So I insult you.'

I scratched at my head. '.drawkcab ecnetnes a epyt ot dluow ti sa esnes hcum sa tuoba sekam taht ,ellitsaB'

She scowled at me, lowering her hand. 'If you don't understand, I'm not going to explain it to you.'

Boys, welcome to the wonderful world of talking to women about their feelings. As a handy primer, here are a few things you should know:

1) Women have feelings.
2) You will spend the next seventy years or so trying to guess what they're feeling and why.
3) You will be wrong most of the time.
4) I like French fries.

That's about all the help I can give you, I'm afraid. If it's any consolation, at least the women in *your* life don't have anger-management issues and a tendency to carry around five-foot-long magical swords.

'Look,' Bastille said. 'It's not important. What's important is saving Mokia. If you didn't notice, that was my *sister* who just got towed away unconscious. I'm not going to let the kingdom fall while she's out.'

'But shouldn't a Mokian be king?'

'You are Mokian,' Bastille said. 'And Nalhallan, and Fracois, and Unkulu. You're a Smedry – you're considered a citizen of all kingdoms. Besides, you *do* have Mokian blood in you. The Smedry line and the Mokian royal line has often intermixed. It wasn't odd for your uncle Millhaven to marry a Mokian. His wife is a third cousin of Mallo's, and your great-great-grandfather was the son of a Mokian prince.'

I blinked. Bastille, it should be noted, rarely shows her

princessly nature. She has a tendency to rip up anything pink, her singing sounds remarkably like the sound produced when you drop a rock on the tail of a wildebeest, and the last time a sweet flock of forest animals showed up and tried to help her clean, she chased them for the better part of an hour, swinging her sword and cursing like a sailor.

But she *does* think like a king's daughter sometimes. And she was force-fed all kinds of princessly information as a child, including long, boring lists of royal family trees. She knows which prince married which hypercountess and which superduke is cousins with which earl.

Yes. In the Free Kingdoms, we have royal titles like superdukes and hypercountesses. It's complicated.

'So ... I really *am* in the royal line,' I said, shocked.

'Of course you are. You're a Smedry – you're related to three quarters of the kings and queens out there.'

'But not you, right?'

'What? No. Not in any important way. We might be fourteenth, upside-down übercousins or something.'

I eyed her, trying to figure out what the gak an 'upside-down übercousin' was. Sounded like the kind of drink a kid my age wasn't allowed to order.

It should be stressed that Bastille and I are certainly *not* directly related. At least, we weren't at that point.

'All right,' I said. 'But I don't know anything about running a war.'

'Fortunately, I do. Troop morale and logistics were part of my training as a princess, and I have practice with battlefield tactics as part of my Crystin training.'

'Great! You can take over for me, then!'

She shook her head, eyes going wide, face getting a little white. 'Don't be stoopid.'

'Er, why not?'

As I think about it, that was kind of a stoopid answer, which was fitting, if you think about it. Me, I try not to think about anything. Oooh ... shiny ...

Bastille grimaced. 'You need to ask? I'm not what this people need. I'm not inspiring. *You* are. You're a king. I'm a general. They're different, different sets of skills.' She nodded toward the Mokian soldiers standing atop the walls. A lot of them didn't look much like warriors. Oh, they had war paint and spears. But not many of them were muscular.

'Mokia is a kingdom of scholars and craftspeople, Alcatraz,' Bastille said softly. 'Why do you think the Librarians attacked here first? They've been besieged for months now, their country at war for years. Many of the trained soldiers have already been knocked unconscious or killed. Do you have any idea what the loss of both the king and queen could mean? They're demoralized, wounded, and beaten down.'

She lifted her finger, tapping me in the chest again. 'They need someone to lead them. They need someone *spectacular*, someone miraculous. Someone who can keep them fighting for just a little longer, until your grandfather arrives with help.'

'And, uh, that someone is me?'

'Yes,' she said, almost grudgingly. 'I told you a few months back that I believed in you. Well, I do. I believe in what you can be when you're confident. Not when you're *arrogant*, but when you're confident. When you decide to do something, really decide, you do amazing things. I wish you could be that person a little more often.'

I scratched my head. 'I think that person is a lie, Bastille. I'm not confident. I just get lucky.'

'You get lucky a lot. Particularly when we really need it. You saved your father, you got the Sands back, you rescued the kings.'

'That last one was mostly you,' I said with a grimace.

'The idea that got us free was yours,' she said, 'and you spotted Archedis.'

I shrugged. 'It seems that when I get desperate, my mind works better. I'm not sure if that's something to be proud of or not.'

'Well, it's what we've got,' Bastille said, 'so we're going to work with it. I'll organize the troops. *You* be confident, give the Mokians the sense that someone's in charge. Together, we'll hold this city together until the Old Smedry gets here.'

'He'll probably be late, you know.'

'Oh, I'm certain he will be,' Bastille said. 'The question isn't, "Will he be late?" The question is, "How late is he going to be?"'

I nodded grimly.

'You ready to be a king?' she asked.

I hesitated just briefly. 'Yes.'

'Good,' she said, spinning as screams erupted from the center of the city. 'Because I think another group of Librarians just tunneled in.'

070706

D on't yawn.
   I shouldn't have agreed to be king. If you've been following
these books, you know that my early experiences set me up to fail.
Being a celebrity made me think that I was much more important
than I really was, and success led me to take more responsibility
than I should have. That all meant I fell really far when I did fall.

You yawning yet? No? Good. You most definitely *don't* want to
part your lips, suck in that sweet air, and feel the relaxing release
as you stretch and let your mouth open wide. You itch to do it;
you've been reading for a while now, and you're getting a little
groggy. But don't yawn. Really, don't do it.

Accepting the crown of Mokia, if even for a short time, was
the culminating peak of my spiral to fame. The events of this
siege became infamous. In fact, I didn't realize what I'd done until
long afterward. (After leaving Mokia, after all, I returned to the
Hushlands.)

Some Hushlanders think we yawn to increase oxygen to the
brain, but researchers have recently discounted this theory. In this
case, they're right. In the Free Kingdoms, it's been known for a
long time that yawns frighten away bloogynaughts. You know what
bloogynaughts are, don't you? They're those things that sneak up
on people while they're reading books, lurking just behind them,
watching them, edging closer and closer until they're right there.
Behind you. Breathing on your neck. About ready to grab you. A
yawn would scare it away. If only you could yawn . . .

Why did I agree to be king? I should have said no. And yet I
didn't. I let them make me king. I let Bastille persuade me. I let
them set me up high.

Why? Well, perhaps for the same reason that – when reading

the paragraphs above – you had a powerful urge to yawn or even glance over your shoulder. Talk about something long enough, and people will start thinking about it. It's kind of like a twisted, funky kind of mind control. Bastille was a princess, my family had once held thrones, and I was related distantly to pretty much every monarch in the Free Kingdoms. I guess I wanted to feel what it was like to be king.

(In the end, I discovered that being a king feels pretty much like being a regular person, only people shoot at you more often.)

Bastille and I charged through the city, racing toward the screams. Mokian men and women threw down the things they had been working on and rallied to the breach. Bastille slipped her sunglasses on, and I nodded to her. She took off at a much faster speed, leaving me behind as she used her enhanced Crystin speed to dart toward the disturbance.

I ran much more slowly, but I made a fair showing of it. The last half a year or so had been very good for my constitution. If you want to practice for a footrace, I'd highly recommend the Alcatraz Smedry training regimen. It involves being chased by Librarians, half-metal monsters, evil apparitions, sentient romance novels, fallen Knights of Crystallia, and the occasional evil chicken named Moe. Our success rate in training footrace winners is 95 percent. Unfortunately, our survival rate is about 5 percent, so it kind of balances everything out.

A group of Mokians filled in around me, running at my same speed. At first I thought they were joining me to rush to the scene of the disturbance. However, they were keeping too close. I realized with shock that they were an honor guard, of the type that run around protecting kings and saying, 'Who dares disturb the king?' and stuff like that. That made me feel important.

Even running as fast as we could, we arrived too late to help with the fighting. The Librarians had come out of a large, gopher-hole-like pit in the ground of a large green field near what I'd later learn was Mokian Royal University. Some bodies lay on the ground, and it made my stomach twist to see how many were

Mokian. At least they weren't dead. Of course, being in a coma was even worse, in many ways.

You may be shocked at how 'civilized' war is out in the Free Kingdoms. However, realize that they do what they do for a reason. If the Librarians could capture Tuki Tuki, they could get the antidote for the sleeping sickness – and they'd get nearly their entire army back to keep fighting, moving inward, to conquer more of the Free Kingdoms. It made sense for the Librarians to encourage the use of the coma-guns and coma-spears.

This latest group of Librarian infiltrators, strangely, looked like they'd surrendered soon after climbing out of the hole. Why hadn't they fought longer? They stood with their hands up, surrounded by ragged Mokian fighters. Bastille watched nearby, arms folded, looking dissatisfied. Likely because she hadn't gotten a chance to stab anyone.

The Mokians should have been happy to have won the skirmish so easily. But most of them just looked exhausted. The field was lit by torches on long poles rammed into the ground, and boulders still struck the dome protecting the city. Each one seemed to crack it a little bit more.

'We can't hold out!' said one of the spear-wielding Mokians. 'Look! They know they can surrender if we rally to fight them. There are so many of them that they're content to lose an entire team to knock out a few of us.'

'It's probably a distraction,' another soldier said. 'They're digging in other places too.'

'They're going to overrun us.'

'We've lost.'

'We—'

'Stop!' Bastille bellowed, waving her arms and getting their attention. '*Stop being stupid!*' She folded her arms, as if that was all she intended to say. Which, knowing Bastille, might just be the case.

'We *haven't* lost,' I said, stepping forward. 'We can win. We just need to hold out a little longer.'

'We can't!' one of the soldiers said. 'There are only a few

thousand of us left. There aren't enough people to patrol the streets to look for tunnelers. Most of us have been awake for three days straight!'

'And so you'd give up?' I demanded, looking at them. 'That's how they win. By making us give up. I've *lived* in Librarian lands. They don't win because they conquer, they win because they make people stop caring, stop wondering. They'll tire you out, then feed you lies until you start repeating them, if only because it's too hard to keep arguing.'

I looked around at the men and women in their islander wraps, holding spears that burned. They seemed ashamed. The field was shockingly quiet; even the captive Librarians didn't say anything.

'This is how they win,' I repeated. 'They *need* you to give in. They *have* to make you stop fighting. They don't rule the Hushlands with chains, fire, and oppression. They rule it with comfort, leisure, and easy lies. It's easy to accept the normal and avoid thinking about the difficult and the strange. Life can be so much simpler if you stop dreaming.

'But *that* is how we defeat them. They can never win, so long as we refuse to believe in their lies. Even if they take Tuki Tuki, even if Mokia falls, even if *all* of the Free Kingdoms become theirs. They will never win so long as we refuse to believe. Don't give up, and you will not lose. I promise you that.'

Around me, the Mokians began to nod. Several even smiled, holding their spears more certainly.

'But what will we do?' a female warrior asked. 'How will we survive?'

'My grandfather is coming,' I said. 'We just have to last a little longer. I'll talk to my counselors ...' I hesitated. 'Er, I have counselors, don't I?'

'We're right here, Your Majesty,' a voice said. I glanced backward, to where three Mokians stood in official-looking wraps, wearing small, colorful caps on their heads. I vaguely remembered them joining me as I ran for the disturbance.

'Great,' I said. 'I'll talk to my counselors, and we'll figure something out. You soldiers, your job is to keep *hoping*. Don't give up.

Don't let them win your hearts, even if they look like they'll win the city.'

Looking back on that speech, it seems incredibly stoopidalicious. Their kingdom was about to fall, their king and queen were casualties, and what was I telling them? 'Just keep believing!' Sounds like the title of a cheesy eighties rock ballad.

People believe in themselves all the time yet still fail. Wanting something badly enough doesn't really change anything, otherwise I'd be a Popsicle. (Read book one.)

Yet in this case, my advice was oddly accurate. The Librarians have always preferred to rule in secret. Biblioden himself taught that to enslave someone, you were best off making them comfortable. Mokia couldn't fall, not completely, unless the Mokians allowed themselves to be turned into Hushlanders.

Sounds impossible, right? Who would *let* themselves be turned into Hushlanders? Well, you didn't see how tired the Mokians were, how much the extended war had beaten them down. It occurred to me at that moment that maybe the Librarians could have won months ago. They'd kept on fighting precisely because they knew they didn't just have to win, they had to *overwhelm*. Kind of how you might keep playing a video game against your little brother, even though you know you can win at any moment, because you're planning the biggest, most awesome, most *crushing* combo move ever.

Except the Librarians were doing it with the hearts of the people of Mokia. And that made me angry.

The soldiers rushed off to get back to their other duties. I eyed the Librarian captives. Had they surrendered too easily? The Mokians didn't seem terribly threatening. Perhaps Bastille had surprised them; facing a bunch of soldiers who hadn't slept in days was one thing, but a fully trained Crystin was another.

I turned to my advisers. There were three of them, two men and a woman. The first man was tall and thin, with a long neck and spindly arms. He was kind of shaped like a soda bottle. The woman next to him was shorter and had a compact look to her, arms pulled in at her sides, hunched over, chin nestled down level with her shoulders. She looked kind of like a can of soda. The final man was large, wide, and thick-bodied. He was husky, with a small head, and kind of looked like ... well, a large two-liter soda bottle.

'Someone get me something to drink,' I barked to my honor guard, then walked up to the soda-pop triplets. 'You're my advisers?'

'We are,' said soda-can woman. 'I'm Mink, the large fellow to my right is Dink, and the man to my left is Wink.'

'Mink, Dink, and Wink,' I said, voice flat. (Like soda that's been left out too long.)

'No relation,' Dink added.

'Thanks for clearing that up,' I said. 'All right, advise me.'

'We should give up,' Dink said.

'Good speech,' Mink added, 'but it sounded too much like a rock ballad.'

'That jacket looks good on you,' Wink said.

'Er, thank you, Wink,' I said, confused.

'Oh, Wink got caught in an unfortunate Librarian disharmony grenade,' Mink added. 'Messed up his brain a little bit. He gives great advice ... it's just not always on the topic you want at the moment.'

'Never get involved in a land war in Asia,' Wink added.

'Great,' I said. 'So you think there's no way out of this?'

'The dome is going to crack soon,' Dink said, shaking his head.

'These burrows are coming more frequently,' Mink said. 'They'll keep digging into our city, knocking more and more people into comas until there's nobody left to fight back.'

'Always wear a hat when feeding pigeons,' Wink added.

All three of us looked at him. Wink shrugged. 'Think about it for a moment. You'll figure out why.'

'So,' Bastille said, walking up, arms folded, 'you're saying that if we can keep the dome from falling and protect against the people digging in, we can hold out.'

The three advisers looked at one another. 'I guess,' Mink said. 'But how are you going to do *that*?'

'Alcatraz will figure something out,' Bastille said.

'I will?'

'You'd better.'

'Never trust a three-fingered lion tamer.'

'Why are you so sure I'll figure something out?'

'Because that's what you *do*.'

'And if I can't this time?'

'If you run out of toothpaste, you can make your own by mixing two parts baking soda with one part salt and some water.'

'I just said that you would.'

'Well, I'll bet it would help if we could destroy those robots.'

'How?'

'An onion a day keeps *everyone* away.'

'Teddy bears! We could use those purple bear grenades, the type that destroy nonliving things.'

'We don't have enough of them.'

'Don't the Mokians have any?'

'I checked. They used all of theirs.'

'Always throw paper first.'

'Hey, guys! What are you doing?'

'Aydee, Alcatraz is going to come up with a brilliant plan to stop the robots.'

'Cool!'

'You're always so bubbly.'

'Kind of like soda pop.'

'Someone needs to get you a drink, Alcatraz.'

'I know.'

'Boom!'

'Did you just say, "Boom", Alcatraz?'

'No, that was the rock hitting the ceiling. We *really* need to stop those!'

'Arr!'

'Wait, what?'

'It's me, Kaz. I was going to say, "Are you guys done jabbering yet?" But I stubbed my toe.'

'Arr!'

'Kaz!'

'That time it wasn't me. It was Sexybeard the pirate.'

'Hey, guys. Arr.'

'Whatever.'

'Fool me once, shame on you. Fool me twice, shame on me. Fool me three times, and I'll hire you as my lawyer.'

'Wait, I'm lost.'

'That's not surprising for you, Kaz.'

'Who's talking?'

'I am.'

'Who are you?'

'Aluki.'

'When did *you* get here?'

'Oh, a page back or so. Looked like a real dangerous conversation to get into.'

'Alcatraz, the rocks! We have to stop them.'

'We need more teddy bears. Wow. Never thought I'd ever use *that* sentence.'

'Nobody *has* more bears.'

'Yes ... but I just thought of something to fix that.'

'Should I be scared?'

'Probably.'

'Always remember, foursight is what Oculators have when wearing their Lenses.'

'Shiver me timbers!'

'All right, Aydee. I've got a question for you. It's going to be a hard one. The hardest math problem you've ever seen.'

'Er ... I don't know ...'

'Alcatraz, are you sure you want to do this?'

'No.'

'Great. That's comforting.'

'It's the best thing I've got right now. Aydee, I'm going to ask you a math question, and I want you to keep the number in your head. Only spit it out when we get done, all right?'

'Okay ...'

'Take one and add fourteen.'

'Er ...'

'Then take away nine.'

'Right.'

'Then multiply by seventy-four.'

'Um ...'

'Then subtract three.'

'Well ...'

'Then take the square root of that.'

'What's a square root?'

'Then take one third of that.'

'Got it.'

'Then multiply by negative one.'

'Okay.'

'*What?*'

'Hush, Bastille. Then add the number of inches in a foot.'

'That's easy.'

'It is? I'm lost.'

'Quiet, Kaz. Then add eleven billion.'

'Okay ...'

'Then subtract eleven and one billion.'

'This is getting hard.'

'Then take the square root of that.'

'Oh, I remember! A square root is a carrot that doesn't know how to dance, right?'

'Batten down the hatches!'

'Then subtract one. That's *exactly* the number of purple bear grenades we have left. How many have we got, Aydee?'

'Uh ... er ... um ...'

'I think her brain is going to explode, Al.'

'Hush. You can do it, Aydee. I know you can.'

'I ... carry the one ... multiply by i. Take the complex derivative of Avogadro's number ... I've got it, Alcatraz! Five thousand, three hundred and fifty-seven. Wow! I didn't know we had that many bears!'

Kaz, Bastille, and I glanced at one another. Then we looked

at Kaz's pack, which held the bears. He took it off in a flash, throwing it away.

He was just fast enough. The pack ripped apart and a mountain of teddy bears burst free – 5,357 of them, to be precise. They flooded out, piling on top of one another, making a mountain of purple exploding teddy bears as large as a building.

'Aydee, you're amazing,' I said.

'Thanks! I think I'm getting better at math. I hope it doesn't ruin my Talent.'

'I think you're fine,' Bastille said dryly, picking herself up off the ground from where she'd ducked, anticipating the explosion of teddy bears.

'That's a big ol' mound of bears,' Kaz said, folding his arms. 'I think it's time to hunt us some robots.'

'Be careful, Your Majesty,' Wink warned. 'Some robots are unbearable.'

'Your Majesty,' Mink said, brushing off her wrap. 'Perhaps you should decide what to do with the prisoners first.'

I glanced to the side. The guards were still standing there, watching over the group of suit-, skirt-, and bow-tie-wearing Librarians. The Mokians looked very anxious. The Librarians seemed bored.

'Do we have a dungeon or something?' I asked. 'We should . . .' I trailed off, noticing something odd. Frowning, I stepped forward. One of the captive Librarians, huddled near the middle, was hiding her face, looking pointedly away from me. She had blond hair and an angular face. As she tried to keep hidden, I caught her eyes and recognized them for certain.

'*Mother?*' I asked, shocked.

$6.02214179 \times 10^{23}$

Are you surprised? My mother showed up completely un-expectedly in Tuki Tuki when I just happened to be there fighting? How unforeseeable!

What? You're not surprised? Why not? Is it because my mother has unexpectedly shown up in *every single one of these books so far*? (It's a mathematical law: One point is a point, two points a line, three points a plane, four points a cliché. I think Archimedes discovered it first.)

This plays into one of the big problems for writers. You see, we tend to skip the boring parts. If we didn't, our novels would be filled of sections like this one:

I got up in the morning and brushed my teeth, then went to the bathroom and took a shower. Nothing exciting happened. I ate breakfast. Nothing exciting happened. I went out to get the newspaper. I saw a squirrel. It wasn't very exciting. Then I came in and watched cartoons. They were boring. I scratched my armpit. Then I went to the bathroom again. Then I took a nap. My evil Librarian mot×her did not show up and harass me. That evening, I clipped my toenails. Yippee.

See? You're asleep now, aren't you? That was mind-numbingly, excruciatingly boring. In fact, you're not even reading this, are you? You're dozing. I could make fun of your stoopid ears and you would never know.

HEY, YOU! WAKE UP!

There. You back? Good. Anyway, we don't include all of that stuff because it tends to put people to sleep. I spent months in between books two and three doing pretty much nothing other than going to the bathroom and scratching my armpits.

I tend to write about the exciting stuff. (This introduction excepted. Sorry.) And that's the stuff that my mother tends to be part of. So it's hard to keep it surprising when she shows up, since every section I write about tends to be one where she gets involved.

So let's start this again. This time, do me the favor of at least *pretending* to be surprised. Maybe hit yourself on the head with the book a few times to daze yourself. That'll make it easier for you to exclaim in surprise when she shows up. (Remember, you should be acting this all out.)

Ahem.

'*Mother?*' I asked, shocked.

'Hello, Alcatraz,' the woman said, sighing. Shasta Smedry – also known as 'Ms. Fletcher' or many other aliases – wore a sharp black business suit and had her hair in a bun. She wore thin, horn-rimmed spectacles, though she wasn't an Oculator. Her face had a kind of pinched look to it, as if she were perpetually smelling something unpleasant.

'What are you *doing* here?' I demanded, stepping up to the Mokian guards, who stood in a ring around the Librarians. I didn't get too close. My mother isn't the safest person to be around.

'Really, Alcatraz, I would have thought you'd be more observant. What am I doing? Obviously, I'm helping to conquer this meaningless, insignificant city.'

I eyed her, and her image *wavered* slightly. I was shocked by that, but I was currently wearing my Oculator's Lenses. They read auras of things with Oculatory power, but they could do other, strange things. Things like give me a nudge to notice something I should have seen.

In this case, I realized what I should do. I took the Oculator's Lenses off and tucked them away. Then I got out my single Truthfinder's Lens, which was suspended in a set of spectacles that was missing the other Lens. I slipped this on, smiling at my mother.

She shut her mouth, looking dissatisfied. She knew what that Lens was. She wouldn't be able to lie, at least not without me spotting it.

'Let me repeat the question,' I said. 'What are you doing here?'

My mother folded her arms. Unfortunately, there was an easy way to defeat the Truthfinder's Lens: by not talking. But fortunately, keeping my mother from saying snide remarks is like keeping me from saying stoopid ones: theoretically possible, but never observed in the wild.

'You're a fool,' Shasta finally said. Puffs of white smoke came from her mouth, visible only to my single Truthfinder-covered eye. She was telling the truth – or, at least, what she saw as the truth. 'This city is doomed.' More white. 'Why did you come here, Alcatraz? You should have stayed safe in Nalhalla.'

'Safe? In a city where you kidnapped me and nearly let your Librarian allies slaughter my friends?'

'That was unfortunate,' Shasta said. 'I didn't wish for it to happen.' All true, surprisingly.

'You let it happen anyway. And now you've followed me here. Why?'

'I didn't follow you here,' she snapped. 'I—' She cut off, as if realizing she'd said too much.

She stopped as I smiled. The first statement had been true. She *wasn't* there because of me. She'd come for other reasons. But why? I doubted it was because she simply wanted to see Tuki Tuki captured. When my mother was involved, things were always a whole lot deeper than they seemed.

'Have you seen my father?' I asked.

She looked away, obviously determined not to say anything. Above, the rocks kept beating against the dome. A chunk of glass broke free, tumbling down to the city a short distance away. I could hear it shatter, like a thousand icicles falling off a rooftop at once.

There wasn't time to chat with my mother right now. 'Throw them in my dungeons,' I said to Aluki. 'I ... er, I do have dungeons, don't I?'

'Not really,' Aluki said. 'We've been keeping prisoners in the university catacombs. They have Expander's Glass reinforcing the walls, which would make it almost impossible for the Librarians to tunnel in and rescue them.'

'Very well. Throw them in the university basement and lock them away,' I said. I pointed at my mother. 'Except her. Lock her someplace *extra* safe. And search her. She stole a book from Nalhalla that we will want to recover.'

'I don't have that anymore,' Shasta said. Unfortunately, the Lens said she was telling the truth. She was also smiling slyly, as if she knew something important.

She couldn't have read it, I thought. *Not without a pair of Translator's Lenses. And she didn't come here to get my pair; she didn't know I would be here.*

The soldiers led Shasta and the other Librarians away. As they did, I noticed one of them watching me. He was an older man and didn't look anything like a soldier. He wore a tuxedolike suit with a cravat at the neck, and he had a short, graying beard flecked with black. He had keen, sagacious eyes.

'Search that one too,' I said, grabbing Aluki's arm and pointing the man out. 'I don't like how he looks at me.'

'Yes, Your Majesty,' Aluki said.

'You don't like how he "looked" at you?' Bastille asked, walking up to me.

'There's something about him,' I said. 'He's odd. I mean, the only reason to wear a cravat is to look distinguished and intriguing. It's kind of like using *sagacious* in a sentence; it's less about what it actually means, and more about making you look smart.'

Bastille frowned, but Kaz nodded, as if understanding. Aydee had run over to the bears and was gleefully counting them out into piles of ten. She gave each one a hug and a name before setting it aside. It was kind of cute, if you ignored the fact that each and every one of those bears was a live grenade.

My three counselors stood, speaking quietly next to the large pile of bears.

Bastille followed my gaze. 'That was dangerous, what you did, Smedry.'

'What? Multiplying the bears?' I shrugged. 'It could have gone the other direction, I suppose, and Aydee's Talent could have made our stock vanish. But I figured that we only had a few bears left, and that wasn't enough to do what we needed to. So what did we have to lose?'

'I'm not worried about what we could have lost,' Bastille said. 'I'm worried about what we could have *gained*.'

'Wait? Huh?' (You say stuff like that a lot when you're as dumb as I am.)

'Shattering Glass, Smedry! What would have happened if Aydee had said we had fifty thousand bears? What if she'd said four or five *million* bears! We'd have been buried in them. You could have destroyed the city, smothering everyone inside of it.'

I cringed, an image popping into my head of purple teddy bears washing over the city. Of the Mokians being crushed beneath the weight of a sea of pleasant plushness. A tsunami of teddies doing the Librarians' work for them. A blitzkrieg of bears, a torrent of toys, an … um … upheaval of ursines.

Or, in simpler terms, a *shattering* lot of bears.

'Gak!' I said.

'That's right,' Bastille said. She wagged a finger at me. 'Smedry Talents are dangerous, particularly in the young. I'd have thought that you – of all people – would realize this.'

'Oh, don't be such a bubble in the glass, Bastille,' Kaz said, smacking me on the arm. 'You did great, kid. That kind of bear firepower is *just* the kind of thing Tuki Tuki needed.'

'It was risky,' Bastille said, folding her arms.

'Yeah, but I don't think it was as dangerous as you say. Aydee's got one of the most powerful Prime Talents around, but I doubt she'd have been able to make *millions* of bears. Likely, she couldn't have destroyed the city – at best, she'd have just crushed those of us here in this field.'

'Very comforting,' Bastille said dryly.

'Well, you know what my pop says. "Danger, risks, and lots of fun. The Smedry way!"'

Kaz, as I've mentioned, is a scholar of magical forces. He knew more about Talents than anyone else alive. In fact, that's probably what he'd been doing here when he'd visited Tuki Tuki originally – studying at the university.

'My lord,' Mink – the soda-can counselor – said, approaching. 'This boon of bears is quite timely, but how are we going to use it to destroy those robots? They're protected by the Librarian army!'

'And don't forget the tunnels,' Dink said.

'And always wash behind your ears,' Wink added.

'I need three things from you,' I said, thinking quickly. 'Some backpacks that will hold several of those bears, six of your fastest warriors, and some really long stilts.'

The counselors looked at one another.

'Go!' I said, waving. 'That dome is about to fall!'

The three scattered, scrambling to do as I asked.

Bastille suddenly turned eastward, toward the ocean. Toward Nalhalla. Her eyes opened. 'Alcatraz, I think the knights are actually coming.'

'What? You can see them?' I looked eagerly.

'I can't see them,' Bastille said. 'I can *feel* them.' She tapped the back of her neck, where the Fleshstone was set into her skin, hidden by her silvery hair. It connected her to the Crystin Mindstone, which then connected her to all of the other Knights of Crystallia.

I didn't see why they were so keen on the thing. I mean, it was because of that very connection that the Knights had all fallen to Archedis's tricks back in Nalhalla. He'd done something to the Mindstone, and it – connected to all of the Crystin – had knocked them out. Seemed like a liability to me.

Of course, that connection *also* had the ability to turn thirteen-year-old girls into superknight kung-fu killing machines. So it wasn't all bad.

'You can sense the other knights?' I said frowning.

'Only in the most general of terms,' she said. 'We ... well, we don't talk about it. If a lot of them feel the same thing at once, I will notice it. And if a lot of them start moving at once, I can feel it. A large number of knights just left Nalhalla.'

'They *just* left Nalhalla,' I said, groaning inside. 'The trip here will take hours and hours.'

'We have to hold out,' Bastille said fervently. 'Alcatraz, your plan is working! For once.'

'Assuming we can survive for a few more hours,' Kaz said. 'You have a plan about that, kid?'

'Well,' I said. 'Kind of. Bastille, how good are you with stilts?'

'Um … okay, I guess.' She hesitated. 'I should be worried, shouldn't I?'

'Probably.'

She sighed. 'Ah well. It can't possibly be worse than death by teddy-bear avalanche.' She hesitated. 'Can it?'

I just smiled.

Four Teens And A Pickle

In March 1225, two years before his death, Genghis Khan sat down to breakfast to dine on a bowl of warm hearts cut from the chests of his enemies. At that time, he was ruler of the largest empire in the history of the world. He reached up, scratched his nose, and said something extremely profound.

'Zaremdaa, en ajil shall mea baina.'

He knew what he was talking about. As do I. Trust me, I've been a king before. (No, really, I have. Sometime, check out volume four of my autobiography, page 669.)

I was only king of one city, really, and only for a short time. But it was ridiculously, insanely, bombastically tough to do the job right. Tougher than trying to get hit in the head with a baseball shot out of a cannon. Tougher than trying to climb a hundred-foot cliff using a rope made of used dental floss. Tougher, even, than trying to figure out where my stoopid metaphors come from.

I've never understood one thing: Why do all of these megalomaniac dictators, secret societies, mad scientists, and totalitarian aliens *want* to rule the world? I mean really? Don't they know what a pain in the neck it is to be in charge? People are always making unreasonable demands of kings. 'Please save us from the invading Vandal hordes! Please make sure we have proper sanitation to prevent the spread of disease! Please stop beheading our wives so often; it's ruining the rugs!'

Being a king is like getting your driver's license. It sounds really cool, but when you finally get your license, you realize that all it *really* means is that your parents can now make you drive your brothers or sisters to soccer practice.

Like Genghis Khan said, 'Zaremdaa, en ajil shall mea baina.' Or, translated, 'Sometimes, this job sucks.' But really, hasn't *everyone* said that at some point?

'Zaremdaa, en ajil shall mea baina!' Bastille said from way up high.

'What was that?' I called up. 'I don't speak Mongolian.'

'I said, sometimes my job really sucks!'

'You're doing great!'

'That doesn't mean that this doesn't *suck!*' Bastille called.

You see, at this point, Bastille was balanced atop a set of stilts, which were in turn taped to another set of stilts, which were in turn taped to *another* set of stilts. Those were on top of a chair, which was on top of a table. And all of that was balanced on top of the Mokian university's science building. (It was a large, island-bungalow-style structure. You know, the kind of place you'd expect to find Jimmy Buffett singing, Warren Buffett vacationing, or a pulled-pork buffet being served.)

'Do you see anything?' I called up to her.

'My entire life flashing before my eyes?'

'Besides that.'

'It's really easy to see who's balding from up here.'

'Bastille!' I said, annoyed.

'Sorry,' she called down. 'I'm just trying to distract myself from my impending death.'

'You weren't so nervous when I suggested this!'

'I was on the *ground* then!'

I raised an eyebrow. I hadn't realized that Bastille was scared of heights. She hadn't acted like this before. Of course, other times she'd been up high, she'd been in a flying vehicle. Not strapped to three sets of stilts and balancing high in the air.

For all her complaining, she was doing a remarkable job, and *she* had been the one to suggest taping the stilts together to get her up higher. Besides, she was wearing her glassweave jacket, which would save her if she did fall. Her Crystin abilities allowed her to keep her balance, despite the height and the instability of her position. It was rather remarkable.

Of course, that didn't stop me from wanting to tease her. 'You aren't feeling dizzy, are you?'

'You aren't helping.'

'Man, I think the breeze is picking up ...'

'Shut up!'

'Is that an earthquake?'

'I'm going to kill you slowly when I get down from here. I'll do it with a hairpin. I'll go for your heart, by way of your foot.'

I smiled. I shouldn't have taunted her. The situation was dire, and there was little cause for laughter in Tuki Tuki. The dome was cracking even further, and my counselors – the two kind of useful ones, at least – said they thought it would last only another fifteen minutes or so.

But seeing Bastille in a situation like she was – where she was uncomfortable and nervous – was very rare. I just ... well, I had to do it. And that, by the way, is the definition of stoopiderlifluous: being so stoopid as to taunt Bastille while she's out of arm's reach, assuming she won't get revenge very soon after.

As I smirked, Kaz rounded the building and trotted up to me, wearing his dark Warrior's Lenses. He'd gotten two small pistols somewhere and wore them strapped to his chest. They looked like flint-and-powder models, perhaps taken from the Mokian stores.

'Everything's ready,' he said. 'Mokians all over the city are climbing atop buildings, looking for the first sign of Librarian holes opening.' He glanced up at Bastille. 'I see you found a way to get even higher,' he called at her. 'Reason number fifty-six and a half: Short people know when to stay on the ground. We're closer to it, we appreciate it more. What is it with you tall people and extreme heights?'

'Kaz, I'm a thirteen-year-old girl,' Bastille called down. 'I'm only, like, a couple of inches taller than you are.'

'It's the principle of the thing,' he called back. Then he looked at me. 'So, are you going to explain this plan of yours, kid?'

'Well, we've got two problems. The rocks hitting the shield and the tunnels digging up. We can't stop the rocks because there's an army between us and the robots. But the Librarians are conveniently digging tunnels from their back lines up into our city. So one of the problems presents a solution to the other.'

'Ah,' Kaz said thoughtfully. 'So those fellows ...' He nodded to the six Mokian runners Aluki had gotten for me. They stood in a line, ready to dash away, bearing backpacks filled with stuffed bears.

I nodded. 'Usually, after the Librarians are fought off from the hole they dig, the Mokians collapse the tunnel. But this time, as soon as the hole is spotted, we'll move everyone out of the area. The emptiness will make the Librarians think that they haven't been spotted, and they'll rush out to cause mayhem. These six men will then sneak down the tunnel and run out behind Mokian lines, then take down the robots. A single one of these bears to the leg should make the robot collapse.'

'Wow,' Kaz said. 'That's actually a good plan.'

'You sound surprised.'

Kaz shrugged. 'You're a Smedry, kid. Half our ideas are insane. The other half are insane but brilliant at the same time. Deciding which is which can be trouble sometimes.'

'I'll tell you how to decide,' Bastille called down. 'Look and see which one involves *me* having to climb up a hundred feet in the air and balance on stilts. Shattering Smedrys!'

'How can she even *hear* us from up there?' Kaz muttered.

'I have very good ears!' Bastille called.

'Here,' I said, picking up a backpack. 'I made one of these for each of us too. There are two of each kind of bear in there. I figure we should all have some, just in case.'

Kaz nodded, throwing on his backpack. I shrugged mine on as well.

'You realize,' Kaz said softly, 'that the soldiers you send out to stop those robots won't be coming back.'

'What? They could run back in the tunnel, and ...'

And I trailed off, realizing how stoopid it sounded. The Librarians might get surprised by my tricky plan – *might* – but they'd never let the Mokian soldiers escape back into the tunnel after destroy-ing the robots. Even if all of this worked out exactly as I wanted, those six men and women weren't returning. At best, they'd get captured. Maybe knocked out by Librarian coma-bullets.

I hadn't even considered this. Perhaps because I didn't want to. Go back and read the beginning of this chapter. Maybe now you'll start to understand what I was saying.

I glanced at the six soldiers. Their faces were grim but determined. They carried their backpacks over their shoulders, and each held a spear. They were younger soldiers, four men and two women, who Aluki had said were their fastest runners. I could see from their eyes that they understood. As I regarded them, they nodded to me one at a time. They were ready to sacrifice for Mokia.

They had seen what my request would demand of them, even if I hadn't. Suddenly, I felt very stoopiderlifluous.

'I should cancel the plan,' I said suddenly. 'We can think of something else.'

'Something that doesn't risk the lives of your soldiers?' Kaz said. 'Kid, we're at *war*.'

'I just …' I didn't want to be the one responsible for them going into danger. But there was nothing to be done about it. I sighed, sitting down.

Kaz joined me. 'So now …' he said.

'Now we wait, I guess.' I glanced upward nervously. The rocks continued to fall; the glass's cracks glowed faintly, making the dark night sky look like it was alight with lightning. Fifteen minutes. If the Librarians didn't burrow in during the next fifteen minutes, the dome would shatter and the Librarian armies would rush in. Most of the Mokians – the ones I didn't have watching for tunnels – were already gathered on the wall, anticipating the attack.

I blinked, realizing for the first time how tired I was. It was well after eleven at this point, and the excitement of everything had kept me going. Now I just had to wait. In many ways, that seemed like the worst thing imaginable. Waiting, thinking, worrying.

Isn't it odd, how waiting can be both boring and nervewracking at the same time? Must have something to do with quantum physics.

A question occurred to me, something I'd been wondering for a while. Kaz seemed the perfect person to ask. I shook off some of my tiredness. 'Kaz,' I said, 'has any of the research you've done indicated that the Talents might be . . . alive?'

'What?' Kaz said, surprised.

I wasn't sure how to explain. Back in Nalhalla – when we'd been in the Royal Archives (not a library) – my Talent had done some odd things. At one point, it had seemed to *reach* out of me. Like it was alive. It had stopped my cousin Folsom from accidentally using his own Talent against me.

'I'm not sure what I mean,' I said lamely.

'We've done a *lot* of research on Talents,' Kaz said, drawing his little circle diagram in the dirt, the one that divided up different Talents into types and power ranges. 'But we don't really *know* much.'

'The Smedry line is the royal line of Incarna,' I said. 'An ancient race of people who mysteriously vanished.'

'They didn't vanish,' Kaz said. 'They destroyed themselves, somehow, until only our line remained. We lost the ability to read their language.'

'The Forgotten Language,' I said. 'We didn't forget it. Alcatraz the First *broke* it. The entire language. So that people couldn't read it. Why?'

'I don't know,' Kaz said. 'The Incarna were the first to get Talents.'

'They brought them down into themselves, somehow,' I said, thinking back to the words of Alcatraz the First, which I'd discovered in his tomb in the Library of Alexandria. 'It was like . . . Kaz, I think what they were trying to do was create people who could *mimic* the power of Oculatory Lenses. Only without having to use the Lenses.'

Kaz frowned. 'What makes you say that?'

'My tongue moving while breath moves out of my lungs and through my throat, vibrating my vocal cords and—'

'I *meant*,' Kaz said. 'Why do you think that the Talents are like Lenses?'

'Oh. Right. Well, a lot of the Talents do similar things to Lenses. Like Australia's Talent and Disguiser's Lenses. I did some reading on it while I was in Nalhalla. There are a lot of similiarities. Shatterer's Lenses can break other glass if you look at it; that's kind of like my Talent. And then there are Traveler's Lenses, which can push a person from one point to another and ignore obstructions in between. That's kind of like what you do. I wonder if there are Lenses that work like Grandpa's power, slowing things or making them late.'

'There are,' Kaz said thoughtfully. 'Educator's Lenses. When you put them on, it slows time.'

'That's an odd name.'

'Not really. Have you ever known anything that can slow down time like a boring class at school?'

'Good point,' I said.

All in all, there were thousands of different kinds of glass that had been identified. A lot of them – like the Traveler's Lenses – were impractical to use. They were either too dangerous, took too much energy to work, or were so rare that complete Lenses of them were nearly impossible to forge.

'Some glass is called technology,' I said, 'but that's just because it can be powered by brightsand. But all glass can be powered by Oculators. I've done it before.'

'I know,' Kaz said. 'The boots. You said you were able to give them an extra jolt of power.'

'I did it again,' I said. 'With Transporter's Glass in Nalhalla.'

'Curious,' Kaz said. 'But Al, nobody else can do that. What makes you think this involves the Incarna?'

'Well, neurons in my brain transmit an electrochemical signal to one another and—'

'I *mean*,' Kaz interrupted. 'Why do you think this has something to do with the Incarna?'

'Because,' I said. 'I just have a feeling about it. Partially Alcatraz the First's writings, partially instinct. The Incarna knew about all these kinds of glass, but they wanted more. They wanted to have these powers innate inside of people. And so somehow, they made it happen – they *gave* us Talents. They turned us into Lenses, kind of.'

I frowned. 'Maybe it's not the fact that I'm an Oculator that lets me power glass. Maybe it's the fact that I'm an Oculator *and* a Smedry. That's much rarer, isn't it?'

'I only know of four who are both,' Kaz said. 'You, Pop, your father, and Australia.'

'Has any research been done into people like us powering glass?'

'Not that I know of,' he confessed.

'I'm right, Kaz,' I said. 'I can *feel* it. The Incarna did something to themselves, something that ended with the creation of the Smedry Talents.'

Kaz nodded slowly.

'Aren't you going to ask what makes me feel this way?'

'Wasn't planning on it.'

"Cuz I've got this really great comment prepared on unconscious mind interacting with the conscious mind and releasing chemical indicators in the form of hormones that influence an emotional response.'

'Glad I didn't ask, then,' Kaz noted.

'Ah well.'

Now, it may seem odd to you that I – a boy of merely thirteen years – figured out all that stuff about the Incarna, when scholars had been trying for centuries to discover it. I had some advantages, though. First, I had the unusual position of being a Smedry, an Oculator, and a holder of the Breaking Talent. From what I can determine, there hadn't been someone who had possessed all three for thousands of years. I might have been the only one other than Alcatraz the First.

Because of that unusual combination, I'd done some strange things. (You've seen me do some of them in these books.) I'd seen things others hadn't, and that had led me to conclusions they couldn't have made. Beyond that, I'd *read* what many of the other scholars – like Kaz – had written. That's part of what I'd spent my time doing in Nalhalla while I waited for the fourth book to start.

There's a saying in the Hushlands: 'If I have seen further it is only by standing on the shoulders of giants.' Newton said it first. I'm not sure how he got hit on the head with an apple while standing up so high in the air, but the quote is quite good.

I had all of their research. I had my own knowledge. Between it all, I happened to figure out the right answer.

Kaz nodded to himself, slowly. 'I think you might be on to something, kid. Some scholars have noticed the connection between types of Smedry Talents and types of glass. They've even tried to put the glasses onto the Incarnate Wheel. But your explanation goes a step further.'

He tapped the diagram he'd drawn on the floor. 'I like it. Things tend to make sense once you figure out all of the pieces. We call Smedry Talents "magic". But I've never liked that word. They work according to their own rules. Take Aydee's power, for instance.'

'It seems pretty magical,' I admitted. 'Creating five thousand bears out of thin air?'

'She didn't create them out of nothing,' Kaz said. 'She's got a spatial Talent, one that changes how things are in space with relation to other things. Like my Talent. I get lost. This moves me from one place to another. Your father loses things, not himself. He can tuck something into his pocket, and it will be gone the next moment. But when he really needs it, he'll "find" it in the pocket of a completely different outfit.

'Aydee's Talent is actually very similar to these. Those bears, they didn't come from nowhere. She moved them from someplace. Out of a storehouse or factory; perhaps she drained the armory back in Nalhalla. That's how it always works. She's not magically making them appear; she's moving them here, and she's putting something back in their place – usually just empty air.'

'Like Transporter's Glass,' I said.

'Yes, actually,' Kaz said. 'Now that you mention it, that *is* very similar.' He tapped the ground again. 'So, if I get you right, you're saying that the Incarna turned people into Lenses. But something went wrong.'

'Right,' I said. 'That's why the Talents are hard to control, why they do such odd things some of the time.'

'And that's what your father is chasing, I warrant,' Kaz said. 'Didn't he say he wanted to give every person Smedry Talents?'

'Yeah,' I said. 'He announced it in a big press conference, to all of Nalhalla.'

'He wants the secret,' Kaz said.

'And my mother does too,' I guessed. 'It's hidden in the Forgotten Language. The trick, the method the Incarna used to turn *people* into *Lenses*. Kind of.'

'And this whole issue with the Translator's Glass was based on that,' Kaz said, growing excited. 'Your mother and he were searching for this same secret, and they knew they needed to be able to read the Forgotten Language to find it. So they searched out the Sands of Rashid . . .'

'And broke up because of differences in how they'd use the abilities once they found them,' I said, glancing toward the university building proper. Where my mother was locked up. 'I have to talk to her, interrogate her. Maybe I can figure out if this is all correct.'

Above us, Bastille began to swear.

I looked up; Bastille was pointing urgently. 'Alcatraz! The earth is moving in a yard three streets over! I think Librarians are tunneling in over there!'

Kaz leaped to his feet, and the six Mokian runners came alert. I glanced at the university, the place of my mother's impromptu prison. An interrogation would have to wait.

'Let's go!' I said, dashing in the direction Bastille had pointed.

8675309

By now, you're probably confused at what chapter this is. Some people I let read the book early were a little confused by the chapter numbers. (Wimps.)

I did this intentionally. See, I knew it would drive Librarians crazy. Despite our many efforts to hide these books as innocent 'fantasy' novels in the bookstores and libraries, the Librarians have proven too clever (or at least too meticulous) for us. They are reading my biographies, and perhaps learning too much about me. So it was time to employ some careful misdirection.

I considered writing the whole book in 133t, but felt that would give me too much m4d ski11z. So it came to the chapter numbers. As you have probably noticed, Librarians don't conform to most people's stereotypes. Most of them don't even *have* stereos. Beyond that, they're not sweet, book-loving scholars; they're maniacal cultists bent on ruling the world. They don't like to shush people. (Unless it means quieting them permanently by sinking them in the bay with their feet tied to an iron shelving cart.) In fact, most Librarians I've seen are quite fond of loud explosions, particularly the types that involve a Smedry at the center.

People don't become Librarians because they want to force people to be quiet, or because they love books, or because they want to help people. No, people become Librarians for only one reason: They like to put things in order. Librarians are *always* organizing stuff. They can't help it. You'll see them for hours and hours sitting on little stools in libraries, going over each and every book on their shelf, trying to decide if it should be moved over one or two slots. It drives them crazy when we normal people wander into their libraries and mess stuff up.

And so, I present to you the perfect Librarian trap. They'll come along, pick up this book, and start to read it, thinking they're so smart for discovering my autobiography. The chapter titles will be completely messed up. That, of course, will make their brains explode. So if you have to wipe some gray stuff off the book, you know who read it before you.

Sorry about that.

Once again, I charged through the city, small retinue in tow. Being king sure seemed to involve running around in the dark a lot.

'Kid,' Kaz said, jogging beside me, 'I should be on the strike team to attack the robots.'

'What?' I exclaimed. 'No, Kaz. I need you here.'

'No, you don't. You're doing just fine on your own.'

'But—'

'Kid, with these Warrior's Lenses on, I can run faster than any of those Mokian soldiers.'

That was true; Warrior's Lenses augmented a person's physical abilities. Kaz had no trouble keeping up with the rest of us, despite his shorter legs.

Warrior's Lenses were one of the few types that could be used by anyone, not just Oculators. It's proof that the world is so unfair that I, to this day, have never had a chance to use Warrior's Lenses. (Well, except that once, but we won't talk about that.) They're supposedly beneath Oculators, or something like that.

'So give the Lenses to someone else,' I said stubbornly.

'Wouldn't work,' he replied. 'They take a lot of training to learn to use. I'll bet there aren't more than a few dozen Mokian soldiers who can use them. Otherwise, the entire army would be wearing them.'

Oh. Well, that made sense. Unfortunately.

'Besides, kid,' Kaz said, 'I can use my Talent to escape from behind the Librarian lines. I might even be able to pull a few of the other runners with me. If you send me, it'll save lives.'

Now *that* was a good argument. If Kaz could get some of the runners out, then that would alleviate my conscience big time.

'Are you sure you can get out?' I said softly as we ran. 'Your Talent has been unpredictable lately ...'

'Oh, I'll be able to get out,' Kaz said. 'I just can't promise when I'll get back. The Talents ... seem like they've *all* been acting up lately. Aydee's goes off at the mere mention of a number, and from what Bastille tells me, your father is losing things more and more often. Something's up.'

I nodded, thinking again of how my Talent had seemed to *snap* out of my body at Folsom.

'All right, you're on the team,' I said. Something occurred to me at that moment. 'But after you get lost, don't try to come back here. Go to Grandpa Smedry instead. I want you to deliver a message for me.'

'Sure thing,' Kaz said.

'Tell him that we really, *really* need him here by midnight. If he doesn't arrive by then, we're doomed.'

'Midnight?' Kaz said. 'That's only a few minutes away.'

'Just do it.'

Kaz shrugged. 'Okay.'

We reached an intersection between two rows of pastoral homes and hesitated. Which way to go? Only Bastille knew. A second later, she raced by, leading the way to the right. We followed her; it certainly hadn't taken her long to get down from the stilts and catch up.

At the end of a row of houses, she slowed and raised a hand. We bunched up behind her, and Kaz quietly informed the youngest – and most nervous-looking – of the Mokian runners that he'd been booted from the strike team. The youth looked very relieved.

'There,' Bastille hissed, pointing at a section of ground several houses down. We peeked around the corner, watching as some shovels broke up out of the ground. The grass lowered, and a few moments later, a few Librarians' heads peeked out.

'Go get Aluki and his soldiers,' I whispered to the young runner that Kaz had relieved. 'Warn him about these infiltrators; he'll need to take care of them once the strike team has sneaked into the tunnel.'

The runner nodded, dashing off. I peeked back around the corner. The Librarians were timidly glancing about, as if surprised to find no resistance. Several of them climbed out of the hole, slinking to the wall of the nearest hutlike house. They waved for the others, and soon the entire group had exited the hole. They ran off down a side street, carrying their rifles and looking for mayhem. In a lot of ways, these Librarian infiltration groups were suicide missions, just like my strike team. The difference being that the Librarians anticipated taking the city very soon, and finding the Mokian coma antidote.

'All right,' I said, waving. 'Go!'

Kaz and the five runners charged around the side of the building, running toward the hole. I waited anxiously. Were the Librarians far enough away? Would they notice what we were doing?

Bastille waited beside me, though I could tell she itched to leap forward and join the strike team. Fortunately, her primary duty was to protect me, so she restrained herself.

The strike team reached the hole and Kaz waved the runners to jump in. Suddenly, something flashed in the hole.

'Rifle fire!' Bastille said.

She was moving a moment later, bolting down the hole. One of our runners collapsed backward, twitching. The others leaped for the ground, taking cover, and two Librarians peeked out of the hole, holding rifles.

Kaz whipped out a pistol and shot one in the face – it let out a blast of light, knocking the Librarian unconscious. Bastille – running inhumanly fast – arrived and kicked the other Librarian in the face.

I blinked. Things happened so *quickly* in battle. By the time I thought to jog out, the two Librarian guards had been disabled. Unfortunately, one of our runners was down.

'Woodpeckers!' Kaz cursed. 'We should have known they'd be smart enough to leave a rear guard.' He checked on the runner who'd been shot. He was unconscious. We'd need the antidote to awaken him.

'There will probably be guards at the end of the tunnel as well,' one of the Mokians said. 'And while we're fast, we're not the best soldiers in the army.'

Kaz nodded. 'If you fight and make a disturbance, the Librarians will cut off our exit out of the tunnel. Sparrows!'

'Kaz, where did you pick up all that fowl language?' Bastille asked.

'Sorry. Spent two weeks trapped in an ornithologist's convention during my last time lost.'

And that is a story all unto itself.

'Well,' I said, 'we'll just have to hope that ...' I trailed off as I noticed Bastille and Kaz sharing a look. Then, shockingly, Bastille pulled the bear-containing backpack off of the unconscious runner. She slung it over her shoulder, then looked at me.

'Stay here,' she said.

'Bastille, no! You can't go.'

'I have the best chance at knocking out guards at the exit of the tunnel quietly. My speed and strength will let me get to those robots faster than the others. I need to go.'

'But you're supposed to protect me!'

She pointed upward, at the glass dome. 'It's only minutes away from breaking. This *is* the best way to protect you.'

She secured her Warrior's Lenses. 'Take care of yourself,' she said. 'You'd better not die. I'm getting a little fond of you. Besides, if I fall, you'll need to get me the antidote.'

With that, she jumped down into the hold. I scrambled up to the edge, looking down. The drop wasn't a deep one; it quickly turned to the side as the tunnel pointed out toward the Librarian army. The runners jumped in after her. Kaz patted my arm. 'I'll try to get her out, kid,' he said.

He followed the others down into the hole, backpack carried over one arm, a pistol carried warily in the other hand. He disappeared into the darkness.

I stared after them for several heartbeats, trying to sort through my emotions. I had sent a team out on a suicide mission. Me. They were following my orders. And *Kaz* and *Bastille* were with them.

Was this what it was to be a king? This terrible guilt?

It felt like someone had slathered all of my internal organs with honey, then let a jar full of ants loose inside there.

It felt like someone had shoved firecrackers up my nose, then set them off with a flamethrower.

It felt like being forced to eat a hundred rotting fish sticks.

In other words, it didn't feel so good.

I turned and took off at a dash, running as quickly as I could. I passed Aluki and his soldiers fighting a pitched battle with the Librarians who'd left the tunnel. Running with all I had, I eventually reached the steps to the top of the wooden wall. I leaped up them. Then, out of breath, puffing, I slammed up against the front of the wall, looking out.

I arrived just in time to see the strike team erupt out of the other side of the tunnel. Bastille had dealt with the Librarian guards in her characteristically efficient way, and the soldiers outside of the tunnel didn't hear anything. They stood by stoopidly as the team of six runners poured out of the tunnel and scattered in different directions.

A boulder crashed against the dome. Another chunk of glass broke free and fell inward, crushing a nearby home.

Come on, I thought anxiously, watching the runners. Mokians gathered around me, cheering on the runners. I noticed absently that my three 'advisers' were among them.

The six runners seemed so insignificant compared with the Librarian army. I found myself holding my breath, wishing there was something – anything – I could do to help. But I was inside the dome, and they far outside of it, an army between us. I could barely see them …

See them.

You're an Oculator, stoopid! Bastille's voice seemed to scream into my mind. I cursed to myself, fumbling in the pocket of my jacket, pulling out a set of glasses with a purple-and-green tint.

My Bestower's Lenses. Hurriedly, I pulled off my Oculator's Lenses and shoved on the Bestower's Lenses instead. Bastille had said, 'They let you give something of yourself to someone else.'

Let's see what these babies can do, I thought with determination.

The strike team spread out, one heading for each of the robots. Those robots were distant enough from one another that each runner had to pick one robot and make for it. Fortunately, that put them running away from the bulk of the army, so they had to contend with only the small number of Librarians who were walking about near the back lines.

That was still a lot of Librarians. Hundreds. Bastille shoved one aside as he tried to attack her, then swung her sword into the stomach of a second.

The sword, it should be noted, did not have a magical 'stunning' setting like the spears did. Ew.

Bastille continued on, but one of the Mokian runners was quickly getting surrounded. He looked kind of like a running back from American football, galloping down the field with a group of Librarian thugs trying to tackle him, a teddy bear held protectively in the crook of his arm.

I focused on him, channeling strength through my Bestower's Lenses. I suddenly felt weak, and my legs started quivering. But I remained focused, and the Mokian took off in a burst of speed, getting ahead of the Librarians, who stumbled and tripped into a mess of arms and legs.

I quickly sought out the other runners. Kaz dodged to the side of a group of Librarians, neatly using his pistol to pick off the one running at him from the front. But one of the other Mokians had gotten herself into a predicament. A crowd of Librarians was in front of her, shoulder to shoulder. They seemed intent on capturing her, rather than shooting her down, which was good.

She looked desperate, and she crouched down to try a final leap before crashing into the Librarians. I focused on her, then jumped into the air, channeling the leap through my Bestower's Lenses into her. She jumped, and my jump added to hers. She bounded into the air, narrowly leaping over the shocked Librarians' heads, while I jumped only an inch or so.

I hit the ground, smiling. Another of the runners was slamming into a group of Librarians blocking him; with my help, he pushed straight through, knocking them to the ground.

I've been told that I shouldn't have been able to accomplish what I did with those Lenses. Theoretically, I would have added only a little bit of strength – as much as a thirteen-year-old boy could – to the Mokians. My strength added to that of the willowy runner shouldn't have let him knock down three toughened Librarian thugs.

But it did. This time, for once in my narrative, I'm not lying. However, that bit about the giant, enchanted ninja wombat was totally made up.

My heart thumped; I felt like I was down there, running for my life. I jumped back and forth between the six runners, eyes flicking here, then there, granting them whatever I could. At one point, one of the runners was confronted by a group of Librarians leveling guns.

You can do it! I thought at the runner, sending all of the courage I could muster.

The runner suddenly looked ten times more confident. He stared down the guns and managed to dodge between them as I granted him extra dexterity, leeching it from myself. He got to the Librarian gunners and leaped over their heads as I enhanced his ability to jump.

The rest of the Librarian armies had noticed what was happening. Hundreds of soldiers charged away from the front lines, yelling. But most were too far away.

Bastille reached her robot. I held my breath as she tossed her grenade bear.

It hit.

I couldn't hear the explosion, but it vaporized the entire section of metal beneath the robot's knee. The robot teetered, holding a rock that it had been about to throw. Then it toppled backward.

Even inside of Tuki Tuki, we felt the vibrations of it hitting the ground. A monstrous, powerful *thump*. To me, it felt like the fall of Goliath himself. (If Goliath had been felled by a purple teddy bear.)

The Mokians on the wall around me let out a loud cheer of victory. On the far side of the Librarian field, Kaz reached his robot. Though he and Bastille had taken the two robots farthest away on either side, their Warrior's Lenses had let them arrive first.

Kaz tossed his bear into the robot's calf, then hurried away in a dash as the monstrous creation fell to the ground, crushing trees beneath it with an awful sound. Kaz jumped into the air in pleasure, probably letting out a whoop of joy at felling the biggest big person of them all. I could almost hear him scream out: 'Reason number three thousand forty-seven! Little people don't feel the need to build their robots as tall as buildings! Ha!'

He took off at a gallop toward the other runners. I smiled broadly, checking on the others.

And that was when the first Mokian I had helped got shot in the back.

16

*S*toopid, elegant, skinny, odd, extravagant.

These words all share something, something you're not expecting. If you can figure it out, I'll give you a cookie. (Answer is at the beginning of the next chapter.)

I'll give you a hint: It has to do with the meaning of the word *awful.*

'No!' I said, watching as the Mokian tumbled to the ground, dropping his bear and rolling to a stop. The Librarians rushed up behind him, surrounding him then prodding him with their rifles. He was out cold.

Just like that, the plan fell apart. Another robot dropped as one of the three remaining runners hit their target. Another soon followed, leaving only two robots up. But that was enough. Another rock fell, and a chunk of glass nearby cracked free.

I looked up. There were so many cracks in the dome that I could barely see the sky.

'I'd guess one more rock will drop it,' Mink the adviser said from beside me. 'Two at the most.'

'We can't let that happen!' I said. The two remaining robots were lifting arms to throw. Another of the runners fell – one that had already destroyed her robot – blasted in the side by Librarians.

Guns were firing all over now, flashing in the night like the lights of some insane disco. I guess the Librarians finally realized what we were doing – at first, they likely thought we were just trying to get messengers out.

A Mokian still ran for one of the remaining robots. Gun blasts fell around him. 'Run!' I said, focusing on him. Giving him strength, speed, jumping ability, everything I could leech out of myself. He dodged about on fleet feet, inhumanly fast. But a contingent of Librarian riflemen set up just beside him.

'NO!' I screamed even louder, letting out a *jolt* of something through my Lenses. I could almost see it. A black arrow that streaked through the air, striking the Mokian.

The Librarians pulled triggers. And their guns exploded.

I froze, shocked, as the Mokian runner leaped one final bound over a fallen log then threw his bear. It smacked into the robot's leg, exploding. The robot tried to throw its boulder, but didn't have the leverage, and the stone fell to the ground out of its grasp. The robot followed, crashing to the ground.

The Mokian skidded to the ground, and a Librarian shot him a moment later, knocking him out.

That was my Talent, I realized. *For a brief moment, I used the Lenses to grant that runner my Talent. It broke the guns when they tried to fire on him.*

The last remaining robot tossed its boulder. We all held our breath as it flew, then smashed into the dome, crashing through it completely and falling into the city. Shards of glass rained down on us. It left a gaping hole in the roof.

Outside, the Librarians cheered. Behind them, I noticed three scrambling forms congregating. Kaz had met up with the two remaining Mokian runners. Kaz hesitated just briefly, but obviously realized that he couldn't wait any longer. A Librarian's rifle shot hit the ground next to them, spraying up dirt and smoke, giving Kaz the moment of disorientation he needed to engage his Talent. As the smoke passed, the three of them were gone, carried to safety.

The last robot leaned down to get another boulder. The hole in the ceiling was bad enough; this final boulder would shatter the dome entirely. Around me, the Mokians hushed as the final robot raised the enormous rock. The Librarians below lined up, moving back into their attack lines, preparing to assult Tuki Tuki.

My eyes caught something. Motion. There, rushing across the ground behind the Librarian lines, was a small determined figure with silver hair. Bastille.

There was still hope.

The Mokians noticed her, pointing. Bastille – belligerent Bastille – had ignored safety, choosing to run for that last robot instead of trying to get to Kaz. She charged with sword strapped to her back, Warrior's Lenses on, dashing with Crystin speed through, around, and sometimes *over* confused Librarian soldiers.

'She's not going to make it,' Aluki said softly. The robot raised its boulder. 'It's too late ...'

He was right. That robot would throw before Bastille arrived. 'She needs more time. I need to get down there.' My heart beating quickly, I moved by instinct, shoving my way through the Mokians and rushing down the steps to the ground. I ran up to the gate out of the city.

'Open the gate!' I cried.

The guards looked at me, dumbfounded. I didn't have time to argue, so I brushed past them and slammed my hands against the gate, sending my Talent into it. The bar holding the gate closed shattered into about a million splinters, the force of the explosion sending the gate swinging open.

I rushed out the door and realized something important. Something life changing. Something amazing.

I needed a battle cry.

'Rutabaga!' I screamed.

It's the first thing that came to mind, I'm afraid. Anyway, I dashed out across the grassy ground, running to the edge of the glass dome. Outside, the robot snapped its massive arms forward, launching the boulder.

I came right up to the glass of the protective shield. Taking a deep breath, I placed my hands against it and sent a surge of power into it.

The dome in front of me let out a wave of light, a ripple of energy. I closed my eyes, holding my hands to the smooth surface, power surging through me like luminescent blood pumping into the glass.

For a moment, I felt like I *was* the glass dome protecting the city. I strengthened the dome, giving it an extra boost, like I'd done with the Transporter's Glass months before.

The rock hit.

And it bounced off, the dome unharmed. I opened my eyes to find the entire thing glowing with a brilliant, beautiful light.

Power was flowing through me at an alarming rate. It seemed to be towing bits of me along with it, my strength, my soul even. I could feel the Talent coiled inside, wanting to snap forth and *destroy* the very thing I was trying to protect. I had to forcibly hold it back.

At no point in my life up to this moment had my dual nature – Oculator and Smedry – been so pointedly manifest to me. In one hand I held the power to save Mokia, and in the other hand the power to destroy it.

I forced myself to release the glass, stumbling backward, exhausted and drained. I felt like I'd just run a marathon while carrying Atlas on my shoulders. And boy, that guy's gained *weight* over the years. (Due to all those new stars we've discovered in the sky, you see.)

I fell backward to the ground, exhausted, Mokians swarming around me. I waved them away, letting Aluki help me back to my feet. The robot was getting another boulder. Where was Bastille?

She'd been caught by a large group of Librarians. She fought desperately, waving her sword around her, fending off the soldiers. She seemed to glance in our direction, then she turned, pulling a bear from her backpack and snapping it into the air.

The maneuver exposed her back to the Librarians.

'Bastille ...' I said, raising a hand. I tried to send her strength through the Bestower's Lenses, but I was too weak. A dozen different shots from Librarian guns hit her at once.

Bastille dropped.

The bear soared.

I held my breath as the robot raised its rock. I didn't have the strength to protect the city again.

And .....

And ....

And ...

And ..

And .

And ..

And ...

And ....

And .....

The bear hit dead-on. A large section of the robot's leg vaporized and it teetered, then toppled to the side, dropping its rock.

Around me, the Mokians let out relieved breaths. I wasn't paying attention. I was just looking at Bastille, lying unconscious on the ground. The Librarians were raising their guns in excitement, as if they'd just felled some fearsome beast. Which I guess they had.

The Librarians pulled Bastille's jacket off of her and began shooting it over and over with their guns. That confused me until I realized they must have recognized it as glassweave. These soldiers belonged to the Order of the Shattered Lens, and they hated glass of all types. They took off her Lenses and shot those a few times too.

Of course, their hatred of glass didn't explain why they felt the need to start kicking Bastille in the stomach as she lay there unconscious. I watched, teeth clenched tightly, seething hatred and anger as they beat on Bastille for a few minutes. I almost ran right out there to go for her, but Aluki caught my arm. We both knew that there was no good in it. I'd just get myself captured too.

The Librarians then picked her up and hauled her away as a prize of war. It was a special victory for them, catching a Knight of Crystallia. They took her to a tent at the back of the battlefield, where they stored all of the important captives they'd put into comas. I felt a coward for having let her go out there without me, and for not going to get her back when she fell.

'Your Majesty?' Aluki said to me. The Mokians around me had grown quiet. They seemed to be able to sense my mood. Perhaps it was because I was unconsciously causing the ground around me to crack and break.

I was alone. No Grandpa, no Bastille, no Kaz. Sure, I had Aluki and his soldiers, not to mention Aydee back in the city. But for the first time in a long while, I felt alone, without guidance.

At this point, you're probably expecting me to say something bitter. Something like, 'I never should have become so dependent on others. That only set me up to fail.'

Or maybe, 'Losing Bastille was inevitable, after I was put in charge. I should never have taken the kingship.'

Or maybe you want me to say, 'Help, there is a snake eating my toes and I forgot to take the jelly out of the oven.' (If so, I can't believe you wanted me to say that. You're a sick, sick person. I mean, what does that even mean? Weirdo.)

Anyway, I will say none of those things here. The fact that you were expecting them means I've trained you well enough.

Now excuse me while I fetch my snake repellant.

'Are you all right, Your Majesty?' Aluki asked again, timid.

'We *will* win this battle,' I said. I felt a strange sense of determination shoving away my feelings of shame and loss. 'And we *will* get the antidote. We no longer have an option in this regard.' I turned to regard the soldiers. 'We will find a way to get Bastille out, and then wake her up. I am *not* going to fail her.'

Solemnly, the soldiers nodded. Oddly, in that moment, I finally *felt* like a Smedry, maybe even a king, for the first time.

'The city is protected for the time being,' I said. 'Though we still have to worry about the tunnels. I want people back to their posts watching the city for Librarian incursions. We're going to last. We're going to win. I vow it.'

'Your Majesty,' Aluki said, nodding upward. 'They knocked a hole in the dome. They'll find a way to exploit that.'

'I know,' I said. 'We'll deal with that when it happens. Have someone watch to see what the Librarians do next. Ask my advisers if they can think of any way to patch that hole.'

'Yes, Your Majesty,' Aluki said. 'Er ... what will you be doing?'

I took a deep breath. 'It's time to confront my mother.'

NCC-1701

In the year 1288, if you were to pass by an old acquaintance on the way to Ye Olde Chain Mail Shoppe and call him 'nice,' you'd actually be calling him an idiot.

If it were the year 1322 instead – and you were on your way to the bookshop to pick up the new wacky comedy by a guy named Dante – when you called someone 'nice' you would be saying that they were timid.

In 1380, if you called someone 'nice,' you'd be saying they were fussy.

In 1405, you'd be calling them dainty.

In 1500, you'd be calling them careful.

By the 1700s – when you were off to do some crowd surfing at the new Mozart concert – you'd be using the word *nice* to mean 'agreeable.'

Sometimes, it's difficult to understand how much change there is all around us. Even language changes, and the same word can mean different things depending on how, where, and when it was said. The word *awful* used to mean 'deserving of awe' – full of awe. The same as awesome. Once, the word *brave* meant 'cowardly.' The word *girl* meant a child of either gender.

(So next time you're with a mixed group of friends, you should call them 'girls' instead of 'guys.' Assuming you're not too brave, nice, nice, nice, or nice.)

People change too. In fact, they're always changing. We like to pretend that the people we know stay the same, but they change moment by moment as they come to new conclusions, experience new things, think new thoughts. Perhaps, as Heraclitus said, you can never step in the same river twice … but I think a more powerful metaphor would have been this: You can never meet the same person twice.

The Mokians hadn't actually put my mother in the university with the other prisoners. I'd told them to put her in a place that was very secure, and they didn't have a prison. (It may surprise you to learn this. Mokia is exactly the sort of place the Librarians don't want you to believe in. A paradise where people are learned, where arguments don't turn into fistfights, but instead debates over warm tea and grapes.)

No, the Mokians didn't have a prison. But they *did* have a zoo.

It was actually more of a research farm, a place where exotic animals could be kept and studied in the name of science. My mother, Shasta Smedry, was confined in a large cage with thick bars that looked like it had once been used to house a tiger or other large cat. It had a little pool for water, a tree to climb in, and several large rock formations.

Unfortunately, the Mokians had removed the tiger before locking my mother in. That was probably for the tiger's safety.

I walked up to the cage, two Mokian guards at my side. Shasta sat inside on a small rock, legs crossed primly, wearing her Librarian business suit with the ankle-length gray skirt and high-necked white blouse. She had on horn-rimmed glasses. They weren't magical, according to my Oculator's Lenses. I checked just to be certain.

'Mother,' I said flatly, stepping up to the cage.

'Son,' she replied.

I should note that this felt very, *very* odd. I'd once confronted my mother in a situation almost exactly like this, during my very first Library infiltration. Except then, my mother had been the one outside the bars, and I had been the one behind them.

I didn't feel any safer having it this way.

'I need to know the formula for the antidote,' I told her. 'The one that will overcome the effects of the Librarian coma-guns.'

'It's a pity, then,' she said, 'that I don't have it.'

I narrowed my eyes. 'I don't believe you.'

'Hmm ... If only there were a way for you to tell if I were speaking lies or not.'

I blushed, then dug out my Truthfinder's Lens. I looked through it.

She spoke directly at me. 'I don't know the antidote.'

The words puffed from her mouth like white clouds. She was telling the truth. I felt a sinking feeling.

'I'm not from the Order of the Shattered Lens,' my mother continued. 'They wouldn't entrust one such as me with something that important – they wouldn't let *any* foot soldier know it. That secret will be very carefully guarded, as will the secret of the antidote to the Mokian stun-spears.'

I looked at my guards. Aluki nodded. 'Very few know our formula, Your Majesty. One was the queen, and the other is the—'

'Don't say it,' I said, eyeing my mother.

She just rolled her eyes. 'You think I care about this little dispute, Alcatraz? I haven't the faintest interest in the outcome of this siege.'

It was the truth.

I gritted my teeth in annoyance. 'Then why did you sneak in?'

She just smiled at me. An insufferable, knowing smile. She'd been the one to suggest I get out my Truthfinder's Lens. She wasn't going to be tricked into saying anything condemning. At least, not unless I shocked her or distracted her.

'I know what you and Father are doing,' I said. 'The Sands of Rashid, the book you both wanted from Nalhalla.'

'You don't know anything.'

'I know that you're seeking the secret of Smedry Talents,' I said. 'You married my father to get access to a Talent, to study them, and perhaps to get close to the whole family. It was always about the Talents. And now you are looking to discover the way that the Incarna people got *their* Talents in the first place.'

She studied me. Something I'd said actually seemed to make her hesitate, look at me in a new way. 'You've changed, Alcatraz.'

'Yeah, I put a new pair on this morning.'

She rolled her eyes again, then stood up. 'Put away that Lens, leave your guards behind, and let's have a chat.'

'What? Why would I do that!'

'Because you should obey your mother.'

'My mother is a ruthless, malevolent, egocentric Librarian bent on controlling the world!'

'We all have our faults,' she said, strolling away from me, following the line of bars to the right. 'Do as I request, or I'll remain silent. The choice is yours.'

I ground my teeth, but there didn't seem to be any other choice. Reluctantly, I put the Truthfinder's Lens away and waved the guards to remain behind as I hurried after Shasta. I wouldn't be able to tell if she was lying or not, at least not for certain. But hopefully I could still learn something from her. Why had she joined the group infiltrating Tuki Tuki? Perhaps she knew something, some way to save us.

As I moved to join her, an alarm rang through the city – one of the scouts we'd posted had seen a tunnel opening. Hopefully, the soldiers would be able to deal with it. I walked up to where Shasta stood, far enough from Aluki and the other guard to be out of earshot. I suspected that she wanted me away from the other two so she could manipulate me into letting her go free.

That wasn't going to happen. I hadn't forgotten how she'd given Himalaya up to be executed, nor how she'd sold me – her own son – to Blackburn, the one-eyed Dark Oculator. Or how she killed Asmodean. (Okay, so she didn't really do that last one, but I wouldn't put it past her.)

'What is it you think you know about the Smedry Talents?' she said to me, arms folded. Her smirk was gone; she looked serious now, perhaps somewhat ominous. The effect was spoiled by the giant tiger chew toy in the grass beside her.

'Kaz and I talked it through,' I said. 'The Incarna wanted to turn *people* into *Lenses*.'

She sniffed. 'A crude way of putting it. They discovered the source of magical Lenses. Every person's soul has a *power* to it, an *energy*. Lenses don't actually have any inherent energy; what they do is focus the energy of the Oculator, distort it, change it into something useful. Like a prism refracting light.'

She looked at me. 'The eyes are the key,' she said. 'Poets have called them windows to the soul. Well, windows go both directions – someone can look into your eyes and see your soul, but when you look at someone, the energy of your soul shines forth. If there are Lenses in front of that energy, it distorts into something else. In some cases, it changes what is going *in* to your eyes, letting you see things you couldn't normally. In other cases, it changes what comes *out*, creating bursts of fire or wind.'

'That's nonsense,' I said. 'I've had Lenses that worked even after I took them off.'

'Your soul was still feeding them,' she said. 'For some kinds of glass, looking through them is important. For others, being near your soul alone is enough, and merely touching them can activate them.'

'Why are you telling me this?'

'You will see,' she said cryptically.

I didn't trust her. I don't think anyone with half a brain would trust Shasta Smedry.

'So what of the Incarna?' I asked.

'They wanted to harness this energy of the soul,' she said. 'Every person's soul vibrates with a distinctive tone, just like pure crystal will create a tone if rubbed the right way. The Incarna felt they could change the soul's vibration to manifest its energy. Men would not "become Lenses," as you put it. Instead, they'd be able to use the power of their soul vibrations.'

The power of their soul vibrations? That sounds like a seventies disco song, doesn't it? I really need to start a band or something to play all of these hits.

'All right,' I said. 'But something went wrong, didn't it? The Talents were flawed. Instead of getting the powers the Incarna anticipated, they ended up with a bunch of people who could barely control their abilities.'

'Yes,' she said, looking at me, thoughtful. 'You've considered this a great deal.'

I felt a surge of rebellious pride. My mother – known as Ms. Fletcher during my childhood – had very rarely given me anything resembling a compliment.

'You want the Talents for yourself,' I said, forcing myself to keep focused. 'You want to use them to give the Librarian armies extra abilities.'

She rolled her eyes.

'Don't try to claim otherwise,' I said. 'You want to keep the Talents for yourself; my father wants to give them to everyone. That's what you and he argued about, isn't it? When you discovered the way to collect the Sands of Rashid, you disagreed on how the Talents were to be used.'

'You could say that,' she said.

'My father wanted to bless people with them; you wanted to keep them for the Librarians.'

'Yes,' she said frankly.

I froze, blinking. I hadn't expected her to actually answer me on that. 'Oh. Er. Well. Hmm.' Maybe I should have paid more attention to the 'ruthless, malevolent, egocentric Librarian bent on controlling the world' part of her description.

'Now that we're past the obvious part,' Shasta said dryly, 'shall we continue with our conversation about the Incarna?'

'All right,' I said. 'So what went wrong? Why are the Talents so hard to control?'

'We don't actually know,' she said. 'The sources – the few I've had read to me with the Translator's Lenses – are contradictory. It seems that some *thing* became tied up in the Talents, some source of energy or power that the Incarna were using to change their soul vibrations. It tainted the Talents, made them work in a way that was more destructive and more unpredictable.'

The Dark Talent ... I thought, again remembering those haunting words I'd read in the tomb of Alcatraz the First.

'You asked why I tell you this,' Shasta said, studying me looking through the bars. 'Well, you have proven very ... persistent in interfering with my activities. Your presence here in Tuki Tuki means I cannot afford to discount you any longer. It is time for an alliance.'

I blinked in shock. *'Excuse* me?'

'An alliance. Between you and me, to serve the greater good.'

'And by serving the greater good, you mean serving yourself.'

She raised an eyebrow at me. 'Don't tell me you haven't figured it out yet. I thought you were clever.'

'Pretend I'm stoopiderifous instead,' I said.

'What happened to the Incarna?'

'They fell,' I said. 'The culture was destroyed.'

'By what?'

'We don't know. It must have been something incredible, something sweeping, something …'

And I got it. Finally. I should have seen it much earlier; you probably did. Well, you're smarter than I am.

I suspected something might be wrong during my father's speech in Nalhalla, when he announced that he wanted to give everyone a Talent. But I hadn't realized the full scope of it, the full danger of it.

'Something destroyed the Incarna,' I found myself saying. 'Something so fearsome that my ancestor Alcatraz the First broke his own language to keep anyone from repeating it …'

'It was this,' Shasta said softly, intensely. 'The secret of the Talents. Think of what it would be like. Every person with a Talent? The Smedry clan alone has a terrible reputation for destruction, accidents, and insanity. Philosophers have guessed that the Talents – the wild nature of them, the unpredictability of your lives when you are young – is what makes you all so reckless.'

'And if everyone had them …' I said. 'It would be chaos. Everyone would be getting lost, multiplying bears, breaking things….'

'It destroyed the Incarna,' Shasta said. 'Attica refused to believe my warnings. He *insists* that the information must be given to all, that it's a "Librarian" ideal to withhold it from the world. But sometimes, complete freedom of information isn't a good thing. What if every person on the planet had the ability, resources, and knowledge to make a nuclear weapon? Would that be a good thing? Sometimes, secrets are *important*.'

I wasn't sure I agreed with that ... but she made a compelling argument. I looked at her, and realized that she sounded – for once in her life – completely honest. She had her arms folded, and seemed distraught.

I suspected that she still loved my father. The Truthfinder's Lens had given me a hint of that months before. But she worked hard to stop him, to steal the Translator's Lenses, to keep the Sands of Rashid from him. Even going so far as to use her own son as a decoy and trap to catch those Sands.

Hesitantly, I pulled out the Truthfinder's Lens. She wasn't looking at me, she was staring off. 'This information is *too dangerous*,' she said, and the words were true – at least, she believed they were.

'If I could stop anyone from getting the knowledge, I would,' she continued. She seemed to have forgotten for the moment that I was even there. 'The book we found in Nalhalla? I burned it. Gone forever. But that's not going to stop Attica. He'll find a way unless I stop him somehow. Biblioden was right. This *must* be contained. For the good of everyone. For the good of my son. For the good of Attica himself ...'

My Lens showed that it was all truth. I lowered it, and in a moment of terrible realization, I understood something. My mother wasn't the bad guy in all of this.

My father was.

Was it possible that the Librarians might actually be *right*?

4815162342

Standing there in that abandoned zoo, I had a moment of understanding. A terrible one that was both awesome and awful, regardless of the definitions you use.

It was much like the moment I'd had when I first saw the map of the world, hanging in that library in my hometown. It had shown continents I didn't expect to see. Confronting it had forced my mind to expand, to reach, to stretch and grab hold of space it hadn't known about previously.

After spending so much time with Grandpa Smedry and the others, I had understandably come to see things as they did. The Smedry way was to be bold almost to the point of irresponsibility. We were an untamed bunch, meddling in important events, taking huge risks. We did a lot of good, but that was because we were carefully channeled by the Knights of Crystallia and our own sense of honor.

But what if *everyone* acted like that? My mother's analogy was a good one. If every person was given a bomb big enough to destroy a city, most would probably be responsible with it. But it took only one mistake to ruin everything.

Were the Librarians *right* to want to contain some information?

I thought they might have been. But, of course, they were wrong about a lot of other things. They controlled too much, and they sought to enforce their way by conquering people. They lied, they distorted, and they suppressed.

But it was still possible for them to be right on occasion, when members of my family were wrong. And it was *very* possible that my mother – arrogant, conniving, and dismissive as she was – was doing something noble, while my father was being reckless.

If he got what he wanted, it could destroy the world.

Standing there, thinking about it, everything changed. Or perhaps I changed, and the world stayed the same. Or maybe we both changed.

Sometimes, I wished that darn river of Heraclitus's would just *stay still*. So long as it wasn't moving, it was easy to figure it out, get a perspective on it.

But that's not how life is. And sometimes, the people who used to be your enemies become your allies instead.

'I see that you understand,' Shasta said.

'I do.'

'Then do we have a truce?' she asked. 'You and I will work together to stop him?'

'I have to think about it first.'

'Don't take too long,' she said, glancing upward. 'Tuki Tuki is doomed. We'll need to get to the catacombs and do our business there quickly, then escape before the city falls.'

'I'm *not* abandoning Tuki Tuki!' I snapped.

'There's no use fighting now,' she said, pointing upward. 'Not with that hole in the dome. The Order of the Shattered Lens has ro-bats. They'll be flying through there to drop on the city in moments.'

'Wait,' I said. 'Ro-bats. Are those, by chance, giant robotic bats?'

'Of course.'

'That's the most stoopiderific thing I've ever heard of.'

'Oh, and what would you call them?'

'Woe-bots, of course,' I said. 'Since they bring woe and destruction. Duh.'

She rolled her eyes.

'Either way, I'm not going to leave. The Mokians are depending on me. They *need* me.'

'Alcatraz,' she said, folding her arms. 'We are working for the preservation of *humankind itself*. Compared to that, one city is unimportant. Do you think it was easy for me to treat you like I did, all those years? It was because I knew that something more important was at stake!'

'Right,' I said, walking away. 'You should win an award for your downright *wonderful* mothering instincts, Shasta.'

'Alcatraz!'

I walked away. Too many things didn't make sense; I had to sort through them. As I walked, Aydee Ecks and Aluki ran up to me, she with her backpack full of bears on her shoulder, him holding his flaming spear.

'Your Majesty,' Aluki said urgently. 'Lady Aydee just brought us word. The scouts have spotted something outside the city. We're in trouble.'

'Giant robotic bats?' I asked.

'Yes.'

'How many?'

'Hundreds, Alcatraz!' Aydee said. 'I started to do the math but Aluki stopped me....'

'Probably for the best,' I said.

'They must have been waiting until the dome broke open to surprise us,' Aluki said. 'Your Majesty, they'll be able to drop *thousands* of troops through that hole! We have no kind of air force. We'll be destroyed in minutes!'

'I ...'

Aluki and Aydee looked at me, eyes urgent. Needful.

'I don't know what to do,' I whispered, hand to my head.

'You have to know what to do,' Aluki said. 'You're *king*!'

'That doesn't mean I have all of the answers!' I said. My mother's revelation had shocked me, unhinged me.

Change. A man can be confident one moment – and then, with one discovery, be shocked to the point that he's completely uncertain. If my mother was working for what was right, and my father was the one trying to destroy the world ...

I'd *saved* him. If everything went wrong, it would be *my* fault. What else had I been horribly wrong about?

But could I trust what my mother had said?

She's right, I thought, with a growing feeling of horror. The words she'd said when I watched her with the Truthfinder's Lens ... the things my father had said ... what I'd read ... my own feelings and experiences with the Dark Talent. All of these things mixed and churned together in me, blended like some nefarious smoothie from a gym counter in Hades.

The Dark Talent, *my* Talent, wanted everyone to be like the Smedrys. Somehow, I knew that Alcatraz the First had contained it within our family, limiting its damage and power. He was the reason why if someone became a Smedry, they got a Talent – but once one became too distant from the family line, children stopped being born with Talents. You only got to be a Smedry if you were cousins to the main line that ran from my grandfather to my father, to me.

It was contained, but my father wanted to let it out. In the face of that, I felt so insignificant. So flawed.

'Alcatraz ...' Aydee said hopefully. 'We need a plan.'

'I don't *have* a plan!' I said, perhaps more loudly than I should have. 'Leave me alone. I just ... I need to think!'

I rushed away, my pack of bears over my shoulder, leaving them standing there stunned. Yes, it was a bitter and childish re-action. But keep in mind that I *was* a child. The Free Kingdomers treat people like they act, regardless of their age, but I was still a thirteen-year-old boy. It was easy to get overwhelmed. Particularly when you learn you may have accidentally doomed the entire world to destruction.

It sounds a little odd when you say it, doesn't it? A kid like me, destroying the world? It makes for a ridiculous image.

(How ridiculous? Well, I'd say about as ridiculous as the image of a bunch of Canadian Mounties sitting on the backs of lizards while throwing cheese at one another. But that's kind of a tangent. Besides, that part isn't even in this book.)

Everything was twisted on its head. I should have surrendered Tuki Tuki. I should have ... I didn't know what I should have done. Stayed in the Hushlands, with my blankets pulled over my head, and never gone with Grandpa Smedry.

I'd probably have ended up shot for that, but at least I wouldn't have put the whole world in danger.

I looked up. Gigantic steel bats were flying through the night sky toward the hole in Tuki Tuki's dome. Each carried some fifty Librarians on their backs.

But what could I do about that?

I turned a corner, walking down a grassy path between two zoo buildings, leaving so that Aluki and Aydee couldn't stare at me with those disappointed eyes. Overhead, terrible screeches began to sound in the air.

At that moment, the ground shook beneath my feet. I looked around, anxious, worrying that the Librarians had found more robots to toss boulders at the city. However, I quickly realized that the entire city wasn't shaking, just the patch of ground *directly* beneath me.

A hole opened up under my feet. I yelped, tumbling down into a hole dug by another Librarian infiltration team.

They'd just happened to come up right where I was standing.

???

I'm afraid it's time to contradict myself. I know, this is very surprising. After all, I'm *never* inconsistent in these books. But it's time to make an exception. Just this once. Please forgive me.

Don't act this chapter out.

I know you've been following along since I told you to, acting out every single event in this book. When I saved the city by powering the dome, you were there, face pressed up against the window of your room. When I had my conversation with my mother, you were repeating the same words to your mother. (She was pretty confused, eh?) When Bastille and the crew were throwing teddy bears at robots, I presume that you ran through your house with stuffed bears, throwing them at anything that moved. And when I got out all of the boxes of macaroni and cheese in my house and mailed them to myself, you did the same thing, sending it all to me care of my publisher.

Oh. You didn't read that part? It happened between Chapters 24601 and 070706. Really, I promise. You should go act it out right now. I can wait.

Anyway, *do not* act out this chapter. You'll see why.

My fall ended abruptly as I crashed into a bunch of surprised Librarians. I struggled, cursing. Everything was jumbled together in the dark, dirty tunnel. There were limbs all over the place; it was like I'd fallen into a bin filled with mannequin arms.

Something looped around me, something made of wire and rope, and as I tried to scream out, something else got stuffed in my mouth.

About thirty seconds later, the group of Librarian soldiers slung me out of their hole, bound up in a net, a gag around my mouth. It had happened so quickly that I was still dazed.

The Librarians were wearing the standard bow ties and business suits – the men extraordinarily muscular, the women looking lean and dangerous – but their suits were camouflaged. They carried guns and moved with a sleek, threatening air. This was a particularly dangerous group of infiltrators – though, oddly, they didn't wear Warrior's Lenses.

I tried to scream out and give warning to Aluki and Aydee, who were waiting just around the corner. But the gag was firmly in place. The Librarians began to chat tersely with one another, speaking a language I didn't recognize. That surprised me, but it really shouldn't have. Not all Librarians in the Hushlands are from English-speaking countries.

I calmed myself, breathing in and out. My Talent would get me out of a stoopid net, no problem. I just had to do it at the right time, when they weren't looking.

Several of the Librarians scouted around the sides of the alley-way, peeking out, while two others – a brutish man and a woman with red hair – knelt down and began to go through my pockets. The woman pulled off my backpack, yanking it out through a hole in the net, while the man held my hands together and wrapped them with a tight string.

The woman pulled open the backpack, rifling through it. She raised an eyebrow at the bears, but stuffed them back inside. Next she began searching through the pockets of my jacket.

That's when I got nervous. If they found my Lenses ... It was time to escape. My Talent would probably surprise them, give me a chance to run. I took a deep breath through the gag and activated the Breaking Talent.

Nothing happened.

Well, okay. That was kind of a lie. Lots of things happened. Some birds flew by, a beetle crawled past, the grass converted carbon dioxide into sugar by means of the sun's energy. My heart beat (very quickly), the Librarians chatted (very quietly), and the Earth rotated (very unnoticeably).

I guess what I meant, then, is this: As far as my Talent was concerned, nothing happened.

It didn't engage. Nothing broke. I felt a moment of desperation and tried again. The Talent refused. It was like I could … feel it in there, seething, angry at me. Almost like it was *offended* by the things I'd talked about with my mother.

It had been a long time since I'd had trouble getting my Talent to do what I wanted it to. I had flashbacks to earlier years in my life, when it ran rampant, breaking everything I didn't want to but unable to break things I did want to.

I squirmed in my bindings, and the beefy Librarian pushed me down harder. He had a cruel, twisted face.

The woman said something, sounding surprised as she pulled my pair of Oculator's Lenses out of my pocket. I hadn't put them back on after using my Truthfinder's Lens on my mother.

The Librarians nearby all got dark expressions on their faces. The woman pulled something from her pocket – a kind of small gun. She pointed it at the Lenses in her hand.

They vaporized, turning to dust, then even that dust seemed to burn away. She shook the frames – which were intact – and inspected them, then tossed them aside.

That's right! I thought. *The Order of the Shattered Lens has the army. They hate all kinds of glass.* That made me even more frantic. I squirmed enough that the big guy holding me down grumbled, and pulled something out of his pocket. Another type of gun.

My eyes opened wide, and I froze as he pointed it down and pulled the trigger.

And then I died.

No, really. I died. Dead, dead, dead.

What's that, you say? How could I be dead? I survived long enough to write this book, you claim?

Well … um … I *could* be writing it as a ghost. So there.

BOO!

Anyway, you're right. The gun didn't kill me. It fired some kind of dart into the ground next to me, attached by a rope. He fired another dart on the other side, and the rope tightened, holding the net – and therefore me – to the ground. The woman got out a knife and cut my jacket off of me.

That's right. My favorite green jacket, the one I'd been wearing since I'd left the Hushlands.

This, I thought with sudden fierceness, *means war!*

(And please don't tell Bastille that I was nearly as broken up about losing my jacket as I was when she got knocked unconscious.)

The two Librarians retreated, one carrying the remnants of my jacket. They left me squirming on the ground, pinned against the grass, gagged. I was desperate by this point. Up above, the flying bats were descending into the city, bearing Librarian soldiers. People screamed throughout the city, yelling, a sense of panic to their voices.

This is the point where, usually, I come up with some brilliant plan to save everyone. I tried hard, searching through my options. But nothing occurred to me. I was pinned down, my Talent refused to work, and I had no Lenses. About a billion Librarian soldiers were descending on Tuki Tuki, and dawn was still hours away.

Why is it I always ended up in these kinds of scrapes? My life over the past six months seemed to me like one bumbling disaster after another. I wasn't any good at fighting the Librarians, I was just good at getting kidnapped, locked up, knocked out, and covered in tar.

Just like my Talent, my wits failed me. It happens, sometimes, particularly when your victories seem so accidental, like mine often do. Besides, even if I could somehow escape the net, Tuki Tuki was still doomed. I couldn't stop thousands of Librarian soldiers.

It was hopeless.

To the side, the Librarians emptied my jacket pockets. They lifted up the Translator's Lenses.

And, with a flash, destroyed them.

My inheritance was gone. One of the most powerful sets of Lenses ever created, something my father had searched for more than a decade to gather. And these Librarians had destroyed them without ever knowing what they meant.

Well, so be it.

Now, at this point, you're probably pretty frustrated with me. 'Alcatraz,' you're probably screaming, 'you can do it, little guy!' Or maybe you're screaming, 'Hey, Bozo, stop being so depressed and *do* something!'

If you're yelling either of those things, might I remind you that you're talking to a book? It can't really respond to you. Do you talk to inanimate things often? (Man, you really are a weirdo.)

Anyway, whenever I'd been put in a situation like this before, I'd thought of some kind of brilliant plan at the last moment. However, it's really tough to be brilliant on command. Sometimes, you get trapped, and there just *isn't* any way out.

I lay, pinned down, staring up at the sky. What had I really accomplished since I'd met my grandfather? I'd rescued my father, and in doing so had unwittingly helped him in his crazy quest to give everyone Smedry Talents. In Nalhalla, I'd gotten back my father's Translator's Lenses for him. Another step toward helping him destroy the world.

And now, here I was in Mokia. I'd accepted the *throne*, becoming king. For what? So I could convince them to keep on fighting when they should have surrendered? So I could make Bastille fall in combat?

The Librarians vaporized my Courier's Lenses next. Then they got out my Bestower's Lenses and my single Truthfinder's Lens. The Librarians vaporized one of the Bestower's Lenses.

There, I thought. *I've finally done it. I've failed.*

Above, in the air, Librarians dove into the city on the backs of their robotic bats.

And behind them, something appeared from the darkness.

Tiny at first, but growing larger. Shadowy vehicles, flying through the night.

More Librarians, I thought. *That's obviously what that is. More Librarians, flying in gigantic glass birds. That makes perfect sense. My, those Librarians look awfully strange, wearing armor and carrying swords like that. One might even think that they're actually ...*

I sat upright, shocked. Or, well, I *would* have sat upright, save for that whole pinned-to-the-ground-and-tied-up thing. So, anyway, I lay pinned to the ground, tied up, but I did it feeling completely shocked.

There, swooping down out of the darkness, was a fleet of twenty glass vehicles with Knights of Crystallia riding on their backs. They dove behind the bats, dropping into the city. The sounds of yelling, fighting, and cheers of war rose in the air.

It had worked. My stoopid plan had worked.

Perhaps I should explain. Do you remember back right before Kaz ran off to attack the robots? You should, it was only, like, two chapters ago. (Too busy talking to books to pay attention to reading them, eh?) Anyway, I sent him with a message for my grandfather. 'Tell him that we really, *really* need him here by midnight. If he doesn't arrive by then, we're doomed!'

You might have ignored the message. Of course we wanted my grandfather to arrive immediately; it was obvious.

But Kaz's explanation of Talents had changed my perception of them. The way we, as Smedrys, see the world affects how the Talents work. Like Aydee – if she *thinks* there are thousands of teddy bears, then there are. Reality doesn't matter as much as the Smedry's view of reality.

Aydee's and Grandpa's Talents are very similar. She moves things through space and puts them where she thinks they should be. Grandpa moves things through time, putting them *when* he thinks they should be – so long as that *when* is something he perceives as being late.

Does your brain hurt yet? 'Cuz if it does, try being me. Anyway, here's the short of it: You might think Grandpa's Talent works only when he's late. But that's not true. It works when he *thinks* he's late.

There was no way he was going to get the knights to Tuki Tuki on time. His Talent wouldn't let it happen. But if he *thought* that he was already late ... If I could persuade him that he needed to be there at midnight ...

Then he might just arrive at twelve thirty instead.

In the sky above, a bird flew by with a distinctive, white-haired man in a tuxedo riding on the back, waving a sword wildly like he was a conductor leading an orchestra. I smiled despite myself. I'd gotten my grandfather to arrive early – all by tricking him into thinking he was late.

But I was still captured. None of the knights came near to where I was laying. The Librarians around me looked to the sky with shock, guns out. The one holding my Lenses – the single remaining Bestower's Lens and my one Truthfinder's Lens – dropped them for the moment.

The fighting in the city grew louder.

This left me feeling very odd. I'd been convinced I couldn't save Tuki Tuki. But I *had* saved it. Or, at least, I'd taken a large step toward doing so. I hadn't failed them as king.

The *me* from the past had been clever enough to come up with a plan, even if the *me* from the future hadn't been able to. (Not *me* from the far future, that's the one writing these books, I mean the *me* from the slight future, the *me* tied up, which is actually the *me* from the past, as the *me* from right now is the one writing. Actually, that *me* is the past *me* too, by the time you read this. And actually—)

'Shut up!' I said to myself. Or, at least, I tried to. Being still gagged, it came out as 'Shusmalgul pulup!'

There wasn't time to think about my failures, my past, or my future. Because my Librarian captors were focused on me again. One lowered a gun, pointing at my head.

I felt a moment of panic. These were Librarians of the Shattered Lens. They were the most devoted, the most fanatical of all Librarians. And they hated Oculators passionately.

They knew what I was, and they weren't about to let me get rescued. The lead Librarian cocked his pistol. It didn't look like one of the fancy, laser pistols used in the war. Just an old-fashioned Hushlander pistol, the kind that shot out a bullet and made you very, very dead.

I tried my Talent. Nothing. I struggled but was pinned tight. I could wriggle my right hand, but that was it.

One of the Librarians said something, as if objecting to the murder of a tied-up kid.

The Librarian with the gun barked something back, quieting the opposition. He looked at me, eyes grim.

I panicked. I couldn't fail now! Not when everything was confused. I needed to *know*. Was my father right, or was my mother? What was this all about? I'd gotten the knights to Tuki Tuki. I couldn't die now! I couldn't! I—

The Librarians had dropped my backpack right beside me.

I blinked, realizing for the first time that a string was peeking out through the back zipper. One of the pull-tag pins for the bears tucked inside; I could see a bit of purple fur peeking out behind the tag.

Frantic, I strained my fingers out and pulled the tag, yanking it. The backpack lurched up against me, but the tag pulled free.

The Librarian pulled the trigger.

There was a *crack* in the air as the gun fired.

Something flashed in my eyes, the backpack exploding, vaporizing, the bullet vanishing in the air. The explosion washed over me, and – as I'd planned – it destroyed the net, the tag, and everything tying me down.

Of course, it *also* vaporized my clothing.

∞

Now, perhaps, you can see why I asked you not to act out that last chapter. If you decided not to take my advice, then I really can't be blamed if you get in trouble for tying yourself to the ground and running around naked for the rest of the afternoon.

Anyway, what just happened is something we call a teddy bear on the mantle. This is an ancient storytelling rule that says, 'If there's an exploding teddy bear that can destroy people's clothing in a given book, that teddy bear *must* be used to destroy someone's clothing by the end of the book.' Coincidentally, this is actually the only time a book has included a teddy bear that can destroy people's clothing, and hence is the first, last, and only application of this literary law.

The blast radius of the bear grenade wasn't large enough to hit the Librarians. (Pity). However, it was just large enough to vaporize the ends of their guns. It also dropped me into a crater in the ground that was some five feet deep. I could see the Librarians above, standing, dumbfounded by what had happened.

I felt a surge of adrenaline. Not because I was still in danger, but because I was now lying stark naked in the middle of a war zone. And though the weather was tropical, the night air still felt rather chilly on my skin.

I scrambled free of the hole, blushing furiously, dashing past the Librarians. I stopped only long enough to scoop up my jacket – with the Bestower's Lens and the Truthfinder's Lens lying on top of it.

The Librarians finally began shouting and giving chase. The explosion had shocked them, but a naked Smedry seemed to have shocked them even further. I tried holding my jacket down to obscure the most delicate parts of my anatomy, but that made it really awkward to run. Keeping my skin intact was more important than keeping it covered, and I started running through the zoo as quickly as I could, holding the jacket and Lenses in my right hand.

So it was that I tore around a corner, completely in the buff, and ran smack-dab into the middle of Aluki, Aydee, twenty Mokian soldiers of both genders, and Draulin, Bastille's mother.

It was not my finest moment.

'Librarian commando superspy assassins!' I cried out, hiding behind Draulin, who wore her full Crystin plate armor and helm. 'Following me! Gak!'

The group turned to look in the direction I'd come from. No Librarians followed. We all waited for a few tense moments, then finally Draulin looked back at me. 'Er, Lord Smedry? Are you all right?'

'Do I *look* all right?' I asked.

'No, you look naked,' Aydee said.

'Gak!' I said, quickly covering myself with my jacket, tying the sleeves around my waist. It had been cut off of me, though, so it didn't stay on real well.

'Ah,' Aluki said, nodding. 'I know this story. His Majesty is pretending to wear invisible clothing to show how stoopid we all are.'

'I don't think that's how the story goes,' Draulin said, eyeing me appraisingly, 'not do I believe that Lord Smedry is taking part in such an elaborate scheme. Those are grenade powder marks on his arms.'

I looked down, noticing that the explosion had dusted my arms with a bit of burned gunpowder. 'Er, yes,' I said, holding the jacket in place. 'And I *was* being chased by Librarians.'

'It is well that we came, then,' Draulin said. 'Come with me, Lord Smedry. Aluki, you should take your soldiers and warn the perimeter guard that a group of Librarian infiltrators are haunting the zoo. They likely saw us up here and decided not to confront us directly.'

The Mokian saluted, taking his soldiers and rushing away. Draulin steered me and Aydee toward a field behind us, where a glass bird was waiting, this one shaped like an owl. I hurried forward eagerly, hoping to find some kind of clothing inside. We found Kaz waiting for us, a big grin on his face.

I hurried up to him. 'Kaz! You did it! You got the message to your father!'

He shrugged modestly. 'I should have realized why you chose the words you did, kid. The moment I spoke them to him, the ships all seemed to *speed up*, instantly.' He eyed me. 'You may have just revolutionized the way we think of Talents. If my pop's Talent can be tricked into making him *early* . . . Well, it will change everything.'

'It's what we were already doing with Aydee,' I said as Draulin and Aydee herself climbed into the glass ship. We stood in a kind of cargo bay at the base of the owl. 'She's the one who sparked the idea in my head, actually.'

The girl smiled pleasantly at that, though she obviously had no idea what I was talking about. It was her ability to keep getting fooled that make her Talent work.

Though . . . as Draulin sent Aydee off to the head of the owl to help pilot, I thought I saw a twinkle of understanding in the girl's eyes. Could she understand? Did she *know exactly* what was happening when we tricked her into adding things wrong? Sometimes, living with a Smedry Talent requires a person to develop in very odd ways. As a child, I'd learned that everyone would hate me for breaking things and had compensated by pushing people away.

Could Aydee have learned to trick herself into ignoring numbers and speaking randomly, off the top of her head, when asked to add something?

Perhaps I was reading too much into that simple glance. I didn't really *know* what she was thinking, all those years ago. Here, wait a second. I'll go talk to her.

. . .

Okay, I asked her and she says yup, that's *exactly* what she does. Also, she said, 'If you're writing about the fall of Tuki Tuki, you'd better make certain to include that part where we caught you frolicking in the zoo naked. I think you were seriously going crazy there, cousin.'

Ahem. Let it be known that I was *not* frolicking. And the naked part ended the moment a Mokian woman in the glass owl brought me one of those colorful islander wraps they wear, and so I tied it on. There is NO MORE NUDITY. You can proceed with acting out the rest of this, if you want.

I stood on my head while singing 'The Star-Spangled Banner' and juggling seventeen live trout with my feet.

Oh, wait. I hope you weren't wearing only a Mokian wrap like me. Sorry about that.

Aluki rushed up the gangplank a moment later, holding his spear. 'The Librarians have liberated the captives in the zoo and the university! That's what they must have gone to do after letting you go, Your Majesty.'

'Shattering Glass!' I said. My mother was free now. Her captivity hadn't lasted long.

And I *still* didn't know what I believed and what I didn't. However, as I looked out of the cargo bay of the *Owlport*, I saw several Librarians fly their mechanical bats right into the walls of the glass dome. It shattered finally, falling in. The larger forces of Librarians outside the city surged into Tuki Tuki.

The city was burning. Huts aflame. People fought and warred in the night. Screams rang in the air. Shadowy groups moved against one another, struggling. In the background, an enormous force of Librarians – with hulking battle robots and wicked rifles – marched in through the open gap.

At that moment, I understood what it was to be in the middle of a war. And I came to a horrifying revelation.

The Knights of Crystallia were no cavalry come to rescue. Two hundred people, no matter how skilled, could not turn the tide of this entire war.

Tuki Tuki was going to fall anyway.

'Let us be going,' Draulin said, waving to a Mokian who was in contact with the flight deck.

'Going?' Kaz said as the gangplank was raised.

'Back to Nalhalla,' Draulin said, folding her armored arms. 'We came here to get Alcatraz, after all. Now we can go back.'

'What? No!' Kaz said. 'We have to fight! That's why we brought you here, Draulin! Lower that gangplank!'

I simply stared out at the horrific scene.

Draulin stepped up beside me. 'I'm not certain if I should curse you for forcing us into this nightmare,' she said to me, 'or if I should bless you for giving us the excuse to come and fight. Many of us wanted to, even though we knew it was hopeless. To fight in one great battle against the Librarians, rather than suffering as they slice us apart kingdom by kingdom.'

'Draulin?' Kaz said. 'Blasted woman. You knights are all—'

'She's right,' I said as the owl began to lift off. 'I can see it. Even with the knights, Mokia can't win. If you'd thought you could make a difference, you would have come and helped, wouldn't you?'

'It was a difficult decision to make,' Draulin said, and I could see that her eyes were solemn. Agonized. 'It was the decision of a surgeon with two patients, one less wounded than the other. Do you abandon the more wounded, let them die while helping the one you can save? Or do you try to help the more wounded, and risk losing them both? We thought Tuki Tuki beyond help. Many of us still wanted to come help.'

'So you're just giving up?' Kaz demanded.

'Of course not,' Draulin said. 'Now that we're here, we will fight. And die. But *my duty* is to get Alcatraz – and you other two – to safety. My brothers and sisters will fight.'

And fail. The owl got higher, and I could see just how big the Librarian army was.

I'd done it again. I'd thought I was saving Tuki Tuki, but I hadn't. Just like helping my father had been turned against me, I found my efforts here twisted on their heads. Not only would Tuki Tuki fall, but the majority of the Knights of Crystallia would be destroyed as well.

I'd accomplished nothing.

When I was young, trying not to break things had only made it worse. Fix Joan and Roy dinner, but burn down their kitchen. Polish my foster father's car, but break it apart instead. It was all coming back to me, the times when the Talent dominated my life.

Things change. Perspectives change. The knights hadn't been cowards for refusing to help Tuki Tuki. They'd made a difficult decision, the right decision. But *I'd* forced them to come anyway, turning a huge disaster into a colossal one.

'We're just going to … leave them?' Kaz said.

'This ship has the king and queen on board,' Draulin said. 'There's a chance that we might be able to bring them out of their coma in Nalhalla.' She didn't sound like she believed it was very likely. 'You've accomplished what you wished. Now, at the very least, allow me to salvage something from the fall of this city.'

My heart was a tempest of emotions, my mind a tempest of thoughts. I didn't know what to feel or think. How could everything have turned upside down so quickly? The arrival of the Knights of Crystallia was supposed to save things, not make it worse.

'What of my father?!' Kaz said.

'Lord Smedry is leading the evacuation of the children and the wounded,' Draulin said. 'He will leave with them.'

In the midst of my heart arguing with my mind arguing with my soul, one single thought pressed through the others. Something I could grab on to, something I could hold on to, something *real*.

Bastille was still down there. And she needed me.

I ran through the *Owlport*, leaving Draulin and Kaz behind. The ship rose high, passing through the hole in the dome – the one atop the city, not the one that had been broken in the side. Glass rooms passed beneath my feet and to my sides, but most of these Nalhallan vehicles were constructed with the same general layout. I burst into the flight deck a moment later, Draulin and Kaz chasing behind me, calling out, sounding confused.

Aydee and a Nalhallan man I didn't recognize were in the piloting seats. 'My name is Alcatraz Smedry,' I said loudly, 'and I'm taking command of this vessel.'

The man blinked at me in shock, but Aydee just shrugged. 'Okay, I guess.'

'Fly us down there,' I said, pointing at the Librarian army camp outside the city. I could see the place where they'd taken Bastille.

'Lord Smedry,' Draulin said, voice disapproving. 'What are you doing?'

'Saving your daughter.'

Draulin showed a moment of indecision. 'She'd want you safe, she is a knight and—'

'Tough,' I said. 'Aydee, take us down.'

'All right ...' Aydee said, steering the *Owlport*. The vehicle wasn't terribly maneuverable – it was meant as a troop transport – and kind of lumbered through the air as Aydee flew it down toward the Librarian camp.

Most of the Librarians were invading Tuki Tuki, and the Librarian camp itself was relatively quiet. There were some guard posts and a couple of thousand Librarians as a reserve force. The prisoner tent was at the back portion of the camp, and the flaps began to blow as the *Owlport* flew down low.

A dozen or so guards raced out of the building. 'Hey, Aydee,' I said. 'If we've got six plus six guards, how many is that?'

'Er ... four?'

'Good enough,' I said, and suddenly there were only four guards, the other eight having been sent away somewhere by Aydee's Talent. Hopefully they wouldn't cause too much trouble there. 'Draulin, Kaz, four guards for you.'

'Sounds good to me,' Kaz said, Warrior's Lenses in place. He raised his pistols as the *Owlport* settled down, face forward, resting on its belly.

Draulin gave me a suffering look, but opened a side door with steps down to the ground, and then followed Kaz out. They charged to engage the Librarian guards.

That was mostly a distraction. I took the other door out and slid down the wing. The floor of the camp was made up of packed-down jungle leaves and fronds, trampled flat by Librarian feet during the months of their siege. They rustled as I ran around to the back of the tent and slipped in.

The Librarians had left their captives lying in rows. I found Bastille near the center of the row, lying asleep in her tight white shirt and uniform pants. There were several dozen others in the tent, all Mokians. Officers or generals who the Librarians had considered valuable as prisoners.

I felt horrible for leaving them behind, but there wasn't much I could do. It was foolish of me to come even for Bastille, since we probably wouldn't be able to wake her up. But with Tuki Tuki falling, with all of the mistakes I'd made, I had to try to do *something*.

I slung Bastille over my shoulder and – teetering (she's kind of heavy, but don't tell her I said that) – I jogged back out the way I had come. Draulin was dusting off her hands, Kaz holstering his pistols, the four Librarian guards unconscious on the ground before them.

And then a cannonball crashed through the *Owlport*, smashing in the side, blowing off one of the wings.

I stumbled to a halt. Another cannonball followed, smashing off the owl's feet and toppling the massive vehicle to its side. I could hear Aydee inside crying out as it fell. A Librarian cannon team had set up nearby. The reserve force of Librarian soldiers was running out in front of it.

'No!' I cried.

Draulin shot me a withering gaze, something that said, 'This is your fault, Smedry.' Then she pulled out her sword and rushed at the Librarians. 'Run!' she yelled at me. 'Lose yourself in the forest!'

I just stood there. I couldn't carry Bastille with me, and I wouldn't leave her.

Draulin charged against an army of several hundred. That seemed a metaphor for everything that had gone wrong in this whole siege. But instead of making me feel sick or depressed like it had earlier, this just made me feel *angry*.

'Go away!' I screamed at the advancing Librarians. 'Leave us alone!'

Something stirred inside of me, something that felt *immense*. Like an enormous serpent, shifting, moving, awakening.

'I want everything to make sense again!' I screamed. Saving Bastille had turned out like everything else. Draulin and Aydee would get captured because of me, and Bastille would remain in a coma.

I'd failed Bastille.

I'd failed the Mokians.

I'd failed the entirety of the Free Kingdoms.

It was too much. It seemed to well up inside of me. Rocks around me began to shatter, popping like popcorn. The tent behind me frayed, the bits of threads that made it coming undone and falling apart.

There had been a time when I hadn't known how to control my Talent. When I hadn't *tried* to. I went back to that time.

Alcatraz the First had named the Breaking Talent the 'Dark Talent.' Well, sometimes darkness can serve us, work for us. It welled up inside me, bursting free, rising above me like an enormous and terrible cloud.

Reports of that day are conflicting. Some people say they could see the Talent take shape, like an enormous serpent with burning eyes, insubstantial and incorporeal. Others only felt the massive earthquake I caused, shaking the ground all around, breaking enormous rifts around Tuki Tuki.

I didn't notice any of that. I was in the middle of what felt like an intense storm, spinning around me like a cyclone. It tried to get free, tried to rip completely out of me, and I held to it, clinging, trying to force it back inside.

Reports say it lasted only for the length of two heartbeats. It felt like hours to me as I struggled, both terrified and in awe of the thing I'd let loose. With a heave of strength, I pulled it back into me. In a second, it was contained.

I blinked, standing in the night. There were a dozen enormous cracks in the ground around me. The Librarians who had been running for me had been knocked to the ground.

Unfortunately, the fighting in Tuki Tuki was still going on, however. I wasn't done. I took the thing inside of me and suddenly knew what to do with it. I reached down, pulling the single remaining Bestower's Lens from the pouch at my pocket. I knelt beside Bastille, who lay on the ground beside me. I brushed back her hair and exposed her Fleshstone. It was crystalline and pure, translucent, like an enormous diamond set into the skin of her neck.

That stone connected all of the Knights of Crystallia together. I raised the Bestower's Lens and looked into the Fleshstone, *willing* my Talent to pass into the stone.

It refused to move. It seethed within me, angry that I had stopped it from destroying. I gritted my teeth, angry, but I was feeling exhausted from all that had happened. I couldn't force it.

So I tried a different tactic. *I need to trick it*, I thought. Grandpa had to be tricked into thinking he was late so that he could arrive early. Aydee had to be confused by numbers so that she could add wrong.

What did I need to make my Talent work? *I need to think it's breaking something important*, I realized. Always, during my childhood, the Talent had acted to shatter, destroy, or break things that were very important to me or to those who cared for me. As I realized this, I found myself hating it again. But there was no time for that.

I focused on the Fleshstone, and I thought about how much I cared for Bastille. How important she'd become to me recently, and how if that stone broke, she'd die. The Talent – gleeful for something to destroy – snapped from me, but I raised the Bestower's Lens and channeled it, sending the Talent into Bastille's Fleshstone.

I felt an immediate *draining* within me as something very powerful was pulled through that Lens and sent into the stone on Bastille's neck.

It sapped me, sucked away what strength I had left. Everything went dark, and I collapsed.

∞ + 1

Three hours later, the sun rose over a broken city.

I sat up in my bed, looking out the window. Tuki Tuki was in shambles; many of the huts had collapsed. Broken spears, bits of metal, and shards of glass lay peppering the lawns of fallen homes. Bits of trash blew in the wind.

There were no bodies, but I could see blood. The bodies had been removed.

'Ah, lad, you're awake.'

I turned to find my grandfather sitting in the chair beside my bed. I was in the palace, one of the few buildings that hadn't fallen during the earthquake.

'What happened?' I asked softly, raising a hand to my head. It throbbed.

'You saved us,' he said. He seemed … oddly subdued. For my grandfather, at least. 'My, my, lad,' he said. 'That was something incredible you did! I'm … not even sure what it was, but it was something incredible indeed!'

'What do you mean?' I asked.

'The Librarian weapons fell apart,' Grandpa said. 'In the middle of the battle. Every gun, grenade, cannon, robot, everything they had. It all just … well, lad, it *broke*.'

I could hear drums. The Mokians were having a celebration. How could they celebrate when their city was in shambles?

Because they still have a city, I thought. *Broken though it is.*

'How are you feeling, lad?' Grandpa asked, scooting his chair closer to me.

'Fine, actually,' I replied. 'Tired. No, *exhausted*. But remarkably good.'

'Well, that's great. Fantastic, in fact! Excellent to hear.' He seemed hesitant about something. 'I don't want to push, lad, but … do you mind me asking what you did?'

'Well,' I said, 'I knew that the Fleshstones on the necks of the Crystin are all connected. And once, when using the Bestower's Lenses you gave me, I loaned someone else my Talent. So I figured … well, if I gave my Talent to all of the Knights at once, while they were fighting, it would work for them like it did for me. It would destroy the weapons of the Librarians when they tried to fire.'

My grandfather seemed disturbed. 'Ah …' he said. 'Yes, very clever, very clever.'

'It wasn't supposed to be clever,' I said, grimacing. 'It just kind of … *happened*. But it looks like it worked.'

'Oh, it worked,' Grandpa said. 'Maybe better than you thought…'

'What?' I asked.

'Well, lad, here's the thing. You didn't just break the weapons of the Librarians who were fighting here. You broke them all, every weapon being wielded by a Librarian *anywhere* in Mokia. In one moment, they all shattered, broke, fell apart.' Grandpa raised a hand to his head, scratching at the fluffy white hair there. 'They've retreated, called off the war, and gone back to the Hushlands. The Mokians have named you a national hero.'

I sat back, stunned.

'Already the news is spreading through the Free Kingdoms,' Grandpa said. 'This is the first time the Librarians have been turned back from taking a kingdom they were besieging. It's being called a miracle. You're a hero, lad. Everyone is talking about it.'

'I …' I felt odd. I should have felt like celebrating, jumping up and screaming for joy. But I still felt troubled and worried. Something inside of me had changed. Being forced to confront my conceptions of what was right and what was wrong, who was good and who was evil, had changed me.

I didn't want to celebrate, I wanted to hide. The world was a scary place. My Talent terrified me suddenly, even after I'd used it to save so many.

'Lad,' Grandpa said. 'Do you know when the Talents ... might come back?'

I felt a chill. 'What do you mean?'

'None of them work anymore,' Grandpa said. 'Me, Kaz, Aydee ... no more Talents. They're gone.'

Hesitantly, I reached out and touched the bed frame, engaging my Talent. But nothing happened. It wasn't like before, when I felt reluctance within me. Now there was just a void, an emptiness where my Talent had once been.

I let it out, I thought. *It can't be! I contained it, kept it from destroying! I pulled it back in!*

But I'd done something else. I'd ... well, somehow, I'd *broken the Smedry Talents.*

'I don't know,' I said. 'I don't know anything.'

'Ah. Well, then, lad, you should rest. Rest indeed ...'

When I next awoke, I had a stream of visitors. Aluki, Aydee, Kaz, then countless Mokians wishing to show their appreciation for me saving their city.

I tried to explain that I'd *destroyed* their city, but they weren't listening. The Librarians had retreated; Mokia was safe. What was left of it, at least.

I kept waiting to see if Bastille, the king, or the queen would come to see me. None of them did, though someone did bring me a cheese sandwich and insist that I eat it, thereby fulfilling the holy prophecy of the Author's Foreword, as was spoken by Alcatraz Smedry.

Finally, I asked the question I'd been dreading and got the answer I'd feared. Those who'd been knocked unconscious during the war were still in comas. The Librarians had fled, taking the antidote with them.

Mokian scientists were confident they could find a cure, given enough time. But in the end, I had failed Bastille after all. And Mokia too – more than half of their population were still unconscious.

I didn't say this to the Mokians. Instead, I nodded and accepted thanks. I couldn't really explain how I felt. I wasn't the same person anymore. Too much had happened. Too much had changed.

I was finally free of the Talent, and that terrified me. Where was it? What had I done?

When I remembered that I'd lost my Translator's Lenses, that only made me feel sicker.

My final visitor of the day was a very unexpected one. She sauntered in, accompanied by my grandfather and two guards. Shasta Smedry, my mother. She still wore her Librarian business suit and skirt. Her blond hair was down, and they'd taken her glasses as a precaution.

My mother could have been a pretty woman if she'd wanted to be. That had never seemed to matter to her.

'Lad,' Grandpa said, 'she insisted that we bring her to you. I'm not sure if it was a good idea.'

'It's all right,' I said, focusing on Shasta. 'You should be gone. The Librarians who kidnapped me went back and freed all of you.'

'Yes, they did,' she said. 'And I waited behind to get captured again.'

I frowned.

'I think your father is going to come here,' Shasta said, eyeing her guards with a raised eyebrow. 'The catacombs of the Mokian Royal University are said to have walls that are inscribed with the Forgotten Tongue. I thought Attica would try to get to them before the city fell. Alcatraz the First was said to have spent much time in this area, and so there's a high probability that the writings were his.'

'Well, that's not an issue any longer,' Grandpa Smedry said. 'The Mokian university is no more. The entire thing was swallowed up in the earthquake, crushed flat, the catacombs pulverized.'

'Is that so?' Shasta said flatly.

'Indeed,' Grandpa said, meeting her stare. There didn't seem to be much affection between them. Of course, they were in-laws, so what did you expect?

'Where will he go next?' I asked.

Shasta turned to me. She drew her lips into a line.

'I'll go with you,' I found myself saying.

'What!' Grandpa said, 'Trembling Taylers, Lad! What are you talking about?'

'We need to find my father,' I said firmly. 'I think he's going to try something stoopid. Something very, very stoopid.'

'But—'

'You,' I said to Shasta, 'me, and my grandfather. Just the three of us, and anyone else you approve. You have my word.'

She seemed amused at that. 'Very well. There are rumors of an enclave of Forgotten Language texts in the heart of Librarian power. I suspect we'll find your father there. The place is carefully guarded, however, and even one such as I will have difficulty sneaking in.'

'Lad, I don't know about this,' Grandpa said.

'The heart of Librarian power?' I asked, ignoring him. 'Where is that?'

'They call it the Library of Congress,' Shasta said. 'But it's really something far grander. The Highbrary, a bunker the size of a city, hidden underneath Washington D.C., in the United States, deep within the Hushlands.'

That got my grandfather's attention. 'The *Highbrary*?' he asked. He got an almost dreamy look in his eyes. 'My, my,' he said. 'I've *always* wanted to infiltrate that place....'

That's my grandfather for you. He might have lost his Talent, but he was still a Smedry.

'The Highbrary will contain the formulas for all Librarian weapon antidotes,' Shasta said, almost teasingly. 'If you want to cure your friends, it is the place to go.'

Grandpa looked even more eager, but he held himself back. 'The lad and I will discuss it, Shasta. If we agree to this little endeavor, then you'll be coming as a prisoner, carefully watched over. That's the only way I'd agree to it.'

Shasta smiled again, glancing at me. 'Very well,' she said, then waved to her guards – as if they were attendants – and had them lead her from the room.

My grandfather looked shaken. He sat down on the stool beside my bed again. 'That woman ...'

'We need to go with her,' I said. 'My father can't be allowed to try to give everyone Smedry Talents. Grandpa, I think that the *Talents* might be what destroyed the Incarna! I think—'

'Yes,' Grandpa said. 'Yes, you're probably right.'

'What? You know already?'

'I've guessed it, lad,' Grandpa said. 'And feared it, after you told me what you found in the tomb of Alcatraz the First.'

'Do you think my father can really do it?' I asked.

'If it were anyone else,' Grandpa said, 'I'd say no. But your father ... well, he's a special man, capable of extraordinary things. Yes, I think he might just be able to do it, if he wants to.'

'He's got the only remaining pair of Translator's Lenses,' I said. 'Mine were destroyed.'

'Ah. I wondered why we didn't find them on you.'

'He's going to the Highbrary. You know what we have to do, Grandfather.'

He looked at me, then nodded. 'Yes. But let's at least sleep on it a day and then decide.'

I nodded back to him, and he stood, withdrawing, leaving me to listen to the sounds of the Mokian drums outside. They'd celebrate all day, as per their tradition.

And then, on the morrow, they'd mourn for those who were dead. Celebrations first, sorrows second.

I didn't have time for either one. Mokia had been a diversion, a distraction, both for myself and my mother. My father, Attica Smedry, had a huge head start, and what he was planning could destroy us all.

The Dark Talent was free, and the entire Smedry clan had lost their powers. An enormous fleet of Librarian soldiers was returning to the Hushlands with tales of what the Talents could do.

I think this is a good place to end, don't you?

AUTHOR'S AFTERWORD

Now you know the truth of why I'm lauded as a hero.

Sure, the things I did in previous volumes of my autobiography helped my reputation. But this was the event that everyone still talks about, the liberation of Mokia, the single-handed defeat of dozens of Librarian armies scattered throughout the Free Kingdoms.

My reputation was secure. I'd go down in history as one of the most influential people to ever live, and I'd be remembered as one of the greatest Mokian kings of all time. (If one of the shortest to rule – I was able to give up the throne to Princess Kamali the next day, when she came back to take over for me.) Sure, Bastille was in trouble – but you know that everything turns out all right with her in the end. After all, I've mentioned several times that she's often standing here in our house, reading over my shoulder as I write these things. All in all, I saved the day, defeated the Librarian armies, and permanently turned the tide of the war.

The funny thing is, in doing all these marvelous things, I'd changed into a completely different person. Your hero is no longer with us. The very act of heroism changed him. I'd walked into Mokia as one person, and I walked out of it as a vastly different one. That's nothing surprising; all people change.

Some changes happen slowly, like a rock being weathered away by the rain. Others happen quickly, suddenly. An earthquake shakes a city. A heart stops beating. A discovery is made, and a lightbulb turns on for the first time.

The Librarians ... they try to keep us from changing. They want everything to remain the same inside the Hushlands. You remember when I talked about how they make all cars and planes look the same? Well, they do that with everything.

In this case, it's not because they're oppressive. It's because they're afraid. Change frightens them. It's unknown, uncertain, like Smedrys and magic. They want everyone to assume that things can't change.

But they can. I did. Alcatraz the hero was no more. If he ever was a hero in the first place. You've seen that most of what I accomplished happened by accident, luck, and a few random ideas that turned out to work. But even if you thought that sort of thing made him a hero, you need to realize that the person you worship is gone.

These four books are the parts everyone knows about. But the last volume, that's the part nobody understands. Nobody thinks to ask, 'What happened to him after he saved us from the Librarians?'

I'll show you. Finally, you'll see. It will be amazing, eye-opening, awful, awesome, stoopiderific, stoopidalicious, stoopiderlifluous, stoopidanated, and crapaflapnasti all at the same time. It involves an altar. Yes, that really did happen. I didn't just make it up. That altar scene is one of the most important events in my life. It happens in the next book, I promise, no lies this time.

Maybe someday I'll actually write that book.

'I will not read the last page of novels first,' I said, and then punched myself in the face.

'I promise, I'll never again read the last page of novels first,' I said, then smacked myself on the head with a book.

'I really, really, *really* regret reading the last page of this novel first!' I said, then let my sibling cousin, or best friend (take your pick) give me a wedgie.

(This page is, of course, here for those of you who skip to the end of the book and read it first. Naughty, naughty! Fortunately, you're acting out the book like you're supposed to, right? Well, let that be a lesson to you.)

THE END

ABOUT THE AUTHOR

'Brandon Sanderson' is the pen name of Alcatraz Smedry. His Hushlander editor forced him to use a pseudonym, since these memoirs are being published as fiction.

Alcatraz actually knows a person named Brandon Sanderson. That man, however, is a fantasy writer, and is therefore prone to useless bouts of delusion in literary form. Alcatraz has it on good authority that Brandon Sanderson is actually illiterate and dictates his thick, overly long fantasy tomes to his potted plant, Count Duku.

It is widely assumed that Brandon went mad several years ago, but few people can tell because his writing is so strange anyway. He spends his time going to science fiction movies, eating popcorn and goat cheese (separately), and trying to warn people about the dangers of the Great Kitten Conspiracy.

He's had his library card revoked on seventeen different occasions.

ACKNOWLEDGEMENTS

Thanks to my agents, Joshua Bilmes (who single-handedly transformed this manuscript from being a whimsical idea into a full-blown super-project) and Steve Mancino, who exceeded my expectations wildly in finding the book a home.

And, speaking of that home, Anica Rissi – my editor at Scholastic – took fantastic care of this book, helping make it the best book possible. Her tireless work is well appreciated, and the same goes for all of the wonderful people over at Scholastic.

As for alpha readers, I'd like to thank Stacy Whitman, Heather Kirby, Kristina Kugler, Peter and Karen Ahlstrom, Kaylynn ZoBell, Isaac Thegn Skarstedt, Ethan Skarstedt, Leif Ethan Skarstedt, Benjamin R. Olsen, Matisse Hales, Lauren Sanderson, Alan Layton, Janette Layton, Nathan Hatfield, Krista Olsen, C. Lee Player, Eric J. Ehlers, and Emily Sanderson. Special thanks to my grandmother, Beth Sanderson, for suggesting this project.

Also, I'd like to give a special acknowledgment to Janci Patterson who worked tirelessly to slay the typo demons in this manuscript. (Not that I didn't manage to sneak a few more in afterward.)

Finally, a thanks to all of the evil librarians out there. It's partially their fault that I ended up being a writer instead of something useful, like a plumber or a foghorn repair technician. It's poetic justice that I would now use my nefarious talent to expose you all for what you really are.

– Brandon Sanderson

ACKNOWLEDGEMENTS

I want to thank my awesome agent, Joshua Bilmes, for being, well, awesome. Thanks also to my editor at Scholastic, Jennifer Rees, whose pleasant personality and editorial know-how make the process of publishing a book so much easier. Peter and Karen Ahlstrom were kind enough to read the manuscript and give me excellent suggestions. Janci Patterson also gave me feedback that was very valuable, even though her comments were written in glaring pink ink! I'd like to thank my lovely wife, Emily Sanderson, who helped with this book in ways too numerous to list here. Finally, a special thank-you goes to Mrs. Bushman's sixth-grade students (you know who you are!) who have been so enthusiastic about my books.

– Brandon Sanderson

ACKNOWLEDGMENTS

For help with these books, I proclaim the following people honorary Bazooka Bunnies:

The Indefinable Peter Ahlstrom, for whom the book is dedicated. He's believed in me longer than anyone else on the list. Without his help, my books would be a lot worse.

Emily Sanderson, who (despite my various lunacies) still loves me, puts up with me, and even married me.

Karen Ahlstrom, who gives great advice, and who also puts up with Peter reading her my books for date night.

Janci Olds, who tells me what I need to hear about my writing. Bastille may be based on her just a tad, but don't tell her, because she might end up chasing me around with a sword.

Kristina Kugler, who taught her two-year-old daughter to put her fingers up to her mouth and wiggle them when someone asks, 'What does Cthulu say?' (Does she need a better reason than that for an acknowledgment? Well, okay, she read the book too and gave lots of great feedback.)

Joshua Bilmes, who fights for these books. He's our own personal Knight of Crystallia.

Jen Rees, who provides a sharp red pencil to fight off the goblins of bad writing.

Thank you all!